G000300132

Three Famous du Maurier Novels

DAPHNE DU MAURIER

Three Famous du Maurier Novels

THE KING'S GENERAL

THE FLIGHT OF THE FALCON

THE HOUSE ON THE STRAND

LONDON
VICTOR GOLLANCZ LTD
1982

This edition © Victor Gollancz Ltd 1982
The King's General Copyright Daphne du Maurier 1946
The Flight of the Falcon © Daphne du Maurier 1965
The House on the Strand © Daphne du Maurier 1969

British Library Cataloguing in Publication Data

Du Maurier, Daphne
    Three famous du Maurier novels.
    I. Title   II. du Maurier, Daphne. The king's
    general   III. du Maurier, Daphne. The flight
    of the falcon   IV. du Maurier, Daphne. The
    house on the strand
    823'.912[F]   PR6007.U47

ISBN 0-575-03215-4

Photoset by Rowland Phototypesetting Ltd,
Bury St Edmunds, Suffolk and printed in Great Britain
by the Pitman Press, Bath

Contents

THE KING'S GENERAL

CHAPTER ONE

SEPTEMBER, 1653. THE LAST OF SUMMER. The first chill winds of autumn. The sun no longer strikes my eastern window as I wake, but, turning laggard, does not top the hill before eight o'clock. A white mist hides the bay sometimes until noon, and hangs about the marshes too, leaving, when it lifts, a breath of cold air behind it. Because of this, the tall grass in the meadow never dries, but long past midday shimmers and glistens in the sun, the great drops of moisture hanging motionless upon the stems. I notice the tides more than I did once. They seem to make a pattern to the day. When the water drains from the marshes, and little by little the yellow sands appear, rippling and hard and firm, it seems to my foolish fancy, as I lie here, that I too go seaward with the tide, and all my old hidden dreams that I thought buried for all time are bare and naked to the day, just as the shells and the stones are on the sands.

It is a strange, joyous feeling, this streak back to the past. Nothing is regretted, and I am happy and proud. The mist and cloud have gone, and the sun, high now and full of warmth, holds revel with my ebb-tide. How blue and hard is the sea as it curls westward from the bay, and the Blackhead, darkly purple, leans to the deep water like a sloping shoulder. Once again—and this I know is fancy—it seems to me that the tide ebbs always in the middle of the day, when hope is highest and my mood is still. Then, half-consciously, I become aware of a shadow, of a sudden droop of the spirit. The first clouds of evening are gathering beyond the Dodman. And the surge of the sea, once far-off and faint, comes louder now, creeping towards the sands. The tide has turned. Gone are the white stones and the cowrie shells. The sands are covered. My dreams are buried. And as darkness falls the flood tide sweeps over the marshes and the land is covered. Then Matty will come in to light the candles and to stir the fire, making a bustle with her presence, and if I am short with her, or do not answer, she looks at me with a shake of her head, and reminds me that the fall of the year was always my bad time. Even in the distant days, when I was young, the menace of it became an institution, and Matty, like a fierce clucking hen, would chase away the casual visitor. "Miss Honor can see nobody to-day." My family soon learnt to understand, and left me in peace. Though peace is an ill word to describe the moods of black despair that used to grip me.

Ah, well . . . they're over now. Those moods at least. Rebellion of the spirit against the chafing flesh, and the moments of real pain when I could not rest. Those were the battles of youth. And I am a rebel no longer. The middle years have me in thrall, and there is much to be said for them. Resignation brings its own reward. The trouble is that I cannot read now as I used to do. At twenty-five, at thirty, books were my great consolation. Like a true scholar, I worked away at my Latin and Greek, so that learning was part of my existence. Now it seems profitless. A cynic when I was young, I am in danger of becoming a worse one now I am old. So Robin says. Poor Robin. God knows I must often make a poor companion. The years have not spared him either. He has aged much this year. Possibly his anxiety over me. I know they discuss the future, he and Matty, when they think I sleep. I can hear their voices droning in the parlour. But when he is with me he feigns his little air of cheerfulness, and my heart bleeds for him. My brother. Looking at him as he sits beside me, coldly critical as I always am towards the people I love, I note the pouches beneath his eyes, and the way his hands tremble when he lights his pipe. Can it be that he was ever light of heart and passionate of mind? Did he really ride into battle with a hawk on his wrist, and was it only ten years ago that he led his men to Braddock Down, side by side with Bevil Grenvile, flaunting that scarlet standard with the three gold rests in the eyes of the enemy? Was this the man I saw once, in the moonlight, fighting his rival for a faithless woman?

Looking at him now, it seems a mockery. My poor Robin, with his greying locks shaggy on his shoulders. Yes, the agony of the war has left its mark on both of us. The war—and the Grenviles. Maybe Robin is bound to Gartred still, even as I am to Richard. We never speak of these things. Ours is the dull drab life of day by day. Looking back, there can be very few amongst our friends who have not suffered. So many gone, so many penniless. I do not forget that Robin and I both live on charity. If Jonathan Rashleigh had not given us this house we should have had no home, with Lanrest gone, and Radford occupied. Jonathan looks very old and tired. It was that last grim year of imprisonment in St Mawes that broke him, that and John's death. Mary looks much the same. It would take more than a civil war to break her quiet composure and her faith in God. Alice is still with them, and her children, but the feckless Peter never visits her. I think of the time when we were all assembled in the long gallery, and Alice and Peter sang, and John and Joan held hands before the fire—they were all so young, such children. Even Gartred with her calculated malevolence could not have charged the atmosphere that evening. Then Richard, my Richard, broke the spell deliberately with one of his devastating cruel remarks, smiling as he did so, and the gaiety went, and the careless joy vanished from the evening. I hated him for doing it, yet understood the mood that prompted him.

Oh, God confound and damn these Grenviles, I thought afterwards, for harming everything they touch, for twisting happiness into pain with a mere inflection of the voice. Why were they made thus, he and Gartred, so that cruelty for its own sake was almost a vice to be indulged in, affording a sensuous delight? What evil genius presided at their cradle? Bevil had been so different. The flower of the flock, with his grave courtesy, his thoughtfulness, his rigid code of morality, his tenderness to his own and to other people's children. And his boys take after him. There is no vice in Jack or Bunny that I have ever seen. But Gartred. Those serpent's eyes beneath the red-gold hair, that hard voluptuous mouth. How incredible it seemed to me, even in the early days when she was married to my brother Kit, that anyone could be deceived by her. Her power to charm was overwhelming. My father and my mother were jelly in her hands, and as for poor Kit, he was lost from the beginning, like Robin later. But I was never won, not for a moment. Well, her beauty is marred now, and I suppose for ever. She will carry that scar to the grave, a thin scarlet line from eye to mouth where the blade slashed her. Rumour has it that she can still find lovers, and her latest conquest is one of the Careys, who has come to live near her at Bideford. I can well believe it. No neighbour would be safe from her if he had a charm of manner, and the Careys were always presentable. I can even find it in my heart to forgive her, now that everything is over. The idea of her dallying with George Carey—she must be at least twenty years the elder—brings a flash of colour into a grey world. And what a world! Long faces and worsted garments, bad harvests and sinking trade, everywhere men poorer than they were before, and the people miserable. The happy aftermath of war. Spies of the Lord Protector in every town and village, and if a breath of protest against the State is heard the murmurer is borne straightway to gaol. The Presbyterians hold the reins in their grasping hands, and the only men to benefit are upstarts like Frank Buller and Robert Bennett and our old enemy, John Robartes, all of them out for what they can get and damn the common man. Manners are rough, courtesy a forgotten quality. We are each one of us suspicious of our neighbour. Oh, brave new world! The docile English may endure it for a while, but not we Cornish. They cannot take our independence from us, and in a year or so, when we have licked our wounds, we'll have another rising, and there'll be more blood spilt and more hearts broken. But we shall still lack our leader. Ah, Richard—my Richard—what evil spirit in you urged you to quarrel with all men, so that even the King is your enemy now? My heart aches for you in this last disgrace. I picture you sitting lonely and bitter at your window, gazing out across the dull flat lands of Holland, and putting the final words to the Defence that you are writing, of which Bunny brought me a rough draft when he came to see me last.

"Oh, put not your trust in Princes, nor in any child of man, for there is no help in them." Bitter, hopeless words, that will do no good, and only breed further mischief. "Sir Richard Grenvile, for his presuming loyalty, must be by a public declaration defamed as a Banditto and his very loyalty understood a crime. However, seeing it must be so, let God be prayed to bless the King with faithful councillors, and that none may be prevalent to be any way hurtful to him or to any of his relations. As for Sir Richard Grenvile, let him go with the reward of an old soldier of the King's. There is no present use for him. When there shall be the Council will think on it, if not too late. *Vale.*"

Resentful, proud, and bitter to the end. For this is the end. There will be no recovery for you now; you have destroyed yourself for ever. Feared and hated by friend and foe. The King's General in the West. The man I love. It was after the Scillies fell to the Parliament, and both Jack and Bunny were home for a while, having visited Holland and France, that they rode over from Stowe to see the Rashleighs at Menabilly, and came down to Tywardreath to pay their respects to me. We talked of Richard, and almost immediately Jack said, "My uncle is greatly altered—you would hardly know him. He sits for hours in silence, looking out of the window of his dismal lodging watching the eternal rain—God, how it rains in Holland—and he has no wish for company. You remember how he used to quip and jest with us, and with all youngsters? Now if he does speak it is to find fault, like a testy old man, and crab his visitor."

"The King will never make use of him again, and he knows it," said Bunny. "The quarrel with the Court has turned him sour. It was madness to fan the flame of his old enmity with Hyde."

Then Jack, with more perception, seeing my eyes, said quickly: "Uncle was always his own worst enemy. Honor knows that. He is damnably lonely, that's the truth of it. And the years ahead are blank."

We were all silent for a moment. My heart was aching for Richard, and the boys perceived it. Presently Bunny said in a low tone: "My uncle never speaks of Dick. I suppose we shall never know now what wretched misfortune overtook him."

I felt myself grow cold, and the old sick horror grip me. I turned my head so that the boys should not see my eyes.

"No," I said slowly. "No, we shall never know."

Bunny drummed with his fingers on the table, and Jack played idly with the pages of a book. I was watching the calm waters of the bay and the little fishing boats creeping round the Blackhead from Gorran Haven. Their sails were amber in the setting sun.

"If," pursued Bunny, as though arguing with himself, "he had fallen into the hands of the enemy, why was the fact concealed? That is what always puzzles me. The son of Richard Grenvile was a prize indeed." I did not answer. I felt Jack move restlessly beside me, and I knew he was aware of my distress. "There is little use," he said, "in going over the past. We are making Honor tired." Soon after they kissed my hands and left, promising to come and see me again before they returned to France. I watched them gallop away, young, and free, and untouched by the years that had gone. One day the King would come back to his waiting country, and Jack and Bunny, who had fought so valiantly for him, would be rewarded. I could picture them at Stowe, and up in London at Whitehall, growing sleek and prosperous, with a whole new age of splendour opening before them, the civil war forgotten.

I lay there in my chair, watching the deepening shadows, and presently Robin came in and sat beside me, enquiring in his gruff tender way if I was tired, regretting that he had missed the Grenvile brothers, and going on to tell me of some small pother in the court-house at Tywardreath. I made a pretence of listening, aware with a queer sense of pity how the trifling everyday events were now his one concern. I thought how once he and his companions had won immortality for their gallant and so useless defence of Pendennis Castle in those tragic summer months in '46—how proud we were of them, how full our hearts—and here he was rambling on about five fowls that had been stolen from a widow in St Blazey. Perhaps I was no cynic after all, but rotten with sentiment.

It was then that the idea came first to me that, by writing down the events of those few years, I would rid myself of a burden. The war, and how it changed our lives; how we were all caught up in it, and broken by it, and our lives hopelessly intermingled one with another. Gartred and Robin, Richard and I, the whole Rashleigh family, pent up together in that house of secrets—small wonder that we came to be defeated. Even to-day Robin goes every Sunday to dine at Menabilly, but not I. My health pleads its own excuse. Knowing what I know, I could not return. Menabilly, where the drama of our lives was played, is vivid enough to me three miles distant here in Tywardreath. The house stands as bare and desolate as it did when I saw it last in '48. Jonathan has neither the heart nor the money to restore it to its former condition. He and Mary and the grandchildren live in one wing only. I pray God they will always remain in ignorance of that final tragedy.

Two people will carry the secret to the grave, Richard and I. He sits in Holland, many hundred miles away, and I lie upon my couch in Tywardreath, and the shadow of the buttress is upon us both. When Robin rides each Sunday to Menabilly I go with him, in imagination, across the park, and come to the high walls surrounding the house. The courtyard lies open, the west front stares down at me. The last rays of the sun shine into my old room above the gate-house, for the lattice is open, but the windows of the room beside it are closed. Ivy tendrils creep across it. The smooth stone of the buttress outside the window is encrusted with lichen. The sun vanishes, and the west front takes once more to the shadows. The Rashleighs eat and sleep within, and go by candlelight to bed, and to dream; but I, down here three miles away in Tywardreath, wake in the night to the sound of a boy's voice calling my name in terror, to a boy's hands beating against the walls, and there in the pitch-black night before me, vivid, terrible, and accusing, is the ghost of Richard's son. I sit up in bed, sweating with horror, and faithful Matty, hearing me stir, comes to me and lights the candle.

She brews me a warm drink, rubs my aching back, and puts a shawl about my shoulders. Robin, in the room adjoining, sleeps on undisturbed. I try to read a while, but my thoughts are too violent to allow repose. Matty brings me paper and a pen, and I begin to write. There is so much to say, and so little time in which to say it. For I do not fool myself about the future. My own instinct, quite apart from Robin's face, warns me that this autumn will be the last. So while my Richard's Defence is discussed by the world and placed on record for all time amongst the archives of this seventeenth century, my apologia will go with me to the grave, and by rotting there with me, unread, will serve its purpose.

I will say for Richard what he never said for himself, and I will show how, despite his bitter faults and failings, it was possible for a woman to love him with all her heart and mind and body and I that woman. I write at midnight, then, by candlelight, while the church clock at Tywardreath chimes the small hours, and the only sound I hear is the sigh of the wind beneath my window and the murmur of the sea as the tide comes sweeping across the sands to the marshes below St Blazey bridge.

CHAPTER TWO

THE FIRST TIME I saw Gartred was when my eldest brother Kit brought her home to Lanrest as his bride. She was twenty-two, and I, the baby of the family except for Percy, a child of ten. We were a happy, sprawling family, very intimate and free, and my father, John Harris, cared nothing for the affairs of the world, but lived for his horses, his dogs, and the peaceful concerns of his small estate. Lanrest was not a large property, but it lay high amidst a sheltering ring of trees, looking down upon the Looe Valley, and was one of those placid, kindly houses that seem to slumber through the years, and we loved it well. Even now, thirty years after, I have only to close my eyes and think of home, and there comes to my nostrils the well-remembered scent of hay, hot with the sun, blown by a lazy wind; and I see the great wheel thrashing the water down at the mills at Lametton, and I smell the fusty, dusty golden grain. The sky was always white with pigeons. They circled and flew above our heads, and were so tame that they would take grain from our hands. Strutting and cooing, puffed and proud, they created an atmosphere of comfort. Their gentle chattering amongst themselves through a long summer's afternoon brought much peace to me in the later years, when the others would go hawking, and ride away laughing and talking, and I could no longer follow them.

But that is another chapter. I was talking of Gartred as I saw her first. The wedding had taken place at Stowe, her home, and Percy and I, because of some childish ailment or other, had not been present at it. This, very foolishly, created a resentment in me from the first. I was undoubtedly spoilt, being so much younger than my brothers and sisters, who made a great pet of me, as did my parents too, but I had it firmly in my mind that my brother's bride did not wish to be bothered with children at her wedding, and that she feared we might have some infection.

I can remember sitting upright in bed, my eyes bright with fever, remonstrating with my mother. "When Cecilia was married, Percy and I carried the train," I said (Cecilia was my eldest sister), "and we all of us went to Mothercombe, and the Pollexefens welcomed us, although Percy and I both made ourselves sick with over-eating." All my mother could say in reply was that this time it was different, and Stowe was quite another place to Mothercombe, and the Grenviles were not the Pollexefens—which seemed to me the most feeble of arguments—and she would never forgive herself if we took the fever to Gartred. Everything was Gartred. Nobody else mattered. There was a great fuss and commotion too about preparing the spare chamber for when the bride and bridegroom should come to stay. New hangings were bought, and rugs, and tapestries, and it was all because Gartred must not be made to feel Lanrest was shabby or in poor repair. The servants were made to sweep and dust, the place was put into a bustle, and everyone made uncomfortable in the process.

If it had been because of Kit, my dear easy-going brother, I should never have grudged it for a moment. But Kit himself might not have existed. It was for Gartred. And like all children I listened to the gossip of the servants. "It's on account of his being heir to Sir Christopher at Radford that she's marrying our young master," was the sentence I heard, amidst the clatter in the kitchens. I seized upon this piece of information and brooded on it, together with the reply from my father's steward: "It's not like a Grenvile to match with a plain Harris of Lanrest."

The words angered me, and confused me too. Why should a Harris of Lanrest be a poor bargain for a Grenvile? It was true that Kit was heir to our Uncle Christopher at Radford—a great barracks of a place the other side of Plymouth—but I had never thought much of the fact until now. For the first time I realised, with something of a shock, that marriage was not the romantic fairy legend I had imagined it to be, but a great institution, a bargain between important families, with the tying up of property. When Cecilia married John Pollexefen, whom she had known since childhood, it had not struck me in this way, but now, with my father riding over to Stowe continually and holding long conferences with lawyers, and wearing a worried frown between his brows, Kit's marriage was becoming like some frightening affair of State, which, if worded wrong, would throw the country into chaos.

Eavesdropping again, I heard the lawyer say: "It is not Sir Bernard Grenvile who is holding out about the settlement, but the daughter herself. She has her father wound round her finger."

I pondered over this awhile, and then repeated it to my sister Mary. "Is it usual," I asked, with no doubt irritating precocity, "for a bride to argue thus about her portion?"

Mary did not answer for a moment. Although she was twenty, life had barely brushed her as yet, and I doubt if she knew more than I did. But I could see that she was shocked. "Gartred is the only daughter," she said, after a moment. "It is perhaps necessary for her to discuss the settlements."

"I wonder if Kit knows of it," I said. "I somehow do not think he would like it."

Mary then bade me hold my tongue, and warned me that I was fast becoming a shrew, and no one would admire me for it. I was not to be discouraged, though, and while I refrained from mentioning the marriage settlement to my brothers, I went to plague Robin—my favourite even in those days—to tell me something of the Grenviles. He had just ridden in from hawking and stood in the stable yard, his dear handsome face flushed and happy, the falcon on his wrist, and I remember drawing back, scared always by the bird's deep, venomous eyes and the blood on her beak. She would permit no one to touch her but Robin, and he was stroking her feathers.

"I am pleased it is Kit and not you that has gone away to find a bride for himself," I said, while the bird watched me from beneath great hooded lids, and Robin smiled, and reached out his other hand to touch my curls, while the falcon ruffled in anger.

"If I had been the eldest son," said Robin gently, "I would have been the bridegroom at this wedding." I stole a glance at him and saw that his smile had gone, and in its place a look of sadness. "Why, did she like you best?" I asked. He turned away then, and, placing the hood over his bird, gave her to the keeper. When he picked me up in his arms he was smiling again. "Come and pick cherries," he said, "and never mind my brother's bride."

"But the Grenviles?" I persisted as he bore me on his shoulders to the orchard. "Why must we be so mighty proud about them?"

"Bevil Grenvile is the best fellow in the world," said Robin. "Kit and Jo and I were at Oxford with him. And his sister is very beautiful." More than that I could not drag from him. But my brother Jo, to whose rather sarcastic, penetrating mind I put the same question later in the day, expressed surprise at my ignorance. "Have you reached the ripe age of ten, Honor," he enquired, "without knowing that in Cornwall there are only two families who count for anything—the Grenviles and the Arundells? Naturally, we humble Harris brood are overwhelmed that our dear brother Kit has been honoured by the august hand of the so ravishing Gartred." Then he buried his nose in a book and there was an end of the matter.

The next week they were all gone to Stowe for the wedding. I had to hug my soul in patience until their return, and then, as I feared, my mother pleaded fatigue, as did the rest of them, and everyone seemed a little jaded and out of sorts with so much feasting and rejoicing, and only my third sister Bridget unbent to me at all. She was in raptures over the magnificence of Stowe and the hospitality of the Grenviles. "This place is like a steward's lodge compared to Stowe," she told me. "You could put Lanrest in one pocket of the grounds there, and it would not be noticed. Two servants waited behind my chair at supper, and all the while musicians played to us from the gallery."

"But Gartred, what of Gartred?" I said with impatience.

"Wait while I tell you," she said. "There were more than two hundred people staying there, and Mary and I slept together in a chamber bigger far than any we possess here. There was a woman to tend us, and dress our hair. And the bedding was changed every day, and perfumed."

"What else, then?" I asked, consumed with jealousy.

"I think Father was a little lost," she whispered. "I saw him from time to time with the other people, endeavouring to talk, but he looked stifled, as though he could not breathe. And all the men were so richly attired, somehow he seemed drab beside them. Sir Bernard is a very fine-looking man. He wore a blue velvet doublet slashed with silver, the day of the wedding, and Father was in his green that fits him a little too well. He over-tops him too—Sir Bernard, I mean—and they looked odd standing together."

"Never mind my father," I said. "I want to hear of Gartred."

My sister Bridget smiled, superior with her knowledge.

"I liked Bevil the best," she said; "and so does everyone. He was in the midst of it all, seeing that no one lacked for anything. I thought Lady Grenvile a little stiff, but Bevil was the soul of courtesy, gracious in all he did." She paused a moment. "They are all auburn-haired, you know," she said with some inconsequence. "If we saw anyone with auburn hair it was sure to be a Grenvile. I did not care for the one they called Richard," she added with a frown.

"Why not? Was he so ugly?" I asked.

"No," she answered, puzzled. "He was more handsome than Bevil. But he looked at us all in a mocking, contemptuous way, and when he trod on my gown in the crush he made no apology. 'You are to blame,' he had the impudence to tell me, 'for letting it trail thus in the dust.' They told me at Stowe he was a soldier."

"But there is still Gartred," I said. "You have not described her." And then, to my mortification, Bridget yawned, and rose to her feet. "Oh, I am too weary to tell you any more," she said. "Wait until the morning. But Mary, and Cecilia, and I are all agreed upon one thing, that we would sooner resemble Gartred than any other woman." So in the end I had to form my own judgment with my own eyes. We were all gathered in the hall to receive them—they had gone first from Stowe to my uncle's estate at Radford—and the dogs ran out into the courtyard as they heard the horses.

We were a large party, because the Pollexefens were with us too, Cecilia had her baby Joan in her arms, and we were all happy and laughing and talking because we were one family and knew one another so well. Kit swung himself down from the saddle—he looked very debonair and gay—and I saw Gartred. She murmured something to Kit, who laughed and coloured, and held his arms to help her dismount, and in a flash of intuition I knew she had said something to him which was part of their life together, and had nought to do with us, his family. Kit was not ours any more, but belonged to her.

I hung back, reluctant to be introduced, and suddenly she was beside me, her cool hand under my chin. "So you are Honor?" she said. The inflection in her voice suggested that I was small for my age, or ill-looking, or disappointing in some special way, and she passed on through to the big parlour, taking precedence of my mother with a confident smile, while the remainder of the family followed like fascinated moths. Percy, being a boy and goggle-eyed at beauty, went to her at once, and she put a sweetmeat in his mouth. She has them ready, I thought, to bribe us children, as one bribes strange dogs. "Would Honor like one too?" she said, and there was a note of mockery in her voice, as though she knew instinctively that this treating of me as a baby was what I hated most. I could not take my eyes from her face. She reminded me of something, and suddenly I knew. I was a tiny child again at Radford, my uncle's home, and he was walking me through the glass-houses in the gardens. There was one flower, an orchid, that grew alone; it was the colour of pale ivory, with one little vein of crimson running through the petals. The scent filled the house, honeyed, and sickly sweet. It was the loveliest flower I had ever seen. I stretched out my hand to stroke the soft velvet sheen, and swiftly my uncle pulled me by the shoulder. "Don't touch it, child. The stem is poisonous."

I drew back, frightened. Sure enough, I could see the myriad hairs bristling, sharp and sticky, like a thousand swords.

Gartred was like that orchid. When she offered me the sweetmeat I turned away, shaking my head, and my father, who had never spoken to me harshly in his life, said sharply, "Honor, where are your manners?" Gartred laughed and shrugged her shoulder. Everyone present turned reproving eyes upon me, and even Robin frowned. My mother bade me go upstairs to my room. That was how Gartred came to Lanrest.

The marriage lasted for three years, and it is not my purpose now to write about it. So much has happened since to make the later life of Gartred the more vivid, and in the battles we have waged the early years loom dim now and unimportant. There was always war between us, that much is certain. She young, and confident, and proud, and I a sullen child, peering at her from behind doors and screens, and both of us aware of a mutual hostility. They were more often at Radford and Stowe than at Lanrest, but when she came home I swear she cast a blight upon the place. I was still a child, and I could not reason, but a child, like an animal, has an instinct that does not lie.

There were no children of the marriage. That was the first blow, and I know this was a disappointment to my parents, because I heard them talk of it. My sister Cecilia came to us regularly for her lying-in, but there was never a rumour of Gartred. She rode and went hawking as we did, she did not keep her room or complain of fatigue, which we had come to expect from Cecilia. Once my mother had the hardihood to say, "When I first wed, Gartred, I neither rode nor hunted, for fear I should miscarry," and Gartred, trimming her nails with a tiny pair of scissors made of mother-of-pearl, looked up at her, and said, "I have nothing within me to lose, madam, and for that you had better blame your son." Her voice was low and full of venom, and my mother stared at her for a moment, bewildered, then rose and left the room in distress. It was the first time the poison had touched her. I did not understand the talk between them, but I sensed that Gartred was bitter against my brother, for soon afterwards Kit came in and, going to Gartred, said to her in a tone loaded with reproach, "Have you accused me to my mother?" They both looked at me, and I knew I had to leave the room. I went out into the garden, and fed the pigeons, but the peace was gone from the place. From that moment everything went ill with them, and with us all. Kit's nature seemed to change. He wore a harassed air, wretchedly unlike himself, and a coolness grew up between him and my father, who had hitherto agreed so well.

Kit showed himself suddenly aggressive to my father, and to us all, finding fault with the working of Lanrest and comparing it to Radford, and in contrast to this was his abject humility before Gartred, a humility that had nothing fine about it but made him despicable to my intolerant eyes. The next year he stood for West Looe in Parliament, and they went often to London, so we did not see them much, but when they came to Lanrest there seemed to be this continual strain about their presence, and once there was a heated quarrel between Kit and Robin one night when my parents were from home. It was midsummer, stifling and warm, and I played truant from my nursery and crept down to the garden in my nightgown. The household were abed. I remember flitting like a little ghost before the windows. The casement of the guest chamber was open wide, and I heard Kit's voice, louder than usual, lifted in argument. Some devil interest in me made me listen. "It is always the same," he said, "wherever we go. You make a fool of me before all men, and now to-night before my very brother. I tell you I cannot endure it any longer."

I heard Gartred laugh, and I saw Kit's shadow reflected on the ceiling by the quivering candlelight. Their voices were low for a moment, and then Kit spoke again for me to hear.

"You think I remark nothing," he said. "You think I have sunk so low that to keep you near me, and to be allowed to touch you sometimes, I will shut my eyes to everyone. Do you think it was pleasant for me at Stowe to see how you looked upon Antony Denys that night when I returned so suddenly from London? A man with grown children, and his wife scarce cold in her grave? Are you entirely without mercy for me?" That terrible pleading note I so detested had crept back into his voice again, and I heard Gartred laugh once more.

"And this evening," he said, "I saw you, smiling across the table at him, my own brother." I felt sick, and rather frightened, but curiously excited, and my heart thumped within me as I heard a step beside me on the paving, and looking over my shoulder I saw Robin stand beside me in the darkness. "Go away," he whispered to me. "Go away at once." I pointed to the open window. "It is Kit and Gartred," I said. "He is angry with her for smiling at you."

I heard Robin catch at his breath, and he turned, as if to go, when suddenly Kit's voice cried out loud and horrible, as though he, a grown man, was sobbing like a child. "If that happens I shall kill you. I swear to God I shall kill you." Then Robin, swift as an arrow, stooped to a stone, and taking it in his hand he flung it against the casement, shivering the glass to fragments.

"God damn you for a coward then," he shouted. "Come and kill me instead." I looked up and saw Kit's face, white and tortured, and behind him Gartred with her hair loose on her shoulders. It was a picture to be imprinted always on my mind, those two at the window, and Robin suddenly different from the brother I had always known and loved, breathing defiance and contempt.

I turned and ran, with my fingers in my ears, and crept up to bed. What passed between them further I never knew. Day broke, and all was as before except that Robin rode away soon after breakfast and did not return until after Kit and Gartred took their departure to Radford, some five days later. Whether anyone else in the family knew of the incident I never discovered. I was too scared to ask, and since Gartred had come amongst us we had all lost our old manner of sharing troubles, and had each one of us grown more polite and secretive.

Next year, in '23, the smallpox swept through Cornwall like a scourge, and few families were spared. In Liskeard the people closed their doors, and the shopkeepers put up their shutters and would do no trade, for fear of the infection.

In June my father was stricken, dying within a few days, and we had scarcely recovered from the blow before messages came to us from my uncle at Radford to say that Kit had been seized with the same dread disease, and there was no hope of his recovery.

Father and son thus died within a few weeks of one another, and Jo, the scholar, became the head of the family. We were all too unhappy with our double loss to think of Gartred, who had fled to Stowe at the first sign of infection and so escaped a similar fate, but when the two wills came to be read, both Kit's and my father's, we learnt that although Lanrest, with Radford later, passed to Jo, the rich pasture lands of Lametton and the Mill were to remain in Gartred's keeping for her lifetime.

She came down with her brother Bevil for the reading, and even Cecilia, the gentliest of my sisters, remarked afterwards with shocked surprise upon her composure, her icy confidence, and the niggardly manner with which she saw to the measuring of every acre down at Lametton. Bevil, married himself now and a near neighbour to us at Killigarth, did his utmost to smooth away the ill-feeling that he sensed amongst us, and although I was still little more than a child I remember feeling unhappy and embarrassed that he was put to so much awkwardness on our account. It was small wonder that he was loved by everyone, and I wondered, to myself, what opinion he held in his secret heart about his sister, or whether her beauty mazed him as it did every man.

When affairs were settled, and they went away, I think we all of us breathed relief that no actual breach had come to pass, causing a feud between the families, and the fact that Lanrest belonged to Jo was a weight off my mother's mind, though she said nothing.

Robin remained from home during the whole period of the visit, and maybe no one but myself could guess the reason.

The morning before she left some impulse prompted me to hesitate before her chamber, the door of which was open, and look at her within. She had claimed that the contents of the room belonged to Kit, and so to her, and the servants had been employed the day before in taking down the hangings, and removing the pieces of furniture she most desired. At this last moment she was alone, turning out a little secretaire that stood in one corner. She did not observe that I was watching her, and I saw the mask off her lovely face at last. The eyes were narrow, the lip protruding, and she wrenched at a little drawer with such force that the part came to pieces in her hands. There were some trinkets at the back of the drawer, none I think of great value, but she had remembered them. Suddenly she saw my face reflected in the mirror.

'If you leave to us the bare walls, we shall be well content,'' I said as her eyes met mine. My father would have whipped me for it had he been alive, and my brothers too, but we were alone.

"You always played the spy, from the first,'' she said softly, but because I was not a man she did not smile.

"I was born with eyes in my head,'' I said to her.

Slowly she put the jewels in a little pouch she wore hanging from her waist. "Take comfort and be thankful you are quit of me now," she said. "We are not likely to see one another again."

"I hope not," I told her. Suddenly she laughed. "It were a pity," she said, "that your brother did not have a little of your spirit."

"Which brother?" I asked.

She paused a moment, uncertain what I knew, and then, smiling, she tapped my cheek with her long slim finger. "All of them," she said, and then she turned her back on me, and called to her servant from the adjoining room. Slowly I went downstairs, my mind on fire with questions, and coming into the hallway I saw Jo fingering the great map hanging on the wall. I did not talk to him, but walked out past him into the garden.

She left Lanrest at noon, with a great train of horses and servants from Stowe to carry her belongings. I watched them, from a hiding-place in the trees, pass away up the road to Liskeard in a cloud of dust.

"That's over," I said to myself. "That's the last of them. We have done with the Grenviles."

But Fate willed otherwise.

CHAPTER THREE

MY EIGHTEENTH BIRTHDAY. A bright December day. My spirits soaring like a bird as, looking out across the dazzling sea from Radford, I watched His Majesty's fleet sail into Plymouth Sound.

It concerned me not that the expedition now returning had been a failure, and that far away in France La Rochelle remained unconquered; these were matters for older people to discuss.

Here in Devon there was laughing and rejoicing and the young folk held high holiday. What a sight they were—some eighty ships or more, crowding together between Drake's Island and the Mount, the white sails bellying in the west wind, the coloured pennants streaming from the golden spars. As each vessel drew opposite the fort at Mount Batten, she would be greeted with a salvo from the great guns, and, dipping her colours in a return salute, let fly her anchor, and bring up opposite the entrance to the Cattwater. The people gathered on the cliffs waved and shouted, and from the vessels themselves came a mighty cheer, while the drums beat and the bugles sounded, and the sides of the ships were seen to be thronged with soldiers. The sun shone upon their breast-plates and their swords, which they waved to the crowds in greeting, and gathered on the poop would be the officers—flashes of crimson, blue and Lincoln green, as they moved amongst the men.

Each ship carried on her mainmast the standard of the officer in command, and as the crowd recognised the colours and the arms of a Devon leader, or a Cornishman, another great shout would fill the air, and be echoed back to us from the cheering fellows in the vessel. There was the two-headed eagle of the Godolphins, the running stag of the Trevannions from Caerhayes, the six swallows of the numerous Arundell clan, and—perhaps loveliest of all—the crest of the Devon Champernownes, a sitting swan holding in her beak a horseshoe of gold.

The little ships, too, threaded their way amongst their larger sisters, and I recognised vessels I had last seen lying in Looe Harbour or in Fowey, now weather-stained and battered, but bearing triumphantly aloft the standards of the men who had built them and manned them and commissioned them for war—among them the wolf's head of our neighbour Trelawney, and the Cornish chough of the Menabilly Rashleighs.

The leading ship, a great three-masted vessel, carried the commander of the expedition, the Duke of Buckingham, and when she was saluted from Mount Batten she replied with an answering salvo from her own six guns, and we could see the Duke's pennant fluttering from the mast-head. She dropped anchor, swinging to the wind, and the fleet followed her, and the rattle of nearly a hundred cables through a hundred hawsers must have filled the air from where we stood on the cliffs below Radford. Slowly their bows swung round, pointing to Cawsand and the Cornish coast, and their sterns came into line, the sun flashing in their windows and gleaming upon the ornamental carving, the writhing serpents and the lions' paws.

And still the bugles echoed across the water and the drums thundered. Suddenly there was silence, the clamour and the cheering died away, and on the flagship commanded by the Duke of Buckingham someone snapped forth an order in a high, clear voice. The soldiers who had crowded the bulwarks were there no longer, they moved as one man, forming into line amidships, there was no jostling, no thrusting into position. There came another order, and the single tattoo of a drum, and in one movement it seemed the boats were manned and lowered into the water, the coloured blades poised as though to strike, and the men who waited on the thwarts sat rigid as automatons.

"I thought as much," said a fellow below me. "There's only one man in the West who could turn an unruly rabble into soldiers fit for His Majesty's bodyguard. There go the Grenvile coat-of-arms—do you see them, hoisted beneath the Duke of Buchingham's standard?" Even as he spoke I saw the scarlet pennant run up to the mast-head, and as it streamed into the wind and flattened the sun shone upon the three gold rests.

The boats drew away from the ship's side, the officers seated in the stern sheets, and suddenly it was high holiday again, with crowded Plymouth boats putting out from the Cattwater to greet the fleet—the whole Sound dotted at once with little craft—and the people watching upon the cliffs began to run towards Mount Batten, calling and shouting, pushing against one another to be the first to greet the landing boats. The spell was broken, and we returned to Radford.

"A fine finish to your birthday," said my brother with a smile. "We are all bidden to a banquet at the Castle, at the command of the Duke of Buckingham." He stood on the steps of the house to greet us, having ridden back from the fortress at Mount Batten. Jo had succeeded to the estates at Radford, my Uncle Christopher having died a few years back, and much of our time now was spent between Plymouth and Lanrest. Jo had become, indeed, a person of some importance, in Devon especially, and besides being Under-Sheriff for the county he had married an heiress into the bargain, Elizabeth Champernowne, whose pleasant manner and equable disposition made up for her lack of looks. My sister Bridget, too, had followed Cecilia's example and married into a Devon family, and Mary and I were the only daughters left unwed.

"There will be ten thousand fellows roaming the streets of Plymouth to-night," jested Robin. "I warrant if we turned the girls loose amongst them they'd soon find husbands."

"Best clip Honor's tongue then," replied Jo, "for they'll soon forget her blue eyes and her curls once she begins to flay them."

"Let me alone—I can look after myself," I told them.

For I was still the spoilt darling, the *enfant terrible*, possessing boundless health and vigour, and a tongue that ran away with me. I was, moreover (and how long ago it seems), the beauty of the family, though my features, such as they were, were more impudent than classical, and I still had to stand on tiptoe to reach to Robin's shoulder. I remember, that night, how we embarked below the fortress and took boat across the Cattwater to the castle. All Plymouth seemed to be upon the water, or on the battlements, while away to westward gleamed the soft lights of the fleet at anchor, the stern windows shining, and the glow from the poop lanterns casting a dull beam upon the water. When we landed, we found the townsfolk pressing about the castle entrance, and everywhere were the soldiers, laughing and talking, encircled with girls, who had decked them with flowers and ribbons for festivity. There were casks of ale standing on the cobbles beside the braziers, and barrow loads of pies, and cakes, and cheeses, and I remember thinking that the maids who roystered there with their soldier lovers would maybe have more value from their evening than we who must behave with dignity within the precincts of the castle.

In a moment we were out of hearing of the joyful noises of the town, and the air was close and heavy with rich scent, and velvet, and silk, and spicy food, and we were in the great banqueting hall with voices sounding hollow and strange beneath the vaulted roof. Now and again would ring out the clear voice of a gentleman-at-arms, "Way for the Duke of Buckingham," and a passage would be cleared for the commander as he passed to and fro amongst the guests, holding court even as His Majesty himself might do.

The scene was colourful and exciting, and I—more accustomed to the lazy quiet of Lanrest—felt my heart beat and my cheek flush, and to my youthful fancy it seemed to me that all this glittering display was somehow a tribute to my eighteenth birthday. "How lovely it is! Are you not glad we came?" I said to Mary, and she, always reserved among strangers, touched my arm and murmured, "Speak more softly, Honor. You draw attention to us," and was for drawing back against the wall. I pressed forward, greedy for colour, devouring everything with my eyes, smiling even at strangers and caring not at all that I seemed bold, when suddenly the crowd parted, a way was cleared, and here was the Duke's retinue upon us, with the Duke himself not half a yard away. Mary was gone, and I was left alone to bar his path. I remember standing an instant in dismay, and then, losing my composure, I curtsied low, as though to King Charles himself, while a little ripple of laughter floated above my head. Raising my eyes, I saw my brother Jo, his face a strange mixture of amusement and dismay, come forward from amongst those who thronged the Duke, and bending over me he helped me to my feet, for I had curtsied so low that I was hard upon my heels and could not rise. "May I present my sister Honor, your Grace?" I heard him say. "This is, in point of fact, her eighteenth birthday, and her first venture into society."

The Duke of Buckingham bowed gravely, and, lifting my hand to his lips, wished me good fortune. "It may be your sister's first venture, my dear Harris," he said graciously, "but with beauty such as she possesses you must see to it that it is not the last." He passed on in a wave of perfume and velvet, with my brother beside him, frowning at me over his shoulder, and as I swore under my breath (or possibly not under my breath, but indiscreetly, and a stable oath learnt from Robin at that) I heard someone say behind me, "If you care to come out on to the battlements, I will show you how to do that as it should be done." I whipped round, scarlet and indignant, and, looking down upon me from six foot or more, with a sardonic smile upon his face, was an officer still clad in his breast-plate of silver, worn over a blue tunic, with a blue and silver sash about his waist. His eyes were golden brown, his hair dark auburn, and I saw that his ears were pierced with small gold rings, for all the world like a Turkish bandit.

"Do you mean you would show me how to curtsy or how to swear?" I said to him in fury.

"Why both, if you wish it," he answered. "Your performance at the first was lamentable, and at the second merely amateur."

His rudeness rendered me speechless, and I could hardly believe my ears. I glanced about me for Mary, or for Elizabeth, Jo's serene and comfortable wife, but they had withdrawn in the crush, and I was hemmed about with strangers. The most fitting thing, then, was to withdraw with dignity. I turned on my heel, and pushed my way through the crowd, making for the entrance, and then I heard the mocking voice behind me once again, "Way for Mistress Honor Harris of Lanrest," proclaimed in high clear tones, while people looked at me astonished, falling back in spite of themselves, and so a passageway was cleared. I walked on with flaming cheeks, scarce knowing what I was doing, and found myself, not in the great entrance as I had hoped, but in the cold air upon the battlements, looking out on to Plymouth Sound, while away below me, in the cobbled square, the townsfolk danced and sang. My odious companion was with me still, and he stood now, with his hand upon his sword, looking down upon me with the same mocking smile on his face.

"So you are the little maid my sister so much detested," he said.

"What the devil do you mean?" I asked.

"I would have spanked you for it had I been her," he said.

Something in the clip of his voice and the droop of his eye struck a chord in my memory. "Who are you?" I said to him.

"Sir Richard Grenvile," he replied, "a colonel in His Majesty's army, and knighted some little while ago for extreme gallantry in the field." He hummed a little, playing with his sash.

"It is a pity," I said, "that your manners do not match your courage."

"And that your deportment," he said, "does not equal your looks."

This reference to my height—always a sore point, for I had not grown an inch since I was thirteen—stung me to fresh fury. I let fly a string of oaths that Jo and Robin, under the greatest provocation, might have loosed upon the stableman, though certainly not in my presence, and which I had only learnt through my inveterate habit of eavesdropping; but if I hoped to make Richard Grenvile blanch I was wasting my breath. He waited until I had finished, his head cocked as though he were a tutor hearing me repeat a lesson, and then he shook his head.

"There is a certain coarseness about the English tongue that does not do for the occasion," he said. "Spanish is more graceful, and far more satisfying to the temper. Listen to this." And he began to swear in Spanish, loosing upon me a stream of lovely-sounding oaths that would certainly have won my admiration had they come from Jo or Robin. As I listened I looked again for that resemblance to Gartred, but it was gone. He was like his brother Bevil, but with more dash, and certainly more swagger, and I felt he cared not a tinker's curse for anyone's opinion but his own.

"You must admit," he said, breaking off suddenly, "that I have you beaten." His smile, no longer sardonic but disarming, had me beaten too, and I felt my anger die within me. "Come and look at the fleet," he said, "a ship at anchor is a lovely thing."

We went to the battlements and stared out across the Sound. It was still and cloudless and the moon had risen. The ships were motionless upon the water, and they stood out in the moonlight carved and clear. The men were singing, and the sound of their voices was borne to us across the water, distinct from the rough jollity of the crowds in the streets below.

"Were your losses very great at La Rochelle?" I asked him.

"No more than I expected, in an expedition that was bound to be abortive," he answered, shrugging his shoulders. "Those ships yonder are filled with wounded men who won't recover. It would be more humane to throw them overboard." I looked at him in doubt, wondering if this was a further instalment of his peculiar sense of humour. "The only fellows who distinguish themselves were those in the regiment I have the honour to command," he continued, "but as no other officer but myself insists on discipline, it was small wonder that the attack proved a failure."

His self-assurance was as astounding to me as his former rudeness.

"Do you talk thus to your superiors?" I asked him.

"If you mean superior to me in matters military, such a man does not exist," he answered, "but superiors in rank, why yes, invariably. That is why, although I am not yet twenty-nine, I am already the most detested officer in His Majesty's army." He looked down at me, smiling, and once again I was at a loss for words.

I thought of my sister Bridget, and how he had trodden upon her dress at Kit's wedding, and I wondered if there was anyone in the world who liked him. "And the Duke of Buckingham?" I said. "Do you speak to him in this way too?" "Oh, George and I are old friends," he answered. "He does what he is told. He gives me no trouble. Look at those drunken fellows in the courtyard there. My heaven, if they were under my command I'd hang the bastards." He pointed down to the square below, where a group of brawling soldiers were squabbling around a cask of ale, accompanied by a pack of squealing women.

"You might excuse them," I said, "pent up at sea so long."

"They may drain the cask dry, and rape every woman in Plymouth, for all I care," he answered, "but let them do it like men and not like beasts, and clean their filthy jerkins first."

He turned away from the battlement in disgust.

"Come now," he said. "Let us see if you can curtsy better to me than you did to the Duke. Take your gown in your hands, thus. Bend your right knee, thus. And allow your somewhat insignificant posterior to sink upon your left leg, thus."

I obeyed him, shaking with laughter, for it seemed to me supremely ridiculous that a colonel in His Majesty's army should be teaching me deportment upon the battlements of Plymouth Castle.

"I assure you it is no laughing matter," he said gravely. "A clumsy woman looks so damnably ill-bred. There now, that is excellent. Once again. Perfection. You can do it if you try. The truth is you are an idle little baggage, and have never been beaten by your brothers." With appalling coolness, he straightened my gown and rearranged the lace around my shoulders.

"I object to dining with untidy women," he murmured.

"I have no intention of sitting down with you to dine," I replied with spirit.

"No one else will ask you, I can vouch for that," he answered. "Come, take my arm. I am hungry if you are not."

He marched me back into the castle, and to my consternation I found that the guests were already seated at the long tables in the banqueting hall, and the servants were bearing in the dishes. We were conspicuous as we entered, and my usual composure fled from me. It was, it may be remembered, my first venture in the social world. "Let us go back," I pleaded, tugging at his arm. "See, there is no place for us; the seats are all filled."

"Go back? Not on your life. I want my dinner," he replied.

He pushed his way past the servants, nearly lifting me from my feet. I could see hundreds of faces staring up at us, and heard a hum of conversation, and for one brief moment I caught a glimpse of my sister Mary, seated next to Robin, away down in the centre of the hall. I saw the look of horror and astonishment in her eyes, and her mouth frame the word "Honor" as she whispered to my brother. I could do nothing but hurry forward, tripping over my gown, borne on the relentless arm of Richard Grenvile to the high table at the far end of the hall where the Duke of Buckingham sat beside the Countess of Mount Edgcumbe, and the nobility of Cornwall and Devon, such as they were, feasted with decorum above the common herd. "You are taking me to the high table," I protested, dragging at his arm with all my force.

"What of it?" he asked, looking down at me in astonishment. "I'm damned if I'm going to dine anywhere else. Way there, please, for Sir Richard Grenvile." At his voice the servants flattened themselves against the wall, and heads were turned, and I saw the Duke of Buckingham break off from his conversation with the Countess. Chairs were pulled forward, people were squeezed aside, and somehow we were seated at the table a hand's stretch from the Duke himself, while the Lady Mount Edgcumbe peered round at me with stony eyes. Richard Grenvile leant forward with a smile. "You are perhaps acquainted with Honor Harris, Countess," he said, "my sister-in-law. This is her eighteenth birthday." The Countess bowed, and appeared unmoved. "You can disregard her," said Richard Grenvile to me. "She's as deaf as a post. But for God's sake smile, and take that glassy stare from your eye." I prayed for death, but it did not come to me. Instead I took the roast swan that was heaped upon my platter.

The Duke of Buckingham turned to me, his glass in his hand. "I wish you very many happy returns of the day," he said.

I murmured my thanks, and shook my curls to hide my flaming cheeks.

"Merely a formality," said Richard Grenvile in my ear. "Don't let it go to your head. George has a dozen mistresses already, and is in love with the Queen of France."

He ate with evident enjoyment, vilifying his neighbours with every mouthful, and because he did not trouble to lower his voice I could swear that his words were heard. I tasted nothing of what I ate or drank, but sat like a bewildered fish throughout the long repast. At length the ordeal was over, and I felt myself pulled to my feet by my companion. The wine, which I had swallowed as though it were water, had made jelly of my legs, and I was obliged to lean upon him for support. I have scant memory indeed of what followed next. There was music, and singing, and some Sicilian dancers, strung about with ribbons, performed a tarantella, but their final dizzy whirling was my undoing, and I have a shaming recollection of being assisted to some inner apartment of the castle, suitably darkened and discreet, where Nature took her toll of me, and the roast swan knew me no more. I opened my eyes and found myself upon a couch, with Richard Grenvile holding my hand, and dabbing my forehead with his kerchief.

"You must learn to carry your wine," he said severely.

I felt very ill, and very ashamed, and tears were near the surface.

"Ah, no," he said, and his voice, hitherto so clipped and harsh, was oddly tender. "You must not cry. Not on your birthday."

He continued dabbing at my forehead with the kerchief.

"I have n-never eaten roast swan b-before," I stammered, closing my eyes in agony at the memory.

"It was not so much the swan as the burgundy," he murmured. "Lie still now, you will be easier by and by."

In truth, my head was still reeling, and I was as grateful for his strong hand as I would have been for my mother's. It seemed to me in no wise strange that I should be lying sick in a darkened unknown room with Richard Grenvile tending me, proving himself so comforting a nurse.

"I hated you at first. I like you better now," I told him.

"It's hard that I had to make you vomit before I won your approval," he answered. I laughed, and then fell to groaning again, for the swan was not entirely dissipated. "Lean against my shoulder, so," he said to me. "Poor little one, what an ending to an eighteenth birthday." I could feel him shake with silent laughter, and yet his voice and hands were strangely tender, and I was happy with him.

"You are like your brother Bevil after all," I said.

"Not I," he answered. "Bevil is a gentleman, and I a scoundrel. I have always been the black sheep of the family."

"What of Gartred?" I asked.

"Gartred is a law unto herself," he replied. "You must have learnt that when you were a little child, and she was wedded to your brother."

"I hated her with all my heart," I told him.

"Small blame to you for that," he answered me.

"And is she content, now that she is wed again?" I asked him.

"Gartred will never be content," he said. "She was born greedy, not only for money, but for men too. She had an eye to Antony Denys, her husband now, long before your brother died."

"And not only Antony Denys," I said.

"You had long ears for a little maid," he answered.

I sat up, rearranging my curls, while he helped me with my gown.

"You have been kind to me," I said, grown suddenly prim, and conscious of my eighteen years. "I shall not forget this evening."

"Nor I either," he replied.

"Perhaps," I said, "you had better take me to my brothers."

"Perhaps I had," he said.

I stumbled out of the little dark chamber to the lighted corridor. "Where were we all this while?" I asked in doubt, glancing over my shoulder. He laughed, and shook his head.

"The good God only knows," he answered; "but I wager it is the closet where Mount Edgcumbe combs his hair." He looked down at me smiling, and, for one instant, touched my curls with his hands. "I will tell you one thing," he said, "I have never sat with a woman before while she vomited."

"Nor I so disgraced myself before a man," I said with dignity.

Then he bent suddenly, and lifted me in his arms like a child. "Nor have I ever lain hidden in a darkened room with anyone so fair as you, Honor, and not made love to her," he told me, and, holding me for a moment against his heart, he set me on my feet again.

"And now, if you permit it, I will take you home," he said.

That is, I think, a very clear and truthful account of my first meeting with Richard Grenvile.

CHAPTER FOUR

WITHIN A WEEK of the encounter just recorded I was sent back to my mother at Lanrest, supposedly in disgrace for my ill-behaviour, and once home I had to be admonished all over again, and hear for the twentieth time how a maid of my age and breeding should conduct herself. It seemed that I had done mischief to everyone. I had shamed my brother Jo by that foolish curtsy to the Duke of Buckingham, and further had offended his wife Elizabeth by taking precedence of her and dining at the high table, to which she had not been invited. I had neglected to remain with my sister Mary during the evening, had been observed by sundry persons cavorting oddly on the battlements with an officer, and had finally appeared some time after midnight from the private rooms within the castle in a sad state of disarray.

Such conduct would, my mother said severely, condemn me possibly for all time in the eyes of the world, and had my father been alive he would more than likely have packed me off to the nuns for two or three years, in the hopes that my absence for a space of time would cause the incident to be forgotten. As it was—and here invention failed her, and she was left lamenting that, as both my married sisters Cecilia and Bridget were expecting to lie-in again and could not receive me, I would be obliged to stay at home.

It seemed to me very dull after Radford, for Robin had remained there, and my young brother Percy was still at Oxford. I was therefore alone in my disgrace. I remember it was some weeks after I returned, a day in early spring, and I had gone out to sulk by the apple-tree, that favourite hiding-place of childhood, when I observed a horseman riding up the valley. The trees hid him for a space, and then the sound of horse's hoofs drew nearer, and I realised that he was coming to Lanrest. Thinking it was Robin, I scrambled down from my apple-tree and went to the stables, but when I arrived there I found the servant leading a strange horse to the stall—a fine grey—and I caught a glimpse of a tall figure passing into the house. I was for following my old trick of eavesdropping at the parlour door, but just as I was about to do so I observed my mother on the stairs.

"You will please go to your chamber, Honor, and remain there until my visitor has gone," she said gravely.

My first impulse was to demand the visitor's name, but I remembered my manners in time, and, afire with curiosity, went silently upstairs. Once there I rang for Matty, the maid who had served me and my sisters for some years now,

and had become my special ally. Her ears were nearly as long as mine, and her
nose as keen, and her round, plain face was now alight with mischief. She
guessed what I wanted her for before I asked her. "I'll bide in the hallway when
he comes out, and get his name for you," she said. "A tall big gentleman he
was, a fine man."

"No one from Bodmin," I said, with sudden misgiving, for fear my mother
should, after all, intend to send me to the nuns.

"Why, bless you, no," she answered. "This is a young master, wearing a
blue cloak slashed with silver."

Blue and silver. The Grenvile colours.

"Was his hair red, Matty?" I asked in some excitement.

"You could warm your hands at it," she answered.

This was an adventure, then, and no more dullness to the day. I sent Matty
below, and paced up and down my chamber in great impatience. The interview
must have been a short one, for very soon I heard the door of the parlour open,
and the clear clipped voice that I remembered well taking leave of my mother,
and I heard his footsteps pass away through the hallway to the courtyard. My
chamber window looked out on to the garden, and I thus had no glimpse of
him, and it seemed eternity before Matty reappeared, her eyes bright with
information. She brought forth a screwed-up piece of paper from beneath her
apron, and with it a silver piece. "He told me to give you the note, and keep the
crown," she said.

I unfolded the note, furtive as a criminal.

"Dear Sister," I read, "although Gartred has exchanged a Harris for a
Denys, I count myself still your brother, and reserve for myself the right of
calling upon you. Your good mother, it seems, thinks otherwise, tells me you
are indisposed, and has bidden me good-day in no uncertain terms. It is not my
custom to ride some ten miles or so to no purpose, therefore you will direct
your maid forthwith to conduct me to some part of your domain where we can
converse together unobserved, for I dare swear you are no more indisposed
than is your brother and servant, Richard Grenvile."

My first thought was to send no answer, for he took my compliance so much
for granted, but curiosity and a beating heart got the better of my pride, and I
bade Matty show the visitor the orchard, but that he should not go too directly,
for fear of being seen from the house. When she had gone, I listened for my
mother's footsteps, and sure enough they sounded up the stairs, and she came
into the room. She found me sitting by the window, with a book of prayers
open on my knee. "I am happy to see you so devout, Honor," she said.

I did not answer, but kept my eyes meekly upon the page.

"Sir Richard Grenvile, with whom you conducted yourself in so unseemly
a fashion a week ago in Plymouth, has just departed," she continued. "It
seems he has left the army for a while, and intends to reside near to us at
Killigarth, standing as Member of Parliament for Fowey. A somewhat sudden
decision."

Still I did not answer. "I have never heard any good of him," said my
mother. "He has always caused his family concern, and been a sore trial to his

brother Bevil, being constantly in debt. He will hardly make us a pleasant neighbour."

"He is, at least, a very gallant soldier," I said warmly.

"I know nothing about that," she answered, "but I have no wish for him to ride over here, demanding to see you, when your brothers are from home. It shows great want of delicacy on his part."

With that she left me, and I heard her pass into her chamber and close the door. In a few moments I had my shoes in my hands and was tiptoeing down the stairs into the garden. Then I flew like the wind to the orchard, and was safe in the apple-tree before many minutes had passed. Presently I heard someone moving about under the trees, and parting the blossom in my hiding-place I saw Richard Grenvile stooping under the low branches. I broke off a piece of twig and threw it at him. He shook his head, and looked about him. I threw another, and this one hit him a sharp crack upon the nose. "God damn it," he began, and, looking up, he saw me laughing at him from the apple-tree. In a moment he had swung himself up beside me, and with one arm around my waist had me pinned against the trunk. The branch cracked most ominously.

"Get down at once—the branch will not hold us both," I said.

"It will, if you keep still," he told me.

One false move would have seen us both upon the ground, some ten feet below, but to remain still meant that I must continue to lie crushed against his chest, with his arm about me, and his face not six inches away from mine.

"We cannot possibly converse in such a fashion," I protested.

"Why not? I find it very pleasant," he answered.

Cautiously he stretched his leg along the full length of the branch to give himself more ease, and pulled me closer.

"Now, what have you to tell me?" he said, for all the world as though it were I who had demanded the interview and not he.

I then recounted my disgrace, and how my brother and sister-in-law had sent me packing home from Plymouth, and it seemed as if I must now be treated as a prisoner in my own home.

"And it is no use your coming here again," I added, "for my mother will never let me see you. It seems you are a person of ill repute."

"How so?" he demanded.

"You are constantly in debt—those were her words."

"The Grenviles are never not in debt. It is the great failing of the family. Even Bevil has to borrow from the Jews."

"You are a sore trial to him, and to all your relatives."

"On the contrary, it is they who are a sore trial to me. I can seldom get a penny out of them. What else did your mother say?"

"That it showed want of delicacy to come here asking to see me when my brothers are from home."

"She is wrong. It showed great cunning, born of long experience."

"And as for your gallantry in the field, she knows nothing about that."

"I hardly suppose she does. Like all mothers, it is my gallantry in other spheres that concerns her at the present."

"I don't know what you mean," I said.

"Then you have less perception than I thought," he answered, and, loosening his hold upon the branch, he flicked at the collar of my gown. "You have an earwig running down your bosom," he said.

I drew back, disconcerted, the abrupt change from the romantic to the prosaic putting me out of countenance.

"I believe my mother to be right," I said stiffly. "I think there is very little to be gained from our further acquaintance, and it would be best to put an end to it now." It was difficult to show dignity in my cramped position, but I made some show of sitting upright, and braced my shoulders.

"You cannot descend unless I let you," he said, and in truth I was locked there, with his legs across the branch. "The moment is opportune to teach you Spanish," he murmured.

"I have no wish to learn it," I answered.

Then he laughed, and, taking my face in his hands, he kissed me very suddenly, which, being a novelty to me, and strangely pleasant, rendered me, for a few moments, incapable of speech or action. I turned away my head, and began to play with the blossoms. "You can go now, if you desire it," he said. I did not desire it, but had too much pride to tell him so. He swung himself to the ground, and lifted me down beside him.

"It is not easy," he said, "to be gallant in an apple-tree. Perhaps you will tell your mother." He wore upon his face that same sardonic smile that I had first seen in Plymouth.

"I shall tell my mother nothing," I said, hurt by this abrupt dismissal. He looked down on me for a moment in silence, and then he said, "If you bid your gardener trim that upper branch we would do better another time."

"I am not certain," I answered, "that I wish for another time."

"Ah, but you do," he said, "and so do I. Besides, my horse needs exercise." He turned through the trees, making for the gate where he had left his horse, and I followed him silently through the long grass. He reached for the bridle, and climbed into the saddle. "Ten miles between Lanrest and Killigarth," he said. "If I did this twice a week, Daniel would be in fine condition by the summer. I will come again on Tuesday. Remember those instructions to the gardener." He waved his gauntlet at me and was gone.

I stood staring after him, telling myself that he was quite as detestable as Gartred, and that I would never see him more; but for all my resolutions I was at the apple-tree again on Tuesday.

There followed then as strange, and to my mind as sweet, a wooing as ever maiden of my generation had. Looking back on it now, after a quarter of a century, when the sequel to it fills my mind with greater clarity, it has the hazy unreality of an elusive dream. Once a week, and sometimes twice, he would ride over to Lanrest from Killigarth, and there, cradled in the apple-tree—with the offending branch lopped as he demanded—he tutored me in love, and I responded. He was but twenty-eight, and I eighteen. Those March and April afternoons, with the bees humming above our heads and the blackcap singing, and the grass in the orchard growing longer day by day, there seemed no end to them and no beginning. Of what we discoursed, when we did not kiss, I have forgotten. He must have told me much about himself, for Richard's thoughts were ever centred about his person, more then than latterly, and I had a picture of a red-haired lad rebellious of authority flaunting his elders, staring out across the storm-tossed Atlantic from the towering, craggy cliffs of his north Cornish coast, so different from our southern shore, with its coves and valleys.

We have, I think, a more happy disposition here in south-east Cornwall, for the very softness of the air, come rain or sun, and the gentle contour of the land, make for a lazy feeling of content. Whereas in the Grenvile country, bare of hedgerow, bereft of tree, exposed to all four winds of heaven—winds laden, as it were, with surf and spray—the mind develops with a quick perception, with more fire to it, more anger, and life itself is hazardous and cruel. Here we have few tragedies at sea, but there the coast is strewn with the bleached bones of vessels wrecked without hope of haven. It holds us more than we ever reckon, the few square miles of territory where we are born and bred, and I can understand what devils of unrest surged in the blood of Richard Grenvile.

These thoughts of mine came at a later date, but then, when we were young, they concerned me not, nor him either, and whether he talked to me of soldiering or Stowe, of fighting the French or battling with his own family, it sounded happy in my ears, and all his bitter jests were forgotten when he kissed me and held me close. It seems odd that our hiding-place was not discovered. Maybe in his careless, lavish fashion he showered gold pieces on the servants. Certainly my mother passed her days in placid ignorance.

And then, one day in early April, my brothers rode from Radford, bringing with them young Edward Champernowne, a younger brother of Elizabeth's. I was happy to see Jo and Robin, but in no mood to exchange courtesies with a stranger, and also I was filled with furtive fear that my secret meetings would be discovered. After we had dined, Jo and Robin and my mother, with Edward Champernowne, withdrew to the book-room that had been my father's, and I was left alone to entertain Elizabeth. She made no mention of my discourtesy at Plymouth, for which I was grateful, but proceeded to lavish great praise upon her brother Edward, who, she told me, was but a year older than myself, and had recently left Oxford. I listened with but half an ear, my thoughts full of Richard.

Later in the evening I was summoned to my mother's room. Jo was with her, and Robin too, but Edward Champernowne had gone to join his sister. All three of them wore an air of well-being.

My mother drew me to her, and kissed me fondly, and said at once that great happiness was in store for me, that Edward Champernowne had asked for my hand in marriage, that she and my brothers had accepted, the formalities had been settled, my portion agreed to, with Jo adding to it most handsomely, and nothing remained now but to determine upon the date. I believe I stared at them all a moment stupefied, and then broke out wildly in a torrent of protestation, declaring that I would not wed him, that I would wed no man who was not of my own choice, and that sooner than do it I would throw myself from the roof. In vain my mother argued with me, in vain Jo enthused upon the virtues of young Champernowne, of his steadiness, of his noble bearing, and of how my conduct had been such, a few months back, that it was amazing he should have asked for my hand at all. "You have come to the age, Honor," he said, "when we believe marriage to be the only means to settle you, and in this matter Mother and myself are the best judges."

"I tell you I will not marry him," I said.

Robin had not taken part in the conversation. He sat a little apart, but now he rose and stood beside me.

"I told you, Jo, it would be little use to drive Honor if she had not the inclination," he said. "Give her time to accustom herself to the project, and she will think better of it."

"Edward Champernowne might think better of it too," replied Jo.

"It were best to settle it now while he is here," said my mother.

I looked at their worried, indecisive faces—for they all loved me well and were distressed at my obduracy. "No," I told them, "I would sooner die," and I flounced from the room in feverish anger, and, going to my chamber, thrust the bolt across the door. To my imagination, strained and overwrought, it seemed to me that my brother and my mother had become the wicked parents in a fairy tale, and I the luckless princess whom they were bent on wedding to an ogre, though I believe the inoffensive Edward Champernowne would not have dared lay a finger upon me. I waited till the whole brood of them were abed, and then, changing my gown and wrapping a cloak about me, I stole from the house. For I was bent upon a harebrained scheme, which was no less than walking through the night to Killigarth, and so to Richard. The thunder had passed and the night was clear enough, and I set off with beating heart down the roadway to the river, which I forded a mile or so below Lanrest. Then I struck westward on the road to Pelynt, but the way was rough, and crossed with intersecting lanes, and my mind misgave me for the fool I was, for, without star-lore, I had no knowledge of direction. I was ill-used to walking any distance, and my shoes were thin. The night seemed endless and the road interminable, and the sounds and murmurs of the countryside filled me with apprehension, though I pretended to myself I did not care. Dawn found me stranded by another stream, and encompassed about by woods, and, weary and bedraggled, I climbed a further hill and saw at last my first glimpse of the sea, and the hump of Looe Island away to the eastward.

I knew then that some inner sense had led me to the coast, and I was not walking north, as I had feared, but the curl of smoke through the trees and the sound of barking dogs warned me that I was trespassing, and I had no wish to be caught by keepers.

About six o'clock I met a ploughman tramping along the highway, who stared at me amazed and took me for a witch, for I saw him cross his fingers and spit when I had passed, but he pointed out the lane that led to Killigarth. The sun was high now above the sea, and the fishing vessels strung out in a line in Talland Bay. I saw the tall chimneys of the house of Killigarth, and once again my heart misgave me for the sorry figure I should make before Richard. If he was there alone, it would not matter, but what if Bevil was at home, and Grace, his wife, and a whole tribe of Grenviles that I did not know? I came to the house then like a thief, and stood before the windows uncertain what to do. It wore the brisk air of early morning. Servants were astir. I heard a clatter in the kitchens, and the murmur of voices. Windows were open to the sun, and the sound of laughter came, and men talking.

I wished with all my heart that I was back in my bed-chamber in Lanrest, but there was no returning. I pulled the bell, and heard the clanging echo through the house. Then I drew back, as a servant came into the hall. He wore the Grenvile livery, and had a stern, forbidding air. "What do you want?" he asked of me.

"I wish to see Sir Richard," I said.

"Sir Richard and the rest of the gentlemen are at breakfast," he answered. "Away with you now—he won't be troubled with you." The door of the dining-room was open, and I heard more sound of talk and laughter, and Richard's voice topping the rest.

"I must see Sir Richard," I insisted, desperate now and near to tears, and then, as the fellow was about to lay his hands upon me and thrust me from the door, Richard himself came out into the hall. He was laughing, calling something over his shoulder to the gentlemen within.

"Richard," I called. "Richard, it is I, Honor," and he came forward, amazement on his face. "What the devil—" he began. Then, cursing his servant to be gone, he drew me into a little ante-room beside the hall.

"What is it? What is the matter?" he said swiftly, and I, weak and utterly worn out, fell into his arms and wept upon his shoulder.

"Softly, my little love. Be easy then," he murmured, and held me close and stroked my hair, until I was calm enough to tell my story. "They want to marry me to Edward Champernowne," I stammered—how foolish it sounded to be blurted thus—"and I have told them I will not do so, and I have wandered all night on the roads to tell you of it."

I felt him shake with laughter as he had done that first evening weeks ago when I had sickened of the swan.

"Is that all?" he asked. "And did you tramp twelve miles or more to tell me that? Oh, Honor, my little love, my dear."

I looked up at him, bewildered that he found so serious a matter food for laughter. "What am I to do then?" I said.

"Why, tell them to go to the devil, of course," he answered; "and if you dare not say it, then I will say it for you. Come in to breakfast." I tugged at his hand in consternation, for if the ploughman had taken me for a witch, and the servant for a beggar, God only knew what his friends would say to me. He would not listen to my protests, but dragged me in to the dining-room where the gentlemen were breakfasting, and there was I with my bedraggled gown and cloak and my torn slippers, faced with Ranald Mohun, and young Trelawney, Tom Treffry, and Jonathan Rashleigh, and some half-dozen others that I did not know. "This is Honor Harris of Lanrest," said Richard. "I think you gentlemen are possibly acquainted with her." They one and all stood up and bowed to me, astonishment and embarrassment written plain upon their faces. "She has run away from home," said Richard, in no way put out by the situation. "Would you credit it, Tom, they want to marry her to Edward Champernowne?"

"Indeed," replied Tom Treffry, quite at a loss, and he bent to stroke his dog's ear to hide his confusion.

"Will you have some bacon, Honor?" said Richard, proffering me a platter heaped with fatty pork, but I was too tired and faint to desire anything more than be taken upstairs and put to rest.

Then Jonathan Rashleigh, a man of family and older than Richard and the others, said quietly: "Mistress Honor would prefer to withdraw, I fancy. I would summon one of your serving-women, Richard."

"Damn it, this is a bachelor household," answered Richard, his mouth crammed with bacon. "There isn't a woman in the place."

I heard a snort from Ranald Mohun, who put a handkerchief to his face, and I saw also the baleful eye that Richard cast upon him, and then somehow they one and all made their excuses, and got themselves from the room, and we were alone at last.

"I was a fool to come," I said. "Now I have disgraced you before all your friends."

"I was disgraced long since," he said, pulling himself another tankard of ale; "but it was well you came after breakfast rather than before."

"Why so?" I asked.

He smiled, and drew a document from his breast.

"I have sold Killigarth, and also the lands I hold in Tywardreath," he answered. "Rashleigh gave me a fair price for them. Had you blundered in sooner he might have stayed his hand."

"Will the money pay your debts?" I said.

He laughed derisively. "A drop in the ocean," he said; "but it will suffice for a week or so, until we can borrow elsewhere."

"Why 'we'?" I enquired.

"Well, we shall be together," he answered. "You do not think I am going to permit this ridiculous match with Edward Champernowne?" He wiped his mouth, and pushed aside his plate, as though he had not a care in the world. He held out his arms to me, and I went to him. "Dear love," I said, feeling in sudden very old and very wise, "you have told me often that you must marry an heiress, or you could not live."

"I should have no wish to live if you were wedded to another man," he answered. Some little time was wasted while he assured me of this.

"But, Richard," I said presently, "if I wed you instead of Edward Champernowne, my brother may refuse his sanction."

"I'll fight him if he does."

"We shall be penniless," I protested.

"Not if I know it," he said. "I have several relatives as yet unfleeced. Mrs Abbot, my old Aunt Katherine up at Hartland, she has a thousand pounds or so she does not want."

"But we cannot live thus all our lives," I said.

"I have never lived anyway else," he answered.

I thought of the formalities and deeds that went with marriage, the lawyers and the documents.

"I am the youngest daughter, Richard," I said, hesitating. "You must bear in mind that my portion will be very small."

At this he shouted with laughter, and, lifting me in his arms, carried me from the room. "It's your person I have designs upon," he said. "God damn your portion."

CHAPTER FIVE

OH, WILD BETROTHAL, startling and swift, decided on in an instant without rhyme or reason, and all objections swept aside like a forest in a fire. My mother was helpless before the onslaught, my brothers powerless to obstruct. The Champernownes, offended, withdrew to Radford, and Jo, washing his hands of me, went with them. His wife would not receive me now, since I had refused her brother, and I was led to understand that the scandal of my conduct had spread through the whole of Devon. All the West, it seemed, said I had eloped with Richard Grenvile and was to wed him now through dire necessity. He had shamed me in a room at Plymouth—he had carried me by force to Killigarth—I had lived there as his mistress for three months—all these and other tales were spread abroad, and Richard and I, in the gladness of our hearts, did nought but laugh at them. At this moment of folly his brother Bevil came riding to Lanrest, and, with his usual grace and courtesy, insisted that I should go to Stowe and be married from the Grenvile home. Bevil brought law and order into chaos, his approval lent some shadow of decency to the whole proceeding—a quality which had been lacking hitherto; and within a few days of his taking charge my mother and I were safely housed at Stowe, where Kit had gone as a bridegroom nearly eight years before.

I was too much in love by then to care a whit for anyone, and, like someone who has feasted too wisely and too well, I swam through the great rooms at Stowe a-glow with confidence, smiling at old Sir Bernard, bowing to all his kinsmen, in no more awe of the grandeur about me than I had been of the familiar, dusty corners in Lanrest. I have small recollection now of what I did, or whom I saw—save that there were Grenviles everywhere and all of them auburn-haired, as Bridget had once told me—but I remember standing for hours in a chamber—that of the Lady Grace, Bevil's wife—while her women pinned my wedding-gown upon me, and gathered it, and tuckered it, and pinned it yet again, while she and my mother gave advice, and a heap of children, as it seemed to me, played about the floor.

Richard was not much with me. I belonged to the women, he said, during these last days. We would have enough of one another by and by. These last days—what a world of prophecy.

Nothing, then, remains out of the fog of recollection but that final afternoon in May, and the sun that came and went behind the clouds, and a high wind blowing. I can see now the guests assembled on the lawns, and how we all proceeded to the falconry, for an afternoon of sport was to precede a banquet in the evening.

The falconers came to leash and jess the hawks, and hood them ready for the chase, and as they did this the stable men brought the horses for us, and the dogs who were to flush the game yelped and pranced about their heels. Richard mounted me upon the little chestnut mare that was to be mine hereafter, and, as he turned to speak a moment to his falconer about the hooding of his bird, I looked over my shoulder and saw a conclave of horsemen gathered about the gate to welcome a new arrival. "What now?" said Richard, and the falconer, shading his eyes from the sun, turned to his master with a smile.

"It is Mrs Denys," he said, "from Orley Court. Now you can match your red hawk with her tiercel."

Richard looked up at me and smiled.

"So it has happened after all," he said, "and Gartred has chosen to visit us." They were riding down the path towards us, and I wondered how she would seem to me, my childhood enemy, to whom, in so strange a fashion, I was to be related once again. No word had come from her, no message of congratulation, but her natural curiosity had won her in the end. "Greetings, sister," called Richard, the old sardonic mockery in his voice. "So you have come to dance at my wedding after all."

"Perhaps," she answered. "I have not yet decided. Two of the children are not well at home." She rode abreast of me, that slow smile that I remembered on her face. "How are you, Honor?"

"Well enough," I answered.

"I never thought to see you become a Grenvile."

"Nor I either."

"The ways of Providence are strange indeed. You have not met my husband." I bowed to the stranger at her side, a big, bluff, hearty man, a good deal older than herself. So this was the Antony Denys, who had caused poor Kit so much anguish before he died. Maybe it was his weight that had won her. "Where do we ride?" she asked, turning from me to Richard.

"In the open country, towards the shore," he answered.

She glanced at the falcon on his wrist. "A red hawk," she said, one eyebrow lifted, "not in her full plumage. Do you think to make anything of her?"

"She has taken kite and bustard, and I propose to put her to a heron to-day if we can flush one."

Gartred smiled. "A red hawk at a heron," she mocked. "You will see her check at a magpie and nothing larger."

"Will you match her with your tiercel?"

"My tiercel will destroy her, and the heron afterwards."

"That is a matter of opinion."

They watched each other like duellists about to strike, and I remembered how Richard had told me they had fought with one another from the cradle. I had my first shadow of misgiving that the day would turn in some way to disaster. For a moment I wondered whether I would plead fatigue and stay behind. I rode for pleasure, not for slaughter, and hawking was never my favourite pastime.

Gartred must have observed my hesitation, for she laughed and said: "Your bride loses her courage. The pace will be too strong for her."

"What?" said Richard, his face falling. "You are coming, aren't you?"

"Why, yes," I said swiftly. "I will see you kill your heron."

We rode out to the open country, with the wind blowing in our faces and the sound of the Atlantic coming to us as the long surf rollers spilt themselves with a roar on to the shore far below. At first the sport was poor, for no quarry larger than a woodcock was flushed. Richard's falcon and Gartred's tiercel were still hooded, and not slipped, for we were not yet come upon the heron's feeding ground. My little mare pawed restlessly at the ground, for up to the present we had had no run and the pace was slow. Near a little copse the falconers flushed three magpies and a cast of goshawks were flown at them, but the magpies, making up for lack of wing power by cunning, scuttled from hedge to hedge, and after some twenty minutes or so of hovering by the hawks, and shouting and driving by the falconers, only one was taken.

"Come. This is poor indeed," said Gartred scornfully. "Can we find no better quarry, and so let fly the falcons?"

Richard shaded his eyes from the sun, and looked towards the west. A long strip of moorland lay before us, rough and uneven, and at the far end of it a narrow, soggy marsh, where the duck would fly to feed in stormy weather, and at all seasons of the year, so Richard told me, the sea-birds came, curlews, and gulls, and herons.

"I'll match my horse to yours, and my red hawk to your tiercel," said Richard suddenly, and even as he spoke he let fly the hood of his falcon and slipped her, putting spurs to his horse upon the gesture. Within ten seconds Gartred had followed suit, her grey-winged peregrine soaring into the sun, and she and Richard were galloping across the moors towards the marsh, with the two hawks like black specks in the sky above them. My mare, excited by the clattering hooves of her companions, took charge of me, nearly pulling my arms out of their sockets, and she raced like a mad thing in pursuit of the horses ahead of us, the yelping of the dogs and the cries of the falconers whipping her speed. My last ride. The sun in my eyes, the wind in my face, the movement of the mare beneath me, the thunder of her hooves, the scent of the golden gorse, the sound of the sea. Unforgettable, unforgotten, deep in my soul for all time. I could see Richard and Gartred racing neck to neck, and in the sky the male and female falcons pitched and hovered. When suddenly away from the marsh ahead of us rose a heron, his great grey wings unfolding, his legs trailing. I heard a shout from Richard, and an answering cry from Gartred, and in an instant it seemed the hawks had seen their quarry, for they both began to circle above the heron, climbing higher and still higher, swinging out in rings until they were like black dots against the sun. The watchful heron, rising too, but in a narrower circle, turned down wind, his queer, ungainly body strangely light and supple, and like a flash the first hawk dived to him—whether it was Richard's young falcon or Gartred's tiercel I could not tell—and missed the heron by a hair's breadth. At once, recovering himself, he began to soar again, in ever higher circles, to recover his lost pitch, and the second hawk swooped, missing in like manner.

I tried to rein in my mare, but could not stop her, and now Gartred and Richard had turned eastward too, following the course of the heron, and we were galloping three abreast, the ground rising steadily towards a circle of stones in the midst of the moor.

"Beware the chasm," shouted Richard in my ear, pointing with his whip, but he was past me like the wind and I could not call to him.

The heron was now direct above my head, and the falcons lost to view, and I heard Gartred shout in triumph: "They bind—they bind—my tiercel has her," and, silhouetted against the sun, I saw one of the falcons locked against the heron and the two come swinging down to earth not twenty yards ahead.

I tried to swerve, but the mare had the mastery, and I shouted to Gartred as she passed me, "Which way is the chasm?" but she did not answer me. On we flew towards the circle of stones, the sun blinding my eyes, and out of the darkening sky fell the dying heron and the blood-bespattered falcon, straight into the yawning crevice that opened out before me. I heard Richard shout, and a thousand voices singing in my ears as I fell.

It was thus, then, that I, Honor Harris of Lanrest, became a cripple, losing all power in my legs from that day forward until this day on which I write, so that for some twenty-five years now I have been upon my back, or upright in a chair, never walking any more, or feeling the ground beneath my feet. If anyone therefore thinks that a cripple makes an indifferent heroine to a tale, now is the time to close these pages and desist from reading. For you will never see me wed to the man I love, nor become the mother of his children. But you will learn how that love never faltered, for all its strange vicissitudes, becoming to both of us, in later years, more deep and tender than if we had been wed, and you will learn also how, for all my helplessness, I took the leading part in the drama that unfolded, my very immobility sharpening my senses and quickening my perception, while chance itself forced me to my role of judge and witness. The play goes on, then—what you have just read is but the prologue.

CHAPTER SIX

IT IS NOT my purpose to survey, in these after-years, the suffering, bodily and mental, that I underwent during those early months when my life seemed finished. They would make poor reading. And I myself have no inclination to drag from the depths of my being a bitterness that is best forgotten. It is enough to say that they feared at first for my brain, and I lived for many weeks in a state of darkness. As little by little clarity returned, and I was able to understand the full significance of my physical state, I asked for Richard; and I learnt that, after having waited in vain for some sign from me, some thread of hope from the doctors that I might recover, he had been persuaded by his brother Bevil to rejoin his regiment. This was for the best. It was impossible for him to remain inactive. The assassination at Portsmouth of his friend the Duke of Buckingham was an added horror, and he set sail for France with the rest of the expedition in that final half-hearted attack on La Rochelle. By the time he returned I had sufficient strength of will to make my decision for the future. This was never to see Richard again. I wrote him a letter, which he disregarded, riding down from London express to see me. I would not see him. He endeavoured to force his way into my room, but my brothers barred the way. It was only when the doctors told him that his presence could but injure me further that he realised the finality of all bonds between us. He rode away without a word. I received from him one last letter, wild, bitter, reproachful—then silence.

In November of that year he married Lady Howard of Fitzford, a rich widow, three times wed already, and four years older than himself. The news came to me indirectly, an incautious word let slip from Matty and at once confusedly covered, and I asked my mother the truth. She had wished to hide it from me, fearing a relapse, and I think my calm acceptance of the fact baffled her understanding.

It was hard for her, and for the rest of them, to realise that I looked upon myself now as a different being. The Honor that was had died as surely as the heron that afternoon in May, when the falcon slew him. That she would live for ever in her lover's heart was possible, no doubt, and a lovely fantasy, but the Richard that I knew and loved was made of flesh and blood; he had to endure, even as I had.

I remember smiling, as I lay upon my bed, to think that after all he had found his heiress, and such a notorious one at that. I only hoped that her experience would make him happy, and her wealth insure him some security.

Meanwhile, I had to school myself to a new way of living, and day after day of immobility. The mind must atone for the body's helplessness. Percy returned from Oxford about this time, bringing his books of learning, and with his aid I set myself the task of learning Greek and Latin. He made an indifferent though a kindly tutor, and I had not the heart to keep him long from his dogs and his horses, but at least he set me on the road to reading, and I made good progress. The family were all most good and tender. My sisters and their children, tearful and strung with pity as they were at first, soon became easy in my presence, when I laughed and chatted with them, and little by little I—the hitherto spoilt darling—became the guide and mediator in their affairs, and their problems would be brought to me to solve. I am speaking now of years, and not of months, for all this did not happen in a day.

Matty, my little maid, became from the first moment my untiring slave and bondswoman. It was she who learnt to read the signs of fatigue about my eyes, and hustled my visitors from the room. It was she who attended to my wants, to my feeding and my washing, though after some little while I learnt to do this for myself; and after three years, I think it was, my back had so far strengthened that I was able to sit upright and move my body. I was helpless, though, in my legs, and during the autumn and the winter months, when the damp settled in the walls of the house, I would feel it also in my bones. It caused me great pain at times, and then I would be hard put to it to keep to the standard of behaviour I had set myself. Self-pity, that most insidious of poisons, would filter into my veins, and the black devils fill my mind, and then it was that Matty would stand like a sentinel at the door and bar the way to all intruders. Poor Matty, I cursed her often enough when the dark moods had me in thrall, but she bore with me unflinchingly. It was Robin, my dear good Robin and most constant companion, who first had the thought of making me my chair, and this chair, that was to propel me from room to room, became his pet invention. He took some months in the designing of it, and when it was built, and I was carried to it, and could sit up straight and move the rolling wheels without assistance, his joy I think was even greater than my own.

It made all the difference to my daily life, and in the summer I could even venture to the garden, and propel myself a little distance, up and down before the house, winning some measure of independence. In '32 we had another wedding in the family. My sister Mary, whom we had long teased for her devoutness and sober, gentle ways, accepted the offer of Jonathan Rashleigh of Menabilly, who had lost his first wife in child-bed the year before, and was left with a growing family upon his hands. It was a most suitable match in all respects, Jonathan being then some forty years of age and Mary thirty-two. She was married from Lanrest, and to the wedding, with their father, came his three children, Alice, Elizabeth and John. Later I was to come to know them well, but even now—as shy and diffident children—they won my affection. To the wedding also came Bevil Grenvile, a close friend to Jonathan as he was to all of us, and it was when the celebrating was over, and Mary departed to her new home the other side of Fowey, that I had a chance to speak with him alone. We spoke for a few moments about his own children, and his life at Stowe, and then

I asked him, not without some tremulation, for all my calm assurance, how Richard did.

For a moment he did not answer, and, glancing at him, I saw his brow was troubled. "I had not wished to speak of it," he said at length, "but since you ask me . . . all has gone very ill with him, Honor, ever since his marriage." Some devil of satisfaction rose in my breast, which I could not crush, and "How so?" I asked. "Has he not a son?" For I had heard that a boy was born to them a year or so before, on May 16th to be exact—the same date, ironically enough, as that on which I had been crippled. A new life for the one that is wasted, I had thought at the time, when I was told of it, and, like a spoilt child that had learnt no wisdom after all, I remember crying all night upon my pillow, thinking of the boy who, but for mischance and the workings of destiny, might have been mine. That was a day, if I recollect aright, when Matty kept guard at my door, and I made picture after picture in my mind of Richard's wife propped upon pillows and a baby in her arms, and Richard smiling beside her. The fantasy was one which, for all my disciplined indifference, I found most damnable. But to return to Bevil.

"Yes," he answered. "It is true he has a son, and a daughter too, but whether Richard sees them or not I cannot say. The truth is that he has quarrelled with his wife and treated her in barbarous fashion—even laid violent hands upon her, so she says—and she is now petitioning for a divorce against him. Furtheremore, he slandered the Earl of Suffolk, his wife's kinsman, who brought an action against him in the Star Chamber and won the case, and Richard, refusing to pay the fine—and in truth he could not, possessing not a penny—is likely to be cast into the Fleet prison for debt at any moment." Oh, God, I thought, what a contrast to the life we would have made together. Or was I wrong, and was this symbolic of what might have been? "He was always violent, even as a lad," continued Bevil. "You knew so little of him, Honor; alas! three months of happy wooing is no time in which to judge a man."

I could not answer this, for reason was on his side. But I thought of the spring days, lost to me for ever, and the apple blossom in the orchard. No maid could have had more tender or more intuitive a lover. "How was Richard violent?" I asked. "Irresponsible and wild, perhaps, but nothing worse. His wife must have provoked him."

"As to that, I know nothing," answered Bevil, "but I can well believe it. She is a woman of some malice, and of doubtful morals. She was a close friend to Gartred—perhaps you did not know that—and it was when she was visiting at Orley Court that the match was made between them. Richard—as no one knows better than yourself—could not have been his best self at that time." I said nothing, feeling, behind Bevil's gentle manner, some faint reproach, unconscious though it was. "The truth is," said Bevil, "that Richard married Mary Howard for her money, but once wed found he had no control over her purse or her property, the whole being in the power of trustees who act solely in her interest."

"Then he is no whit better off than he was before?" I asked.

"Rather worse, if anything," replied Bevil, "for the Star Chamber will not release him from his debt for slander, and I have too many claims upon me at this time to help him either."

It was a sorry picture that he painted, and, though to my jealous fancy it was preferable to the idyllic scene of family bliss that I had in imagination conjured, it was no consolation to learn of his distress. That Richard should ill use his wife because he could not trifle with her property was an ugly fact to face, but, having some inkling of his worse self, I guessed this to be true. He had married her without love, and in much bitterness of heart, and she, suspecting his motive, had taken care to disappoint him. I held to my resolve, though, and sent him no word of sympathy or understanding. Nor was it my own pride and self-pity that kept me from it, but a firm belief that such a course was wisest. He must lead his own life, in which I had no further part.

He remained, we heard later, for many months in prison, and then in the autumn of the following year he left England for the continent, where he saw service with the King of Sweden.

How much I thought of him, and yearned for him, during those intervening years does not matter to this story. I was weakest during the long watches of the night, when my body pained me. During the day I drilled my feelings to obedience, and what with my progress in my studies—I was by way of becoming a fair Greek scholar—and my interest in the lives of my brothers and sisters, the days and the seasons passed with some fair measure of content.

Time heals all wounds, say the complacent, but I think it is not so much time that does it as determination of the spirit. And the spirit can often turn to devil in the darkness. Five, ten, fifteen years; a large slice out of a woman's life, and a man's too, for that matter. I was a maid, and a rebellious, disorderly one at that, when I was first crippled; but in the year of '42, when the war that was to alter all our lives broke forth, I was a woman of some two and thirty years, the "good Aunt Honor" to my numerous nephews and nieces, and a figure of some importance to the family at large.

A person who is for ever chair-bound or bed-ridden can become a tyrant if she so desires, and, though I never sought to play the despot, I came to be, after my mother died, the one who made decisions, whose authority was asked for on all occasions, and in some strange fashion it seemed that a legendary quality was woven about my personality, as though my physical helplessness must give me greater wisdom.

I accepted the homage with my tongue in my cheek, but was careful not to destroy the fond illusion. The young people liked me, I think, because they knew me to be a rebel still, and when there was strife within the family I was sure to take their part. Cynical on the surface, I was an incurable romantic underneath, and if there were messages to be given, or meetings to arrange, or secrets to be whispered, my chamber at Lanrest would become trysting-place, rendezvous, and confessional in turn. Mary's stepchildren, the Rashleighs, were my constant visitors, and I found myself involved in many a youthful squabble, defending their escapades with a ready tongue, and soon acting as go-between to their love affairs. Jonathan, my brother-in-law, was a good, just man, but stern; a firm believer in the settled marriage as against the impulsive prompting of the heart. No doubt he was right, but there was something distasteful to my mind in the bargaining between parents and the counting of every farthing, so that when Alice, his eldest daughter, turned thin and pale for languishing after that young rake, Peter Courtney—the parents disputing for months whether they should wed or no—I had them both to Lanrest and bade them be happy while the chance was theirs, and no one was a whit the wiser.

They married in due course, and although it ended in a separation (for this I blame the war), at least they had some early happiness together, for which I hold myself responsible.

My godchild Joan was another of my victims. She was, it may be remembered, the child of my sister Cecilia, and some ten years my junior. When John Rashleigh, Mary's stepson, came down from Oxford to visit us, he found Joan at my bedside, and I soon guessed which way the wind was blowing. I had half a thought of sending them to the apple-tree, but some inner sentimentality forbade me, and I suggested the bluebell wood instead. They were betrothed within a week, and married before the bluebells had faded, and not even Jonathan Rashleigh could find fault with the marriage settlement.

But the war years were upon us before we were aware, and Jonathan, like all the county gentlemen, my brothers included, had more anxious problems before him. Trouble had been brewing for a long while now, and we in Cornwall were much divided in opinion, some holding that His Majesty was justified in passing what laws he pleased (though one and all grumbled at the taxes) and others holding to it that Parliament was right in opposing any measure that smacked of despotism. My brothers held firmly for the King, and Jo was already in a position of authority, for his business was to superintend the defences of the coast—and as the months passed tempers became shorter and friendships grew colder, an unpleasing spirit of distrust walking abroad. Civil war was talked of openly, and each gentleman in the county began to look to his weapons, his servants, and his horses, so that he could make some contribution to the cause he favoured when the moment came. The women too were not idle, many—like Cecilia at Mothercombe—tearing strips of bed-linen into bandages, and packing their store-rooms with preserves for fear of siege. Arguments were fiercer then, I do believe, than later when the fighting was amongst us. Friends who had supped with us the week before became of a sudden suspect, and long-forgotten scandals were brought forth to blacken their names, merely because of the present opposition of their views.

The whole business made me sick at heart, and this whipping up of tempers between neighbours who for generations had lived at peace seemed a policy of the devil. I hated to hear Robin, my dearly loved brother, with his tenderness for dogs and horses, slander Dick Buller for upholding Parliament, vowing he took bribes and made spies of his own servants, when Dick and he had gone hawking together not six months before. While Rob Bennett, another of our neighbours and a friend of Buller's, began to spread damning rumours in return about my brother-in-law Jonathan Rashleigh, saying that Jonathan's father and elder brother, who had died very suddenly within a week of one another many years before, during the smallpox scourge, had not succumbed to the disease at all, but had been poisoned. These tales showed how in a few months we had changed from neighbours into wolves at one another's throats.

At the first open rupture between His Majesty and Parliament in '42 my brothers Jo and Robin, and most of our closest friends, including Jonathan Rashleigh, his son-in-law, Peter Courtney, the Trelawneys, the Arundells, and, of course, Bevil Grenvile, declared for the King. There was an end at once to family life and any settled way of living. Robin went off to York to join His Majesty's army, taking Peter Courtney with him, and almost immediately they were both given command of a company. Peter, showing much dash and courage in his first action, was knighted on the field.

My brother Jo and my brother-in-law Jonathan went about the county raising money, troops and ammunition for the royal cause. The first was no easy matter, for Cornwall was a poor county at the best of times and lately the taxes had well-nigh broken us; but many families, with little ready money to spare, gave their plate to be melted down to silver, a loyal if wasteful gesture. My attitude to the war was somewhat cynical, for, holding no belief in great causes, and living alone now at Lanrest with only Matty and the servants to tend me, I felt myself curiously detached. The successes of the first year did not go to my head, as they did to the rest of my family, for I could not believe, as they were inclined to, that Parliament would give way so easily. For the Parliamentarians had many powerful men at their command, and much money—all the rich merchants of London were strongly in their favour— besides which I had an uneasy suspicion, which I kept to myself, that their army was incomparably the better of the two. God knows our leaders wanted nothing in courage, but they lacked experience. Equipment, too, was poor, and discipline non-existent in the ranks.

By the autumn the war was getting rather too close for comfort, and the two armies were ranged east and west along the Tamar. I had an uneasy Christmas, and in the third week of January I learnt that the worst had happened, and the enemy had crossed the Tamar into Cornwall. I was at breakfast when the news was brought us, and by none other than Peter Courtney, who had ridden hot-foot from Bodmin to warn me that the opposing army was even now on the road to Liskeard. He, with his regiment, which was under the command of Sir Ralph Hopton, was drawn up to oppose them, and Hopton was at the moment holding a council of war at Boconnoc, only a few miles distant. "With any luck," he told us, "the fighting will not touch you, here at Lanrest, but will be between Liskeard and Lostwithiel. If we can break them now and drive them out of Cornwall the war will be as good as won."

He looked handsome, flushed and excited, his dark curls falling about his face. "I have no time to go to Menabilly," he told me. "Should I fall in battle, will you tell Alice that I love her well?"

He was gone like a flash, and I and Matty, with the two elderly manservants and three lads—all that were left to us—were alone, unarmed and unprepared. There was nothing to do but to get the cattle and the sheep in from pasture and secure them in the farmstead, and bolt and bar ourselves within the house. Then we waited, all gathered round the fireside in my chamber upstairs. Once or twice, opening the casement, we thought we heard the sound of cannon shot, dull and intermittent, strangely distant in the cold clear air of January. Somewhere about three in the afternoon one of the farm lads came running to the house and hammered loud upon the entrance door. "The enemy are routed," he called excitedly, "the whole pack of them scattering like whipped dogs along the road to Liskeard. There's been a great battle fought to-day on Braddock Down." More stragglers appeared who had taken refuge in the hedges, and one and all told the same story, that the King's men had won a victory, fighting like furies, and taking nearly a thousand prisoners.

Knowing that rumour was a lying jade, I bade the household bide awhile, and keep the doors fast until the story should be proved, but before nightfall we knew the victory was certain, for Robin himself came riding home to cheer us, covered in dust, with a bloodstained bandage on his arm, and with him the Trelawney brothers and Ranald Mohun. They were all of them laughing and triumphant, for the two Parliament divisions had fled in dire disorder straight for Saltash, and would never, said Jack Trelawney, show their faces more this side the Tamar. "And this fellow," he said, clapping Robin on the shoulder, "rode into battle with a hawk on his wrist, which he let fly at Ruthin's musketeers, and, by God, the bird so startled them that the lot of them shot wide, and started taking to their legs before they'd spent their powder."

"It was a wager I had with Peter," smiled Robin; "and if I lost the forfeit was my spurs, and that I should be godfather to his next baby."

They rocked with laughter, caring not a whit for the spilt blood and the torn bodies they had trampled, and then sat down, all of them, and drank great jugs of ale, wiping the sweat from their foreheads and discussing every move of the battle they had won like gamesters after a cock-fight.

Bevil Grenvile had been the hero of the day in this, his first engagement, and they described to us how he had led the Cornish foot down one hill and up another in so fierce a charge that the enemy could not withstand them.

"You should have seen him, Honor," said Robin, "with his servants and his tenants drawn up in solemn prayer before him, his sword in his hand, his dear honest face lifted to the sky. They were all clad in the blue and silver livery, as if it were high holiday. And down the hill they followed him, shouting 'A Grenvile! A Grenvile!' with his servant Tony Paine waving his crimson standard with the three gold rests upon it. My God, I tell you, it made me proud to be a Cornishman."

"It's in his blood," said Jack Trelawney. "Here's Bevil been a country squire for all his life, and you put a weapon in his hand and he turns tiger. The Grenviles are all alike at heart."

"I wish to heaven," said Ranald Mohun, "that Richard Grenvile would return from slaughtering the savages in Ireland and come and join his brother." There was a moment's awkward silence, while some of them remembered the past and recollected my presence in the room, and then Robin rose to his feet and said they must be riding back to Liskeard. Thus, in south-east Cornwall, war touched us for a brief space in '43 and so departed, and many of us who had not even smelt the battle talked very big of what we

had heard and seen, while those who had taken part in it, like Robin, boasted
that the summer would see the rebels in Parliament laying down their arms for
ever.

Alas! his optimism was foolish and ill-judged. Victories we had indeed that
year, throughout the west as far as Bristol, with our own Cornishmen covering
themselves with glory, but we lost, in that first summer, the flower of our
Cornish manhood.

Sydney Godolphin, Jack Trevannion, Nick Slanning, Nick Kendal, one by
one their faces come back to me as I review the past, and I remember the
sinking feeling in the heart with which I would take up the list of the fallen that
would be brought to me from Liskeard. All of them were men of noble conduct
and high principle, whom we could ill spare in the county, and whose loss
would make its mark upon the army. The worst tragedy of the year, or so it
seemed to us, was when Bevil Grenvile was slain at Lansdowne. Matty came
running to my chamber with the tears falling down her cheeks. "They've killed
Sir Bevil," she said. Bevil, with his grace and courtesy, his sympathy and
charm, who was worth all the other Cornish leaders put together. I felt it as if he
had been my own brother, but I was too stunned to weep for him. "They say,"
said Matty, "that he was struck down by a pole-axe, just as he and his men had
won the day and the enemy were scattering. And big Tony Paine, his servant,
mounted young Master Jack upon his father's horse, and the men followed the
lad, all of them fighting mad with rage and grief to see their master slain."

Yes, I could picture it. Bevil killed on an instant, his head split in two by
some damned useless rebel, while his boy Jack, barely fourteen, climbed on to
Bevil's white charger that I knew so well, and with the tears smarting his eyes
brandished a sword that was too big for him. And the men, with the blue and
silver colours, following him down the hill, their hearts black with hatred for
the enemy. Oh, God, the Grenviles, there was some quality in the race, some
white, undaunted spirit bred in their bones and surging through their blood
that put them, as Cornishmen and leaders, way ahead above the rest of us.

So, outwardly triumphant and inwardly bleeding, we Royalists watched the
year draw to its close, and 1644—that fateful year for Cornwall—opened with
His Majesty master of the west, but the large and powerful forces of the
Parliament in great strength elsewhere, and still unbeaten.

In the spring of the year a soldier of fortune, returning from Ireland, rode to
London to receive payment for his services. He gave the gentlemen in
Parliament to understand that in return for this he would join forces with them,
and they, pleased to receive so doughty a warrior amongst their ranks, gave
him £600 and told him their plans for the spring campaign. He bowed and
smiled—a dangerous sign had they but known it—and straightway set forth in
a coach and six, with a host of troopers following him and a banner carried in
front of him. The banner was a great map of England and Wales on a crimson
ground, with the words "England Bleeding" written across it in letters of gold.
When this equipage arrived at Bagshot Heath, the leader of it descended from
his coach, and, calling his troopers about him, calmly suggested that they
should all now proceed to Oxford and fight for His Majesty, and not against

him. The troopers, nothing loath, accepted, and the train proceeded on its way to Oxford, bearing with it a quantity of money, arms, and silver plate, bequeathed by Parliament, and all the minutes of the secret council that had just been held in London.

The name of this soldier of fortune who had hoodwinked the Parliament in so scurrilous a fashion was Richard Grenvile.

CHAPTER SEVEN

ONE DAY TOWARDS the end of April, Robin came over from Radford to see me, urging me to leave Lanrest and to take up residence, for a time at any rate, with our sister Mary Rashleigh at Menabilly. Robin was at that time commanding a regiment of foot, for he had been promoted colonel under Sir John Digby, and was taking part in the long-drawn-out siege of Plymouth, which alone among the cities in the west still held out for Parliament.

"Jo and I are both agreed," said Robin, "that while the war continues you should not continue to live here alone. It is not fit for any woman, let alone one as helpless as yourself. Deserters and stragglers are constantly abroad, robbing on the highway, and the thought of you here, with a few old men and Matty, is a constant disturbance to our peace of mind."

"There is nothing here to rob," I protested, "with the plate gone to the Mint at Truro; and as to harm to my person—a crippled woman can give little satisfaction."

"That is not the point," said Robin. "It is impossible for Jo and Percy and me to do our duty, remembering all the while that you are here alone."

He argued for half a day before I reluctantly gave way, and then with an ill-grace and much disturbance in my mind. For fifteen years—ever since I had been crippled—I had not left Lanrest, and to set forth now to another person's house, even though that person was my own sister, filled me with misgiving.

Menabilly was already packed with Rashleigh relatives, who had taken refuge with Jonathan, seizing the war as an excuse, and I had no wish to add to their number. I had a great dislike of strangers, or of conversing with anyone for the sake of courtesy; besides, I was set now in my ways, my days were my own, I followed a personal routine.

"You can live at Menabilly exactly as you do here at Lanrest," protested Robin, "save that you will be more comfortable. Matty will attend you, you will have your own apartment and your meals brought to you, if you do not wish to mix with the company. Set on the hill there, with the sea air blowing and the fine gardens for you to be wheeled about in, nothing could be more pleasant, to my opinion."

I disagreed, but, seeing his anxiety, I said no more; and within a week my few belongings were packed, the house was closed, and I was being carried in a litter to Menabilly.

How disturbing it was, and strange, to be on the road again. To pass through Lostwithiel, to see the people walking in the market-place—the normal daily life of a community from which I had been so long absent, living in my own world at Lanrest. I felt oddly nervous and ill at ease, as I peered through the curtains of my litter; as if I had been suddenly transplanted to a foreign land, where the language and the customs were unknown to me. My spirits rose as we climbed the long hill out of the town, and when we came abreast of the old redoubt at Castledore, and I saw the great blue bay of Tywardreath spread out before me, I thought that maybe after all the change of place and scene might yet be bearable. John Rashleigh came riding along the highway to meet me, waving his hat, a broad smile on his thin, colourless face. He was just twenty-three, and the tragedy of his life was that he had not the health or strength to join the army, but must bide at home and take orders from his father, for he had been cursed from babyhood with a malignant form of ague that kept him shivering and helpless sometimes for days on end. He was a dear, lovable fellow, with a strong sense of duty, yet in great awe of his father; and his wife—my god-daughter Joan—with her merry eyes and mischievous prattle, made him a good foil. Riding with him now was his companion and second cousin, Frank Penrose, a young man of the same age as himself, who was employed by my brother-in-law as secretary and junior agent about the estate.

"All is prepared for you, Honor," smiled John as he rode beside my litter. "There are over twenty of us in the house at present, and the lot of them have gathered in the courtyard to greet you. To-night a dinner is to be given for your reception."

"Very well, then," I answered. "You may tell these fellows to turn back again towards Lostwithiel."

At this he confessed that Joan had bade him tease me, and all the company were in the east wing of the house, and no one would worry me. "My stepmother has put you," he said, "in the gatehouse, for she says you like much light and air, and the chamber there has a window looking both ways, over the outer courtyard to the west, and on to the inner court that surrounds the house. Thus you will see all that goes on about the place, and have your own private peep-show."

"It sounds," I answered, "like a garrison, with twenty people crammed within the walls."

"Nearly fifty altogether, counting the servants," laughed John, "but they sleep head to toe up in the attics."

My spirits sank again, and as we turned down from the highway into the park, and I saw the great stone mansion at the end of it, flanked by high walls and outbuildings, I cursed myself for a fool for coming. We turned left into the outer court, surrounded by bakehouses and larders and dairies, and passing under the low archway of the gatehouse—my future dwelling—drew up within the inner court. The house was four-square, built around the court, with a big clock tower or belfry at the northern end, and the entrance to the south. On the steps stood Mary now to greet me, and Alice Courtney, her eldest step-daughter, and Joan, my godchild, both of them with their babies tugging at their skirts.

"Welcome, dearest Honor, to Menabilly," said Mary, her dear face puckered already in nervousness that I should hate it. "The place is full of children, Honor—you must not mind," smiled Alice, who since her marriage to Peter had produced a baby every year. "We are thinking out a plan to attach a rope of your own to the bell in the belfry," said Joan, "so that if the noise becomes too deafening you can pull it in warning, and the household will be silenced."

"I am already established, then, as a dragon," I replied, "which is all to the good, for I mean to do as I please, as Robin may have warned you." They carried me into the dark panelled hall, and, ignoring the long gallery which ran the whole length of the house, and from which I could hear the ominous sound of voices, bore me up the broad staircase and along a passage to the western wing. I was, I must confess, immediately delighted with my apartment, which, though low-ceilinged, was wide and full of light. There were windows at each end, as John had said—the western one looking down over the archway to the outer court and the park beyond, and the eastern one facing the inner court. There was a small room to the right for Matty, and nothing had been forgotten for my comfort.

"You will be bothered by no one," said Mary. "The apartments beyond the dressing-room belong to the Sawles—cousins of Jonathan's—who are very sober and retiring and will not worry you. The chamber to your left is never occupied."

They left me then, and with Matty's aid I undressed and got myself to bed, a good deal exhausted from my journey, and glad to be alone. The first few days passed in becoming accustomed to my new surroundings and settling down, like a hound to a change of kennel.

My chamber was very pleasant, and I had no wish to leave it; also, I liked the chiming of the clock in the belfry, and, once I had told myself firmly that the quiet of Lanrest must be forgotten, I came to listen to the comings and goings that were part of this big house, the bustle in the outer court, the footsteps passing under the arch below me, and even—though I would have denied the accusation—taking a peep from my curtains at the windows opposite that, like mine, looked down upon the inner court, and from which, now and again, people would lean, talking to others within. At intervals during the day the young people would come and converse with me, and I would get a picture of the other inmates of the house, the two families of Sawle and Sparke, cousins to the Rashleighs, between whom there was, it seemed, a perpetual bickering. There were the grandchildren, too, to keep in order—Alice had three small daughters and Joan a boy and girl, with another baby expected in the autumn—so in one way and another Menabilly was a colony to itself, with a different family in every wing.

By the fifth day I was sufficiently at home, and mistress of my nerves, to leave my chamber and take to my chair. With John propelling it, and Joan and Alice on either side, and the children running before, we made a tour of the domain. The gardens were extensive, surrounded by high walls, and laid out to the eastward on rising ground, which, when the summit was reached, looked down over dense woodland across to further hills and the highway that ran to Fowey, three miles distant. To the south lay pasture land and farm buildings and another pleasure garden, also walled, which had above it a high causeway leading to a summer-house, fashioned like a tower with long leaded windows, commanding a fine view of the sea and the Gribben Head.

"This," said Alice, "is my father's sanctum. Here he does his writing and accounts, and from the windows can observe every ship that passes, bound for Fowey." She tried the door to the summer-house, but it was locked. "We must ask him for the key when he returns," she said. "It would be just the place for Honor and her chair when the wind is too fresh upon the causeway." John did not answer, and it occurred to him perhaps, as it had to me, that his father might not want me for companion. We made a circle of the grounds, returning by the steward's house and the bowling-green, and so through the warren at the back to the outer court. I looked up at the gatehouse, already familiar with the vase of flowers set in my window, and noticed for the first time the barred window of the apartment next to mine, and the great buttress that jutted out beside it.

"Why is that apartment never used?" I asked idly. John waited a moment or two before replying. "My father goes to it at times," he said. "He has furniture and valuables shut away."

"It was my uncle's room," said Alice, hesitating, with a glance at John. "He died very suddenly, you know, when we were children."

Their manner was diffident, and I did not press the question, remembering all at once Jonathan's elder brother, who had died within eight days of his old father, supposedly of smallpox, and about whom the Parliamentarian Rob Bennett had spread his poison rumour.

We then went below the archway, and I schooled myself to an introduction to the Rashleigh cousins. They were all assembled in the long gallery, a great dark panelled chamber with windows looking out on to the court and eastward to the gardens. There were fireplaces at either end, with the Sawles seated before the first and the Sparkes circled round the other, glaring at one another like animals in a cage, while in the centre of the gallery my sister Mary held the balance with her other stepdaughter, Elizabeth, who was twice a Rashleigh, having married her first cousin a mile away at Combe. John propelled me up the gallery and with fitting solemnity presented me to the rival factions.

There were but two Sawles to three Sparkes, and my godchild Joan had made a pun upon their names, saying that what the Sparkes possessed in flame, the Sawles made up in soul. The latter were indeed a dour, forbidding couple, old Nick Sawle doubled up with rheumatics and almost as great a cripple as I was myself, while Temperance, his wife, came of Puritan stock, as her name suggested, and was never without a prayer-book in her hand. She fell to prayer as soon as she observed me—God knows I had never had that effect before on man or woman—and when she had finished asked me if I knew that we were all of us, saving herself, damned to eternity. It was a startling greeting, but I replied cheerfully enough that this was something I had long suspected, whereupon she proceeded to tell me in a rapid whisper, with many spiteful glances at the further fireplace, that Anti-Christ was come into the world. I looked over my shoulder and saw the rounded shoulders of Will Sparke, who was engaged in a harmless game of chequers with his sisters. "Providence has sent you among us to keep watch," hissed Temperance Sawle, and tore to shreds the characters of her cousins, piece by piece. Half-stupefied, I made a signal to John, who propelled me to the Sparkes—two sisters and a brother. Will was one of those unfortunate high-voiced old fellows with a woman's mincing ways, whom I felt instinctively must be malformed beneath his clothes. His tongue seemed as two-edged as that of his cousin Temperance, and he fell to jesting with me at once about the habits of the Sawles, as though I were an ally. Deborah made up in masculinity what her brother lacked, being heavily moustached and speaking from her shoes, while Gillian, the younger sister, was all coy prettiness in spite of her forty years, bedecked with rouge and ribbons, and with a high thin laugh that pierced my eardrum like a sword.

The air seemed purer somehow in the gatehouse than the gallery, and after I had visited the apartments of Alice and Joan and Elizabeth, and watched the romping of the children, and the kicking of the babies, I was thankful enough to retire to my own chamber and blissful solitude. Matty brought me my dinner—this being a privilege to which I clung—and was full of gossip, as was her nature, about the servants in the house and what they said of their masters. Jonathan, my brother-in-law, was respected, feared, but not much loved. They were all easier when he was from home. He kept an account of every penny spent, and any servant wasting food or produce was instantly dismissed. Mary, my sister, was more liked, though she was said to be a tyrant in the still-room. The young people were all in high favour, especially Alice, whose sweet face and temper would have endeared her to the devil himself, but there was much shaking of heads over her handsome husband, Peter, who had a hot eye for a fine leg, as Matty put it, and was apt to put his arm round the kitchen girls if he had the chance. I could well believe this, having flung a pillow at Peter often enough myself for taking liberties.

"Master John and Mistress Joan are also liked," said Matty, "but they say Master John should stand up more to his father." Her words put me in mind of the afternoon, and I asked her what she knew of the apartment next to mine. "It is a lumber room, they tell me," she answered. "Mr Rashleigh has the key, and has valuables shut away."

My curiosity was piqued, though, and I bade her search for a crack in the door. She put her face to the keyhole, but saw nothing. I gave her a pair of scissors, both of us giggling like children, and she worked away at the panelling for ten minutes or so until she had scraped a wide enough crack at which to place one eye. She knelt before it for a moment or two, then turned to me in disappointment. "There's nothing there," she said. "It is a plain chamber,

much the same as this, with a bed in one corner, and hangings on the wall." I
felt quite aggrieved, having hoped—in my idiot romantic fashion—for a heap
of treasure. I bade her hang a picture over the crack, and turned to my dinner.
But later, when Joan came to sit with me at sunset, and the shadows began to
fall, she said suddenly, with a shiver, "You know, Honor, I slept once in this
room when John had the ague, and I did not care for it."

"Why so?" I asked, drinking my wine.

"I thought I heard footsteps in the chamber next door."

I glanced at the picture over the crack, but it was well hidden.

"What sort of footsteps?" I said.

She shook her head, puzzled. "Soft ones," she said, "like someone walking
with slippered soles for fear he may be heard."

"How long ago was this?" I asked.

"During the winter," she said. "I did not tell anyone."

"A servant perhaps," I suggested, "who had no business to be there."

"No," she said, "none of the servants has a key—no one has but my
father-in-law, and he was from home then." She waited a moment, and then
she said, glancing over her shoulder, "I believe it is a ghost."

"Why should a ghost walk at Menabilly?" I answered. "The house has not
been built fifty years."

"People have died here, though," she said, "John's old grandfather and his
uncle John." She watched me with bright eyes, and, knowing my Joan, I
wagered there was more to come.

"So you too have heard the poison story," I said, drawing a bow at venture.
She added, "But I don't believe it, it would be wicked, horrible. He is too
good and kind a man. But I do think it was a ghost that I heard, the ghost of
the elder brother that they called Uncle John."

"Why should he pace the room with padded soles?" I asked.

She did not answer for a moment, and then, guiltily, she whispered: "They
never speak of it—John made me promise not to tell—but he was mad, a
hopeless idiot, and they used to keep him shut up in the chamber there."

This was something I had never heard before. I found it horrible.

"Are you certain?" I said.

"Oh, yes," she replied. "There is a bit about it in old Mr Rashleigh's
will—John told me. Old Mr Rashleigh, before he died, made my father-in-law
promise to look after the elder brother, give him food and drink, and shelter in
the house. They say the chamber there was set aside for him, built in a special
way; I don't exactly know. And then he died, you see, very suddenly of the
smallpox. John and Alice and Elizabeth don't remember him—they were only
babies."

"What a disagreeable tale," I said. "Give me some more wine, and let's
forget it." After a while she went away, and Matty came to draw the curtains. I
had no more visitors that night. But as the shadows lengthened, and the owls
began to hoot down in the warren, I found my thoughts returning to the idiot
Uncle John, shut up in the chamber there, year after year, from the first
building of the house, a prisoner of the mind as I was of the body.

But in the morning I heard news that made me forget, for a while, this talk of footsteps in the night.

CHAPTER EIGHT

THE DAY BEING fine, I ventured forth in my chair once more upon the causeway, returning to the house at midday to find that a messenger had ridden to Menabilly, during my absence, bearing letters from Plymouth and else- where to members of the household, and the family were now gathered in the gallery discussing the latest information from the war. Alice was seated in one of the long windows overlooking the garden, reading aloud a lengthy epistle from her Peter. "Sir John Digby has been wounded," she said, "and the siege is now to be conducted by a new commander, who has them all by the ears at once. Poor Peter—this will mean an end to hawking excursions and supper parties. They will have to wage the war more seriously." She turned the page of scrawled writing, shaking her head. "And who is to command them?" enquired John, who once more was acting as attendant to my chair. "Sir Richard Grenvile," answered Alice.

Mary was not in the gallery at the time, and, since she was the only person at Menabilly to know of the romance long finished and forgotten, I was able to hear mention of his name without embarrassment. For it is a strange truth, as I had by then discovered, that we only become aware of hot discomfort when others are made awkward for our sakes.

I knew, from something that Robin had let slip, that Richard was come into the west, his purpose being to raise troops for the King, so I understood, and to be placed now in command of the siege of Plymouth meant promotion. He had already become notorious, of course, for the manner in which he had hood- winked Parliament and joined His Majesty. "And what," I heard myself saying, "does Peter think of his new commander?" Alice folded up her letter. "As a soldier, he admires him," she answered "but I think he has not a great opinion of him as a man."

"I have heard," said John, "that he hasn't a scruple in the world, and once an injury is done to him he will never forget it or forgive."

"I believe," said Alice, "that when in Ireland he inflicted great cruelty on the people—though some say it was no more than they deserved. But I fear he is very different from his brother."

It made strange hearing to have the lover who had held me once against his heart discussed in so calm and cool a fashion.

At this moment Will Sparke came up to us, also with a letter in his hand. "So Richard Grenvile is commanding now at Plymouth," he said. "I have the news here from my kinsman in Tavistock, who is with Prince Maurice. It seems the Prince thinks highly of his ability, but, my heaven—what a scoundrel."

I began to burn silently, my old love and loyalty rising to the surface.

"We were just talking of him," said John.

"You heard his first action on coming west, I suppose?" said Will Sparke, warming like all his kind to malicious gossip. "I had it direct from my kinsman at the time. Grenvile rode straight to Fitzford, his wife's property, turned out the caretakers, seized all the contents, had the agent flung into gaol, and took all the money owed by the tenants to his wife for his own use."

"I thought," said Alice, "that he had been divorced from his wife."

"So he is divorced," replied Will. "He is not entitled to a penny from the property. But that is Richard Grenvile for you."

"I wonder," I said calmly, "what has happened to his children?"

"I can tell you that," said Will. "The daughter is with the mother in London—whether she has friends in Parliament or not I cannot say. But the lad was at Fitzford with his tutor when Grenvile seized the place, and by all accounts is with him now. They say the poor boy is in fear and trembling of his father, and small blame to him."

"No doubt," I said, "he was brought up to hate him by his mother."

"Any woman," retorted Will, "who had been as ill used as she, unhappy lady, would hardly paint her spouse in pretty colours."

Logic was with him, as it always was with the persons who maligned Richard, and presently I bade John carry me upstairs to my apartment. But the day that had started so well when I set forth upon the causeway turned sour on me, and I lay on my bed for the rest of it, telling Matty I would see no visitors.

For fifteen years the Honor that had been lay dead and buried, and here she was struggling beneath the surface once again at the mere mention of a name that was best forgotten. Richard in Germany, Richard in Ireland, was too remote a person to swim into my daily thoughts. When I thought of him, or dreamt of him—which was often—it was always as he had been in the past. And now he must break into the present, a mere thirty miles away, and there would be constant talk of him, criticism and discussion, and I should be forced to hear his name bandied and besmirched, as Will Sparke had bandied it this morning. "You know," he had said, before I went upstairs, "the Roundheads call him Skellum Grenvile, and have put a price upon his head. The nickname suits him well, and even his own soldiers whisper it behind his back."

"And what does it signify?" I asked.

"Oh," he said. "I thought you were a German scholar, Mistress Harris, as well as learned in the Greek and Latin." He paused. "It means a vicious beast," he sniggered.

Oh, yes, there was much reason for me to lie moodily on my bed, with the memory of a young man smiling at me from the branches of an apple-tree, and the humming of the bees in the blossom.

Fifteen years . . . he would be forty-four now, ten years older than myself.

"Matty," I said, before she lit the candles, "bring me a mirror."

She glanced at me suspiciously, her long nose twitching.

"What do you want a mirror for?" she asked.

"God damn you, that's my business," I answered.

We snapped at one another continually, she and I, but it meant nothing. She brought me the mirror, and I examined my appearance as though seeing myself as a stranger would.

There were my two eyes, my nose, my mouth, much as they had always been, but I was fuller in the face now than I had been as a maid—sluggish from lying on my back, I told myself. There were little lines, too, beneath my eyes, lines that had grown there from pain when my legs hurt me. I had less colour than I had once. My hair was the best point, for this was Matty's special pride, and she would brush it for hours to make it glossy. I handed back the mirror for Matty with a sigh. "What do you make of it?" she asked.

"In ten years," I said, "I'll be an old woman."

She sniffed and began to fold my garments on a chair.

"I'll tell you one thing," she said, drawing in her underlip.

"What's that?"

"You're fairer now as a woman than you ever were as a prinking, blushing maid, and I'm not the only one that thinks it."

This was encouraging, and I had an immediate vision of a long train of suitors all tiptoeing up the stairs to pay me homage. A pretty fancy, but where the devil were they?

"You're like an old hen," I said to Matty, "who always thinks her poorest chick the loveliest. Go to bed."

I lay there for some time, thinking of Richard, wondering too about his little son, who must be a lad now of fourteen. Could it be true, as Will Sparke had said, that the boy went in fear of his father? Supposing we had wedded, Richard and I, and this had been our son. Would we have sported with him as a child, danced him upon our knees, gone down with him on all fours on the ground and played at tigers? Would he have come running to me with muddied hands, his hair about his face, laughing? Would he be auburn-haired like Richard? Would we all three have ridden to the chase, and Richard have shown him how to sit straight in the saddle? Vain, idle supposition, drenched in sentiment, like buttercups by the dew on a wet morning.

I was half asleep, muzzy with a dream, when I heard a movement in the next chamber. I raised my head from the pillow, thinking it might be Matty in the dressing-room, but the sound came from the other side. I held my breath and waited. Yes, there it was again. A stealthy footstep padding to and fro. I remembered in a flash the tale that Joan had told me of the mad Rashleigh uncle, confined in there for years. Was it his ghost in truth that stole there in the shadows? The night was pitchy, for it was only quarter moon, and no glimmer came to me from either casement. The clock in the belfry struck one. The footsteps ceased, then proceeded once again, and for the first time too I was aware of a cold current of air coming to my apartment from the chamber beyond.

My own casements were closed, save the one that looked into the inner court, and this was only open to a few inches; besides, the draught did not come from that direction. I remembered then that the closed-up door into the empty chamber did not meet the floor at its base, but was raised two inches or so from the ground, for Matty had tried to look under it before she made the crack with the scissors. It was from beneath this door that the current of air blew now—and to my certain knowledge there had never been a draught from there before.

Something, then, had happened in the empty chamber next to mine to cause the current. The muffled tread continued, stealthy, soft, and with the sweat running down my face I thought of the ghost stories my brothers had recounted to me as a child, of how an earth-bound spirit would haunt the place he hated, bringing with him from the darker regions a whisper of chill dank air. One of the dogs barked from the stables, and this homely sound brought me to my senses. Was it not more likely that a living person was responsible for the cold current that swept beneath the door, and that the cause of it was the opening of the barred window that, like my western one, looked out on to the outer court? The ghost of poor idiot Uncle John would have kept me in my bed for ever, but a living soul, treading furtively in the night hours in a locked chamber, was something to stir the burning curiosity of one who, it may be remembered, had from early childhood shown a propensity to eavesdrop where she was not wanted.

Secretly, stealthily, I reached out my hand to the flint that Matty from long custom left beside my bed, and lit my candle. My chair was also within reach. I pulled it close to me, and, with the labour that years of practice had never mitigated, lowered myself into it. The footsteps ceased abruptly. So I am right, I thought in triumph. No ghost would hesitate at the sound of a creaking chair. I waited perhaps for as long as five minutes, and then the intruder must have recovered himself, for I heard the faint noise of the opening of a drawer. Softly I wheeled myself across the room. Whoever is there, I smiled grimly, is not aware that a cripple can be mobile, granted she has a resourceful brother with a talent for invention. I came abreast the door and waited once again. The picture that Matty had hung over the crack was on a level with my eye. I blew out my candle, trusting to fortune to blunder my way back to bed when my curiosity was satisfied. Then, very softly, holding my breath, I lifted the picture from the nail, and, framing my face with my hands for cover, I peered with one eye into the slit. The chamber was in half darkness, lit by a single candle on a bare table. I could not see to right or left—the crack was not large enough—but the table was in a direct line with my eye. A man was sitting at the table, his back turned to me. He was booted and spurred, and wore a riding-cloak about his shoulders. He had a pen in his hand, and was writing on a long white slip of paper, consulting, now and again, another list propped up before him on the table. Here was flesh and blood indeed, and no ghost; the intruder was writing away as calmly as though he were a clerk on a copying-stool. I watched him come to the end of the long slip of paper, and then he folded it, and, going to the cabinet in the wall, opened the drawer with the same sound I had heard before. The light was murky, as I have said, and, with his back turned to me and his hat upon his head, I could make little of him except that his riding-cloak was a dark crimson. Then he moved out of my line of vision, taking the candle, and walked softly to the far corner of the room.

I heard nothing after that, and no further footsteps, and while I waited puzzled, with my eye still to the crack, I became aware suddenly that the draught of air was no longer blowing beneath the door. Yet I had heard no sound of a closing window. I bent down from my chair, testing the bottom of the door with my hand, but no current came. The intruder, therefore, had by some action unperceived by me cut off the draught, making his exit at the same time. He had left the chamber, as he had entered it, by some entrance other than the door that led into the corridor. I blundered back across my room in clumsy fashion, having first replaced the picture on its nail, and knocking into a table on the way woke that light sleeper, Matty. "Have you lost your senses," she scolded, "circling round your chamber in the pitch-black?" And she lifted me like a child and dumped me in my bed.

"I had a nightmare," I lied, "and thought I heard footsteps. Is there anyone moving in the courtyard, Matty?"

She drew aside the curtain. "Not a soul," she grumbled, "not even a cat scratching on the cobbles. Everyone is asleep."

"You will think me mazed, I don't doubt," I answered, "but venture with your candle a moment into the passage, and try the door of the locked apartment next to this."

"Mazed it is," she snapped. "This comes of looking into the mirror on a Friday night." In a moment she was back again. "The door is locked as it always is," she said, "and, judging by the dust upon the latch, it has not been opened for months, or more."

"No," I mused. "That is just what I supposed."

She stared at me, and shook her head.

"I'd best brew you a hot cordial," she said.

"I do not want a hot cordial," I answered.

"There's nothing like it for putting a stop to bad dreams," she said. She tucked in my blankets, and, after grumbling a moment or two, went back to her own room. But my mind was far too lively to find sleep for several hours. I kept trying to remember the formation of the house, seen from without, and what it was that struck me as peculiar the day before, when John had wheeled me in my chair towards the gatehouse. It was past four in the morning when the answer came to me. Menabilly was built four-square around the courtyard, with clean, straight lines and no protruding wings. But at the north-west corner of the house, jutting from the wall outside the fastened chamber, was a buttress, running tall and straight from the roof down to the cobbles. Why in the name of heaven, when old John Rashleigh built his house in 1600, did he build the north-west corner with a buttress? And had it some connection with the fact that the apartment behind was designed for the special use of his idiot eldest son?

Some lunatics are harmless, some are not. But even the worst, the truly animal, are given air and exercise at certain periods of the day, and would hardly be paraded through the corridors of the house itself. I smiled to myself in the darkness, for I had guessed, after three restless hours of tossing on my back, how the intruder had crept into the apartment next to mine without using the locked door into the passage. He had come, and he had gone, as poor uncle John had doubtless done nearly half a century before, by a hidden stairway in the buttress. But why he had come, and what was his business, I had yet to discover.

CHAPTER NINE

It TURNED TO RAIN the next morning, and I was unable to take my usual airing in the grounds. But later in the day the fitful sun peeked through the low clouds and, wrapping my cloak about me, I announced to Matty my intention of going abroad.

John Rashleigh was out riding round the farms on the estate, with the steward Langdon, whose house it was I had observed beyond the bowling-green. Thus I had not my faithful chair attendant. Joan came with me instead, and it was an easy enough matter to persuade her to wheel me first through the archway to the outer court, where I made pretence of looking up to admire my quarters in the gatehouse.

In reality, I was observing the formation of the buttress, which ran, as I thought it did, the whole length of the house on the north-west corner, immediately behind it being the barred chamber.

The width of the buttress was a little over four feet, so I judged, and, if it was hollow behind a false façade of stone, could easily contain a stair. There was, however, no outlet to the court—this was certain. I bade Joan wheel me to the base, on pretence of touching the lichen which already, after only fifty years, was forming on the stone, and I satisfied myself that the outside of the buttress at any rate was solid. If my supposition was correct, then there must be a stairway within the buttress leading underground, far beneath the foundations of the house, and a passage running some distance to an outlet in the grounds. Poor uncle John. It was significant that there was no portrait of him in the gallery, alongside the rest of the family. If so much trouble was taken by his father that he should not be seen, he must have been an object of either fear or horror. We left the outer court and, traversing the warren, came by the path outside the steward's lodge. The door was open to the parlour, and Mrs Langdon, the steward's wife, was standing in the entrance, a comfortable, homely woman, who, on being introduced to me, insisted that I take a glass of milk. While she was absent, we glanced about the trim room, and Joan, laughing, pointed to a bunch of keys that hung on a nail beside the door. "Old Langdon is like a gaoler," she whispered. "As a rule he is never parted from that bunch, but dangles them at his belt. John tells me he has a duplicate of each key belonging to my father-in-law."

"Has he been steward long?" I asked.

"Oh, yes," said Joan. "He came here as a young man when the house was built. There is no corner of Menabilly that he does not know."

I wager then, I thought to myself, that he knows too the secret of the buttress, if there is a secret. Joan, with a curiosity much like mine, was examining the labels on the keys. "Summer-house," she read, and with a mischievous smile at me, she slipped it from the bunch, and dangled it before my eyes. "You expressed a wish to peep into the tower on the causeway, did you not?" she teased. At this moment Mrs Langdon returned with the milk, and, fearful of discovery, Joan, like a guilty child, reddened and concealed the key within her gown. We chatted for a few moments, while I drank my milk in haste and Joan gazed with great innocence at the ceiling. Then we bade the good woman farewell and turned into the gardens, through the gate in the high wall.

"Now you have done for yourself," I said. "How in the world will you return the key?"

Joan was laughing under her breath. "I'll give it to John," she said. "He must devise some tale or other to satisfy old Langdon. But, seeing that we have the key, Honor, it would be a pity not to make some use of it." She was an accomplice after my own heart, and a true godchild. "I make no promise," I murmured. "Wheel me along the causeway, and we will see which way the wind is blowing."

We crossed the gardens, passing the house as we did so, and waved to Alice at the window of her apartment above the gallery. I caught sight, too, of Temperance Sawle, peering like a witch from the side-door, evidently in half a mind to risk the damp ground and join us. "I am the best off in my chair," I called to her. "The walks are wringing wet, and clouds coming up again from the Gribben."

She bolted like a rabbit within doors again, and I saw her pass into the gallery, while Joan, smothering her laughter, propelled me through the gate on to the causeway.

It was only when mounted thus some ten feet from the ground that the fine view of the sea could be obtained, for down on the level the sloping ground masked all sight of it. Menabilly, though built on a hill, lay therefore in a saucer, and I commented on the fact to Joan as she wheeled me towards the towered summer-house at the far end of the causeway. "Yes," she said, "John has explained to me that the house was so built that no glimpse of it should be sighted from the sea. Old Mr Rashleigh lived in great fear of pirates. But, if the truth be told, he was not above piracy himself, and in the old days, when he was alive, there were bales of silk, and bars of silver, concealed somewhere within the house, stolen from the French and brought hither by his own ships, and then landed down at Pridmouth yonder."

In which case, I thought privately, a passage known to no one but himself, and perhaps his steward, would prove of great advantage.

But we had reached the summer-house, and Joan, glancing first over her shoulder to see that no one came, produced her key, and turned it in the lock. "I must tell you," she confessed, "that there is nothing great to see. I have been here once or twice, with my father-in-law, and it is nought but a rather musty room, the shelves lined with books and papers, and a fine view from the windows." She wheeled me through the door, and I glanced about me, half hoping, in a most childish manner, to find traces of piracy. But all was in order. The walls of the summer-house were lined with books, save for the windows, which, as she said, commanded the whole stretch of the bay to the Gribben and to the east showed the steep coast road that led to Fowey. Anyone, on horse or on foot, approaching Menabilly from the east would be observed by a watcher at the window, likewise a vessel sailing close in-shore. Old Mr Rashleigh had shown great cunning as a builder.

The flagged floor was carpeted, save in one corner, by my brother-in-law's writing table, where a strip of heavy matting served for his feet. It was in keeping with his particular character that the papers on his desk were neatly documented, and filed in order. Joan left me in my chair to browse among the books, while she herself kept watch out on the causeway. There was nothing much to tempt my interest. Books of law, dry as dust, books of accountancy, and many volumes docketed as "County Affairs", no doubt filed when Jonathan was Sheriff for the Duchy of Cornwall. On a lower shelf, near to his writing-table, were volumes labelled "My Town House" and another "Menabilly", while close beside these he had "Marriage Settlements" and "Wills". He was nothing if not methodical in his business.

The volume marked "Wills" was nearest to me, and surprisingly tempting to my hand. I looked over my shoulder and saw through the window that Joan, humming a tune, was busily engaged in picking posies for her children. I reached out my hand and took the volume. Page after page was covered in my brother-in-law's meticulously careful hand. I turned to the entries headed by the words "My father, John Rashleigh. Born, 1554. Died, May 6th, 1624." Folded close to this—perhaps it had slipped in by accident—was an account of a case brought to the Star chamber in the year 1616 by one Charles Bennett against the above John Rashleigh. This Charles Bennett, I remembered, was father to Robert Bennett, our neighbour at Looe, who had spread the poison rumour. The case, had I time to peruse it, would have made good reading, for it was of a highly scandalous nature; Charles Bennett accused John Rashleigh of "leading a most incontinent course of life, lying with divers women, over forty-five in number, uttering blasphemies, etc., etc., and his wife dying through grief at his behaviour, she being a sober virtuous woman." I was somewhat surprised after this, glancing at the end, to find that John Rashleigh had been acquitted. What a lovely weapon, though, to hold over the head of my self-righteous brother-in-law when he made boast, as he sometimes did, of the high morals of his family. But I turned a page and came to the will I had been seeking. So old John Rashleigh had not done too badly for his relatives. Nick

Sawle had got fifty pounds (which I dare say Temperance had snatched from him) and the Sparkes had benefited to the same extent. The poor of Fowey had some twenty pounds bestowed upon them. It is really most iniquitous, I told myself, that I should be prying thus into matters that concern me not at all, but I read on. All lands in Cornwall, his house in Fowey, his house at Menabilly, and the residue of his estate to his second son Jonathan, his executor. And then the codicil at the end: "Thirty pounds annuity out of Fowey to the use of my eldest son John's maintenance, to be paid after the death of my second son Jonathan, who during his life will maintain him and allow him a chamber with meat and drink and apparel." I caught a glimpse of Joan's shadow passing the window, and with a hurried, guilty movement I shut the volume and put it back upon the shelf.

There was no doubt then about the disability of poor uncle John. I turned my chair from the desk, and as I did so the right wheel stuck against some obstruction on the ground beneath the heavy matting. I bent down from my chair to free the wheel, turning up the edge of the mat as I did so. I saw then that the obstruction was a ring in the flagstone, which, though flat to the ground and unnoticeable possibly to a foot treading upon it, had been enough to obstruct the smooth running of my chair.

I leant from my chair as far as I could, and, seizing the ring with my two hands, succeeded in lifting the stone some three inches from the ground, before the weight of it caused me to drop it once again—but not before I had caught a glimpse of the sharp corner of a step descending into darkness. I replaced the mat just as my godchild came into the summer-house.

"Well, Honor," she said, "have you seen all you have a mind to for the present?"

"I rather think I have," I answered, and in a few moments she had closed the door, turned the key once more in the lock, and we were bowling back along the causeway. She prattled away about this and that, but I paid but scant attention, for my mind was full of my latest discovery. It seemed fairly certain that there was a pit or tunnel underneath the flagstone in the summer-house, and the placing of a mat on top of it, and the position of the desk, suggested that the hiding of it was deliberate. There was no rust about the ring-bolt to show disuse, and the ease with which I, helpless in my chair, had lifted the stone a few inches proved to me that this was no cobwebby corner of concealment long forgotten. The flagstone had been lifted frequently, and recently. I looked over my shoulder down the pathway to the beach, or Pridmouth Cove, as Joan had termed it. It was narrow and steep, flanked with stubby trees, and I thought how easy it would be for an incoming vessel, anchored in deep water, to send a boat ashore with some half-dozen men, who could climb up the path to where it ended beneath the summer-house on the causeway, and for a watcher at the window of the summer-house to relieve the men of any burden they should bear upon their backs. Was this what old John Rashleigh had foreseen when he built his tower, and did bales of silk and bars of silver lie stacked beneath the flagstone some forty years before? It seemed very probable, but whether the step beneath the flagstone had any connection with my suspicions of the buttress it was difficult to say. One thing was certain. There was a secret entrance to Menabilly through the chamber next to mine, and someone had passed that way only the night before, for I had seen him with my own eyes.

"You are silent, Honor," said Joan, breaking in upon my thoughts. "What are you thinking of?"

"I have just come to the opinion," I answered, "that I was somewhat rash to leave Lanrest, where each day was alike, and come amongst you all at Menabilly, where something different happens every day."

"I wish I thought as you did," she replied. "To me the days and weeks seem much the same, with the Sawles backbiting at the Sparkes, and the children fretful, and my dear John grousing all the while that he cannot go fighting with Peter and the rest."

We came to the end of the causeway, and were about to turn in through the gate into the walled gardens when her little son Jonathan, a child of barely three years, came running across the path to greet us. "Uncle Peter is come," he cried, "and another gentleman, and many soldiers. We have been stroking the horses."

I smiled up at his mother. "What did I tell you?" I said. "Not a day passes but there is some excitement at Menabilly."

I had no wish to run the gauntlet of the long windows in the gallery, where the company would be assembled, and bade Joan wheel me to the entrance in the front of the house, which was usually deserted at this time of the day, when no one was within the dining-chamber. Once indoors, one of the servants could carry me to my apartment in the gatehouse, and later I could send for Peter, always a favourite with me, and have his news of Robin. We passed in then through the door, little Jonathan running in front, and at once we heard laughter and talk coming from the gallery. The wide arched door to the inner courtyard was open, and we could see some half-dozen troopers with their horses watering at the well beneath the belfry. There was much bustle and clatter, a pleasant, lively sound, and I saw one of the troopers look up to a casement in the attic and wave his hand in greeting to a blushing kitchen-girl. He was a big, strong-looking fellow with a broad grin on his face, and then he turned, and signalled to his companions to follow him, which they did, each one leading his horse away from the well and following him through the archway beneath my gatehouse to the outer courtyard and the stables.

It was when they turned thus and clattered through the court that I noticed how each fellow wore upon his shoulder a scarlet shield, with three gold rests upon it. For a moment I thought my heart would stop beating, and I was seized with sudden panic.

"Find one of the servants quickly," I said to Joan. "I wish to be carried straightway to my room."

But it was too late. Even as she sent little Jonathan scampering hurriedly towards the servants' quarters, Peter Courtney came out into the hall, his arm about his Alice, in company with two or three brother officers. "Why, Honor," he cried. "This is a joy indeed. Knowing your habits, I feared to find you hiding in your apartment, with Matty standing like a dragon at the door.

Gentlemen, I present to you Mistress Honor Harris, who has not the slightest desire to make your acquaintance." I could have slain him for his lack of discretion, but he was one of those gay light-hearted creatures with a love of jesting and poking fun, and no more true perception than a bumble-bee. In a moment his friends were bowing before my chair and exchanging introductions, and Peter, still laughing and talking in his haphazard, strident way, was pushing my chair through to the gallery. It seemed full of people—Sawles, and Sparkes, and Rashleighs all chatting at the top of their voices, and at the far end by the window I caught sight of Mary in conversation with someone whose tall back and broad shoulders were painfully, almost terrifyingly familiar. Mary's expression, preoccupied and distrait, told me that she was at that moment wondering if I had returned from my promenade, for I saw her eyes search the gardens; and then she saw me, and her brow wrinkled in a well-known way and she began talking sixteen to the dozen. Her loss of composure gave me back my own. What in hell's name do I care, after fifteen years, I told myself. There is no need to swoon at an encounter. God knows I have breeding enough to be mistress of the situation, here in Mary's house at Menabilly, with nigh a score of people in the room.

Peter, impervious to any doubtful atmosphere, propelled me slowly towards the window, and out of the corner of my eye I saw my sister Mary, overcome by cowardice, do something that I dare swear I might have done myself had I been her, and that was to murmur a hasty excuse to her companion about summoning the servants to bring further refreshment, before she fled from the gallery without looking once in my direction. Richard turned and saw me. And as he looked at me it was as if my whole heart moved over in my body and was mine no longer.

"Sir," said Peter, "I am pleased to present to you my dearly loved kinswoman, Mistress Honor Harris of Lanrest."

"My kinswoman also," said Richard—and then he bent forward and kissed my hand.

"Oh, is that so, sir?" said Peter vaguely, looking from one to the other of us. "I suppose all we Cornish families are in some way near related. Let me fill your glass, sir. Honor, will you drink with us?"

"I will," I answered. In truth, a glass of wine seemed to me my only salvation at the moment. While Peter filled the glasses I had my first long look at Richard. He had altered. There was no doubt of it. He had grown much broader, for one thing, not only in the body, but about the neck and shoulders. His face was somewhat heavier than it had been. There was a brown, weather-beaten air about him that was not there before, and lines beneath his eyes. It was, after all, fifteen years. And then he turned to me, giving me my glass, and I saw that there was only one white streak in his auburn hair, high above the temple, and the eyes that looked at me were quite unchanged.

"Your health and fortune," he said quietly, and, draining his glass, he held it out, with mine, to be refilled. I saw the little telltale pulse beating on his right temple, and I knew then that the encounter was as startling and as moving to him as it was to me.

"I did not know," he said, "that you were at Menabilly."

I saw Peter glance at him curiously, and I wondered if this was the first time he had ever seen his commanding officer show any sign of nervousness or strain. The hand that held the glass trembled very slightly, and the voice that spoke was hard, queerly abrupt.

"I came here a few days since from Lanrest," I answered, my voice perhaps as oddly flat as his. "My brothers said I must not live alone while the war continues."

"They showed wisdom," he replied. "Essex is moving westward all the time. It is very probable we shall see fighting once again this side the Tamar." At this moment Peter's small daughters came running to his knees, shrieking with joy to see their father, and Peter, laughing an apology, was swept into family life upon the instant, taking one apiece upon his shoulder and moving down the gallery in triumph. Richard and I were thus left alone beside the window. I looked out on to the garden, noting the trim yew hedges and the smooth lawns, while a score of trivial observations ran insanely through my head.

"How green the grass is after the morning rain," and "It is something chilly for the time of year" were phrases I had never yet used in my life, even to a stranger, but they seemed, at that moment, to be what was needed to the occasion. Yet though they rose unbidden to my tongue, I did not frame them, but continued looking out upon the garden in silence, with Richard as dumb as myself. And then in a low voice, clipped and hard, he said:

"If I am silent you must forgive me. I had not thought, after fifteen years, to find you so damnably unchanged."

This streak back from the indifferent present to the intimate past was a new shock to be borne, but a curiously exciting one.

"Why damnably?" I said, watching him over the rim of my glass.

"I had become used, over a long period, to a very different picture," he said. "I thought of you as an invalid, wan and pale, a sort of shadow without substance, hedged about with doctors and attendants. And instead I find— this." He looked me then full in the face with a directness and a lack of reserve that I remembered well.

"I am sorry," I answered, "to disappoint you."

"You misinterpret me," he said. "I have not said I was disappointed. I am merely speechless." He drained his glass once more and put it back upon the table. "I shall recover," he said, "in a moment or two. Where can we talk?"

"Talk?" I asked. "Why, we can talk here, I suppose, if you wish to."

"Amidst a host of babbling fools and screaming children—not on your life," he answered. "Have you not your own apartments?"

"I have," I replied with some small attempt at dignity, "but it would be considered somewhat odd if we retired there."

"You were not used to quibble at similar suggestions in the past," he said.

This was something of a blow beneath the belt, and I had no answer for him.

"I would have you remember," I said, with lameness, "that we have been strangers to one another for fifteen years."

"Do you think," he said, "that I forget it for a moment?"

At this juncture we were interrupted by Temperance Sawle, who, with baleful eyes, had been watching us from a distance, and now moved within our orbit. "Sir Richard Grenvile, I believe," she said.

"Your servant, ma'am," replied Richard with a look that would have slain anyone less soul-absorbed than Temperance.

"The Evil One seeks you for his own," she announced. "Even at this moment I see his talons at your throat, and his jaws open to devour you. Repent, repent, before it is too late."

"What the devil does she mean?" said Richard.

I shook my head, and pointed to the heavens, but Temperance, warming to her theme, continued:

"The mark of the Beast is on your forehead," she declared. "The men you lead are become as ravening wolves. You will all perish, every one of you, in the bottomless pit."

"Tell the old fool to go to hell," said Richard.

I offered Mistress Sawle a glass of wine, but she flinched as if it had been boiling oil. "There shall be a weeping and a gnashing of teeth," she continued.

"My God, you're right," said Richard, and, taking her by the shoulders, he twisted her round like a top, and walked her across the room to the fireplace and her husband.

"Keep this woman under control," he ordered, and there was an immediate silence, followed by a little flutter of embarrassed conversation. Peter Courtney, very red about the neck, hurried forward with a brimming decanter. "Some more wine, sir?" he said.

"Thank you, no, I've had about as much as I can stand," said Richard. I noticed the young officers, all with their backs turned, examining the portraits on the walls with amazing interest. Will Sparke was one of the little crowd about the fireplace, staring hard at the King's general, his mouth wide open.

"A good day for catching flies, sir," said Richard pleasantly.

A little ripple of laughter came from Joan, hastily suppressed as Richard turned his eyes upon her. He beckoned then to John Rashleigh, who had returned but a few moments ago from his day's ride, and was now hovering at the entrance to the gallery somewhat mud-stained and splashed, bewildered by the unexpected company. "Hi, you," called Richard. "Will you summon one of your fellow servants, and carry Mistress Harris's chair to her apartment? She has had enough of the company downstairs."

"That is John Rashleigh, sir," whispered Peter hurriedly, "the son of the house, and your host in his father's absence."

"Ha! My apologies," said Richard, walking forward with a smile. "Your dress being somewhat in disorder, I mistook you for a menial. My own young officers lose their rank if they appear so before me. How is your father?"

"Well, sir, I believe," stammered John in great nervousness.

"I am delighted to hear it," said Richard. "Tell him so, when you see him. And tell him too that now I am come into the west I propose to visit here very frequently—the course of the war permitting it."

"Yes, sir."

"You have accommodation for my officers, I suppose, and for a number of my men out in the park, should we wish to bivouac at any time?"

"Yes, indeed, sir."

"Excellent. And now I propose to dine upstairs with Mistress Harris, who is a close kinswoman of mine, a fact of which you may not be aware. What is the usual method with her chair?"

"We carry it, sir—it is quite a simple matter." John gave a nod to Peter, who, astonishingly subdued for him, came forward, and the pair of them seized an arm of my chair on either side.

"It would be an easier matter," said Richard, "if the occupant were bodily removed, and carried separately." And before I could protest he had placed his arms about me and had lifted me from the chair. "Lead on, gentlemen," commanded Richard.

The strange procession proceeded up the stairs, watched by the company in the gallery and by some of the servants too, who, with their backs straight against the wall and their eyes lowered, permitted us to pass. John and Peter tramped on ahead, with the chair between them, step by step, both of them red about the neck; while I, with my head on Richard's shoulder, and my arms tight about him for fear of falling, thought the way seemed over-long.

"I was in error just now," said Richard in my ear. "You have changed after all."

"In what way?" I asked.

"You are two stone heavier," he answered.

And so we came to my chamber in the gatehouse.

CHAPTER TEN

I CAN RECOLLECT that supper as if it were yesterday. I lay on my bed with the pillows packed behind me, and Richard was seated on the end of it, with the low table in front of us both.

It might have been a day since we had parted, instead of fifteen years. When Matty came into the room bearing the platters, her mouth pursed and disapproving—for she had never understood how we came to lose one another, but imagined he had deserted me because of my crippled state—Richard burst out laughing on the instant, calling her "old go-between", which had been his nickname for her in those distant days, and asked her how many hearts she had broken since he saw her last. She was for replying to him shortly, but it was no use. He would have none of it, and, taking the platters from her and putting them on the table, he soon had her reconciled—blushing from head to toe—while he poked fun at her broadening figure and the frizzed curl on her forehead. "There are some half-dozen troopers in the court," he told her, "waiting to make your acquaintance. Go and prove to them that Cornish women are better than the frousts in Devon," and she went off, closing the door behind her, guessing no doubt that for the first time in fifteen years I had no need of her services.

He fell to eating right away, for he was always a good trencher-man, and soon cleared all that had been put before us, while I—still weak with the shock of seeing him—toyed with the wishbone of a chicken. He started walking about the chamber before he had finished, a habit I remembered well, with a great bone in one hand and a pie in the other, talking all the while about the defences at Plymouth, which his predecessor had allowed to become formidable instead of razing them to the ground on first setting siege to the place. "You'd hardly credit it, Honor," he said, "but there's that fat idiot Digby been sitting on his arse nine months before the walls of Plymouth, allowing the garrison to sortie as they please, fetch food and firewood and build up barricades, while he played cards with his junior officers. Thank God a bullet in his head will keep him to his bed a month or two, and allow me to conduct the siege instead."

"And what do you propose to do?" I asked.

"My first two tasks were simple," he replied, "and should have been done last October. I threw up a new earthwork at Mount Batten, and the guns I have placed there so damage the shipping which endeavours to pass through the Sound that the garrison are hard put to it for supplies. Secondly, I have cut off their water-power, and the mills within the city can no longer grind flour for the inhabitants. Give me a month or two to play with, and I'll have 'em starved." He took a great bite out of his pie, and winked at me.

"And the blockade by land, is that effective now?" I questioned.

"It will be, when I've had time to organise it," he answered. "The trouble is that I've arrived to find that most of the officers in my command are worse than useless—I've sacked more than half of them already. I have a good fellow in charge at Saltash, who sent the rebels flying back to Plymouth with several fleas in their ears when they tried a sortie a week or two back, a sharp engagement in which my nephew Jack—Bevil's eldest boy, you remember him—did very well. Last week we sprang a little surprise on one of their outposts close to Maudlyn. We beat them out of their position there, and took a hundred prisoners. I rather think the gentlemen of Plymouth sleep not entirely easy in their beds."

"Prisoners must be something of a problem," I said. "It is hard enough to find forage in the country for your own men. You are obliged to feed them, I suppose?"

"Feed them be damned," he answered. "I send the lot to Lydford Castle, where they are hanged without trial for high treason." He threw his drumstick out of the window, and tore the other from the carcase.

"But, Richard," I said, hesitating, "that is hardly justice, is it? I mean—they are only fighting for what they believe to be a better cause than ours?"

"I don't give a fig for justice," he replied. "The method is effective, and that's the only thing that matters."

"I am told the Parliament has put a price upon your head already," I said. "I am told you are much feared and hated by the rebels."

"What would you have them do, kiss my backside?" he asked. He smiled, and came and sat beside me on the bed.

"The war is too much with us; let us talk about ourselves," he said. I had not wished for that, but hoped to keep him busy with his siege of Plymouth.

"Where are you living at the moment?" I parried. "In tents about the fields?"

"What would I be doing in a tent," he mocked, "with the best houses in Devon at my disposal? Nay, my headquarters are at Buckland Abbey, which my grandfather sold to Francis Drake half a century ago, and I do not mind telling you that I live there very well. I have seized all the sheep and cattle upon the estate, and the tenants pay their rents to me, or else are hanged. They call me the Red Fox behind my back, and the women, I understand, use the name as a threat to their children when they misbehave, saying 'Grenvile is coming. The Red Fox will have you.'"

He laughed, as if this was a fine jest, but I was watching the line of his jaw, which was heavier than before, and the curve of his mouth that narrowed at the corners.

"It was not thus," I said softly, "that your brother Bevil's reputation spread throughout the west."

"No," he said, "and I have not a wife as Bevil had, nor a home I love, nor a great brood of happy children."

His voice was harsh suddenly, and strangely bitter. I turned my face away, and lay back on my pillows.

"Do you have your son with you at Buckland?" I asked quietly.

"My spawn?" he said. "Yes, he is somewhere about the place with his tutor."

"What is he like?"

"Dick? Oh, he's a little handful of a chap, with mournful eyes. I call him 'whelp' and make him sing to me at supper. But there's no sign of Grenvile in him—he's the spit of his God-damned mother."

The boy we would have played with, and taught, and loved. I felt suddenly sad, and oddly depressed, that his father should dismiss him with this careless shrug of a shoulder.

"It went wrong with you then, Richard, from the beginning," I said.

"It did," he answered.

There was a long silence, for we had entered upon dangerous ground.

"Did you never try," I asked, "to make some life of happiness?"

"Happiness was not in question," he said. "That went with you, a factor you refused to recognise."

"I am sorry," I said.

"So am I," he answered.

The shadows were creeping across the floor. Soon Matty would come to light the candles.

"When you refused to see me, that last time," he said, "I knew that nothing mattered any more but bare existence. You have heard the story of my marriage, with much embellishment, no doubt, but the bones of it are true."

"Had you no affection for her?"

"None whatever. I wanted her money, that was all."

"Which you did not get."

"Not then. I have it now. And her property, and her son—whom I fathered in a moment of black insensibility. The girl is with her mother up in London. I shall get her too one day, when she can be of use to me."

"You are very altered, Richard, from the man I loved."

"If I am so, you know the reason why."

The sun had gone from the windows, the chamber seemed bleak and bare. Every bit of those fifteen years were now between us. Suddenly he reached out his hand to mine, and, taking it, held it against his lips. The touch I so well remembered was very hard to bear.

"Why in the name of God," he said, rising to his feet, "were you and I marked down for such a tragedy?"

"It is no use being angry," I said. "I gave that up long ago. At first, yes, but not now. Not for many years. Lying on my back has taught me some discipline—but not the kind you engender in your troops."

He came and stood beside my bed, looking down upon me.

"Has no one told you," he said, "that you are more lovely now than you were then?"

I smiled, thinking of Matty and the mirror.

"I think you flatter me," I answered, "or maybe I have more time, now I lie idle, to play with paint and powder."

No doubt he thought me cool and at my ease, and had no knowledge that his tone of voice ripped wide the dusty years and sent them scattering.

"There is no part of you," he said, "that I do not now remember. You had a mole in the small of your back which gave you much distress. You thought it ugly—but I liked it well."

"Is it not time," I said, "that you went downstairs to join your officers? I heard one of them say you were to sleep this night at Grampound."

"There was a bruise on your left thigh," he said, "caused by that confounded branch that protruded halfway up the apple-tree. I compared it to a dark-sized plum, and you were much offended."

"I can hear the horses in the courtyard," I said. "Your troopers are preparing for the journey. You will never reach your destination before morning."

"You lie there," he said, "so smug and so complacent on your bed, very certain of yourself now you are thirty-four. I tell you, Honor, I care not two straws for your civility."

And he knelt then at my bed with his arms about me and the fifteen years went whistling down the wind.

"Are you still queasy when you eat roast swan?" he whispered.

He wiped away the silly childish tears that pricked my eyes, and laughed at me, and smoothed my hair.

"Beloved half-wit, with your God-damned pride," he said, "do you understand now that you blighted both our lives?"

"I understood that at the time," I told him.

"Why then, in the name of heaven, did you do it?"

"Had I not done so, you would soon have hated me, as you hated Mary Howard."

"That is a lie, Honor."

"Perhaps. What does it matter? There is no reason now to harp back on the past."

"There I agree with you. The past is over. But we have the future with us. My marriage is annulled; you know that, I suppose. I am free to wed again."

"Then do so, to another heiress."

"I have no need of an heiress now, with all the estates in Devon to my plunder. I have become a gentleman of fortune to be looked upon with favour by the spinsters of the west."

"There are many you might choose from, all agog for husbands."

"In all probability. But I want one spinster only, and that yourself."

I put my two hands on his shoulders and stared straight at him. The auburn hair, the hazel eyes, the little pulse that beat in his right temple. He was not the only one with recollections. I had my memories too, and could—had I the mind and lack of modesty—have reminded him of a patch of freckles that had been as much a matter for discussion as the mole upon my back.

"No, Richard."

"Why?"

"Because I will not have you wedded to a cripple."

"You will never change your mind?"

"Never."

"And if I carry you by force to Buckland?"

"Do so, if you will, I can't prevent you. But I shall still be a cripple." I leant back on my pillows, faint suddenly, and exhausted. It had not been a light thing to bear, this strain of seeing him, of beating down the years. Very gently he released me, and smoothed my blankets, and when I asked for a glass of water he gave me one in silence. It was nearly dark, and the clock in the belfry had struck eight a long while since. I could hear the jingling of harness from the courtyard, and the scraping sound of horses.

"I must ride to Grampound," he said at length.

"Yes," I said.

He stood for a moment looking down on to the court. The candles were lighted now throughout the house. The west windows of the gallery were open, sending a beam of light into my chamber. There was sound of music. Alice was playing her lute, and Peter singing.

Richard came once more and knelt beside my bed.

"I understand," he said, "what you have tried so hard to tell me. There can never be, between us, what there was once. Is that it?"

"Yes," I said.

"I knew that all along, but it would make no difference," he said.

"It would," I said, "after a little while."

"I shall always love you," said Richard, "and you will love me too. We cannot lose each other now, not since I have found you again. May I come and see you often, that we may be together?"

"Whenever you wish," I answered.

There came a burst of clapping from the gallery, and the voices of the officers and the rest of the company asking for more. Alice struck up a lively jiggling air upon her lute—a soldier's drinking song, much whistled at the moment by our men—and they one and all chimed in upon the chorus, with the troopers in the courtyard making echo to the song.

"Do you have as much pain now as when you were first hurt?" he said.

"Sometimes," I answered, "when the air is damp. Matty calls me her weather-glass."

"Can nothing be done for it?"

"She rubs my legs and my back with lotion that the doctors gave her. But it is of little use. You see, the bones were all smashed and twisted, and they cannot knit together."

"Will you show me, Honor?"

"It is not a pretty sight, Richard."

"I have seen worse in battle."

I pulled aside my blanket and let him look upon the crumpled limbs that he had once known whole and clean. He was thus the only person in the world to see me so, except Matty and the doctors. I put my hands over my eyes, for I did not care to see his face.

"There is no need for that," he said. "Whatever you suffer, you shall share with me, from this day forward." He bent then, and kissed my ugly twisted legs, and after a moment covered me again with the blanket. "Will you promise," he said, "never to send me from you again?"

"I promise," I said.

"Farewell, then, sweetheart, and sleep sound this night."

He stood for a moment, his figure carved clear against the beam of light from the windows opposite, and then turned and went away down the passage. Presently I heard them all come out into the courtyard and mount their horses; there was the sound of leave-taking and laughter, Richard's voice high above the others telling John Rashleigh he would come again. Suddenly clipped and curt, he called an order to his men, and they went riding through the archway beneath the gatehouse where I lay, and I heard the sound of the hoof-beats echo across the park.

CHAPTER ELEVEN

T̲HAT R̲ICHARD G̲RENVILE should become suddenly, within a few hours, part of my life again was a mental shock that for a day or two threw me out of balance. The first excitement over and the stimulation of his presence that evening fading away, reaction swung me to a low ebb. It was all too late. No good could come of it. Memory of what had been, nostalgia for the past coupled with sentiment, had stirred us both to passion for a moment; but reason came with daylight. There could never be a life for us together, only the doubtful pleasure of brief meetings, which the hazards of war might at any time render quite impracticable. What then? For me a lifetime of lying on my back, waiting for a chance encounter, for a message, for a word of greeting; and for him, after a space, a nagging irritation that I existed in the background of his life, that he had not visited me for three months and must make some effort to do so, that I expected some message from him which he found difficult to send—in short, a friendship that would become as wearisome to him as it would be painful to me.

Although his physical presence, his ways, his tenderness—however momentary—had been enough to engender in me once again all the old love and yearning in my heart, cold criticism told me he had altered for the worse. Faults that I had caught glimpses of in youth were now increased tenfold. His pride, his arrogance, his contempt for anyone's opinion but his own—these were more glaring than they had ever been. His knowledge of military matters was great, that I well believed, but I doubted if he would ever work in harmony with the other leaders, and his quick temper was such that he would have every royalist leader by the ears, and in the end give offence to His Majesty himself.

The callous attitude to prisoners—dumped within Lydford Castle and hung without trial—showed me that streak of cruelty I had always known was in his nature; and his contemptuous dismissal of his little son, who must, I felt sure, be baffled and bewildered at the sudden change in his existence, betrayed a deliberate want of understanding that was almost vile. That suffering and bitterness had turned him hard, I granted. Mine was the fault, perhaps; mine was the blame.

But the hardness had bitten into his nature now, and it was too late to alter it. Richard Grenvile at forty-four was what fate, and circumstance, and his own will, had made him.

So I judged him without mercy, in those first days after our encounter, and was within half a mind of writing to him once again, putting an end to all further meetings. Then I remembered how he had knelt beside my bed, and I had shared with him my terrible disfigurement, and he, more tender than any father, more understanding than any brother, had kissed me and bade me sleep.

If he had this gentleness and intuition with me, a woman, how was it that he showed to others, even to his son, a character at once so proud and cruel, so deliberately disdainful?

I felt torn between two courses, lying there on my bed in the gatehouse. One was to see him no more, never, at any time. Leave him to carve his own future, as I had done before. And the other was to ignore the great probability of my own personal suffering, spurn my own weak body which would be tortured incessantly by his physical presence, and give to him wholeheartedly and without any reservation all the small wisdom I had learnt, all the love, all the understanding that might yet bring to him some measure of peace.

This second course seemed to me more positive than the first, for if I renounced him now, as I had done before, it would be through cowardice, a sneaking fear of being hurt in more intolerable a fashion, if it were possible, than I had been fifteen years ago.

Strange how all arguments in solitude, sorted, sifted, and thrashed in the quiet of one's own chamber, shrivel to nothing when the subject of them is close once more instead of separated by distance. And so it was with Richard, for when he rode to Menabilly on his return from Grampound to Plymouth, and, coming out on to the causeway to seek me, found me in my chair looking out towards the Gribben, and kissed my hand with all the old fire, and love, and ardour—haranguing me straightforth upon the gross inefficiency of every Cornishman he had so far encountered except those under his immediate command—I knew that we were bound together for all time, and I could not send him from me. His faults were my faults, his arrogance my burden, and he stood there, Richard Grenvile, what my tragedy had made him.

"I cannot stay long," he said to me. "I have word from Saltash that those damned rebels have made a sortie in my absence, effected a landing at Cawsand, and taken the fort at Inceworth. The sentries were asleep, of course, and if the enemy haven't shot them, I will. I'll have my army purged before I'm finished."

"And no one left to fight for you, Richard," I said.

"I'd sooner have hired mercenaries from Germany or France than own these soft-bellied fools," he answered. And he was gone in a flash, leaving me half-happy, half-bewildered, with an ache in my heart that I knew now was to be for ever part of my existence.

That evening my brother-in-law, Jonathan Rashleigh, returned to Menabilly, having been some little while in Exeter on the King's affairs. He had come by way of Fowey, having spent, so he informed us, the last few days at his town house there on the quay, where he had found much business to transact, and some loss amongst his shipping, for the Parliament had at this time command of the sea and seized every vessel they could find, and it was hard for any unarmed merchant ship to run the gauntlet.

Some feeling of constraint came upon the place at his return, of which even I, secure in my gatehouse, could not but be aware.

The servants were more prompt about their business, but less willing. The grandchildren, who had run about the passages in his absence, were closeted in their quarters with the doors well shut. The voices in the gallery were more subdued. It was indeed obvious that the master had returned. Alice, and John, and Joan found their way more often to the gatehouse, as if it had become in some way a sanctuary. John looked harassed and preoccupied, and Joan whispered to me in confidence that his father found fault with his running of the estate and said he had no head for figures.

I could see that Joan was burning to enquire about my friendship with Richard Grenvile, which they must have thought strangely sudden, and I saw Alice look at me, though she said nothing, with a new warm glance of understanding. "I knew him well long ago, when I was eighteen," I told them, but to plunge back into the whole history was not my wish. I think Mary had given them a hint or two, in private. She herself said little of the visit, beyond remarking he had grown much stouter, a true sisterly remark, and then she showed me the letter he had left for Jonathan, which ended with these words:

"I here conclude, praying you to present once more my best respects to your good wife, being truly glad she is yours, for a more likely good wife was in former time hardly to be found, and I wish my fortune had been as good—but patience is a virtue, and so I am your ready servant and kinsman, Richard Grenvile."

Patience is a virtue. I saw Mary glance at me as I read the lines.

"You do not intend, Honor," she said in a low voice, "to take up with him again?"

"In what way, Mary?"

"Why, wed with him, to be blunt. This letter is somewhat significant."

"Rest easy, sister. I shall never marry Richard Grenvile or any man."

"I should not be comfortable, nor Jonathan either, if Sir Richard should come here and give an impression of intimacy. He may be a fine soldier, but his reputation is anything but that."

"I know, Mary."

"Jo writes from Radford that they say hard things of him in Devon."

"I can well believe it."

"I know it is not my business, but it would sadden me much, it would greatly grieve us all, if—if you bound yourself to him in some way."

"Being a cripple, Mary, makes one strangely free of bonds."

She looked at me doubtfully, and then said no more, but I think the bitterness was lost on her.

Presently Jonathan himself came up to pay his respects to me. He hoped I was comfortable, that I had everything I needed, and did not find the place too noisy after the quiet of Lanrest.

"And you sleep well, I trust, and are not disturbed at all?"

His manner, when he asked this, was somewhat odd, a trifle evasive, which was strange for him, who was so self-possessed a person.

"I am not a heavy sleeper," I told him. "A creaking board or a hooting owl is enough to waken me."

"I rather feared so," he said abruptly. "It was foolish of Mary to put you in this room, facing as it does a court on either side. You would have been better in the south front, next to our own apartments. Would you prefer this?"

"Indeed, no. I am very happy here."

I noticed that he stared hard at the picture on the door, hiding the crack, and once or twice seemed as if he would ask a question, but could not bring himself to the point; then, after chat upon no subject in particular, he took his leave of me.

That night, between twelve and one, since I was wakeful, I sat up in bed to drink a glass of water. I did not light my candle, for the glass was within my reach. But as I replaced it on the table I became aware of a cold draught of air blowing beneath the door of the empty room. That same chill draught I had noticed once before. I waited, motionless, for the sound of footsteps, but none came. And then, faint and hesitating, came a little scratching sound upon the panel of the door where I had hung the picture. Someone, then, was in the empty room, clad in his stockinged feet, with his hands upon the door.

The sound continued for five minutes, certainly not longer, and then ceased as suddenly as it had started, and once again the tell-tale draught of air was cut in a trice, and all was as before. A horrid suspicion formed then in my mind, which in the morning became certainty. When I was dressed, and in my chair and Matty busy in the dressing-room, I wheeled myself to the door and lifted the picture from the nail. It was as I thought. The crack had been filled in. I knew then that my presence in the gatehouse had been a blunder on the part of my sister, and that I caused annoyance to that unknown visitor who prowled by night in the adjoining chamber.

The secret was Jonathan Rashleigh's, and not mine to know. Suspecting my prying eyes, he had given orders for my peephole to be covered. I pondered then upon the possibility, which had entered my head earlier, that Jonathan's elder brother had not died of the smallpox some twenty years before, but was still alive—in some horrid state of preservation, blind and dumb—living in animal fashion in a lair beneath the buttress, and that the only persons to know of this were my brother-in-law and his steward Langdon, and some stranger— a keeper possibly—clad in a crimson cloak.

If it were indeed so, and my sister Mary and her stepchildren were in ignorance of the fact, while I, a stranger, had stumbled upon it, then I knew I must make some excuse and return home to Lanrest, for to live day by day with a secret of this kind upon my conscience was something I could not do. It was too sinister, too horrible.

I wondered if I should confide my fears to Richard, when he next came, or whether, in his ruthless fashion, he would immediately give orders to his men to break open the room and force the buttress, so bringing ruin perhaps to my brother-in-law and host.

Fortunately, the problem was solved for me in a very different way, which I will now disclose. It will be remembered that on the day of Richard's first visit my godchild Joan had mischievously borrowed the key of the summer-house, belonging to the steward, and allowed me to explore the interior. The flurry and excitement of receiving visitors had put all thoughts of the key from her little scatter-brained head, and it was not until two days after my brother-in-law's return that she remembered the key's existence.

She came to me with it in her hand, in great perturbation, for, she said, John was already so much out of favour with his father for some neglect on the estate that she was loath now to tell him of her theft of the key, for fear it should bring him into greater trouble. As for herself, she had not the courage to take the key back to Langdon's house and confess the foolery. What was she then to do?

"You mean," I said, "what am I to do? For you wish to absolve yourself of all responsibility, isn't that so?"

"You are so clever, Honor," she pleaded, "and I so ignorant. Let me leave the key with you, and so forget it. Baby Mary has a cough, and poor John a touch of his ague. I really have so much on my mind."

"Very well, then," I answered, "we will see what can be done."

I had some idea of taking Matty into my confidence, and weaving a tale by which Matty would visit Mrs Langdon and say she had found the key thrown down on a path in the Warren, which would be plausible enough, and while I turned this over in my mind I dangled the key between my fingers. It was of medium size, not larger, in fact, than the one in my own door. I compared the two, and found them very similar. A sudden thought then struck me, and, wheeling my chair into the passage, I listened for a moment, to discover who stirred about the house. It was a little before nine o'clock, with the servants all at their dinner and the rest of the household either talking in the gallery or already retired to their rooms for the night. The moment seemed well-chosen for a very daring gamble, which might, or might not, prove nothing to me. I turned down the passage and halted outside the door of the locked chamber. I listened again, but no one stirred. Then very stealthily I pushed the key into the rusty lock. It fitted. It turned. And the door creaked open. I was so carried away for a moment by the success of my own scheme that I was nonplussed. I sat in my chair, uncertain what to do. But that there was a link between this chamber and the summer-house now seemed definite, for the key turned both locks.

The chance to examine the room might never come again, and, for all my fear, I was devoured with horrid curiosity. I edged my chair within the room, and kindling my candle—for it was of course in darkness, with the windows barred—I looked about me. The chamber was simple enough. Two windows, one to the north and the other to the west, both with iron bars across them. A bed in the far corner, a few pieces of heavy furniture, and the table and chair I had already seen from the crack. The walls were hung about with a heavy arras, rather old, and worn in many parts. It was indeed a disappointing room, with little that seemed strange in its appointments. It had the faded musty smell that always clings about disused apartments. I laid the candle on the table, and wheeled myself to the corner that gave upon the buttress. This too had an arras hanging from the ceilings, which I lifted—and found nothing but bare stone behind it. I ran my hands over the surface, but could find no join. The wall seemed smooth to my touch. But it was murky, and I could not see, so I returned to the table to fetch my candle, first listening at the door to make certain that the servants were still at supper. It was while I waited there, with an eye to the passage that turned at right angles, running beneath the belfry, that I felt a sudden breath of cold air on the back of my head.

I looked swiftly over my shoulder, and noticed that the arras on the wall beside the buttress was blowing to and fro, as though a cavity had opened, letting through a blast of air, and even as I watched, I saw, to my great horror, a hand appear from behind a slit in the arras and lift it to one side. There was no time to wheel my chair into the passage, no time even to reach my hand out to the table and blow the candle. Someone came into the room with a crimson cloak about his shoulders, and stood for a moment, with the arras pushed aside and a great black hole in the wall behind him. He considered me a moment, and then spoke. "Close the door gently, Honor," he said, "and leave the candle. Since you are here it is best that we should have an explanation, and no further mischief."

He advanced into the room, letting the arras drop behind him, and I saw then that the man was my brother-in-law, Jonathan Rashleigh.

CHAPTER TWELVE

I FELT LIKE a child caught out in some misdemeanour, and was hot with shame and sick embarrassment. If he then was the stranger in the crimson cloak, walking his house in the small hours, it was not for me to question it. To be discovered thus, prying in his secrets, with the key not only of this door, but of his summer-house as well, was surely something he could never pardon.

"Forgive me," I said. "I have acted very ill."

He did not answer at once, but first made certain that the door was closed. Then he lit further candles, and, laying aside his cloak, drew a chair up to the table.

"It was you," he said, "who made a crack there in the panel? It was not there before you came to Menabilly."

His blunt question showed me what a shrewd grasp he had of my gaping curiosity, and I confessed that I was indeed the culprit. "I will not attempt to defend myself," I said. "I know I had no right to tamper with your walls. There was some talk of ghosts, otherwise I would not have done it. And one night during last week I heard footsteps."

"Yes," he said. "I had not thought to find your chamber occupied. I heard you stir, and guessed then what had happened. We are somewhat pushed for room, as you no doubt realise, otherwise you would not have been put into the gatehouse."

He waited a moment, and then, looking closely at me, he said: "You have understood, then, that there is a secret entry to this chamber."

"Yes."

"And the reason you are here this evening is that you wished to find whither it led?"

"I knew it must be within the buttress."

"How did you come upon that key?"

This was the very devil, but there was nothing for it but to tell him the whole story, putting the blame heavily upon myself and saying little of Joan's share in the matter. I said that I had looked about the summer-house, and admired the view, but as to my peering at his books, and his father's will and lifting the heavy mat and finding the flagstone—nay, he would have to put me on the rack before I confessed to that.

He listened in silence, regarding me coldly all the while, and I knew what an interfering fool he must consider me.

"And what do you make of it, now you know that the nightly intruder is none other than myself?" he questioned.

Here was a stumbling-block. For I could make nothing of it. And I did not dare voice that secret, very fearful supposition that I kept hidden at the back of my mind.

"I cannot tell, Jonathan," I answered, "except that you use this entry for some purpose of your own, and that your family know nothing of it." At this he was silent, considering me slowly, and then, after a long pause, he said to me: "John has some knowledge of the subject, but no one else, except my steward Langdon. Indeed, the success of the royal cause we have at heart would gravely suffer should the truth become known."

This last surprised me. I did not see that his family secrets could be of any concern to His Majesty. But I said nothing.

"Since you already know something of the truth," he said, "I will acquaint you further, desiring you first to keep all knowledge of it to yourself."

I promised, after a moment's hesitation, being uncertain what dire secret I might now be asked to share.

"You know," he said, "that at the beginning of hostilities I, with certain other gentlemen, was appointed by His Majesty's Council to collect and receive the plate given to the royal cause in Cornwall, and arrange for it to be taken to the Mint at Truro and there melted down?"

"I knew you were Collector, Jonathan—no more than that."

"Last year another Mint was erected at Exeter, under the supervision of my kinsman, Sir Richard Vyvyan, hence my constant business with that city. You will appreciate, Honor, that to receive a great quantity of very valuable plate, and be responsible for its safety until it reaches the Mint, is a heavy burden upon my shoulders."

"Yes, Jonathan."

"Spies abound, as you are well aware. Neighbours have long ears, and even a close friend can turn informer. If some member of the rebel army could but lay his hands upon the treasure that so frequently passes into my keeping, Parliament would be ten times the richer, and His Majesty ten times the poorer. Therefore all cartage of the plate has to be done at night, when the roads are quiet. Also it is necessary to have depots throughout the county, where the plate can be stored until the necessary transport can be arranged. These depots must be secret. As few people as possible must know their whereabouts. It is therefore imperative that the houses or buildings that serve as depots should contain hiding-places, known only to their owners. Menabilly, as you have already discovered, has such a hiding-place."

I found myself getting hot under the skin, not at the implied sarcasm of his words, but because his revelation was so very different from what I—with excess of imagination—had supposed.

"The buttress against the far corner of this room," he continued, "is hollow in the centre. A flight of narrow steps leads to a small room, built in the thickness of the wall and beneath the courtyard, where it is possible for a man to stand, and sit, though it is but five feet square. This room is connected with a passage, or rather tunnel, which runs under the house and so beneath the causeway to an outlet in the summer-house. It is in this small buttress room that I have been accustomed, during the past year, to hide the plate.

"When the plate is brought to this depot," he went on, "or taken away, we work by night, my steward, John Langdon, and I. The wagons wait down at Pridmouth, and we bring the plate from the buttress room, along the tunnel to the summer-house, and so down to the cove in one of my hand-carts, where it is placed in the wagons. The men who conduct the procession from here to Exeter are all trustworthy, but none of them, naturally, know whereabouts at Menabilly I have kept the plate hidden. That is not their business. No one knows that but myself and Langdon, and now you, Honor, who—I regret to say—have really no right at all to share the secret."

I said nothing, for there was no possible defence.

"John knows the plate has been concealed in the house, but has never enquired where. He is, as yet, ignorant of the room beneath the buttress, as well as the tunnel to the summer-house."

Here I risked offence by interrupting him.

"It was providential," I said, "that Menabilly possessed so excellent a hiding-place."

"Very providential," he agreed. "Had it not been so I could hardly have set about the business. You wonder, no doubt, why the house should have been so constructed?"

I confessed to some small wonder on the subject.

"My father," he said briefly, "had certain—how shall I put it?—shipping transactions, which necessitated privacy. The tunnel was therefore useful in many ways."

In other words, I said to myself, your father, dear Jonathan, was nothing more or less than a pirate of the first order, whatever his standing and reputation in Fowey and the county.

"It happened also," he said in a lower tone, "that my unfortunate eldest brother was not in full possession of his faculties. This was his chamber, from the time the house was built in 1600 until his death, poor fellow, twenty-four years later. At times he was violent, hence the reason for the little cell beneath the buttress, where lack of air and close confinement soon rendered him unconscious and easy then to handle."

He spoke naturally, and without restraint, but the picture that his words conjured up turned me sick. I saw the wretched, shivering maniac choking for air in the dark room beneath the buttress, with the four walls closing in upon him. And now this same room stacked with silver plate like a treasure-house in a fairy-tale.

Jonathan must have seen my change of face, for he looked kindly at me and rose from his chair.

"I know," he said, "it is not a pretty story. It was a relief to me, I must admit, when the smallpox that carried off my father took my brother too. It was not a happy business caring for him, with young children in the house. You have heard, no doubt, the malicious tales that Robert Bennett spread abroad?"

I mentioned vaguely that some rumour had come to my ears.

"He took the disease some five days after my father," said Jonathan. "Why he should have taken it, while my wife and I escaped, we shall never know. But so he did, and, becoming violent at the same time with one of his periodic fits, stood not a chance. It was over very quickly."

There were sounds of the servants moving from the kitchens.

"You will return now to your apartment," he said, "and I will go back the way I came. You may give me John Langdon's key. If in future you hear me come to this apartment, you will understand what I am about. I keep accounts here of the plate temporarily in my possession, which I refer to from time to time. I need hardly tell you that not a word of what has this night passed between us must be spoken about to any other person."

"I give you my solemn promise, Jonathan."

"Good-night, then, Honor."

He helped me turn my chair into the passage, and then, very softly, closed the door behind me. I reached my own room a few moments before Matty came upstairs to draw the curtains.

CHAPTER THIRTEEN

Although there were never any ties of affection between my brother-in-law and myself, I certainly held him in greater respect and regard after our encounter of that evening. I knew now that "the King's business" on which he travelled to and fro was no light matter, and it was small wonder he was often short-tempered with his family. I respected him too for having taken me into his confidence, after my unwarrantable intrusion into his locked chamber. I was left only with a sneaking regret that he had not shown me the staircase in the buttress or the cell beneath it, but this would have been too much to expect. I had a vivid picture, though, of the flapping arras and the black gulf behind. Meanwhile, the progress of the war was causing each one of us no small concern. Our western army was under the supreme command of the King's nephew, Prince Maurice, who was in great need of reinforcements, especially of cavalry, if he was ever to strike a decisive blow against the enemy. But the plan of the summer campaign appeared unsettled, and although Maurice's brother, Prince Rupert, endeavoured to persuade the King to send some two thousand horse into the west there was the usual obstruction from the Council, and the cavalry were not forthcoming. This, of course, we heard from Richard, who, fuming with impatience because he had as yet none of the guns that had been promised him, told us with grim candour that our western army was anyhow worn with sickness, and quite useless, and that Prince Maurice himself had but one bee in his bonnet, which was to sit before Lyme Regis, waiting for the place to open up to him.

"If Essex and the rebel army choose to march west," said Richard, "there is nothing to stop him, except a mob of sick men all lying on their backs, and a handful of drunken generals. I can do nothing, with my miserable two men and a boy squatting before Plymouth." Essex did choose to march west, and was in Weymouth and Bridport by the third week of June, and Prince Maurice, with great loss of prestige, retreated in haste to Exeter.

Here he found his aunt, the Queen, who had arrived in a litter from Bristol, being fearful of the approaching enemy, and it was here at Exeter that she gave birth to her youngest child, which did not lessen the responsibilities of Prince Maurice and his staff. He decided that the wisest course was to get her away to France as speedily as possible, and she set forth for Falmouth, very weak and nervous, two weeks after the baby had been born.

My brother-in-law Jonathan was among those who waited on her as she passed through Bodmin on her way south, and came back telling a very pitiful tale of her appearance, for she was much worn and shaken by her ordeal. "She may have advised His Majesty ill on many an occasion," said Jonathan, "but at least she is a woman, and I tremble to think of her fate if she fell into the hands of the rebels." It was a great relief to all the Royalists in Cornwall when she reached Falmouth without mishap, and embarked for France.

But Essex and the rebel army were gathering in numbers all the while, and we felt it was but a matter of weeks before he passed through Dorset into Devon, with nothing but the Tamar then between him and Cornwall. The only one who viewed the approaching struggle with relish was Richard. "If we can but draw the beggar into Cornwall," he said, "a country of which he knows nothing, and whose narrow lanes and high hedges would befog him completely, then, with the King's and Rupert's army coming up in the rear and cutting off all retreat, we will have him surrounded and destroyed."

I remember him rubbing his hands gleefully, and laughing at the prospect like a boy on holiday, but the idea did not much appeal to Jonathan and other gentlemen, who were dining at Menabilly on that day. "If we have fighting in Cornwall, the country will be devastated," said Francis Bassett, who with my brother-in-law was engaged at that time in trying to raise troops for the King's service, and finding it mighty hard. "The land is too poor to feed an army—we cannot do it. The fighting must be kept the other side of the Tamar, and we look to you and your troops, Grenvile, to engage the enemy in Devon and keep us from invasion."

"My good fool," said Richard—at which Francis Bassett coloured, and we all felt uncomfortable—"you are a country squire, and I respect your knowledge of cattle and pigs. But for God's sake leave the art of war to professional soldiers like myself. Our aim at present is to destroy the enemy, which we cannot do in Devon, where there is no hope of encirclement. Once across the Tamar he will run his head into a noose. My only fear is that he will not do so, but will use his superior cavalry on the open Devon moors against Maurice and his hopeless team of half-wits, in which case we shall have lost one of the greatest chances this war has yet produced."

"You are prepared, then," said Jonathan, "to see Cornwall laid waste, people homeless, and much sickness and suffering spread abroad? It does not appear to be a prospect of much comfort."

"Damn your comfort," said Richard. "It will do my fellow countrymen a world of good to see a spot of bloodshed. If you cannot suffer that for the King's cause, then we may as well treat with the enemy forthwith."

There was some atmosphere of strain in the dining-chamber when he had spoken, and shortly afterwards my brother-in-law gave the signal for dispersal. It was an oddity I could not explain even to myself that since Richard had come back into my life I could face company with greater equanimity that I had done before, and had now formed the habit of eating downstairs rather than in my chamber. Solitude was no longer my one aim. After dining, since it was still light, he took a turn with me upon the causeway, making himself attendant to my chair.

"If Essex draws near to Tavistock," he said, "and I am forced to raise the siege of Plymouth and retreat, can I send the whelp to you?"

I was puzzled for a moment, thinking he alluded to his dog.

"What whelp?" I asked. "I did not know you possessed one."

"The south-west makes you slow of brain," he said. "My spawn, I mean— my pup, my son and heir. Will you have him here under your wing and put some sense into his frightened head?"

"Why, yes, indeed, if you think he would be happy with me."

"I think he would be happier with you than with any other person in the world."

"Have you spoken to Jonathan?"

"Yes. He is willing. But I wonder what you will make of Dick. He is a scrubby object."

"I will love him, Richard, because he is your son."

"I doubt that sometimes when I look at him. He has a shrinking, timid way with him, and his tutor tells me that he cries for a finger scratch. I would exchange him any day for young Joe Grenvile, a kinsman, whom I have as aide-de-camp at Buckland. He is up to any daring scheme, that lad, and a fellow after my own heart, like Bevil's eldest boy."

"Dick is barely turned fourteen," I said to him. "You must not expect too much. Give him a year or two to learn confidence."

"If he has taken after his mother, then I'll turn him off and let him starve," said Richard. "I won't have frog's spawn about me."

"Perhaps," I said, "your example does not greatly encourage him to take after yourself. Were I a child I would not want a red fox for a father."

"He is the wrong age for me," said Richard: "too big to dandle, and too small to talk to. He is yours, Honor, from this day forward. I declare I will bring him over to you this day week."

And so it was arranged, with Jonathan's permission, that Dick Grenvile and his tutor, Herbert Ashley, should add to the numbers at Menabilly. I was strangely happy and excited the day they were expected, and went with my sister Mary to inspect the room that had been put to their service beneath the clock-tower.

I took pains with my toilet, wearing my blue gown that was my favourite, and bidding Matty brush my hair for half the morning. And all the while I told myself what a sentimental fool I was to waste such time and trouble for a little lad who would not look at me. It was about one o'clock that I heard the horses trotting across the park, and I called in a fever to Matty to fetch the servants to carry me downstairs, for I wished to be in the garden when I greeted them, for I have a firm belief that it is always easier to become acquainted with anyone out of doors, in the sun, than shut fast within four walls.

I was seated, then, in the walled garden beneath the causeway, when the gate opened and a lad came walking across the lawn towards me. He was taller than I had imagined, with the flaming Grenvile locks, and an impudent snub-nose, and a swagger about him that reminded me instantly of Richard. And then, as he spoke, I realised my mistake. "My name is Joe Grenvile," he said. "They have sent me from the house to bring you back. There has been a slight mishap. Poor Dick tumbled from his horse as we drew rein in the courtyard—the stones were somewhat slippery—and he has cut his head. They have taken him to your chamber, and your maid is washing off the blood."

This was very different from the picture I had painted, and I was at once distressed that the arrival should have gone awry.

"Is Sir Richard with you?" I asked as he wheeled me down the path.

"Yes," said young Joe, "and in a great state of irritation, cursing poor Dick for incompetence, which made the little fellow worse. We have to leave again within the hour. Essex has reached Tiverton, you know, and Taunton Castle is also in the rebel's hands. Prince Maurice has withdrawn several units from our command, and there is to be a conference at Okehampton, which Sir Richard must attend. Ours are the only troops that are now left outside Plymouth."

"And you find all this greatly stirring, do you, Joe?" I asked.

"Yes, madam. I can hardly wait to have a crack at the enemy myself."

We turned in at the garden entrance, and found Richard pacing up and down the hall. "You would hardly believe it possible," he said, "but the whelp must go and tumble from his horse, right on the very doorstep. Sometimes I think he has softening of the brain, to act in so boobish a fashion. What do you think of Joe?" He clapped the youngster on the shoulder, who looked up at him with pride and devotion. "We shall make a soldier of this chap, anyway," he said. "Go and draw me some ale, Joe, and a tankard for yourself. I'm as thirsty as a drowning man."

"What of Dick?" I asked. "Shall I not go to him?"

"Leave him to the women and his useless tutor," said Richard. "You'll soon have enough of him. I have one hour to spend at Menabilly, and I want you to myself." We went to the little ante-room beyond the gallery, and there he sat with me while he drank his ale, and told me that Essex would be at Tavistock before the week was out.

"If he marches on Cornwall, then we have him trapped," said Richard, "and if the King will only follow fast enough on his heels the game is ours. It will be unpleasant while it lasts, my sweetheart, but it will not be for long, that I can promise you."

"Shall we see fighting in this district?" I asked, with some misgiving.

"Impossible to answer. It depends on Essex, whether he strikes north or south. He will make for Liskeard and Bodmin, where we shall try to hold him. Pray for a dirty August, Honor, and they will be up to their eyes in mud. I must go. I sleep to-night in Launceston, if I can make it." He put his tankard on the table, and, first closing the door, knelt beside my chair. "Look after the little whelp," he said, "and teach him manners. If the worst should happen and there be fighting in the neighbourhood, hide him under your bed. Essex would take any son of mine as hostage. Do you love me still?"

"I love you always."

"Then cease listening for footsteps in the gallery, and kiss me as though you meant it."

It was easy for him, no doubt, to hold me close for five minutes and have me in a turmoil with his love-making, and then ride away to Launceston, his mind aflame with other matters; but for me, left with my hair and gown in disarray, and no method of escape, and long hours stretching before me to think about it all, it was rather more disturbing. I had chosen the course, though—I had let him come back into my life, and I must put up with the fever he engendered in me which could never more be stilled.

So, calling to his aide-de-camp, he waved his hand to me and rode away to Launceston, where, I told myself with nagging jealousy, he and young Joe would in all probability dine overwell and find some momentary distraction before the more serious business of to-morrow, for I knew my Richard too well to believe he lived a life of austerity simply because he loved me.

I patted my curls, and smoothed my lace collar, then pulled the bellrope for a servant, who, with the aid of another, bore me in my chair to my apartments. I did not pass through the front of the house, as was my custom, but through the back rooms beneath the belfry, and here in a passage I found Frank Penrose, my brother-in-law's cousin and dependant, engaged in earnest conversation with a young man of about his own age who had a sallow complexion and retreating chin, and who appeared to be recounting the story of his life.

"This is Mr Ashley, Mistress Honor," said Frank with the smarming manner peculiar to him. "He has left his charge resting in your apartment."

Mr Ashley bowed and scraped his heels.

"Sir Richard informed me you are the boy's godmother, madam," he said, "and that I am to take my commands from you. It is, of course, rather irregular, but I will endeavour to adapt myself to the circumstances." You are a fool, I thought, and a prig, and I don't think I am going to like you, but aloud I said: "Please continue, Mr Ashley, as you have been accustomed to at Buckland. I have no intention of interfering in any way, except to see that the boy is happy." I left them both bowing and scraping, and ready to pull me to pieces as soon as my back was turned, and so was brought to the gatehouse. I met Matty coming forth with a basin of water, and strips of bandage on her arm.

"Is he much hurt?" I asked.

Her lips were drawn in the tight line that I knew meant disapproval of the whole proceeding.

"More frightened than anything else," she said. "He'll fall to pieces if you look at him."

The servants set me down in the room and withdrew, closing the door. He was sitting hunched up in a chair beside the hearth, a white shrimp of a boy with great dark eyes and tight black locks, his pallor worsened by the bandage on his head. He watched me nervously, biting his nails all the while.

"Are you better?" I said gently.

He stared at me for a moment, and then said, with a queer jerk of his head: "Has he gone?"

"Has who gone?" I asked.

"My father."

"Yes. He has ridden away to Launceston with your cousin."

He considered this a moment. "When will he be back?" he asked.

"He will not be back. He has to attend a meeting at Okehampton to-morrow or the following day. You are to stay here for the present. Did he not tell you who I am?"

"I think you must be Honor. He said I was to be with a lady who was beautiful. Why do you sit in that chair?"

"Because I cannot walk. I am a cripple."

"Does it hurt?"

"No. Not very much. I am used to it. Does your head hurt you?"

He touched the bandage warily. "It bled," he said. "There is blood under the bandage."

"Never mind, it will soon heal."

"I will keep the bandage on or it will bleed afresh," he said. "You must tell the servant who washed it not to move the bandage."

"Very well," I said, "I will tell her."

I took a piece of tapestry and began to work on it so that he should not think I watched him, and would grow accustomed to my presence.

"My mother used to work at tapestry," he said after a lengthy pause. "She worked a forest scene with stags running."

"That was pretty," I said.

"She made three covers for her chairs," he went on. "They were much admired at Fitzford. You never came to Fitzford, I believe?"

"No, Dick."

"My mother had many friends, but I did not hear her speak of you."

"I do not know your mother, Dick. I only know your father."

"Do you like him?" The question was suspicious, sharply put.

"Why do you ask?" I said, evading it.

"Because I don't. I hate him. I wish he would be killed in battle." The tone was savage, venomous. I stole a glance at him, and saw him once more biting at the back of his hand.

"Why do you hate him?" I asked quietly.

"He is a devil, that's why. He tried to kill my mother. He tried to steal her house and money, and then kill her."

"Why do you think that?"

"My mother told me."

"Do you love her very much?"

"I don't know. I think so. She was beautiful. More beautiful than you. She is in London now, with my sister. I wish I could be with her."

"Perhaps," I said, "when the war is finished with, you will go back to her."

"I would run away," he said, "but for London being so far, and that I might get caught in the fighting. There is fighting everywhere. There is no talk of anything at Buckland but the fighting. I will tell you something."

"What is that?"

"Last week I saw a wounded man brought into the house upon a stretcher. There was blood upon him."

The way he said this puzzled me, his manner was so shrinking.

"Why," I asked, "are you so much afraid of blood?"

The colour flamed into his pale face. "I did not say I was afraid," he answered quickly.

"No, but you do not like it. Neither do I. It is most unpleasant. But I am not fearful if I see it spilt."

"I cannot bear to see it spilt at all," he said, after a moment. "I have always been thus, since I was a little child. It is not my fault."

"Perhaps you were frightened as a baby."

"That's what my mother brought me up to understand. She told me that when she had me in her arms once my father came into the room and quarrelled violently with her upon some matter, and that he struck her on the face, and she bled. The blood ran on to my hands. I cannot remember it, but that is how it was."

I began to feel very sick at heart, and despondent, but was careful that he should not notice it.

"We won't talk about it any more then, Dick, unless you want to. What shall we discuss instead?"

"Tell me what you did when you were my age, how you looked, and what you said; and had you brothers and sisters?"

And so I wove him a tale about the past, thus making him forget his own, while he sat watching me; and by the time Matty came, bringing us refreshment, he had lost enough of his nervousness to chat with her too, and make big eyes at the pasties, which soon disappeared, while I sat and looked at his little chiselled features, so unlike his father's, and the close black curls upon his head. Afterwards I read to him for a while, and he left his chair and came and curled on the floor beside my chair, like a small dog who would make friends in a strange house, and when I closed the book he looked up at me and smiled—and the smile for the first time was Richard's smile and not his mother's.

CHAPTER FOURTEEN

FROM THAT DAY forward Dick became my shadow. He arrived early, with my breakfast, never my best moment of the day, but because he was Richard's son I suffered him. He then left to do his lessons with the sallow Mr Ashley while I made my toilet, and later in the morning came to walk beside my chair upon the causeway.

He sat beside me in the dining-chamber, and brought a stool to the gallery when I went there after dinner; seldom speaking, always watchful, he hovered continually about me like a small phantom.

"Why do you not run and play in the gardens?" I asked. "Or ask Mr Ashley to take you down to Pridmouth? There are fine shells there on the beach, and as the weather is warm you could swim if you had the mind. There's a young cob, too, in the stables you could ride across the park."

"I would rather stay with you," he said.

And he was firm on this, and would not be dissuaded. Even Alice, who had the warmest way with children I ever saw, failed with him, for he would shake his head and take his stool behind my chair.

"He has certainly taken a fancy to you, madam," said the tutor, relieved, I am sure, to find his charge so little trouble. "I have found it very hard to interest him."

"He is your conquest," said Joan, "and you will never more be rid of him. Poor Honor. What a burden to the end of your days!"

But it did not worry me. If Dick was happy with me, that was all that mattered, and if I could bring some feeling of security to his poor lonely little heart and puzzled mind I should not feel my days were wasted. Meanwhile, the news worsened, and some five days after Dick's arrival word came from Fowey that Essex had reached Tavistock, and the siege of Plymouth had been raised, with Richard withdrawing his troops from Saltash, Mount Stampford, and Plympton, and retreating to the Tamar bridges.

That evening a council was held in Tywardreath amongst the gentry in the district, at which my brother-in-law presided, and one and all decided to muster what men and arms and ammunition they could, and ride to Launceston to help defend the county.

The following morning saw the preparations for departure. All those on the estate who were able-bodied and fit to carry arms paraded before my brother-in-law with their horses, their kit packed on the saddles, and amongst them were the youngest of the house-servants who could be spared and all the grooms. Jonathan, his son-in-law, John Rashleigh of Coombe, and Oliver Sawle from Penrice—brother to old Nick Sawle—and many other gentlemen from round about Fowey and St Austell gathered at Menabilly before setting forth, while my poor sister Mary went from one to the other with her face set in a smile which I knew was sadly forced, handing them cake and fruit and pasties to cheer them on their way. John was left with many long instructions, which I could swear he would never carry in his head, and then we watched them set off across the park, a strange, pathetic little band full of ignorance and high courage, the tenants wielding their muskets as though they were hay-forks, and with considerably more danger to themselves than to the enemy they might encounter. It was '43 all over again, with the rebels not thirty miles away, and although Richard might declare that Essex and his army were running into a trap, I was disloyal enough to wish they might keep out of it.

Those last days of July were clammy warm. A sticky breeze blew from the south-west that threatened rain and never brought it, while a tumbled sea rolled past the Gribben white and grey. At Menabilly we made a pretence of continuing as though all were as usual, and nothing untoward likely to happen, and even forced a little gaiety when dining that we must wait upon ourselves, now that there were none but womenfolk to serve us. But for all this deception, intended to convey a sense of courage, we were tense and watchful—our ears always pricked for the rumble of cannon or the sound of horses. I can remember how we all sat beside the long table in the dining-chamber, the portrait of His Majesty gazing calmly down upon us from the dark panelling above the open hearth, and how at the end of a strained, tedious meal Nick Sawle, who was the eldest amongst us, conquered his rheumatics and rose to his feet in great solemnity, saying, "It were well that, in this time of stress and trouble, we should give a toast unto His Majesty. Let us drink to our beloved King, and may God protect him, and all who have gone forth from this house to fight for him."

They all then rose to their feet too, except myself, and looked up at his portrait—those melancholy eyes, that small obstinate mouth—and I saw the tears run down Alice's cheeks as she thought of Peter, and sad resignation come to Mary's face, her thoughts with Jonathan. Yet none of them, gazing at the King's portrait, dreamed of blaming him for the trouble that had come upon them. God knows I had no sympathy for the rebels, who each one of them was out for feathering his own nest and building up a fortune, caring nothing for the common people whose lot they pretended would be bettered by their victory, but nor could I, in my heart, recognise the King as the fountain of all truth, but thought of him always as a stiff, proud man, small in intelligence as he was in stature, yet commanding, by his grace of manner, his dignity, and his moral virtue, a wild devotion in his followers that sprang from their warm hearts and not their reason.

We were a quiet, subdued party who sat in the long gallery that evening. Even the sharp tongue of Temperance Sawle was stilled, her thin features pinched and anxious, while the Sparkes forewent their usual game of chequers and sat talking in low voices. "Have the rebels crossed the Tamar?" This was, I think, the thought in all our minds, and while Mary, Alice and Joan worked at their tapestry, and I read in a soft voice to Dick, my brain was busy all the while reckoning the shortest distance that the enemy would take, and whether they would cross by Saltash or by Gunnislake. John had left the dining-chamber as soon as the King's health had been drunk, saying he could stand this waiting about no longer, but must ride to Fowey for news. He returned about nine o'clock, with the report that the town was well-nigh empty, with so many ridden to north to join the army, but that those who were left were standing at their doors, glum and despondent, saying that word had come that Grenvile and his troops had been defeated at Newbridge below Gunnislake, while Essex and some ten thousand men were riding towards Launceston. I remember Will Sparke leaping to his feet at hearing this, and breaking out into a tirade against Richard, his shrill voice sharp and nervous. "What have I been saying all along?" he cried. "When it comes to a test like this, the fellow is no commander. The pass at Gunnislake should be easy to defend, no matter the strength of the opponent, and here is Grenvile pulled out and in full retreat without having struck a blow to defend Cornwall. Heaven, what a contrast to his brother."

"It is only rumour, cousin Will," said John with an uncomfortable glance in my direction. "There was no one in Fowey able to swear to the truth of it."

"I tell you, everything is lost," said Will. "Cornwall will be ruined and overrun, even as Sir Francis Bassett said the other day. And if it is so, then Richard Grenvile will be to blame for it."

I watched young Dick swallow the words with eager eyes, and, pulling at my arm, he whispered, "What is it he says? What has happened?"

"John Rashleigh hears that the Earl of Essex has passed into Cornwall," I told him softly, "finding little opposition. We must wait until the tale is verified."

"Then my father has been slain in battle?"

"No, Dick. Nothing has been said of that. Do you wish me to continue reading?"

"Yes, please, if you will do so."

And I went on with the tale, taking no notice of his biting of his hand, for my anxiety was such that I could have done the same myself. Anything might have happened during these past forty-eight hours, Richard left for slain upon the steep road down from Gunnislake and his men fled in all directions, or taken prisoner, perhaps, and at this moment being put to torture in Launceston Castle that he might betray the plan of battle. It was always my fault to let imagination do its worst, and although I guessed enough of Richard's strategy to know that a retreat on the Tamar bank was probably his intention from the first, in order to lure Essex into Cornwall, yet I longed to hear the opposite, and that a victory had been gained that day and the rebels pushed back into Devon.

I slept but ill that night, for to be ignorant of the truth is, I shall always believe, the worst sort of mental torture, and to a powerless woman, who cannot forget her fears in taking action, there is no remedy. The next day was as hot and airless as the one preceding, and when I came down after breakfast I wondered if I looked as haggard and careworn to the rest of the company as they looked to me. And still no news. Everything was strangely silent—even the jackdaws who usually clustered in the trees down in the warren had flown and settled elsewhere. Shortly before noon Mary, coming from her sun parlour across the hall, cried, "There is a horseman riding through the park towards the house." Everyone began talking at once and pushing to the windows, and John, white about the lips, went to the courtyard to receive whomever it should be.

The rider clattered into the inner court, with all of us watching from the windows, and though he was covered from head to foot with dust, and had a great slash across his boot, I recognised him as young Joe Grenvile.

"I have a message for Mistress Harris," he said, flinging himself from his horse. My throat went dry, and my hands wet. He is dead, I thought, for certain.

"But the battle? How goes the battle?" and "What of the rebels?" "What has happened?" Questions on all sides were put to him, with Nick Sawle on one side, and Will Sparke on the other, so that he had to push his way through them to reach me in the hall.

"Essex will be in Bodmin by nightfall," he said briefly. "We have just had a brush above Lostwithiel with Lord Robartes and his brigade, who have now turned back to meet him. We ourselves are in hot retreat to Truro, where Sir Richard plans to raise more troops. I am come from the road but to bring this message to Mistress Harris."

"Essex at Bodmin?" A cry of alarm went up from all the company, and Temperance Sawle went straightway on her knees and called upon her Maker. But I was busy tearing open Richard's letter.

"My sweet love," I read, "the hook is nicely baited, and the poor misguided fish gapes at it with his mouth wide open. He will be in Bodmin at night, and most probably in Fowey to-morrow. His chief adviser in the business is that crass idiot, Jack Robartes, whose mansion at Lanhydrock I have just had infinite pleasure in pillaging. They will swallow the bait hook, line, and sinker. We shall come up on them from Truro, and His Majesty, Maurice, and Ralph Hopton from the east. The King has already advanced as far as Tavistock, so the fish will be most prettily landed. Your immediate future at Menabilly being somewhat unpleasant, it will be best if you return the whelp to me, with his tutor. I have given Joe instructions on the matter. Keep to your chamber, my dear love, and have no fear. We will come to your succour as soon as may be. My respects to your sister and the company.
"Your devoted servant Richard
"Grenvile."

I placed the letter in my gown, and turned to Joe.

"Is the General well?" I asked.

"Never better," he grinned. "I have just left him eating roast pork on the road to Grampound, while his servant cleaned his boots. The troops are in high fettle. If you hear rumours of our losses at Newbridge, pay no attention to them; the higher the figure they are put at by the enemy, the better pleased will be Sir Richard."

I motioned then that I would like to speak with him apart, and he withdrew alone with me to the sun-parlour.

"What is the plan for Dick?" I asked.

"Sir Richard thinks it best if the boy and Mr Ashley embark by fishing-boat for St Mawes, if arrangements can be made with one of the fellows at Polkerris. They can keep close in shore, and once around the Dodman the passage will not be long."

"When should they depart?"

"As soon as possible. I will see to it, and go with them to the beach. Then I shall return to join Sir Richard, and with any luck catch up with him on the Grampound–Truro road. The trouble is that the roads are already choked with people in headlong flight from Essex, all making for the west, and it will not be long now before the rebel cavalry reach the district."

"There is, then, no time to lose," I answered. "I will ask Mr John Rashleigh to go with you to Polkerris—he will know the men there who are most likely to be trusted."

I called John to come to me, and hurriedly explained the plan, whereupon he set forth straightway to Polkerris with Joe Grenvile, while I sent word to Herbert Ashley that I wished to speak to him. He arrived looking very white about the gills, for rumour had run riot in the place that the Grenvile troops were flying in disorder with the rebels on their heels and the war was irrevocably lost. He looked much relieved when I told him that he and Dick were to depart upon the instant, by sea and not by road, and went immediately to pack their things, promising to be ready within the hour. The task then fell upon me to break the news to my shadow. He was standing by the side-door, looking out on to the garden, and I beckoned him to my side.

"Dick," I said to him, "I want you to be brave and sensible. The neighbour-hood is likely to be surrounded by the enemy before another day, and Menabilly will be seized. Your father thinks it better you should not be found here, and I have arranged, therefore, with Mr Rashleigh, that you and your tutor should go by boat to St Mawes, where you will be safe."

"Are you coming too?" he asked.

"No, Dick. This is a very sudden plan, made only for yourselves. I, and the rest of the company, will remain at Menabilly."

"Then so will I."

"No, Dick. You must let me judge for you. And it is best for you to go."

"Does it mean that I must join my father?"

"That I cannot tell. All I know is that the fishing boat is to take you to St Mawes."

He said nothing, but looked queerly sulky and strange, and after a moment or two went up to join his tutor.

I had a pain at the pit of my stomach all the while, for there is nothing so contagious as panic, and the atmosphere of sharp anxiety was rife in the air. In the gallery little groups of people were gathered, all with strained eyes and drawn faces, and Alice's children, aware of tension, chose—poor dears—this moment to be fretful, and were clinging to her skirts crying bitterly.

"There is time yet to reach Truro if only we had conveyance," I heard Will say, his face grey with fear, "but Jonathan took all the horses with him, and the farm wagons would be too slow. Where has John gone? Is it not possible for him to arrange in some manner that we be conducted to Truro?"

His sisters watched him with anxious eyes. Then Nick Sawle, drawing himself up proudly, said in a loud voice: "My wife and I propose to stay at Menabilly. If cowards care to clatter on the roads as fugitives, they are welcome to do so, but I find it a poor return to our Cousin Jonathan to desert his house like rats in a time of trouble."

My sister Mary looked towards me in distress. "What do you counsel, Honor?" she said. "Should we set forth, or should we stay? Jonathan gave me no commands. He assured me that the enemy would not cross the Tamar, or, at the worst, be turned back after a few miles."

"My God," I said, "if you care to hide in the ditches with the driven cattle, then by all means go, but I swear you will fare worse upon the road than you are likely to do at home. Better to starve under your own roof than in the hedges."

"We have plenty of provisions," said Mary, snatching a ray of hope. "We are not likely to want for anything, unless the siege be long." She turned in consultation to her stepdaughters, who were all of them still occupied in calming the children, and I thought it wisest not to spread further consternation by telling her that once the rebels held the house they would make short work of her provisions.

The clock in the belfry had just struck three when Dick and his tutor came down ready for departure. The lad was still sulky, and turned his head from me when I would say good-bye. This was better than the rebellious tears I had expected, and with a cheerful voice I wished him a speedy journey, and assured him that a week or less would see the end of all our troubles. He did not answer, and I signed to Herbert Ashley to take his arm and to start walking across the park with Frank Penrose, who would conduct them to Polkerris, and there fall in with John Rashleigh and Joe Grenvile, who must by this time have matters well arranged.

Anxiety and strain had brought an aching back upon me, and I desired nothing so much as to retire to the gatehouse and lie upon my bed. I sent for Matty, and she, with the help of Joan and Alice, carried me upstairs. I lay upon my bed, wishing with all my heart that I were a man and could ride with Joe Grenvile on the road to Truro, instead of lying there, a woman and a cripple, waiting for the relentless tramp of enemy feet. I had been there but an hour, I suppose, snatching brief oblivion, when I heard once more the sound of a horse galloping across the park, and, calling to Matty, enquired who it should be. She went to the casement and looked out.

"It's Mr John," she said, "in great distress by his expression. Something has gone amiss." My heart sank at her words. Perhaps, after all, the fishermen at Polkerris could not be tempted to set sail. In a moment or two I heard his footstep on the stairs and he flung into my room, forgetting even to knock upon the door.

"We have lost Dick," he said. "He has vanished, and is nowhere to be found." He stood staring at me, the sweat pouring down his face, and I could see that his whole frame was trembling.

"What do you mean? What has happened?" I asked swiftly, raising myself in my bed.

"We were all assembled on the beach," he said, his breath coming quickly, "and the boat was launched. There was a little cuddy below deck, and with my own eyes I saw Dick descend to it, his bundle under his arm. There was no trouble to engage the boat, and the men—both of them stout fellows, well known to me—were willing. Just before they drew anchor we heard a clatter on the cobbles beside the cottages, and some lads came running down in great alarm to tell us that the first body of rebel horse had cut the road from Castledore to Tywardreath, and that Polmear hill was already blocked with troops. At this the men began to make sail, and young Joe Grenvile turned to me with a wink and said, 'It looks as if I must go by water too.' Before I could answer him, he had urged his horse into the sea and was making for the sand flats half a mile away to the westward. It was half tide, but he had reached them, and turned in his saddle to wave to us. He'll be on Gosmoor by now, and half way to St Austell."

"But Dick?" I said. "You say you have lost Dick?"

"He was in the boat," he said stubbornly. "I swear he was in the boat. But we turned to listen to the lads and their tale of the troops at Tywardreath, and then with one accord we watched young Joe put his horse to the water and swim for it. By heaven, Honor, it was the boldest thing I have ever seen a youngster do, for the tide can run swiftly between Polkerris and the flats. And then Ashley the tutor, looking about him, called for Dick, but could not find him. We searched the vessel from stem to stern, but he wasn't there. He was not on the beach. He was not anywhere. For God's sake, Honor, what are we to do now?"

I felt as helpless as he did, and sick with anxiety, for here was I having failed utterly in my trust, and the rebel troops were not two miles away.

"Where is the boat now?" I asked.

"Lying off the Gribben, waiting for a signal from me," said John, "with that useless tutor aboard, with no other thought in his mind but getting to St Mawes. But even if we find the boy, Honor, I fear it will be too late."

"Search the cliffs in all directions," I said, "and the grounds, and the park and pasture. Was anything said to the lad upon the way?"

"I cannot say. I think not. I only heard Frank Penrose tell him that by nightfall he would be with his father."

So that was it, I thought. A moment's indiscretion, but enough to turn Dick from his journey, and make him play truant like a child from school. I could do nothing in the search, but bade John set forth once more with Frank Penrose, saying no word to anyone of what had happened. And, calling to Matty, I bade her take me to the causeway.

CHAPTER FIFTEEN

ONCE ON THE high ground, I had as good a view of the surrounding country as I could wish, and I saw Frank Penrose and John Rashleigh strike out across the park to the beacon fields, and then divide. All the while I had a fear in my heart that the boy had drowned himself, and would be found with the rising tide floating face downwards in the wash below Polkerris cliffs. There was no sign of the boat, and I judged it to be to the westward, beyond Polkerris and the Gribben.

Back and forth we went along the causeway, with Matty pushing my chair, and still no sign of a living soul, nothing but the cattle grazing on the farther hills, and the ripple of a breeze blowing the corn upon the skyline.

Presently I sent Matty within doors for a cloak, for the breeze was freshening, and on her return she told me that stragglers were already pouring into the park from the roads, women, and children, and old men, all with makeshift bundles on their backs, begging for shelter, for the route was cut to Truro and the rebels were everywhere. Many of them were already kindling fires down in the Warren and making rough shelter for the night.

"As I came out just now," said Matty, "a litter borne by four horses came to rest in the courtyard, and a lady within demanded harbourage for herself and her young daughters. I heard the servant say they had been nine hours upon the road."

"Go back, Matty," I said, "and see what you can do to help my sister. None of the servants have any sense left in their heads."

She had not been gone more than ten minutes before I saw two figures coming across the fields towards me. One of them, seeing me upon the causeway, waved his arm, while with the other he held fast to his companion.

It was John Rashleigh, and he had Dick with him.

When they reached me I saw the boy was dripping wet, and scratched about the face and hands by brambles, but for once he was not bothered by the sight of blood, but stared at me defiantly.

"I will not go," he said. "You cannot make me go."

John Rashleigh shook his head at me, and shrugged his shoulders in resignation. "It's no use, Honor," he said. "We shall have to keep him. There's a wash on the beaches now, and I've signalled to the boat to make sail and take the tutor across the bay to Mevagissy or Gorrau, where he must make shift for himself. As for this lad, I found him halfway up the cliff, a mile from Polkerris—he had been waist-deep in water for the past three hours. God only knows what Sir Richard will say to the bungle we have made."

"Never mind Sir Richard. I will take care of him," I said, "when—and if—we ever clap eyes on him again. That boy must return to the house with me and be shifted into dry clothes before anything else is done with him."

Now, the causeway at Menabilly is set high, as I have said, commanding a fine view both to east and to west, and at this moment, I know not why, I turned my head towards the coast road that descended down to Pridmouth from Coombe and Fowey, and I saw, silhouetted on the skyline above the valley, a single horseman. In a moment he was joined by others, who paused an instant on the hill, and then, following their leader, plunged down the narrow roadway to the cove. John saw them too, for our eyes met, and we looked at one another long and silently, while Dick stood between us, his eyes downcast, his teeth chattering.

Richard in the old days was wont to tease me for my south-coast blood, so sluggish, he averred, compared with that which ran through his own north-coast veins, but I swear I thought, in the next few seconds, as rapidly as he had ever done or was likely yet to do.

"Have you your father's keys?" I said to John.

"Yes," he said.

"All of them?"

"All of them."

"Then open the door of the summer-house."

He obeyed me without question—thank God his stern father had taught him discipline—and in an instant we stood at the threshold with the door flung open.

"Lift the mat from beneath the desk there," I said, "and raise the flagstone." He looked at me then in wonder, but went without a word to do as I had bidden him. In a moment the mat was lifted, and the flagstone too and the flight of steps betrayed to view. "Don't ask me any questions, John," I said. "There is no time. A passage runs underground from those steps to the house. Take Dick with you now, first replacing the flagstone above your heads, and crawl with him along the passage to the further end. You will come to a small room, like a cell, and another flight of steps. At the top of the steps is a door, which opens, I believe, from the passage end. But do not try to open it until I give you warning from the house."

I could read the sense of what I said go slowly to his mind, and a dawn of comprehension come into his eyes.

"The chamber next to yours?" he said. "My uncle John."

"Yes," I said. "Give me the keys. Go quickly."

There was no trouble now with Dick. He had gathered from my manner that danger was deadly near and the time for truancy over. He bolted down into the hole like a frightened rabbit. I watched John settle the mat over the flagstone, and then, descending after Dick, he lowered the stone above his head and disappeared. The summer-house was as it had been, empty, and untouched. I leant over in my chair and turned the key in the lock, and then put the keys inside my gown. I looked out to the eastward and saw that the skyline was empty. The troopers would have reached the cove by now, and, after they had watered their horses at the mill, would climb up the further side and be at Menabilly within ten minutes. The sweat was running down my forehead clammy cold, and as I waited for Matty to fetch me—and God only knew how much longer she would be—I thought how I would give all I possessed in the world at that moment for one good swig of brandy.

Far out on the beacon hills I could see Frank Penrose still searching hopelessly for Dick, while in the meadows to the west one of the women from the farm went calling to the cows, all oblivious of the troopers who were riding up the lane.

And at that moment my godchild Joan came hurrying along the causeway to fetch me, her pretty face all strained and anxious, her soft dark hair blowing in the wind.

"They are coming," she said. "We have seen them from the windows. Scores of them, on horseback, riding now across the park."

Her breath caught in a sob, and she began running with me along the causeway, so that I too was caught in a sudden panic and could think of nothing but the wide door of Menabilly still open to enfold me. "I have searched everywhere for John," she faltered, "but I cannot find him. One of the servants said they saw him walking out towards the Gribben. Oh, Honor—the children—what will become of us? What is going to happen?"

I could hear shouting from the park, and out on the hard ground beyond the gates came the steady rhythmic beat of horses trotting; not the light clatter of a company, but line upon line of them, the relentless measure of a regiment, the jingle of harness, the thin alien sound of a bugle.

They were waiting for us by the windows of the gallery, Alice, and Mary, the Sawles, the Sparkes, a little tremulous gathering of frightened people, united now in danger, and two other faces that I did not know, the peaky, startled faces of strange children with lace caps upon their heads and wide lace collars. I remembered then the unknown lady who had flung herself upon my sister's mercy, and as we turned into the hall, slamming the door behind us, I saw the horses that had drawn the litter still standing untended in the courtyard, save that the grooms had thrown blankets upon them, coloured white and crimson, and stamped at the corners with a dragon's head. A dragon's head . . . but even as my memory swung back into the past I heard her voice, cold and clear, rising above the others in the gallery. "If only it can be Lord Robartes, I can assure you all no harm will come to us. I have known him well these many years, and am quite prepared to speak on your behalf."

"I forgot to tell you," whispered Joan. "She came with her two daughters, scarce an hour ago. The road was held, and they could not pass St Blazey. It is Mrs Denys of Orley Court."

Her eyes swung round to me. Those same eyes, narrow, heavy-lidded, that I had seen often in my more troubled dreams, and her gold hair, golder than it had been in the past, for art had taken counsel with Nature and outstripped it. She stared at the sight of me, and for a second I caught a flash of odd discomfort like a flicker in her eyes, and then she smiled her slow, false, well-remembered smile, and, stretching out her hands, she said, "Why, Honor, this is indeed a pleasure. Mary did not tell me that you too were here at Menabilly."

I ignored the proffered hand, for a cripple in a chair can be as ill-mannered as she pleases, and as I stared back at her in my own fashion, with suspicion and foreboding in my heart, we heard the horses ride into the courtyard and the bugles blow. Poor Temperance Sawle went down upon her knees, the children whimpered, and my sister Mary, with her arm about Joan and Alice, stood very white and still. Only Gartred watched with cool eyes, her hands playing gently with her girdle.

"Pray hard and pray fast, Mrs Sawle," I said. "The vultures are gathering."

And, since there was no brandy in the room, I poured myself some water from a jug, and raised my glass to Gartred.

CHAPTER SIXTEEN

I T WAS WILL SPARKE, I remember, who went to unbar the door—though he had been the first to bolt it earlier—and as he did so he excused himself in his high-pitched, shaking voice, saying, "It is useless to start by offending them. Our only hope lies in placating them."

We could see through the windows how the troopers dismounted, staring about them with confident, hard faces beneath their close-fitting skull helmets, and it seemed to me that one and all they looked the same, with their cropped heads and their drab brown leather jerkins, and this ruthless similarity was both startling and grim. In a moment we heard their heavy footsteps in the house, clamping through the dining-chamber and up the stairs, and into the gallery returned Will Sparke, a nervous smile on his face, which was drained of all colour. Behind him came three officers, the first a burly man with a long nose and heavy jaw, wearing a green sash about his waist. I recognised him at once as Lord Robartes, the owner of Lanhydrock, who in former days had gone riding and hawking with my brother Kit, but was not much known to the rest of us. He was now our enemy, and could dispose of us as he wished. "Where is the owner of the house?" he asked.

"My husband is from home," said Mary, coming forward, "and my stepson somewhere in the grounds."

"Is everyone living in the place assembled here?"

"All except the servants."

"You have no malignants in hiding?"

"None."

Lord Robartes turned to the staff officer at his side.

"Make a thorough search of the house and grounds," he said. "Break down any door you find locked, and test the panelling for places of concealment. Give orders to the farm-people to round up all sheep and cattle and other livestock, and place men in charge of them, and the granaries. We will take over this gallery and all other rooms on the ground-floor for our personal use. Troops to bivouac in the park."

"Very good, sir." The officer stood to attention, and then departed about his business. Lord Robartes drew up a chair to the table and the remaining officer gave him paper and a quill.

"Now, madam," he said to Mary, "give me your full name and the name and occupation of each member of your household."

One by one he had us documented, looking at each victim keenly as though the very admission of name and age betrayed some sign of guilt. Only when he came to Gartred did his manner relax something of its hard suspicion. "A foolish time to journey, Mrs Denys," he said. "You would have done better to remain at Orley Court."

"There are so many soldiery abroad of little discipline and small respect," said Gartred languidly. "It is not very pleasant for a widow with young daughters to live alone, as I do. I hoped by travelling south to escape the fighting."

"You thought wrong," he answered, "and I am afraid you must abide by the consequences of such an error. You will have to remain here in custody with Mrs Rashleigh and her household."

Gartred bowed, and did not answer. Lord Robartes rose to his feet. "When the apartments above have been searched you may go to them," he said, addressing Mary and the rest of us, "and I must request you to remain in them until further orders. Exercise once a day will be permitted in the garden here, under close escort. You must prepare your food as, and how, you are able. We shall take command of the kitchens, and certain stores will be allotted to you. Your keys, madam."

I saw Mary falter, and then, slowly and reluctantly, she unfastened the string from her girdle. "Can I not have entry there myself?" she asked. "No, madam. The stores are no longer yours, but the possession of the Parliament, like everything pertaining to this estate."

I thought of the jars of preserves upon Mary's shelves, the honeys, and the jams, and the salted pilchards in the larders, and the smoked hams, and the sides of salted mutton. I thought of the bread in the bakeries, the flour in the bins, the grain in the granaries, the young fruit setting in the orchards. And all the while I thought of this, the sound of heavy feet came tramping from above, and out in the grounds came the bugle's cry.

"I thank you, madam. I must warn you, and the rest of the company, that any attempt at escape, any contravention of my orders, will be punished with extreme severity."

"What about milk for the children?" said Joan, her cheeks very flushed, her head high. "We must have milk, and butter, and eggs. My little son is delicate, and inclined to croup."

"Certain stores will be given you daily, madam—I have already said so," said Lord Robartes. "If the children need more nourishment, you must do without yourselves. I have some five hundred men to quarter here, and their needs come before yours, or your children's. Now you may go to your apartments."

This was the moment I had waited for, and, catching Joan's eye, I summoned her to my side. "You must give up your apartment to Mrs Denys," I murmured, "and come to me in the gatehouse. I shall move my bed into the adjoining chamber." Her lips framed a question, but I shook my head. She had sense enough to accept it, for all her agitation, and went at once to Mary with the proposition, who was so bewildered by the loss of her keys that her natural hospitality had deserted her.

"I beg of you to make no move because of me," said Gartred, smiling, her arms about her children. "May and Gertie and I can fit in anywhere. The house is something like a warren—I remember it of old."

I looked at her thoughtfully, and remembered then how Kit had been at Oxford at the same time as my brother-in-law, when old Mr Rashleigh was still alive, and that during the days of Jonathan's first marriage Kit had ridden over to Menabilly often from Lanrest.

"You have been here before then?" I said to Gartred.

"Why, bless me, yes," she yawned. "Some five-and-twenty years ago Kit and I came for a harvest supper, and lost ourselves about the passages." But at this moment Lord Robartes, who had been conferring with his officer, turned from the door.

"You will now, please," he said, "retire to your apartments."

We went out the further door, where the servants were huddled like a flock of startled sheep, and Matty and two others grasped the arms of my chair. Already the troopers were in the kitchens, in full command, and the round of beef that had been roasting for our dinner was being cut into great slices and served out amongst them, while down the stairs came three more of them, two fellows and a non-commissioned officer, bearing loads of Mary's precious stores in their arms. Another had a great pile of blankets, and a rich embroidered cover that had been put aside until winter in the linen room.

"Oh, but they cannot have that," said Mary. "Where is an officer? I must speak to someone of authority."

"I have authority," replied the sergeant, "to remove all linen, blankets, and covers that we find. So keep a cool temper, lady, for you'll find no redress." They stared us coolly in the face, and one of them favoured Alice with a bold, familiar stare, and then whispered something in the ear of his companion.

Oh, God, how I hated them upon the instant. I, who had regarded the war with irony and cynicism hitherto, and a bitter shrug of the shoulder, was now filled with burning anger when it touched me close. Their muddied boots had trampled the floors, and upstairs wanton damage could at once be seen where they had thrust their pikes into the panelling and stripped the hangings from the walls. In Alice's apartments the presses had been overturned and the contents spilled upon the floor, and already a broken casement hung upon its hinge with the glass shattered. Alice's nurse was standing in the centre of the room, crying and wringing her hands, for the troopers had carried off some of the children's bedding, and one clumsy oaf had trodden his heel upon the children's favourite doll and smashed its head to pieces. At the sight of this, their precious toy, the little girls burst into torrents of crying, and I knew then the idiot rage that surges within a man in wartime and compels him to commit murder.

I took one glance, and then bade Matty and her companions bear me to my room. It had suffered like disturbance, with the bed tumbled and the stuffing ripped from the chairs for no rhyme or reason, and they had saved me the trouble of unlocking the barred chamber, for the door was broken in and pieces of planking strewn about the floor. The arras was torn in places, but the arras that hung before the buttress was still and undisturbed.

I thanked God in my heart for the cunning of old John Rashleigh, and desiring Matty to set me down beside the window I looked out into the courtyard, and saw the soldiers all gathered below, line upon line of them, with their horses tethered, and the tents gleaming white already in process of erection in the park, with the campfires burning, and the cattle lowing as they were driven by the soldiers to a pen, and all the while that God-damned bugle blowing, high-pitched and insistent, in a single key. I turned from the window, and told Matty that Joan and her children would now be coming to the gatehouse, and I would remain here, in the chamber that had been barred.

"The troopers have made short work of mystery," said Matty, looking about her, and at the broken door. "There was nothing put away here after all, then."

When the two rooms were in order, and the servants had helped Matty to repair the door, thus giving me my privacy from Joan, I sent them from me to give assistance to Joan on making place for Gartred in the southern front. All was now quiet, save for the constant tramping of soldiers in the court below, and the comings and goings beneath me in the kitchens. Very cautiously I drew near the north-east corner of my new apartment, and lifted the arras. I ran my hands over the stone wall, as I had done that time before in the darkness when Jonathan had discovered me, and once again I could find no outlet, no division in the stone.

I realised then that the means for entry must be from without only, a great handicap to us, who used it now, but no doubt cunningly intended by the builder of the house, who had no desire for his idiot eldest son to come and go at pleasure. I knocked with my fists against the wall, but they sounded not at all. I called "John" in a low voice, expecting no answer; nor did I receive one.

This, then, was a new and hideous dilemma, for I had warned John not to attempt an entry to the chamber before I warned him, since I was confident at the time that I would be able to find the entrance from inside. This I could not do, and John and Dick were in the meantime waiting in the cell below the buttress for a signal from me. I placed my face against the wall, crying "John . . . John . . ." as loudly as I dared, but I guessed, with failing heart, that the sound of my voice would never carry through the implacable stone. Hearing footsteps in the corridor I let the arras fall and returned to the window, where I made a pretence of looking down into the court. I heard movements in my old apartment in the gatehouse, and a moment later a loud knocking on the door between. "Please enter," I called, and the roughly-repaired door was pushed aside, tottering on its hinge, and Lord Robartes himself came into the room, accompanied by one of his officers and Frank Penrose, with his arms bound tight behind him.

"I regret my sudden intrusion," said Lord Robartes, "but we have just found this man in the grounds. He volunteered information I find interesting, which you may add to, if you please."

I glanced at Frank Penrose, who, half frightened out of his wits, stared about him like a hare, passing his tongue over his lips. I did not answer, but waited for Lord Robartes to continue.

"It seems you have had living here, until to-day, the son of Skellum

Grenvile," he said, watching me intently, "as well as his tutor. They were to have left by fishing-boat for St Mawes a few hours since. You were the boy's godmother and had the care of him, I understand. Where are they now?"

"Somewhere off the Dodman, I hope," I answered.

"I am told that as the boat set sail from Polkerris the boy could not be found," he replied, "and Penrose here and John Rashleigh went in search of him. My men have not yet come upon John Rashleigh or the boy. Do you know what has become of them?"

"I do not," I answered. "I only trust they are aboard the boat."

"You realise," he said harshly, "that there is a heavy price upon the head of Skellum Grenvile, and to harbour him or any of his family would count as treason to Parliament. The Earl of Essex has given me strict orders as to this."

"That being the case," I said, "you had better take Mrs Denys into closer custody. She is Sir Richard's sister, as you no doubt know."

I had caught him off his guard with this, and he looked at me nonplussed. Then he began tapping on the table in sudden irritation. "Mrs Denys has, I understand, little or no friendship with her brother," he said stiffly. "Her late husband, Mr Antony Denys, was known to be a good friend to Parliament and an opposer of Charles Stuart. Have you nothing further to tell me about your godson?"

"Nothing at all," I said, "except that I have every belief that he is upon that fishing-boat, and with the wind in the right quarter he will be, by this time, nearly halfway to St Mawes."

He turned his back on me at that and left the room, with the luckless Frank Penrose shuffling at his heels, and I realised, with relief, that the agent was ignorant as to Dick's whereabouts, like everybody else in Menabilly, and for all he knew my tale might be quite true and both Dick and John some ten miles out at sea. Not one soul, then, in the place knew the secret of the buttress but myself, for Langdon the steward had accompanied my brother-in-law to Launceston. This was a great advantage, making betrayal an impossibility. But I still could not solve the problem of how to get food and drink and reassurance to the two fugitives I had myself imprisoned. And another fear began to nag at me, with recollection of my brother-in-law's words: "Lack of air and close confinement soon rendered him unconscious and easy to handle." Uncle John, gasping for breath in the little cell beneath the buttress. How much air, then, came through to the cell from the tunnel beyond? *Enough for how many hours?*

Once again, as earlier in the day, the sweat began to trickle down my face, and half-unconsciously I wiped it away with my hand. I felt myself defeated. There was no course for me to take. A little bustle from the adjoining room, and a child's cry, told me that Joan and her babies had come to my old apartment, and in a moment she came through, with little Mary whimpering in her arms and small Jonathan clinging to her skirts.

"Why did you move, Honor dear?" she said. "There was no need." And like Matty she gazed about the room in curiosity. "It is very plain and bare," she added; "nothing valuable at all. I am much relieved, for those brutes would have got it. Come back in your own chamber, Honor, if you can bear with the babies."

"No," I said. "I am well enough."

. "You look so tired and drawn," she said, "but I dare swear I do the same. I feel I have aged ten years these last two hours. What will they do to us?"

"Nothing," I said, "if we keep to our rooms."

"If only John would return," she said, tears rising to her eyes. "Supposing he has had some skirmish on the road, and has been hurt? I cannot understand what can have become of him."

The children began to whimper, hearing the anxiety in her voice, and then Matty, who loved children, came and coaxed the baby, and proceeded to undress her for her cot, while little Jonathan, with a small boy's sharp nervous way, began to plague us all with questions: Why did they come to their Aunt Honor's room? And who were all the soldiers? And how long would they stay?

The hours wore on with horrid dragging tedium, and the sun began to sink behind the trees at the far end of the park, while the air was thick with smoke from the fires lit by the troopers.

All the time there was tramping below, and orders called, and the pacing to and fro of horses. The children were restless, turning continually in their cots and calling for either Matty or their mother, and when Joan was not hushing them she was gazing from my window, reporting fresh actions of destruction, her cheeks aflame with indignation. "They have rounded up all the cattle from the beef park and the beacon fields, and driven them into the park here, with a pen about them," she said, "and they are dividing up the steers now into another pen." Suddenly she gave a little cry of dismay. "They have slaughtered three of them," she said. "The men are quartering them already by the fires. Now they are driving the sheep." We could hear the anxious baaing of the ewes to the sturdy lambs, and the lowing of the cattle. I thought of the five hundred men encamped there in the park, and the many hundreds more between us and Lostwithiel, and how they and their horses must be fed, but I said nothing. Joan shut the window, for the smoke from the camp fires blew thick about the room and the noise of the men shouting and calling orders made a vile and sickening clamour. The sun set in a dull crimson sky, and the shadows lengthened.

About half-past eight Matty brought us a small portion of a pie upon one plate, with a carafe of water. Her lips were grimly set.

"This for the two of you," she said. "Mrs Rashleigh and Lady Courtney fare no better. Lady Courtney is making a little broth for the children's breakfast, in case they give us no eggs."

Joan ate my piece of pie as well as hers, for I had no appetite. I could think of one thing only, that it was now nearly five hours since her husband and Richard's son had lain hidden in the buttress. Matty brought candles, and presently Alice and Mary came to say good night, poor Mary looking suddenly like an old woman from anxiety and shock.

"They're axing the trees in the orchard," she said. "I saw them myself, sawing the branches, and stripping the young fruit that has scarce formed. The servants have been told by the soldiers that to-morrow they are going to cut the corn, strip all the barley from Eighteen Acres, and the wheat from the Great Meadow. And it wants three weeks to harvest." The tears began to course down her cheeks, and she turned to Joan. "Why does John not come?" she said in useless reproach. "Why is he not here to stand up for his father's home?"

"If John was here he could do nothing," I said swiftly before Joan could lash back in anger. "Don't you understand, Mary, that this is war? This is what has been happening all over England, and we in Cornwall are having our first taste of it."

Even as I spoke there came a great burst of laughter from the courtyard, and a tongue of flame shot up to the windows. The troopers were roasting an ox in the clearing above the Warren, and because they were too idle to search for firewood they had broken down the doors from the dairy and the bakery, and were piling them upon the fire.

"There must have been thirty officers or more at dinner in the gallery," said Alice quietly. "We saw them from our windows afterwards walk up and down the terrace before the house. One or two were Cornish—I remember meeting them before the war—but most of them were strangers."

"They say the Earl of Essex is in Fowey," said Joan, "and has set up his headquarters at Place. Whether it is true or not I do not know."

"The Treffrys will not suffer," said Mary bitterly. "They have too many relatives fighting for the rebels. You won't find Bridget has her stores pillaged, and her larders ransacked."

"Come to bed, Mother," said Alice gently. "Honor is right—it does no good to worry. We have been spared so happily until now. If my father and Peter are safe somewhere, with the King's army, nothing else can matter."

They went to their own apartments, and Joan to the children next door, while Matty—all oblivious of my own hidden fears—helped me undress for bed.

"There's one discovery I've made this night, anyway," she said grimly, as she brushed my hair.

"What is that, Matty?"

"Mrs Denys hasn't lost her taste for gentlemen."

I said nothing, waiting for what would follow.

"You and the others had pie for your suppers," she said, "but there was roast beef and burgundy taken up to Mrs Denys, and places set for two upon the tray. Her children were put together in the dressing-room, and had a chicken between them."

I realised that Matty's partiality for eavesdropping and her nose for gossip might stand us in good stead in the immediate future.

"And who was the fortunate who dined with Mrs Denys?" I asked.

"Lord Robartes himself," said Matty with sour triumph.

My first suspicion became a certainty. It was not mere chance that had so strangely brought Gartred to Menabilly after five-and-twenty years. She was here for a purpose.

"Lord Robartes is not an ill-looking man," I said. "I might invite him to share cold pie with me another evening."

Matty snorted, and lifted me to bed. "I'd like to see Sir Richard's face if you did," she snapped.

"Sir Richard would not mind," I answered. "Not if there was something to be gained from it."

I feigned a lightness I was far from feeling, and when she had blown the candles and was gone I lay back in my bed with my nerves tense and strained. The flames outside my window died away, and slowly the shouting and the laughter ceased, and the tramping of feet, and the movement of the horses, and the calling bugles. I heard the clock in the belfry strike ten, then eleven, and then midnight. The people within the house were still and silent, and so was the alien enemy. At a quarter after midnight a dog howled in the far distance, and as though it were a signal I felt suddenly upon my cheek a current of cold chill air. I sat up in bed and waited. The draught continued, blowing straight from the torn arras on the wall. "John," I whispered, and "John," I whispered again. I heard a movement from behind the arras like a scratching mouse. Slowly, stealthily, I saw the hand come from behind the arras, lifting it aside, and a figure step out, dropping on all fours and creeping to my bed. "It is I, Honor," I said, and the cold, froggy hand touched me, icy cold, and the hands clung to me, and the dark figure climbed on to my bed, and lay trembling beside me.

It was Dick, the clothes still dank and chill upon him, and he began to weep, long and silently, from exhaustion and from fear.

I held him close, warming him as best as I could, and when he was still I whispered, "Where is John?"

"In the little room," he said, "below the steps. We sat there, waiting, hour after hour, and you did not come. I wanted to turn back, but Mr Rashleigh would not let me." He began to sob again, and I drew the covers over his head.

"He has fainted, down there on the steps," he said. "He's lying there now, his head between his hands. I got hold of the long rope that hangs there, above the steps, and pulled at it, and the hinged stone gave way, and I came up into this room. I did not care—I could not stay there longer, Honor. It's black as pitch, and closer than a grave." He was still trembling, his head buried in my shoulder. I went on lying there, wondering what to do, whether to summon Joan and thus betray the secret to another, or wait until Dick was calmer and then send him back there with a candle to John's aid. And as I waited, my heart thumping, my ears strained to all sounds, I heard from without the tiptoe of a footstep in the passage, the noise of the latch of the door gently lifted and then let fall again as the door was seen to be fastened, and a moment's pause; then the footstep tiptoeing gently away once more, and the soft, departing rustle of a gown. Someone had crept to the chamber in the stillness of the night, and that someone was a woman.

I went on lying there with my arms wrapped close about the sleeping boy and the clock in the belfry struck one, then two, then three. . . .

CHAPTER SEVENTEEN

As THE FIRST grey chinks of light came through the casement I roused Dick, who lay sleeping with his head upon my shoulder like a baby, and when he had blinked a moment, and got his wits restored to him, I bade him light the candle and creep back again to the cell. Since John was by nature far from strong anything might have happened. Never, in all the fifteen years I had been crippled, had I so needed the use of my legs as now, but I was helpless. In a few moments Dick was back again, his little ghost's face looking more pallid than ever in the grey morning light. "He is awake," he said, "but very ill, I think. Shaking all over, and seeming not to know what has been happening. His head is burning hot, but his limbs are cold."

At least he was alive, and a wave of thankfulness swept over me. But from Dick's description I realised what had happened. The ague, that was his legacy from birth, had attacked John once again with its usual ferocity, and small wonder, after more than ten hours crouching beneath the buttress. I made up my mind swiftly. I bade Dick bring the chair beside my bed, and with his assistance I lowered myself into it. Then I went to the door communicating with the gatehouse chamber, and very gently called for Matty.

In a moment or two she came from the little dressing-room, her round plain face yawning beneath her night-cap, and would have chided me for rising had I not placed my finger on my lips. The urgency of the situation was such that my promise to my brother-in-law must finally be broken, though little of it held as it was. And without Matty it would be impossible to act. She came in, then, her eyes round with wonder when she saw Dick. "You love me, Matty, I believe," I said to her. "Now I ask you to prove that love as never before. This boy's safety and life are in our hands." She nodded, saying nothing.

"Dick and Mr John have been hiding since last evening," I said. "There is a staircase and a little room built within the thickness of these walls. Mr John is ill. I want you to go to him and bring him here. Dick will show you the way."

He pulled aside the arras, and now for the first time I saw how the entrance was effected. A block of stone, about four feet square, worked on a hinge, moved by a lever and a rope, if pulled from beneath the narrow stair. This gave an opening just wide enough for a man to crawl through. When it was shut the stone was so closely fitting that it was impossible to find it from within the chamber, nor could it be pushed open, for the lever held it. The little stairway, set inside the buttress, twisted steeply to the cell below, which had height enough for a man to stand upright. More I could not see, craning from my chair, save for a dark heap that must be John, lying on the lower step.

There was something weird and fearful in the scene, with the grey light of morning coming through the casement, and Matty, a fantastic figure in her nightclothes and cap, edging her way through the gap in the buttress. As she disappeared with Dick I heard the first high call of the bugle from the park, and I knew that for the rebel army the day had now begun. Soon the soldiers within the house would also be astir, and we had little time in hand. It was, I believe, some fifteen minutes before they were all three within the chamber, though it seemed an hour, and in those fifteen minutes the daylight had filled the room and the troopers were moving in the courtyard down below. John was quite conscious, thank God, and his mind lucid, but he was trembling all over and in a high fever, fit for nothing but his own bed and his wife's care. We took rapid consultation, in which I held firmly to one thing, and that was that no further person, not even Joan his wife nor Mary his stepmother, should be told how he had come into the house, or that Dick was with us still.

John's story, then, was to be that the fishing-boat came in to one of the coves beneath the Gribben, where he put Dick aboard, and that on returning across the fields he had seen the arrival of the troopers, and hid until nightfall. But, his fever coming upon him, he decided to return, and therefore climbed in by the lead piping and the creeper that ran along the south front of the house outside his father's window. For corroboration of this John must go at once to his father's room, where his stepmother was sleeping, and waken her, and win her acceptance of the story. It was like a nightmare to arrange, with Joan in the adjoining chamber, through which he must pass to gain the southern portion of the house. For if he went by the passage beneath the belfry he might risk encounter with the servants or the troopers. Matty went first, and since there was no question from Joan, or any movement from the children, we judged them to be sleeping, and poor John, his body on fire with fever, crept swiftly after her. I thought of the games of hide-and-seek I had played with my brothers and sisters at Lanrest as children, and how now that it was played in earnest there was no excitement but a sickening strain, which brought sweat to the forehead and a pain to the belly. When Matty returned, and reported John in safety in his father's rooms, the first stage of the proceeding was completed. The next I had to break to Dick with great misgiving and an assumption of sternness and authority I was far from feeling. It was that he could remain with me, in my apartment, but must be prepared to stay, perhaps for long hours at a time, within the secret cell beneath the buttress, and have a palliasse there to sleep upon if need be, should there be visitors to my room.

He fell to crying at once, as I had expected, beseeching me not to let him stay alone in the dark cell. He would go mad, he said—he could not stand it, he would rather die.

I was well-nigh desperate, now that the house was beginning to stir, and the children to talk in the adjoining chamber.

"Very well, then," I said. "Open the door, Matty. Call the troopers. Tell them that Richard Grenvile's son is here and wishes to surrender himself to their mercy. They have sharp swords, and the pain will soon be over." God forgive me that I could find it in my heart so to terrify the lad, but it was his only salvation.

The mention of the swords, bringing the thought of blood, sent the colour draining from his face, as I knew it would, and he turned to me, his dark eyes desperate, and said, "Very well. I will do as you ask me." It is those same dark eyes that haunt me still, and will always do so, to the day I die.

I bade Matty take the mattress from my bed, and the stool beside the window, and some blankets, and bundle them through the open gap on to the stair. "When it is safe for you to come, I will let you know," I said. "But how can you," said Dick, "when the gap is closed?" Here I was forced back again into the old dilemma of the night before. I could have wept with strain and weariness, and looked at Matty in despair. "If you do not quite close the gap," she said, "but let it stay open three inches, Master Dick, with his ear put close to it, will hear your voice."

We tried it, and although I was not happy with the plan it seemed the one solution. We found, too, that with a gap of two or three inches he could hear me strike with a stick upon the floor, once, twice, or thrice, which we arranged as signals. Thrice meant real danger, and then the stone must be pulled flush to the wall.

He had gone to his cell, with his mattress and his blankets and half a loaf that Matty had found for him, as the clock in the belfry struck six, and almost immediately little Jonathan from the adjoining room came pushing through the door, his toys under his arm, calling in loud tones for me to play with him. The day had started. When I look back now, to the intolerable strain and anguish of that time, I wonder how in God's name I had the power to endure it. For I had to be on guard, not only against the rebels, but against my friends too, and those I loved. Mary, Alice and Joan must all three remain in ignorance of what was happening, and their visits to my chamber, which should have been a comfort and a consolation in this time of strain, merely added to my anxiety.

What I would have done without Matty I do not know. It was she, acting sentinel as she had done in the past, who kept them from the door when Dick was with me, and, poor lad, I had to have him often, for the best part of the day. Luckily, my crippled state served as a good excuse, for it was known that often in the past I had "bad days", and had to be alone, and this lie was now my only safeguard. John's story had been accepted as full truth, and since he was quite obviously ill, and in high fever, he was allowed to remain in his father's rooms with Joan to care for him and was not removed to closer custody.

I remember Matty saying to me on that first day, Friday, the second of August: "How long will they be here, Miss Honor? When will the Royalist army come to relieve us?"

And I, thinking of Richard down at Truro, and His Majesty already, so the rumour ran, entering Launceston, told her four days at the longest. But I was wrong. For four whole weeks the rebels were our masters.

It is nearly ten years since that August of '44, but every day of that age-long month is printed firm upon my memory.

The first week was hot and stifling, with a glazed blue sky and not a cloud upon it, and in my nostrils now I can recapture the smell of horse-flesh and the stink of sweating soldiery, borne upwards to my open casement from the fetid court below. Day in, day out, came the jingle of harness, the clattering of hooves, the march of tramping feet, and the grinding sound of wagon wheels, and ever insistent, above the shouting of orders and the voices of the men, the bugle call, hammering its single note.

Imprisonment made cronies of us all, and no sooner had Alice and her brood departed than the Sparke sisters would come enquiring for me with some wild rumour to unfold, gleaned from the frightened servants, of how the house was to be burnt down with all its inmates when Essex gave the order—but not till the women had been ravaged. I dare say I was the only woman in the house to be unmoved by such a threat, for God knows I could not be more bruised and broken than I was already. But for Deborah and Gillian it was another matter, and Deborah, whom I judged to be even safer from assault than I was myself, showed me with trembling hands the silver bodkin with which she would defend her honour. Their brother Will was become a sort of toady to the officers, but as soon as their backs were turned he was whispering some slander about them, and repeating snatches of conversation he had overheard, bits and pieces that were no use to anyone. Once or twice Nick Sawle came tapping slowly to my room, leaning on his two sticks, a look of lost bewilderment and muddled resentment in his eye because the rebels had not been flung from Menabilly within four-and-twenty hours of their arrival, and I was forced to listen to his theories that His Majesty must be now at Launceston, now at Liskeard, now back again at Exeter. While he argued his poor wife Temperance stared at him dully, in a kind of trance, her religious eloquence pent up at last from shock and fear so that she could do no more than clutch her Prayer Book without quoting from it.

Once a day we were allowed within the garden, for some thirty minutes, and I would leave Matty in my room on an excuse and have Alice push my chair. The poor gardens were laid waste already, with the yew trees broken and the flower beds trampled, and up and down the muddied paths we went, stared at by the sentries at the gate and by the officers gathered at the long windows in the gallery. Their appraising, hostile eyes burnt through our backs, but must be endured for the sake of the fresh air we craved, and sometimes their laughter came to us. Their voices were hard and ugly, for they were mostly from London and the eastern counties, except the staff officers of Lord Robartes— and I never could abide the London twang, made doubly alien now through enmity. Never once did we see Gartred when we took our exercise, though her two daughters, reserved and unfriendly, played in the far corner of the garden, watching us and the children with blank eyes.

"I don't know what to make of it," said Alice, in my ear. "She is supposed to be a prisoner like us, but she is not treated so. I have watched her, from my window, walk in the walled garden beneath the summer-house, talking and smiling to Lord Robartes, and the servants say he dines with her most evenings."

"She only does what many other women do in wartime," I said, "and turns the stress of the day to her advantage."

"You mean she is for the Parliament?" asked Alice.

"Neither for the Parliament, nor for the King, but for Gartred Denys," I answered. "Do you not know the saying—to race with the hare and run with the hounds? She will smile on Lord Robartes, and sleep with him too if she has a mind, just as long as it suits her. He would let her leave to-morrow, if she asked him."

"Why, then," said Alice, "does she not do so, and return in safety to Orley Court?"

"That," I answered, "is what I would give a great deal to find out." And as we paced up and down, up and down, before the staring, hostile eyes of the London officers, I thought of the footstep I had heard at midnight in the passage, the soft hand on the latch, and the rustle of a gown. Why should Gartred, while the house slept, find her way to my apartment in the north-east corner of the building and try my door, unless she knew her way already? And granting that she knew her way, what then was her motive?

It was ten days before I had my answer.

On Sunday, August the eleventh, came the first break in the weather. The sun shone watery in a mackerel sky, and a bank of cloud gathered in the south-west. There had been much coming and going all the day, with fresh regiments of troopers riding to the park, bringing with them many carts of wounded, who were carried to the farm buildings before the house. Their cries of distress were very real and terrible, and gave to us, who were their enemies, a sick dread and apprehension.

For the first time we were given soup only for our dinner, and a portion of stale bread, and this, we were told, would be the best we could hope for from henceforward. No reason was given, but Matty, with her ears pricked, had hung about the kitchens with her tray under her arm, and gleaned some gossip from the courtyard.

"There was a battle yesterday on Braddock Down," she said. "They've lost a lot of men." She spoke softly, for with our enemies about us we had grown to speak in whispers, our eyes upon the door.

I poured half my soup into Dick's bowl, and watched him drink it greedily, running his tongue round the rim like a hungry dog. "The King is only three miles from Lostwithiel," she said. "He and Prince Maurice have joined forces, and set up their headquarters at Boconnoc. Sir Richard has advanced, with nigh a thousand men from Truro, and is coming up on Bodmin from the west. 'Your fellows are trying to squeeze us dry,' said the trooper in the kitchen, 'like a bloody orange. But they won't do it.'"

"And what did you answer him?" I said to Matty.

She smiled grimly, and cut Dick the largest slice of bread. "I told him I'd pray for him, when Sir Richard got him," she answered.

After eating, I sat in my chair looking out across the park and watched the clouds gathering thick and fast. There were scarce a dozen bullocks left in the pen, out of the fine herd there had been the week before, and only a small flock of sheep. The rest had all been slaughtered. These remaining few would be gone within the next eight-and-forty hours. Not a stem of corn remained in the far meadows. The whole had been cut and ground, and the ricks pulled. The grass in the park was now bare earth where the horses had grazed upon it. Not a tree stood in the orchard beyond the Warren. If Matty's tale was true, and the King and Richard to east and west of Lostwithiel, then the Earl of Essex and ten thousand men were pent up in a narrow strip of land some nine miles long, with no way of escape except the sea.

Ten thousand men, with provisions getting low, and only the bare land to live on, while three armies waited in their rear.

There was no laughter to-night from the courtyard, no shouting, and no chatter; only a blazing fire as they heaped the cut trees and the kitchen benches upon it, the doors torn from the larder and the tables from the stewards' room, and I could see their sullen faces lit by the leaping flames.

The sky darkened, and slowly, silently, the rain began to fall. And as I listened to it, remembering Richard's words, I heard the rustle of a gown and a tap upon my door.

CHAPTER EIGHTEEN

DICK WAS GONE in a flash to his hiding-place, and Matty clearing his bowl and platter. I sat still in my chair, with my back to the arras, and bade them enter who knocked upon the door.

It was Gartred. She was wearing, if I remember right, a gown of emerald green, and there were emeralds round her throat and in her ears. She stood a moment within the doorway, a half smile on her face. "The good Matty," she said, "always so devoted. What ease of mind a faithful servant brings."

I saw Matty sniff, and rattle the plates upon her tray, while her lips tightened in ominous fashion.

"Am I disturbing you, Honor?" said Gartred, that same smile still on her face. "The hour is possibly inconvenient—you go early no doubt to bed?"

All meaning is in the inflexion of the voice, and when rendered on paper words seem plain and harmless enough. I give the remarks as Gartred phrased them, but the veiled contempt, the mockery, the suggestion that, because I was crippled, I must be tucked down and in the dark by half-past nine, this was in her voice, and in her eyes as they swept over me.

"My going to bed depends upon my mood, as doubtless it does with you," I answered. "Also it depends upon my company."

"You must find the hours most horribly tedious," she said, "but then no doubt you are used to it by now. You have lived in custody so long that to be made prisoner is no new experience. I must confess I find it unamusing." She came closer in the room, looking about her, although I had given her no invitation.

"You have heard the news, I suppose?" she said.

"That the King is at Boconnoc, and a skirmish was fought yesterday in which the rebels got the worst of it? Yes, I have heard that," I answered. The last of the fruit, picked before the rebels came, was standing on a platter in the window. Gartred took a fig and began to eat it, still looking about her in the room. Matty gave a snort of indignation which passed unnoticed, and taking her tray went from the chamber with a glance at Gartred's back that would have slain her had it been perceived.

"If this business continues long," said Gartred, "we none of us here will find it very pleasant. The men are already in an ugly mood. Defeat may turn them into brutes."

"Very probably," I said.

She threw away the skin of her fig and took another.

"Richard is at Lanhydrock," she said. "Word came to-day through a captured prisoner. It is rather ironic that we have the owner of Lanhydrock in possession here. Richard will leave little of it for him by the time this campaign is settled, whichever way the battles goes. Jack Robartes is black as thunder."

"It is his own fault," I said, "for advising the Earl of Essex to come into Cornwall, and run ten thousand men into a trap."

"So it is a trap?" she said. "And my unscrupulous brother the baiter of it? I rather thought it must be."

I did not answer. I had said too much already. And Gartred was in quest of information. "Well, we shall see," she said, eating her fig with relish, "but if the process lasts much longer the rebels will turn cannibal. They have the country stripped already between here and Lostwithiel, and Fowey is without provisions. I shudder to think what Jack Robartes would do to Richard if he could get hold of him."

"The reverse holds equally good," I told her.

She laughed, and squeezed the last drop of juice into her mouth.

"All men are idiots," she said, "and more especially in wartime. They lose all sense of values."

"It depends," I said, "upon the meaning of values."

"I value one thing only," she said. "My own security."

"In that case," I said, "you showed neglect of it when you travelled upon the road ten days ago."

She watched me under heavy lids and smiled. "Your tongue hasn't blunted with the years," she said, "nor tribulation softened you. Tell me, do you still care for Richard?"

"That is my affair," I said.

"He is detested by his brother officers. I suppose you know that," she said, "and loathed equally in Cornwall as in Devon. In fact, the only creatures he can count his friends are sprigs of boys, who daren't be rude to him. He has a little train of them, nosing his shadow."

Oh, God, I thought, you bloody woman, seizing upon the one insinuation in the world to make me mad. I watched her play with her rings.

"Poor Mary Howard," she said; "what she endured. You were spared intolerable indignities, you know, Honor, by not being his wife. I suppose Richard has made great play lately of loving you the same, and no doubt he does, in his curious vicious fashion. Rather a rare new pastime, a woman who can't respond."

She yawned, and strolled over to the window. "His treatment of Dick is really most distressing," she said. "The poor boy adored his mother, and now I understand Richard intends to rear him as a freak, just to spite her. What did you think of him when he was here?"

"He was young, and sensitive, like many other children," I said.

"It was a wonder to me he was ever born at all," said Gartred, "when I think of the revolting story Mary told me. However, I will spare your feelings, if you still put Richard on a pedestal. I am glad, for the lad's sake, that Jack Robartes did not find him here at Menabilly. He has sworn an oath to hang any relative of Richard's."

"Except yourself," I said.

"Ah, I don't count," she answered. "Mrs Denys of Orley Court is not the same as Gartred Grenvile." Once more she looked up at the walls, and then again into the courtyard.

"This is the room, isn't it," she said, "where they used to keep the idiot? I can remember him mouthing down at Kit when we rode here five-and-twenty years ago."

"I have no idea," I said. "The subject is not discussed among the family."

"There was something odd about the formation of the house," she said carelessly. "I cannot recollect exactly what it was. Some cupboard, I believe, where they used to shut him up when he grew violent, so Kit told me. Have you discovered it?"

"There are no cupboards here," I said, "except the cabinet over yonder."

"I am so sorry," she said, "that my coming here forced you to give your room to Joan Rashleigh. I could so easily have made do with this one, which one of the servants told me was never used until you took it over."

"It was much simpler," I said, "to place you and your daughters in a larger room, where you can entertain visitors to dinner."

"You always did like servants' gossip, did you not?" she answered. "The hobby of all old maids. It whips their appetite to imagine what goes on behind closed doors."

"I don't know," I said. "I hardly think my broth tastes any better for picturing you hip to hip with Lord Robartes."

She looked down at me, her gown in her hands, and I wondered who had the greater capacity for hatred, she or I.

"My being here," she said, "has at least spared you all, so far, from worse unpleasantness. I have known Jack Robartes for many years."

"Keep him busy, then," I said. "That's all we ask of you."

I was beginning to enjoy myself at last, and, realising it, she turned towards the door. "I cannot guarantee," she said, "that his good temper will continue. He was in a filthy mood to-night at dinner, when he heard of Richard at Lanhydrock, and has gone off now to a conference at Fowey with Essex and the chiefs of staff."

"I look to you, then," I said, "to have him mellow by the morning." She stood with her hand on the door, her eyes sweeping the hangings on the wall. "If they lose the campaign," she said, "they will lose their tempers too. A defeated soldier is a dangerous animal. Jack Robartes will give orders to sack Menabilly, and destroy inside and without."

"Yes," I said. "We are all aware of that."

"Everything will be taken," she said, "clothes, jewels, furniture, food—and not much left of the inhabitants. He must be a curious man, your brother-in-law, Jonathan Rashleigh, to desert his home, knowing full well what must happen to it in the end."

I shrugged my shoulders. And then, as she left, she gave herself away. "Does he still act as Collector for the Mint?" she said. Then for the first time I smiled, for I had my answer to the problem of her presence.

"I cannot tell you," I said. "I have no idea. But if you wait long enough for the house to be ransacked, you may come upon the plate you think he has concealed. Good night, Gartred."

She stared at me a moment, and then went from the room. At last I knew her business, and had I been less preoccupied with my own problem of concealing Dick, I might have guessed it sooner. Whoever won or lost the campaign in the west, it would not matter much to Gartred, she would see to it that she had a footing on the winning side. If there were pickings to be scavenged in the aftermath of battle, Gartred Denys would not stay at home in Orley Court. I remembered her grip upon the marriage settlement with Kit, I remembered that last feverish search for a lost trinket on the morning she left Lanrest, a widow, and I remembered too the rumours I had heard since she was widowed for the second time, how Orley Court was much burdened with debt and must be settled among her daughters when they came of age. Gartred had not yet found a third husband to her liking, but in the meantime she must live. The silver plate of Cornwall would be a prize indeed, could she lay hands on it.

This, then, was her motive, with suspicion already centred on my room. She did not know the secret of the buttress, but memory had reminded her that there was, within the walls of Menabilly, some such hiding-place. And with sharp guesswork, she had reached the conclusion that my brother-in-law would make a wartime use of it. That the hiding-place might also conceal her nephew had, I was certain, never entered her head. Nor—and this was supposition on my part—was she working in partnership with Lord Robartes. She was playing her own game, but if she found she could not get what she wanted by playing a lone hand—then she would lay her cards upon the table and damn the consequences.

This, then, was what we had to fear, and no one in the house knew of it but myself. So Sunday, August the eleventh, came and went, and we woke next morning to another problematical week in which anything might happen, with the three Royalist armies squeezing the rebels tighter hour by hour, the strip of country left to them becoming daily more bare and devastated, and a steady, sweeping rain turning all the roads to mud.

Gone was the hot weather, the glazed sky, and the sun. A high, blustering wind broke across the park, and from my tightly shut casement I could see the dripping tents, the horses tethered line upon line beneath the trees at the far end, their heads disconsolate, while the men stood about in huddled, melancholy groups, their fires dead as soon as kindled. Many of the wounded died in the farm buildings. Mary saw the burial parties go forth at dawn, a silent, grey procession in the early morning mist, and we heard they took them to the Long Mead, the valley beneath the woods at Pridmouth.

No more wounded came to the farm buildings, and we guessed from this that the heavy weather had put a stop to fighting. But we heard also that His Majesty's army now held the east bank of the Fowey River, from St Veep down to the fortress at Polruan, which commanded the harbour entrance. The rebels in Fowey were thus cut off from their shipping in the Channel and could receive no supplies by sea, except from such small boats as could land at Pridmouth or Polkerris or on the sand flats at Tywardreath, which the heavy run from the south-west now made impossible. There was little laughter or chatter now from the mess-room in the gallery, so Alice said, and the officers, with grim faces, clumped back and forth from the dining-chamber, which Lord Robartes had taken for his own use, while every now and then his voice would be raised in anger, as a messenger would ride through the pouring rain bearing news of some fresh disaster.

Whether Gartred moved about the house or not I do not know. Alice said she thought she kept to her own chamber. I saw little of Joan, for poor John's ague was still unabated, but Mary came from time to time to visit me, her face each day more drawn and agonised as she learnt of further devastation to the estate. More than three hundred of the sheep had already been slaughtered, thirty fatted bullocks, and sixty store bullocks. All the draught oxen taken, and all the farm horses, some forty of them in number. A dozen or so hogs were left out of the eighty there had been, and these would all be gone before the week was out. The last year's corn had vanished the first week of the rebel occupation, and now they had stripped the new, leaving no single blade to be harvested. There was nothing left, of course, of the farm wagons, or carts, or farming tools—these had all been taken. And the sheds where the winter fuel had been stored were as bare as the granaries. There was, in fact—so the servants in fear and trembling reported to Mary—scarcely anything remaining of the great estate that Jonathan Rashleigh had left in her keeping but a fortnight since. The gardens spoilt, the orchards ruined, the timber felled, the livestock eaten. Whichever way the war in the west should go, my brother-in-law would be a bankrupt man.

And they had not yet started upon the house or the inhabitants. Our feeding was already a sore problem. At midday we all gathered to the main meal of the day. This was served to us in Alice's apartments in the east wing, while John lay ill in his father's chamber, and there some twenty of us herded side by side, the children clamouring and fretful, while we dipped stale bread in the mess of watery soup provided, helped sometimes by swollen beans and cabbage. The children had their milk, but no more than two cupfuls for the day, and already I noticed a staring look about them, their eyes over-large in the pale faces, while their play had become listless, and they yawned often. The old people suffered like the children, and complained fretfully with the same misunderstanding of what war brings.

It was solely with Matty's aid that I was able to feed Dick at all. By some means, fair or foul, which I did not enquire into, she had made an ally of the second scullion, to whom she pulled a long story about her ailing, crippled mistress, with the result that further soup was smuggled to my chamber beneath Matty's apron and no one the wiser for it. It was this same scullion who fed us with rumours, too—most of them disastrous to his own side—which made me wonder if a bribe would make him a deserter. At mid-week we heard that Richard had seized Restormel Castle by Lostwithiel, and that Lord Goring, who commanded the King's horse, held the bridge and the road below St Blazey. Essex was now pinned up in our peninsula, some seven miles long and two broad, with ten thousand men to feed, and the guns from Polruan trained on Fowey Harbour. It could not last much longer. Either Essex and the rebels must be relieved by a further force marching to him from the east, or he must stand and make a fight of it. And we would sit, day after day, with cold hearts and empty bellies, staring out upon the sullen soldiery as they stood huddled in the rain outside their tents, while their leaders within the house held councils of despondency. Another Sunday came, and with it a whisper of alarm among the rebels that the country people were stealing forth at night and doing murder. Sentries were found strangled at their posts, men woke to find their comrades with cut throats, others would stagger to headquarters from the high road, their hands lopped from their wrists, their eyes blinded. The Cornish were rising.

On Tuesday, the twenty-seventh, there was no soup for our midday dinner, only half a dozen loaves amongst the twenty of us. On Wednesday one jugful of milk for the children, instead of three, and the milk much watered.

On Thursday Alice and Joan and Mary, and the two Sparke sisters and I, divided our bread amongst the children, and made for ourselves a brew of herb tea with scalding water. We were not hungry. Desire for food left us when we saw the children tear at the stale bread and cram it in their mouths, then turn and ask for more which we could not give to them. And all the while the south-west wind tore and blustered in the teeming sky, and the rebel bugle that had haunted us so long sounded across the park like a challenge of despair.

CHAPTER NINETEEN

O<small>N</small> F<small>RIDAY</small>, <small>THE THIRTIETH</small> of August, I lay all day upon my bed, for to gather with the others now would be a farce, and in any case I had not the strength to do so. My cowardly soul forbade me watch the children beg and cry for their one crust of bread. Matty brewed me a cup of tea, and it seemed wrong to swallow even that. Hunger had made me listless, and, heedless of danger, I let Dick come and lie upon his mattress by my bed, while he gnawed a bone that Matty had scavenged for him. His eyes looked larger than ever in his pale face, and his black curls were lank and lustreless. It seemed to me that in his hunger he grew more like his mother, and sometimes, looking down on him, I would fancy she had stepped into his place and it was Mary Howard I fed and sheltered from the enemy, and she who licked the bones with little pointed teeth and tore at the strips of flesh with small, eager paws.

Matty herself was hollow-eyed and sallow. Gone were the buxom hips and the apple cheeks. Whatever food she could purloin from her friend the scullion—and there was precious little now for the men themselves—she smuggled to Dick or to the children.

During the day, while I slipped from one racking dream into another, with Dick curled at my feet like a puppy, Matty leant up against the window, staring at the mist that had followed now upon the rain, and hid the tents and horses from us.

The hoof-beats woke me shortly after two, and Matty, opening the window, peered down into the outer court and watched them pass under the gatehouse to the courtyard. Some dozen officers, she said, with an escort of troopers, and the leader on a great black horse wearing a dark grey cloak. She slipped from the room to watch them descend from their horses in the inner court, and came back to say that Lord Robartes had stood himself on the steps to receive them, and they had all passed into the dining-chamber with sentries before the doors.

Even my tired brain seized the salient possibility—that this was the last council to be held, and that the Earl of Essex had come to it in person. I pressed my hands over my eyes to still my aching head. "Go find your scullion," I said to Matty. "Do what you will to him, but make him talk." She nodded, tightening her lips, and before she went she brought another bone to Dick, from some lair within her own small room, and, luring him with it like a dog to his kennel, got him to his cell beneath the buttress.

Three, four, five, and it was already murky, the evening drawing in early because of the mist and rain, when I heard the horses pass beneath the archway once again, and so out across the park. At half-past five Matty returned. What she had been doing those intervening hours I never asked her from that day to this, but she told me the scullion was without, and wished to speak to me. She lit the candles, for I was in darkness, and as I raised myself upon my elbow I questioned her with my eyes, and she gave a jerk of her head towards the passage.

"If you give him money," she whispered, "he will do anything you ask him." I bade her fetch my purse, which she did, and then, going to the door, she beckoned him within. He stood blinking in the dim light, a sheepish grin on his face—but that face, like ours, was lean and hungry.

I beckoned him to my bed, and he came near, with a furtive glance over his shoulder. I gave him a gold piece, which he pocketed instantly. "What news have you?" I asked.

He looked at Matty, and she nodded. He ran his tongue over his lips.

" 'Tis only rumour," he said, "but it's what they're saying in the courtyard." He paused, and looked again towards the door.

"The retreat begins to-night," he said. "There'll be five thousand of them marching through the darkness to the beaches. You'll hear them, if you listen. They'll come this way, down to Pridmouth and Polkerris. The boats will take them off when the wind eases."

"Horses can't embark in small boats," I said. "What will your generals do with their two thousand horse?"

He shook his head, and glanced at Matty. I gave him another gold piece.

"I had but a word with Sir William Balfour's groom," he said. "There's talk of breaking through the Royalist lines to-night, when the foot retreat. I can't answer for the truth of it, nor could he."

"What will happen to you and the other cooks?" I asked.

"We'll go by sea, same as the rest," he said.

"Not likely," I said. "Listen to the wind."

It was soughing through the trees in the Warren, and the rain spattered against my casement.

"I can tell you what will happen to you," I said. "The morning will come, and there won't be any boats to take you from the beaches. You will huddle there, in the driving wind and rain with a thundering great south-west sea breaking down at Pridmouth and the country people coming down on you all from the cliffs with pitch-forks in their hands. Cornish folk are not pleasant when they are hungry."

The man was silent, and passed his tongue over his lips once again.

"Why don't you desert?" I said. "Go off to-night, before worse can happen to you. I can give you a note to a Royalist leader."

"That's what I told him," said Matty. "A word from you to Sir Richard Grenvile would see him through to our lines."

The man looked from one to the other of us, foolish, doubtful, greedy. I gave him a third gold piece. "If you break through to the King's army," I said, "within an hour, and tell them there what you have just told me—about the horse trying to run for it before morning—they'll give you plenty more of these gold pieces, and a full supper into the bargain." He scratched his head, and looked again at Matty. "If the worst comes to the worst and you're held prisoner," I told him, "it would be better than having the bowels torn out of you by Cornishmen."

It was this last word that settled him. "I'll go," he said, "if you'll write a word for me."

I scribbled a few words to Richard, which were as like as not never to reach his hands (nor did they do so, as I afterward discovered), and bade the fellow find his way through the woods to Fowey if he could, and in the growing darkness get a boat to Bodinnick, which was held by the Royalists, and there give warning of the rebel plan.

It would be too late, no doubt, to do much good, but it was at least a venture worth the trying. When he had gone, with Matty to speed him on his way, I lay back on my bed and listened to the rain, and as it fell I heard in the far distance, from the high road beyond the park, the tramp of marching feet. Hour after hour they sounded, tramp, tramp, without a pause, through the long hours of the night. When the morning broke, misty, and wet, and grey, they were still marching there upon the high road, bedraggled, damp, and dirty, hundred upon hundred straggling in broken lines across the park and making for the beaches.

Order was gone by midday on Saturday, discipline was broken, for as a watery sun gleamed through the scurrying clouds we heard the first sounds of gun-fire from Lostwithiel, as Richard's army broke upon them from the rear. We sat at our windows, hunger at last forgotten, with the rain blowing in our weary faces, and all day long they trudged across the park, a hopeless tangle now of men and horses and wagons; voices yelling orders that were not once obeyed, men falling to the ground in weariness and refusing to move further, horses, carts, and the few cattle that remained all jammed and bogged together in the sea of mud that once had been a park. The sound of the gun-fire drew nearer, and the rattle of musket-shots, and one of the servants, climbing to the belfry, reported that the high ground near Castledore was black with troops and smoke and flame, while down from the fields came little running figures, first a score, then fifty, then a hundred, then a hundred more, to join the swelling throng about the lanes and in the park.

And the rain went on, and the retreat continued.

At five o'clock word went round the house that we were every one of us to descend to the gallery. Even John, from his sick-bed, must obey the order. The rest had little strength to drag their feet, and I found difficulty in holding to my chair. Nothing had passed our lips now but weak herb tea for two whole days. Alice looked like a ghost, for I think she had denied herself entirely for the sake of her three little girls. Her sister Elizabeth was scarcely better, and her year-old baby in her arms was as still as a waxen doll. Before I left my chamber I saw that Dick was safe within his cell, and this time, in spite of protestations, I closed the stone that formed the entrance.

A strange band we were, huddled there together in the gallery, with wan faces; the children strangely quiet, and an ominously heavy look about their hollow eyes. It was the first time I had seen John since that morning a month ago, and he seemed most wretchedly ill, his skin a dull yellow colour, and shaking still in every limb. He looked across at me as though to ask a question, and I nodded to him, summoning a smile. We sat there waiting, no one with the heart or strength to speak. A little apart from us, near the centre window, sat Gartred with her daughters. They too were thinner and paler than before, and I think had not tasted chicken now for many days, but, compared to the poor Rashleigh and Courtney babies, they were not ill-nourished.

I noticed that Gartred wore no jewels and was very plainly dressed, and somehow the sight of this gave me a strange foreboding. She took no notice of us, beyond a few words to Mary on her entrance, and seated beside the little table in the window she proceeded to play patience. She turned the cards with faces uppermost, considering them with great intentness. This, I thought, is the moment she has been waiting for for over thirty days.

Suddenly there was a tramping in the hall and into the gallery came Lord Robartes, his boots splashed with mud, the rain running from his coat. His staff officers stood beside him, and one and all wore faces grim and purposeful.

"Is everybody in the household here?" he called harshly.

Some sort of murmur rose from amongst us, which he took to be assent.

"Very well, then," he said, and, walking towards my sister Mary and her stepson John, he stood confronting them.

"It has come to my knowledge," he said, "that your malignant husband, madam, and your father, sir, have concealed upon the premises large quantities of silver, which should by right belong to Parliament. The time has ended for any trifling or protestation. Pressure is being brought to bear upon our armies at this moment, forcing us to a temporary withdrawal. The Parliament needs every ounce of silver in the land, to bring this war to a successful conclusion. I ask you, madam, therefore, to tell me where the silver is concealed."

Mary, God bless her ignorance, turned up her bewildered face to him.

"I know nothing of any silver," she said, "except the few pieces of plate we have kept of our own, which you now possess, having my keys."

"I talk of great quantities, madam, stored in some place of hiding, until it can be transported by your husband to the Mint."

"My husband was Collector for Cornwall, that is true, my lord. But he has never said a word to me about concealing it at Menabilly."

He turned from her to John. "And you, sir? No doubt your father told you all his affairs?"

"No," said John firmly. "I know nothing of my father's business, nor have I any knowledge of a hiding-place. My father's only confidant is his steward, Langdon, who is with him at present. No one here at Menabilly can tell you anything at all."

For a moment Lord Robartes stared down at John, then, turning away, he called to his three officers. "Sack the house," he said briefly. "Strip the hangings and all furnishings. Destroy everything you find. Take all jewels, clothes, and valuables. Leave nothing of Menabilly but the bare walls."

At this poor John struggled to his feet. "You cannot do this," he said. "What authority has Parliament given you to commit such wanton damage? I protest, my lord, in the name of common decency and humanity." And my sister Mary, coming forward, threw herself upon her knees. "My Lord Robartes," she said, "I swear to you by all I hold most dear that there is nothing concealed within my house. If it were so I would have known of it. I do implore you to show mercy to my home."

Lord Robartes stared down at her, his eyes hard.

"Madam," he said, "why should I show your house mercy, when none was shown to mine? Both victor and loser pay the penalty in civil war. Be thankful that I have heart enough to spare your lives." And with that he turned on his heel and went from us, taking his officers with him and leaving two sentries at the door.

Once again he mounted his horse in the courtyard and rode away, back to the useless rearguard action that was being fought in the hedges and ditches up at Castledore, with the mizzle rain still falling thick and fast. We heard the major he had left in charge snap forth an order to his men—and straightway they started tearing at the panelling in the dining-chamber. We could hear the woodwork rip, and the glass shatter as they smashed the mullioned windows. At this first warning of destruction Mary turned to John, the tears ravaging her face. "For God's sake," she said, "if you know of any hiding-place, tell them of it, so that we save the house. I will take full blame upon myself when your father comes." John did not answer. He looked at me. And no one of the company there present saw the look save Gartred, who at that moment raised her head. I made no motion of my lips. I stared back at him, as hard and merciless as Lord Robartes. He waited a moment, then answered very slowly, "I know nought of any hiding-place."

I think had the rebels gone about their work with shouts and merriment, or even drunken laughter, the destruction of the house would have been less hard to bear. But because they were defeated troops, and knew it well, they had cold savage murder in their hearts, and did what they had to do in silence.

The door of the gallery was open, with the two sentries standing on guard beside it, and no voices were uplifted, no words spoken. There was only the sound of the ripping wood, the breaking of the furniture, the hacking to pieces of the great dining-table, and the grunts of the men as they lifted their axes.

We heard them climb the stairs and break into the south rooms, and as they tore down the door of Mary's chamber she began to weep long and silently, and Alice took her in her arms and hushed her like a child. The rest of us did nothing, but sat like spectres, inarticulate. Then Gartred looked towards me from her window. "You and I, Honor, being the only members of the company without a drop of Rashleigh blood, must pass the time somehow. Tell me, do you play piquet?"

"I haven't played it since your brother taught me, sixteen years ago," I answered.

"The odds are in my favour, then," she said. "Will you risk a partie?" As she spoke she smiled, shuffling her cards, and I guessed the double meaning she would bring to it.

"Perhaps," I said, "there is more at stake than a few pieces of silver."

We heard them tramping overhead, and the sound of the splitting axe, while the shivering glass from the casements fell to the terrace outside.

"You are afraid to match your cards against mine?" said Gartred.

"No," I said. "No, I am not afraid."

I pushed my chair towards her and sat opposite to her at the table. She handed the cards for me to cut and shuffle, and when I had done so, I returned them to her for the dealing, twelve apiece. There started then the strangest partie of piquet that I have ever played, before or since, for while Gartred risked a fortune I wagered for Richard's son, and no one knew it but myself. The rest of the company, dumb and apathetic, were too weak even to wonder at us, and if they did it was with shocked distaste and shuddering dislike, that we—because we did not belong to Menabilly—could show ourselves so heartless.

"Five cards," called Gartred.

"What do they make?" I said.

"Making nine."

"Good."

"Five."

"A quart major, nine. Three knaves."

"Not good."

She led with the ace of hearts, to which I played the ten, and as she took the trick we heard the rebels wrenching the tapestry from the bedroom walls above. There was a dull smouldering smell, and a wisp of smoke blew past the windows of the gallery.

"They are setting fire," said John quietly, "to the stables and the farm-buildings before the house."

"The rain will surely quench the flames," whispered Joan. "They cannot burn fiercely, not in the rain."

One of the children began to wail, and I saw gruff Deborah take her on her knee and murmur to her. The smoke of the burning buildings was rank and bitter in the steady rain, and the sound of the axes overhead and the tramping of the men was as though they were felling trees in a thick forest, instead of breaking to pieces the great four-poster bed where Alice had borne her babies. They threw the glass mirror out on to the terrace, where it splintered to a thousand fragments, and with it came the broken candle-sticks, the tall vases, and the tapestried chairs.

"Fifteen," said Gartred, leading the king of diamonds, and "Eighteen," I answered, trumping it with my ace.

Some of the rebels, with a sergeant in charge of them, came down the staircase, and they had with them all the clothing they had found in Jonathan's and Mary's bedroom, and her jewels too, and combs, and the fine figured arras that had hung upon the walls. This they loaded in bundles upon the pack-horses that waited in the courtyard. When they were fully laden a trooper led them through the archway, and two more took their place. Through the broken windows of the wrecked dining-chamber we could see the disordered rebel bands still straggling past the smouldering farm buildings towards the meadows and the beach, and as they gazed up at the house, grinning, their fellows at the house windows, warming to their work and growing reckless, shouted down to them with jeers and cat-calls, throwing out the mattresses, the chairs, the tables—all they could lay hands upon which would make fodder for the flames that rose reluctantly in the slow drizzle from the blackened farm buildings.

There was one fellow making a bundle of all the clothing and the linen. Alice's wedding-gown, and the little frocks she had embroidered for her children, and all Peter's rich apparel that she had kept with such care in her press till he should need it. The tramping ceased from overhead, and we heard them pass into the rooms beneath the belfry. Some fellow, in mockery, began to toll the bell, and the mournful clanging made a new sound in our ears, mingling with the shouting and yelling and rumble of wagon wheels that still came to us from the park, and the ever-increasing bark of cannon-shot, now barely two miles distant.

"They will be in the gatehouse now," said Joan. "All your books and your possessions, Honor, they will not spare them any more than ours." There was reproach in her voice, and disillusion, that her favourite aunt and godmother should show no sign of grief. Still the bell tolled and the ceilings shook with heavy, murderous feet, and down into the inner court now they threw the debris from the west part of the building, portraits, and benches, rugs and hangings, all piled on top of one another in hideous confusion, while those below discarded the less valuable, and fed them to the flames.

We started upon the third hand of the partie. "A tierce to a king," called Gartred, and "Good," I replied, following her lead of spades. And all the while I knew that the rebels had now come to the last room of the house, and were tearing down the arras before the buttress. I saw Mary raise her grief-stricken face and look towards us. "If you would but say one word to the officer," she said to Gartred, "he might prevent the men from further damage. You are a friend of Lord Robartes, and have some sway with him. Is there nothing you can do?"

"I could do much," said Gartred, "if I were permitted. But Honor tells me it is better for the house to fall about our ears. Fifteen, sixteen, seventeen, and eighteen. My trick, I fancy."

She wrote her score on the tablets by her side.

"Honor," said Mary, "you know that it will break Jonathan's heart to see his home laid desolate. All that he has toiled and lived for, and his father before him, for nearly fifty years. If Gartred can in some way save us, and you are trying to prevent her, I can never forgive you, nor will Jonathan, when he knows of it."

"Gartred can save no one, unless she likes to save herself," I answered, and began to deal for the fourth hand.

"Five cards," called Gartred.

"*Equalë*," I answered.

"A quart to a king."

"A quart to a knave."

We were in our fifth and last game, each winning two apiece, when we heard them tramping down the stairs, with the major in the lead. The terrace and the courtyard were heaped high with wreckage, the loved possessions and treasures of nearly fifty years, even as Mary had said, and what had not been packed upon the horses was left now to destroy. They set fire to the remainder, and watched it burn, the men leaning upon their axes and breathing hard now that the work was over. When the pile was well alight the major turned his back upon it, and coming into the gallery clicked his heels and bowed derisively to John.

"The orders given me by Lord Robartes have been carried out with implicit fidelity," he announced. "There is nothing left within Menabilly House but yourselves, ladies and gentlemen, and the bare walls."

"And you found no silver hidden?" asked Mary.

"None, madam, but your own—now happily in our possession."

"Then this wanton damage, this wicked destruction, has been for nothing?"

"A brave blow has been struck for Parliament, madam, and that is all that we, her soldiers and her servants, need consider."

He bowed and left us, and in a moment we heard him call further orders, and horses were brought, and he mounted and rode away even as Lord Robartes had done an hour before. The flames licked the rubble in the courtyard, and save for their dull hissing, and the patter of the rain, there was suddenly no other sound. A strange silence had fallen upon the place. Even the sentries stood no longer by the door.

I looked up at Gartred, and this time it was I who smiled, and I who spread my cards upon the table.

"Discard for *carte blanche*," I said softly, and, adding ten thus to my score, I led her for the first time, and with my next hand drew three aces to her one, and gained the partie.

She rose then from the table without a word, save for one mock curtsy to me, and calling her daughters to her, went upstairs. I sat alone, shuffling the cards as she had done, while out into the hall faltered the poor weak members of our company to gaze about them, stricken at the sight that met their eyes.

The panels ripped, the floors torn open, the windows shattered from their frames, and all the while the driving rain, that had neither doors nor windows now to bar it, blew in upon their faces, soft and silent, with great flakes of charred timber and dull soot from the burning rubble in the courtyard. The last rebels had retreated to the beaches, save for the few who still made the stand at Castledore, and there was no trace of them left now at Menabilly but the devastation they had wrought, and the black, churning slough that once was road and park. As I sat there, listening, still shuffling the cards in my hands, I heard, for the first time, a new note above the cannon and the musket shot and the steady pattering rain. Not clamouring or insistent, like the bugle that had haunted me so long, but quick, triumphant, coming ever nearer, the sharp, brisk tattoo of the Royalist drums.

CHAPTER TWENTY

THE REBEL ARMY capitulated to the King in the early hours of Sunday morning. There was no escape by sea for the hundreds of men herded on the beaches. Only one fishing-boat put forth from Fowey bound for Plymouth, in the dim light before dawn, and she carried in her cabin the Lord General the Earl of Essex, and his adviser, Lord Robartes. So much we learnt later, and we learnt too that Matty's scullion had proved faithful to his promise and borne his message to Sir Jacob Astley at Bodinnick on the Friday evening. But by that time word had reached His Majesty, the out-posts upon the road were warned and the Parliament horse had successfully broken through the Royalist lines, and made good their escape to Saltash. So, by a lag in time, over two thousand rebel horse got clean away to fight another day, a serious mishap which was glossed over by our forces in the heat and excitement of the big surrender, and I think the only one of our commanders to go nearly hopping mad at the escape was Richard Grenvile.

It was, I think, most typical of his character that when he sent a regiment of his foot to come to our succour on that Sunday morning, bringing us food from their own wagons, he did not come himself, but forwarded me this brief message, stopping not to consider whether I lived or died, or whether his son was with me still:

"You will soon learn," he wrote, "that my plan has only partially succeeded. The horse have got away, all owing to that besotted idiot Goring lying in a stupor at his headquarters, and permitting—you will scarcely credit it—the rebels to slip through his lines without as much as a musket shot at their backsides. May God preserve us from our own commanders. I go now in haste to Saltash in pursuit, but have little hope of overtaking the sods, if Goring, with his cavalry, has already failed."

First a soldier, last a lover, my Richard had no time to waste over a starving household and a crippled woman who had let a whole house be laid waste about her for the sake of the son he did not love. So it was not the father after all who carried the fainting lad into my chamber once again, and laid him down, but poor sick John Rashleigh, who, crawling for the second time into the tunnel beneath the summer-house, found Dick unconscious in the buttress cell, tugged at the rope, and so opened the hinged stone into the room.

This was about nine o'clock on the Saturday night, after the house had been abandoned by the rebels, and we were all too weak to do much more than smile at the Royalist foot when they beat their drums under our gaping windows on the Sunday morning.

The first necessity was milk for the children and bread for ourselves, and later in the day, when we had regained a little measure of our strength and the soldiers had kindled a fire for us in the gallery—the only room left liveable—we heard once more the sound of horses, but this time heartening and welcome, for they were our own men coming home. I suppose I had been through a deal of strain those past four weeks, something harder than the others because of the secret I had guarded; and so, when it was over, I suffered a strange relapse, accentuated, maybe, by natural weakness, and had not the strength for several days to lift my head. The scenes of joy and reunion, then, were not for me. Alice had her Peter, Elizabeth her John of Coombe, Mary had her Jonathan, and there was kissing, and crying, and kissing again, and all the horrors of our past days to be described, and the desolation to be witnessed. But I had no shoulder on which to lean my head, and no breast to weep upon. A truckle bed from the attic served me for support, this being one of the few things that the rebels had not destroyed.

I recollect that my brother-in-law bent over me when he returned, and praised me for my courage, saying that John had told him everything and I had acted as he would have done himself, had he been home. But I did not want my brother-in-law. I wanted Richard. And Richard had gone to Saltash, chasing rebels. All the rejoicing came as anticlimax. The bells pealing in Fowey Church, echoed by the bells at Tywardreath, and His Majesty summoning the gentlemen of the county to his headquarters at Boconnoc and thanking them for their support—he presented Jonathan with his own lace handkerchief and Prayer Book—and a sudden wild thanksgiving for deliverance and for victory, seemed premature to me, and strangely sour. Perhaps it was some fault in my own character, some cripple quality, but I turned my face to the wall, and my heart was heavy. The war was not over, for all the triumphs in the west. Only Essex had been defeated, and his eight thousand men. There were many thousands in the north and east of England who had yet to show their heels. "And what is it all for?" I thought. "Why can they not make peace? Is it to continue thus, with the land laid waste, and houses devastated, until we are all grown old?"

Victory had a hollow sound, with our enemy Lord Robartes in command at Plymouth, still stubbornly defended, and there was something narrow and parochial in thinking the war over because Cornwall was now free. It was the second day of our release, when the menfolk had ridden off to Boconnoc to take leave of His Majesty, that I heard the sound of wheels in the outer court, and preparation for departure, and then those wheels creaking over the cobbles and disappearing through the park. I was too tired then to question it, but later in the day, when Matty came to me, I asked her who it was that went away from Menabilly in so confident a fashion. "Who else could it be," Matty answered, "but Mrs Denys?" So Gartred, like a true gambler, had thought best to cut her losses and be quit of us.

"Did she see Dick," I asked, "before she left?"

"Aye," said Matty. "He went up to her at breakfast and saluted her. She stared at him amazed—I watched her. And then she asked him, 'Did you come in the morning with the infantry?' and he grinned like a little imp, and answered: 'I have been here all the time.'"

"Imprudent lad," I said. "What did she say to him?"

"She did not answer for a moment, Miss Honor, and then she smiled—you know her way—and said, 'I might have known it. You may tell your gaoler you are not worth one bar of silver.'"

"And was that all?"

"That was all. She went soon after. She'll never come again to Menabilly." And Matty rubbed my sore back with her hard, familiar hands. But Matty was wrong, for Gartred did come again to Menabilly, as you shall hear, and the man who brought her was my own brother. But I run ahead of my story, for we are still in September, '44.

That first week, while we recovered our strength, my brother-in-law and his steward set to work to find out what it would cost to make good the damage that had been wrought upon his house and his estate. The figure was colossal, and beyond his means. I can see him now, seated in one corner of the gallery, reading from his great account book, every penny he had lost meticulously counted and entered in the margin. It would take months, nay years, he said, to restore the house and bring back the estate to its original condition. While the war lasted no redress would be forthcoming. After the war, so he was told, the Crown would see that he was not the loser. I think Jonathan knew the value of such promises, and, like me, he thought the rejoicings in the west were premature. One day the rebels might return again, and next time the scales be turned.

In the meantime, all that could be done was to save what was left of the harvest—and that but one meadow of fourteen acres which the rebels had left uncut but the rain had well-nigh ruined.

Since his house in Fowey had been left bare in the same miserable fashion as Menabilly, his family, in their turn, were homeless, and the decision was now made amongst us to divide. The Sawles went to their brother at Penrice, and the Sparkes to other relatives in Tavistock. The Rashleighs themselves, with the children, split up among near neighbours until a wing of Menabilly should be repaired. I was for returning to Lanrest until I learnt, with a sick heart, that the whole house had suffered a worse fate than Menabilly and was wrecked beyond hope of restoration.

There was nothing for it but to take shelter for the time being with my brother Jo at Radford, for although Plymouth was still held by Parliament the surrounding country was safe in Royalist hands, and the subduing of the garrison and harbour was only, according to our optimists, a matter of three months at the most.

I would have preferred, had the choice been offered me, to live alone in one bare room at Menabilly rather than repair to Radford and the stiff household of my brother, but alas! I had become in a few summer months but another of the vast number of homeless people, turned wanderer through war, and must swallow pride and be grateful for hospitality, from whatever direction it might come.

I might have gone to my sister Cecilia at Mothercombe or my sister Bridget at Holbeton, both of whom were pleasanter companions than my brother Jo, whose official position in the county of Devon had turned him somewhat cold and proud, but I chose Radford for the reason that it was close to Plymouth—and Richard was once more Commander of the Siege. What hopes I had of seeing him, God only knew, but I was sunk deep now in the mesh I had made for myself, and waiting for a word from him, or a visit of an hour had become my sole reason for existence.

"Why cannot you come with me to Buckland?" pleaded Dick, for the tutor, Herbert Ashley, had been sent to fetch him home. "I would be content at Buckland, and not mind my father, if you could come too and stand between us."

"Your father," I answered him, "has enough work on his hands without keeping house for a crippled woman."

"You are not crippled," declared the boy with passion. "You are only weak about the legs, and so must sit confined to your chair. I would tend you, and wait upon you, hour by hour with Matty, if you would but come with me to Buckland."

I smiled, and ran my hand through his dark curls.

"You shall come and visit me at Radford," I said, "and tell me of your lessons. How you fence, and how you dance, and what progress you make in speaking French."

"It will not be the same," he said, "as living here with you in the house. Shall I tell you something? I like you best of all the people that I know—next to my own mother."

Ah, well, it was an achievement to be second once again to Mary Howard. The next day he rode away in company with his tutor, turning back to wave to me all the way across the park, and I shed a useless, sentimental tear when he was gone from me.

What might have been—what could have been. These are the saddest phrases in our English tongue. And back again, pell-mell, would come the fantasies: the baby I had never borne, the husband I would never hold. The sickly figures in an old maid's dream, so Gartred would have told me.

Yes, I was thirty-four, an old maid and a cripple; but sixteen years ago I had had my moment, which was with me still, vivid and enduring, and by God I swear I was happier with my one lover than Gartred ever had been with her twenty.

So I set forth upon the road again and turned my back on Menabilly, little thinking that the final drama of the house must yet be played with blood and tears, and I kissed my dear Rashleighs one and all and vowed I would return to them as soon as they could have me.

Jonathan escorted me in my litter as far as Saltash, where Robin came to meet me. I was much shaken, not by the roughness of the journey, but by the sights I had witnessed on the road. The aftermath of war was not a pleasant sight to the beholder. The country was laid waste, for one thing, and that was the fault of the enemy. The corn was ruined, the orchards devastated, the houses smoking. And in return for this the Cornish people had taken toll upon the rebel prisoners. There were many of them still lying in the ditches, with the dust and flies upon them. Some without hands and feet, some hanging downwards from the trees. And there were stragglers who had died upon the road, in the last retreat, too faint to march from Cornwall—and these had been set upon and stripped of their clothing and left for the hungry dogs to lick.

I knew then, as I peered forth from the curtains of my litter, that war can make beasts of every one of us, and that the men and women of my own breed could act even worse in warfare than the men and women of the eastern counties. We had, each one of us, because of the civil war, streaked back two centuries in time, and were become like those half savages of the fourteen hundreds who, during the Wars of the Roses, slit each other's throats without compunction.

At Saltash there were gibbets in the market square, with the bodies of rebel troopers hanging upon them scarcely cold, and as I turned my sickened eyes away from them I heard Jonathan enquire of a passing soldier what faults they had committed.

He grinned, a fine tall fellow, with the Grenvile shield on his shoulder. "No fault," he said, "except that they are rebels, and so must be hanged, like the dogs they are."

"Who gave the order, then?"

"Our general, of course. Sir Richard Grenvile."

Jonathan said nothing, but I saw that he looked grave, and I leant back upon my cushions, feeling, because it was Richard's doing and I loved him, that the fault was somehow mine and I was responsible. We halted there that night, and in the morning Robin came, with an escort, to conduct me across the Tamar and so through the Royalist lines outside the Plymouth defences, round to Radford.

Robin looked well and bronzed, and I thought again with cynicism how men, in spite of protestations about peace, are really bred to war and thrive upon it. He was not under Richard's command, but was colonel of foot under Sir John Berkeley, in the army of Prince Maurice, and he told us that the King had decided not to make a determined and immediate assault upon Plymouth after all, but leave it to Grenvile to subdue by slow starvation, while he and Prince Maurice marched east out of Devon towards Somerset and Wiltshire, there to join forces with Prince Rupert and engage the Parliament forces which were still unsubdued. I thought to myself that Richard would reckon this bad strategy, for Plymouth was no pooping little town, but the finest harbour in all England next to Portsmouth, and for His Majesty to gain the garrison, and have command also of the sea, was of very great importance. Slow starvation had not conquered it before; why then should it do so now? What Richard needed for assault was guns and men. But I was a woman, and not supposed to have knowledge of these matters.

No one hated cruelty more than I did, nor deplored the streak of it in Richard with greater sickness of heart, but as we travelled towards Radford, making a great circuit of the forts around Plymouth, I noticed with secret pride that the only men who carried themselves like soldiers were those who wore the Grenvile shields on their shoulders. Some of Goring's horse were quartered by St Budeaux and they were lolling about the village, drinking with the inhabitants, while a sentry squatted on a stool, his great mouth gaping in a yawn, his musket lying at his feet. From the nearby inn came a group of officers, laughing and very flushed, but the sentry did not leap to his feet when he observed them. Robin joined the officers a moment, exchanging greetings, and as we passed through the village he told me that the most flushed of the group was Lord Goring himself, a very good fellow, and a most excellent judge of horses.

"Does that make him a good commander?" I asked.

"He is full of courage," said Robin, "and will ride at anything. That is all that matters." And he proceeded to tell me about a race which had been run the day before, under the very nose of the rebels, and how Lord Goring's chestnut had beaten Lord Wentworth's roan by half a neck. "Is that how Prince Maurice's army conducts its war?" I asked. Robin laughed—he too thought it all very fine sport.

But the next post we passed was held by Grenvile men. And here there was a barrier across the road, with armed sentries standing by it, and Robin had to show his piece of paper, signed by Sir John Berkeley, before we could pass through. An officer barked an order to the men, and they removed the barrier. There were perhaps a score of them standing by the postern, cleaning their equipment; they looked lean and tough, with an indefinable quality about them that stamped them Grenvile men. I would have known them on the instant had I not seen the scarlet pennant by the postern door, with the three golden rests staring from the centre, capped by a laughing gryphon.

We came at length by Plymstock to Radford, and my brother's house, and as I was shown to my apartments looking north over the river towards the Cattwater and Plymouth I thought of my eighteenth birthday long ago, and how Richard had sailed into the Sound with the Duke of Buckingham. It seemed a world ago, and I another woman. My brother was now a widower, for Elizabeth Champernowne had died a few years before the war in childbed, and my youngest brother Percy, with his wife Phillipa, had come to live with him and look after Jo's son, John, a child of seven, since they themselves were childless. I had never cared much for Radford, even as a girl, and now within its austere barrack precincts I found myself homesick, not so much for Lanrest and the days that were gone, but for my last few months at Menabilly. The danger I had known there, and the tension I had shared, had, in some strange fashion, rendered the place dear to me. The gatehouse between the court-yards, the long gallery, the causeway that looked out to the Gribben and the sea, seemed to me now, in retrospect, my own possession. The fighting did not touch them here at Radford, for all its proximity to Plymouth, and the talk was of the discomfort they had to bear by living within military control.

Straight from a sacked house and starvation, I wondered that they should think themselves ill-used, with plenty of food upon the table; but no sooner had we sat down to dinner (I had not the face to demand it, the first evening, in my room) than Jo began to hold forth, with great heat, upon the dictatorial manners of the army. "His Majesty has thought fit," he said, "to confer upon Richard Grenvile the designation of General in the West. Very good. I have no word to say against the appointment. But when Grenvile trades upon the title to commandeer all the cattle within a radius of thirty miles or more to feed his army, and rides roughshod over the feelings of the county gentry with the one sentence 'Military necessities come first', it is time that we all protested."

If Jo remembered my old alliance with Richard, the excitement of the moment had made him conveniently forget it. Nor did he know that young Dick had been in my care at Menabilly the past weeks. Robin, too, full of his own commander, Berkeley, was pleased to agree with Jo. "The trouble with Grenvile," said Robin, "is that he insists upon his fellows being paid. The men in his command are like hired mercenaries. No free quarter, no looting, no foraging as they please, and all this comes very hard upon the pockets of people like yourself, who must provide the money."

"Do you know," continued Jo, "that the Commissioners of Devon have been obliged to allot him one thousand pounds a week for the maintenance of his troops? I tell you, it hits us very hard."

"It would hit you harder," I said, "if your house was burnt down by the Parliament."

They stared at me in surprise, and I saw young Phillipa look at me in wonder for my boldness. Woman's talk was not encouraged at Radford. "That, my dear Honor," said Jo coldly, "is not likely to happen." And, turning his shoulder to me, he harped on the outraged Devon gentry, and how this new-styled General in the West had coolly told them he had need of all their horses and their muskets in this siege of Plymouth, and if they did not give them to him voluntarily he would send a company of his soldiers to collect them.

"The fellow is entirely without scruples, no doubt of that," said Percy, "but in fairness to him I must say that all the country people tell me they would rather have Grenvile's men in their villages than Goring's. If Grenvile finds one of his own fellows looting, he is shot upon the instant. But Goring's men are quite out of control, and drunk from dawn to dusk."

"Oh, come," frowned Robin, "Goring and his cavalry are entitled to a little relaxation, now that the worst is over. No sense in keeping fellows standing to attention all day long."

"Robin is right," said Jo. "A certain amount of licence must be permitted, to keep the men in heart. We shall never win the war otherwise."

"You are more likely to lose it," I said, "by letting them loll about the villages with their tunics all undone."

The statement was rendered the more unfortunate by a servant entering the room upon this instant and announcing Sir Richard Grenvile. He strode in with his boots ringing on the stone flags, in that brisk way I knew so well, totally unconscious of himself or the effect he might produce, and with a cool nod to Jo, the master of the house, he came at once to me and kissed my hand.

"Why the devil," he said, "did you come here and not to Buckland?" That he at once put me a disadvantage amongst my relatives did not worry him. I murmured something about my brother's invitation, and attempted to introduce him to the company. He bowed to Phillipa, but turned back immediately to me.

"You've lost that weight that so improved your person," he said. "You're as thin as a church mouse."

"So would you be," I answered, "if you'd been held prisoner by the rebels for four weeks."

"The whelp is asking for you all day long," said Richard. "He dins your praises in my ears till I am sick of them. I have him outside, with Joseph. Hi! spawn!" He turned on his heels, bawling for his son. I think I never knew of any man, save Richard, who could in so brief a moment fill a room with his presence and become, as it were, the master of a house that was in no way his. Jo stood at his own table, his napkin in his hand, and Robin too, and Percy, and they were like dumb servants waiting for the occasion, while Richard took command. Dick crept in cautiously, timid and scared as ever, his dark eyes lighting at the sight of me, and behind him strode young Joseph Grenvile, Richard's kinsman and aide-de-camp, his features and his colouring so like his General's as to make me wonder and not for the first time, God forgive my prying mind, whether Richard had been purposely vague about the relationship between them, and whether he was not as much his son as Dick was. God damn you, I thought, begetting sons about the countryside before I was even crippled. "Have you all dined?" said Richard, reaching for a plum. "These lads and I could eat another dinner." Jo, with heightened colour and a flea in his ear, as the saying goes, called the servants to bring back the mutton. Dick squeezed himself beside me, like a small dog regaining his lost mistress, and while they ate Richard declaimed upon the ill-advisability of the King having marched east without first seeing Plymouth was subdued.

"It's like talking to a brick wall, God bless him," said Richard, his mouth full of mutton. "He knows no more of warfare than this dead sheep I swallow." I saw my brothers look at one another askance, that a general should dare to criticise his king. "I'll fight in his service until there's no breath left in my body," said Richard, "but it would make it so much simpler for the country if he would ask advice of soldiers. Put some food into your belly, spawn. Don't you want to grow as fine a man as Jo here?" I saw Dick glance under his eyes at Joseph with a flicker of jealousy. Jo then was the favourite, no doubt about that. What a world of difference between them, too—the one so broad-shouldered, big, and auburn-haired; the other little, with black hair and eyes. I wonder, I thought grudgingly, what buxom country girl was Joseph's mother, and if she still lived, and what had happened to her? But while I pondered the question, as jealous as young Dick, Richard continued talking. "It's that damned lawyer who's to blame," he said; "that fellow Hyde, an upstart from God knows what snivelling country town, and now jumped into favour as Chancellor of the Exchequer. His Majesty won't move a finger without asking his advice. I hear Rupert has all but chucked his hand in, and returned to Germany. Depend upon it, it's fellows like this who will lose the war for us."

"I have met Sir Edward Hyde," said my brother. "He seemed to me a very able man."

"Able my arse," said Richard. "Anyone who jiggles with the Treasury must be double-faced to start with. I've never met a lawyer yet who didn't line his own pockets before he fleeced his clients." He tapped young Joseph on the shoulder. "Give me some tobacco," he said. The youngster produced a pipe and pouch from his coat. "Yes, I hate the breed," said Richard, blowing a cloud of smoke across the table, "and nothing affords me greater pleasure than to see them trounced. There was a fellow called Braband, who acted as attorney for my wife against me in the Star Chamber in the year '33—a neighbour of yours, Harris, I believe?"

"Yes," said my brother coldly, "and a man of great integrity devoted to the King's cause in this war."

"Well, he'll never prove that now," said Richard. "I found him creeping about the Devon lanes disguised the other day, and seized the occasion to arrest him as a spy. I've waited eleven years to catch that blackguard."

"What have you done to him, sir?" asked Robin.

"He was disposed of," said Richard, "in the usual fashion. No doubt he is doing comfortably in the next world."

I saw young Joseph hide his laughter in his wine-glass, but my three brothers gazed steadfastly at their plates.

"I dare say," said my eldest brother slowly, "that I should be very ill-advised if I attempted to address to you, General, a single word of criticism, but . . ."

"You would, sir," said Richard, "be extremely ill-advised." And, laying his hand a moment on Joseph's shoulder, he rose from the table. "Go on, lads, and get your horses. Honor, I will conduct you to your apartment. Good evening, gentlemen."

I felt that whatever reputation I might have for dignity in the eyes of my family was gone to the winds for ever as he swept me to my room. Matty was sent packing to the kitchen, and he laid me on my bed and sat beside me.

"You had far better," he said, "return with me to Buckland. Your brothers are all asses. As for the Champernownes, I have a couple of them on my staff, and both are useless."

"And what would I do at Buckland," I said, "among a mass of soldiers? What would be thought of me?"

"You could look after the whelp," he said, "and minister to me in the evening. I get very tired of soldiers' company."

"There are plenty of women," I said, "who could give you satisfaction."

"I have not met any," he said.

"Bring them in from the hedgerows," I said, "and send them back again in the morning. It would be far less trouble than having me upon your hands from dawn till dusk."

"My God," he said, "if you think I want to bounce about with some fat female after a hard day's work sweating my guts out before the walls of

Plymouth, you flatter my powers of resilience. Keep still, can't you, while I kiss you?"

Below the window, in the drive, Jo and Dick paced the horses up and down. "Someone," I said, "will come into the room."

"Let them," he answered. "What the hell do I care?"

I wished that I could have the same contempt for my brother's house as he had. It was dark by the time he left, and I felt as furtive as I had done at eighteen when slipping from the apple-tree.

"I did not come to Radford," I said weakly, "to behave like this."

"I have a very poor opinion," he answered, "of whatever else you came for."

I thought of Jo and Robin, Percy and Phillipa, all sitting in the hall below, and the two lads pacing their horses under the stars.

"You have placed me," I said, "in a most embarrassing position."

"Don't worry, sweetheart," he said. "I did that to you sixteen years ago." As he stood there, laughing at me, with his hand upon the door, I had half a mind to throw my pillow at him.

"You and your double-faced attorneys," I said. "What about your own two faces? That boy out there—your precious Joseph—you told me he was your kinsman?"

"So he is," he grinned.

"Who was his mother?"

"A dairy-maid at Killigarth. A most obliging soul. Married now to a farmer, and mother of his twelve sturdy children."

"When did you discover Joseph?"

"A year or so ago, on returning from Germany, and before I went to Ireland. The likeness was unmistakable. I took some cheeses and a bowl of cream off his mother, and she recalled the incident, laughing with me, in her kitchen. She bore no malice. The boy was a fine boy. The least I could do was to take him off her hands. Now I wouldn't be without him for the world."

"It is the sort of tale," I said sulkily, "that leaves a sour taste in the mouth."

"In yours, perhaps," he said, "but not in mine. Don't be so mealy-mouthed, my loved one."

"You lived at Killigarth," I said, "when you were courting me."

"God damn it," he said, "I didn't ride to see you every day."

I heard them all in a moment laughing beneath my window, and then mount their horses and gallop away down the avenue, and as I lay upon my bed, staring at the ceiling, I thought how the blossom of my apple-tree, so long dazzling and fragrant white, had a little lost its sheen and was become, after all, a common apple-tree; but that the realisation of this, instead of driving me to torments as it would have done in the past, could now, because of my four-and-thirty years, be borne with equanimity.

CHAPTER TWENTY-ONE

I WAS FULLY PREPARED, the following morning, to have my brother call upon me at an early hour and inform me icily that he could not have his home treated as a bawdy house for soldiery. I knew so well the form of such a discourse. The honour of his position, the welfare of his young son, the delicate feelings of Phillipa, our sister-in-law, and although the times were strange and war had done odd things to conduct, certain standards of behaviour were necessary for people of our standing. I was in fact already planning to throw myself upon my sister Cecilia's mercy over at Mothercombe, and had my excuses already framed, when I heard the familiar sound of tramping feet. I bid Matty look from the window, and she told me that a company of infantry was marching up the drive, wearing the Grenvile shields. This, I felt, would add fuel to the flames that must already be burning in my brother's breast.

Curiosity, however, was too much for me, and, instead of remaining in my apartment like a child who had misbehaved, I bade the servants carry me downstairs to the hall. Here I discovered my brother Jo in heated argument with a fresh-faced young officer, who declared coolly, and with no sign of perturbation, that his General, having decided that Radford was most excellently placed for keeping close observation on the enemy battery at Mount Batten, wished to commandeer certain rooms of the house for himself as a temporary headquarters, and would Mr John Harris be good enough to show the officer a suite of rooms commanding a north-western view?

Mr Harris, added the officer, would be put to no inconvenience, as the General would be bringing his own servants, cooks, and provisions. "I must protest," I heard my brother say, "that this is a highly irregular proceeding. There are no facilities here for soldiers, I myself am hard-pressed with work about the county, and . . ."

"The General told me," said the young officer, cutting him short, "that he had a warrant from His Majesty authorising him to take over any place of residence in Devon or Cornwall that should please him. He already has a headquarters at Buckland, Werrington, and Fitzford, and there the inhabitants were not permitted to remain, but were forced to find room elsewhere. Of course, he does not propose to deal thus summarily with you, sir. May I see the rooms?"

My brother stared at him tight-lipped for a moment, then, turning on his heel, escorted him up the stairs which I had just descended. I was very careful to avoid his eye.

During the morning the company of foot proceeded to establish themselves in the north wing of the mansion, and, watching from the long window in the hall, I saw the cooks and pantry boys stagger towards the kitchen entrance bearing plucked fowls, and ducks, and sides of bacon, besides crate after crate of wine. Phillipa sat at my side, stitching her sampler.

"The King's General," she said meekly, "believes in doing himself well. I have not seen such fare since the siege of Plymouth started. Where do you suppose he obtains all his supplies?"

I examined my nails, which were in need of trimming, and so did not have to look her in the face.

"From the many houses," I answered, "that he commandeers."

"But I thought," said Phillipa, with maddening persistency, "that Percy told us Sir Richard never permitted his men to loot."

"Possibly," I said with great detachment, "Sir Richard looks upon ducks and burgundy as perquisites of war."

She went to her room soon after, and I was alone when my brother Jo came down the stairs.

"Well," he said grimly, "I suppose I have you to thank for this invasion."

"I know nothing about it," I answered.

"Nonsense. You planned it together last night."

"Indeed we did not."

"What were you doing then, closeted with him in your chamber?"

"The time seemed to pass," I said, "in reviving old memories."

"I thought," he said, after a moment's pause, "that your present condition, my dear Honor, would make talk of your former intimacy quite intolerable, and any renewal of it beyond question."

"So did I," I answered.

He looked down at me, his lips pursed.

"You were always shameless as a girl," he said. "We spoilt you most abominably, Robin, your sisters, and I. And now at thirty-four to behave like a dairy-maid."

He could not have chosen an epithet, to my mind, more unfortunate.

"My behaviour last night," I said, "was very different from a dairy-maid's."

"I am glad to hear it. But the impression, upon us here below, was to the contrary. Sir Richard's reputation is notorious, and for him to remain within a closed apartment for nearly an hour and three-quarters alone with a woman can conjure up, to my mind, one thing and one thing only."

"To my mind," I answered, "it can conjure up at least a dozen."

After that I knew I must be damned for ever, and was not surprised when he left me without further argument, except to express a wish that I might have some respect for his roof.

I felt brazen and unrepentant all the day, and when Richard appeared that evening, in tearing spirits, commanding dinner for two in the apartment his soldiers had prepared for him, I had a glow of wicked satisfaction that my relatives sat below in gloomy silence, while I ate roast duck with the General overhead.

"Since you would not come to Buckland," he said, "I had perforce to come to you."

"It is always a mistake," I said, "to fall out with a woman's brothers."

"Your brother Robin has ridden off with Berkeley's horse to Tavistock," he answered, "and Percy I am sending on a delegation to the King. That leaves only Jo to be disposed of. It might be possible to get him over to the Queen of France."

"And how long," I asked, "will it take before Plymouth falls before you?" He shook his head, and looked dubious.

"They have the whole place strengthened," he said, "since our campaign in Cornwall, and that's the devil of it. Had His Majesty abided by my advice, and tarried here a fortnight only with his army, we would have the place to day. But no. He must listen to Hyde and march to Dorset, and here I am, back again where I was last Easter, with less than a thousand men to do the job."

"You'll never take it then," I asked, "by direct assault?"

"Not unless I can increase my force," he said, "by nearly another thousand. I'm already recruiting hard up and down the county. Rounding up deserters, and enlisting new levies. But the fellows must be paid. They won't fight otherwise, and I don't blame 'em. Why the devil should they?"

"Where," I said, "did you get this burgundy?"

"From Lanhydrock," he answered. "I had no idea Jack Robartes had laid down so good a cellar. I've had every bottle of it removed to Buckland." He held his goblet to the candlelight, and smiled.

"You know that Lord Robartes sacked Menabilly simply and solely because you had pillaged his estate?"

"He is an extremely dull-witted fellow."

"There is not a pin to choose between you where pillaging is concerned. A Royalist does as much damage as a rebel. I suppose Dick told you that Gartred was one of us at Menabilly?"

"What was she after?"

"The Duchy silver plate."

"More power to her. I could do with some of it myself, to pay my troops."

"She was very friendly with Lord Robartes."

"I have yet to meet a man that she dislikes."

"I think it very probable that she acts spy for Parliament."

"There you misjudge her. She would do anything to gain her own ends but that. You forget the old saying: that, of the three families in Cornwall, a Godolphin was never wanting in wit, a Trelawney in courage, or a Grenvile in loyalty. Gartred was born and bred a Grenvile, no matter if she beds with every fellow in the Duchy."

A brother, I thought, will always hold a brief for a sister. Perhaps Robin at this moment was doing the same thing for me.

Richard had risen and was looking through the window towards the distant Cattwater and Plymouth.

"To night," he said quietly, "I've made a gambler's throw. It may come off.

It may be hopeless. If it succeeds, Plymouth can be ours by daybreak."

"What do you mean?"

He continued looking through the window to where the lights of Plymouth flickered.

"I am in touch with the second of command in the garrison," he said softly, "a certain Colonel Searle. There is a possibility that for the sum of three thousand pounds he will surrender the city. Before wasting further lives, I thought it worth my while to assay bribery."

I was silent. The prospect was hazardous, and somehow smelt unclean.

"How have you set about it?" I asked at length.

"Young Jo slipped through the lines to-night at sunset," he answered, "and will, by now, be hidden in the town. He bears upon him my message to the colonel, and a firm promise of three thousand pounds."

"I don't like it," I said. "No good will come of it."

"Maybe not," he said indifferently, "but at least it was worth trying. I don't relish the prospect of battering my head against the gates of Plymouth the whole winter."

I thought of young Jo and his impudent brown eyes.

"Supposing," I said slowly, "that they catch your Joseph?"

Richard smiled. "That lad," he answered, "is quite capable of looking after himself."

But I thought of Lord Robartes as I had seen him last, with muddied boots, and the rain upon his shoulders, sour and surly in defeat, and I knew how much he must detest the name of Grenvile.

"I shall be rising early," said Richard, "before you are awake. If, by midday, you hear a salvo from every gun inside the garrison, you will know that I have entered Plymouth, after one swift and very bloody battle." He took my face in his hands, and kissed it, and then bade me good night. But I found it hard to sleep. The excitement of his presence in the house had turned to anxiety and strain. I knew, with all the intuition in my body, that he had gambled wrong.

I heard him ride off, with his staff, about 5.30 in the morning, and then, dead tired, my brain chasing itself in circles, I fell into a heavy sleep.

When I awoke it was past ten o'clock. A grey day, with a nip of autumn in the air. I had no wish for breakfast, nor even to get up, but stayed there in my bed. I heard the noises of the house, and the coming and going of the soldiers in their wing, and at twelve o'clock I raised myself upon my elbow and looked towards the river. Five past twelve. A quarter-past. Half-past twelve. There was no salvo from the guns. There was not even a musket shot. It rained at two, then cleared, then rained again. The day dragged on, dull, interminable. I had a sick feeling of suspense all the while. At five o'clock Matty brought me my dinner on a tray, which I picked at with faint appetite. I asked her if she had heard of any news, but she said she knew of none. But later, when she had taken away my tray, and come to draw my curtains, her face was troubled.

"What is the matter?" I asked.

"It's what one of Sir Richard's men was saying, down there to the sentry," she answered, "some trouble to day in Plymouth. One of their best young officers taken prisoner by Lord Robartes, and condemned to death by Council of War. Sir Richard has been endeavouring all day to ransom him, but has not succeeded."

"Who is it?"

"I don't know."

"What will happen to the officer?"

"The soldier did not say."

I lay back again on my bed, my hands over my eyes, to dim the candle. Foreboding never played me wrong, not when I was seized with it for a whole night and day. Maybe perception was a cripple quality. Later I heard the horses coming up the drive and the sentries standing to attention. Footsteps climbed the stairs, slowly, heavily, and passed along to the rooms in the northern wing. A door slammed, and there was silence. It was a long while that I waited there, lying on my back. Just before midnight I heard him walk along the passage and his hand fumbled a moment on the latch of my door. The candles were blown, and it was dark. The household slept. He came to my side, and knelt before the bed. I put my hand on his head, and held him close to me. He knelt thus for many moments without speaking.

"Tell me," I whispered, "if it will help you."

"They hanged him," he said, "above the gates of the town where we could see him. I sent a company to cut him down, but they were mown down by gunfire. They hanged him, before my eyes." Now that suspense was broken, and the long day of strain behind me, I was aware of the feeling of detachment that possesses all of us when a crisis has been passed, and the suffering is not one's own.

This was Richard's battle. I could not fight it for him. I could only hold him in the darkness.

"That rat Searle," he said, his voice broken, strangely unlike my Richard, "betrayed the scheme, and so they caught the lad. I went myself beneath the walls of the garrison to parley with Robartes. I offered him any terms of ransom or exchange. He gave me no answer. And while I stood there, waiting, they strung him up above the gate . . ."

He could not continue. He laid his head upon me, and I held his hands that clutched so fiercely at the patchwork quilt upon the bed.

"To-morrow," I said, "it might have been the same. A bullet through the head. A thrust from a pike. An unlucky stumble from his horse. This happens every day. An act of war. Look upon it in that way. Jo died in your service, as he would wish to do."

"No," he said, his voice muffled. "It was my fault. On me the blame, now, to night, for all eternity. An error in judgment. The wrong decision."

"Jo would forgive you. Jo would understand."

"I can't forgive myself. That's where the torture lies."

I thought then of all the things that I would want to bring before him. How he was not infallible, and never had been, and that this stroke of fate was but a grim reminder of the fact. His own harsh measures to the enemy had been repaid, measure for measure. Cruelty begat cruelty, betrayal gave birth to treachery, the qualities that he had fostered in himself these past years had now recoiled upon him.

The men of Parliament had not forgotten his act of perfidy in the spring, when, feigning to be their friend, he had deserted to the King, bearing their secrets. They had not forgotten the executions without trial, the prisoners condemned to death in Lydford Castle, nor the long line of troopers hanging from the gibbets in the market-square in Saltash. And Lord Robartes, with his home Lanhydrock ravaged and laid waste, his goods seized, had seen rough justice and revenge in taking the life of the messenger who bore an offer of bribery and corruption in his pocket.

It was the irony of the Devil, or Almighty God, that the messenger should have been no distant kinsman, but Richard Grenvile's son. All this came before me in that moment when I held Richard in my arms. And now, I thought, we have come to a crisis in his life. The dividing of the ways. Either to learn from this single tragedy of a boy's death that cruelty was not the answer, that dishonesty dealt a returning blow, that accepting no other judgment but his own would in a space of time make every friend an enemy; or to learn nothing, to continue through the months and years deaf to all counsel, unscrupulous, embittered, the Skellum Grenvile with a price upon his head, the red fox who would be pointed to for evermore as lacking chivalry, a hated contrast to his well-beloved brother.

"Richard . . ." I whispered. "Richard, my dear and only love . . ." but he rose to his feet, he went slowly to the window, and, pulling aside the curtains, stood there with the moonlight on his hands that held the sword, but his face in shadow.

"I shall avenge him," he said, "with every life I take. No quarter any more. No pardons. Not one of them shall be spared. From this moment I shall have one aim only in my life, to kill rebels. And to do it as I wish I must have command of the army; otherwise I fail. I will brook no dispute with my equals, I will tolerate no orders from those senior to me. His Majesty made me General in the West, and by God, I swear that the whole world shall know it."

I knew then that his worse self possessed him, soul and body, and that nothing that I could say or do could help him in the future. Had we been man and wife, or truly lovers, I might, through the close day-by-day intimacy, have learnt to soften him; but Fate and circumstance had made me no more than a shadow in his life, a phantom of what might have been. He had come to me to night because he needed me, but neither tears nor protestations nor assurances of my love and tenderness to all eternity would stay him now from the pursuit of the dim and evil star that beckoned to him.

CHAPTER TWENTY-TWO

RICHARD WAS CONSTANTLY at Radford during the six months that followed. Although his main headquarters were at Buckland, and he rode frequently through both Devon and Cornwall raising new recruits, a company of his men was kept at my brother's house throughout.

The reason given that watch must be kept upon the fortresses of Mount Batten and Mount Stamford was true enough, but I could tell from my brother's tightened lips, and Percy and Phillipa's determined discussion upon other matters when the General's name was mentioned, that my presence in the house was considered to be the reason for the somewhat singular choice of residence. And when Richard with his staff arrived to spend a night or two, and I was bidden to a dinner *tête-à-tête* immediately upon his coming into the house, havoc at once was played with what shred of reputation might be left to me. I think, had I thrown my cap over the mills and gone to live with him at Buckland, it might have been better for the lot of us. But this I steadfastly refused to do, and even now, in retrospect, I cannot give the reason, for it will not formulate itself in words. Always, at the back of my mind, was the fear that by sharing his life with too great intimacy, I would become a burden to him, and the love we bore for one another slip to disenchantment. Here at Radford he could seek me out upon his visits, and being with me would bring him peace and relaxation, tonic and stimulation; whatever mood he would be in, weary or high-spirited, I could attune myself accordingly. But had I made myself persistently available, in some corner of his house, little by little he would have felt the tug of an invisible chain, and the lovely freedom that there was between us would exist no more. The knowledge of my crippled state, so happily glossed over and indeed forgotten when he came to me at Radford, would have nagged me, a perpetual reproach, had I lived beneath his roof at Buckland. The sense of helplessness, of ugly inferiority, would have worked like a maggot in my mind, and even when he was most gentle and most tender I should have thought, with some devil flash of intuition: "This is not what he is wanting."

That was my greatest fault; I lacked humility. Though sixteen years of discipline had taught me to accept crippledom and become resigned to it, I was too proud to share the stigma of it with my lover. Oh, God, what I would have given to have walked with him and ridden, to move and turn before him, to have liveliness and grace.

Even a gipsy in the hedges, a beggar-woman in the gutters, had more dignity than I. He would say to me, smiling over his wine, "Next week you shall come to me at Buckland. There is a chamber, high up in the tower, looking out across the valley to the hills. This was once my grandfather's, who fought in the *Revenge*, and when Drake purchased Buckland he used the chamber as his own, and hung maps upon the wall. You could lie there, Honor, dreaming of the past, and the Armada. And in the evening I would come to you, and kneel beside your bed, and we would make believe that the apple-tree at Lanrest was still in bloom, and you eighteen."

I could see the room as he described it. And the window looking to the hills. And the tents of the soldiers below. And the pennant flying from the tower, scarlet and gold. I could see too the other Honor, walking by his side upon the terrace, who might have been his lady.

And I smiled at him, and shook my head. "No, Richard," I said, "I will not come to Buckland."

And so the autumn passed, and a new year came upon us once again. The whole of the west country was held firmly for the King, save Plymouth, Lyme, and Taunton, which stubbornly defied all attempt at subjugation, and the two seaports, relieved constantly by the Parliament shipping, were still in no great danger of starvation. So long as these garrisons were unsubdued the west could not be counted truly safe for His Majesty, and although the Royalist leaders were of good heart, and expressed great confidence, the people were already sick and tired of war, which had brought them nothing but loss and high taxation. I believe it was the same for Parliament, and that troops deserted from the army every day. Men wanted to be home again, upon their rightful business. They had no wish to fight for King or Parliament. "A plague on both your houses" was the common cry. In January Richard became Sheriff for Devon, and with this additional authority he could raise fresh troops and levies, but the way he set about it was never pleasing to the Commissioners of the county. He rode roughshod over their feelings, demanding men and money as a right, and for the smallest pretext he would have a gentleman arrested and clapped into gaol, until such time as a ransom would be paid.

This would not be hearsay from my brother, but frank admissions on the part of Richard himself. Always unscrupulous where money was concerned, now that he had an army to pay, any sense of caution flew to the winds. Again and again I would hear his justification: "The country is at war. I am a professional soldier, and I will not command men who are not paid. While I hold this appointment for His Majesty, I will undertake to feed, clothe, and arm the forces at my disposal, so that they hold themselves like men and warriors and do not roam the countryside, raping and looting and in rags, like the disorderly rabble under the so-called command of Berkeley, Goring, and the rest. To do this I must have money. And to get money I must demand it from the pockets of the merchants and the gentry of Cornwall and Devon." I think he became more hated by them every day, but by the common people more respected. His troops won such credit for high discipline that their fame spread far abroad to the eastern counties, and it was, I believe, because of this that the first seeds of jealousy began to sow themselves in the hearts and the minds of his brother commanders. None of them were professionals like himself, but men of estate and fortune, who by their rank had immediately, upon the outbreak of the war, been given high commands, and expected to lead newly-raised armies into battle. They were gentlemen of leisure, of no experience, and, though many of them were gallant and courageous, warfare to them consisted of a furious charge upon blood horses, dangerous and exciting, with more speed to it than a day's hawking, and, when the fray was over, a return to their quarters to eat, and drink and play cards, while the men they had led could fend for themselves. Let them loot the villages, and strip the poor inhabitants—it saved the leaders a vast amount of unpleasantness, and the trouble that must come from organisation. But it was irritating, I imagine, to hear how Grenvile's men were praised, and how Grenvile's men were paid and fed and clothed, and Sir John Berkeley, who commanded the troops at Exeter, and was for ever hearing complaints from the common people about Lord Goring's cavalry, and Lord Wentworth's foot, was glad enough, I imagine, to report to his supreme commander, Prince Maurice, that, even if Grenvile's men were disciplined, the Commissioners of Devon and Cornwall had no good word to say of Grenvile himself, and that, in spite of all the fire-eating and hanging of rebel prisoners, Plymouth was still not taken.

"They expect me," Richard would say, "to hurl my fellows at the defences without any regard for their lives, and, having lost three-quarters of them in one assault, recruit another five hundred the following week. Had I command of unlimited forces, and of God's quantity of ammunition, a bombardment of three days would reduce Plymouth to ashes. But with the little I have at my disposal I cannot hope to reduce the garrison before the spring."

His blockade of Plymouth was complete by land, but, the rebels having command of the Sound, provisions and relief could be brought to them by sea, and this was the real secret of their success. All that Richard, as commander of the siege, could do was to wear out the defenders by constant surprise attack upon the outward positions, in the hope that in time they would, from very weariness, surrender.

It was a hopeless, gruelling task, and the only people to win glory and praise for their stout hearts were the men who were besieged within the city.

It was shortly after Christmas that Richard decided to send Dick to Normandy, with his tutor, Herbert Ashley.

"It's no life for him at Buckland," he said. "Ever since Jo went I've had a guard to watch him, day and night, and the thought of him, so close to the enemy should they try a sally, becomes a constant anxiety. He can go to Caen, or Rouen; and when the business is well over I shall send for him again."

"Would you never," I said with diffidence, "consider returning him to London, to his mother?"

He stared at me as though I had lost my senses.

"Let him go back to that bitch-faced hag," he said, astounded, "and become more of a little reptile than he is already? I would sooner send him this moment to Robartes, and let him hang."

"He loves her," I said. "She is his mother."

"So does a pup snuggle to the cur that suckled him," he answered, "but soon forgets her smell, once he is weaned. I have but one son, Honor, and if he can't be a credit to me and become the man I want, I have no use for him."

He changed the subject abruptly, and I was reminded once again how I had chosen to be friend, not wife, companion and not mistress, and to meddle with his child was not my business. So Dick rode to Radford to bid me good-bye, and put his arms about me, and said he loved me well. "If only," he said, "you could have come with me into Normandy."

"Perhaps," I said, "you will not remain there long. And, anyway, it will be fresh and new to you, and you will make friends there, and be happy."

"My father does not wish me to make friends," he said. "I heard him say as much to Mr Ashley. He said that in Caen there were few English, and therefore it would be better to go there than to Rouen, and that I was to speak to no one, and go nowhere, without Mr Ashley's knowledge or permission. I know what it is. He is afraid that I might fall in with some person who should be friendly to my mother."

I had no answer to this argument, for I felt it to be true. "I shall not know you," I said, summoning a smile, "the next time that I lay my eyes upon you. You will be a young man, with lovelocks on your shoulders, and a turn for poetry, in six months' time."

"Fine poetry I shall write," he sulked, "conversing in French day by day with Mr Ashley."

And so Dick and the timid, unconvincing Herbert Ashley set sail for Normandy, the last day of December, taking with them a bill of exchange for twenty pounds, which was all that the General in the West could spare them, Dick taking besides my love and blessing, which would not help at all. And while they rocked upon the Channel between Falmouth and St Malo, would not fail. I can see him now, in his room in that north block at Radford, poring over his map of the Plymouth defences. When I asked to look at it he tossed it to me with a laugh, saying no woman could make head or tail of his marks and crosses.

And he was right, for never had I seen a chart more scribbled upon with dots and scratches. But even my unpractised eye could note that the network of defences was formidable indeed, for before the town and garrison could be attacked a chain of outer forts, or "works" as he termed them, had first to be breached. He came and stood beside me, and with his pen pointed to the scarlet crosses on the map.

"There are four works here to the north, in line abreast," he said, "the Pennycomequick, the Maudlyn, the Holiwell, and the Lipson forts. I propose to seize them all. Once established there, we shall turn the guns against the garrison itself. My main strength will fall upon the Maudlyn works, the others being more in the nature of a feint to draw their fire." He was in high spirits, as always before a big engagement, and, suddenly, folding his map, he said to me: "You have never seen my fellows, have you, in their full war-paint, prior to a battle? Would you like to do so?"

I smiled. "Do you propose to make me your aide-de-camp?"

"No. I am going to take you round the posts."

It was three o'clock, a cold fine afternoon in January. One of the wagons was fitted as a litter and, with Richard riding at my side, we set forth to view his army.

It was a sight that even now, when all is over and done with and the Siege of Plymouth a forgotten thing except for the official records in the archives of the town, I can call before me with wonder and with pride. The main body of his army was drawn up in the fields behind the little parish of Egg Buckland, and since there had been no warning of our coming the men were not summoned to parade, but were going about their business in preparation for the attack ahead.

The first signal that the General had come in person was a springing to attention of the guards before the camp, and straightway there came a roll upon the drums from within, followed by a second more distant, and then a third, and then a fourth, so that in the space of a few moments, so it seemed to me, the air around me rang with a tattoo, as the drums of every company sounded the alert. And swiftly, unfolding in the crisp cold air, the scarlet pennant broke from the pole-head, with the golden rests staring from the centre.

Two officers approached and, saluting with their swords, stood before us. This Richard acknowledged with a half gesture of his hand, and then my chair was lifted from the wagon, and, with a stalwart young corporal to propel me, we proceeded round the camp.

I can smell now the wood smoke from the fires as the blue rings rose into the air, and I can see the men, bending over their washtubs, or kneeling before the cooking-pots, straightening themselves with a jerk as we approached, and standing to attention like steel rods. The foot were quartered separately from the horse, and these we inspected first, great brawny fellows of five foot ten or more, for Richard had disdain for little men and would not recruit them. They had a bronzed, clean look about them, the result, so Richard said, of living in the open.

I had fresh in my mind a picture of the rebel regiment who had taken Menabilly. Although they had worn a formidable air upon first sight, with their close helmets and uniform jerkins, they had soon lost their sheen, and as the weeks wore on they became dirty-looking and rough, and with the threat of defeat had one and all reverted to a London mob in panic.

Richard's men had another stamp upon them, and, though they were drawn mostly from the farms and moors of Cornwall and of Devon, rustic in speech and origin, they had become knit, in the few months of his command, into a professional body of soldiers, quick of thought and limb, with an admiration for their leader that showed at once in the upward tilt of their heads as he addressed them and the flash of pride in their eyes.

The horse were drawn up on the further field, and we watched them being groomed and watered for the night, fine sleek animals—many of them seized from rebel estates, as I was fully aware—and they stamped on the hard ground, the harness jingling, their breath rising in the cold air like the smoke from the fires.

The sun was setting, fiery red, beyond the Tamar into Cornwall, and as it sank beyond the hills it threw a last dull sullen glow upon the forts of Plymouth to the south of us. We could see the tiny figures of the rebel sentries, like black dots, upon the outer defences, and I wondered how many of the Grenvile men about me would make themselves a sacrifice to the spitting thunder of the rebel guns.

Lastly, as evening fell, we visited the forward posts, and here there was no more cleaning of equipment, no grooming of horses, but men stripped bare for battle, silent, motionless, and we talked in whispers, for we were scarce two hundred yards from the enemy defences.

The silence was grim, uncanny. The assault force seemed dim figures in the gathering darkness, for they had blackened their faces to make themselves less visible, and I could make out nothing of them but white eyes, gleaming, and the show of teeth when they smiled. Their breastplates were discarded for a night attack, and in their hands they carried pikes, steely sharp. I felt the edge of one of them and shuddered.

At the last post we visited the men were not so prompt to challenge us as hitherto, and I heard Richard administer a sharp reproof to the young officer in charge. The colonel of the regiment of foot, in command of the post, came forth to excuse himself, and I saw that it was my old suitor of the past, Jo's brother-in-law, Edward Champernowne. He bowed to me, somewhat stiffly, and then turned to Richard. I heard him stammer several attempts at explanation, and the two withdrew to a little distance. On his return Richard was silent, and we straightway turned back towards my wagon and the escort, and I knew that the review was finished.

"You must return alone to Radford," he said. "I will send the escort with you. There will be no danger."

"And the coming battle?" I asked. "Are you confident, and pleased?"

He paused a moment before replying. "Yes," he answered, "yes, I am hopeful. The plan is sound, and there is nothing wanting in the men. If only my seconds were more dependable." He jerked his head towards the post from which we had just lately come. "Your old lover, Edward Champernowne," he said, "I sometimes think he would do better to command a squad of ducks. He has a flickering of reason when his long nose is glued upon a map, ten miles from the enemy, but give him a piece of work to do upon the field a hundred yards away, and he is lost."

"Can you not replace him with some other?" I questioned.

"Not at this juncture," he said. "I have to risk him now."

He kissed my hand and smiled, and it was not until he had turned his back on me and vanished that I remembered I had never asked him whether the reason for his not returning with me to Radford was because he proposed to lead the assault in person.

I jogged back in the wagon to my brother's house, my spirits sinking. Shortly before daybreak, next morning, the attack began. The first we heard of it at Radford was the echo of the guns across the Cattwater—whether from within the garrison or from the outer defences we could not tell—but by midday we had the news that three of the works had been seized and held by the Royalist troops, and the most formidable of the forts, the Maudlyn, stormed by the commanding General in person. The guns were turned, and the men of Plymouth felt for the first time their own fire fall upon the walls of the city. I could see nothing from my window but a pall of smoke hanging like a curtain in the sky, and now and again, the wind being northerly, I thought I heard the sound of distant shouting from the besieged within the garrison.

At three o'clock, with barely three hours of daylight left, the news was not so good. The rebels had counter-attacked, and two of the forts had been recaptured. The fate of Plymouth now depended upon the rebels gaining back the ground they had lost and driving the Royalists from their foothold all along the line, and most especially from the Maudlyn works. I watched the setting sun, as I had done the day before, and I thought of all those, both rebel men and Royalist, whose lives had been held forfeit within these past four-and-twenty hours. We dined in the hall at half-past five, with my brother Jo seated at the head of his table, as was his custom, and Phillipa at his right hand and his little motherless son, young John, upon his left. We ate in silence, none of us having much heart for conversation, while the battle only a few miles away hung thus in the balance. We were nearly finished when my brother Percy, who had ridden down to Plymstock to get news, came bursting in upon us.

"The rebels have gained the day," he said grimly, "and driven off Grenvile with the loss of three hundred men. They stormed the fort on all sides, and finally recaptured it, barely an hour ago. It seems that Grenvile's covering troops, who should have come to his support and turned the scale to success, failed to reach him. A tremendous blunder on the part of someone."

"No doubt the fault of the General himself," said Jo drily, "in having too much confidence."

"They say, down in Plymstock, that the officer responsible has been shot by Grenvile for contravention of orders," said Percy, "and is lying now in his tent with a bullet through his head. Who it is they could not tell me, but we shall hear anon."

I could think of nothing but those three hundred men who were lying now upon their faces under the stars, and I was filled with a great war-sickness, a loathing for guns and pikes and blood and battle-cries. The brave fellows who had smiled at me the night before, so strong, so young and confident, were now carrion for the sea-gulls who swooped and dived in Plymouth Sound, and it was Richard, my Richard, who had led them to their death. I could not blame him. He had only, by attacking, done his duty. He was a soldier. . . .

As I turned away to call a servant for my chair, a young secretary, employed by my elder brother on the Devon Commission, came into the room, much agitated, with a request to speak to him.

"What is the matter?" said Jo tersely. "There is no one but my family present."

"Colonel Champernowne lies at Egg Buckland, mortally wounded," said the secretary. "He was not hurt in battle, but pistolled by the General himself on returning to headquarters."

There was a moment of great silence. Jo rose slowly from his chair, very white and tense, and I saw him turn round and look at me, as did my brother

Percy. In a moment of perception I knew what they were thinking. Jo's brother-in-law, Edward Champernowne, had been my suitor seventeen years before, and they both saw, in this sudden terrible dispute after the heat of battle, no military cause, but some private jealous wrangle, the settling of a feud.

"This," said my elder brother slowly, "is the beginning of the end for Richard Grenvile."

His words fell upon my ear cold as steel, and, calling softly to the servant, I bade him take me to my room.

The next day I left for Mothercombe, to my sister Cecilia, for to remain under my brother's roof one moment longer would have been impossible. The vendetta had begun.

My eldest brother, with the vast family of Champernowne behind him, and supported by the leading families in the county of Devon, most of them members of the Commission, pressed for the removal of Sir Richard Grenvile from his position as Sheriff and commander of the King's forces in the west. Richard retaliated by turning my brother out of Radford and using the house and estate as a jumping-ground for a fresh assault upon Plymouth.

Snowed-up in Mothercombe with the Pollexefens, I knew little of what was happening, and Cecilia, with consummate tact and delicacy, avoided the subject. I myself had had no word from Richard since the night I had bidden him goodbye before the battle, and now that he was engaged in a struggle with foe and former friends as well I thought it best to keep silent. He knew my whereabouts, for I had sent word of it, and should he want me he would come to me.

The thaw burst at the end of March, and we had the first tidings of the outside world for many weeks.

The peace moves between King and Parliament had come to nothing, for the Treaty of Uxbridge had failed, and the war, it seemed, was to be carried on more ruthlessly than ever.

The Parliament, we heard, was forming a new Model Army, likely to sweep all before it, in the opinion of the judges, while His Majesty had sent forth an edict to his enemies saying that unless the rebels repented their end must be damnation, ruin, and infamy. The young Prince of Wales, it seemed, was now to bear the title of supreme commander of all the forces in the west, and was gone to Bristol, but since he was a lad of only fifteen years or so the real authority would be vested in his Advisory Council, at the head of whom was Hyde, the Chancellor of the Exchequer.

I remember John Pollexefen shaking his head as he heard the news. "There will be nothing but wrangles now between the Prince's Council and the generals," he said. "Each will countermand the orders of the other. Lawyers and soldiers never agree. And while they wrangle the King's cause will suffer. I do not like it."

I thought of Richard and how he had once vouchsafed the same opinion. "What is happening at Plymouth?" asked my sister. "Stalemate," said her husband. "A token force of less than a thousand men left to blockade the garrison, and Grenvile with the remainder gone to join Goring in Somerset and lay siege to Taunton. The spring campaign has started."

Soon a year would have come and gone since I had left Lanrest for Menabilly. The snow melted down in the Devon valley where Cecilia had her home, and the crocus and the daffodil appeared. I made no plans. I sat and waited. Someone brought a rumour that there was great disaffection in the High Command, and that Grenvile, Goring, and Berkeley were all at logger-heads.

March turned to April. The golden gorse was in full bloom. And on Easter Day a horseman came riding down the valley, wearing the Grenvile badge. He asked at once for Mistress Harris, and, saluting gravely, handed me a letter.

"What is it?" I asked before I broke the seal. "Has something happened?" My throat felt dry and strange, and my hands trembled. "The General has been gravely wounded," replied the soldier, "in a battle before Wellington House at Taunton. They fear for his life." I tore open the letter, and read Richard's shaky scrawl.

"Dear Heart," he said, "this is the very devil. I am like to lose my leg, if not my life, with a great gaping hole in my thigh, below the groin. I know now what you suffer. Come teach me patience. I love you."

I folded the letter, and, turning to the messenger, asked him where the General lay.

"They were bringing him from Taunton down to Exeter when I left," he answered. "His Majesty had dispatched his own chirurgeon to attend upon Sir Richard. He was very weak, and bade me ride without delay to bring you this."

I looked at Cecilia, who was standing by the window. "Would you summon Matty to pack my clothes," I said, "and ask John if he would arrange for a litter, and for horses? I am going to Exeter."

CHAPTER TWENTY-THREE

WE TOOK THE southern route to Exeter, and at every halt upon the journey I thought to hear the news of Richard's death.

Totnes, Newton Abbot, Ashburton, each delay seemed longer than the last, and when at length after six days I reached the capital of Devon, and saw the great cathedral rising high above the city and the river, it seemed to me I had been weeks upon the road.

Richard still lived. This was my first enquiry, and the only thing that mattered. He was lodging at the hostelry in the cathedral square, where I immediately repaired. He had taken the whole building for his personal use, and had a sentry before the door.

When I gave my name a young officer immediately appeared from within, and something ruddy about his colouring, and familiar in his bearing, made me pause a moment before addressing him correctly. Then his courteous smile gave me the clue.

"You are Jack Grenvile, Bevil's boy," I said, and he reminded me of how he had come once with his father to Lanrest in the days before the war.

"My uncle will be most heartily glad to see you," he said as I was lifted from my litter. "He has talked of little else since writing to you. He has sent at least ten women flying from his side since coming here, swearing they were rough and did not know their business, nor how to dress his wound. Matty shall do it, he said, while Honor talks to me." I saw Matty colour up with pleasure at these words, and assume at once an air of authority before the corporal who shouldered our trunks.

"And how is he?" I asked, as I was set down within the great inn parlour, which had been, judging by the long table in the centre, turned into a messroom for the General's staff.

"Better these last three days than hitherto," replied his nephew, "but at first we thought to lose him. Directly he was wounded I applied to the Prince of Wales to wait on him, and I attended him here from Taunton. Now he declares he will not send me back. Nor have I any wish to go."

At this moment Richard's servant came down the stairs saying the General wished to see Mistress Harris upon the instant. I went first to my room, where Matty washed me and changed my gown, and then, with Jack Grenvile to escort me, I went along the corridor, in my wheeled chair, to Richard's room.

It looked out upon the cobbled square, and as we entered the great bell from the cathedral chimed four o'clock.

"God confound that blasted bell," said a familiar voice, sounding stronger than I had dared to hope, from the dark-curtained bed in the far corner. "A dozen times I have asked the Mayor of this damned city to have it silenced, and nothing has been done. Harry, for God's sake make a note of it."

"Sir," answered hurriedly a tall youth at the foot of the bed, scribbling a word upon his tablets.

"And move these pillows, can't you? Not that way, you clumsy lout; behind my head, thus. Where the devil is Jack? Jack is the only lad who knows how I like them placed."

"Here I am, Uncle," said his nephew, "but you will not need me now. I have brought you someone with gentler hands than I."

He pushed my chair towards the bed, smiling, and I saw Richard's hand reach out to pull back the curtains.

"Ah!" he said, sighing deeply. "You have come at last." He was deathly white. And his eyes had grown larger, perhaps in contrast to the pallor of his face. His auburn locks were clipped short, giving him a strangely youthful look. For the first time I noticed in him a resemblance to Dick. I took his hand and held it.

"I did not wait," I said, "once I had read your letter."

He turned to the two lads standing at the foot of the bed, his nephew and the one he had named Harry.

"Get out, both of you," he said, "and if that damned chirurgeon shows his face, tell him to go to the devil."

"Sir," they replied, clicking their heels, and I could swear that as they left the room young Jack Grenvile winked an eye at his companion.

Richard lifted my hand to his lips, and then cradled it beside his cheek. "This is a good jest," he said, "on the part of the Almighty. You and I both smitten in the thigh."

"Does it pain you much?" I asked.

"Pain me? My God, splinters from a cannon-ball, striking below the groin, burn something fiercer than a woman's kiss. Of course it pains me."

"Who has seen the wound?"

"Every chirurgeon in the army, and each one makes more mess of it than his fellow."

I called for Matty, who was waiting outside the door, and she came in at once with a basin of warm water and bandages and towels.

"Goodday to you, mutton-face," said Richard. "How many corporals have you bedded with *en route?*"

"No time to bed with anyone," snapped Matty, "carried at the rate we were, with Miss Honor delaying only to sleep a few snatched hours every night. Now we've come here to be insulted."

"I'll not insult you, unless you tie my bandages too tight."

"Come, then," she said. "Let's see what they have done to you."

She unfolded the bandages with expert fingers, and exposed the wound. It was deep, in truth, the splinters having penetrated the bone and lodged there. With every probe of her fingers he winced and groaned, calling her every name under the sun, which did not worry her.

"It's clean, that's one thing," she said. "I fully expected to find it gangrenous. But you'll have some of those splinters to the end of your days, unless you let them take your leg off."

"They'll not do that," he answered. "I'd rather keep the splinters and bear the pain."

"It will give you an excuse, at any rate, for your bad temper," she replied. She washed the wound, and dressed it once again, and all the while he held my hand as Dick might do. Then she finished, and he thumbed his finger to his nose as she left the room.

"Over three months," he said, "since I have seen you. Are the Pollexefens as unpleasant as the rest of your family?"

"My family were not unpleasant till you made them so."

"They disliked me from the first. Now they pursue their dislike across the county. You know the Commissioners of Devon are in Exeter as this moment, with a list of complaints a mile long to launch at me?"

"I did not know."

"It's all a plot, hatched by your brother. Three members of the Prince's

Council are to come down from Bristol and discuss the business with the Commissioners; and as soon as I am fit enough to move I am to go before them. Jack Berkeley, commanding here at Exeter, is up to his neck in the intrigue."

"And what exactly is the intrigue?"

"Why, to have me shifted from my command, of course, and for Berkeley to take my place."

"Would you mind so very much? The blockade of Plymouth has not brought you much satisfaction."

"Jack Berkeley is welcome to Plymouth. But I'm not going to lie down and accept some secondary command, dished out to me by the Prince's Council while I hold authority from His Majesty himself."

"His Majesty," I said, "appears by all accounts to have his own troubles. Who is this General Cromwell we hear so much about?"

"Another God-damned Puritan with a mission," said Richard. "They say he talks with the Almighty every evening, but I think it far more likely that he drinks. He's a good soldier, though. So is Fairfax. Their new Model Army will make mincemeat of our disorganised rabble."

"And, knowing this, you choose to quarrel with your friends?"

"They are not my friends. They are a set of low, back-biting blackguards. And I have told them all so, to their faces."

It was useless to argue with him. And his wound had made him more sensitive on every point. I asked if he had news of Dick, and he showed me a stilted letter from the tutor, as well as copies of instructions that he had sent to Herbert Ashley. There was nothing very friendly or encouraging amongst them. I caught a glimpse of the words, "For his education I desire he may constantly and diligently be kept to the learning of the French tongue; reading, writing, and arithmetic, also riding, fencing, and dancing. All this I shall expect of him, which, if he follow according to my desire for his own good, he shall not want anything. But if I understand that he neglects in any kind what I have herein commanded him to do, truly I will neither allow him a penny to maintain him, nor look on him again as my son." I folded the instructions, and put them back into the case, which he locked and kept beside him.

"Do you think," I said, "to win his affection in that way?"

"I don't ask for his affection," he said. "I ask for his obedience."

"You were not harsh thus with Jo. Nor are you so unrelenting to your nephew Jack."

"Jo was one in a million, and Jack has some likeness to him. That lad fought at Landsown like a tiger, when poor Bevil fell. And he was but fifteen, as Dick is now. All these lads I have affection for because they hold themselves like men. But Dick, my son and heir, shudders when I speak to him, and whimpers at the sight of blood. It does not make for pride in his father."

An argument. A blow. A baby's cry. And fifteen years of poison seeping through a child's blood. There was no panacea that I could think of to staunch the flood of resentment. Time and distance might bring a measure of healing that close contact only served to wound. Once again Richard kissed my hand.

"Never mind young Dick," he said. "It is not he who has a dozen splinters through his thigh."

No man, I think, was ever a worse patient than Richard Grenvile, and no nurse more impervious to his threats and groans and curses than was Matty. My role, if less exacting, called for great equanimity of temperament. Being a woman, I did not have his spurs hurled at my head, as did his luckless officers, but I suffered many a bitter accusation because my name was Harris, and he liked to taunt me too because I had been born and bred in south-east Cornwall, where the women all were hags and scolds, so he averred, and the men cowards and deserters. "Nothing good came out of Cornwall yet," he said, "save from the north coast." And seeing that this failed to rouse me he sought by other means to make me rankle, a strange and unprofitable pastime for a sick man, but one I could understand in full measure, for I had often wished so to indulge myself some seventeen years before, but had never the courage of my moods.

He kept his bed for some five weeks, and then, by the end of May, was sufficiently recovered to walk in his chamber with a stick, and at the same time curse his harassed staff for idleness.

The feathers flew when he first came downstairs, for all the world like a turkey-fight, and I never saw high-ranking officers more red about the ears than the colonels and the majors he addressed that May morning. They looked at the door with longing eyes, like schoolboys, with but one thought in their mind, to win freedom from his lashing tongue, or so I judged from their expressions. But when, after I had taken my airing in the square, I conversed with them, sympathy on the tip of my tongue, they one and all remarked upon the excellence of the General's health and spirits.

"It does one good," said a colonel of foot, "to see the General himself again. I hardly dared to hope for it, a month since."

"Do you bear no malice then," I said, "for his words to you this morning?"

"Malice?" said the colonel, looking puzzled. "Why should I bear malice? The General was merely taking exercise."

The ways of professional soldiers were beyond me.

"It is a splendid sign," said Richard's nephew Jack, "when my uncle gives vent to frowns and curses. It mostly means he is well pleased. But see him smile, and speak with courtesy, and you may well reckon that the luckless receiver of his favours is halfway to the guard-room. I once saw him curse a fellow for fifteen minutes without respite, and that evening promote him to the rank of captain. The next day he received a prisoner, a country squire, I think, from Barnstaple, who owed him money, and my uncle plied him with wine, and smiles, and favours. He was hanging from a tree at Buckland two hours afterwards."

I remember asking Richard if these tales were true. He laughed. "It pleases my staff," he said, "to weave a legend about my person." But he did not deny them.

Meanwhile, the Prince's Council had come to Exeter to have discussion with the Devon Commissioners and to hear the complaints they had to make

against Sir Richard Grenvile. It was unfortunate, I felt, that the head of the
Prince's Council was that same Sir Edward Hyde whom Richard had described
to me at Radford as a jumped-up lawyer. I think the remark had been repeated
to him, for when he arrived at the hostelry to call upon Richard, accompanied
by Lords Culpepper and Capel, I thought his manner very cold and formal,
and I could see he bore little cordiality towards the general who had so
scornfully dubbed him upstart. I was presented to them, and immediately
withdrew. What they thought of me I neither knew nor cared. It would be but
another scandalous tale to spread, that Sir Richard Grenvile had a crippled
mistress.

What in truth transpired behind those closed doors I never discovered. As
soon as the three members of the Prince's Council tried to speak they would be
drowned by Richard, with a tirade of accusations against the Governor of the
city, Sir John Berkeley, who, so he avowed, had done nothing for nine months
now but put obstructions in his path.

"Let Berkeley take over Plymouth, if he so desires it," Richard declared.
(This he told me afterwards.) "God knows it troubles me to be confined to
blocking up a place, when there is likely to be action in the field. Give me power
to raise men in Cornwall and in Devon, without fear of obstruction, and I will
place an army at the disposal of the Prince of Wales that will be a match for
Cromwell's Puritans." Whereupon he formally handed over his resignation as
commander of the Siege of Plymouth, and sent the lords of the Council packing
off back to Bristol to receive the Prince's authority sanctioning him to a new
command. "I handled them," he said to me gleefully, "with silken gloves. Let
Jack Berkeley stew at Plymouth, and good luck to him." And he drank a bottle
and a half of burgundy at supper, which played havoc with his wound next
morning.

I have forgotten how many days we waited for the royal warrant to arrive,
confirming him in the appointment to raise troops, but it must have been ten
days or more. At last Richard declared that he would not kick his heels waiting
for a piece of paper that few people would take the trouble to read, and he
proceeded to raise recruits for the new army. His staff were dispatched about
the countryside rounding up the men who had been idle, or had deserted and
gone home, during his illness. All were promised pay and clothing. And as
Sheriff of Devon (for this post he had not resigned with his command) Richard
ordered his old enemies, the Commissioners, to raise fresh money for the
purpose. I guessed this would bring a hornets' nest about his ears again, but I
was only a woman, and it was not my business.

I sat one day beside my window, looking out on to the cathedral, and I saw
Sir John Berkeley, who had not yet gone to Plymouth, ride away from the
hostelry looking like a thundercloud. There had been a stormy meeting down
below, and, according to young Jack, Sir John had got the worst of it.

"I yield to no man," said Richard's nephew, "in my admiration for my
uncle. He has the better of his opponents every time. But I wish he would
guard his tongue."

"What," I asked wearily, "are they disputing now?"

"It is always the same story," said Jack. "My uncle says that as Sheriff of the county he can compel the Commissioners to pay his troops. Sir John declares the contrary. That it is to him, as Governor of the city and commander before Plymouth, that the money should be paid. They'll fight a duel about it before they have finished." Shortly afterwards Richard came to my room white with passion. "My God," he said, "I cannot stand this hopeless mess an instant longer. I shall ride at once to Bristol to see the Prince."

"You are not well enough to ride," I said.

"I can't help that. I won't stay here and have that hopeless nincompoop Jack Berkeley obstruct every move I make. He is hand-in-glove with your blasted brother, that's the trouble."

"You began the trouble," I said, "by making an enemy of my brother. All this has come about because you shot Edward Champernowne."

"What would you have had me do—promote the sod?" he stormed. "A weak-bellied rat who caused the death of three hundred of my finest troops because he was too lily-livered to face the rebel guns and come to my support? Shooting was too good for him. A hundred years ago he would have been drawn and quartered."

The next day he left for Barnstaple, where the Prince of Wales had gone to escape the plague at Bristol, and I was thankful that he took his nephew Jack as aide-de-camp. He had three men to hoist him into the saddle, and he still looked most damnably unwell. He smiled up at me as I leant from my window in the hostelry, and saluted with his sword. "Have no fear," he said, "I'll return within a fortnight. Keep well. Be happy."

But he never did return, and that was the end of my sojourn as a nurse and comforter at Exeter. On the eighteenth of June the King and Prince Rupert were heavily defeated by General Cromwell at Naseby, and the rebel army, under the supreme command of General Fairfax, was marching once again towards the west. The whole of the Royalist strategy had now to be changed to meet this new menace, and, while rumours ran rife that Fairfax was coming upon Taunton, I had a message from Richard to say that he had been ordered by the Prince of Wales to besiege Lyme and had the commission of field-marshal in his pocket.

"I will send for you," he said, "when I have fixed my headquarters. In the meantime, rest where you are. I think it very likely that we shall all of us, before the summer is out, be on the run again." This news was hardly pleasant hearing, and I bethought me of the relentless marching feet that I had heard a year ago at Menabilly. Was the whole horror of invasion to be endured once again? I did as he bade me, and stayed at Exeter. I had no home, and one roof was as good to me now as another. If I lacked humility, I also had no pride. I was nothing more nor less, by this time, than a camp-follower. A pursuivant of the drum.

On the last day of June Jack Grenvile came for me, with a troop of horse to bear my litter. Matty and I were already packed and ready. We had been waiting since the message a fortnight before.

"Where are we bound?" I said gaily. "For Lyme or London?"

"For neither," he said grimly. "For a tumbled-down residence in Ottery St Mary. The General has thrown up his commission."

He could tell me little of what had happened, except that the bulk of the new forces that had been assigned to Richard's new command, and were to rendezvous at Tiverton, had suddenly been withdrawn by the orders of the Prince's Council and diverted to the defence of Barnstaple, without a word of explanation to the General. We came to Ottery St Mary, a sleepy Devon village where the inhabitants stared at the strange equipage that drew up before the manor house as though the world were suddenly grown crazy—in which they showed good reason. In the meadows behind the village were drawn Richard's own horse and foot, who had followed him from the beginning. Richard himself was seated in the dining-chamber of his headquarters, his wounded leg propped upon a chair before him.

"Greetings," he said maliciously, "from one cripple to another. Let us retire to bed and see who has the greatest talent for invention."

"If that," I said, "is your mood, we will discuss it presently. At the moment I am tired, hungry and thirsty. But would you care to tell me what the devil you are doing in Ottery St Mary?"

"I am become a free man," he answered, smiling, "beholden to neither man nor beast. Let them fight the new Model Army in their own fashion. If they won't give me the troops, I do not propose to ride alone with nephew Jack against Fairfax and some twenty thousand men."

"I thought," I said, "that you were become field-marshal."

"An empty honour," he said, "signifying nothing. I have just returned the commission to the Prince of Wales in an empty envelope, desiring him to place it up a certain portion of his person. What shall we drink for supper, hock or burgundy?"

CHAPTER TWENTY-FOUR

T HAT WAS, I THINK, the most fantastic fortnight I have ever known. Richard, with no command and no commission, lived like a royal prince in the humble village of Ottery St Mary, the people for miles around bringing their produce to the camp, their corn, their cattle, in the firm belief that he was the supreme commander of His Majesty's troops from Lyme to Land's End. For payment he referred them graciously to the Commissioners of Devon. The first Sunday after his arrival he caused an edict to be read in the church of Ottery St Mary and other churches in the neighbouring parishes, desiring that all those persons who had been plundered by the Governor of Exeter, Sir John

Berkeley, when quartering troops upon them, should bring to him, Sir Richard Grenvile, the King's General in the West, an account of their losses, and he would see that they were righted.

The humble village folk, thinking that a saviour had come to dwell amongst them, came on foot from a distance of twenty miles or more, each one bearing in his hands a list of crimes and excesses committed, according to them, by Lord Goring's troopers and Sir John Berkeley's men, and I can see Richard now, standing in the village place before the church, distributing largesse in princely fashion from a sum of money he had discovered behind a panel in his headquarters, a house belonging to an unfortunate squire with vague Parliamentary tendencies, whom Richard had immediately arrested. On the Wednesday, since it was fine, he held a review of his troops—the sight being free to the villagers—and the drums sounded, and the church bells pealed, and in the evening bonfires were lit and a great supper was served at the headquarters to the officers, at which I presided like a queen.

"We may as well be merry," said Richard, "while the money lasts." I thought of that letter to the Prince of Wales, which must by now have reached the Prince's Council, and I pictured the Chancellor of the Exchequer, Edward Hyde, opening the paper before the assembly.

I thought also of Sir John Berkeley, and what he would say when he heard about the edict in the churches, and it seemed to me that my rash and indiscreet lover would be wiser if he struck his camp and hid in the mists on Dartmoor, for he could not bluff the world much longer in Ottery St Mary.

The bluff was superb while it lasted, and, since the Parliamentary squire whom we had superseded kept a well-stocked cellar, we soon had every bottle sampled, and Richard drank perdition to the supporters of both Parliament and Crown.

"What will you do," I asked, "if the Council sends for you?"

"Exactly nothing," he answered, "unless I have a letter, in his own handwriting, from the Prince of Wales himself."

And, with a smile that his nephew would call ominous, he opened yet another bottle.

"If we continue thus," I said, turning my glass down upon the table, "you will become as great a sot as Goring."

"Goring cannot stand after five glasses," said Richard. "I can drill a whole division after twelve." And, rising from the table, he called to the orderly who stood without the door. "Summon Sir John Grenvile," he said. In a moment Jack appeared, also a little flushed, and gay about the eyes.

"My compliments," said Richard, "to Colonels Roscarrock and Arundell. I wish the troops to be paraded on the green. I intend to drill them."

His nephew did not flicker an eyelid, but I saw his lips quiver.

"Sir," he said, "it is past eight o'clock. The men have been dismissed to their quarters."

"I am well aware of the fact," replied his uncle. "It was for the purpose of rousing them that drums were first bestowed upon the army. My compliments to Colonels Roscarrock and Arundell."

Jack clicked his heels and left the room. Richard walked slowly, and very solemnly, towards the chair where lay his sling and sword. He proceeded to buckle them about his waist.

"The sling," I said softly, "is upside down."

He bowed gravely in acknowledgement, and made the necessary adjustment. And from without the drums began to beat, sharp and alert, in the gathering twilight.

I was, I must confess, only a trifle less dazed about the head than I had been on that memorable occasion long before, when I had indulged too heavily in burgundy and swan. This time—and it was my only safeguard—I had my chair to sit in, and I can remember, through a sort of haze, being propelled towards the village green with the drums sounding in my ears and the soldiers running from all directions to form lines upon the grass sward. Villagers leant from their casements, and I remember one old fellow in a nightcap shrieking out that Fairfax was come upon them and they would all be murdered in their beds.

It was, I dare swear, the one and only occasion in the annals of His Majesty's army when two regiments have been drawn up and drilled by their commanding general in the dusk after too good a dinner.

"My God," I heard Jack Grenvile choke behind me, whether in laughter or emotion I never discovered, "this is magnificent. This will live for ever." And when the drums were silent I heard Richard's voice, loud and clear, ring out across the village green.

It was the fitting climax to a crazy fourteen days. . . .

At breakfast the next morning a messenger came riding to the door of the headquarters with the news that Bridgwater had been stormed and captured by Fairfax and his rebel forces, that the Prince's Council had fled to Launceston, and that the Prince of Wales bade Sir Richard Grenvile depart instantly with what troops he had and come to him in Cornwall.

"Is the message a request or a command?" asked my general.

"A command, sir," replied the officer, handing him a document, "not from the Council, but from the Prince himself."

Once again the drums were sounded, but this time for the march, and as the long line of troops wound their way through the village and on to the highway to Okehampton I wondered how many years would pass before the people of Ottery St Mary forgot Sir Richard Grenvile and his men. We followed, Matty and I, within a day or two, with an escort to our litter and orders to proceed to Werrington Park, near Launceston, which was yet another property that Richard had seized, without a scruple, from the owner of Buckland Monochorum, Francis Drake. We arrived to find Richard, in fair spirits, restored to the Prince's favour, after a very awkward three hours before the Council. It might have been more awkward, had not the Council been in so immediate a need of his services.

"And what has been decided?" I asked.

"Goring is to go north, to intercept the rebels," he said, "while I remain in Cornwall and endeavour to raise a force of some three thousand foot. It would have been better if they had sent me to deal with Fairfax, as Goring is certain to make a hash of it."

"There is no one but you," I said, "who can raise troops in Cornwall. Men will rally to a Grenvile, but none other. Be thankful that the Council sent for you at all, after your impudence."

"They cannot afford," said Richard, "to do without me. And anyway, I don't give a fig for the Council and that snake, Hyde. I am only doing this business to oblige the Prince. He's a lad after my own heart. If His Majesty continues to haver as he does at present, with no coherent plan of strategy, I am not at all sure that the best move would not be to hold all Cornwall for the Prince, live within it like a fortress, and let the rest of England go to blazes."

"You have only to phrase that a little differently," I said, "and a malicious friend who wished you ill would call it treason."

"Treason be damned," he said. "It is but sound common sense. No man has greater loyalty to His Majesty than I, but he does more to wreck his own cause than any who serve under him."

While Matty and I remained at Werrington, Richard travelled the length and breadth of Cornwall recruiting troops for the Prince's army. It was no easy business. The last invasion had been enough for Cornishmen. Men wished only to be left alone to tend their land and business. Money was as hard to raise as it had been in Devon, and with some misgiving I watched Richard use the same high-handed measures with the Commissioners of the Duchy as he had with those of the sister county. Those who might have yielded with some grace to tact gave way grudgingly to pressure, and Richard during that summer and early autumn of 1645 made as many enemies amongst the Cornish landowners as he had done in Devon.

On the north coast men rallied to his call because of his link with Stowe; the very name of Grenvile sounded like a clarion. They came to him from beyond the border even, from Appledore and Bideford, and down the length of that storm-bound Atlantic coast from Hartland point to Padstowe. They were his best recruits. Clear-eyed, long-limbed, wearing with pride the scarlet shield with the three gold rests upon their shoulders. Men from Bude and Stratton and Tintagel, men from Boscastle and Camelford. And with great cunning Richard introduced his prince as Duke of Cornwall, who had come into the west to save them from the savage rebel hordes beyond the Tamar.

But further south he met with rebuffs. Danger seemed more remote to people west of Truro, and even the fall of Bristol to Fairfax and the Parliament, which came like a clap of doom on September 10th, failed to rouse them from their lethargy.

"Truro, Helston, and St Ives," said Richard, "are the three rottenest towns in Cornwall," and he rode down, I remember, with some six hundred horse to quell a rising of the townsfolk, who had protested against a levy he had raised the week before.

He hanged at least three men, while the remainder were either fined or imprisoned. He took the opportunity, too, of visiting the castle at St Mawes, and severely reprimanding its commander, Major Bonython, because he had failed to pay the soldiers under his command within the garrison.

"Whoever I find half-hearted in the Prince's cause must change his tune or suffer disciplinary action," declared Richard. "Whoever fails to pay his men shall contribute from his own pocket, and whoever shows one flicker of disloyalty to me, as commander, or to the Prince I serve, shall answer for it with his life."

I heard him say this myself, in the market-place at Launceston before a great crowd assembled there, the last day of September, and, while his own men cheered so that the echo came ringing back to us from the walls of the houses, I saw few smiles upon the faces of the townsfolk gathered there.

"You forget," I said that night to him at Werrington, "that Cornishmen are independent, and love freedom better than their fellows."

"I remember one thing," he answered, with that thin, bitter smile of his which I knew too well, "that Cornishmen are cowards, and love their comfort better than their King."

As autumn drew on, I began to wonder if either freedom or comfort would belong to any of us by the end of the year.

Chard, Crediton, Lyme, and finally Tiverton fell before Fairfax in October, and Lord Goring had done nothing to stop them. Many of his men deserted and came flocking to join Richard's army, for they had greater faith in him as a commander. This led to further jealousy, further recriminations, and it looked as though Richard would fall as foul with Goring as he had done with Sir John Berkeley three months earlier. There was constant fault-finding, too, by the Prince's Council in Launceston, and scarcely a day would pass without some interfering measure from the Chancellor, Edward Hyde.

Money was getting scarce again, and the equipping of the army for the winter another nightmare for my General. Boots and stockings were worn through and hard to replace, while the most vital necessity of all, ammunition, was very low in stock, the chief reason for this being that the Royalist magazine for the western forces had been captured at the beginning of the autumn by the rebels, when they took Bristol, and all that Richard had at his disposal were the small reserves at Bodmin and Truro.

Then suddenly, without any warning, Lord Goring threw up his command and went to France, giving as the reason that his health had cracked and he could no longer shoulder any responsibility.

"The rats," said Richard slowly, "are beginning, one by one, to desert the sinking ship." Goring took several of his best officers with him, and the command in Devon was given to Lord Wentworth, an officer with little experience, whose ideas of discipline were even worse than Goring's. He immediately went into winter quarters at Bovey Tracey, and declared that nothing could be done against the enemy until the spring. It was at this moment, I think, that the Prince's Council first lost heart and realised the full magnitude of what might happen. They were fighting a losing cause. Preparations were made to move from Launceston and go further west to Truro. This, said Richard grimly when he told me, could mean but one thing. They wanted to be near Falmouth, so that when the crisis came the Prince of Wales and the leaders of the Council could take ship to France. It was then I asked him bluntly what he wished to do. "Hold a line," he answered, "from Bristol Channel to the Tamar, and keep Cornwall for the Prince. It can be done. There is no other answer."

"And His Majesty?"

Richard did not answer for a moment. He was standing, I remember well, with his back turned to the blazing log fire and his hands behind his back. He had grown more worn and lined during the past few months, the result of the endless anxieties that pressed upon him, and the silver streak that ran through his auburn locks had broadened above his brow. The raw November weather nipped his wounded leg, and I guessed, with my experience, what he must suffer. "There is no hope for His Majesty," he said at length, "unless he can come to some agreement with the Scots and raise an army from them. If he fails, his cause is doomed."

Forty-three, forty-four, forty-five, and, approaching us, forty-six. For over three years men had fought and suffered and died for that proud stiff little man and his rigid principles. Everything seemed doubtful suddenly, and grim and hopeless. "Richard," I said, and he caught the inflection in my voice and came beside me. "Would you too," I asked, "leave the sinking ship?"

"Not," he said, "if there is any chance of holding Cornwall for the Prince."

"But if the Prince should sail for France," I persisted, "and the whole of Cornwall be overrun—what then?"

"I would follow him," he answered, "and raise a French army of fifty thousand men, and land again in Cornwall."

He came and knelt beside me, and I held his face between my hands.

"We have been happy in our strange way, you and I," I said.

"My camp-follower," he smiled. "My trailer of the drum."

"You know that I am given up as lost to all perdition by good persons," I said. "My family have cast me off, and do not speak of me. Even my dear Robin is ashamed of his sister. I had a letter from him this very morning. He is serving with Sir John Digby before Plymouth. He implores me to leave you, and return to the Rashleighs at Menabilly."

"Do you want to go?"

"No. Not if you still need me."

"I shall always need you. I shall never part with you again. But if Fairfax comes you would be safer in Menabilly than in Launceston."

"That is what was said to me last time, and you know what happened."

"Yes, you suffered for four weeks, and the experience made a woman of you." He looked down at me in his cruel mocking way, and I remembered how he had never thanked me yet for succouring his son. "Next time it might be for four years," I said, "and I think I would be white-haired at the end of it."

"I shall take you with me, if I lose my battle," he said. "When the crisis comes, and Fairfax crosses the Tamar, I will send you and Matty to Menabilly. If we win the day, so far so good. If we lose, and I know the cause is lost, then I will come riding to you at your Rashleigh's, and we will get a fishing-boat from Polkerris and sail across the Channel to St Malo, and find Dick."

"Do you promise?"

"Yes, sweetheart. I promise."

And when he had reassured me, and held me close, I was somewhat comforted, yet always, nagging at my mind, was the reminder that I was not only a woman but a cripple, and would make a sorry burden to a fugitive.

The next day the Prince's Council summoned him to Truro, and asked him there, before the whole assembly, what advice he could give them for the defence of Cornwall against the enemy, and how the safety of the Prince of Wales could be best assured. He did not answer them at once, but the next day, in his lodging, he composed a letter to the Secretary-at-War, and gave full details of the plan, so far only breathed to me in confidence, of what he believed imperative to be done. He showed me the draft of it on his return, and much of what he proposed filled me with misgiving; not because of its impracticability, but because the kernel of it was so likely to be misconstrued. He proposed, in short, to make a treaty with the Parliament, by which Cornwall would become separate from the remainder of the country and be ruled by the Prince of Wales, as Duke of the Duchy. The Duchy would contain its own army and its own fortifications, and control its own shipping. In return, the Cornish would give a guarantee not to attack the forces of the Parliament. Thus gaining a respite, the people of Cornwall, and especially the western army, would become so strong that in the space of a year or more they would be in ripe condition to give effective aid unto His Majesty once more. (This last, it may be realised, was not to be one of the clauses in the treaty.) Failing an agreement with Parliament, then Richard advised that a line be held from Barnstaple to the English Channel, and ditches dug from the north coast to the Tamar, so that the whole of Cornwall became virtually an island. On this river bank would be the first line of defence, and all the bridges would be destroyed. This line, he averred, could be held for an indefinite period, and any attempt at an invasion be immediately repulsed.

When he had finished his report, and sent it to the Council, he returned to me at Werrington, to await an answer. Five days, a week, and no reply. And then at last a cold message from the Chancellor and the Secretary-at-War, to say that the plan had been considered, but had not found approval. The Prince's Council would thus consider other measures, and acquaint Sir Richard Grenvile when his services would be required.

"So," said Richard, throwing the letter on to my lap, "a smack in the eye for Grenvile, and a warning not to rise above his station. The Council prefers to lose the war in their own fashion. Let them do so. Time is getting short, and if I judge Fairfax rightly neither snow nor hail nor frost will hamper him in Devon. It would be wise, my Honor, if you sent word of warning to Mary Rashleigh, and told her that you would spend Christmas with her."

The sands were running out. I could tell it by his easy manner, his shrugging of his shoulders.

"And you?" I said, with that old sick twist of foreboding in my heart.

"I will come later," he said, "and we will see the New Year in together, in that room above the gatehouse."

And so, on the third morning of December, I set forth once again, after eighteen months, for my brother-in-law's house of Menabilly.

CHAPTER TWENTY-FIVE

MY SECOND COMING was very different from my first. Then it had been spring, with the golden gorse in bloom and young John Rashleigh coming to meet me on the highway before the park. War had not touched the neighbourhood, and in the park were cattle grazing, and flocks of sheep with their young lambs, and the last of the blossom falling from the fruit trees in the orchards. Now it was December, a biting wind cutting across the hills and valleys, and no young, laughing cavalier came out to greet me. As we turned in at the park gates I saw at once that the walls were still tumbled, and had not been repaired since the destruction wrought there by the rebels. Where the acres dipped to the sea above Polkerris a labourer with a team of oxen ploughed a single narrow enclosure, but to east and west the land was left uncultivated. What should be rich brown ploughland was left to thistle. A few lean cattle grazed within the park, and even now, after a full year or more had come and gone, I noticed the great bare patches of grassland where the rebel tents had stood, and the blackened roots of the trees they had felled for firewood.

As we climbed the hill towards the house, I could see the reassuring curl of smoke rise from the chimneys and could hear the barking of the stable dogs, and I wondered, with a strange feeling of sadness and regret, whether I should be as welcome now as I had been eighteen months before. Once again my litter passed into the outer court, and, glancing up at my old apartment in the gatehouse, I saw that it was shuttered and untenanted, even as the barred room beside it, and that the whole west wing wore the same forlorn appearance. Mary had warned me in her letter that only the eastern portion of the house had as yet been put in order, and they were living in some half a dozen rooms, for which they had found hangings and the bare necessities of furniture. Once more into the inner court, with a glance upward at the belfry and the tall weather-vane, and then—reminiscent of my former visit—came my sister Mary out upon the steps, and I noticed, with a shock, that her hair had gone quite white. Yet she greeted me with her same grave smile and gentle kiss, and I was taken straightway to the gallery, where I found my dear Alice strung about as always with her mob of babies, and the newest of the brood, just turned twelve months, clutching at her knee in her first steps. At once, as they plied me with refreshment, I had to hear all the news of the past year—of how Jonathan had not yet received one penny piece from the Crown to help him in the restoration of his property, and how whatever had been done he had done himself, with the aid of his servants and tenants.

"Cornwall is become totally impoverished," said my sister sadly, "and everyone dissatisfied. The harvest of this summer could not make up for all we lost last year, and each man with an estate to foster says the same. Unless the war ends swiftly we shall be ruined."

"It may end swiftly," I answered, "but not as you would wish it."

I saw Mary glance quickly at Alice, and Alice made as though to say something, and then desisted. And I realised that as yet no mention had been made of Richard, my relationship to him being something that the Rashleighs possibly preferred should be ignored. I had not been questioned once about the past twelve months.

"They say, who know about these things," said Mary, "that His Majesty is very hopeful, and will soon send an army to the west to help us drive Fairfax out of Devon."

"His Majesty is too preoccupied in keeping his own troops together in the Midlands," I answered, "to concern himself about the west."

"You do not think," said Alice anxiously, "that Cornwall is likely to suffer invasion once again?"

"I do not see how we are to avoid it."

"But . . . we have plenty of troops, have we not?" said Mary, still shying from mention of their General. "I know we have been taxed hard enough to provide for them."

"Troops without boots or stockings make poor fighters," I said, "especially if they have no powder for their muskets."

"Jonathan says everything has been mismanaged," said Mary. "There is no supreme authority in the west to take command. The Prince's Council say one thing—the commanders say another. I, for my part, understand nothing of it. I only wish it were well over."

I could tell from their expressions—even Alice's, usually so fair and generous—that Sir Richard Grenvile had been as badly blamed at Menabilly as elsewhere for his high-handed ways and indiscretions, and that unless I broached his name now there would be an uneasy silence on the subject for the whole duration of my visit. Not one of them would take the first step, and there would be an awkward barrier between us all, making for discomfort. "Perhaps," I said, "having dwelt with Richard Grenvile for the past eight months, ever since he was wounded, I am prejudiced in his favour. I know he has many faults, but he is the best soldier that we have in the whole of His Majesty's army. The Prince's Council would do well to listen to his advice, on military matters if on nothing else."

They neither of them said anything for a moment, and then Alice, colouring a little, said, "Peter is with your brother Robin, you know, under Sir John Digby, before Plymouth. He told us, when he was last here, that Sir Richard constantly sent orders to Sir John, which he has no right to do."

"What sort of orders, good or bad?" I asked.

"I hardly think the orders themselves were points of dispute," said Alice. "They were possibly quite necessary. But the very fact that he gave them to Sir John, who is not subordinate, caused irritation."

At this juncture my brother-in-law came to the gallery and the discussion broke, but I wondered, with a heavy heart, how many friends were now left to my Richard among those who had at first sworn fealty to his leadership. After I had been at Menabilly a few days, my brother-in-law himself put the case more bluntly. There was no discreet avoidance, on his part, of Richard's name. He asked me straight out if he had recovered from his wound, as he had heard report from Truro that on the last visit to the Council the General had looked far from well, and very tired.

"I think he is tired," I said, "and unwell. And the present situation gives him little cause for confidence or good spirits."

"He has done himself irreparable harm here in Cornwall," said my brother-in-law, "by commanding assistance rather than requesting it."

"Hard times require hard measures," I said. "It is no moment to go cap in hand for money to pay troops when the enemy is in the next county."

"He would have won far better response had he gone about his business with courtesy and an understanding of the general poverty of all of us. The whole Duchy would have rallied to his side had he but half the understanding that was his brother Bevil's."

And to this I could give no answer, for I knew it to be true. . . .

The weather was cold and dreary, and I spent much of my time within my chamber, which was the same that Gartred had been given eighteen months before. It had suffered little in the general damage, for which, I suppose, thanks had to be rendered to her. It was a pleasant room, with one window to the gardens, still shorn of their glory, and the new grass seeds that had been sown very clipped yet and thin, and two windows to the south, from where I could see the causeway sloping to rising ground and the view upon the bay. I was content enough, yet strangely empty; for it comes hard to be alone again after eight months in company with the man you love. I had shared his troubles and misfortunes, and his follies too. His moods were become familiar, loved and understood. The cruel quip, the swift malicious answer to a question, and the sudden, fleeting tenderness, so unaccountable, so warming, that would change him in one moment from a ruthless soldier to a lover.

When I was with him the days were momentous and full; now they had all the chill drabness of December, when as I took my breakfast the candles must be lit, and for my brief outing on the causeway I must be wrapped in cloak and covers. The fall of the year, always to me a moment of regret, was now become a period of tension and foreboding.

At Christmas came John and Joan from Fowey, and Peter Courtney, given a few days' grace from Sir John Digby in the watch on Plymouth, and we all made merry for the children's sake, and maybe for our own as well. Fairfax was forgotten, and Cromwell too, the doughty second-in-command who led his men to battle, so we were told, with a prayer upon his lips. We roasted chestnuts before the two fires in the gallery, and burnt our fingers snatching sugar plums from the flames, and I remember too an old blind harper who was given shelter for the night on Christmas Eve, and came and played to us in the soft candlelight. Since the wars there were many such wanderers upon the road, calling no home their own, straggling from village to village, receiving curses more often than silver pieces. Maybe the season had made Jonathan more generous, for this old fellow was not turned away, and I can see him now, in his threadbare jerkin and torn hose, with a black shade over his eyes, sitting in the far corner of the gallery, his nimble fingers drumming the strings of his harp, his quavering old voice sweet and true. I asked Jonathan if he were not afraid of thieves in these difficult times, and, shaking his head, he gestured grimly to the faded tapestries on the panels, and the worn chairs. "I have nothing left of value," he said. "You yourself saw it all destroyed a year since." And then, with a half-smile and a lowered voice: "Even the secret chamber and the tunnel contain nothing now but rats and cobwebs."

I shuddered, thinking suddenly of all I had been through when Dick had hidden there, and I turned with relief to the sight of Peter Courtney playing leap-frog with his children, the sound of their merry laughter rising above the melancholy strains of the harper's lament. The servants came to fasten the shutters, and for a moment my brother-in-law stood before the window looking out upon the lead sky, so soon to darken, and together we watched the first pale snowflakes fall. "The gulls are flying inland," he said. "We shall have a hard winter." There was something ominous in his words, harmless in themselves, that rang like a premonition of disaster. Even as he spoke the wind began to rise, echoing in the chimneys, and circling above the gardens wheeled the crying gulls, who came so seldom from their ledges in the cliffs, and with them the scattered flocks of redwing from the north, birds of passage seeking sanctuary.

Next morning we woke to a white world, strangely still, and a sunless sky teeming with further snow to come, while clear and compelling through the silence came the Christmas bells from the church at Tywardreath.

I thought of Richard, alone with his staff at Werrington, and I feared that he would never keep his promise now, with the weather broken and snowdrifts maybe ten feet deep upon the Bodmin moors.

But he did come, at midday on the ninth of January, when for four-and-twenty hours a thaw had made a slush of the frozen snow and the road from Launceston to Bodmin was just passable to an intrepid horseman. He brought Jack Grenvile with him, and Jack's younger brother, Bunny, a youngster of about the age of Dick, with a pugnacious jaw and merry eyes, who had spent Christmas with his uncle and now never left his side, vowing he would not return to Stowe again to his mother and his tutor, but would join the army and kill rebels. As I watched Richard tweak his ear, and laugh and jest with him, I felt a pang of sorrow in my heart for Dick, lonely and unloved, save for that dreary Herbert Ashley, across the sea in Normandy, and I wondered if it must always be that Richard should show himself so considerate and kind to other lads, winning their devotion, and remain a stranger to his own son.

My brother-in-law, who had known Bevil well, bade welcome Bevil's boys,

and after a first fleeting moment of constraint—for the visit was unexpected—
he welcomed Richard, too, with courtesy. Richard looked better, I thought—
the hard weather suited him—and after five minutes his was the only voice we
heard in the long gallery, a sort of hush coming upon the Rashleigh family with
his presence, and my conscience told me that his coming had put an end to their
festivity. Peter Courtney, the jester-in-chief, was stricken dumb upon the
instant, and I saw him frown to Alice to chide their eldest little girl, who,
unafraid, ventured to Richard's side and pulled his sash.

None of them were natural any more because of the General, and, glancing at
my sister Mary, I saw the well-known frown upon her face as she wondered
about her larder, and what fare she could provide, and I guessed too that she
was puzzling as to which apartment could be given to him, for we were all
crammed into one wing as it was. "You are on your way to Truro, I suppose?"
she said to him, thinking he would be gone by morning. "No," he answered. "I
thought, while the hard weather lasted, I might bide with you a week at
Menabilly, and shoot duck instead of rebels."

I saw her dart a look of consternation at Jonathan, and there was a silence,
which Richard found not at all unusual, as he was unused to other voices but
his own, and he continued cursing with great heartiness the irritating slowness
of the Cornish people. "On the north coast," he said, "where these lads and
myself were born and bred, response is swift and sudden, as it should be. But
the Duchy falls to pieces south of Bodmin, and the men become like snails."
The fact that the Rashleighs had been born in south-east Cornwall did not
worry him at all. "I could never," he continued, "have resided long at
Killigarth. Give a fellow a command at Polperro or at Looe on Christmas Day,
and with a slice of luck it will be obeyed by midsummer."

Jonathan Rashleigh, who owned land in both places, stared steadily before
him. "But whistle a fellow overnight at Stratton," said Richard, "or from
Morwenstowe, or Bude, and he is at your side by morning. I tell you frankly
that had I none other but Atlantic men in my army I would face Fairfax
to-morrow with composure. But at the first sight of cold steel, the rats from
Truro and beyond will turn and run."

"I think you underestimate your fellow countrymen and mine," said
Jonathan quietly.

"Not a bit of it. I know them all too well."

If, I considered, the conversation of the week was to continue in this strain,
the atmosphere of Menabilly would be far from easy. But Jack Grenville, with a
discretion born of long practice, tapped his uncle on the shoulder. "Look, sir,"
he said. "There are your duck." Pointing to the sky above the garden, still grey
and heavy with unfallen snow, he showed the teal in flight, heading to the
Gribben. Richard was at once a boy again, laughing, jesting, clapping his
hands upon his nephew's shoulders, and in a moment the men of the household
fell under the spell of his change of mood, and John, and Peter, and even my
brother-in-law were making for the shore. We women wrapped ourselves in
cloaks and went out upon the causeway to watch the sport, and it seemed to me
that the years had rolled away, as I saw Richard, with Peter's goshawk on his

wrist, turn to laugh at me. The boys were running across the thistle park to the long mead in the Pridmouth valley, shouting and calling to one another, and the dogs were barking.

The snow still lay upon the fields, and the cattle in the beef park nosed hungrily for fodder. The flocks of lapwing, growing tame and bold, wheeled screaming round our heads. For a brief moment the sun came from the white sky and shone upon us, and the world was dazzling. "This," I thought, "is an interlude, lasting a single second. I have my Richard, Alice has her Peter, Joan her John. Nothing can touch us for to day. There is no war. The enemy are not in Devon, waiting for the word to march."

In retrospect, the events of '44 seemed but an evil dream that could never be repeated, and as I looked across the valley to the further hill, and saw the coast road winding down the fields of Tregares and Culver Close to the beach at Pridmouth, I remembered the troopers who had appeared there, on the skyline, on that fateful August day. Surely Richard was mistaken? They could not come again? There was a shouting from the valley, and up from the marshes rose the duck, with the hawks above them, circling, and I suddenly shivered for no reason. Then the sun went blank, and a cat's paw rippled the sea, while a great shadow passed across the Gribben hill. Something fell upon my cheek, soft and clammy white. It was snowing once again.

That night we made a circle by the fire in the gallery, while Jonathan and Mary retired early to their room.

The blind harper had departed with the New Year, so there was none to make music for us save Alice and her lute, and Peter with his singing, while the two Grenvile brothers, Jack and Bunny, whistled softly together—a schoolboy trick learnt from their father Bevil long ago, when the great house at Stowe had rung with singing and with music. John heaped logs upon the fire, and blew the candles, and the flames lit the long room from end to end, shining on the panelling and on the faces of us, one and all, as we sat around the hearth.

I can see Alice as she was that night, fingering her lute, looking up adoringly at her Peter, who was to prove, alas! so faithless in the years to come, while he, with his constraint before his General melting with the firelight and the late hour, threw back his head and sang to us:

> *"And wilt thou leave me thus?*
> *Say nay, say nay, for shame.*
> *To save thee from the blame*
> *Of all my grief and grame,*
> *And wilt thou leave me thus?*
> *Say nay! Say nay!"*

I saw Joan and John hold hands and smile; John, with his dear honest face, who would never be unfaithful and a deserter to his Joan, as Peter would to Alice, but was destined to slip away from her for all that, to the land from which no one of us returns, in barely six years' time.

"And wilt thou leave me thus,
And have no more pity
Of him that loveth thee?
Alas! thy cruelty.
And wilt thou leave me thus?
Say nay! Say nay!"

Plaintive and gentle were Alice's fingers upon the lute, and Jack and Bunny, cupping their mouths with their hands, whistled softly to her lead. I stole a glance at Richard. He was staring into the flames, his wounded leg propped on a stool before him. The flickering firelight cast shadows on his features, distorting them to a grimace, and I could not tell whether he smiled or wept.

"You used to sing that once, long ago," I whispered, but if he heard me he made no move; he only waited for the last verse of Peter's song. Then he laid aside his pipe, blowing a long ribbon of smoke into the air, and reached across the circle for Alice's lute.

"We are all lovers here, are we not?" he said. "Each in our own fashion, except for these sprigs of boys." He smiled maliciously, and began to drum the strings of the lute:

"Your most beautiful bride who with garlands is crowned
And kills with each glance as she treads on the ground,
Whose lightness and brightness doth shine in such splendour,
That none but the stars
Are thought fit to attend her,
Though now she be pleasant and sweet to the sense,
Will be damnably mouldy a hundred years hence."

He paused, cocking an eye at them, and I saw Alice shrink back in her chair, glancing uncertainly at Peter. Joan was picking at her gown, biting her lips. Oh, God, I thought, why do you break the spell? Why do you hurt them? They are none of them much more than children.

"Then why should we turmoil in cares and in fears,
Turn all our tranquill'ty to sighs and to tears?
Let's eat, drink, and play till the worms do corrupt us,
'Tis certain, Post Mortem,
Nulla voluptas,
For health, wealth, and beauty, wit, learning and sense,
Must all come to nothing a hundred years hence."

He rippled a final chord upon the strings, and, rising to his feet, handed the lute to Alice with a bow.

"Your turn again, Lady Courtney," he said. "Or would you prefer to play at spillikins?"

Someone—Peter, I think it was—forced a laugh, and then John rose to light the candles. Joan leant forward and raked apart the fire, so that the logs no longer burnt a flame. They flickered dully, and went dark. The spell was broken.

"It is snowing still," said Jack Grenvile, opening a shutter. "Let us hope it falls twenty foot in depth in Devon, and stifles Fairfax and his merry men."

"It will more likely stifle Wentworth," said Richard, "sitting on his arse in Bovey Tracey."

"Why does everyone stand up?" asked young Bunny. "Is there to be no more music?" But no one answered. The war was upon us once again, the fear, the doubt, the nagging insecurity, and all the quiet had vanished from the evening.

CHAPTER TWENTY-SIX

———————

I SLEPT UNEASILY that night, passing from one troubled dream into another, and at one moment I thought to hear the sound of horses' hooves riding across the park. Yet my windows faced east, and I told myself it was but fancy, and the wind stirring in the snow-laden trees. But when Matty came to me with breakfast she bore a note in her hands from Richard, and I learnt that my fancy was in truth reality, and that he, and the two Grenviles and Peter Courtney, had all ridden from the house shortly after daybreak.

A messenger had come to Menabilly with the news that Cromwell had made a night attack on Lord Wentworth in Bovey Tracey, and, finding the Royalist army asleep, had captured four hundred of the horse, while the remainder of the foot who had not been captured had fled to Tavistock in complete disorder and confusion. "Wentworth has been caught napping," Richard had scribbled on a torn sheet of paper, "which is exactly what I feared would happen. What might have been a small reverse is likely to turn into disaster if a general order is given to retreat. I propose riding forthwith to the Prince's Council, and offering my services. Unless they appoint a supreme commander to take over Wentworth's rabble, we shall have Fairfax and Cromwell across the Tamar." Mary need not have worried after all. Sir Richard Grenvile had passed but a single night under her roof, and not the week that she had dreaded. . . .

I rose that morning with a heavy heart, and, going downstairs to the gallery, found Alice in tears, for she knew that Peter would be foremost in the fighting when the moment came. My brother-in-law looked grave, and departed at midday, also bound for Launceston, to discover what help might be needed from the landowners and gentry in the event of invasion. John, with Frank Penrose, set forth to warn the tenants on the estate that once again their services might be needed, and the day was wretchedly reminiscent of that other day in August, nearly eighteen months before. But now it was not midsummer, but midwinter. And there was no strong Cornish army to lure the rebels into a trap, with another Royalist army marching in the rear.

Our men stood alone—with His Majesty three hundred miles away or more, and General Fairfax was a very different leader from the Earl of Essex. He would walk into no trap, but if he came would cross the Tamar with a certainty.

In the afternoon Elizabeth from Coombe came to join us, her husband having gone, and told us that the rumour ran in Fowey that the siege of Plymouth had been raised and that Digby's troops, along with Wentworth's, were retreating fast to the Tamar bridges.

We sat before the smouldering fire in the gallery, a little group of wretched women, and I stared at that same branch of ash that had burnt so brightly the preceding night, when our men were with us, and was now a blackened log amongst the ashes.

We had faced invasion before, had endured the brief horrors of enemy occupation, but we had never known defeat. Alice and Mary were talking of the children, the necessity this time of husbanding supplies beneath the floor-boards of the rooms, as though a siege was all that was before us. But I said nothing, only stared into the fire. And I wondered who would suffer most, the men who died swiftly in battle or those who would remain to face imprisonment and torture. I knew then that I would rather Richard fought and died than stayed to fall into the hands of Parliament. It did not bear much thinking what they would do to Skellum Grenvile if they caught him.

"The King will march west, of course," Elizabeth was saying. "He could not leave Cornwall in the lurch. They say he is raising a great body of men in Oxfordshire, this moment. When the thaw breaks . . ."

"Our defences will withstand the rebels," Joan said. "John was talking to a man in Tywardreath. Much has been accomplished since last time. They say we have a new musket—with a longer barrel—I do not know exactly, but the rebels will not face it, so John says. . . ."

"They have no money," said Mary. "Jonathan tells me the Parliament is desperate for money. In London the people are starving. They have no bread. The Parliament are bound to seek terms from the King, for they will be unable to continue the war. When the spring comes . . ."

I wanted to put my fingers in my ears and muffle the sound of their voices. On and on, one against the other, the old false tales that had been told so often. It cannot go on. . . . They must give in. . . . They are worse off than we. . . . When the thaw breaks, when the spring comes. . . . And suddenly I saw Elizabeth look towards me—she had less reserve than Alice, and I did not know her so well—and ask, "What does Sir Richard Grenvile say? You must hear everything of what goes on. Will he attack and drive the rebels back to Dorset?"

Her ignorance, and theirs, was so supreme that I had not the heart nor the will to enlighten her.

"Attack?" I said. "With what forces do you suggest that he attacks?"

"Why, with those at his disposal," she answered. "We have many able-bodied men in Cornwall."

I thought of the sullen bands I had seen sulking in the square at Launceston, and the handful of brawny fellows in the fields below Werrington, wearing the Grenvile shield on their shoulders.

"A little force of pressed men," I said, "and volunteers, against some fifty thousand trained soldiers?"

"But man for man we are superior," urged Elizabeth. "Everyone says that. The rebels are well equipped, no doubt, but when our fellows meet them face to face, in fair fight, in open country . . ."

"Have you not heard," I said softly, "of Cromwell, and the new Model Army? Do you not realise, that never in England, until now, has there been raised an army like it?"

They stared at me, nonplussed, and Elizabeth, shrugging her shoulders, said I had greatly altered since the year before, and was now become defeatist. "If we all talked in that fashion," she said, "we would have been beaten long ago. I suppose you have caught it from Sir Richard. I do not wonder that he is unpopular."

Alice looked embarrassed, and I saw Mary nudge Elizabeth with her foot.

"Don't worry," I said. "I know his faults far better than you all. But I think if the Council of the Prince would only listen to him this time, we might save Cornwall from invasion."

That evening, on going to my room, I looked out on the weather, and saw that the night was clear and the stars were shining. There would be no more snow, not yet awhile. I called Matty to me, and told her my resolve. This was to follow Richard back to Werrington, if transport could be got for me at Tywardreath, and to set forth at noon the following day, passing the night at Bodmin, and so to Werrington the day after. By doing this I would disobey his last instructions, but I had, in my heart, a premonition that unless I saw him now I would never see him more. What I thought, what I feared, I cannot tell. But it came to me that he might fall in battle, and that by following him I would be with him at the last.

The next morning was fine, as I expected, and I rose early, and went down to breakfast, and informed the Rashleigh family of my plan. They one and all begged me to remain, saying it was folly to travel the roads at such a season, but I was firm; and at length John Rashleigh, dear, faithful friend, arranged matters for me, and accompanied me as far as Bodmin.

It was bitter cold upon the moors, and I had little stomach for my journey, as, with Matty at my side, I left the hostelry at Bodmin at daybreak. The long road to Launceston stretched before us, bleak and dreary, with great snow-drifts on either side of us, and one false step of our horses would send the litter to destruction. Although we were wrapped about with blankets, the nipping, nagging wind penetrated the curtains, freezing our faces, and when we halted at Five Lanes for hot soup and wine to warm us I had half a mind to go no further, but find lodging for the night at Altarnun. The man at the inn, though, put an end to my hesitation. "We have had soldiers here these past two days," he said, "deserters from the army before Plymouth. Some of Sir John Digby's men. They were making for their homes in west Cornwall. They were not going to stay on the Tamar banks to be butchered, so they told me."

"What news had they?" I asked, my heart heavy.

"Nothing good," he answered. "Confusion everywhere. Orders, and counter-orders. Sir Richard Grenvile was down on Tamarside, inspecting bridges, giving instructions to blow them when the need arose, and a colonel of foot refused to take the order, saying he would obey none other than Sir John Digby. What is to become of us if the generals start fighting amongst themselves?"

I felt sick, and turned away. There would be no biding for me this night at Altarnun. I must reach Werrington by nightfall.

On, then, across the snow-covered moors, wind-swept and desolate, and every now and then we would pass straggling figures making for the west, their apparel proclaiming to the world that once they were King's men, but now deserters. They were blue from cold and hunger, and yet they wore a brazen, sullen look, as though they cared no longer what became of them, and some of them shouted as we passed, "To hell with the war. We're going home," and shook their fists at my litter, jeering, "You're driving to the devil."

The short winter afternoon soon closed in, and by the time we came to Launceston, and turned out of the town to St Stephens, it was grown pitch-dark, and snowing once again. An hour or so later I would have been snow-bound on the road, with nothing but waste moorland on either side of me. At last we came to Werrington, which I had not thought to see again, and when the startled sentry at the gates recognised me, and let the horses pass through the park, I thought that even he, a Grenvile man, had lost his look of certainty and pride, and would become, granted ill-fortune, no better than the deserters on the road.

We drew up into the cobbled court, and an officer came forth whose face was new to me. His expression was blank when I gave him my name, and he told me that the General was in conference and could not be disturbed. I thought that Jack might help me, and asked therefore if Sir John Grenvile, or his brother Mr Bernard, could see Mistress Honor Harris on a matter of great urgency.

"Sir John is no longer with the General," answered the officer. "The Prince of Wales recalled him to his entourage yesterday. And Bernard Grevile has returned to Stowe. I am the General's aide-de-camp at present." This was not hopeful, for he did not know me, and as I watched the figures of the soldiers, passing backwards and forwards in the hall within the house, and heard the tattoo of a drum in the far distance, I thought how ill-timed and crazy was my visit, for what could they do with me, a woman and a cripple, in this moment of great stress and urgency?

I heard a murmur of voices. "They are coming out now," said the officer. "The conference is over." I caught sight of Colonel Roscarrock, whom I knew well, a loyal friend of Richard's, and in desperation I leant from my litter and called to him. He came to my side at once, in great astonishment, but at once, with true courtesy, covered his consternation and gave orders for me to be carried into the house. "Ask me no questions," I said. "I have come at a bad moment. I can guess that. Can I see him?" He hesitated for a fraction of a minute. "Why, of course," he said, "he will want to see you. But I must warn you, things are not going well for him. We are all concerned . . ." He broke off in confusion, looking most desperately embarrassed and unhappy.

"Please," I said, avoiding his eyes, "please tell him I am here." He went at once into the room that Richard used as his own, and where we had sat together, night after night, for over seven months. He stayed a moment, and then came for me. My chair had been lifted from the litter, and he took me to the room, then closed the door. Richard was standing by the table. His face was hard, set in the firm lines that I knew well. I could tell that of all things in the world I was, at that moment, the farthest from his thoughts.

"What the devil," he said wearily, "are you doing here?"

It was not the welcome that I yearned for, but was that which I deserved.

"I am sorry," I said. "I could not rest, once you were gone. If anything is going to happen—which I know it must—I want to share it with you. The danger, I mean. And the aftermath."

He laughed shortly, and tossed a paper on to my lap.

"There'll be no danger," he said, "not for you, or me. Perhaps, after all, it is as well you came. We can travel west together."

"What do you mean?" I said.

"That letter—you can read it," he said. "It is a copy of a message I have just sent to the Prince's Council, resigning from His Majesty's army. They will have it in an hour's time."

I did not answer for a moment. I sat quite cold and still.

"What do you mean?" I asked at length. "What has happened?" He went to the fire and stood with his hands behind his back. "I went to them," he said, "as soon as I returned from Menabilly. I told them that, if they wished to save Cornwall and the Prince, they must appoint a supreme commander. Men are deserting in hundreds, discipline is non-existent. This would be the only hope, the last and final chance. They thanked me. They said they would consider the matter. I went away. I rode next morning to Gunnislake and Callington. I inspected the defences. There I commanded a certain colonel of foot to blow a bridge when need arose. He disputed my authority, saying his orders were to the contrary. Would you like to know his name?"

I said nothing. Some inner sense had told me.

"It was your brother, Robin Harris," he said. "He even dared to bring your name into a military matter. 'I cannot take orders from a man,' he said, 'who has ruined the life and reputation of my sister. Sir John Digby is my commander, and Sir John has bidden me to leave this bridge intact.'"

Richard stared at me an instant, and then began to pace up and down the strip of carpet by the fire.

"You would hardly credit it," he said; "such lunacy, such gross incompetence. It matters not that he is your brother, that he drags a private quarrel into the King's business. But to leave the bridge for Fairfax, to have the impertinence to tell me, a Grenvile, that John Digby knows his business best . . ."

I could see Robin, very red about the neck, with beating heart and swelling anger, thinking, dear damned idiot, that by defying his commander he was somehow defending me and downing, in some bewildering hothead fashion, the seducer of his sister.

"What then?" I asked. "Did you see Digby?"

"No," he answered. "What would be the use, if he defied me, as your brother did? I returned here to Launceston, to take my commission from the Council as supreme commander, and thus show my powers to the whole army, and be damned to them."

"And you have the commission?"

He leant to the table, and, seizing a small piece of parchment, held it before my eyes. "The Council of the Prince," he read, "appoints Lord Hopton in supreme command of His Majesty's forces in the west, and desires that Sir Richard Grenvile should serve under him as Lieutenant-General of the foot."

He read slowly, with deadly emphasis and scorn; and then tore the document to tiny shreds and threw the pieces in the fire. "That is my answer to them," he said. "They may do as they please. To morrow you and I will return to shoot duck at Menabilly." He pulled the bell beside the fire, and his new aide-de-camp appeared. "Bid the servants bring some supper," he said. "Mistress Harris has travelled long, and has not dined."

When the officer had gone I put out my hand to Richard.

"You can't do this," I said. "You must do as they tell you."

He turned round on me in anger. "Must?" he said. "There is no must. Do you think that I shall truckle to that damned lawyer at this juncture? It is he who is at the bottom of this, he who is to blame. I can see him, with his bland attorney's manner, talking to the members of the Council. 'This man is dangerous,' he says to them, 'this soldier, this Grenvile. If we give him the supreme command he will take precedence of us, and send us about our business. We will give Hopton the command. Hopton will not dare to disobey. And when the enemy cross the Tamar, Hopton will withstand them just long enough for us to slip across to Guernsey with the Prince.' That is how the lawyer talks; that is what he has in mind. The traitor, the damned disloyal coward."

He faced me, white with anger.

"But, Richard," I persisted, "don't you understand, my love, my dear, that it is you they will call disloyal at this moment? To refuse to serve under another man, with the enemy in Devon? It is you who will be pointed at, reviled? You, and not Hyde?"

He would not listen; he brushed me away with his hand.

"This is not a question of pride, but concerns my honour," he said. "They do not trust me. Therefore I resign. Now, for God's sake, let us dine, and say no more. Tell me, was it snowing still at Menabilly?"

I failed him that last evening. Failed him miserably. I made no effort once to enter in his mood, that switched now so suddenly from black anger to forced jollity. I wanted to talk about the future, about what he proposed to do, but he would have none of it. I asked what his officers thought, what Colonel

Roscarrock had said, and Colonels Arundell and Fortiscue? Did they too uphold him in his grave, unorthodox decision? But he would not speak of it. He bade the servants open another bottle of wine, and with a smile he drained it all, as he had done seven months before at Ottery St Mary. It was nearly midnight when the new aide-de-camp knocked upon the door, bearing a letter in his hand.

Richard took it, and read the message; then with a laugh threw it in the fire. "A summons from the Council," he said, "to appear before them at ten to morrow, in the castle court at Launceston. Perchance they plan some simple ceremony, and will dub me Earl. That is the customary reward for soldiers who have failed."

"Will you go?" I asked.

"I shall go," he said, "and then proceed with you to Menabilly."

"You will not relent?" I asked. "Not swallow your pride, or honour, as you call it, and consent to do as they demand of you?"

He looked at me a moment, and he did not smile.

"No," he said slowly. "I shall not relent."

I went to bed, to my old room, next to his, and left the door open between our chambers, should he be restless, and wish to come to me. But at past three in the morning I heard his footstep on the stair, and he did not speak or call to me.

I slept one hour perhaps, or two. I do not remember. It was still snowing when I woke, and dull and grey. I bade Matty dress me in great haste, and sent word to Richard, asking if he would see me.

He came instead to my room, and with great tenderness told me to stay abed, at any rate until he should return from Launceston.

"I will be gone an hour," he said; "two at the utmost. I shall but delay to tell the Council what I think of them, and then come back to breakfast with you. My anger is all spent. This morning I feel free, and light of heart. It is an odd sensation, you know, to be at long last without responsibility." He kissed my two hands, and then went away. I heard the sound of the horses trotting away across the park. There was a single drum, and then silence. Nothing but the footsteps of the sentry, pacing up and down before the house. I went and sat in my chair beside the window, with a rug over my knees. It was snowing steadily. There would be a white carpet in the castle green at Launceston. Here, at Werrington, the world was desolate. The deer stood huddled under the trees down by the river. At midday Matty brought me meat, but I did not fancy it. I went on sitting at the window, gazing out across the park, and presently the snow had covered all trace of the horses, and the soft white flakes began to freeze upon the glass of the casement, clouding my view. It must have been past three when I heard the sentry standing to attention, and once again the muffled tattoo of a drum. Some horses were coming to the house by the northern entrance, and because my window did not face that way I could not see them. I waited. Richard might not come at once—there would be many matters to see to in that room downstairs. At a quarter-to-four there came a knock upon my door, and a servant demanded, in a hushed tone, if Colonel

Roscarrock could wait on Mistress Harris. I told him, "Certainly," and sat there, with my hands clasped on my lap, filled with the apprehension that I knew too well.

He came, and stood before the door, disaster written plainly on his face.

"Tell me," I said. "I would know the worst at once."

"They have arrested him," he said slowly, "on a charge of disloyalty to the Prince and to His Majesty. They seized him there, before us, his staff, and all his officers."

"Where have they imprisoned him?"

"There, in Launceston Castle. The Governor and an escort of men were waiting to take him. I rode to his side and begged him to give fight. His staff, his command, the whole army, I told him, would stand by him, if he would but give the word. But he refused. 'The Prince,' he said, 'must be obeyed.' He smiled at us there, on the castle green, and bade us be of good cheer. Then he handed his sword to the Governor, and they took him away."

"Nothing else?" I asked. "No other word, no message of farewell?"

"Nothing else," he said, "except he bade me take good care of you, and see you safely to your sister."

I sat quite still, my heart numb, all feeling and all passion spent.

"This is the end," said Colonel Roscarrock. "There is no other man in the army fit to lead us but Richard Grenvile. When Fairfax chooses to strike, he will find no opposition. This is the end."

Yes, I thought. This is the end. Many had fought and died, and all in vain. The bridges would not be blown now, the roads would not be guarded nor the defences held. When Fairfax gave the word to march, the word would be obeyed, and his troops would cross the Tamar, never to depart. The end of liberty in Cornwall, for many months, for many years, perhaps for generations. And Richard Grenvile, who might have saved his country, was now a prisoner, of his own side, in Launceston Castle.

"If we had only time," Colonel Roscarrock was saying, "we could have a petition signed by every man and woman in the Duchy, asking for his release. We could send messengers, in some way, to His Majesty himself, imploring pardon, insisting that the sentence of the Council is unjust. If we had only time . . ."

If we had only time, when the thaw breaks, when the spring comes. . . . But it was that day, the nineteenth of January, and the snow was falling still.

CHAPTER TWENTY-SEVEN

MY FIRST ACTION was to leave Werrington, which I did that evening, before Sir Charles Trevannion, on Lord Hopton's staff, came to take over for his commander. I no longer had any claim to be there, and I had no wish to embarrass Charles Trevannion, who had known my father well. I went therefore to the hostelry in Broad Street, Launceston, near to the castle, and Colonel Roscarrock, after he had installed me there, took a letter for me to the Governor, requesting an interview with Richard for the following morning. He returned at nine o'clock, with a courteous but firm refusal. No one, said the Governor, was to be permitted to see Sir Richard Grenvile, by strict order of the Prince's Council. "We intend," said Colonel Roscarrock to me, "sending a deputation to the Prince himself at Truro. Jack Grenvile, I know, will speak for his uncle, and many more besides. Already, since the news has gone abroad, the troops are murmuring, and have been confined to their quarters for twenty-four hours in consequence. I can tell, by what the Governor said, that rioting is feared." There was no more I could ask him to do that day—I had already trespassed too greatly on his time already—so I bade him a good night and went to bed, to pass a wretched night, wondering all the while in what dungeon they had lodged Richard, or if he had been given lodging according to his rank.

The next day, the twentieth, driving sleet came to dispel the snow, and I think, because of this, and because of my unhappiness, I have never hated any place so much as Launceston. The very name sounded like a gaol. Just before noon Colonel Roscarrock called on me with the news that there were proclamations everywhere about the town that Sir Richard Grenvile had been cashiered from every regiment he had commanded, and was dismissed from His Majesty's army—and all without court martial.

"It cannot be done," he said with vehemence. "It is against every military code and tradition. There will be a mutiny in all ranks at such gross injustice. We are to hold a meeting of protest today, and I will let you know directly it is over what is decided." Meetings and conferences—somehow I had no faith in them. Yet how I cursed my impotence, sitting in my hired room above the cobbled street in Launceston.

Matty, too, fed me with tales of optimism. "There is no other talk about the town," she said, "but Sir Richard's imprisonment. Those who grumbled at his severity before are now clamouring for his release. This afternoon a thousand people went before the Castle and shouted for the Governor. He is bound to let him go, unless he wants the castle burnt about his ears."

"The Governor is only acting under orders," I said. "He can do nothing. It is to Sir Edward Hyde and the Council that they should direct their appeals."

"They say in the town," she answered, "that the Council have gone back to Truro, so fearful they are of mutiny."

That evening, when darkness fell, I could hear the tramping of many feet in the market square, and distant shouting, while flares and torches were tossed into the sky. Stones were thrown at the windows of the town hall, and the landlord of my hostelry, fearing for his own, barred the shutters early, and the doors.

"They've put a double guard at the Castle," he told Matty, "and the troops are still confined to their quarters."

How typical it was, I thought with bitterness, that now, in his adversity, my Richard should become so popular a figure. Fear was the whip that drove the people on. They had no faith in Lord Hopton or any other commander. Only a Grenvile, they believed, could keep the enemy from crossing the Tamar.

When Colonel Roscarrock came at last to see me, I could tell from his weary countenance that nothing much had been accomplished. "The General has sent word to us," he said, "that he will be no party to release by force. He asks for a court martial, and a chance to defend himself before the Prince, and to be heard. As to us, and to his army, he bids us serve under Lord Hopton."

Why in God's name, I wondered, could he not have done the same himself but twelve hours since?

"So there will be no mutiny?" I said. "No storming of the castle?"

"Not by the army," said Colonel Roscarrock in dejection. "We have taken an oath to remain loyal to Lord Hopton. You have heard the latest news?"

"No?"

"Dartmouth has fallen. The Governor, Sir Hugh Pollard, and over a thousand men are taken prisoner. Fairfax has a line across Devon now, from north to south."

This would be no time, then, to hold courts martial.

"What orders have you," I asked wearily, "from your new commander?"

"None as yet. He is at Stratton, you know, in the process of taking over and assembling his command. We expect to hear nothing for a day or two. Therefore I am at your disposal. And I think—forgive me—there is little purpose in your remaining here at Launceston." Poor Colonel; Roscarrock. He felt me to be a burden, and small blame to him. But the thought of leaving Richard a prisoner in Launceston Castle was more than I could bear.

"Perhaps," I said, "if I saw the Governor myself?" But he gave me little hope. The Governor, he said, was not the type of man to melt before a woman. "I will go again," he assured me, "to-morrow morning, and ascertain at least that the General's health is good, and that he lacks for nothing." And with that assurance he left me, to pass another lonely night, but in the morning I woke to the sound of distant drums, and then heard the clattering of horses and troopers pass my window, and I wondered whether orders had come from Lord Hopton at Stratton during the night and if the army was on the march again. I sent Matty below for news, and the landlord told her that the troops had been on the move since before daybreak. "All the horse," he said, "had ridden away north already."

I had just finished breakfast when a runner brought me a hurried word, full of apology, from Colonel Roscarrock, saying that he had received orders to proceed at once to Stratton, as Lord Hopton intended marching north to Torrington, and that if I had any friend or relative in the district it would be best for me to go to them immediately. I had no friend or relative, nor would I seek them if I had, and, summoning the landlord, I told him to have me carried to Launceston Castle, for I wished to see the Governor. I set forth, therefore, well wrapped against the weather, with Matty walking by my side and four fellows bearing my litter, and when I came to the castle gate I demanded to see the captain of the guard. He came from his room, unshaven, buckling his sword, and I thought how Richard would have dealt with him.

"I would be grateful," I said to him, "if you could give a message from me to the Governor."

"The Governor sees no one," he said at once, "without a written appointment."

"I have a letter here, in my hands," I said. "Perhaps it could be given to him."

He turned it over, looking doubtful, and then looked at me again. "What exactly, madam, is your business?" he said.

He looked not unkindly, for all his blotched appearance, and I took a chance. "I have come," I said, "to enquire after Sir Richard Grenvile." At this he handed back my letter.

"I regret, madam," he said, "but you have come on a useless errand. Sir Richard is no longer here."

Panic seized me on the instant, and I pictured a sudden, secret execution. "What do you mean?" I asked. "No longer here?"

"He left this morning under escort for St Michael's Mount," replied the captain of the guard. "Some of his men broke from their quarters last night and demonstrated here before the castle. The Governor judged it best to remove him from Launceston." At once the captain of the guard, the castle walls, the frowning battlements, lost all significance. Richard was no more imprisoned there. "Thank you," I said. "Good day," and I saw the officer stare after me, and then return to his room beneath the gate.

St Michael's Mount. Some seventy miles away, in the western toe of Cornwall. At least he was far removed from Fairfax, but how in the world was I to reach him there? I returned to the hostelry, with only one thought in my head now, and that to get from Launceston as soon as possible.

As I entered the door the landlord came to meet me, and said that an officer had called to enquire for me, and was even now waiting my return. I thought it must be Colonel Roscarrock, and went at once to see—and found instead my brother Robin. "Thank God," he said, "I have sight of you at last. As soon as I had news of Sir Richard's arrest, Sir John gave me leave of absence to ride to Werrington. They told me at the house you had been gone two days."

I was not sure whether I was glad to see him. It seemed to me, at this moment, that no man was my friend unless he was friend to Richard also. "Why have you come?" I said coolly. "What is your purpose?"

"To take you back to Mary," he said. "You cannot possibly stay here."

"Perhaps," I answered, "I have no wish to go."

"That is neither here nor there," he said stubbornly. "The entire army is in process of reorganising, and you cannot remain in Launceston without protection. I myself have orders to join Sir John Digby at Truro, where he has gone with a force to protect the Prince in the event of invasion. My idea is to leave you at Menabilly on my way thither."

I thought rapidly. Truro was the headquarters of the Council, and if I went to the town there was a chance, faint yet not impossible, that I could have an audience with the Prince himself.

"Very well," I said to Robin, shrugging my shoulders, "I will come with you, but on one condition. And that is that you do not leave me at Menabilly, but let me come with you all the way to Truro."

He looked at me doubtfully. "What," he said, "is to be gained by that?"

"Nothing gained, nor lost," I answered; "only, for old time's sake, do what I demand."

At that he came and took my hand, and held it a minute.

"Honor," he said, his blue eyes full upon my face, "I want you to believe me when I say that no action of mine had any bearing on his arrest. The whole army is appalled. Sir John himself, who had many a bitter dispute with him, has written to the Council, appealing for his swift release. He is needed, at this moment, more than any other man in Cornwall."

"Why," I said bitterly, "did you not think of it before? Why did you refuse to obey his orders about the bridge?"

Robin looked startled for a moment, and then discomforted.

"I lost my temper," he admitted. "We were all rankled that day, and Sir John, the best of men, had given me my orders. You don't understand, Honor, what it has meant to me, and Jo, and all your family, to have your name a byword in the county. Ever since you left Radford last spring to go to Exeter people have hinted, and whispered, and even dared to say aloud the foulest things."

"Is it so foul," I said, "to love a man, and go to him when he lies wounded?"

"Why are you not married to him, then?" said Robin. "If you had been, in God's conscience, you would have earned the right now to share in his disgrace. But to follow from camp to camp, like a loose woman. . . . I tell you what they say, Honor, in Devon. That he well earns his name of Skellum to trifle thus with a woman who is crippled."

Yes, I thought, they would say that in Devon. . . .

"If I am not Lady Grenvile," I said, "it is because I do not choose to be so."

"You have no pride, then, no feeling for your name?"

"My name is Honor, and I do not hold it tarnished," I answered him.

"This is the finish. You know that?" he said, after a moment's pause. "In spite of a petition, signed by all our names, I hardly think the Council will agree to his release. Not unless they receive some counter-order from His Majesty."

"And His Majesty," I said, "has other fish to fry. Yes, Robin, I understand. And what will be the outcome?"

"Imprisonment at His Majesty's pleasure, with a pardon, possibly, at the end of the war."

"And what if the war does not go the way we wish, but the rebels gain Cornwall for the Parliament?"

Robin hesitated, so I gave the answer for him.

"Sir Richard Grenvile is handed over, a prisoner, to General Fairfax," I said, "and sentenced to death as a criminal of war." I pleaded fatigue, then, and went to my room, and slept easily for the first time for many nights, for no other reason but because I was bound for Truro, which was some thirty miles distant from St Michael's Mount.

The snow of the preceding days had wrought havoc on the road, and we were obliged to go a longer route, by the coast, for the moors were now impassable. Thus, with many halts and delays, it was well over a week before we came to Truro, only to discover that the Council was now removed to Pendennis Castle, at the mouth of the Fal, and Sir John Digby and his forces were now also within the garrison.

Robin found me and Matty a lodging at Penryn, and went at once to wait on his commander, bearing a letter from me to Jack Grenvile, whom I believed to be in close attendance on the Prince. The following day Jack rode to see me—and I felt as though years had passed since I had last set eyes upon a Grenvile. Yet it was barely three weeks since he, and Richard, and young Bunny, had ridden all three to Menabilly. I nearly wept when he came into the room.

"Have no fear," he said at once. "My uncle is in good heart, and sturdy health. I have received messages from him from the Mount, and he bade me write you not to be anxious for him. It is rather he who is likely to be anxious on your part, for he believes you with your sister, Mrs Rashleigh."

I determined then to take young Jack into my confidence.

"Tell me first," I said, "what is the opinion on the war?"

He made a face, and shrugged his shoulders. "You see we are at Pendennis," he said quietly. "That, in itself, is ominous. There is a frigate at anchor in the roads, fully manned and provisioned, with orders to set sail for the Scillies when the word is given. The Prince himself will never give the word—he is all for fighting to the last—but the Council lacks his courage. Sir Edward Hyde will have the last word, not the Prince of Wales."

"How long, then, have we till the word be given?"

"Hopton and the army have marched to Torrington," answered Jack, "and there is a hope—but I fear a faint one—that by attacking first Hopton will take the initiative, and force a decision. He is a brave fellow, but lacks my uncle's power, and the troops care nothing for him. If he fails at Torrington, and Fairfax wins the day—then you may expect that frigate to set sail."

"And your uncle?"

"He will remain, I fear, at the Mount. He has no other choice. But Fairfax is a soldier, and a gentleman. He will receive fair treatment." This was no answer for me. However much a soldier and a gentleman Fairfax himself might be, his duty was to Parliament, and Parliament had decreed in '43 that Richard Grenvile was a traitor.

"Jack," I said, "would you do something for me, for your uncle's sake?"

"Anything in the world," he answered, "for the pair of you."

Ah, bless you, I thought, true son of Bevil. . . .

"Get me an audience with the Prince of Wales," I said to him.

He whistled, and scratched his cheek, a very Grenvile gesture.

"I'll do my best, I swear it," he said, "but it may take time and patience, and I cannot promise you success. He is so hemmed about with members of the Council, and dares do nothing but what he is told to do by Sir Edward Hyde. I tell you, Honor, he's led a dog's life until now. First his mother, and now the Chancellor. When he does come of age and can act for himself, I'll wager he'll set the stars on fire."

"Make up some story," I urged. "You are his age, and a close companion. You know what would move him. I give you full licence."

He smiled—his father's smile. "As to that," he said, "he has only to hear your story, and how you followed my uncle to Exeter, to be on tenterhooks to look at you. Nothing pleases him better than a love-affair. But Sir Edward Hyde—he's the danger."

He left me, with an earnest promise to do all he could, and with that I was forced to be content. Then came a period of waiting that seemed like centuries, but was, in all reality, little longer than a fortnight. During this time Robin came several times to visit me, imploring me to leave Penryn and return to Menabilly. Jonathan Rashleigh, he said, would come himself to fetch me, would I but send the word.

"I must warn you, in confidence," he said, "that the Council have little expectation of Hopton's withstanding Fairfax. The Prince, with his personal household, will sail for Scilly. The rest of us within the garrison will hold Pendennis until we are burnt out of it. Let the whole rebel army come. We will not surrender."

Dear Robin. As you said that, with your blue eyes blazing and your jaw set, I forgave you for your enmity for Richard, and the silly, useless harm you did in disobeying him.

Death or glory, I reflected. That was the way my Richard might have chosen. And here was I, plotting one thing only, that he should steal away like a thief in the night.

"I will go back to Menabilly," I said slowly, "when the Prince of Wales sets sail for the Scillies."

"By then," said Robin, "I shall not be able to assist you. I shall be inside the garrison, at Pendennis, with our guns turned east upon Penryn."

"Your guns will not frighten me," I said, "any more than Fairfax's horse, thundering across the moors from the Tamar. It will look well, in after-years, in the annals of the Harris family, to say that Honor died in the last stand in '46."

Brave words, spoken in hardihood, ringing so little true. . . .

On the fourteenth of February, the feast of St Valentine, that patron saint of lovers, I had a message from Jack Grenvile. The wording was vague, and purposely omitted names.

"The snake is gone to Truro," he said, "and my friend and I will be able to receive you, for a brief space, this afternoon. I will send an escort for you. Say nothing of the matter to your brother."

I went alone, without Matty, deeming in a matter of such delicacy it were better to have no confidante at all.

True to his word, the escort came, and Jack himself awaited me at the entrance to the castle. No haggling this time with a captain of the guard. But a swift word to the sentry, and we were through the arch and within the precincts of the garrison before a single soul, save the sentry, was a whit the wiser.

The thought occurred to me that this perhaps was not the first time Jack Grenvile had smuggled a woman into the fortress. Such swift handling came possibly from long experience. Two servants in the Prince's livery came to carry me, and after passing up some stairs (which I told myself were back ones, and suitable to my person), I was brought to a small room within a tower, and placed upon a couch. I would have relished the experience were not the matter upon which I sought an audience so deadly serious. There was wine and fruit at my elbow, and a posy of fresh flowers, and His Highness, I thought, for all his mother, has gained something by inheriting French blood.

I was left for a few moments to refresh myself, and then the door opened again and Jack stood aside, to let a youngster of about his own age pass before him. He was far from handsome, more like a gipsy than a prince, with his black locks and swarthy skin, but the instant he smiled I loved him better than all the famous portraits of his father that my generation had known for thirty years. "Have my servants looked after you," he said at once, "and given you all you want? This is garrison fare, you know—you must excuse it." And as he spoke I felt his bold eyes look me up and down in cool, appraising fashion, as though I were a maid and not fifteen years his senior. "Come, Jack," he said, "present me to your kinswoman," and I wondered what the devil of a story Jack had spun.

We ate and drank, and all the while he talked he stared, and I wondered if his boy's imagination was running riot on the thought of his notorious and rebellious general making love to me, a cripple. "I have no claim to trespass on your time, sir," I said at length, "but Sir Richard, Jack's uncle, is my dear friend, and has been so now over a span of years. His faults are many, and I have not come to dispute them. But his loyalty to yourself has never, I believe, been the issue in question."

"I don't doubt it," said the prince, "but you know how it was. He got up against the Council, and Sir Edward in particular. I like him immensely myself, but personal feeling cannot count in these matters. There was no choice but to sign that warrant for his arrest."

"Sir Richard did very wrong not to serve under Lord Hopton," I said. "His worse fault is his temper, and much, I think, had gone wrong that day to kindle it. Given reflection, he would have acted otherwise."

"He made no attempt, you know, sir," cut in Jack, "to resist arrest. The whole staff would have gone to his aid, had he given them the word. That I have on good authority. But he told all of them he wished to abide by your Highness's command."

The Prince rose to his feet and paced up and down the room.

"It's a wretched affair all round," he said. "Grenvile is the one fellow who might have saved Cornwall, and all the while Hopton fights a hopeless battle up in Torrington. I can't do anything about it, you know—that's the devil of it. I shall be whisked away myself before I know what is happening."

"There is one thing you can do, sir, if you will forgive my saying so," I said.

"What then?"

"Send word to the Mount that when you and the Council sail for the Scillies Sir Richard Grenvile shall be permitted to escape at the same time; and commandeer a fishing-boat for France."

The Prince of Wales stared at me a moment, and then that same smile I had remarked upon his face before lit his whole ugly countenance. "Sir Richard Grenvile is most fortunate," he said, "to have so *fidèle* an ally as yourself. If I am ever in his shoes, and find myself a fugitive, I hope I can rely on half so good a friend."

He glanced across at Jack. "You can arrange that, can't you?" he said. "I will write a letter to Sir Arthur Bassett at the Mount, and you can take it there, and see your uncle at the same time. I don't suggest we ask for his company in the frigate when we sail, because I hardly think the ship would bear his weight, alongside Sir Edward Hyde." The two lads laughed, for all the world like a pair of schoolboys caught in mischief. Then the Prince turned, and, coming to the couch, bent low and kissed my hand.

"Have no fear," he said. "I will arrange it. Sir Richard shall be free the instant we sail for the Scillies. And when I return—for I shall return, you know, one day—I shall hope to see you, and him also, at Whitehall." He bowed, and went, forgetting me, I dare say, for ever more, but leaving with me an impression of black eyes and gipsy features that I have not forgotten to this day. . . .

Jack escorted me to the castle entrance once again. "He will remember his promise," he said. "That I swear to you. I have never known him go back on his word. To-morrow I shall ride with that letter to the Mount."

I returned to Penryn, worn-out and utterly exhausted now that my mission was fulfilled. I wanted nothing but my bed, and silence. Matty received me with sour looks and the grim, pursed mouth that spelt disapproval. "You have wanted to be ill for weeks," she said. "Now that we are here, in a strange lodging, with no comforts, you decide to do so. Very well. I'll not answer for the consequences."

"No one asks you to," I said, turning my face to the wall. "For God's sake, if I want to, let me sleep, or die."

Two days later Lord Hopton was defeated outside Torrington, and the whole western army in full retreat across the Tamar. It concerned me little, lying in that lodging at Penryn with a high fever. On the twenty-fifth of

February Fairfax had marched and taken Launceston, and on the second of March had crossed the moors to Bodmin.

That night the Prince of Wales, with his Council, set sail in the frigate *Phœnix*—and the war in the west was over. . . .

The day Lord Hopton signed the treaty in Truro with General Fairfax my brother-in-law, Jonathan Rashleigh, by permission of the Parliament, came down to Penryn to fetch me back to Menabilly. The streets were lined with soldiers, not ours, but theirs, and the whole route from Truro to St Austell bore signs of surrender and defeat. I sat, with stony face, looking out of the curtains of my litter, while Jonathan Rashleigh rode by my side, his shoulders bowed, his face set in deep, grim lines.

We did not converse. We had no words to say. We crossed St Blazey bridge and Jonathan handed his pass to the rebel sentry at the post, who stared at us with insolence and then jerked his head and let us pass. They were everywhere. In the road, in the cottage doors at Tywardreath, at the barrier, at the foot of Polmear hill. This was our future then, for ever more, to ask, in deep humility, if we might travel our own roads. That it should be so worried me no longer, for my days of journeying were over. I was returning to Menabilly to be no longer a camp-follower, no longer a lady of the drum, but plain Honor Harris, a cripple on her back. And it did not matter to me, I did not care.

For Richard Grenvile had escaped to France.

CHAPTER TWENTY-EIGHT

DEFEAT, AND THE aftermath of war. . . . Not pleasant for the losers. God knows that we endure it still—and I write in the autumn of 1653—but in the year '46 we were new to defeat, and had not yet begun to learn our lesson. It was, I think, the loss of freedom that hit the Cornish hardest. We had been used, for generations, to minding our own affairs, and each man lived after his fashion. Landlords were fair, and usually well-liked, with tenant and labourer living in amity together. We had our local disagreements, as every man will with his neighbour, and our family feuds, but no body of persons had ever before interfered with our way of living, nor given us commands. Now all was changed. Our orders came to us from Whitehall, and a Cornish County Committee, way up in London, sat in judgment upon us. We could no longer pass our own measures and decide, by local consultation, what was suited to each town and village. The County Committee made our decisions for us.

Their first action was to demand a weekly payment from the people of Cornwall to the revenue, and this weekly assessment was rated so high that it was impossible to find the money, for the ravages of war had stripped the country bare. Their next move was to sequester the estate of every landlord who had fought for the King. Because the County Committee had not the time nor the persons to administer these estates, the owners were allowed to dwell there, if they so desired, but had to pay to the Committee, month by month, the full and total value of the property. This crippling injunction was made the harder because the estates were assessed at the value they had held before the war, and now that most of them were fallen into ruin, through the fighting, it would take generations before the land gave a return once more.

A host of petty officials who were paid fixed salaries by the Parliament, and were the only men at these times to have their pockets well-lined, came down from Whitehall to collect the sums due to the County Committee; and these agents were found in every town and borough, forming themselves in their turn into committees and sub-committees, so that no man could buy as little as a loaf of bread without first going cap in hand to one of these fellows and signing his name to a piece of paper. Besides these civil employers of the Parliament, we had the military to contend with, and whosoever should wish to pass from one village to another must first have a pass from the officer in charge, and then his motives questioned, his family history gone into, detail for detail, and as likely as not find himself arrested for delinquency at the end of it.

I truly believe that Cornwall was, in that first summer of '46, the most wretched county in the kingdom. The harvest was bad—another bitter blow to landlord and labourer alike—and the price of wheat immediately rose to fantastic prices. The price of tin, on the contrary, fell low, and many mines closed down on this account. Poverty and sickness were rife by the autumn, and our old enemy the plague appeared, killing great numbers in St Ives and in the western districts. Another burden was the care of the many wounded and disabled soldiers, who, half-naked and half-starved, roamed the villages, begging for charity. There was no single man or woman or little child who benefited in any way by this new handling of affairs by Parliament, and the only ones to live well were those Whitehall agents who poked their noses into our affairs from dawn till dusk, and their wealthy masters, the big Parliamentary landlords. We had grumbled in the old days at the high taxes of the King, but the taxes were intermittent. Now they were continuous. Salt, meat, starch, lead, iron—all came under the control of Parliament, and the poor man had to pay accordingly.

What happened up-country I cannot say—I speak for Cornwall. No news came to us, much beyond the Tamar. If living was hard, leisure was equally restricted. The Puritans had the upper hand of us. No man must be seen out-of-doors upon a Sunday unless he were bound for church. Dancing was forbidden—not that many had the heart to dance, but youngsters have light hearts and lighter feet—and any game of chance or village festival was frowned upon. Gaiety meant licence, and licence spelt the abomination of the Lord. I often thought how Temperance Sawle would have rejoiced in the brave new world, for all her Royalist traditions, but poor Temperance fell an early victim to the plague.

The one glory of that most dismal year of '46 was the gallant, though alas! so useless, holding of Pendennis Castle for the King through five long months of siege. The rest of us were long conquered and subdued, caught fast in the meshes of Whitehall, while Pendennis still defied the enemy. Their commander was Jack Arundell, who had been in the old days a close friend as well as kinsman to the Grenviles, and Sir John Digby was his second-in-command. My own brother Robin was made a major-general under him. It gave us, I think, some last measure of pride in our defeat, that this little body of men, with no hope of rescue and scarce a boatload of provisions, should fly the King's flag from March the second until August the seventeenth, and that even then they wished to blow themselves and the whole garrison to eternity, rather than surrender. But starvation and sickness had made weaklings of the men, and for their sakes only did Jack Arundell haul down his flag. Even the enemy respected their courage, and the garrison were permitted to march out, so Robin told us afterwards, with the full honours of war, drums beating, colours flying, trumpets sounding. . . . Yes, we have had our moments, here in Cornwall. . . . When they surrendered, though, our last hopes vanished, and there was nothing now to do but sigh, and look into the black well of the future.

My brother-in-law, Jonathan Rashleigh, like the rest of his Royalist landlords, had his lands sequestered by the County Committee, and was told, when he went down to Truro in June, that he must pay a fine of some one thousand and eighty pounds to the Committee before he could redeem them. His losses, after the '44 campaign, were already above eight thousand, but there was nothing for it but to bow his head to the victors and agree to pay the ransom during the years to come. He might have quitted the country and gone to France, as many of our neighbours did, but the ties of his own soil were too strong, and in July, broken and dispirited, he took the National Covenant, by which he vowed never again to take arms against the Parliament. This bitter blow to his pride, self-inflicted though it was, did not satisfy the Committee, and shortly afterwards he was summoned to London and ordered to remain there, nor to return to Cornwall until his full fine was paid. So yet another home was broken, and we, at Menabilly, tasted the full flavour of defeat. He left us, one day in September, when the last of the poor harvest had been gathered in, looking a good ten years older than his five-and-fifty years, and I knew then, watching his eyes, how loss of freedom can so blight the human soul that a man cares no longer if he lives or dies.

It remained for Mary, my poor sister, and John, his son, so to husband his estate that the debt could month by month be paid, but we well knew that it might take years, even the remainder of his life. His last words to me, before he went to London, were kind and deeply generous. "Menabilly is your home," he said, "for as long a time as you should so desire it. We are one and all sufferers in this misfortune. Guard your sister for me; share her troubles. And help John, I pray you. You have a wiser head than all I leave behind."

A wiser head. . . . I doubted it. It needed a pettifogging mind, with every low lawyer's trick at the finger's end, to break even with the County Committee and the paid agents of the Parliament. There was none to help us. My brother

Robin, after the surrender of Pendennis, had gone to Radford, to my brother Jo, who was in much the same straits as ourselves, while Peter Courtney, loathing inactivity, left the West Country altogether, and the next we heard from him was that he had gone abroad to join the Prince of Wales. Many young men followed this example—living was good at the French Court. I think, had they loved their homes better, they would have stayed behind and shared the burdens of defeat with their womenfolk.

Alice spoke never a word of blame, but I think her heart broke when we heard that he had gone. . . .

It was strange, at first, to watch John and Frank Penrose work in the fields side by side with the tenants, for every hand was needed if the land was to be tilled entirely and yield a full return. Even our womenfolk went out at harvesting—Mary herself, and Alice, and Elizabeth, while the children, thinking it fine sport, helped to carry the corn. Left to ourselves, we would have soon grown reconciled and even well content with our labours, but the Parliament agents were for ever coming to spy upon us, to question us on this and that, to count the sheep and cattle, to reckon, it almost seemed, each ear of corn, and nothing must be gathered, nothing spent, nothing distributed amongst ourselves, but all laid before the smug, well-satisfied officials in Fowey town, who held their licence from the Parliament. The Parliament . . . the Parliament. . . . From day to day the word rang in our ears. The Parliament decrees that produce shall be brought to market only upon a Tuesday. . . . The Parliament has ordered that all fairs shall henceforth be discontinued. . . . The Parliament warns every inhabitant within the above-prescribed area that no one, save by permission, shall walk abroad one hour after sunset. . . . The Parliament warns each householder that every dwelling will be searched each week for concealed firearms, weapons, and ammunition, from this day forward, and any holder of the same shall be immediately imprisoned. . . .

"The Parliament," said John Rashleigh wearily, "decrees that no man may breathe God's air, save by a special licence, and that one hour in every other day. My God, Honor, no man can stand this long."

"You forget," I said, "that Cornwall is only one portion of the kingdom. The whole of England, before long, will suffer the same fate."

"They will not, they cannot, endure it," he said.

"What is their alternative? The King is virtually a prisoner. The party with the most money and the strongest army rules the country. For those who share their views life is doubtless very pleasant."

"No one can share their views and call his soul his own."

"There you are wrong. It is merely a matter of being accommodating, and shaking hands with the right people. Lord Robartes lives in great comfort at Lanhydrock. The Treffrys—being related to Hugh Peters and Jack Trefusis—live very well at Place. If you chose to follow their example and truckle to the Parliament, doubtless you would find life here at Menabilly so much the easier."

He stared at me suspiciously. "Would you have me go to them and fawn, while my father lives a pauper up in London, watched every moment of his day? I would sooner die."

I knew he would sooner die, and loved him for it. Dear John, you might have had more years beside your Joan, and be alive to-day, had you spared yourself, and your poor health, in those first few months of aftermath. . . . I watched him toil, and the women too, and there was little I could do to help but figure the accounts, an unpaid clerk, with smudgy fingers, and tot up the debts we owed on quarter-days. I did not suffer as the Rashleighs did, pride being, I believe, a quality long lost to me, and I was sad only in their sadness. To see Alice, gazing wistfully from a window, brought a pain to my heart, and when Mary read a letter from her Jonathan, deep shadows beneath her eyes, I think I hated the Parliament every whit as much as they did.

But that first year of defeat was, in some queer fashion, quiet and peaceful to me who bore no burden on my shoulders. Danger was no more. Armies were disbanded. The strain of war was lifted. The man I loved was safe across the sea, in France, and then in Italy, in the company of his son, and now and then I would have word of him from some foreign city, in good heart and spirits, and missing me, it would seem, not at all. He talked of going to fight the Turks with great enthusiasm, as if, I thought with a shrug of my shoulder, he had not had enough of fighting after three hard years of civil war. "Doubtless," he wrote, "you find your days monotonous in Cornwall." Doubtless I did. To women who have known close siege and stern privation, monotony can be a pleasant thing. . . . A wanderer for so many months, it was restful to find a home at last, and to share it with people that I loved, even if we were all companions in defeat.

God bless the Rashleighs, who permitted me those months at Menabilly. The house was bare and shorn of its former glory, but at least I had a room I called my own. The Parliament could strip the place of its possessions, take the sheep and cattle, glean the harvest, but they could not take from me, nor from the Rashleighs, the beauty that we looked on every day. The devastation of the gardens was forgotten when the primroses came in spring, and the young green budded on the trees. We, the defeated, could still listen to the birds on a May morning, and watch the clumsy cuckoo wing his way to the little wood beside the Gribben hill. The Gribben hill. . . . I watched it, from my chair upon the causeway, in every mood from winter to midsummer. I have seen the shadows creep, on an autumn afternoon, from the deep Pridmouth valley to the summit of the hill, and there stay a moment, waiting on the sun.

I have seen too the white sea-mists of early summer turn the hill to fantasy, so that it becomes, in a single second, a ghost land of enchantment, with no sound coming but the wash of breakers on the hidden beach, where, at high noon, the children gather cowrie shells. Dark moods too of bleak November, when the rain sweeps in a curtain from the south-west. But, quietest of all, the evenings of late summer, when the sun has set, and the moon has not yet risen, but the dew is heavy in the long grass.

The sea is very white and still, without a breath upon it, and only a single thread of wash upon the covered Cannis rock. The jackdaws fly homeward to their nests in the Warren. The sheep crop the short turf, before they rub together beneath the stone wall by the winnowing place. Dusk comes slowly to the Gribben hill, the woods turn black, and suddenly, with stealthy pad, a fox creeps from the trees in the thistle park, and stands watching me, his ears pricked. . . . Then his brush twitches and he is gone, for here is Matty tapping along the causeway to bring me home; and another day is over. Yes, Richard, there is comfort in monotony. . . .

I return to Menabilly to find all have gone to bed, and the candles extinguished in the gallery. Matty carries me upstairs, and as she brushes my hair, and ties the curling rags, I think I am almost happy. A year has come and gone, and though we are defeated we live, we still survive. I am lonely, yes, but that has been my portion since I turned eighteen. And loneliness has compensations. Better to live inwardly alone than together in constant fear. And as I think thus, my curling rag in my hand, I see Matty's round face looking at me from the mirror opposite.

"There were strange rumours in Fowey to-day," she says quietly.

"What rumours, Matty? There are always rumours."

She moistens a rag with her tongue, then whips it round a curl. "Our men are creeping back," she murmurs. "First one, then two, then three. Those who fled to France a year ago."

I rub some lotion on my hands, and face.

"Why should they return? They can do nothing."

"Not alone, but if they band together, in secret, one with another. . . ."

I sit still, my hands in my lap, and suddenly I remember a phrase in the last letter that came to me from Italy.

"You may hear from me," he said, "before the summer closes, by a different route. . . ." I thought him to mean he was going to fight the Turks.

"Do they mention names?" I say to Matty, and for the first time for many months a little seed of anxiety and fear springs to my heart. She does not answer for a moment—she is busy with a curl. Then at last she speaks, her voice low and hushed.

"They talk of a great leader," she says, "landing in secret at Plymouth from the continent. He wore a dark wig, they said, to disguise his colouring. But they did not mention names. . . ."

A bat brushes itself against my window, lost and frightened, and close to the house an owl shrieks in warning. And it seemed to me, that moment, that the bat was no airey-mouse of midsummer, but the scared symbol of all hunted things.

CHAPTER TWENTY-NINE

Rumours. Always rumours. Never anything of certainty. This was our portion during the winter of '47–'48. So strict was the Parliamentary hold on news that nothing but the bare official statements were given to us down in Cornwall, and these had no value, being simply what Whitehall thought good for us to know.

So the whispers started, handed from one to the other, and when the whispers came to us fifth-hand we had to sift the welter of extravagance to find the seed of truth. The Royalists were arming. This was the firm base of all the allegations. Weapons were being smuggled into the country from France, and places of concealment were found for them. Gentlemen were meeting in one another's houses. The labourers were conversing together in the field. A fellow at a street-corner would beckon to another, for the purpose, it would seem, of discussing market prices; there would be a question, a swift answer, and then the two would separate, but information had been passed, and another link forged.

Outside the parish church of Tywardreath would stand a Parliamentary soldier, leaning on his musket, while the busybody agent, who had beneath his arm a fold of documents listing each member of the parish and his private affairs, gave him "Good morning"; and while he did so the old sexton, with his back turned, prepared a new grave, not for a corpse this time, but for weapons. . . . They could have told a tale, those burial grounds of Cornwall. Cold steel beneath the green turf and the daisies, locked muskets in the dark family vaults. Let a fellow climb to repair his cottage roof against the rains of winter, and he will pause an instant and glance over his shoulder, and, thrusting his hand under the thatch, feel for the sharp edge of a sword. These would be Matty's tales. Mary would come to me, with a letter from Jonathan in London. "Fighting is likely to start again at any moment," would be his guarded words. "Discontent is rife, even here, against our masters. Many Londoners who fought in opposition to the King would swear loyalty to him now. I can say no more than this. Bid John have a care whom he meets and where he goes. Remember, I am bound to my oath. If we meddle in these matters he and I will answer for it with our lives."

Mary would fold the letter anxiously and place it in her gown. "What does it mean?" she would say. "What matters does he refer to?" And to this there could be one answer only. The Royalists were rising.

Names that had not been spoken for two years were now whispered by cautious tongues. Trelawney. . . . Trevannion. . . . Arundell. . . . Bassett. . . . Grenvile. . . . Yes, above all, Grenville. He had been seen at Stowe, said one. Nay, that was false, it was not Stowe, but at his sister's house near Bideford. The Isle of Wight, said another. The red fox was gone to Carisbroke to take secret council of the King. He had not come to the West Country. He had been seen in Scotland. He had been spoken to in Ireland. Sir Richard Grenvile was returned. Sir Richard Grenvile was in Cornwall. . . .

I made myself deaf to these tales. For once too often, in my life, I had had a bellyful of rumours. Yet it was strange no letter came any more from Italy, or from France. . . .

John Rashleigh kept silent on these matters. His father had bidden him not meddle, but to work, night and day, at the husbanding of the estate, so that the groaning debt to Parliament could be paid. But I could guess his thoughts. If there were in truth a rising, and the Prince landed, and Cornwall was freed once more, there would be no debt to pay. If the Trelawneys were a party to the plan, and the Trevannions also, and all those in the county who swore loyalty to the King in secret, then was it not something like cowardice, something like shame, for a Rashleigh to remain outside the company? Poor John. He was often restless and sharp-tempered, those first weeks of spring, after ploughing was done. And Joan was not with us to encourage him, for her twin boys, born the year before, were sickly, and she was with them, and the elder children, at Mothercombe in Devon. Then Jonathan fell ill up in London, and though he asked permission of the Parliament to return to Cornwall they would not grant it, so he sent for Mary, and she went to him.

Alice was the next to leave. Peter wrote to her from France, desiring that she should take the children to Trethurfe, his home, which was—so he had heard—in sad state of repair, and would she go there, now spring was at hand, and see what could be done. She went, the first day of March, and it suddenly became strangely quiet at Menabilly. I had been used so long to children's voices that now to be without them, and the sound of Alice's voice calling to them, and the rustle of Mary's gown, made me more solitary than usual, even a little sad. There was no one but John now for company, and I wondered what we should make of it together, he and I, through the long evenings.

"I have half a mind," he said to me the third day we sat together, "to leave Menabilly in your care, and go to Mothercombe."

"I'll tell no tales of you if you do," I said to him.

"I do not like to go against my father's wishes," he admitted, "but it's over six months now since I have seen Joan and the children, and not a word comes to us here of what is passing in the country. Only that the war has broken out again. There is fighting in places as far apart as Wales and the Eastern Counties. I tell you, Honor, I am sick of inactivity. For very little I would take horse and ride to Wales."

"No need to ride to Wales," I said quietly, "when there is likely to be a rising in your own county."

He glanced at the half-open door of the gallery. A queer, instinctive move, unnecessary when the few servants that we had could all be trusted. Yet since we had been ruled by Parliament this gesture would be force of habit. "Have you heard anything?" he said guardedly. "Some word of truth, I mean, not idle rumour?"

"Nothing," I answered, "beyond what you hear yourself."

"I thought perhaps Sir Richard . . ." he began, but I shook my head.

He sighed, and glanced once more towards the door.

"If only," he said, "I could be certain what to do. If there should be a rising, and I took no part in it, how lacking in loyalty to the King I would seem, and what dishonour it would be to the name of Rashleigh."

"If there should be a rising and it failed," I said, "how damp your prison walls, how uneasy your head upon your shoulders."

He smiled, for all his earnestness. "Trust a woman," he said, "to douse a fellow's ardour."

"Trust a woman," I replied, "to keep war out of her home."

"Do you wish to sit down indefinitely, then, under the rule of Parliament?" he asked.

"Not so. But spit in their faces, before the time is ripe, and we shall find ourselves one and all under their feet for ever."

Once again he sighed, rumpling his hair and looking dubious.

"Get yourself permission," I said, "and go to Mothercombe. It's your wife you need, and not a rising. But I warn you, once you are in Devon you may not find it so easy to return."

This warning had been repeated often during the past weeks. Those who had gone into Devon or to Somerset upon their lawful business, bearing a permit from the local Parliamentary officials, would find great delay upon the homeward journey, much scrutiny and questioning, and this would be followed by a search for documents or weapons, and possibly a night or more under arrest. We, the defeated, were not the only ones to hear the rumours. . . .

The Sheriff of Cornwall at this time was a neighbour, Sir Thomas Herle of Prideaux, near St Blazey, who, though firm for Parliament, was a just and fair man. He had done all he could to mitigate the heavy fine placed upon the Rashleigh estate, through respect for my brother-in-law, but Whitehall was too strong for his local powers. It was he now, in kindness, who granted John Rashleigh permission to visit his wife at Mothercombe in Devon, and so it happened, this fateful spring, that I was, of all our party, the only one remaining at Menabilly. A woman and a cripple—it was not likely that such a one could foster, all alone, a grim rebellion. The Rashleighs had taken the oath. Menabilly was now above suspicion. And though the garrison at Fowey and other harbours on the coast were strengthened, and more troops quartered in the towns and villages, our little neck of land seemed undisturbed. The sheep grazed on the Gribben hill. The cattle browsed in the beef park. The wheat was sown in eighteen acres. And smoke from a single fire—my own—rose from the Menabilly chimneys. Even the steward's house was desolate, now old John Langdon had been gathered to his fathers, for with the crushing burden on the estate his place had not been filled. His keys, once so important and mysterious, were now in my keeping, and the summer-house, so sacred to my brother-in-law, had become my routine shelter on a windy afternoon. I had no wish these days to pry into the Rashleigh papers. Most of the books were gone, stored in the house or packed and sent after him to London. The desk was bare and empty. Cobwebs hung from the walls. Green patches of mould showed upon the ceiling. But the torn matting on the floor still hid the flagstone with the iron ring. . . . I saw a rat once creep from his corner and stare at me a moment with beady, unwinking eyes. A great black spider spun a web from a broken pane of glass in the east window, while ivy, spreading from the ground, thrust a tendril to the sill. A few years more, I thought, and Nature would take toll of it all, and no one would remember the flagstone with the ring upon it, or the flight of steps, and the earthy, mouldering tunnel. Well, it had served its purpose. Those days would not return.

I looked out towards the sea, one day in March, and watched the shadows darken, for an instant, the pale ripple of the water beyond Pridmouth. The clock in the belfry struck four o'clock. Matty was gone to Fowey, and should be back by now. I heard a footstep on the path beneath the causeway, and called, thinking it was one of the farm labourers returning home, who could bear a message for me to the house. The footsteps ceased, but there came no word in answer.

I called again, and this time I heard a rustle in the undergrowth. My friend the fox, perhaps, was out upon his prowl. Then I saw a hand fasten to the sill and cling there for an instant, gripping for support. But the walls of the summer-house were smooth, giving no foothold, and in a second the hand had slipped and was gone.

Someone was playing spy upon me. . . . If one of the long-nosed Parliamentary agents who spent their days scaring the wits out of the simple country people wished to try the game on me, he would receive short measure.

"If anyone wishes to speak with Mr Rashleigh, he is from home," I called loudly. "There is no one but myself in charge at Menabilly. Mistress Honor Harris, at your service."

I waited a moment, my eye still on the window, and then a shadow, falling suddenly upon my right shoulder, told me there was someone at the door. I whipped round, in an instant, my hands on the wheels of my chair, and saw the figure of a man, small and slight, clad in plain dark clothes like a London clerk, with a hat pulled low over his face. He stood watching me, his hand upon the lintel of the door.

"Who are you?" I said. "What do you want?" There was something in his manner which struck a chord. . . . The way he hesitated, standing on one foot, then bit his thumb-nail. . . . I groped for the answer, my heart beating, when he whipped his hat from his close black curls, and I saw him smile, tremulous at first, uncertain, until he saw me smile too and stretch my arms towards him.

"Dick . . ." I whispered. He came and knelt by me at once, covering my hands in kisses.

I forgot the intervening years, and had in my arms a little frightened boy who gnawed a bone and swore he was a dog and I his mistress. And then, raising his head, I saw he was a boy no longer, but a young man, with hair upon his lip, and curls no longer riotous, but sleek and close. His voice was low and soft, a man's voice.

"Four years," I said. "Have you grown thus in four small years?"

"I shall be eighteen in two months' time," he answered, smiling. "Have you forgotten? You wrote the first year for my birthday, but never since."

"Writing has not been possible, Dick, these past two years."

I could not take my eyes from him, he was so grown, so altered. Yet that way of watching with dark eyes, wary and suspicious, was the same, and the trick of gnawing at his hand.

"Tell me quickly," I said, "before they come to fetch me from the house, what you are doing here, and why."

He looked at me doubtfully. "I am the first to come, then?" he asked. "My father is not here?"

My heart leapt, but whether in excitement or in fear I could not tell. In a flash of intuition, it seemed that I knew everything. The waiting of the past few months was over. It was all to begin afresh. . . . It was all to start again. . . .

"No one is here," I answered, "but yourself. Even the Rashleighs are from home."

"Yes, we knew that," he said. "That is why Menabilly has been chosen."

"Chosen for what?" I asked.

He did not answer. He started his old trick of gnawing at his hand. "They will tell you," he said, blinking his eyelids, "when they come."

"Who are 'they'?" I asked.

"My father, first," he answered, with his eye upon the door, "and Peter Courtney another, and Ambrose Manaton of Trecarrel, and your own brother Robin, and, of course, my Aunt Gartred."

Gartred. . . . At this I felt like someone who has been ill overlong or withdrawn from the world, leading another life. There had been rumours enough, God knows, in south-east Cornwall to stun the senses, but none so formidable as fell now upon my ears.

"I think it best," I said slowly, "if you tell me what has happened since you came to England."

He rose then from his knee, and, dusting the dirt from his clothes with a fastidious hand, swept a place upon the window-sill to sit. "We left Italy last autumn," he said, "and came first of all to London. My father was disguised as a Dutch merchant, and I as his secretary. Since then we have travelled England, from south to north, outwardly as foreign men of business, secretly as agents for the Prince. At Christmas we crossed the Tamar into Cornwall, and went first of all to Stowe. My aunt is dead, you know, and no one was there but the steward, and my cousin Bunny, and the others. My father made himself known to the steward, and since then many secret meetings have been held throughout the county. From Stowe it is but a step to Bideford and Orley Court. There we found my aunt Gartred, who, having fallen out with her Parliamentary friends, was hot to join us, and your brother Robin also."

Truly the world had passed me by at Menabilly. The Parliament had one grace to its credit, that the stoppage of news stopped gossip also.

"I did not know," I said, "that my brother Robin lived at Bideford."

Dick shrugged his shoulders. "He and my aunt are very thick," he answered. "I understand your brother has made himself her bailiff. She owns land, does she not, that belonged to your eldest brother, who is dead?"

Yes, they could have met again that way. Why should I blame Robin, grown weary and idle in defeat?

"And so?" I asked.

"And so the plans matured, the clans gathered. They are all in it, you know, from east to west, the length and breadth of Cornwall. The Trelawneys, the Trevannions, the Bassetts, the Arundells. And now the time draws near. The muskets are being loaded and the swords sharpened. You will have a front seat at the slaughter."

There was a strange note of bitterness in his soft voice, and I saw him clench his hands upon the sill.

"And you?" I asked. "Are you not excited at the prospect? Are you not happy to be one of them?"

He did not answer for a moment, and when he did I saw his eyes look large and black in his pale face, even as they had done as a boy four years before.

"I tell you one thing, Honor," he said passionately. "I would give all I possess in the world, which is precious little, to be out of it."

The force with which he spoke shocked me for an instant, but I took care that he should not guess it.

"Why so?" I asked. "Have you no faith that they will succeed?"

"Faith?" he said wearily. "I have no faith in anything. I begged him to let me stay in Italy, where I was content after my own fashion, but he would not let me. I found that I could paint, Honor. I wished to make painting my trade. I had friends, too, fellows of my age, for whom I felt affection. But no. Painting was womanish, a pastime fit for foreigners. My friends were womanish too, and would degrade me. If I wished to live, if I hoped to have a penny to my name, I must follow him, do his bidding, ape his ways, grow like my Grenvile cousins. God in heaven, how I have come to loathe the very name of Grenvile!"

Eighteen, but he had not changed. Eighteen, but he was still fourteen. This was the little boy who had sobbed his hatred of his father.

"And your mother?" I asked gently.

He shrugged his shoulders. "Yes, I have seen her," he said listlessly, "but it's too late now to make amends. She cares nothing for me. She has other interests. Four years ago she would have loved me still. Not now. It's too late. His fault. Always his fault."

"Perhaps," I said, "when—when this present business is concluded, you will be free. I will speak for you. I will ask that you may return to Italy, to your painting, to your friends."

He picked at the fringe of his coat with his long slim hands—too long, I thought, too finely slim for a Grenvile.

"There will be fighting," he said slowly, "men killing one another for no purpose, save to spill blood. Always to spill blood. . . ."

It was growing dim in the summer-house, and still I had heard no more about their plans. The fear that I read in his eyes found an echo in my heart, and the old strain and anxiety was with me once again. "When did you leave Bideford?" I asked.

"Two days ago," he answered. "Those were my orders. We were to proceed separately, each by a different route. Lady Courtney has gone to Trethurfe, I presume?"

"She went at the beginning of the month."

"So Peter intended. It was part of the ruse, you see, for emptying the house. Peter has been in Cornwall and amongst us since before Christmas."

Another prey for Gartred? A second bailiff to attend on Orley Court? And Alice here, with wan cheeks, and chin upon her hand, at an open window. . . . Richard did not choose his serviteurs for kindness.

"Mrs Rashleigh was inveigled up to London for the same purpose," said Dick. "The scheme has been cunningly planned, like all schemes of my father's. And the last cast of all, to rid the house of John, was quite in keeping with his character."

"John went of his own accord," I answered, "to see his wife at Mothercombe in Devon."

"Aye, but he had a message first," said Dick, "a scrap of paper, passed to him in Fowey, saying that his wife was over-fond of a neighbour, living in her father's house. I know, because I saw my father pen the letter, laughing as he did so, with aunt Gartred at his back."

I was silent at that. God damn them both, I thought, for cruelty. And I knew Richard's answer, even as I accused him in my thoughts: "Any means, to secure the end that I desire."

Well, what was to come was no affair of mine. The house was empty. Let them make of it a place of assignation. I could not stop them. Let Menabilly become, in one brief hour, the headquarters of the Royalist rising. Whether they succeeded or failed was not my business. "Did your father," I said, "send any word to me? Did he know that I was here?"

Dick stared at me blankly for a moment, as though I were in truth the half-wit I now believed myself to be.

"Why, yes, of course," he said. "That is why he picked on Menabilly, rather than on Caerhayes. There was no woman at Caerhayes to give him comfort."

"Does your father," I said, "still need comfort after two long years in Italy?"

"It depends," he answered, "what you intend by comfort. I never saw my father hold converse with Italian women. It might have made him better-tempered, if he had."

I saw Richard, in my mind's eye, pen in hand, with a map of Cornwall spread on a table before him. And dotted upon the map were the houses by the coast that offered sanctuary. Trelawne . . . too deeply wooded. Penrice . . . not close enough to the sea. Caerhayes . . . yes, good landing ground for troops, but not a single Miss Trevannion. Menabilly . . . with a beach, and a hiding-place, and an old love into the bargain, who had shared his life before and might be induced, even now, after long silence, to smile on him a moment after supper. And the pen would make a circle round the name of Menabilly. So I was become cynic in defeat. The rule of Parliament had taught me a lesson. But as I sat there watching Dick and thinking how little he resembled his father, I knew that all my anger was but a piece of bluff deceiving no one, not even my harder self, and that there was nothing I wanted in the world so much as to play hostess once more to Richard by candlelight, and to live again that life of strain and folly, anguish and enchantment.

CHAPTER THIRTY

It FELL ON me to warn the servants. I summoned each one to my chamber in turn. "We are entering upon dangerous days," I said to them. "Things will pass here at Menabilly which you will not see, and will not hear. Visitors will come and go. Ask no questions. Seek no answer. I believe you are, one and all, faithful subjects of His Majesty?"

This was sworn upon the Book of Common Prayer.

"One incautious word that leaves this house," I said, "and your master up in London will lose his life, and ourselves also, in all probability. That is all I have to say. See that there is clean linen on the beds, and sufficient food for guests. But be deaf and dumb and blind to those who come here."

It was on Matty's advice that I took them thus into my confidence. "Each one can be trusted," she said, "but a word of faith from you will bind them together, and not all the agents in the West Country will make them blab."

The household had lived sparsely since the siege of '44, and there were few comforts for our prospective visitors. No hangings to the walls, no carpets on the floors in the upper chambers. Straw mattresses in place of beds. They must make what shift they could, and be grateful.

Peter Courtney was the first to come. No secrecy for him. He flaunted openly his pretended return from France, dining with the Treffrys at Place upon the way and loudly announcing his desire to see his children. Gone to Trethurfe? But all his belongings were at Menabilly. Alice had misunderstood his letter. . . .

Nothing wan or pale about Peter. He wore a velvet coat that must have cost a fortune. Poor Alice and her dowry. . . .

"You might," I said to him, "have sent her a whisper of your safe return. She would have kept it secret."

He shrugged a careless shoulder. "A wife can be a cursed appendage in times like these," he said, "when a man must live from day to day, from hand to mouth. To tell the truth, Honor, I am so plagued with debts that one glimpse of her reproachful eyes would drive me crazy."

"You look well on it," I said. "I doubt if your conscience worries you unduly." He winked, his tongue in his cheek, and I thought how the looks that I had once admired were coarsened now with licence and good living. Too much French wine, too little exercise.

"And what are your plans," I asked, "when Parliament is overthrown?"

Once again he shrugged his shoulders. "I shall never settle at Trethurfe," he said. "Alice can live there if she pleases. As for myself, why, war has made me restless."

He whistled under his breath and strolled towards the window.

The next to come was Bunny Grenvile. Bunny, at seventeen, already head and shoulders taller than his cousin Dick. Bunny with snub nose and freckles. Bunny with eager, questing eyes, and a map of the coast under his arm. "Where are the beaches? Where are the landing-places? No, I want no refreshment. I have work to do. I want to see the ground." And he was off to the Gribben, a hound to scent, another budding soldier, like his brother Jack.

"You see," said Dick cynically, his black eyes fastened on me, "how all Grenvile men but me are bred with a nose for blood? You despise me, don't you, because I do not go with him?"

"No, Dick," I answered gently.

"Ah, but you will in time. Bunny will win your affection, as he has won my father's. Bunny has courage. Bunny has guts. Poor Dick has neither. He is only fit for painting, like a woman." He threw himself on his back upon the couch, staring upward at the ceiling.

Our third arrival was Mr Ambrose Manaton—a long-familiar name to me, for my family of Harris had for generations past had lawsuits with the Manatons respecting that same property of theirs, Trecarrel. What it was all about I could not say, but I know my father never spoke to any of them. There was an Ambrose Manaton who stood for Parliament before the war at Launceston. This man was his son. He was, I suppose, a few years older than Peter Courtney, some four-and-thirty years. Sleek and suave, with a certain latent charm. He wore his own fair hair, curling to his shoulders. Thinking it best spoken and so dismissed for ever, I plunged into the family dispute as soon as I set eyes on him. "Our families," I said, "have waged a private war for generations. Something to do with property. Since I am the youngest daughter, you are safe with me. I can lay claim to nothing."

"I could not refuse so fair a pleader, if you did," he answered.

I considered him thoughtfully as he kissed my hand. Too ready with his compliment, too easy with his smile. What exactly, I wondered, was his part in this campaign? I had not heard of him ever as a soldier. Money? . . . Property? . . . Those lands at Trecarrel and at Southhill that my father could not claim? Richard had no doubt assessed the value. A Royalist rising cannot be conducted without funds. Did Ambrose Manaton, then, hold the purse? I wondered what had induced him to risk his life and fortune. He gave me the clue a moment afterwards.

"Mrs Denys has not yet arrived?"

"Not yet. You know her well?"

"We found ourselves near neighbours in north Cornwall and north Devon." The tone was easy, the smile confident. Oh, Richard, my love of little scruple. So Gartred was the bait to catch the tiger.

What in the name of thunder had been going on all these long winter months at Bideford? I could imagine, with Gartred playing hostess. Well, I was hostess now at Menabilly. And the straw mattresses upstairs would be hard cheer after the feather beds of Orley Court. "My brother, General Harris, acts as bailiff to Mrs Denys, so I understand?"

"Why, yes, something of the sort," said Ambrose Manaton. He studied the toe of his boot. His voice was a shade over-casual.

"Have you seen your brother lately?" he asked.

"Not for two years. Not since Pendennis fell."

"You will see a change in him then. His nerves have gone to pieces. The result of the siege, no doubt."

Robin never had a nerve in his body. Robin rode to battle with a falcon on his wrist. If Robin was changed, it was not the fault of five months' siege. . . .

They came together, shortly before dark. I was alone in the gallery to receive them. The rule of Parliament had fallen light on Gartred. She was, I think, a little fuller in the bosom, but it became her well. And, chancing Fate, she had let Nature do its damndest with her hair, which was no longer gleaming gold, but streaked with silver white, making her look more lovely and more frail.

She tossed her cloak to Robin as she came into the room, proclaiming in that first careless gesture all that I cared to know of their relationship. The years slipped backward in a flash, and she was a bride of twenty-three, already tired of Kit, her slave and bondsman, who had not the strength of will to play the master.

It might have been Kit once again, standing there in the gallery at Menabilly, with a dog's look of adoration in his eyes.

But Ambrose Manaton was right. There was not only adoration in Robin's eyes. There was strain too, doubt, anxiety. And the heavy jowl and puffy cheeks betrayed the easy drinker. Defeat and Gartred had taken toll of my brother.

"We seem fated, you and I, to come together at moments of great crisis," I said to Gartred. "Do you still play piquet?"

I saw Robin look from one to the other of us, mystified, but Gartred smiled, drawing off her lace gloves.

"Piquet is out of fashion," she answered. "Dice is a later craze, but must be done in secret, since all games of chance are frowned upon by Parliament."

"I shall not join you, then," I said. "You will have to play with Robin or with Ambrose Manaton."

Her glance at me was swift, but I let it pass over my head.

"I have at least the consolation," she said, "of knowing that for once we shall not play in opposition. We are all partners on a winning side."

"Are we?" I said. It was only four years since she had come here as a spy for Lord Robartes.

"If you doubt my loyalty," said Gartred, "you must tell Richard when he comes. But it is rather late to make amends. I know all the secrets." She smiled again, and as I looked at her I felt like a knight of old, saluting his opponent before combat.

"I have put you," I said, "in the long chamber overhead, which Alice has with her children when she is home."

"Thank you," she said.

"Robin is on your left," I said, "and Ambrose Manaton upon your right, at the small bedroom at the stairs' head. With two strong men to guard you, I think it hardly likely you'll be nervous."

She gave not a flicker of the eyelid, but, turning to Robin, gave him some commands about her baggage. He went at once to obey her, like a servant.

"It has been fortunate for you," I said, "that the menfolk of my breed have proved accommodating."

"It would be more fortunate still," she answered, "if they could be at the same time less possessive."

"A family failing," I replied, "like the motto of our house, 'What we have, we hold.'"

She looked at me a moment thoughtfully. "It is a strange power," she said, "this magnetism that you have for Richard. I give you full credit."

I bowed to her from my chair. "Give me no credit, Gartred," I answered. "Menabilly is but a name upon a map, that will do as well as any other. An empty house, a nearby shore."

"And a secret hiding-place into the bargain," she said shrewdly.

But now it was my time to smile.

"The Mint had the silver long ago," I said, "and what was left has gone to swell the Parliament exchequer. What are you playing for this time, Gartred?"

She did not answer for a moment, but I saw her cat's eyes watching Robin's shadow in the hall.

"My daughters are grown up," she said. "Orley Court becomes a burden. Perhaps I would like a third husband and security."

Which my brother could not give to her, I thought, but which a man some fifteen years younger than herself, with lands and fortune, might be pleased to do. Mrs Harris . . . Mrs Denys . . . Mrs Manaton? "You broke one man in my family," I said. "Take care that you do not seek to break another."

"You think you can prevent me?"

"Not I. You may do as you please. I only give you warning."

"Warning of what?"

"You will never play fast and loose with Robin, as you did with Kit. Robin would be capable of murder."

She stared at me a moment, uncomprehending. And then my brother came into the room.

We made strange company for dinner. Gartred, her silver hair bejewelled, at the head of the table, and those two men on either side of her, my brother with hand ever reaching to the decanter, his eyes feasting on her face, while Ambrose Manaton, cool and self-possessed, kept up a flow of conversation in her right ear, excluding Robin, about the corrupt practices of Parliament—which made me suspect he must have a share in it, from knowing so much detail. On my left sat Peter Courtney, who from time to time caught Gartred's eye and smiled in knowing fashion. But as he did the same to the serving-maid who passed his plate, and to me when I chanced to glance his way, I guessed it to be habit rather than conspiracy. I knew my Peter. Dick glowered in the centre, throwing black looks towards his cousin opposite as he rattled on about the letters he had received from his brother Jack, who was grown so high in favour with the Prince of Wales in France that they were never parted. And as I looked at each in turn, seeing they were served with food and wine, playing the hostess in this house that was not mine, frowned upon, no doubt, by the ghost of old John Rashleigh, I thought, with some misgiving, that had Richard sought his hardest in the county he could not have found six people more likely to fall out and disagree than those who sat around the table now.

Gartred, his sister, had never wished him well. Robin, my brother, had disobeyed his orders in the past. Peter Courtney was one of those who had muttered at his leadership. Dick, his son, feared and hated him. Ambrose Manaton was an unknown quantity, and Bunny, his nephew, a pawn who could read a map. Were these to be the leaders of the rising? If so, God help poor Cornwall and the Prince of Wales.

"My uncle," Bunny was saying, arranging the salt cellars in the fashion of a fort, "never forgets an injury. He told me once, if a man does him an ill turn, he will serve him with a worse one."

He went on to describe some battle of the past, to which no one listened, I think, except Peter, who did so from good nature. But the words Bunny had spoken so lightly rang strangely in my head. "My uncle never forgets an injury."

He must have been injured by all of us at one time or other, seated at the table now at Menabilly. What a time to choose to pay old scores, Richard, my lover, mocking and malevolent. The eve of a rising, and these six people in it to the hilt.

There was something symbolic in the empty chair beside me.

Then we fell silent, for the door suddenly opened and he stood there, watching us, his hat upon his head, his long cloak hanging from his shoulders. Gone was the auburn hair I loved so well, and the curled wig that fell below his ears gave him a dark, satanic look that matched his smile.

"What a bunch of prizes," he said, "for the Sheriff of the Duchy if he chose to call. Each one of you a traitor."

They stared at him, blankly—even Gartred, for once, slow to follow his swift mind. But I saw Dick start and gnaw his fingernails. Then Richard tossed his hat and cloak to the waiting servant in the hall and came to the empty chair at my right side.

"Have you been waiting long?" he said to me.

"Two years and three months," I answered him.

He filled the glass from the decanter at his side.

"In January, '46," he said to the company, "I broke a promise to our hostess here. I left her one morning at Werrington, saying I would be back again to breakfast with her. Unfortunately, the Prince of Wales willed otherwise. And I breakfasted instead in Launceston. Castle. I propose to make amends for this to-morrow."

He lifted his glass, draining it in one measure, then put out his hand to mine, and held it on the table.

"Thank God," he said, "for a woman who does not give a damn for punctuality."

CHAPTER THIRTY-ONE

It was like Werrington once more. The old routine. The old haphazard sharing of our days and nights. He would burst into my chamber as I breakfasted, my toilet undone, my hair in curl rags, while he paced about the room talking incessantly, touching my brushes, my combs, my bracelets on the table, cursing all the while at some delay in the plans he was proposing. Trevannion was too slow. Trelawney the elder too cautious. And those who were to lead the insurrection farther west had none of them big names—they were all small fry, lacking the right qualities for leadership. "Grose of St Buryan, Maddern of Penzance, Keigwin of Mousehole," said Richard; "none of them held a higher rank than captain in '46, and have never led troops into action. But we have to use them now. It is a case of *faute de mieux*. The trouble is that I can't be in fifty places at the same time."

Like Werrington once more. A log fire in the dining-chamber. A heap of papers scattered on the table, and a large map in the centre. Richard seated in his chair, with Bunny, instead of Jack, at his elbow. The red crosses on the beaches where the invading troops should land. Crinnis. . . . Pentewan. . . . Veryan. . . . The beacons on the headlands to warn the ships at sea. The Gribben. . . . The Dodman. . . . The Nare. . . . My brother Robin standing by the door, where Colonel Roscarrock would have stood. And Peter Courtney riding into the courtyard, bearing messages from Jonathan Trelawney.

"What news from Talland?"

"All well. They will wait upon our signal. Looe can easily be held. There will be no opposition there to matter."

The messages sifted, one by one. Like all defeated peoples, those who had crumbled first in '46 were now the most eager to reel. Helston. . . . Penzance. . . . St Ives. . . . The confidence was supreme. Grenvile, as commander in chief, had but to give the word.

I sat in my chair by the fireside, listening to it all, and I was no longer in the dining-chamber at Menabilly, but back at Werrington, at Ottery St Mary, at Exeter. . . . The same problems, the same arguments, the same doubting of the commanders, the same swift decisions. Richard's pen pointing to the Scillies. "This will be the main base for the Prince's army. No trouble about seizing the islands. Your brother Jack can do it with two men and a boy." And Bunny, grinning, nodded his auburn head. "Then the main landings to be where we have our strongest hold. A line between here and Falmouth, I should fancy, with St Mawes the main objective."

The big conferences would be held at night. It was easier then to move about the roads. The Trelawneys from Trelawne, Sir Charles Trevannion from Caerhayes, the Arundells from Trerice, Sir Arthur Bassett from Tehidy. I would lie in my chamber overhead and hear the drone of voices from the dining-room below, and always that clear tone of Richard's, overtopping them all. Was it certain that the French would play? This was the universal doubt, expressed by the whole assembly, that Richard would brush impatiently aside. 'God damn the French. What the hell does it matter if they don't? We can do without them. Never a Frenchman yet but was not a liability to his own side."

"But," murmured Sir Charles Trevannion, "if we at least had the promise of their support, and a token force to assist the Prince in landing, the moral effect upon Parliament would be as valuable as ten divisions put against them."

"Don't you believe it," said Richard. "The French hate fighting on any soil but their own. Show a frog an English pike, and he will show you his backside. Leave the French alone. We won't need them once we hold the Scillies and the Cornish forts. The Mount . . . Pendennis . . . St Mawes . . . Bunny, where are my notes giving the present disposition of the enemy troops? Now, gentlemen . . ."

And so it would continue. Midnight, one, two, three o'clock. What hour they went, and what hour he came to bed, I would not know, for exhaustion would lay claim to me long since.

Robin, who had proved his worth in those five weeks at Pendennis, had much responsibility upon his shoulders. The episode of the bridge had been forgotten. Or had it? I would wonder sometimes, when I watched Richard's eye upon him. Saw him smile for no reason. Saw him tap his pen upon his chin.

"Have you the latest news from Helston?"

"Here, sir. To hand."

"I shall want you to act as deputy for me to-morrow at Penrose. You can be away two nights; no more. I must have the exact number of men they can put upon the roads between Helston and Penryn."

"Sir . . ." And I would see Robin hesitate a moment, his eyes drift towards the door leading to the gallery, where Gartred's laugh would suddenly ring loud and clear. Later his flushed face and bloodshot eye told its own tale.

"Come, Robin," Richard would say curtly, after supper, "we must burn the midnight candle once again. Peter has brought me messages in cypher from Penzance, and you are my expert. If I can do with four hours' sleep, so can the rest of you."

Richard, Robin, Peter, Bunny, crowded round the table in the dining-room, with Dick standing sentinel at the door, watching them wearily, resentfully. Ambrose Manaton by the fire, consulting a great sheaf of figures. "All right, Ambrose," Richard would say, "I shan't need your assistance over this problem. Go and talk high finance to the women in the gallery."

And Ambrose Manaton smiling, bowing his thanks. Walking from the room with a shade too much confidence, humming under his breath.

"Will you be late?" I said to Richard.

"H'm . . . H'm . . ." he answered absently. "Fetch me that file of papers, Bunny." Then of a sudden, looking up at Dick, "Stand straight, can't you? Don't slop over your feet," he said harshly.

Dick's black eyes blinking, his slim hands clutching at his coat. He would open the door for me to pass through in my chair, and all I could do to give him confidence was to smile and touch his hand. No gallery for me. Three makes poor company. But upstairs to my chamber, knowing that the voices underneath would drone for four hours more. An hour, perhaps, would pass, while I read on my bed, and then the swish of a skirt upon the landing as Gartred passed into her room. Silence. Then that tell-tale creaking stair. The soft closing of a door. But beneath me in the dining-room the voices would drone on till after midnight.

One evening, when the conference broke early and Richard sat with me awhile before retiring, I told him bluntly what I heard.

He laughed, trimming his finger-nails by the open window.

"Have you turned prude, sweetheart, in your middle years?" he said.

"Prudery be damned," I answered. "But my brother hopes to marry her. I know it, from his hints and shy allusions about rebuilding the property at Lanrest."

"Then hope will fail him," replied Richard. "Gartred will never throw herself away upon a penniless soldier. She has other fish to fry, and small blame to her."

"You mean," I asked, "the fish she is in the process of frying at this moment?"

"Why, yes, I suppose so," he answered, with a shrug. "Ambrose has a pretty inheritance from his Trefusis mother, besides what he will come into when his father dies. Gartred would be a fool if she let him slip from her."

How calmly the Grenviles seized fortunes for themselves.

"What exactly," I said, "does he contribute to your present business?" He cocked an eye at me, and grinned.

"Don't poke your snub nose into my affairs," he said. "I know what I'm about. I'll tell you one thing, though: we'd have difficulty in paying for this affair without him."

"So I thought," I answered.

"Taking me all round," he said, "I'm a pretty cunning fellow."

"If you call it cunning," I said, "to play one member of your staff against another. For my part, I would call it knavery."

"Good generalship," he said.

"Gerry-mandering," I answered.

"A *ruse de guerre*," he countered.

"Pawky politics," I argued.

"Ah, well," he said, "if the manœuvre serves my purpose it matters not how many lives be broken in the process."

"Take care they're broken afterwards, and not before," I said.

He came and sat beside me on the bed.

"I think you mislike me much, now my hair is black," he suggested.

"It becomes your beauty, but not your disposition."

"Dark foxes leave no trail behind them."

"Red ones are more lovable."

"When the whole future of a country is at stake, emotions are thrown overboard."

"Emotions, but not honour."

"Is that a pun upon your name?"

"If you like to take it so.'

He took my hands in his and pressed them backwards on the pillow, smiling. "Your resistance was stronger at eighteen," he said.

"And your approach more subtle."

"It had to be, in that confounded apple-tree."

He laid his head upon my shoulder, and turned my face to his.

"I can swear in Italian now, as well as Spanish," he said to me.

"Turkish also?"

"A word or two. The bare necessity."

He settled himself against me in contentment. One eye drooped. The other regarded me malevolently from the pillow.

"There was a woman I encountered once in Naples . . ."

"With whom you passed an hour?"

"Three to be exact."

"Tell the tale to Peter," I yawned. "It doesn't interest me."

He lifted his hands to my hair and took the curlers from it.

"If you placed these rags upon you in the day, it would be more to your advantage and to mine," he mused. "Where was I, though? Ah, yes, the Neapolitan."

"Let her sleep, Richard, and me also."

"I only wished to tell you her remark to me on leaving. 'So it is true, what I have always heard,' she said to me, 'that you Cornishmen are famed for one thing only, which is wrestling?' 'Signorina,' I replied, 'there is a lady waiting for me in Cornwall who would give me credit for something else besides.'" He stretched and yawned and, propping himself on his elbow, blew the candle. "But there," he said, "those southern women were as dull as milk. My vulpine methods were too much for them."

The nights passed thus, and the days as I have described them. Little by little the plans fell into line, the schemes were tabulated. The final message came from the Prince in France that the French fleet had been put at his disposal, and an army, under the command of Lord Hopton, would land in force in Cornwall while the Prince, with Sir John Grenvile, seized the Scillies. The landing was to coincide with the insurrection of the Royalists under Sir Richard Grenvile, who would take and hold the key-points in the Duchy.

Saturday, the thirteenth of May, was the date chosen for the Cornish rising. . . . The daffodils had bloomed, the blossom was all blown, and the first hot days of summer came without warning on the first of May. The sea below the Gribben was glassy calm, the sky deep blue, without a single cloud. The labourers worked in the fields, and the fishing-boats put out to sea from Gorran and Polperro. In Fowey all was quiet. The townsfolk went about their business, the Parliamentary agents scribbled their roll upon roll of useless records to be filed in dusty piles up in Whitehall and the sentries at the castle stared yawning out to sea. I sat out on the causeway, watching the young lambs, and thinking, as the hot sun shone upon my bare head, how in a bare week now the whole peaceful countryside would be in an uproar once again. Men shouting, fighting, dying. . . . The sheep scattered, the cattle driven, the people running homeless on the roads. Gunfire once again, the rattle of musketry. The galloping of horses, the tramp of marching feet. Wounded men dragging themselves into the hedges, there to die untended. The young corn trampled, the cottage thatch in flames. All the old anxiety, the old strain and terror. The enemy are advancing. The enemy are in retreat. Hopton has landed in force. Hopton has been repulsed. The Cornish are triumphant. The Cornish have been driven back. Rumours, counter-rumours. The bloody stench of war. . . .

The planning was all over now, and the long wait had begun. A week of nerves, sitting at Menabilly with our eyes upon the clock. Richard, in high spirits as always before battle, played bowls with Bunny in the little walled green beside the steward's empty lodge. Peter, in sudden realisation of his flabby stomach muscles, rode furiously up and down the sands at Par to reduce his weight. Robin was very silent. He took long walks alone, down in the woods, and on returning went first to the dining-room, where the wine-decanter stood. I would find him there sometimes, glass in hand, brooding; and when I questioned him he would answer me evasively, his eyes strangely watchful, like a dog listening for the footstep of a stranger. Gartred, usually so cool and indifferent when she had the whip hand in a love affair, showed herself, for the first time, less certain and less sure. Whether it was because Ambrose Manaton was fifteen years her junior, and the possibility of marriage with him hung upon a thread, I do not know, but a new carelessness had come upon her which was, to my mind, the symbol of a losing touch. That she was heavily in debt at Orley Court I knew for certain. Richard had told me as much. Youth lay behind her. And a future without a third husband to support her would be hard going, once her beauty went. A dowager, living in retirement with her married daughters, dependent on the charity of a son-in-law? What an end for Gartred Grenvile! So she became careless. She smiled too openly at

Ambrose Manaton. She put her hand on his at the dining-table. She watched him, over the rim of her glass, with that same greed I had noticed years before when, peeping through her chamber door, I had seen her stuff the trinkets in her gown. And Ambrose Manaton, flattered, confident, raised his glass to her in return.

"Send her away," I said to Richard. "God knows she has caused ill feeling enough already. What possible use can she be to you now, here at Menabilly?"

"If Gartred went, Ambrose would follow her," he answered. "I can't afford to lose my treasurer. You don't know the fellow as I do. He's as slippery as an eel, and as close-fisted as a Jew. Once back with her in Bideford, and he might pull out of the business altogether."

"Then send Robin packing. He will be no use to you, anyway, if he continues drinking in this manner."

"Nonsense. Drink in his case is stimulation, the only way to ginger him. When the day comes I'll ply him so full of brandy that he will take St Mawes Castle single-handed."

"I don't enjoy watching my brother go to pieces."

"He isn't here for your enjoyment. He is here because he is of use to me, and one of the few officers that I know who doesn't lose his head in battle. The more rattled he becomes, here at Menabilly, the better he will fight outside it."

He watched me balefully, blowing a cloud of smoke into the air.

"My God," I said, "have you no pity at all?"

"None," he said, "where military matters are concerned."

"You can sit here, quite contentedly, with your sister behaving like a whore upstairs, holding one string of Manaton's purse and you the other; while my brother, who loves her, drinks himself to death and breaks his heart?"

"To hell with his heart. His sword is all I care about, and his ability to wield it."

And, leaning from the window in the gallery, he whistled his nephew Bunny to a game of bowls. I watched them both, jesting with one another like a pair of schoolboys without a care, casting their coats upon the short green turf. "God damn the Grenviles, one and all," I said, my nerves in ribbons. As I spoke, thinking myself alone, I felt a slim hand touch me on the shoulder, and heard a boy's voice whisper in my ear, "That's what my mother said, eighteen years ago."

And there was Dick behind me, his black eyes glowing in his pale face, gazing out across the lawn towards his father and young Bunny.

CHAPTER THIRTY-TWO

Thursday the eleventh of May dawned as hot and sticky as its predecessors. Eight-and-forty hours to go before the torch of war was lit once more in Cornwall. Even Richard was on edge that morning, when word came from a messenger at noon to say that spies had reported a meeting, a few days since, at Saltash, between the Parliamentary commander in the west, Sir Hardress Waller, and several of the Parliamentary gentlemen, and that instructions had been given to double the guards at the chief towns throughout the Duchy. Some members of the Cornish County Committee had gone themselves to Helston to see if all was quiet.

"One false move now," said Richard quietly, "and all our plans will have been made in vain."

We were gathered in the dining-room, I well remember, save only Gartred, who was in her chamber, and I can see now the drawn, anxious faces of the men as they gazed in silence at their leader. Robin, heavy, brooding; Peter, tapping his hand upon his knee; Bunny, with knitted brows; and Dick, as ever, gnawing at his hand.

"The one thing I have feared all along," said Richard. "Those fellows in the west can't hold their tongues. Like ill-trained redhawks, too keen to sight the quarry. I warned Keigwin and Grose to stay this last week within doors, as we have done, and hold no conferences. No doubt they have been out upon the roads, the whispers have the speed of lightning." He stood by the window, his hands behind his back. We were all, I believe, a little sick with apprehension. I saw Ambrose Manaton rub his hands nervously together, his usual composure momentarily lost to him.

"If anything should go wrong," he ventured, hesitating, "what arrangements can be made for our own security?"

Richard threw him a contemptuous glance. "None," he said briefly. He returned to the table, and gathered up his papers.

"You have your orders, one and all," he said. "You know what you have to do. Let us rid ourselves, then, of all this rubbish, useless to us once the battle starts."

He began to throw the maps and documents into the fire, while the others still stared at him, uncertain.

"Come," said Richard. "You look, the whole damned lot of you, like a flock of crows before a funeral. On Saturday we make a bid for freedom. If any man is afraid let him say so now, and I'll put a halter round his neck for treason to the Prince of Wales."

Not one of us made answer. Richard turned to Robin. "I want you to ride to Trelawne," he said, "and tell Jonathan Trelawney and his son that the rendezvous for the thirteenth is changed. They and Sir Arthur Bassett must join Sir Charles Trevannion at Caerhayes. Tell them to go to-night, skirting the high roads, and accompany them there."

"Sir," said Robin slowly, rising to his feet, and I think I was the only one who saw the flicker of his glance at Ambrose Manaton. As for myself, a weight was lifted from me. With Robin gone from the house, I, his sister, might safely breathe again. Let Gartred and her new lover make what they could of the few hours remaining. I did not care a jot so long as Robin was not there to listen to them.

"Bunny," said his uncle, "you have the boat at Pridmouth standing by in readiness?"

"Sir," said Bunny, his grey eyes dancing. He was, I think, the only one who still believed he played at soldiers.

"Then we shall rendezvous also at Caerhayes," said Richard, "at daybreak on the thirteenth. You can sail to Gorran to-morrow, and give my last directions about the beacon on the Dodman. A few hours on salt-water in this weather will be good practice for your stomach." He smiled at the lad, who answered it with boyish adoration, and I saw Dick lower his head and trace imaginary lines upon the table with slow, hesitating hand.

"Peter?" said Richard.

Alice's husband leapt to his feet, drawn from some pleasant reverie of French wine and women to the harsh reality of the world about him. "My orders, sir?"

"Go to Caerhayes and warn Trevannion that the plans are changed. Tell him the Trelawneys and Bassett will be joining him. Then return here to Menabilly in the morning. And a word of warning, Peter."

"What is that, sir?"

"Don't go a-Courtneying on the way there. There is not a woman worth it, from Tywardreath to Dodman."

Peter turned pink, for all his bravado, but nerved himself to answer "Sir" with great punctiliousness.

He and Robin left the room together, followed by Bunny and by Ambrose Manaton. Richard yawned and stretched his arms above his head, and then, wandering to the hearth, stirred the black embers of his papers in the ashes.

"Have you no commands for me?" said Dick slowly.

"Why, yes," said Richard, without turning his head, "Alice Courtney's daughters must have left some dolls behind them. Go search in the attics, and fashion them new dresses."

Dick did not answer. But he went, I think, a little whiter than before, and, turning on his heel, left the room.

"One day," I said, "you will provoke him once too often."

"That is my intention," answered Richard.

"Does it please you, then, to see him writhe in torment?"

"I hope to see him stand up to me at last, not take it lying down like a coward."

"Sometimes," I said, "I think that after twenty years I know even less about you than I did when I was eighteen."

"Very probably."

"No father in the world would act as harshly to his son as you do to your Dick."

"I only act harshly because I wish to purge his mother's whore blood from his veins."

"You will more likely kindle it."

He shrugged his shoulders and we fell silent a moment, listening to the sound of the horses' hooves echoing across the park as Robin and Peter rode to their separate destinations.

"I saw my daughter up in London, when I lay concealed there for a while," said Richard suddenly.

Foolishly, a pang of jealousy shot through my heart, and I answered like a wasp. "Freckled, I suppose? A prancing miss?"

"Nay. Rather studious and quiet. Dependable. She put me in mind of my mother. 'Bess,' I said to her, 'will you look after me in my declining years?' 'Why, yes,' she answered, 'if you send for me.' I think she cares as little for that bitch as I do."

"Daughters," I said, "are never favourites with their mothers. Especially when they come to be of age. How old is she?"

"Near seventeen," he said, "with all that natural bloom upon her that young people have. . . ." He stared absently before him. This moment, I thought with great lucidity and calm above the anguish, is in a sense our moment of farewell, our parting of the ways, but he does not know it. Now his daughter is of age he will not need me.

"Heigh-ho," he said. "I think I start to feel my eight-and-forty years. My leg hurts damnably to-day, and no excuse for it, with the sun blazing in the sky."

"Suspense," I said, "and all that goes along with it."

"When this campaign is over," he said, "and we hold all Cornwall for the Prince of Wales, I'll say good-bye to soldiering. I'll build a palace on the north coast, near to Stowe, and live in quiet retirement, like a gentleman."

"Not you," I said. "You'd quarrel with all your neighbours."

"I'd have no neighbours," he answered, "save my own Grenvile clan. My God, we'd make a clean sweep of the Duchy. Jack, and Bunny, and I. D'you think the Prince would make me Earl of Launceston?" He laid his hand upon my head an instant and then was gone, whistling for Bunny, and I sat there alone, in the empty dining-room, despondent, oddly sad. . . .

That evening we all went early to our beds, with the thunder that would not come still heavy in the air. Richard had taken Jonathan Rashleigh's chamber for his own, with Dick and Bunny in the dressing-rooms between.

Now Peter and Robin had gone, the one to Caerhayes, the other to Trelawne, I thought, with cynicism, that Ambrose Manaton and Gartred could indulge their separate talents for invention until the morning, should the spirit move them.

A single door between their chambers, and I the only neighbour, at the head of the stairs. I heard Gartred come first, and Ambrose follow her—then all was silent on the landing. Ah well, I thought, wrapping my shawl around me, thank God I can grow old with some complacency. White hairs could come, and lines, and crow's feet, and they would not worry me. I did not have to struggle for a third husband, not having had a first. But it was hard to sleep, with the full moon creeping to my window.

I could not hear the clock in the belfry from my present chamber, as I used to in the gatehouse, but it must have been near midnight, or just after, when I woke suddenly from the light sleep into which I had fallen, it seemed, but a few moments earlier, with a fancy that I had heard someone moving in the dining-room below. Yes, there it was distinctly. The furtive sound of one who blundered his way in darkness, and bumped into a table, or a chair. I raised myself in my bed and listened. All was silent once again. But I was not easy. I put my hand out to my chair and dragged it to me, then listened once again. Then sudden, unmistakable, came the stealthy tread of a footstep on the creaking tell-tale stair. Some intuition, subconscious perhaps from early in the day, warned me of disaster. I lowered myself into my chair, and without waiting to light my candle—nor was there need with the moon casting a white beam on the carpet—I propelled myself across the room and turned the handle of my door.

"Who is there?" I whispered.

There was no answer, and, coming to the landing, I looked down upon the stair and saw a dark figure crouching there, his back against the wall, the moonlight gleaming on the naked sword in his hand. He stood in stockinged feet, his shirt-sleeves rolled above his elbow—my brother Robin, with murder in his eyes. He said nothing to me, only waited to see what I would do.

"Two years ago," I said softly, "you disobeyed an order given you by your commander, because of a private quarrel. That was in January, '46. Do you intend to do the same in May of '48?"

He crept close and stood on the top stair beside me, breathing strangely. I could smell the brandy on his breath.

"I have disobeyed no one," he said. "I gave my message. I parted with the Trelawneys at the top of Polmear hill."

"Richard bade you accompany them to Caerhayes," I said.

"No need to do so, Trelawney told me—two horsemen pass more easily than three. Let me by, Honor."

"No, Robin. Not yet. Give me first your sword."

He did not answer. He stood staring at me, looking, with his tumbled hair and troubled eyes, so like the ghost of our dead brother Kit that I trembled, even as his hands did on his sword. "You cannot fool me," he said, "neither you, nor Richard Grenvile. This business was but a pretext to send me from the house, so that they could be together."

He looked upward to the landing and the closed door of the room beyond the stairs.

"Go to bed, Robin," I said, "or come and sit with me in my chamber. Let me talk to you awhile."

"No," he said. "This is my moment. They will be together now. If you try to prevent me, I shall hurt you also."

He brushed past my chair and made across the landing, tiptoeing, furtive, in his stockinged feet, and whether he was drunk or mad I could not tell. I knew only the purpose in his eyes.

"For God's sake, Robin," I said, "do not go into that room. Reason with them in the morning, if you must, but not now, not at this hour."

For answer he turned the handle, a smile upon his lips both horrible and strange, and I wheeled then, sobbing, and went back into my room and hammered loudly at the dressing-rooms where Dick and Bunny slept.

"Call Richard," I said. "Bid him come quickly, now, this instant. And you too, both of you. There is no time to lose."

A startled voice—Bunny's, I believe—made answer, and I heard him clamber from his bed. But I had turned again, and crossed my room towards the landing, where all was silent still, and undisturbed. Nothing but the moonlight shining strong into the eastern windows. And then there came that sound for which I waited, piercing the silence with its shrill intensity. Not an oath, not a man's voice raised in anger, but the shocking horror of a woman's scream.

CHAPTER THIRTY-THREE

ACROSS THE LANDING, through Ambrose Manaton's empty room to Gartred's chamber beyond. The wheels of my chair turning slowly, for all my labour. And all the while calling, "Richard . . . Richard . . ." with a note in my voice I did not recognise.

Oh, God, that fight there in the moonlight, the cold white light pouring into the unshuttered windows, and Gartred with a crimson gash upon her face clinging to the hangings of the bed. Ambrose Manaton, his silken nightshirt stained with blood, warding off with his bare hands the desperate blows that Robin aimed at him, until, with a despairing cry, he reached the sword that lay among his heap of clothes upon a chair. Their bare feet padded on the boards, their breath came quick and short, and they seemed, the two of them, like phantom figures, lunging, thrusting, now in moonlight and now in shadow, with no word uttered. "Richard . . ." I called again, for this was murder, here before my eyes, with the two men between me and the bed where Gartred crouched, her hands to her face, the blood running down between her fingers.

He came at last, half-clad, carrying his sword, with Dick and Bunny at his heels bearing candles. "An end to this, you God-damned idiots," he shouted, forcing himself between them, his own sword shivering their blades, and there was Robin, his right wrist hanging limp, with Richard holding him, and Ambrose Manaton back against the farther wall, with Bunny by his side.

They stared at one another, Robin and Ambrose Manaton, like animals in battle, chests heaving, eyes bloodshot, and suddenly Robin, seeing Gartred's face, realised what his work had done. He opened his mouth to speak, but no words came. He trembled, powerless to move or utter, and Richard pushed him to a chair and held him there. "Call Matty," said Richard to me. "Get water, bandages. . . ."

Once more I turned to the landing, but already the household were astir, the frightened servants gathering in the hall below, the candles lit. "Go back to bed," said Richard harshly. "No one of you is needed, save Mistress Honor's woman. There has been a trifling accident, but no harm done." I heard them shuffle, whisper, retire to their own quarters, and here was Matty, staunch, dependable, seizing the situation at a glance and fetching bowls of water, strips of clean linen. The room was lit now by some half-dozen candles. The phantom scene was done, the grim reality was with us still.

Those tumbled clothes upon the floor, Gartred's and his. Manaton leaning upon Bunny's arm, staunching the cuts he had received, his fair curls lank and damp with sweat. Robin upon a chair, his head buried in his hands, all passion spent. Richard standing by his side, grim and purposeful. And one and all we looked at Gartred on the bed, with that great gash upon her face from her right eyebrow to her chin. It was then, for the first time, that I noticed Dick.

His face was ashen white, his eyes transfixed in horror, and suddenly he reeled and fell, as the blood that stained the clean white linen spread and trickled on to Matty's hands.

Richard made no move. He said to Bunny, between clenched teeth, his eyes averted from his son's limp body, "Carry the spawn to his bed and leave him." Bunny obeyed, and as I watched him stagger from the room, his cousin in his arms, I thought with cold and deadly weariness: "This is the end. This is finality."

Someone brought brandy. Bunny, I suppose, on his return. We had our measure, all of us. Robin drinking slow and deep, his hands shaking as he held his glass. Ambrose Manaton quick and nervous, the colour that had gone soon coming to his face again. Then Gartred, moaning faintly, with her head on Matty's shoulder, her silver hair still horribly bespattered with her blood.

"I do not propose," said Richard slowly, "to hold an inquest. What has been, has been. We are on the eve of deadly matters, with the whole future of a kingdom now at stake. This is no time for any man to seek private vengeance in a quarrel. When men have sworn an oath to my command, I demand obedience."

Not one of them made answer. Robin gazed, limp and shattered, at the floor.

"We will snatch," said Richard, "what hours of sleep we can, until the morning. I will remain with Ambrose in his room, and Bunny, stay with Robin. In the morning you will go together to Caerhayes, where I shall join you. Can I ask you, Matty, to remain here with Mrs Denys?"

"Yes, Sir Richard," said Matty steadily.

"How is her pulse? Has she lost much blood?"

"She is well enough now, Sir Richard. The bandages are firm. Sleep and rest will work wonders by the morning."

"No danger to her life?"

"No, Sir Richard. The cut was jagged, but not deep. The only damage done is to her beauty." Matty's lips twitched in the way I knew, and I wondered how much she guessed of what had happened.

Ambrose Manaton did not look towards the bed. The woman who lay upon it might have been a stranger. "This is their finish too," I thought. "Gartred will never become Mrs Manaton and own Trecarrel."

I turned my eyes from Gartred, white and still, and felt Richard's hands upon my chair. "You," he said quietly, "have had enough for one night to contend with." He took me to my room, and, lifting me from my chair, laid me down upon my bed.

"Will you sleep?" he said.

"I think not," I answered.

"Rest easy. We shall be gone so soon. A few hours more and it will be over. War makes a good substitute for private quarrels."

"I wonder. . . ."

He left me and went back to Ambrose Manaton, not, I reflected, for love, to share his slumbers, but to make sure his treasurer did not slip from him in the few remaining hours left to us before daylight. Bunny had gone with Robin to his room, and this also, I surmised, was a precaution. Remorse and brandy have driven stronger men than Robin to their suicide.

What hope of sleep had any of us? There was the full moon, high now in the heavens, and you, I thought, shining there in the hushed gardens with your pale cold face above the shadows, have witnessed strange things this night at Menabilly. We Harrises and Grenviles had paid ill return for Rashleigh hospitality. . . .

The hours slipped by, and I suddenly remembered Dick, who slept in the dressing-room next door to me, alone. Poor lad, faint at the sight of blood as he had been in the past, was he now lying, wakeful like me, with shame upon his conscience? I thought I heard him stir, and I wondered if dreams haunted him, as they did me, and if he wished for company. "Dick . . ." I called softly. "Dick . . ." I called again, but there was no answer. Later, a little breeze, rising from the sea, made a draught come to my room from the open window and, playing with the latch upon the door, shook it free, so that it swung to and fro, banging every instant like a loosened shutter.

He must sleep deep, then, if it did not waken him.

The moon went, and the morning light stole in and cleared the shadows, and still the door between our two rooms creaked, and closed, and creaked again, making a nagging accompaniment to my uneasy slumbers. Maddened at last, I climbed to my chair to shut it, and as my hand fastened on the latch I saw through the crack of the door that Dick's bed was empty. He was not in the room. . . .

Numb and exhausted, I stumbled to my bed. "He has gone to find Bunny," I thought. "He has gone to Bunny and to Robin." But before me was the picture of his white, anguished face, and sleep, when it did come, could not banish the memory.

Next morning, when I woke to find the broad sun streaming in my room, the scenes of the hours before held a nightmare quality. I longed for them to dissipate, as nightmares do, but when Matty bore in my breakfast I knew them to be true.

"Yes, Mrs Denys had some sleep," she answered to my query, "and will, to my mind, be little worse for her adventure until she lifts her bandage." Matty, with a sniff, had small pity in her bosom.

"Will the gash not heal in time?" I asked.

"Aye, it will heal," she said, "but she'll bear the scar there for her lifetime. She'll find it hard to trade her beauty now." She spoke with a certain relish, as though the events of the preceding night had wiped away a legion of old scores.

"Mrs Denys," said Matty, "has got what she deserved."

Had she? Was this a chess-board move, long planned by the Almighty, or were we, one and all, just fools to fortune? I knew one thing—since I had seen the gash on Gartred's face, I hated her no longer. . . .

"Were all the gentlemen at breakfast?" I said suddenly.

"I believe so."

"And Master Dick as well?"

"Yes. He came somewhat later than the others, but I saw him in the dining-room an hour ago."

A wave of relief came to me, for no reason except that he was safely in the house. "Help me to dress," I said to Matty.

Friday, the twelfth of May. A hazard might have made it the thirteenth. Some sense of delicacy kept me from Gartred's chamber. Now her beauty was marred, she and I would now hold equal ground, and I had no wish to press the matter home. Other women might have gone to her, feigning commiseration, but with triumph in their hearts, but Honor Harris was not one of them. I sent messages by Matty that she should ask for what she wanted, and left her to her thoughts. . . . I found Robin in the gallery, standing moodily beside the window, his right arm in a sling. He turned his head at my approach, then looked away again in silence.

"I thought you had departed with Bunny to Caerhayes," I said to him.

"We wait for Peter Courtney," he answered dully. "He has not yet returned."

"Does your wrist pain you?" I asked gently.

He shook his head, and went on staring from the window.

"When the shouting is over, and the turmoil done," I said, "we will keep house together, you and I, as we did once at Lanrest."

Still he did not answer, but I saw the tears start in his eyes.

"We have loved the Grenviles long enough," I said, "each in our separate fashion. The time has come when they must learn to live without us."

"They have done that," he said, his voice low, "for nearly thirty years. It is we who are dependent upon them."

These were the last words we ever held upon the subject, Robin and I, from that day unto this. Reserve has kept us silent, though we have lived together for five years. . . .

The door opened and Richard came into the gallery, Bunny at his shoulder like a shadow.

"I cannot understand it," he said, pacing the floor in irritation. "Here it is nearly noon, and no sign yet of Peter. If he left Caerhayes at daybreak, he should have been here long since. I suppose, like every other fool, he has thought best to ignore my orders."

The barb was lost on Robin, who was too far gone in misery to mind. "If you permit me," he said humbly, "I can ride in search of him. He may have stayed to breakfast with the Sawles at Penrice."

"He is more likely behind a haystack with a wench," said Richard. "My God, I will have eunuchs on my staff, next time I go to war. Go then, if you like, but keep a watch upon the roads. I have heard reports of troops through St Blazey. The rumour may be false, and yet . . ." He broke off in the middle of his speech, and resumed his pacing of the room. Presently we heard Robin mount his horse and ride away. The hours wore on, the clock in the belfry struck twelve, and later one. The servants brought cold meat and ale, and we helped ourselves, haphazard, all of us with little appetite, our ears strained for sound. At half-past one there was a footfall on the stairs, slow and laboured, and I noticed Ambrose Manaton glance unconsciously to the chamber overhead, then draw back against the window. The handle of the door was turned, and Gartred stood before us, dressed for travel, one side of her face shrouded with a veil, a cloak around her shoulders. No one spoke as she stood there like a spectre. "I wish," she said at length, "to return to Orley Court. Conveyance must be found for me."

"You ask for the impossible," said Richard shortly, "and no one knows it better now than you. In a few hours the roads will be impassable."

"I'll take my chance of that," she said. "If I fall fighting with the rabble, I think I shall not greatly care. I have done what you asked me to do. My part is played."

Her eyes were upon Richard all the while, and never once on Ambrose Manaton. Richard and Gartred. . . . Robin and I. . . . Which sister had the most to forgive, the most to pay for? God knows I had no answer.

"I am sorry," said Richard briefly. "I cannot help you. You must stay here until arrangements can be made. We have more serious matters on our hands than the transport of a sick widow. . . ."

Bunny was the first to catch the sound of the horse's hooves galloping across the park. He went to the small mullioned window that gave on to the inner court and threw it wide; and as we waited, tense, expectant, the sound drew closer, and suddenly the rider and his horse came through the arch beneath the gatehouse, and there was Peter Courtney, dust-covered and dishevelled, his hat gone, his dark curls straggling on his shoulders. He flung the reins to a startled waiting groom and came straightway to the gallery.

"For God's sake save yourselves! We are betrayed," he said.

I think I did not show the same fear and horror on my face as they did, for, although my heart went cold and dead within me, I knew with wretched certainty that this was the thing I had waited for all day. Peter looked from one to the other of us, and his breath came quick. "They have all been seized," he said. "Jonathan Trelawney, his son, Charles Trevannion, Arthur Bassett and the rest. At ten this morning they came riding to the house, the Sheriff, Sir Thomas Herle, and a whole company of soldiers. We made a fight for it, but there were more than thirty of them. I leapt from an upper window, by Almighty Providence escaping with no worse than a wrenched ankle. I got the first horse to hand, and put spurs to him without mercy. Had I not known the bylanes as I know my own hand, I could not have reached you now. There are soldiers everywhere. The bridge at St Blazey blocked and guarded. Guards on Polmear hill." He looked around the gallery, as though in search of someone. "Robin gone?" he asked. "I thought so. It was he, then, I saw, when I was skirting the sands, engaged in fighting with five of the enemy or more. I dared not go to his assistance. My first duty was to you. What now? Can we save ourselves?"

We all turned now to look at our commander. He stood before us, calm and cool, giving no outward sign that all he had striven for lay crushed and broken. "Did you see their colours?" he asked swiftly. "What troops were they? Of whose command?"

"Some were from Bodmin, sir," said Peter, "the rest advance guards of Sir Hardress Waller's. There were line upon line of them, stretching down the road towards St Austell. This is no chance encounter, sir. The enemy are in strength."

Richard nodded, turning quick to Bunny. "Go to Pridmouth," he said. "Make sail instantly. Set a course due south, until you come in contact with the first outlying vessel of the French fleet. They will be cruising eastward of the Scillies by this time to-morrow evening. Ask for Lord Hopton's ship. Give him this message." He scribbled rapidly upon a piece of paper.

"Do you bid them come?" said Ambrose Manaton. "Can they get to us in time?" He was white to the lips, his hands clenched right.

"Why, no," said Richard, folding his scrap of paper, "I bid them alter course and sail for France again. There will be no rising. The Prince of Wales does not land this month in Cornwall." He gave the paper to his nephew. "Good chance, my Bunny," he said, smiling. "Give greetings to your brother Jack, and with a spice of luck you will find the Scillies fall to you like a plum a little later in the summer. But the Prince must say goodbye to Cornwall for the present."

"And you, uncle?" said Bunny. "Will you not come with me? It is madness to delay if the house is likely to be surrounded."

"I'll join you in my own time," said Richard. "For this once, I ask that my orders be obeyed."

Bunny stared at him an instant, then turned and went, his head high, bidding none of us farewell.

"But what are we to do? Where are we to go?" said Ambrose Manaton, "Oh, God, what a fool I have been to let myself be led into this business. Are the roads all watched?" He turned to Peter, who stood shrugging his shoulders, watching his commander.

"Who is to blame? Who is the traitor? That is what I want to know," said Ambrose Manaton, all composure gone, a new note of suspicion in his voice. "None but ourselves knew the change in rendezvous. How did the Sheriff time his moment with such devilish accuracy that he could seize every leader worth a curse?"

"Does it matter," said Richard gently, "who the traitor was once the deed is done?"

"Matter?" said Ambrose Manaton. "Good God, you take it coolly. Trevannion, the Trelawneys, the Arundells, and Bassett, all of them in the Sheriff's hands, and you ask does it matter who betrayed them? Here are we, ruined men, likely to be arrested within the hour, and you stand there like a fox and smile at me."

"My enemies call me fox, but not my friends," said Richard softly. He turned to Peter. "Tell the fellows to saddle a horse for Mr Manaton," he said, "and for you also. I guarantee no safe conduct for the pair of you, but at least you have a sporting chance, as hares do from a pack of hounds."

"You will not come with us, sir?"

"No. I will not come with you."

Peter hesitated, looking first at him, and then at me.

"It will go ill with you, sir, if they should find you."

"I am well aware of that."

"The Sheriff, Sir Thomas Herle, suspects your presence here in Cornwall. His first challenge, when he came before Caerhayes and called Trevannion, was: 'Have you Sir Richard Grenvile here in hiding? If so produce him, and you shall go free.'"

"A pity, for their sakes, I was not there."

"He said that a messenger had left a note at his house at Prideaux, early before dawn, warning him that the whole party, yourself included, would be gathered later at Caerhayes. Some wretch had seen you, sir, and with devilish intuition guessed your plans."

"Some wretch indeed," said Richard, smiling still, "who thought it sport to try the Judas touch. Let us forget him."

Was it his nephew Jack who, long ago at Exeter, said once to me: "Beware my uncle when you see him smile . . . ?"

Then Ambrose Manaton came forward, his finger stabbing at the air. "It is you," he said to Richard, "you who are the traitor, you who have betrayed us. From first to last, from beginning to the end, you knew it would end thus. The French fleet never were to come to our aid, there never was to be a rising. This is your revenge for that arrest four years ago at Launceston. Oh, God, what perfidy. . . ." He stood before him, trembling, a high note of hysteria in his voice, and I saw Peter fall back a pace, the colour draining from his face, bewilderment, then horror, coming to his eyes.

Richard watched them, never moving, then slowly pointed to the door. The horses had been brought to the courtyard, and we heard the jingle of the harness.

Put back the clock, I whispered savagely, make it four years ago, and Gartred acting spy for Lord Robartes. Let her take the blame. Fix the crime on her. She is the one who will emerge from this unscathed, for all her spoilt beauty. I looked towards her, and saw, to my wonder, that she was looking at me also. Her scarf had slipped, showing the vivid wound upon her cheek. The sight of it, and the memory of the night before, filled me, not with anger or with pity, but despair. She went on looking at me, and I saw her smile.

"It's no use," she said. "I know what you are thinking. Poor Honor, I have cheated you again. Gartred has the perfect alibi."

The horses were galloping from the courtyard. I saw Ambrose Manaton go first, his hat pulled low, his cloak bellying, and Peter follow him, with one brief glance towards our windows.

The clock in the belfry struck two. A pigeon, dazzling white against the sky, fluttered to the court below. Gartred lay back against the couch, the smile on her lips a strange contrast to the gash upon her face. Richard stood by the window, his hands behind his back. And Dick, who had never moved once in all the past half-hour, waited, like a dumb thing, in his corner.

"Do the three Grenviles," I said slowly, "wish to take council, alone, amongst themselves?"

CHAPTER THIRTY-FOUR

RICHARD WENT ON standing by the window. Now that the horses were gone, and the sound of their galloping had died away, it was strangely hushed and still within the house. The sun blazed down upon the gardens, the pigeons pricked the grass seeds on the lawn. It was the hottest hour of a warm summer day, when bumble bees go humming in the limes, and the young birds fall silent. When Richard spoke he kept his back turned to us, and his voice was soft and low.

"My grandfather," he said, "was named Richard also. He came of a long line of Grenviles who sought to serve their country and their king. Enemies he had in plenty, friends as well. It was my misfortune and my loss that he died in battle nine years before my birth. But I remember as a lad asking for tales of him, and looking up at that great portrait which hung in the long gallery at Stowe. He was stern, they said, and hard, and rarely smiled, so I have heard tell, but his eyes that looked down upon me from the portrait were hawk's eyes, fearless and far-seeing. There were many great names in those days: Drake, Raleigh, Sydney—and Grenvile was of their company. He fell mortally wounded, you may remember, on the decks of his own ship, called the *Revenge*. He fought alone, with the Spanish fleet about him, and when they asked him to surrender he went on fighting still, with masts gone, sails gone, the decks torn beneath his feet. The Grenvile of that day had courage, and preferred to have his vessel blown to pieces, rather than sell his life for silver to the pirate hordes of Spain." He fell silent a moment, watching the pigeons on the lawn, and then he went on talking, with his hands behind his back. "My uncle John," he said, "explored the Indies with Sir Francis Drake. He was a man of courage too. They were no weaklings, those young men who braved the winter storms of the Atlantic in search of savage lands beyond the seas. Their ships were frail, they were tossed week after week at the mercy of wind and sea, but some salt tang in their blood kept them undaunted. He was killed there, in the Indies, was my Uncle John, and my father, who loved him well, built a shrine to him at Stowe." There was no sound from any one of us in the gallery. Gartred lay on the couch, her hands behind her head, and Dick stood motionless in his dark corner.

"There was a saying, born about this time," continued Richard, "that no Grenvile was ever wanting in loyalty to his king. We were bred to it, my brothers and I. Gartred too, I think, will well remember those evenings in my father's room at Stowe when he, though he was not a fighting man—for he lived in days of peace—read to us from an old volume with great clasps about it of the wars of the past, and how our forebears fought in them."

A gull wheeled overhead above the gardens, his wings white against the dark blue sky, and I remembered of a sudden the kittiwakes at Stowe, riding the rough Atlantic beneath Richard's home.

"My brother Bevil," said Richard, "was a man who loved his family and his home. He was not bred to war. He desired, in his brief life, nothing so much as to rear his children with his wife's care, and live at peace amongst his neighbours. When war came he knew what it would mean, and did not turn his back upon it. Wrangling he detested, bloodshed he abhorred, but because he bore the name of Grenvile, he knew, in 1642, where his duty lay. He wrote a letter at that time to our friend and neighbour, John Trelawney, who has this day been arrested, as you know, and because I believe that letter to be the finest thing my brother ever penned I asked Trelawney for a copy of it. I have it with me now. Shall I read it to you?"

We did not answer. He felt in his pocket slowly for a paper, and, holding it before the window, read aloud.

"'I cannot contain myself within my doors when the King of England's standard waves in the field upon so just occasion, the cause being such as must make all those that die in it little inferior to martyrs. And for mine own part I desire to acquire an honest name or an honourable grave. I never loved my life or ease so much as to shun such an occasion, which if I should, I were unworthy of the profession I have held, or to succeed those ancestors of mine who have, so many of them, in several ages, sacrificed their lives for their country.'"

Richard folded the letter again, and put it once more into his pocket. "My brother Bevil died at Lansdowne," he said, "leading his men to battle, and his young son, Jack, a lad of but fifteen, straightway mounted his father's horse and charged the enemy. That youngster who has just left us, Bunny, ran from his tutor last autumn, playing truant, that he might place himself at my disposal, and hold a sword for this cause we all hold dear. I have no brief for myself. I am a soldier. My faults are many, and my virtues few. But no quarrel, no dispute, no petty act of vengeance has ever turned me, or will turn me now, from loyalty to my country and my King. In the long and often bloody history of the Grenviles, not one of them, until this day, has proved a traitor."

His voice had sunk now, deadly quiet. The pigeons had flown from the lawns. The bees had hummed their way below the thistle park.

"One day," said Richard, "we may hope that His Majesty will be restored to his throne, or if not he, then the Prince of Wales instead. In that proud day, should any of us live to see it, the name of Grenvile will be held in honour, not only here in Cornwall, but in all England too. I am judge enough of character, for all my other failings, to know that my nephew Jack will prove himself as great a man of peace as he has been a youth of war, nor will young Bunny ever lag behind. They can tell their sons, in the years to come, 'We Grenviles fought to bring about the restoration of our King' and their names will rank in that great book at Stowe my father read to us, beside that of my grandfather Richard, who fought in the *Revenge*." He paused a moment, then spoke lower still.

"I care not," he said, "if my name be written in that book in smaller characters. 'He was a soldier,' they may say. 'The King's general in the west.' Let that be my epitaph. But there will be no other Richard in that book at Stowe. For the King's general died without a son." A long silence followed his last words. He went on standing at the window, and I sat still in my chair, my hands folded on my lap. Soon now it would come, I thought, the outburst, the angry, frightened words; or the torrent of wild weeping. For eighteen years the storm had been pent up, and the full tide of emotion could not wait longer now. This is our fault, I whispered to myself, not his. Had Richard been more forgiving, had I been less proud; had our hearts been filled with love and not hatred, had we been blessed with greater understanding. . . . Too late. Full twenty years too late. And now the little scapegoat of our sins went bleeding to his doom. . . .

But the cry I waited for was never uttered. Nor did the tears fall. Instead, he came out from his corner, and stood alone an instant in the centre of the room. The fear was gone now from the dark eyes, and the slim hands did not tremble.

He looked older than he had done hitherto, older and wiser. As though, while his father had been speaking, a whole span of years had passed him by.

Yet when he spoke, his voice was a boy's voice, young and simple. "What must I do?" he said. "Will you do it for me, or must I kill myself?"

It was Gartred who moved first. Gartred, my lifelong foe and enemy. She rose from her couch, pulling the veil about her face, and came up to my chair. She put her hands upon it, and, still with no word spoken, she wheeled me from the room. We went out into the garden, under the sun, our backs turned to the house, and we said no words to one another, for there were none to say. But neither she nor I, nor any man or woman alive or dead, will ever know what was said, there in the long gallery at Menabilly, by Richard Grenvile to his only son.

That evening the insurrection broke out in the west. There had been no way to warn the Royalists of Helston and Penzance that the leaders in the east had been arrested, and the prospective rising was now doomed to failure. They struck, at the appointed hour, as had been planned, and found themselves faced, not with the startled troops they had expected, but the strong forces, fully prepared and armed, that came post-haste into Cornwall for the purpose. No French fleet beyond the Scillies came coasting to Land's End and the Lizard. There was no landing of twenty thousand men upon the beaches, beneath Dodman and the Nare. And the leaders who should have come riding to the west were shackled, wrist to wrist, in the garrison at Plymouth. No Trelawney, no Arundell, no Trevannion, no Bassett. What was to have been the torch to light all England was no more than a sudden quivering flame, spurting to nothing, spluttering for a single moment in the damp Cornish air. A few shops looted at Penzance . . . a smattering of houses pillaged at Mullion . . . a wild unruly charge upon Goonhilly Down, with no man knowing whither he rode, or wherefore he was fighting . . . and then the last hopeless, desperate stand at Mawgan Creek, with the Parliamentary troops driving the ill-led Royalists to destruction, down over the rocks and stones to the deep Helford River.

The rebellion of '48. The last time men shall ever fight, please God, upon our Cornish soil. . . . It lasted but a week, but for those who died and suffered it lasted for eternity. The battles were west of Truro, so we, at Menabilly, smelt no powder. But every road and every lane was guarded, and not even the servants ventured out of doors. That first evening a company of soldiers, under the command of Colonel Robert Bennett, our old neighbour near to Looe, rode to Menabilly, and made a perfunctory search throughout the house. He found no one present but myself and Gartred. He little knew that, had he come ten minutes earlier, he would have found the greatest prize of all.

I can see Richard now, his arms folded, seated in the dining-chamber with the empty chairs about him, deaf to all my pleading. "When they come," he said, "they shall take me, as I am. Mine is the blame. I am the man for whom my friends now suffer. Very well, then. Let them do their worst upon me, and by surrendering my person I may yet save Cornwall from destruction."

Gartred, with all her old cool composure back again, shrugged her shoulders in disdain. "Is it not a little late now in the day to play the martyr?" she suggested. "What good will your surrender do at this juncture? You flatter yourself, poor Richard, if you think the mere holding of a Grenvile will spare the rest from imprisonment and death. I hate these last-minute gestures, these sublime salutes. Show yourself a man, and escape, the pair of you, as Bunny did." She did not look towards Dick. Nor did I. But he sat there, silent as ever, at his father's side.

"We shall make fine figures on the scaffold, Dick and I," said Richard. "My neck is somewhat thicker, I know, than his, and may need two blows from the axe instead of one."

"You may not have the pleasure, or the parade, of a martyr's execution," said Gartred, yawning, "but instead a knotted rope in a dank dungeon. Not the usual finish for a Grenvile."

"It would be better," said Richard quietly, "if these two Grenviles did die in obscurity."

There was a pause, and then Dick spoke, for the first time since that unforgettable moment in the gallery.

"How do we stand," he said jerkily, "with the Rashleighs? If my father and I are found here by the enemy, will it be possible to prove to them that the Rashleighs are innocent in the matter?"

I seized upon his words for all the world like a drowning woman. "You have not thought of that," I said to Richard. "You have not considered for one moment what will become of them. Who will ever believe that Jonathan Rashleigh, and John too, were not party also to your plan? Their absence from Menabilly is no proof. They will be dragged into the matter, and my sister Mary also. Poor Alice at Trethurfe, Joan at Mothercombe, a legion of young children. They will all of them, from Jonathan in London to the baby on Joan's knee, suffer imprisonment, and maybe death into the bargain, if you are taken here."

It was at this moment that a servant came into the room, much agitated, his hands clasped before him. "I think it best to tell you," he said, "that a lad has come running across the park to say the troopers are gathered at the top of Polmear hill. Some have gone down towards Polkerris. The rest are making for Tregaminion and the park gates."

"Thank you," said Richard, bowing. "I am much obliged to you for your discretion." The servant left the room, hoping, I dare say, to feign sickness in his quarters when the troopers came.

Richard rose slowly to his feet and looked at me.

"So you fear for your Rashleighs?" he said. "And because of them you have no wish to throw me to the wolves? Very well, then. For this once I will prove accommodating. Where is the famous hiding-place that four years ago proved so beneficial to us all?"

I saw Dick flinch and look away from me towards his father. "Dick knows," I answered. "Would you condescend to share it with him?"

"A hunted rat," said Richard, "has no choice. He must take the companion that is thrust upon him."

Whether the place was rank with cobwebs, mould and mildew, I neither knew nor cared. At least it would give concealment while the troopers came. And no one, not even Gartred, knew the secret.

"Do you remember," I said to Dick, "where the passage led? I warn you, no one has been there for four years."

He nodded, deathly pale. And I wondered what bug of fear had seized him now, when but an hour ago he had offered himself, like a little lamb, for slaughter.

"Go then," I said, "and take your father. Now, this instant, while there is still time."

He came then to me, his new-found courage wavering, looking so like the little boy who loved me once that my heart went out to him. "The rope," he said, "the rope upon the hinge. What if it has frayed now with disuse, and the hinge rusted?"

"It will not matter," I said, "you will not need to use it now. I shall not be waiting for you in the chamber overhead."

He stared at me, lost for a moment, dull, uncomprehending, and I verily believe that for one brief second he thought himself a child again. Then Richard broke the spell with his hard, clear voice.

"Well?" he said. "If it must be done, this is the moment. There is no other method of escape."

Dick went on staring at me, and there came into his eyes a strange new look I had not seen before. Why did he stare at me thus? Or was it not me he stared at but some other, some ghost of a dead past that tapped him on the shoulder?

"Yes," he said slowly. "If it must be done, this is the moment. . . ." He turned to his father, opening first the door of the dining-room. "Will you follow me, sir?" he said to Richard.

Richard paused a moment on the threshold. He looked first at Gartred, then back at me again. "When the hounds are in full cry," he said, "and the coverts guarded, the red fox goes to earth."

He smiled, holding my eyes for a single second, and was gone after Dick on to the causeway. . . . Gartred watched them disappear, then shrugged her shoulder. "I thought," she said, "the hiding-place was in the house. Near your old apartment in the gatehouse."

"Did you?" I said.

"I wasted hours, four years ago, searching in the passages, tiptoeing outside your door," she said.

There was a mirror hanging on the wall beside the window. She went to it, and stared, pulling her veil aside. The deep crimson gash ran from her eyebrow to her chin, jagged, irregular, and the smooth contour of her face was gone for ever. I watched her eyes, and she saw me watching them through the misty glass of the little mirror.

"I could have stopped you," she said, "from falling with your horse to the ravine. You knew that, didn't you?"

"Yes," I said.

"You called me, asking for the way, and I did not answer you."

"You did not," I said.

"It has taken a long time to call it quits," she said to me. She came away then from the mirror, and, taking from her sack the little pack of cards I well remembered, sat down by the table, close to my wheeled chair. She dealt the cards face downwards on the table. "We will play patience, you and I, until the troopers come," said Gartred Grenvile.

CHAPTER THIRTY-FIVE

I DOUBT IF Colonel Bennett had searched all Cornwall, whether he could have found a quieter couple when he came, than the two women playing cards in the dining-hall at Menabilly. One with a great scar upon her face, and silver hair; the other a hopeless cripple. Yes, there had been guests with us until to-day, we admitted it. Mr Rashleigh's son-in-law, Sir Peter Courtney, and my own brother, Robin Harris. No, we knew nothing of their movements. They came and went as they pleased. Mr Trelawney had called once, we understood, but we had not seen him. Why was I left alone at Menabilly by the Rashleighs? From necessity and not from choice. Perhaps you have forgotten, Colonel Bennett, that my home at Lanrest was burnt down four years ago—by your orders, someone told me once. A strange action for a neighbour. And why was Mrs Denys from Orley Court near Bideford a guest of mine at the present season? Well, she was once my sister-in-law, and we had long been friends. . . . Yes, it was true my name had been connected with Sir Richard Grenvile in the past. There are gossips in the west country as well as at Whitehall. . . . No, Mrs Denys had never been very friendly with her brother. No, we had no knowledge of his movements. We believed him to be in Naples. Yes, search the house, from the cellars to the attics, search the grounds. Here are the keys. Do what you will. We have no power to stop you. Menabilly is no property of ours. We are merely guests in the absence of Mr Rashleigh. . . .

"Well, you appear to speak the truth, Mistress Harris," he said to me on the conclusion of his visit (he had called me "Honor" once, when we were neighbours near to Looe), "but the fact that your brother and Sir Peter Courtney are implicated in the rising which is now breaking out at Helston and Penzance renders this house suspect. I shall leave a guard behind me, and I rather think, when Sir Hardress Waller comes into the district, he will make a more thorough search of the premises than I have had time to do to-day. Meanwhile. . . ." he broke off abruptly, his eyes drifting, as if in curiosity, back to Gartred.

"Pardon my indelicacy, Madam," he said, "but that cut is recent?"

"An accident," said Gartred, shrugging, "a clumsy movement and some broken glass."

"It has more the appearance of a sword-cut, forgive my rudeness. Were you a man, I would say you had fought a duel, and received the hurt from an opponent."

"I am not a man, Colonel Bennett. If you doubt me, why not come upstairs, to my chamber, and let me prove it to you?" Robert Bennett was a Puritan. He stepped back a pace, colouring to his ears. "I thank you, madam," he said, stiffly. "My eyes are sufficient evidence."

"If promotion came by gallantry," said Gartred, "you would still be in the ranks. I can think of no other officer in Cornwall, or in Devon either, who would decline to walk upstairs with Gartred Denys." She made as though to deal the cards again, but Colonel Bennett made a motion of his hands.

"I am sorry," he said shortly, "but whether you are Mrs Denys or Mrs Harris these days does not greatly matter. What does matter is that your maiden name was Grenvile."

"And so?" said Gartred, shuffling her cards.

"And so I must ask you to come with me, and accept an escort down to Truro. There you will be held, pending investigation, and when the roads are quieter you will have leave to depart to Orley Court."

Gartred dropped her cards into her sack, and rose slowly to her feet. "As you will," she said, shrugging her shoulders. "You have some conveyance, I presume? I have no dress for riding."

"You will have every comfort, madam."

He turned then to me. "You are permitted to remain here until I receive further orders from Sir Hardress Waller. These may be forthcoming in the morning. But I must ask you to be in readiness to move upon the instant, should the order come. You understand?"

"Yes," I answered. "Yes. I understand."

"Very good, then. I will leave a guard before the house, with instructions to shoot on sight should his suspicions be in any way aroused. Good evening. You are ready, Mrs Denys?"

"Yes, I am ready." Gartred turned to me and touched me lightly on the shoulder. "I am sorry," she said, "to cut my visit short. Remember me to the Rashleighs when you see them. And tell Jonathan what I said about the gardens. If he wishes to plant flowering shrubs, he must first rid himself of foxes. . . ."

"Not so easy," I answered. "They are hard to catch. Especially when they go underground."

"Smoke them out," she said. "It is the only way. Do it by night; they leave less scent behind them. Good-bye, Honor."

"Good-bye, Gartred." She went, throwing her veil back from her face to show the vivid scar, and I have not seen her from that day to this.

I heard the troopers ride away from the courtyard and out across the park. Before the two entrance doors stood sentries, with muskets at their sides. And a sentry stood also at the outer gate, and by the steps leading to the causeway. I sat watching them, then pulled the bell-rope by the hearth for Matty.

"Ask them," I said, "if Colonel Bennett left permission for me to take exercise in my chair within the grounds."

She was back in a moment, with the message that I feared.

"He is sorry," she answered, "but Colonel Bennett gave strict orders that you were not to leave the house."

I looked at Matty, and she looked at me.

The thoughts chased round my head in wild confusion. "What hour is it?" I asked.

"Near five o'clock," she answered.

"Four hours of daylight still," I said.

"Yes," she answered.

From the window of the dining-hall I could see the sentry pacing up and down before the gates of the south garden. Now and then he paused to look about him and to chat with his fellow at the causeway steps. The sun, high in the south-west, shone down upon their muskets.

"Take me upstairs, Matty," I said slowly.

"To your own chamber?"

"No, Matty. To my old room beyond the gatehouse. . . ."

I had not been there in all the past two years of my stay at Menabilly. The west wing was still bare, untouched. Desolate and stripped as when the rebels had come pillaging in '44. The hangings were gone from the walls. The room had neither bed, nor chair, nor table. One shutter hung limp from the further window, giving a faint creak of light. The room had a dead, fusty smell, and in the far corner lay the bleached bones of a rat. The west wing was very silent. Very still. No sound came from the deserted kitchens underneath.

"Go to the stone," I whispered. "Put your hands against it." Matty did so, kneeling on the floor. She pressed against the square stone by the buttress, but it did not move.

"No good," she murmured, "it is hard fixed. Have you forgotten that it only opened from the other side?"

Had I forgotten? It was the one thing that I remembered. . . . Smoke them out, said Gartred, it is the only way. Yes, but she did not understand. She thought they were hidden somewhere in the woods. Not behind stone walls, three foot thick. . . .

"Fetch wood and paper," I said to Matty. "Kindle a fire. Not in the chimney, but here, against the wall."

There was a chance—a faint one, God knew well—that the smoke would penetrate the cracks in the stones and make a signal. They might not be there, though. They might be crouching in the tunnel at the farther end, beneath the summer-house.

How slow she was, good Matty, faithful Matty, fetching the dried grass and the twigs. How carefully she blew the fire, how methodically she added twig to twig. "Hurry," I said. "More wood, more flame."

"Patience," she whispered, "it will go, in its own time."

In its own time. Not my time. Not Richard's time. . . .

The room was filled with smoke. It seeped into our eyes, our hair, it clung about the windows. But whether it seeped into the stones we could not tell. Matty went to the window, and opened the crack two inches further. I held a long stick in my hands, poking helplessly at the slow, sizzling fire, pushing the sticks against the buttress wall. "There are four horsemen riding across the park," said Matty suddenly. "Troopers, like those who came just now."

My hands were wet with sweat. I threw away my useless stick and rubbed my eyes, stung and red with smoke. I think I was nearer panic at that moment than any other in my eight-and-thirty years.

"Oh, God," I whispered. "What are we to do?"

Matty closed the window gently. She stamped upon the embers of the fire. "Come back to your chamber," she said. "Later, to-night, I will try here once again. But we must not be found here now." She carried me in her broad arms from the dark, musty room, through the gatehouse to the corridor beyond, and down to my own chamber in the eastern wing. She laid me on my bed, bringing water for my face and hands. We heard the troopers ride into the courtyard, and then the sound of footsteps below. Impervious to man or situation, the clock beneath the belfry struck six, hammering its silly leaden notes with mechanical precision. Matty brushed the soot from my hair and changed my gown, and when she had finished there came a tap upon the door. A servant, with frightened face, whispered that Mistress Harris was wanted down below. They put me in my chair and carried me downstairs. There had been four troopers, Matty said, riding across the park, but only three stood here, in the side hall, looking out across the gardens. They cast a curious glance upon me, as Matty and the servant put me down inside the door of the dining-hall. The fourth man stood by the fireplace, leaning upon a stick. And it was not another trooper like themselves but my brother-in-law, Jonathan Rashleigh.

For a moment I was too stunned to speak. Then relief, bewilderment, and something of utter helplessness swept over me, and I began to cry. He took my hand and held it, saying nothing. In a minute or two I had recovered, and, looking up at him, I saw what the years had done. Two, was it, he had been away in London? It might be twenty. He was, I believe, at that time but fifty-eight. He looked seventy. His hair was gone quite white, his shoulders, once so broad, were shrunk and drooping. His very eyes seemed sunk deep in his skull. "What has happened?" I asked. "Why have you come back?"

"The debt is paid," he said, and even his voice was an old man's voice, slow and weary. "The debt is paid, the fine is now wiped out. I am free to come to Cornwall once again."

"You have chosen an ill moment to return," I answered.

"So they have warned me," he said slowly.

He looked at me, and I knew, I think, in that moment that he had been, after all, a party to the plan. That all the guests who had crept like robbers to his house had come with his connivance, and that he, a prisoner in London, had risked his life because of them.

"You came by road?" I asked him.

"Nay. By ship," he answered. "My own ship, the *Frances*, which plies between Fowey and the continent, you may remember."

"Yes, I remember."

"Her merchandise has helped to pay my debt. She fetched me from Gravesend a week ago, when the County Committee gave me leave to go from London and return to Fowey. We came to harbour but a few hours since."

"Is Mary with you?"

"No. She went ashore at Plymouth, to see Joan at Mothercombe. The guards at Plymouth told us that a rising was feared in Cornwall, and troops were gone in strength to quell it. I made all haste to come to Fowey, fearing for your safety."

"You knew then that John was not here? You knew I was . . . alone?"

"I knew you were . . . alone."

We both fell silent, our eyes upon the door.

"They have arrested Robin," I said softly, "and Peter also, I fear."

"Yes," he said. "So my guards tell me."

"No suspicion can fall upon yourself?"

"Not yet," he answered strangely.

I saw him look towards the window, where the broad back of the sentry blocked the view. Then slowly, from his pocket, he drew a folded paper, and when he opened it I saw that it was a poster, such as they stick upon the walls for wanted men. He read it to me:

"'Anyone who has harboured at any time, or seeks to harbour in the future, the malignant known as Richard Grenvile, shall, upon discovery, be arrested for high treason, his lands sequestered finally and for ever, and his family imprisoned.'"

He folded the paper once again. "This," he said, "is posted upon every wall in every town in Cornwall."

For a moment I did not speak, and then I said, "They have searched this house already. Two hours ago. They found nothing."

"They will come again," he answered, "in the morning."

He went back to the hearth and stood in deep thought, leaning on his stick. "My ship the *Frances*," he said slowly, "anchors in Fowey only for the night. To-morrow, on the first tide, she sails for Holland."

"For Holland?"

"She carries a light cargo as far as Flushing. The master of the vessel is an honest man, faithful to any trust that I might lay upon him. Already in his charge is a young woman whom I thought fit to call my kinswoman. Had matters been other than they are, she might have landed with me, here in Fowey. But Fate and circumstance decided otherwise. Therefore she will proceed to Flushing also, in my ship, the *Frances*."

"I don't see," I said, after a moment's hesitation, "what this young woman has to do with me. Let her go to Holland by all means."

"She would be easier in mind," said Jonathan Rashleigh, "if she had her father with her."

I was still too blind to understand his meaning until he felt in his breast pocket for a note, which he handed to me. I opened it, and read the few words scribbled in an unformed youthful hand. "If you still need a daughter in your declining years," ran the message, "she waits for you, on board the good ship *Frances*. Holland, they say, is healthier than England. Will you try the climate with me? My mother christened me Elizabeth, but I prefer to sign myself your daughter, Bess."

I said nothing for a little while, but held the note there in my hands. I could have asked a hundred questions, had I the time—or inclination. Women's questions, such as my sister Mary might have answered, and perhaps understood. Was she pretty? Was she kind? Had she his eyes, his mouth, his auburn hair? Would she understand his lonely moods? Would she laugh with him when his moods were gay? But none of them mattered, or were appropriate to the moment. Since I should never see her, it was not my affair.

"You have given me this note," I said to Jonathan, "in the hope that I can pass it to her father."

"Yes," he answered.

Once again he looked at the broad back of the sentry by the window.

"I have told you that the *Frances* leaves Fowey on the early tide," he said. "A boat will put off to Pridmouth, as they go from harbour, to lift lobster pots dropped between the shore and the Cannis rock. It would be a simple matter to pick up a passenger in the half-light of morning."

"A simple matter," I answered, "if the passenger is there."

"It is your business," he said, "to see, then, that he is."

He guessed that Richard was concealed within the buttress—so much I could tell from his eyes and the look he fastened now upon me. "The sentries," I said, "keep a watch upon the causeway."

"At this end only," he said softly. "Not at the other."

"The risk is very great," I said, "even by night, even by early morning."

"I know that," he answered, "but I think the person of whom we speak will dare that risk."

Once again he drew the poster from his pocket. "If you should deliver the note," he said quietly, "you could give him this as well." I took the poster in silence, and placed it in my gown.

"There is one other thing that I would have you do," he said to me.

"What is that?"

"Destroy all trace of what has been. The men who will come to-morrow have keener noses than the troops who came to-day. They are scent hounds, trained to the business."

"They can find nothing from within," I answered. "You know that. Your father had the cunning of all time when he built his buttress."

"But from without," he said, "the secret is less sure. I give you leave to finish the work begun by the Parliament in '44. I shall not seek to use the summer-house again."

I guessed his meaning as he stood there watching me, leaning on his stick. "Timber burns fiercely in dry weather," he said to me, "and rubble makes a pile, and the nettles and the thistles grow apace in midsummer. There will be no need to clear those nettles in my lifetime, nor in John's either."

"Why do you not stay," I whispered, "and do this work yourself?"

But even as I spoke the door of the dining-hall was opened and the leader of the three troopers, waiting in the hall, entered the room. "I am sorry, sir," he said, "but you have already had fifteen minutes of the ten allotted to you. I cannot go against my orders. Will you please make your farewell now, and return with me to Fowey?"

I stared at him blankly, my heart sinking in my breast again.

"I thought Mr Rashleigh was a free agent once again?"

"The times being troublesome, my dear Honor," said Jonathan quietly, "the gentlemen in authority deem it best that I should remain at present under surveillance, if not exactly custody. I am to spend the night, therefore, in my town house at Fowey. I regret if I did not make myself more clear." He turned to the trooper. "I am grateful to you," he said, "for allowing me this interview with my sister-in-law. She suffers from poor health, and we have all been anxious for her." And without another word, he went from me and I was left there, with the note in my hand and the poster in my gown, and the lives of not only Richard and his son, but those of the whole family of Rashleigh, depending upon my wits and my sagacity.

I waited for Matty, but she did not come to me, and, impatient at last, I rang the bell beside the hearth. The startled servant who came running at the sound told me that Matty was not to be found—he had sought for her in the kitchens, in her bedroom, but she had not answered. "No matter," I said, and made a pretence of taking up a book and turning the pages. "Will you dine now, madam?" he said to me. "It is nearly seven. Long past your usual hour."

"Why, yes," I said, "if you care to bring it," feigning intensity upon my book, yet all the while counting the hours to darkness, and wondering with an anxious heart what had become of Matty. I ate my meat and drank my wine, tasting them not at all, and as I sat there in the dark panelled dining-hall, with the portrait of old John Rashleigh and his wife frowning down upon me, I watched the shadows lengthen, and the murky evening creep on, and the great banked clouds of evening steal across the sky.

It was close on nine o'clock when I heard the door open with a creak. Turning in my chair I saw Matty standing there, her gown stained green and brown with bracken and with earth. She put her finger to her lips and I said nothing. She came across the room and closed the shutters. As she folded the last one into place, she spoke softly over her shoulder. "He is not ill-looking, the sentry on the causeway."

"No?"

"He knows my cousin's wife at Liskeard."

"Introductions have been made on less than that."

She fastened the hasp of the shutter, and drew the heavy curtain. "It was somewhat damp in thistle park," she said.

"So I perceive," I answered.

"But he found a sheltered place beneath a bush, where we could talk about my cousin's wife. . . . While he was looking for it I waited in the summer-house."

"That," I said, "was understandable."

The curtains were now all drawn before the shutters, and the dining-hall in darkness. Matty came and stood beside my chair. "I lifted the flagstone," she said. "I left a letter on the steps. I said, if the rope be still in place upon the hinge, would they open the stone entrance in the buttress to-night at twelve o'clock. We would be waiting for them."

I felt for her strong, comforting hand and held it between mine.

"I pray they find it," she said slowly. "There must have been a fall of earth since the tunnel was last used. The place smelt of the tomb. . . ."

We clung to one another in the darkness, and as I listened I could hear the steady thumping of her heart.

CHAPTER THIRTY-SIX

I LAY UPON my bed upstairs from half-past nine until a quarter before twelve. When Matty came to rouse me the house was deadly still. The servants had gone to their beds in the attics, and the sentries were at their posts about the grounds. I could hear one of them pacing the walk beneath my window. The treacherous moon, never an ally to a fugitive, rose slowly above the trees in thistle park. We lit no candles. Matty crept to the door and listened. Then she lifted me in her arms, and trod the long, twisting corridor to the empty gatehouse. How bare were the rooms, how silent and accusing; and there was no moonlight here, on the western side, to throw a beam of light upon the floor.

Inside the room that was our destination the ashes of our poor fire, kindled that afternoon, flickered feebly still, and the smoke hung in clouds about the ceiling. We sat down beside the wall in the far corner, and waited. . . . It was uncannily still—the stillness of a place that has not known a footstep or a voice for many years. The quiet of a long-forgotten prison where no sunlight ever penetrates, where all seasons seem alike.

Winter, summer, spring, and autumn, would all come and go, but never here, never in this room. Here was eternal night. And I thought, sitting there beside the cold wall of the buttress, that this must be the darkness that so frightened the poor idiot uncle John when he lay here, long ago, in the first building of the house. Perhaps he lay upon this very spot on which I sat, his hands feeling the air, his wide eyes searching. . . .

Then I felt Matty touch me on the shoulder, and as she did so the stone behind me moved. . . . There came, upon my back, the current of cold air I well remembered, and now, turning, I could see the yawning gulf, and the narrow flight of steps behind, and could hear the creaking of the rope upon its rusty hinge.

Although it was the sound I wanted most in all the world to hear, it struck a note of horror, like the summons from a grave. Now Matty lit her candle, and, throwing the beam on to the steps, I saw him standing there, earth upon his face, his hands, his shoulders, giving him, in that weird, unnatural light, the features of a corpse newly-risen from his grave. He smiled, and the smile had in it something grim and terrible.

"I feared," he said, "you would not come. A few hours more, and it would have been too late."

"What do you mean?" I asked.

"No air," he said. "There is only room here from the tunnel for a dog to crawl. I have no great opinion of your Rashleigh builder."

I leant forward, peering down the steps, and there was Dick huddled at the bottom, his face as ghostly as his father's.

"It was not thus," I said, "four years ago."

"Come," said Richard. "I will show you. A gaoler should have knowledge of the cell where she puts her prisoners."

He took me in his arms, and, crawling sideways, dragged me through the little stone entrance to the steps and down to the cell below. I saw it for the first time, and the last, that secret room beneath the buttress. Six foot high, four square, it was no larger than a closet, and the stone walls, clammy cold with years, felt icy to my touch. There was a little stool against the corner, and by its side an empty trencher, with a wooden spoon. Cobwebs and mould were thick upon them, and I thought of the last meal that had been eaten there, a quarter of a century before, by idiot uncle John. Above the stool hung the rope, near frayed, upon its rusty hinge, and beyond this the opening to the tunnel, a round black hole about eighteen inches high, through which a man must crawl and wriggle if he wished to reach the further end. "I don't understand," I said, shuddering. "It could not have been thus before. Jonathan would never have used it had it been so."

"There has been a fall of earth and stones," said Richard, "from the foundations of the house. It blocks the tunnel, save for a small space through which we burrowed. I think, when the tunnel was used before, the way was cleared regularly with pick and spade. Now that it has not been used for several years, Nature has claimed it for her own again. My enemies can find me a new name. Henceforth I will be badger, and not fox."

I saw Dick's white face watching me. What is he telling me, I wondered, with his dark eyes? What is he trying to say?

"Take me back," I said to Richard. "I have to talk to you."

He carried me to the room above, and it seemed to me, as I sat there breathing deep, that the bare boards and smoky ceiling were paradise compared to the black hole from which we had come. Had I in truth forced Dick to lie there, hour after hour, as a lad four years ago? Was it because of this that his eyes accused me now? God forgive me, but I thought to save his life. We sat there by the light of a single candle, Richard, and Dick, and I, while Matty kept watch upon the door.

"Jonathan Rashleigh has returned," I said.

Dick threw me a questioning glance, but Richard answered nothing.

"The fine is paid," I said. "The County Committee have allowed him to come home. He will be able to live in Cornwall henceforth, a free man, unencumbered, if he does nothing more to rouse the suspicions of the Parliament."

"That is well for him," said Richard. "I wish him good fortune."

"Jonathan Rashleigh is a man of peace," I said, "who, though he loves his King, loves his home better. He has endured two years of suffering and privation. I think he has earned repose now, and he had but one desire—to live amongst his family, in his own house, without anxiety."

"The desire," said Richard, "of almost every man."

"His desire will not be granted," I said, "if it should be proved he was a party to the rising."

Richard glanced at me, then shrugged his shoulders.

"That is something that the Parliament would find difficult to lay upon him," he said. "Rashleigh has been two years in London."

For answer, I took the bill from my gown, and, spreading it on the floor, put the candlestick upon it. I read it aloud, as my brother-in-law had read it to me, that afternoon:

"'Anyone who has harboured at any time, or seeks to harbour in the future, the malignant known as Richard Grenvile, shall, upon discovery, be arrested for high treason, his lands sequestered finally and for ever, and his family imprisoned.'"

I waited a moment, and then I said: "They will come in the morning, Jonathan said, to search again."

A blob of grease from the candle fell upon the paper, and the edges curled. Richard placed it to the flame, and the paper caught and burnt, wisping to nothing in his hands, then fell and scattered.

"You see?" said Richard to his son. "Life is like that. A flicker, and a spark, and then it is over. No trace remains."

It seemed to me that Dick looked at his father as a dumb dog gazes at his master. Tell me, said his eyes, what you are asking me to do.

"Ah, well," said Richard, with a sigh, "there's nothing for it but to run our necks into cold steel. A dreary finish. A scrap upon the road, some dozen men upon us, handcuffs and rope, and then the march through the streets of London, jeered at by the mob. Are you ready, Dick? Yours was the master hand that brought us to this pass. I trust you profit by it now."

He rose to his feet and stretched his arms above his head. "At least," he said, "they keep a sharp axe in Whitehall. I have watched the executioner do justice before now. A little crabbed fellow he was, last time I saw him, but with biceps in his arms like cannon-balls. He only takes a single stroke." He paused a moment, thoughtful. "But," he said slowly, "the blood makes a pretty mess upon the straw."

I saw Dick grip his ankle with his hand, and I turned like a fury on the man I loved. "Will you be silent?" I said. "Hasn't he suffered enough these eighteen years?"

Richard stared down at me, one eyebrow lifted.

"What?" he said smiling. "Do you turn against me too?"

For answer, I threw him the note I was clutching in my hand. It was smeared by now, and scarcely legible. "There is no need for your fox's head to lie upon the block," I said to him. "Read that, and change your tune."

He bent low to the candle, and I saw his eye change in a strange manner as he read, from black malevolence to wonder.

"I've bred a Grenvile after all," he answered softly.

"The *Frances* leaves Fowey on the morning tide," I said. "She is bound for Flushing, and has room for passengers. The master can be trusted. The voyage will be swift."

"And how," asked Richard, "do the passengers go aboard?"

"A boat, in quest of lobsters and not foxes, will call at Pridmouth," I said lightly, "as the vessel sails from harbour. The passengers will be waiting for it. I suggest that they conceal themselves for the remainder of the night till dawn on the cowrie beach near to the Gribben Hill, and when the boat creeps to its pots, in the early morning light, a signal will bring it to the shore."

"It would seem," said Richard, "that nothing could be more easy."

"You agree, then, to this method of escape? Adieu to your fine heroics of surrender?" I think he had forgotten them already, for his eyes were travelling beyond my head to plans and schemes in which I played no part. "From Holland to France," he murmured, "and, once there, to see the Prince. A new plan of campaign better than this last. A landing, perchance, in Ireland, and from Ireland to Scotland. . . ." His eyes fell back upon the note screwed up in his hand. "'My mother christened me Elizabeth,'" he read, "'but I prefer to sign myself your daughter Bess.'"

He whistled under his breath, and tossed the note to Dick. The boy read it, and handed it back in silence to his father.

"Well?" said Richard. "Shall I like your sister?"

"I think, sir," said Dick slowly, "you will like her very well."

"It took courage, did it not," pursued his father, "to leave her home, find herself a ship, and be prepared to land alone in Holland without friends or fortune?"

"Yes," I said, "it took courage, and something else beside."

"What was that?"

"Faith in the man she is proud to call her father. Confidence that he will not desert her, should she prove unworthy."

They stared at one another, Richard and his son, brooding, watchful, as though between them both was some dark secret understanding that I, a woman, could not hope to share. Then Richard put the note into his pocket and turned, hesitating, to the entrance in the buttress. "Do we go," he said, "the same way by which we came?"

"The house is guarded," I said. "It is your only chance."

"And when the watch-dogs come to-morrow," he said, "and seek to sniff our tracks, how will you deal with them?"

"As Jonathan Rashleigh suggested," I replied, "dry timber in midsummer burns easily, and fast. I think the family of Rashleigh will not use their summer-house again."

"And the entrance here?"

"The stone cannot be forced. Not from this side. See the rope there, and the hinge."

We peered, all three of us, into the murky depths. And Dick, of a sudden, reached out to the rope and pulled upon it, and the hinge also. He gave three tugs, and then they broke, useless for ever.

"There," he said, smiling oddly. "No one will ever force the stone again, once you have closed it from this side."

"One day," said Richard, "a Rashleigh will come and pull the buttress down. What shall we leave them for legacy?" His eyes wandered to the bones in the corner. "The skeleton of a rat," he said. And, with a smile, he threw it down the stair.

"Go first, Dick," he said, "and I will follow you."

Dick put his hand out to me, and I held it for a moment.

"Be brave," I said. "The journey will be swift. Once safe in Holland you will make good friends."

He did not answer. He gazed at me with his great dark eyes, then turned to the little stair.

I was alone with Richard. We had had several partings, he and I. Each time I told myself it was the last. Each time we had found one another once again. "How long this time?" I said.

"Two years," he said. "Perhaps eternity."

He took my face in his hands and kissed me long.

"When I come back," he said, "we'll build that house at Stowe. You shall sink your pride at last, and become a Grenvile."

I smiled, and shook my head.

"Be happy with your daughter," I said to him.

He paused at the entrance to the buttress.

"I tell you one thing," he said. "Once out in Holland, I'll put pen to paper, and write the truth about the Civil War. My God, I'll flay my fellow generals, and show them for the sods they are. Perhaps, when I have done so, the Prince of Wales will take the hint and make me at last supreme commander of his forces."

"He is more likely," I said, "to degrade you to the ranks."

He climbed through the entrance and knelt upon the stair, where Dick waited for him.

"I'll do your destruction for you," he said. "Watch from your chamber in the eastern wing, and you will see the Rashleigh summer-house make its last bow to Cornwall, and the Grenviles also."

"Beware the sentry," I said. "He stands below the causeway."

"Do you love me still, Honor?"

"For my sins, Richard."

"Are they many?"

"You know them all."

And as he waited there, his hand upon the stone, I made my last request.

"You know why Dick betrayed you to the enemy?"

"I think so."

"Not from resentment, not from revenge. But because he saw the blood on Gartred's cheek. . . ."

He stared at me thoughtfully, and I whispered: "Forgive him, for my sake, if not for your own."

"I have forgiven him," he said slowly; "but the Grenviles are strangely fashioned. I think you will find that he cannot forgive himself." I saw them both, father and son, standing upon the stair with the little cell below, and then Richard pushed the stone flush against the buttress wall, and it was closed for ever. I waited there beside it for a moment, and then I called for Matty. "It's all over," I said. "Finished now and done with."

She came across the room and lifted me in her arms.

"No one," I said to her, "will ever hide in the buttress cell again." I put my hand on to my cheek. It was wet. I did not know I had been crying. "Take me to my room," I said to Matty.

I sat there, by the far window, looking out across the gardens. The moon was high now—not white as last night, but with a yellow rim about it. Clouds had gathered in the evening, and were banking, curled and dark against the sky. The sentry had left the causeway steps and was leaning against the hatch door of the farm buildings opposite, watching the windows of the house. He did not see me sitting there, in the darkness, with my chin upon my hand.

Hours long it seemed I waited there, staring to the east, with Matty crouching at my side, and at length I saw a little spurt of flame rise above the trees in thistle park. The wind was westerly, blowing the smoke away, and the sentry down below, leaning against the barn, could not see it from where he stood.

Now, I said to myself, it will burn steadily till morning, and when daylight comes they will say poachers have lit a bonfire in the night that spread, catching the summer-house alight, and someone from the estate here must go cap in hand, with apologies for carelessness, to Jonathan Rashleigh in his house at Fowey. Now, I said also, two figures wend their way across the cowrie beach and wait there, in the shelter of the cliff. They are safe, they are together. I can go to bed, and sleep, and so forget them. And yet I went on sitting there, beside my bedroom window, looking out upon the lawns, and I did not see the moon, nor the trees, nor the thin column of smoke rising in the air, but all the while Dick's eyes, looking up at me for the last time, as Richard closed the stone in the buttress wall.

CHAPTER THIRTY-SEVEN

AT NINE IN THE MORNING came a line of troopers riding through the park. They dismounted in the courtyard, and the officer in charge, a colonel from the staff of Sir Hardress Waller at Saltash, sent word up to me that I must dress and descend immediately, and be ready to accompany him to Fowey. I was dressed already, and when the servants carried me downstairs I saw the troopers he had brought prising the panelling in the long gallery. The watchdogs had arrived. . . .

"This house was sacked once already," I said to the officer, "and it has taken my brother-in-law four years to make what small repairs he could. Must his work begin again?"

"I am sorry," said the officer, "but the Parliament can afford to take no chances with a man like Richard Grenvile."

"You think to find him here?"

"There are a score of houses in Cornwall where he might be hidden," he replied. "Menabilly is but one of them. This being so, I am compelled to search the house rather too thoroughly for the comfort of those who dwell beneath its roof. I am afraid that Menabilly will not be habitable for some little while. . . . Therefore I must ask you to come with me to Fowey."

I looked about me, at the place that had been my home now for two years. I had seen it sacked before. I had no wish to witness the sight again. "I am ready," I said to the officer.

As I was placed in the litter, with Matty at my side, I heard the old sound I well remembered, of axes tearing the floor-boards, of swords ripping the wood, and another jester, like his predecessor in '44, had already climbed up to the belfry and hung cross-legged from the beam, the rope between his hands, swinging the great bell from side to side. It tolled us from the gatehouse, tolled us from the outer court. This, I thought to myself in premonition, is my farewell to Menabilly. I shall not live here again.

"We will go by the coast," said the officer, looking in the window of my litter. "The highway is choked with troops, bound for Helston and Penzance."

"Do you need so many," I asked, "to quell but a little rising?"

"The rising will be over in a day or so," he answered, "but the troops have come to stay. There will be no more insurrections in Cornwall, east or west, from this day forward."

And as he spoke the Menabilly bell swung backwards, forwards, in a mournful knell, echoing his words.

I looked up from the path beneath the causeway, and the summer-house that had stood there yesterday, a little tower with its long windows, was now charred rubble, a heap of sticks and stones.

"By whose orders," called the officer, "was that fire kindled?" I heard him take counsel of his men, and they climbed to the causeway to investigate the pile, while Matty and I waited in the litter. In a few moments the officer returned.

"What building stood there?" he asked me. "I can make nothing of it from the mess. But the fire is recent, and smoulders still."

"A summer-house," I said. "My sister, Mrs Rashleigh, loved it well. We sat there often when she was home. This will vex her sorely. Colonel Bennett, when he came here yesterday, gave orders, I believe, for its destruction."

"Colonel Bennett," said the officer, frowning, "had no authority without permission of the Sheriff, Sir Thomas Herle."

I shrugged my shoulders. "He may have had permission. I cannot tell you. But he is a member of the County Committee, and therefore can do much as he pleases."

"The County Committee takes too much upon itself," said the officer. "One day they will have trouble with us in the army." He mounted his horse in high ill-temper, and shouted an order to his men. A civil war within a civil war. Did no faction ever keep the peace amongst themselves? Let the Army and the Parliament quarrel as they pleased; it would help our cause in the end, in the long run. . . . And as I turned and looked for the last time at the smouldering pile upon the causeway, and the tall trees in thistle park, I thought of the words that had been whispered two years ago, in '46; when the snow melts, when the thaw breaks, when the spring comes.

We descended the steep path to Pridmouth. The tide was low, the Cannis rock showed big and clear, and on the far horizon was the black smudge of a sail. The mill-stream gurgled out upon the stones, and ran sharply to the beach, and from the marsh at the farther end a swan rose suddenly, thrashing his way across the water, and, circling in the air a moment, winged his way out to the sea. We climbed the further hill, past Coombe Manor, where the Rashleigh cousins lived, and so down to my brother-in-law's town house on Fowey quay. The first thing I looked for was a ship at anchor in the Rashleigh roads, but none was there. The harbour water was still and grey, and no vessels but little fishing-craft anchored at Polruan. The people on the quayside watched with curiosity as I was lifted from my litter and taken to the house. My brother-in-law was waiting for me in the parlour. The room was dark panelled, like the dining-hall at Menabilly, with great windows looking out upon the quay. On the ledge stood the model of a ship—the same ship that his father had built and commissioned forty years before to sail with Drake against the Armada. She too was named the *Frances*.

"I regret," said the officer, "that for a day or so, until the trouble in the west has quietened down, it will be necessary to keep a watch upon this house. I must ask you, sir, and this lady here, to stay within your doors."

"I understand," said Jonathan. "I have been so long accustomed to surveillance that a few more days of it will not hurt me now."

The officer withdrew, and I saw a sentry take up his position outside the window as his fellow had done the night before at Menabilly. "I have news of Robin," said my brother-in-law. "He is detained in Plymouth, but I think they can fasten little upon him. When this matter has blown over he will be released, on condition that he takes the oath of allegiance to the Parliament, as I was forced to do."

"And then?" I said.

"Why, then he can become his own master, and settle down to peace and quiet. I have a little house in Tywardreath that would suit him well, and you too, Honor, if you should wish to share it with him. That is . . . if you have no other plan."

"No," I said. "No, I have no other plan."

He rose from his chair and walked slowly to the window, looking out upon the quay. An old man, white-haired and bent, leaning heavily upon his stick. The sound of the gulls came to us as they wheeled and dived above the harbour.

"The *Frances* sailed at five this morning," he said slowly.

I did not answer.

"The fishing-lad who went to lift his pots pulled first into Pridmouth for his passenger. He found him waiting on the beach, as he expected. He looked tired and wan, the lad said, but otherwise little the worse for his ordeal."

"One passenger?" I said.

"Why, yes, there was but one," said Jonathan, staring at me. "Is anything the matter? You look wisht and strange."

I went on listening to the gulls above the harbour, and now there were children's voices also, laughing and crying, as they played upon the steps of the quay. "There is nothing the matter," I said. "What else have you to tell me?"

He went to his desk in the far corner, and, opening a drawer, took out a length of rope, with a rusted hinge upon it.

"As the passenger was put aboard the vessel," said my brother-in-law, "he gave the fisher-lad this piece of rope, and bade him hand it, on his return, to Mr Rashleigh. The lad brought it to me as I breakfasted just now. There was a piece of paper wrapped about it, with these words written on the face. "Tell Honor that the least of the Grenviles chose his own method of escape."

He handed me the little scrap of paper.

"What does it mean?" he asked. "Do you understand it?"

For a long while I did not answer. I sat there with the paper in my hands, and I saw once more the ashes of the summer-house blocking for ever more the secret tunnel, and I saw too the silent cell, like a dark tomb, in the thick buttress wall.

"Yes, Jonathan," I said, "I understand."

He looked at me a moment, and then went to the table and put the rope and hinge back in the drawer.

"Well," he said, "it's over now, praise heaven. The danger and the strain. There is nothing more that we can do."

"No," I answered. "Nothing more that we can do."

He fetched two glasses from the sideboard, and filled them with wine from the decanter. Then he handed one to me. "Drink this," he said kindly, his hand upon my arm. "You have been through great anxiety." He took his glass, and lifted it to the ship that had carried his father to the Armada.

"To the other *Frances*," he said, "and to the King's general in the west. May he find sanctuary and happiness in Holland."

I drank the toast in silence, then put the glass back upon the table. "You have not finished it," he said. "That spells ill-luck to him whom we have toasted."

I took the glass again, and this time I held it up against the light so that the wine shone clear and red.

"Did you ever hear," I said, "those words that Bevil Grenvile wrote to Jonathan Trelawney?"

"What words were those?"

Once more we were assembled, four-and-twenty hours ago, in the long gallery at Menabilly. Richard at the window, Gartred on the couch, and Dick, in his dark corner, with his eyes upon his father. "And for mine own part," I quoted slowly, "I desire to acquire an honest name or an honourable grave. I never loved my life or ease so much as to shun such an occasion, which, if I should, I were unworthy of the profession I have held, or to succeed those ancestors of mine who have, so many of them, in several ages, sacrificed their lives for their country."

I drank my wine then to the dregs, and gave the glass to Jonathan.

"Great words," said my brother-in-law, "and the Grenviles were all great men. As long as the name endures, we shall be proud of them in Cornwall. But Bevil was the finest of them. He showed great courage at the last."

"The least of them," I said, "showed great courage also."

"Which one was that?" he asked.

"Only a boy," I said, "whose name will never now be written in the great book at Stowe, nor his grave be found in the little churchyard at Kilkhampton."

"You are crying," said Jonathan slowly. "This time has been hard and long for you. There is a bed prepared for you above. Let Matty take you to it. Come now, take heart. The worst is over. The best is yet to be. One day the King will come into his own again; one day your Richard will return."

I looked up at the model of the ship upon the ledge, and across the masts to the blue harbour water. The fishing-boats were making sail, and the gulls flew above them crying, white wings against the sky.

"One day," I said, "when the snow melts, when the thaw breaks, when the spring comes."

What Happened to the People in the Story

Sir Richard Grenvile. The King's General never returned to England again. He bought a house in Holland, where he lived with his daughter Elizabeth until his death in 1659, just a year before the Restoration. He offered his services to the Prince of Wales in exile (afterwards Charles II), but they were not accepted, due to the ill-feeling between himself and Sir Edward Hyde, later Earl of Clarendon. The exact date of his death is uncertain, but he is said to have died in Ghent, lonely and embittered, with these words only for his epitaph: "Sir Richard Grenvile, the King's General in the West".

Sir John Grenvile (Jack). Bernard Grenvile (Bunny). These two brothers were largely instrumental in bringing about the restoration of Charles II in 1660. They both married, lived happily, and were in high favour with the King. John was created Earl of Bath.

Gartred Denys. She never married again, but left Orley Court and went to live with one of her married daughters, Lady Hampson, at Taplow, where she died at the ripe age of eighty-five.

Jonathan Rashleigh. Suffered further imprisonment for debt at the hands of Parliament, but lived to see the Restoration. He died in 1675, a year after his wife, Mary.

John Rashleigh. He died in 1651, aged only thirty, in Devon, when on the road home to Menabilly after a visit to London about his father's business. His widow Joan lived in Fowey until her death in 1668, aged forty-eight. Her son Jonathan succeeded to his grandfather's estates at Menabilly.

Sir Peter Courtney. He deserted his wife, ran hopelessly into debt, married a second time, and died in 1670.

Alice Courtney. Lived the remainder of her life at Menabilly, and died there in 1659, aged forty. There is a tablet to her memory in the church at Tywardreath.

Ambrose Manaton. Little is known about him, except that he was MP for Camelford in 1668. His estate, Trecarrel, fell into decay.

Robin and Honor Harris. The brother and sister lived in retirement at Tywardreath, in a house provided for them by Jonathan Rashleigh. Honor died on the 17th day of November, 1653, and Robin in June, 1655. Thus they never lived to see the Restoration. The tablet to their memory in the church runs thus: "In memory of Robert Harris, sometime Major-General of His Majesty's forces before Plymouth, who was buried here under the 29th day of June, 1655. And of Honor Harris, his sister, who was likewise here underneath buried, the 17th day of November, in the year of our Lord 1653.

> "*Loyall and stout; thy Crime this—this thy praise,*
> *Thou'rt here with Honour laid—thought without Bayes.*"

Postscript

In the year 1824, Mr William Rashleigh, of Menabilly, in the parish of Tywardreath in Cornwall, had certain alterations made to his house, in the course of which the outer courtyard was removed, and blocked in to form kitchens and a larder. The architect, summoned to do the work, noticed that the buttress against the north-west corner of the house served no useful purpose, and he told the masons to demolish it. This they proceeded to do, and on knocking away several of the stones they came upon a stair, leading to a small room, or cell, at the base of the buttress. Here they found the skeleton of a young man, seated on a stool, a trencher at his feet, and the skeleton was dressed in the clothes of a Cavalier, as worn during the period of the Civil War. Mr William Rashleigh, when he was told of the discovery, gave orders for the remains to be buried with great reverence in the churchyard at Tywardreath. And because he and his family were greatly shocked at the discovery, he ordered the masons so to brick up the secret room that no one in the household should come upon it in future. The alterations of the house continued, the courtyard was blocked in, a larder built against the buttress, and the exact whereabouts of the cell remained for ever a secret held by Mr Rashleigh and his architect. When he consulted family records, Mr Rashleigh learnt that certain members of the Grenvile family had hidden at Menabilly before the rising of 1648, and he surmised that one of them had taken refuge in the secret room and had been forgotten. This tradition has been handed down to the present day.

DAPHNE DU MAURIER.

Acknowledgements

I WISH TO TENDER my grateful thanks to John Cosmo Stuart Rashleigh of Throwleigh, and to William Stuart Rashleigh of Stoketon, for giving me permission to print this blend of fact and fiction. I trust that they, and especially Œnonie Johnson, whose labour in copying family papers proved so helpful, will enjoy this glimpse of their forebears at Menabilly in days long vanished and forgotten.

I am grateful also to Miss Mary Coate, Mr A. L. Rouse, and Mr Tregonning Hooper for their great kindness in lending books and manuscripts.

D. DU M.

THE FLIGHT OF THE FALCON

Author's Note

The Flight of the Falcon is a work of fiction. Although Ruffano was inspired by an existing Italian city the topography, the events described, the inhabitants and every member of the university are purely imaginary.

CHAPTER ONE

WE WERE RIGHT on time. Sunshine Tours informed its passengers on the printed itinerary that their coach was due at the Hotel Splendido, Rome, at approximately 1800 hours. Glancing at my watch, I saw that it wanted three minutes to the hour.

"You owe me five hundred lire," I said to Beppo.

The driver grinned. "We'll see about that in Naples," he said. "In Naples I shall present you with a bill for more than two thousand lire."

Our bets were continuous throughout the tour. We each kept a book, checked the kilometres against the time, and then settled up when either of us felt like paying. The latter generally fell to me, no matter who had come out on top with the betting. As courier, I received the larger tips.

I turned round, smiling, to my load of merchandise. "Welcome to Rome, ladies and gentlemen," I said, "the city of popes, emperors, and Christians thrown to the lions, not to mention movie stars."

A wave of laughter greeted me. Somebody in the back row cheered. They liked this sort of thing. Any facetious remark made by the courier helped to establish the relationship between passengers and pilot. Beppo, as driver, may have been responsible for their safety on the road, but I, as guide, manager, mediator and shepherd of souls, held their lives in my hands. A courier can make or break a tour. Like the conductor of a choir he must, by force of personality, induce his team to sing in harmony; subdue the raucous, encourage the timid, conspire with the young, flatter the old.

I climbed down from my seat, flinging wide the door, and saw the porters and pages hurrying from the swing-doors of the hotel to meet us. I watched my flock descend, sausages from a machine, fifty all told—no need to count the heads, for we had not stopped between Assisi and Rome—and led the way to the reception desk.

"Sunshine Tours, Anglo-American Friendship League," I said.

I shook hands with the reception clerk. We were old acquaintances. I had been on this particular route for two years now.

"Good trip?" he asked.

"Pretty fair," I replied, "apart from the weather. It was snowing in Florence yesterday."

"It's still March," he said. "What do you expect? You people start your season too soon."

"Tell them that at the head office in Genoa," I answered.

Everything was in order. We held block bookings, of course, and because it was early in the season the management had fixed my whole party on the second floor. This would please them. Later in the year we should be lucky to get the fifth, and tucked away in the rear of the building at that.

The clerk watched my party file into the reception lounge. "What have you brought us?" he asked. "The holy alliance?"

"Don't ask me," I shrugged. "They joined forces at Genoa on Tuesday. Some sort of club. Beef and barbarians. The usual treatment in the restaurant at seven-thirty?"

"It's all laid on," he said, "and the relief coach ordered for nine. I wish you joy."

We use certain code-words for our clients in the touring business. The English are beef to us, and the Americans barbarians. It may not be complimentary, but it's apt. These people were running wild on pasture land and prairie when we were ruling the world from Rome. No offence intended.

I turned to greet the respective leaders of my Anglo-American group. "Everything's fine," I said. "Accommodation for all on the second floor. Telephones in every room. Any queries ring down to the desk and they'll put you through to me. Dinner at seven-thirty. I'll meet you here. The reception manager will now show you to your rooms. OK?"

Theoretically, this was where I laid off for an hour and twenty minutes, found my own small lair, had a shower and collapsed, but it seldom worked that way. Nor did it today. My telephone buzzed as soon as I'd taken off my jacket.

"Mr Fabbio?"

"Speaking."

"It's Mrs Taylor here. Utter and complete disaster! I've left every package I bought in Florence in that hotel in Perugia."

I might have known. She had left a coat in Genoa and a pair of overshoes in Siena. She had insisted that these things, almost certainly unnecessary south of Rome, must be telephoned for and forwarded to Naples.

"Mrs Taylor, I'm so sorry. What were in the packages?"

"Breakables, mostly. There were two pictures . . . a statuette of Michelangelo's David . . . some cigarette boxes. . . ."

"Don't worry. I'll take care of it. I'll telephone Perugia right away and see that your packages get to our office in Genoa, and are waiting there for your return."

It depended on how busy they were at reception whether I left them to put through the call and make the enquiry, or dealt with it myself. Better do it myself. It would save time in the long run. I had sized up the Taylor woman as a package-leaver as soon as she joined us. She trailed belongings. Spectacles, head-scarves, picture postcards kept falling out of her outsize handbag. It is an English failing, a fault of the species. Apart from this, beef give very little trouble, though in their desire to seek the sun they blister more readily than other nationalities. Bare-armed, bare-legged, they're into cotton frocks and shorts the first day of the tour, turning brick-red in the process. Then I have to conduct them to the nearest chemist's shop for salves and lotions.

The telephone buzzed once more. Not my call to Perugia, but one of the barbarians. A woman again, naturally. The husbands never bother me.

"Mr Fabbio?"

"Speaking."

"Guess what. It's a boy!"

I did a double-think. Barbarians give you their life history the first evening in Genoa. Which of them was it that was expecting her first grandchild, back in Denver, Colorado? Mrs Hiram Bloom.

"Congratulations, Mrs Bloom. This calls for a special celebration."

"I know it. I'm so excited I don't know what I'm doing." The scream of delight nearly broke my eardrum. "Now, I want just you, and one or two of the others, to meet Mr Bloom and myself in the bar before dinner, to drink the little boy's health. Shall we say seven-fifteen?"

It would cut down my free time to half-an-hour, and that call from Perugia hadn't yet come through. Nothing to be done. Courtesy first and foremost.

"That's very kind of you, Mrs Bloom. I'll be there. All well with your daughter-in-law?"

"She's fine. Just fine."

I hung up before she could read me out the cable. Time for a shave, anyway, and with luck a shower.

You have to be wary about accepting invitations from clients. A birthday or a wedding anniversary is legitimate, or the arrival of a grandchild. Nothing much else, or it tends to make bad blood and you are half-way to ruining your tour. Besides, where drinking is concerned a courier has to watch his intake. Whatever happens to his party, he must remain sober. So must the driver. This is not always easy.

I dealt with the Perugia call while still dripping from the shower, and after struggling into a clean shirt went downstairs to inspect the arrangements made for us in the restaurant. Two long tables in the middle of the room, each seating twenty-five, and in the centre of either table, dwarfing the flowers, the bunched flags of both nations, the Stars and Stripes and the Union Jack. This never fails to please—the clients feel that it gives tone to the proceedings.

A word with the head waiter, promising him to have my party seated by seven-thirty sharp. They liked us to have our main course finished and the dessert served before the other diners wandered in to their tables. It was important for us, too. We worked to a tight schedule, and were due to take off for our tour of "Rome By Night" at nine o'clock.

A final check on time, and then the short celebration drink in the bar. There were only a handful of them gathered to toast baby Bloom, but you could hear them from the entrance hall, where the excluded beef hung about in twos and threes, aloof, disdainful, their faces buried in the English newspapers. The extrovert barbarian roar had turned the Anglo-Saxons dumb.

Mrs Bloom glided towards me, a frigate in full sail. "Now, Mr Fabbio, you'll not refuse champagne?"

"Half a glass, Mrs Bloom. Just to wish long life to your grandson."

There was something touching in her happiness. Generosity exuded from her person. She placed her arm through mine and drew me forward into the group. How kind they were, dear God, how kind . . . Epitomising, in their all-embracing warmth, the barbarian hunger for love. I drew back, suffocated, then, ashamed of myself, let the wave engulf me. Back in Genoa I had many tributes from Mrs Bloom's compatriots. Christmas cards by the score, letters, greetings. Did I remember the trip two years ago? When would I visit them in the States? They often thought of me. They had named their youngest son Armino. The sincerity of those messages shamed me. I never answered them.

"I hate to break this up, Mrs Bloom. But it's just on seven-thirty."

"What you say goes, Mr Fabbio. You're the boss."

The two nations mingled in the entrance hall, halting momentarily as they greeted new acquaintances, the women appraising each other's dresses. Then through to the restaurant drifted my fifty head of cattle, lowing, murmuring, myself the stockman in the rear. There were cries of pleasure at the sight of the flags. For a moment I feared a burst into national song, "The Star-spangled Banner", "God Save the Queen"—it had happened before—but I caught the head waiter's eye and we managed to seat them before patriotism could do its worst. Then to my own small table in the corner. One lone male barbarian, middle-aged, swimmy-eyed, had placed himself at the corner of one of the long tables, from where he could watch me. I had him taped. I knew his kind. He would get no encouragement from the courier, but we might have trouble with him in Naples.

While I ate I did the day's accounts. This was my custom. I shut my ears to the sound of voices and the clatter of plates. If the accounts are not kept up to date you never get straight, and then there is hell to pay with head office. Book-keeping did not bother me. I found it relaxing. And then, when the figures were totted up, the notebook put away, my plate removed, I could sit back, finish my wine and smoke a cigarette. This was the real time of reckoning—no longer of sums to be forwarded every day to Genoa, but of my own motives. How long would it continue? Why was I doing this? What urge drove me, like a stupefied charioteer, on my eternal, useless course?

"We get paid for it, don't we?" said Beppo. "We make good money."

Beppo had a wife and three children in Genoa. Milan—Florence—Rome—Naples—they were all the same to him. A job was a job. Three days off duty at the end of it, home, and bed. He was satisfied. No inner demon broke his rest or asked him questions.

The babble of voices, topped by the barbarians, rose to a roar. My little flock was in full cry. Replete, at ease, their tongues loosened with whatever had filled their glasses, expectant of what the night would bring them—and what could it bring them but a bedding down beside their spouses after peering at buildings old, remote and alien to them, falsely lit for their enjoyment, glimpsed briefly through the windows, steamy with their breath, of a hired coach?—they spilt themselves, for a brief moment, of doubt and care. They were no longer individuals. They were one. They were escaping from all that bound and tied them—but to what?

The waiter bent over me. "The coach is waiting," he said. Ten minutes to nine. Time for them to fetch coats, hats, scarves, powder their faces and relieve themselves. It was not until I had counted the heads, as they climbed into the coach at one minute after nine, that I realised we mustered forty-eight. Two were missing. I checked with the driver—not Beppo, who was free to spend the evening as he pleased, but a man native to the city.

"There were two signore in advance of the rest," he told me. "They walked off together, down the street."

I glanced over my shoulder towards the via Veneto. The Hotel Splendido stands one street away, in comparative peace and quiet, but from the pavement one can see the bright lights and the gay shop-windows, and watch the traffic surge towards the Porta Pinciana. Here, for most women, is greater lure than the Colosseum we were bound for.

"No," said the driver, "they went that way." He pointed left. Then, from around the block, into the via Sicilia, came the hurrying figures. I should have known it. The two retired school-teachers from south London. Forever enquiring, forever critical, they were zealous for reform. It was this couple who had bade me stop the coach on the road to Siena because, they insisted, a man was ill-treating his oxen. It was this couple who, finding a stray cat in Florence, made me waste half-an-hour of our precious time seeking its home. A mother, admonishing her child in Perugia, had been in her turn admonished by the school-teachers. Now, bridling and outraged, they clattered towards me.

"Mr Fabbio . . . Someone should do something. There's a poor old woman, very ill, humped in the doorway of a church round the corner."

I contained myself with difficulty. The churches of Rome give sanctuary to all beggars, down-and-outs and drunks who care to sprawl upon their steps until such time as the police drive them away.

"Don't concern yourselves, ladies. This is quite usual. The police will see to her. Now hurry, please. The coach is waiting."

"But it's absolutely scandalous. . . . In England we . . ."

I took both women firmly by the arm and propelled them towards the coach. "You are not in England, ladies, you are in Rome. In the city of the emperors oxen, cats, children and the aged receive their just reward. The old woman is lucky in that refuse is no longer fed to the lions."

The school-teachers were still choking with indignation as the coach swept left, past the very church where the woman lay.

"There, Mr Fabbio, look . . . there!"

Obedient, I nudged the driver. He slowed down, co-operative, to give me a better view. Those passengers who were seated on the right of the coach stared likewise. The streetlamp showed the figure in relief. I have had moments in my life, as has everyone, when something in memory clicks, when we are aware of a sensation of what the French call "déjà vu". Somewhere, some time, and God alone knew when, I had seen that bowed posture, the ample drapery spread, the arms folded, the head buried under the weight of shawls. But not in Rome. My vision lay elsewhere. The memory was childhood's, blotted out by the years between. As we swept forward to the floodlights and the tourist illusion, one of the lovers on the back seat produced a mouth-organ and broke into the strains of a song long stale to the driver and myself, but popular with barbarian and beef—"Arrivederci Roma".

It was some time after midnight when we drew up at the Hotel Splendido once again. My troupe of fifty, yawning, stretching and I trust satisfied, rolled out of the coach one by one and passed through the swing-doors of the hotel. They had by this time as much individuality as machines mass-produced off an assembly line.

I was dead, and longed above all things for bed. Instructions for the morning, last messages, thanks, good-night from all, and it was over. Oblivion for seven hours. The courier could pass out. When, as I thought, the lift doors had closed on the last of them, I sighed, and lit a cigarette. It was the best moment of the day. Then, from behind a pillar where he must have hovered unobserved, stalked the lone middle-aged barbarian. He swung from the hips, as they all do when they walk, in unconscious identification with their coloured brethren.

"How about a night-cap in my room?" he said.

"Sorry," I answered curtly, "it's against regulations."

"Ah, come off it," he said, "it's after hours."

He rolled forward, and with a half-glance over his shoulder slipped a note into my hand. "Room 244," he murmured, and went.

I turned through the swing-doors into the street. It had happened before, it would happen again; my rebuff and his consequent hostility would be a factor to be reckoned with throughout the tour. It must be borne. The courtesy I owed to my employers in Genoa forbade complaint. But I was not paid by Sunshine Tours to appease the lust or loneliness of clients.

I walked to the end of the block and stood a moment, drinking the cold air. A car or two passed by and vanished. The traffic hummed behind me in the via Veneto, out of sight. I looked across to the church and the figure lay there still, immobile on the doorstep.

I glanced down at the note in my hand. It was ten thousand lire. A hint, I supposed, of favours to come. I went across the street and bent over the sleeping woman. The furtive odour of stale wine, worn clothes, rose to my nostrils. I fumbled for the hidden hand under the enveloping shawls and put the note into it. Suddenly she stirred. She lifted her head. The features were aquiline and proud, the eyes, once large, were now sunken, and the straggling grey hair fell in strands to her shoulders. She must have travelled from some distance, for she had two baskets beside her containing bread and wine, and yet a further woollen shawl. Once again I was seized with that sense of recognition, that link with the past which could not be explained. Even the hand that, warm despite the cold air, held on to mine in gratitude awakened an involuntary, reluctant response. She stared at me. Her lips moved.

I turned, I think I ran. Back to the Hotel Splendido. If she called to me—and I could have sworn she called—then I would not hear. She had the ten thousand lire, and would find food and shelter in the morning. She had nothing to do with me, nor I with her. The draped figure, suppliant, as though in mourning, was an illusion of my brain, and had no connection with a drunken peasant. At all costs I must sleep. Be fresh for the morning, the visit to St Peter's, the Vatican, the Sistine Chapel, the Sant' Angelo. . . .

A courier, a charioteer, has no time. No time.

CHAPTER TWO

I AWOKE WITH a start. Had someone called Beo? I turned on the light, got out of bed, drank a glass of water, looked at my watch. It was 2 a.m. I fell back into bed, but the dream was with me still. The bare impersonal hotel bedroom, my clothes flung on the chair, the account book and the itinerary of the tour beside me on the table were part of a day-by-day existence belonging to another world, not the one into which my dreaming self had inadvertently stumbled. Beo. . . . Il Beato, the blessed one. Childhood's name, given me by my parents and by Marta, because, no doubt, I was an afterthought, a later addition to the family circle, there being eight years between my elder brother Aldo and myself.

Beo. . . . Beo. . . . The cry rang in my ears as it had done in my dream, and I could not rid myself of the sense of oppression and fear. Sleeping, I had been a traveller in time, no longer a courier, and hand-in-hand with Aldo I stood in the side-chapel of the church of San Cipriano in Ruffano, staring above me at the altar-piece. The picture was of the Raising of Lazarus, and out of a gaping tomb came the figure of the dead man, still fearfully wrapped in his shroud—all save his face, from which the bindings had somehow fallen away, revealing staring, suddenly awakened eyes, that looked upon his Lord with terror. The Christ, in profile, summoned him with beckoning finger. Before the tomb, in supplication and distress, her arms bowed, her flowing garment spread, lay a woman, supposedly the Mary of Bethany who, often confused with Mary Magdalena, so adored her Master. But to my childish mind she resembled Marta. Marta, the nurse who fed and dressed me every day, who rode me upon her knee, who rocked me in her arms and called me Beo.

This altar-piece haunted me at night, and Aldo knew it. On Sundays and feast-days, when we accompanied our parents and Marta to church, and instead of going to the Duomo worshipped at the parish-church of San Cipriano, it so happened that we stood on the left of the nave, nearest to the chapel. Unconscious, like all parents, of the dread that possessed their child, they never looked to see that my brother, clasping my hand in his, urged me ever nearer to the wide-flung gates of the side-chapel, until I was compelled to lift my head and stare.

"When we go home," whispered Aldo, "I will dress you as Lazarus, and I shall be the Christ and summon you."

This was the worst of all. More full of terror even than the altar-piece itself. For Aldo, searching in the press where Marta kept the soiled linen before putting it to the wash, would drag out our father's night-shirt, limp and crumpled, and drag it over my head. To my fastidious mind there was, in this, some touch of degradation; and to be wrapped in worn clothes belonging to an adult turned my small stomach sour. Nausea rose in me, but there was no time to rebel. I was thrust into the closet above the stairs, and the door shut. This, oddly enough, I did not mind. The closet was spacious, and on the slatted shelves lay the clean, fresh linen, lavender-sweet. Herein spelt safety. But not for long. The handle of the closet turned. The door softly opened. Aldo cried, "Lazarus, come forth!"

So great was my dread, so disciplined to his commands my spirit, that I dared not disobey. I came forth, and the horror was that I did not know whether I should meet with the Christ or with the Devil, for according to Aldo's ingenious theory the two were one, and also, in some manner which he never explained, interchangeable.

Thus at times my brother, robed in a towel as Christ, bearing a walking-stick for crook, beckoned me with a smile, fed me with sweets, put his arms about me, was kind and loving. But at others, wearing the dark shirt of the Fascist Youth organisation to which he belonged and armed with a kitchen fork, he would represent Satan, and proceed to jab me with his weapon. I did not understand why Lazarus, the poor man raised from the dead, should so have earned the Devil's hate, and why his friend, the Christ, should so basely have deserted him; but Aldo, never at a loss, informed me that the play between God and Satan was unending, they tossed for souls as men in the world, and in the cafés of Ruffano, threw at dice. It was not a comforting philosophy.

Back in bed, in the Hotel Splendido, inhaling a cigarette, I wondered why I had been so suddenly transported to that nightmare world where Aldo was my king. It must have been that, as I drank the health of the small newborn barbarian, unconscious memory confounded him with myself, the timid Beato of a former world; and that, when I saw the woman lying on the church steps, the vision of the altar-piece in the San Cipriano chapel, with the Mary who loved both Lazarus and Christ prostrating herself in supplication before the open tomb, returned to me in undiminished force. Whatever the explanation, it was not welcome.

After a while I fell asleep once more, only to plunge into further torment. The altar-piece became associated with another picture, this time in the ducal palace at Ruffano, where our father held the post of Superintendent, a much respected office. This portrait, on display in the duke's bedchamber, and accounted a masterpiece by all lovers of art, had been painted in the early fifteenth century by a pupil of Piero della Francesca. It had for subject the Temptation, and showed Christ standing on the Temple pinnacle. The artist had composed the Temple to resemble one of the twin towers of the ducal palace, the most notable feature of the whole façade that reared itself in beauty above the city of Ruffano. Furthermore, the face of the Christ, gazing out from the portrait to the hills beyond, had been drawn by the daring artist in the likeness of Claudio, the mad duke, named the Falcon, who in a frenzy had thrown himself from the tower, believing, so the story ran, that he was the Son of God.

For centuries this picture had lain in the dusty cellars of the palace, until it was discovered at some period after the Risorgimento, when much reconstruction of the building took place. Forever afterwards it graced—or, as some scandalised inhabitants of Ruffano murmured, disgraced—the ducal apartment. The picture, like the altar-piece in San Cipriano, both shocked and fascinated me, as my brother Aldo was well aware. He would force me to climb with him, without our father's knowledge, the dangerous twisting stairway of the tower, and opening the ancient doorway leading directly to the turret would lift me, with what seemed superhuman strength, on to the encircling balustrade.

"This was where the Falcon stood," Aldo would say. "This was where the Devil tempted him. 'If thou be the Son of God, cast thyself down; for it is written, He shall give his angels charge concerning thee; and in their hands they shall bear thee up, lest at any time thou dash thy foot against a stone'."

Hundreds of feet below lay the city of Ruffano, the distant piazza de Mercato. The people, the moving vehicles, scurried about their business like ants on some lowly, dusty plain. I would cling to the balustrade, trembling. I don't know what age I was. Six, perhaps, or seven.

"Shall I tell you what the Falcon did?" asked Aldo.

"No," I pleaded, "no. . . ."

"He spread out his arms," said Aldo, "and he flew. His arms were wings, he had become a bird. He soared over the rooftops and the city that was his, and the people stared up at him in wonder."

"It isn't true!" I cried. "He couldn't fly. He was not a bird, he was not a falcon. He was a man, and fell. He fell and died. Father told me so."

"He was a falcon," insisted Aldo, "he was a falcon, and he flew."

In my dream the scene of terror I remembered was repeated once again. I clung to the balustrade, Aldo behind me. Then, with greater power than I had possessed as a child, I flung myself backwards, breaking from his grasp, and ran down, down the narrow twisting stair to where Marta waited, calling "Beo . . . Beo . . .". Her arms were there, ready to receive me, and she wrapped herself round me, holding me close, soothing me and comforting me. Marta, dear Marta. Why, though, in the dream, the odour of old, worn clothes? The smell of wine?

This time, on waking, I could feel my heart thumping in my breast, and I was sweating. The nightmare was too vivid to risk a third encounter. I switched on the light, sat up in bed, took up my notebook, and went over the accounts until, dizzy with exhaustion, I fell into a half-doze, and slept without dreaming until the knock on the door at seven announced the floor-waiter with my rolls and coffee.

The routine of the day began. The night, with all its horror, was a world away. The telephone started buzzing, as it always did, and within ten minutes I was involved in all the small technicalities of the hours ahead; the plans of those who wished to spend the morning shopping and join the rest of us at lunch; the queries of those who desired to see St Peter's but did not want to walk up and down the long galleries of the Vatican. Downstairs to the coach and the waiting Beppo, whose evening, unlike mine, had been spent in the warmth and comfort of his favourite trattoria.

"You know what?" he said. "You and I should change places. You drive the coach, and I make love to the clients."

This was a dig at my morning face, haggard from want of sleep. I told him he would be welcome.

As our cargo mounted, refreshed and eager for the "Rome By Day" that offered herself for their pleasure, I noticed that the lone barbarian, my suitor of last night, now cut me dead.

Our chariot swept left, past the church that had, in fearful fashion, confounded itself with San Cipriano and turned a dream to nightmare. The step was bare, the peasant woman gone. She was even now, I hoped, indulging herself, renewing inward fires with ten thousand lire I had given her. The retired school-teachers had forgotten her existence. They were already thumbing a guide-book and reading to their neighbours those contents of the Villa Borghese—first stop—that must on no account be missed. I was not surprised to discover them, some twenty minutes later, hurrying past the more conventional statuary, to stare with avid eyes at the reclining hermaphrodite.

On, on, the peace of the Pincio behind us, and so down to the piazza del Popolo, across the Tiber to Sant'Angelo, and thence to St Peter's and the Vatican. Then, God be thanked, to lunch.

Beppo, wise fellow, ate his in the coach, read the newspaper, slept; but my part was always that of the conductor, and in the restaurant near St Peter's there was little room or leisure to relax. Mrs Taylor had already lost her umbrella, left, she thought, in the cloakroom at the Vatican. Would I please see to it as soon as possible? We were due to leave for the Baths of Caracalla at 2 p.m., then back on our tracks to the Forum and a long afternoon amongst the ruins. Here it was my policy to let my charges loose to their own devices.

This afternoon it turned out otherwise. I had rescued the lost umbrella, and was crossing the via della Conciliazione to assemble my group, when I noticed that a handful of them had preceded me and were clustered about Beppo, who was reading to them from an open newspaper. He winked at me, enjoying his role of interpreter. His listeners looked shocked. I observed, with misgiving, that the two school-teachers were in the van.

"What's the excitement?" I asked.

"Murder off the via Sicilia," said Beppo, "within a hundred yards or so of the Hotel Splendido. These ladies claim to have seen the victim."

The most vocal of the school-teachers turned to me, outraged. "It's that poor woman," she said, "it must be the same. The driver says she was found stabbed on the church steps at five o'clock this morning. We could have saved her. It's too horrible for words."

I was shocked to silence. My aplomb deserted me. I snatched the paper from Beppo and read for myself. The notice was brief.

"The body of a woman was found at five o'clock this morning on the steps of a church on the via Sicilia. She had been stabbed. The woman appeared to be a vagrant, and had been drinking. A few coins only were found in her possession, and the crime would seem to be without motive. The police are seeking anyone who saw the woman, or noticed anything unusual in the vicinity during the hours of darkness, and who may be able to help their enquiries."

I returned the newspaper to Beppo. The group watched for my reaction.

"This is very regrettable," I said, "but not, I'm afraid, altogether unusual. Crimes of violence occur in every city. One can only hope the criminal will soon be caught."

"But we saw her," clamoured the school-teacher. "Hilda and I tried to speak to her, just before nine o'clock. She was not dead then. She was asleep, and breathing heavily. You saw her from the coach as we went by. Everyone saw her. I wanted you to do something then."

Beppo caught my eye and shrugged. He moved discreetly to the coach and climbed into his driving-seat. This was my business to sort out, not his.

"Madam," I said, "I don't wish to be heartless, but as far as we are concerned the incident is closed. There was little we could have done for the woman then. There is nothing now. The police have her case in hand. Now, we are already behind schedule. . . ."

But argument had broken out amongst the group. The remainder of the party joined us, asking what had happened. Passers-by paused and stared.

"Into the coach," I said firmly. "Into the coach, please, everybody. We are holding up the traffic."

Once seated, babel reigned. The barbarians, Mr Hiram Bloom their spokesman, were of the opinion that it never helped to meddle in other people's business. You only got abuse. The Anglo-Saxons glowered, especially the two school-teachers from south London. A woman had died on the doorsteps of a church, within a few hundred yards of the Pope's own Vatican City, within earshot of British travellers asleep in bed at the Hotel Splendido, and if the Rome police did not know how to do their job it was time a London bobby came to show them.

"So what?" murmured Beppo in my ear. "The police station, or the Baths of Caracalla?"

Beppo was fortunate. He was not involved. It was otherwise for me. No motive, the paper said, ignorant of the true facts. The woman had been murdered, not for the few coins found in her possession, but for the ten thousand lire I had put into her hand. It was as simple as that. Some roaming vagabond, himself with an empty belly, had stumbled across her in the small hours, pocketed the note, and perhaps arousing her, and suddenly terrified for his own life, had silenced her forever. Our petty criminals have small respect for human life. Who would shed tears over a vagrant, and a drunkard one at that? A hand over her mouth, a quick jab, and away.

"I insist," announced the school-teacher, a note of hysteria in her voice, "in reporting to the police. It's my duty to tell them what I know. It may help them to learn that we saw her in the church porch at nine o'clock. If Mr Fabbio refuses to go with me, I shall go alone."

Mr Bloom touched me on the shoulder. "What exactly would it entail?" he said sotto voce. "Any unpleasantness for the rest of the party? Or just a routine statement from you on behalf of these two ladies, and then finish?"

"I don't know," I answered. "Who can ever tell with the police, once they start asking questions?"

I told Beppo to drive on. Dissentient voices rose and fell behind me. Indifferent traffic hemmed us in on either side. Mine must be the decision, for good or ill. One false move and the harmony of my flock would dissolve, and a spirit of ill-feeling and resentment, so fatal to a tour, spring into being.

I reached for my pocket-book and handed a roll of notes to Mr Bloom.

"If you will be so good," I said, "as to take charge of the party, both at the Baths of Caracalla and at the Forum. There are guides who speak English in both places. Beppo will interpret if there should be any difficulty. You are due at the English Tea Rooms near the piazza di Spagna at four-thirty. I will meet you there."

The school-teacher leant forward. "What are you going to do?" she demanded.

"Conduct you and your friend to the police," I told her.

We were for it. There was no retreat. I told Beppo to set us down at the first taxi rank. The two Samaritans and I watched the coach drive away to the Baths of Caracalla. I had seldom regretted a departure more.

Driving to police headquarters my companions were strangely silent. They had not expected so swift an acquiescence to their plans.

"Will the police officers speak English?" asked the more nervous of the two women.

"I doubt it, madam," I replied. "Would you expect your police officers to speak Italian?"

They exchanged glances. I could sense the hostility that froze them to their seats. Also a deep mistrust of Roman law. Police headquarters are forbidding in any city, but I disliked the mission far more than they, to whom, no doubt, it could be counted as an experience of tourism. The sight of uniform, any uniform, makes me want to run. The tramp of feet, the brisk word of command, the cold speculative eye, have disagreeable associations; they remind me of my youth.

We alighted at our destination and I told the taxi to wait. I warned him, speaking clearly so that my companions could understand, that we might be hours.

Our feet sounded hollow as we crossed the courtyard to the police-station within. We were passed from the enquiry-desk to a waiting-room, from the waiting-room to an inner office, where the officer on duty asked our names, addresses, and the nature of our business. On my informing him that the English ladies wished to give information about the woman found murdered on the steps of the church in the via Sicilia, he stared. Then he struck a bell and snapped an order to the man who entered. The atmosphere was chill. After a moment two more police officers entered. Notebooks were produced. All three stared at the now subdued school-teachers. I explained to the officer behind the desk that neither spoke Italian. They were English tourists, I the courier in charge of Sunshine Tours.

"If you have any information material to last night's murder, please give it," he said curtly. "We have no time to waste."

The elder of the two Englishwomen began to speak, pausing, between sentences, for me to act as her interpreter. I used my own discretion as to what to omit in her somewhat incoherent tale. The remark that it seemed to her and her friend disgraceful that in these modern times there was no hospital or asylum in Rome for a starving woman to go to would hardly interest the police.

"You actually touched the woman?" asked the officer.

"Yes," replied the school-teacher. "I touched her shoulder and spoke. She grunted. I felt that she might be ill, and so did my friend. We hurried back to the coach and asked Mr Fabbio here to do something. He said it was not our business, and we were keeping the coach waiting."

The police officer questioned me with a glance. I replied that it was true. And that the time was just after 9 p.m.

"And when you returned from the tour you did not notice whether the woman was still there?" he asked her through my interpretation.

"I'm afraid not. The coach did not pass that way, and we were all very tired."

"In fact, the subject was not mentioned again?"

"No. Actually, my friend and I did bring it up when we were undressing. We said what a disgraceful thing it was that Mr Fabbio had not called an ambulance or informed the police."

Once again the officer glanced in my direction. I thought I detected sympathy. "Will you please thank these ladies for having come forward?" he said. "Their testimony has been helpful. For the records, I must trouble them to identify the clothing worn by the murdered woman, if they can do so."

I had not expected this. Nor had my charges. They turned a little pale.

"Is it necessary?" faltered the younger of the two.

"It appears so," I said.

We followed one of the police officers down a corridor and through to a small room. A white-coated attendant came forward, and after a moment's explanation went to an inner sanctum and brought forth a bundle of clothing and two baskets. My charges turned paler still.

"Yes," said the elder hurriedly, turning aside her head, "yes, I feel sure those were the things. How very dreadful it all is . . ."

The white-coated attendant, officious in his capacity as ghoul, asked if the ladies wished to view the body.

"No," I said, "they are not required to do so. The clothes are identification enough. However, if it would help at all with the enquiry, I am willing to do so on their behalf."

The police agent with us shrugged his shoulders. It was up to me. Neither of the two school-teachers knew what was being discussed. I passed with the attendant into the mortuary. Drawn by some painful and disturbing fascination, I approached the slab on which the body lay. The attendant drew back the covering, revealing the face. It was noble in repose, and younger than it had seemed last night.

I turned away. "Thank you," I said to the attendant.

I informed the officer in charge, on returning to the interview room, that the ladies had recognised the clothes. He thanked them once again.

"I assume," I said, "that these ladies will not be required for further questioning? We leave for Naples tomorrow afternoon."

Gravely the officer noted the fact in his report. "I do not anticipate," he said, "that we shall need their presence again. We have their names and addresses. I wish the ladies and yourself a pleasant resumption of your tour."

I could have sworn that after bowing to the school-teachers his eyelid flickered for an instant in a wink; but not at them, at me.

"Any clue to the victim's identity?" I asked.

He shrugged. "There are hundreds such, as you know, who wander into the city from outside. They are hard to check. Nothing on her of value. The murderer may have been a fellow-vagrant with some motive of revenge, or else a prowler, doing it for kicks. We'll pick him up."

We were dismissed. We walked back, across the courtyard, to the waiting taxi. I handed the ladies in. "The English Tea Rooms," I told the driver.

I looked at my watch. I had judged the time correctly. My charges could settle peacefully to a cup of tea together before the remainder of the party came. When we arrived I paid the taxi off and escorted the pair inside the English Tea Rooms. I settled them at a corner table.

"Now, ladies," I said, "you can relax."

My automatic smile brought no response, save a stiff inclination of the head.

I went out, and walked down the via dei Condotti to a bar. I had to think. I kept seeing the aquiline features, sharpened by death, of the murdered woman. Murdered because I had put ten thousand lire into her hand.

I felt sure now I had not been mistaken. There had been recognition in her eyes the night before, and she had called Beo as I ran away across the street. I had not seen her for over twenty years, but it was Marta.

CHAPTER THREE

_____

W HEN THE POLICE officers were questioning the English school-teachers—I should have spoken then. The opportunity was given me. They had asked whether, when we returned from our tour, we had noticed that the woman was still on the doorstep of the church. This had been the moment. "Yes," I should have said, "yes, I walked to the end of the street and she was there, and I crossed over and put a note for ten thousand lire in her hand."

I could imagine the look of surprise in the police officer's eyes. "A note for ten thousand lire?"

"Yes."

"What time was this?"

"Shortly after midnight."

"Did any of the party see you?"

"No."

"Was the money your own, or did it belong to Sunshine Tours?"

"It had just been given me. A mark of favour."

"You mean a tip?"

"Yes."

"By one of your clients?"

"Yes. But if you ask him, he will deny it."

Then the police officer would have asked for the two English ladies to withdraw. The interrogation would have continued, harder pressed. Not only could I never summon a witness to the fact that the lone barbarian had given me the money and had asked me to his room, but I could not produce a motive for giving away the money that would make sense to the police officer. Nothing made sense.

"You say you were reminded of an altar-piece that frightened you as a child?"

"Yes."

"And because of that you decided to put ten thousand lire into an unknown woman's hand?"

"It happened so quickly. I did not have time to think."

"I suggest to you that you never did have a note for ten thousand lire in your possession, and that you are now inventing this story of putting such a note into the woman's hand because you imagine it will give you an alibi."

"An alibi for what?"

"An alibi for the murder itself."

I paid for my drink and went into the street. It had begun to rain. Umbrellas sprouted like mushrooms to right and left. Girls with splashed legs bumped into me. Tourists, taken by surprise, stood huddled in doorways. My school-teachers were safe in the English Tea Rooms, and with this weather, which had threatened all afternoon, Mr Hiram Bloom would have mustered his party from the Forum and taken them back to Beppo and the waiting coach.

I turned up my coat collar, pulled my hat low and threaded my way through side streets to the via del Tritone and the Rome office of Sunshine Tours. It was almost four, and with any luck my comrade Giovanni might be back at his desk, though he liked to spin out the afternoon break. I was lucky. He was at his usual place in the far corner, speaking down the inevitable telephone. He saw me, raised his hand in greeting and pointed to a chair. The office was comparatively empty, save for a handful of tourists pressing patiently against the centre grille, demanding changes of reservations, hotel bookings, the usual routine.

Giovanni hung up, shook hands with me, and smiled. "Shouldn't you be in Naples?" he said. "No—what am I saying—Naples tomorrow, happily for you and your little bunch. Rome becomes more impossible every day. Good trip?"

"So-so. I can't grumble. Barbarian and beef, all very amiable."

"Girls good-looking?"

"Nothing to raise the blood-pressure. Anyway, do we have time? You try a courier's job."

He laughed and shook his head. "Well, what can I do for you?"

"Giovanni . . . I want your help. I'm in trouble."

He expressed sympathy.

"I want you to find a substitute for me to take the tour on to Naples," I said.

He exploded. "Impossible! Quite impossible in the time. I have no one here in Rome. Besides, head office . . ."

"Head office needn't know. At least, not immediately. Giovanni, surely you can rustle up someone? Supposing I had appendicitis?"

"Have you appendicitis?"

"No, but I can invent one if it will help."

"It won't help. I tell you, Armino, there is nothing I can do—we don't have substitutes hanging about in the office here just because you want a vacation."

"Listen to me, Giovanni. I don't want a vacation. I want you to put me on a northern route. Work an exchange. Just a temporary one, of course. I must go north."

"You mean Milan?"

"No . . . Any tour going towards the Adriatic will do."

"It's too early for the Adriatic, you know that. Nobody goes to the Adriatic until May."

"Well, then, not necessarily a coach, a tour, but a private client, who might consider Ravenna, Venice."

"Too early for Venice too."

"It's never too early for Venice. Giovanni, please."

He began to ruffle through some papers on the desk in front of him. "I can't promise anything. Something may turn up before tomorrow, but time is short. You take off for Naples at 1400 hours tomorrow, and unless I can arrange a double switch it won't work."

"I know, I know. But try."

"It's a woman, I suppose?"

"Of course it's a woman."

"And she can't wait?"

"Let us put it that I can't wait."

He sighed, and picked up his telephone. "If I have any news I'll leave a message at the Splendido for you to ring me. The things we do for our friends. . . ."

I left him, and made my way back to the English Tea Rooms. The rain had ceased and the sun glittered on all of us pedestrians so suddenly reprieved. If

Giovanni could not work the transfer, that was that. I had made the gesture. Gesture towards what? I did not know. Appeasement of the dead, perhaps, or my own conscience. I could still be wrong, the murdered woman not Marta. If so, although in my own mind I was an accessory to her death because I had placed the ten thousand lire in her hand, I was absolved from heavier guilt. If Marta, no. The cry of Beo made me a murderer too, in every sense as guilty as the criminal, as the thief who used the knife.

When I arrived in the piazza di Spagna I saw that my flock had finished tea and were about to mount the coach. I went to join them. I could tell, by the inflated appearance of the school-teachers, that they had recounted their tale. They were the heroines of their brief hour.

No message from Giovanni that evening at the hotel, and after dinner, a replica of the preceding night, but this time with speeches, we crossed over in the relief coach to Trastevere, so that my little flock could glimpse for an hour or so the café life that it pleased them to think was native to the area.

"This is the real Rome," breathed Mrs Hiram Bloom, seating herself at a cramped table in a side-street outside a taverna brightly lit with pseudo-lanterns for her innocent enjoyment. Six musicians, wearing breeches, stockings and Neapolitan caps, appeared with beribboned guitars as if by magic, and my little party swayed in sympathy to their rhythmic strains. There was something endearing in their innocence and pleasure. I felt almost sad that tomorrow, perhaps, they would all be in Naples, no longer in my care. A shepherd has his moments. . . .

No message from Giovanni at the hotel desk when we returned. Nevertheless I slept, and this night, God be thanked, without a single dream.

A call came through from Giovanni a few minutes after nine. "Armino," he said quickly, "look, I think I've fixed it. Two Tedeschi in a Volkswagen, going north. They want an interpreter. You speak German, don't you?"

"I do."

"Seize on to it, then. Herr Turtmann and his frau. Ugly as sin, both clutching maps and guide-books. They don't care where they go, as long as it's north. Sight-seeing fanatics."

"What about my substitute?"

"All arranged. You know my brother-in-law?"

"You have several."

"This one used to work in the American Express. He knows all the answers, and he's raring to go to Naples. He's all right. We can trust him."

I had a moment's doubt. Would Giovanni's brother-in-law botch the trip? Did he know how to handle people? And even if it worked, when the head office in Genoa learnt about the transfer would I lose my job?

"Listen, Giovanni, are you sure?"

He sounded impatient. "Look, take it or leave it. I'm doing you a favour, aren't I? I don't care either way. My brother-in-law is all set, and he's coming up to see you right away so that you can brief him. And I must let Herr Turtmann know. He wants to be off by ten-thirty."

I had just under an hour-and-a-half to hand over to my replacement, get myself down to the office and meet my new clients. It would be a near thing.

"Agreed," I told Giovanni, and hung up.

I drank a second cup of cold coffee and threw my few things into their case. At twenty minutes to ten Giovanni's brother-in-law knocked on the door. I remembered him at once. Eager, with a fine show of talk, I doubted if he carried indigestion tablets for queasy Anglo-Saxon stomachs, or would take an interest in the Bloom grandson. No matter. A courier can't have everything. We sat down side by side on my rumpled bed and I showed him my notes and the itinerary of the tour, plus the passenger-list, to which I added a short description of the idiosyncrasies of each client.

We left the room together, and I let my replacement go over to the reception desk and explain his status. I shook hands and wished him a good trip. As I passed through the swing-doors of the hotel into the street I felt like a nurse running out on her charges. The sensation was peculiar. I had never ratted on a tour before.

A taxi dropped me at the office in the via del Tritone, and as soon as I entered I saw Giovanni wearing his official face, all smiles and courtesy, talking to what were clearly my future clients. There was no mistaking their nationality. Both were middle-aged. Both carried ciné-cameras. He was a large, square-shouldered fellow, with stiff hair like the bristles of a clothes-brush and gold-rimmed spectacles. She was sallow, with hair piled-up under a hat a size too small for her. She wore, for no good reason, long white socks that contrasted with her dark top-coat. I came forward. He shook hands.

"My wife and I are keen photographers," announced Herr Turtmann as soon as Giovanni had introduced us. "We like to photograph in motion, from the car. We understand you can drive."

"Certainly, if you wish it," I said.

"Excellent. Then we can be off at once."

Giovanni bowed at them both, all smiles. Then he winked at me. "I wish you a pleasant trip," he said.

We took a taxi to where they had parked the Volkswagen. The roof was piled high with luggage, as was half the rear seat. The Tedeschi never travel light, and they accumulate possessions as they go.

"You will drive," commanded Herr Turtmann. "My wife and I wish to take pictures as we leave Rome. I leave the choice of route to you, but we should like to pass through Spoleto. They give two stars in my guide-book to the cathedral square."

I settled myself in the driving-seat, Herr Turtmann beside me, his wife tucked away in the back. As we crossed the Tiber they both held ciné-cameras to their eyes, moving them slowly from side to side like a machine-gunner sweeping his field of fire.

When the shooting ceased, which it did from time to time, they fed themselves copiously from paper bags and drank coffee from an outsize thermos flask. They talked little, and the silence suited me. It needed all my attention to pass the lorries on the road, and we had some two hundred and sixty kilometres to cover before we reached the destination I had in mind.

"And tonight?" asked Herr Turtmann suddenly. "Where do we sleep tonight?"

"We sleep at Ruffano," I said.

He rustled the pages of the guide-book on his lap. "There are several monuments with three stars, Gerda," he said over his shoulder to his wife. "We can shoot them all. Ruffano will suit us well."

It was both fitting and ironic that, having left the city where I was born and had spent the first eleven years of childhood in the company of one German, I should return to it more than twenty years later with another. Now, in March, the rolling countryside was purple-grey, stark and uninviting, the sky threatening the snow that had fallen in Florence; then, in the glazed, hot July of '44, the roads north out of Ruffano had been dusty white. The army trucks and vehicles on our route had given way to the Commandant's Mercedes, the flag fluttering from the bonnet. At times, aware of the car's importance, the weary drivers in the trucks would stiffen themselves into a salute, occasionally acknowledged by the Commandant within. If he was too indolent, I saluted for him. It helped to pass the journey, prevented me from feeling sick, and spared me the spectacle of watching my beautiful slut of a mother feeding her conqueror with grapes. Her frequent rather silly laughter, merged with his, offended my sense of what was due to adult dignity.

"I see," remarked Herr Turtmann to his wife, "that in the ducal palace in Ruffano they have the remarkable portrait of the Temptation of Christ, considered blasphemous until quite recently. I always thought it had been removed by our people in the war for safer housing."

I did not tell him that I had watched my father, the Superintendent, and his assistants crate the picture with great care and store it, with some others, in the cellars of the palace, for fear of any such eventuality.

My clients were amenable to a brief snack in Spoleto, with a swift shooting of the piazza and the Duomo façade, and we pressed on through Foligno and beyond, our road forever curling, twisting, amongst the rolling hills, while ahead the mountains, snow-covered, gave warning that my home, some five hundred metres high, might be in the grip of winter still. The first snowflakes fell, or rather we ran into them as we came up from the south; they must have been falling all day. The sky became a pall. The rivers, swollen with the coursing mountain streams, roared through the ravines beside us.

It was nearing seven when I had my first sight of home. To the traveller coming from Rome the city suddenly emerges, cresting the two hills, dwarfing the valleys below. I could not remember ever seeing it under snow. It was magnificent. Forbidding also, as if to warn the intrepid traveller—enter at your peril. How little changed, dear God, how little changed.

Herr Turtmann and his wife, risking the drifting snow, held cameras to the open windows of the car, and for their benefit, as well as to satisfy my own pride, I circled the valley just beneath the walls, to enter by the western gate, the porta del Sangue—the Gate of Blood.

"And rightly so," my father used to say, "since it was through here that Claudio, the first duke, drove his captives to their death."

Snow banked the road as it curved upward, lay thick upon the roof-tops, made phantoms of the trees, and, crowning the minarets of the twin towers of the palace and the Duomo and campanile beyond, turned my city into legend, into dream. I had forgotten there could be such beauty still.

I drove up the via dei Martiri to the city's centre, the piazza della Vita, and there braked. Nothing had altered, save the falling snow that had turned the city dumb, driving the inhabitants within doors. The buildings, a blend of ochre and musty pink, enfolded the piazza, their symmetry broken by the five converging streets. Blank windows above the colonnades stared down on the cobbled stones, their shutters fastened. The shops were closed. I recognised the names. The bookshop, the pharmacy, they were still the same. Dominating all, the shabby, sprawling Hotel dei Duchi, where, as a child, it had been a treat to lunch on Sundays. But later, when it was the Commandant's headquarters, entry was barred. Then, sentries had stood to attention before the door, or stamped their feet. Staff-cars and dispatch-riders' motor-cycles had been drawn up where now I parked Herr Turtmann's Volkswagen. Memory, dammed for over twenty years, was in full spate, and I was flooded by a wave of feeling.

I pushed open the door of the hotel and looked about me, hardly knowing what it was I sought—whether the office of the Commandant, the click of typewriters, or the reception lounge with stiff-backed chairs on which my father and his friends drank Cinzano after Mass. I think it was the last. And the last greeted me, though modernised into some semblance of a tourists' bar, with picture postcard racks, magazines upon the table, and a television-set in the far corner.

The silence was profound. I struck a bell that pealed alarmingly. In old days the proprietor, Signor Longhi, and his wife Rosa were always there to greet my father. He was bright-eyed, kindly, and walked—if I remembered rightly—with a limp; he had been wounded as a young man in the first world war. His wife Rosa, vivacious, plump, had been a redhead. She and my mother used to chatter trivialities, and when my mother was not present Signora Longhi would flirt, though mildly, with my proud father.

Now, in answer to my summons, a little maid appeared. Flustered, she said she thought we could have rooms, but she must first ask the padrona. A loud voice called from above. The padrona herself descended, slowly, because of excessive weight, and wheezing as she came. The eyes, darkly pouched, peered out at me from flabby cheeks; her hair was the streaky auburn of a poor provincial dye. I recognised, with a shock, a middle-aged Signora Longhi.

"You want rooms tonight?" she asked, looking upon me with indifference.

I explained the needs of the Turtmanns and myself and turned away from her, disenchanted. I went out into the snow to fetch my clients and their luggage. The flustered maid, the only apparent porter, followed me. It was out of season, of course, and yet. . . . Somehow the welcome had not been auspicious. The Turtmanns, unmoved, checked in and tramped upstairs, watched by the yawning padrona. The little boy to whom she had once fed sweetmeats was long forgotten.

I saw the Turtmanns settled into a room on the second floor and found the way to my own, a small room overlooking the piazza. Despite the falling snow I unfastened the shutters, opened the windows and stood a moment, drinking the sharp air.

I felt as a phantom would, returning after death. The indifferent buildings slumbered. Suddenly the campanile by the Duomo tolled out the hour. The note, deep-toned, was echoed in a moment by the varying notes from the other churches. San Cipriano, San Michele, San Martino, Sant'Agata, I knew them all, I recognised them all, with the thin high note of San Donato on the hill below the ducal palace the last to sound. This had been the moment when I said my prayers at Marta's knee. I fastened the window, closed the shutters, and found my way to the dining-room below.

CHAPTER FOUR

HERR TURTMANN AND his wife were already eating. They gave no sign for me to join them, and thankfully I sat down at a small table near the serving screen. Another maid, less flustered than her fellow, served as waitress, directed from time to time by the padrona herself, who would come from behind the screen to stare at us, rasp out an order, then disappear. Every mouthful that I ate, each draught of the rough local wine, raisin-coloured, which filled my carafe induced nostalgia. The centre table, laid for a dozen through long custom, was where Aldo had celebrated his fifteenth birthday. Handsome as a stripling god, he raised his glass to our parents, thanking them for the honour they had done him, while the surrounding guests applauded and I, the sibling, stared. My father, fated to die of pneumonia in an Allied prison-camp, toasted his first-born with a smile. My mother, radiant in a lime-green dress, preened her maternal feathers, kissing her hand to husband and to son. The Commandant had not yet loomed on her horizon.

I poured out the last of the wine from my carafe, and as I did so, like an echo to my thoughts, a little, white-haired old man came limping from behind the screen, bearing an illustrated magazine which he took to the Turtmanns' table. He pointed with pride to the leading feature, an article on Ruffano, and to a photograph of himself, the proprietor, Signor Longhi. He left the supplement with the Turtmanns and limped back to my corner.

"Good evening, signore," he said. "I hope everything has been to your satisfaction?"

He had a nervous tremor in his left hand, and this he tried to hide by placing the hand behind his back. It was, I supposed, an ailment of old age; the eager, bright-eyed Signor Longhi was no more. I thanked him for his trouble, and he bowed and disappeared behind the screen, his eyes sweeping over me without recognition. I could not expect otherwise. Why should anyone connect the insignificant courier of today with Signor Donati's youngest of long ago,—"Il Beato" whom adults patted on the head? We were all forgotten, we had all passed on. . . .

Dinner finished, and the Turtmanns escorted to their room, I fetched my coat, opened the front door of the Hotel dei Duchi, and went out into the piazza. Silence, white and still, enveloped me. There were footsteps in the snow, at first clear and firmly printed, the tracks of an individual which soon lost themselves against a drift and vanished. The biting air penetrated my light-weight overcoat. Winter's invasion of spring had caught me, like any other tourist, ill-prepared.

I looked to right and left, forgetting, after more than twenty years, how the main street divided into two on either side of the piazza, each branch to run, almost perpendicular it seemed, to its own summit. I struck left, hazarding a guess, past the great bulk of San Cipriano which loomed at me out of the snow, and immediately knew I was at fault, for the street ran broad and steep, and would emerge eventually on the north-western hill in front of the statue of Duke Carlo. Carlo the Good, the younger brother of mad Claudio, who in his reign of forty years, loved and respected, rebuilt his palace and his city and made Ruffano famous. I turned back to the piazza and struck south up the narrow twisting street to where it opened, suddenly, into the piazza Maggiore, and there, in all its majesty, stood the ducal palace of my boyhood, of my dreams, the rose-pink walls touched by the falling snow.

Idiot tears pricked my eyes—I, the courier, moved like any tourist by a picture-postcard print—and I moved forward, still in a dream, and touched the walls I knew. Here was the entrance door to the quadrangle within, used by my father the Superintendent and ourselves, Aldo and me, but never by the visiting crowds. There were the steps on which I used to jump, and here, beyond, the massive façade of the Duomo, rebuilt in the eighteenth century. Icicles had formed on the fountain in the piazza, hanging like crystals from the lips of the bronze cherubs. I used to drink at this fountain, inspired by a tale of Aldo's that it held all purity and many secrets in its clear waters; if there were secrets, I learnt none of them. I lifted my head to the palace roof and saw brooding there, above the entrance door, the great bronze figure of the Falcon, emblem of the Malebranche, the ducal family, his head snow-capped, his giant wings outspread. Then I turned from the palace and walked on, uphill, past the university, and turned left into the via dei Sogni, the Street of Dreams. No one stirred, not even a prowling cat. Now it was my footprints only that marked the fallen snow, and when I came to the high walls that enclosed my father's house, with the single tree crowning the small garden, a cold wind like a knife cut across the narrow street, so that the snow, still featherlight, drifted in front of me.

Once more I had the strange impression that I was a ghost returned, or not even a ghost, some disembodied spirit of long ago, and that there, in the darkened house, Aldo and I lay sleeping. We used to share a room, until he was promoted to one of his own. Not a chink of light showed tonight from the fastened shutters. I wondered who lived there now, if indeed the house was inhabited at all. Somehow it seemed to me forlorn, reproachful. And the garden wall I always thought so high had shrunk. I crept away like a furtive alley-cat, down past the church of San Martino, and took the short cut of the San Martino steps, descending abruptly to the piazza della Vita once again. I had not, on my reconnaissance, encountered a single soul.

I let myself in at the hotel and went up to my room, undressed, and so to bed. A hundred images raced through my mind, crossing and re-crossing like routes converging on an autostrada. Some memorable, some dim. The present intermingled with the past, my father's face became confused with Aldo's, the very uniforms they had worn when I had seen them last. The uniform which had graced Aldo at nineteen, with the pilot's wings, merged into those of my mother's lovers—the German Commandant, the American Brigadier in Frankfurt with whom we lived for two years. Even the head waiter at the Splendido, a passing acquaintance glimpsed a dozen times and never thought of, turned into the bank manager my mother eventually married, my step-father Enrico Fabbio of Turin, who gave me an education and a name. Too many faces, too many passing strangers, too many hotel bedrooms, hired apartments; none of them mine, nothing I called home. Life an unending journey with no end, flight without purpose. . . .

A shrill bell ringing in the corridor awakened me, and when I turned on my light I saw that it was morning, eight o'clock. I flung back my shutters. The snow had ceased and the sun was shining. Below me in the piazza della Vita people were going about their business. Shops had opened up, the assistants were sweeping away the snow; the familiar long-forgotten pattern of morning in Ruffano had taken on its accustomed shape. The sharp clean smell of the piazza came to my nostrils, the smell I remembered. A woman shook a mat out of a window. A group of men, standing beneath me, argued. A dog, with tail erect, chased a streaking cat, narrowly missed by a swerving car. More traffic than of old, or was it that in war only the military moved? I had no recollection of police on point duty, but one of them stood there now with arm out-stretched, directing the cars across the piazza to the via Rossini and the ducal palace. The young were everywhere, on vespas or on foot, all southward bound, up the hill, and it came to me, with surprise, that the small university of my childhood must have expanded and that the ducal palace, once Ruffano's pride, perhaps no longer reigned supreme.

I turned from the window, dressed, and went along to the dining-room for coffee, thinking to spare the flustered maid an errand. Signor Longhi brought me a tray himself, setting the coffee on the table with trembling hands.

"My apologies, signore," said the old man. "We are short-staffed, and are having alterations to the kitchen before the season opens."

I had been aware since waking of thuds and knocking, the voices of workmen calling to one another, the smell of paint, of mortar.

"Have you owned the hotel long?" I asked him.

"Ah yes," he answered, with some of the eagerness I remembered, "over thirty years, with a break during the Occupation. We had a staff headquarters here for a time. My wife and I went to Ancona. The Hotel dei Duchi was patronised by many well-known people in old days, writers, politicians. I can show you. . . ."

He limped towards a bookcase in the far corner, opened it and removed a visitors' book, which he carried back to my table as tenderly as he would a new-born infant. It opened automatically at a certain page.

"The English Minister, Stanley Baldwin, honoured us once," he said, pointing to the signature. "He stayed one night, was sorry not to stay more. The American film star Gary Cooper—there, on the next page. He was to have made a film here, but nothing came of it."

He turned the pages proudly for my inspection, '36, '37, '38, '39, '40, the years of my childhood, and an impulse rose in me to say, "And Signor Donati, the Superintendent at the palace, you remember him, and the signora? You remember Aldo at fifteen? Do you remember Beo, the small Beato, so small for his age that they took him for four, not seven? Well, here he is. Still small, still insignificant."

I controlled the impulse and went on drinking coffee. Signor Longhi continued to turn the pages of his visitors' book—omitting, I noticed, the years of shame—and so on to the fifties and the sixties, with no more ministers, no more film-stars, the pages filled with the names of a hundred tourists, English, American, German, Swiss, the passing clientèle who came and went, the kind I took under my wing on Sunshine Tours.

A rasping voice summoned him from behind the screen, and he limped away to do his wife's bidding. Furtively, my eye on the screen, I turned to '44, and there it was, bold, with a flourish, the signature of the Commandant, and the months when he made the hotel his staff headquarters. The remaining page was a blank. The Longhis had departed to Ancona . . . I snapped the book to and carried it to the bookcase. That was the place for mementos of the past. The Commandant, with his arrogant step, his bullying voice that swiftly, all too swiftly, thickened to sickly sentiment, he was better under lock and key. But for him and his symbolic presence—a conqueror conquered, a feather in her cap—my mother and I, with my father dead in a prison camp and Aldo shot down in flames, might have gone to Ancona with the Longhis. There had been talk of it. And then? Fruitless speculation. She would have picked another lover on the coast and wandered anyway, trailing her "Beato" with her.

"Are you ready?"

I turned my head. Herr Turtmann and his wife were standing in the doorway, overcoated, booted, strung about with their camera impedimenta.

"At your service, Herr Turtmann."

It was their intention to see the ducal palace and then drive out of Ruffano and pursue their tour north. I helped them stack the luggage and Herr Turtmann gave me the money to pay the bill. Signora Longhi counted the notes, returned the change and yawned. If my mother had not died of cancer of the womb in '56 she would have looked like Rosa Longhi. Her figure too had spread. Her hair was dyed also. Whether from disillusion or because of her illness, she used to scold my stepfather Enrico Fabbio in much the rasping way that the padrona here scolded her lame husband.

"Do you have much competition in Ruffano?" I asked, folding Herr Turtmann's bill.

"The Hotel Panorama," she answered shrugging. "Built three years ago. Everything modern. On the other hill, near the piazza del Duca Carlo. How can we hope to keep going in this dump? My husband is old. I'm tired. The place is beyond us."

Her epitaph spoken, she slumped behind the desk. I went out to join the Turtmanns in the car, another slice of childhood written off.

We left the piazza della Vita and drove up the narrow via Rossini to park outside the ducal palace. Morning had brought reality to my dream world of the preceding night. Other cars were stationed between our destination and the Duomo, pedestrians came and went, vespas roared past us to the university beyond.

At the entrance, a uniformed attendant leant from a boxed-in office. "Do you want a guide?" he called.

I shook my head. "I know where I am," I said.

Our footsteps echoed on the stone floor. I led the way through to the quadrangle, once more a ghost, a wanderer in time. This was where I used to shout, my voice reverberating to the arched colonnade.

"Aldo? Aldo? Wait for me!"

Back would come the answering echo. "I'm here. Follow me. . . ."

I followed now, up the grand staircase to the gallery above, while in every niche and vault stood the Malebranche falcon and the letters "C.M." for the two dukes, Claudio and Carlo. The Turtmanns stumped after me. We paused a moment in the gallery for them to draw breath, and the bench was there, the bench on which Marta used to sit and do her knitting, while I ran backwards and forwards along the gallery in front of her, or sometimes, greatly daring—if Aldo was not there to pounce upon me—travelled the whole circuit, pausing now and again to stare through the great windows that looked down upon the quadrangle below.

"Well?" said Herr Turtmann, staring at me. I withdrew my eyes from the gallery, with its empty bench, and turned right, into the throne room. Oh, God . . . that musty, sullen smell, redolent of ages past, of ancient feuds, of dukes and duchesses long dead, of courtiers, pages. . . . The smell of vaulted ceilings, ochre walls, the heavy, dusty scent of tapestry.

The dead were with me as I walked the familiar room. Not only the spectres of the history I had learnt, the mad Duke Claudio, the beloved Carlo, the gracious duchess and her retinue of ladies; my own dead were beside me too. My father, gracious as a duke himself, showing the palace to visiting historians from Rome or Florence; Marta, shushing if I raised my voice, coaxing me out of earshot of the distinguished guests; Aldo, above all Aldo. Advancing on tiptoe, his finger to his lips.

"He's waiting!"

"Who's waiting?"

"The Falcon. . . . To seize you in his claws, and carry you off."

A babble of sound came from behind me. A party of young people, students doubtless, escorted by a woman lecturer, noised their way into the throne room with us, filling the whole place with their presence. Even the Turtmanns were disturbed. I beckoned them on to the reception rooms beyond. A uniformed guide, stifling his yawn, approached my clients, scenting the prospect of largesse. He had a smattering of English, and took my Tedeschi for barbarians.

"Note-a the ceiling," he said, "the ceiling very fine. Restored by Tolomeo."

I left him to it and slipped away. Ignoring the duchess's apartments I headed for the Room of the Cherubs and the ducal bedchamber. They were empty. An attendant on a window-seat slumbered in a far corner.

Little was changed. Palaces, unlike people, withstand the years. Only the pictures had been moved, brought from their war-time sojourn in the cellars to be displayed now, so I grudgingly admitted, to greater advantage than in my father's day. They were placed more correctly, where the light could play upon them. The Madonna and Child, my mother's favourite, instead of hanging on the wall in comparative obscurity, stood upon an easel, alone in tranquil grandeur. The dull marble busts of a later age, which were in old days grouped about the room, had been removed. There was nothing now to detract from the Madonna. The attendant opened an eye. I went towards him.

"Who is the Superintendent here?" I asked.

"There is no Superintendent," he replied. "The palace is under the supervision of the Arts Council of Ruffano—that is to say the ducal apartments, the pictures, tapestries, and the rooms above. The library on the ground floor is used by members of the university."

"Thank you," I said.

I passed on before he could point out to me the dancing cherubs on the chimney-piece. There was a time when I had names for every one of them. I entered the ducal bedchamber, searching instinctively for the picture on the wall, the "Temptation of Christ" of which Herr Turtmann had spoken to his frau. It was still there. No Arts Council could place this one on an easel.

Unhappy Christ, or, as the artist with ingenious candour had painted him, unhappy Claudio. . . . He stood in his saffron shift, one hand upon his hip, staring at nothing—unless it was at the roof-tops of his visionary world, the world that might be his, should Temptation master him. The Devil, in the guise of friend and counsellor, whispered his message. Behind him the rosy sky foretold a triumphant dawn. The city of Ruffano slept, ready to stir and wake and do his bidding.

"All these things will I give thee, if thou wilt fall down and worship me."

I had forgotten that his eyes were pallid like his golden hair, and that the hair itself, framing the pale face, resembled thorns.

A wave of voices sounded in the rear. The Turtmanns and their persuasive guide, the students and the lecturer were hard upon me. I slipped through to the audience chamber, knowing that the pursuing babblers would not only dally before the picture I had left, but would turn aside to visit the ducal study, the ducal chapel. By slipping a few hundred lire into the guide's hand the Turtmanns might even be permitted a glimpse of the spiral staircase leading to the tower above.

Here in the audience chamber was the hidden entrance to the second tower. The spiral stairway of this one, though a replica of the other, was never in my father's day considered safe. Those tourists who were intrepid enough to brace their muscles and brave vertigo were conducted to the right-hand tower, through the ducal dressing-room.

I went to the wall and lifted the concealing tapestry. The doorway was still there, the key within the lock. I turned it, the door opened. Before me was the stair, curving ever upward to the tower above, below me the descent, three hundred steps or more, to the abyss below. How long was it, I wondered, since anyone had climbed this stair? Cobwebs smeared the little leaded window, and dead flies. The old fear, the old fascination gripped me. I put my hand upon the cold stone step, preparatory to climbing.

"Who is there? It is forbidden to mount the stair!"

I looked over my shoulder. The guide I had left sleeping in the Room of the Cherubs had followed and stood staring at me, his beady eyes narrowed in suspicion.

"What are you doing? How did you get there?" he asked.

I felt the guilt of years. For such an act my father would have commanded bed, and bed without supper, unless it was smuggled up to me by Marta.

"I'm sorry," I said. "I chanced to look behind the tapestry and saw the door."

He waited for me to pass. Then he shut the door, turned the key and replaced the tapestry. I gave him five hundred lire. Mollified, he pointed to the room ahead. "Room of the Popes," he said. "Round the wall are busts of twenty popes. All very interesting."

I thanked him, and passed on. The Room of the Popes had always lacked allure.

I skirted the remaining rooms, the ceramics and the stone reliefs. In old days they had been good for hiding in, for the echo came more clearly. I walked down the great stairway once again, traversed the quadrangle and the entrance passage and went out into the street. I lit a cigarette and leant against the columns of the Duomo, waiting for my clients. A postcard vendor approached me with his wares. I waved him away.

"When does the invasion start?" I asked.

He shrugged. "Any time now," he said, "if the weather mends. The municipality do their best to put Ruffano on the map, but we're poorly placed. Those who are heading for the coast prefer to go direct. We depend mostly on the students for selling this stuff."

He thumbed his postcards and the little bicycle-flags bearing the insignia of the Malebranche Falcon.

"Are there many of them?"

"Students? Over five thousand, they say. A lot of them come in by day, the town can't house them. It's all happened in the last three years. Plenty of opposition from the older folk, the place getting spoilt and so on, the students rowdy. Well, they're young, aren't they? And it's good for trade."

The intake at the university must have doubled, possibly trebled. I could not be sure. The students gave little trouble in the past, as far as I remembered. I had the impression then that they were all studying to be teachers.

My informant ambled off and as I waited for the Turtmanns, smoking my cigarette, I became aware, for the first time for months, for years, that the hour no longer pressed. I was working to no schedule. There was no Sunshine Touring coach drawn up in the piazza in front of me.

The snow was melting rapidly under the hot sun. Children were chasing one another round the fountain. An old woman came to the door of the baker's opposite, her knitting in her hands. More student groups of youths and young women passed into the ducal palace.

I stared up at the Falcon above the palace door, his bronze wings poised for flight. Last night, snow-covered, oblique against the sky, he had seemed menacing, a threat to all who trespassed. This morning, though still the guardian of the palace walls, the spread wings hinted freedom.

The deep-toned bell of the campanile by the Duomo struck eleven. Hardly had the last notes died away when the Turtmanns, gesticulating, slammed the Volkswagen door. They must have emerged without my seeing them, and were now impatient to be gone.

"We have seen all we want to see," barked my client. "We propose to leave the city by the opposite hill, after photographing the statue of Duke Carlo. This will give us longer in Ravenna."

"It's up to you," I said.

We climbed into the car, I in the driving seat, as yesterday. We left the piazza Maggiore and went downhill to the piazza della Vita, and so across the city's centre and up the northern hill to the piazza del Duca Carlo. I realised now why the Longhis had lost business. The new Hotel Panorama, with its view of the city and surrounding country, its gaily-painted balconies, its grass verges and little orange trees, held more glamour for the tourist than the poor Hotel dei Duchi.

"Ha!" said Herr Turtmann. "Look, that is where we should have stayed." He turned on me, angrily.

"Too late, my friend, too late," I murmured in my own tongue.

"What? What is it you say?"

"The Hotel Panorama does not open until Easter," I said smoothly. I stopped the car, and they got out to film the statue of Duke Carlo and the surrounding view. This used to be the regulation walk on Sundays. The local dignitaries, their wives and children and dogs, would parade about the plateau, neatly laid out with trees and shrubs, and bedding plants in summer. Here there was some change, if nowhere else. New houses had been built below the summit, and the orphanage, that once had stood alone in its stark ugliness, was now hemmed in by smarter dwellings. This, I took it, was the affluent quarter of Ruffano, the modern challenge to the more famous southern hill. I got out of the Volkswagen, carrying my small grip, as my clients, having finished the morning's filming, came towards the car.

"This, Herr Turtmann," I said, holding out my hand, "is where I say goodbye. The road to the right out of the piazza will take you downhill to the Porta Malebranche, and so on your way north. Take the coast road to Ravenna, it's very fast."

He and his wife stared at me, and he blinked behind his gold-rimmed spectacles. "You are engaged as our courier and chauffeur," he said. "It was arranged with the agent in Rome."

"A misunderstanding." I bowed. "I undertook to escort you as far as Ruffano, no further. I regret the inconvenience."

I have some respect for the Tedeschi. They know when they are beaten. Had my client been a fellow-countryman, or a Frenchman, he would have burst into a tirade of abuse. Not so Herr Turtmann. He looked at me a moment, his mouth tightened, then he ordered his wife curtly into the car.

"As you please," he said. "I have already paid in advance for your services. The Rome office must reimburse me."

He got in, slammed the door, and started up the engine. In a moment the Volkswagen was on its way, across the piazza del Duca Carlo and out of sight. Out of my life as well. I was no longer a courier. No longer a charioteer. I turned my back on the good Duke Carlo, high above me on his pedestal, and stared south to the opposite hill. The ducal palace of the Malebranche, with its twin towers facing westward, adorned the summit like a crown. I started to walk downhill into the city.

CHAPTER FIVE

At NOON THE piazza della Vita earns its name. The women, their shopping done, have all gone home to prepare the midday meal. The men take over. Crowds of them were assembled there when I reached the centre. Shopkeepers, clerks, loafers, youths, men of business, all talking, gossiping, some merely standing still and staring. It was the custom, it had always been like this. A passing stranger might have thought them members of some organisation about to take over the city. He would have been wrong. These men were the city. This was Ruffano.

I bought a paper and leant against one of the pillars of the colonnade. I searched the pages for the Roman news, and found half-a-dozen lines about the murder in the via Sicilia.

"The identity of the woman murdered two days ago in the via Sicilia has not yet been discovered. It is believed that she came from the provinces. A lorry-driver has stated that he gave a lift to a woman answering to her description after leaving Terni. The police are pursuing their enquiries."

We had passed through Terni yesterday, before turning right to Spoleto. Travelling south from Ruffano to Rome a wanderer, a vagrant, would be glad to seize the chance of a lorry-ride for the remaining distance. Doubtless the lorry-driver had come forward and identified the body, but in any case the description of the dead woman would by this time have been circulated to every city in the country, so that the police could check with their list of missing persons. What, though, if the dead woman was not upon the list? What if, filled with a sudden wanderlust, she had simply left her home? I could not remember if Marta possessed relatives. Surely not. Surely she had devoted herself to my parents after Aldo had been born, and had remained with us ever after. She never talked of brothers, sisters. . . . Her devotion, her whole life, had been given to us.

I put the paper down and stared about me. No faces that I knew, not even amongst the old. Hardly surprising, when I had left Ruffano aged eleven. The day we drove away, my mother and I, in the staff car with the Commandant, Marta had been at Mass. She always went to Mass each morning. Knowing her custom, my mother had timed our exit deliberately.

"I'll leave a note for Marta," she said, "and she can follow later, with all our things. There's no time to bother with them now. The Commandant has to leave immediately."

I did not understand what it was all about. Military persons were always coming and going. The war was apparently over, yet there seemed to be more soldiers than ever before. Germans, not ours. It was beyond me.

"Where are we going with the Commandant?" I asked my mother.

She was evasive. "What does it matter?" she answered impatiently. "Anywhere, as long as it's out of Ruffano. He'll take care of us."

I felt certain Marta would be dismayed when she returned from Mass. She might not want to go. She hated the Commandant. "You are sure Marta will follow?"

"Yes, yes, of course."

And so to leaning out of the staff car, saluting, watching the passing country, thinking of Marta less often each day, being fobbed off in the months to follow with more lies, more evasions. And then forgetting, finally forgetting. Until two days ago. . . .

I crossed the piazza to the church of San Cipriano. It was shut. Of course it was shut. All churches closed at noon. As a courier it was part of my job to reconcile the tourists to this fact. I must bide my time as they did until the afternoon.

Then, suddenly, I saw a man I recognised. He was standing in the piazza, arguing with a group of cronies, a cross-eyed fellow with a long lean face, hardly altered in old age from what he had been at forty-five. He was a cobbler in the via Rossini, and he used to repair our shoes. His sister Maria had been our cook over a period, and a friend of Marta's. This fellow, and his sister if she lived, would surely have kept in touch with her. The question was, how could I approach him without giving myself away? I lit another cigarette and kept my eye on him.

Presently, the argument finished, he moved away. Not up the via Rossini but to the left out of the piazza, threading along the via dei Martiri, and so across it to a narrow street beyond. Feeling like a detective out of a police novel, I followed him. Progress was slow, for he paused now and again to exchange a word with an acquaintance, and I, more furtive than ever, was obliged to stoop to tie a shoe-lace, or stare about me as if a tourist and lost. I could have done with the Turtmanns' cameras to save my face.

He ambled on, and at the further end of the narrow street turned left again. When I caught up with him he was near enough to touch, standing at the top of the steep steps beside the small oratorio of Ognissanti. The steps descend abruptly, almost vertically, to the via dei Martiri below. He stood aside for me to pass.

"Excuse me, signore," he said.

"Pardon me, signore," I countered, "I was simply following my nose, a stranger in Ruffano."

His gaze, cross-eyed, had always been disconcerting. I did not know now whether he looked at me or not.

"The steps of Ognissanti," he said, pointing, "the oratorio of Ognissanti."

"Yes," I said, "so I see."

"You wish to visit the oratorio, signore?" he asked. "My neighbour has the key."

"Another time," I said. "Please don't trouble yourself."

"No trouble at all," he said. "She is sure to be at home. Later on, in the season, she opens the oratorio at regular hours. At the moment it isn't worth her while."

Before I could prevent him he had called up at the window of the small house adjoining the chapel. It opened, and an elderly woman thrust out her head.

"What is it, Signor Ghigi?" she called.

Ghigi, that was it. That was the name above the cobbler's shop. Our cook had been Maria Ghigi.

"A visitor to see the oratorio," he called, then waited for her descent. The window slammed. I felt myself unwelcome.

"I'm sorry to make myself a nuisance," I said.

"At your service, signore," he said.

The cross-eyes were surely searching me. I turned my head. In a moment or two the door opened and the woman emerged, fumbling for her keys. She opened the door of the oratorio and motioned to me to pass. I stared about me, feigning interest. The attraction of the oratorio is a group of martyred saints, modelled in wax. I remembered having been brought here as a child, and being reproved by the attendant for trying to touch the models.

"Very fine," I observed to the couple watching me.

"It is unique," said the cobbler, and then, as if in afterthought, "did the signore say he is a stranger to Ruffano?"

"Yes," I said, "I come from Turin." Instinct made me give my stepfather's city, where my mother had died.

"Ah, Turin," he said, as though disappointed, and added, "You have nothing like this in Turin."

"We have the shroud," I told him, "the shroud that wrapped the Saviour. The marks of the sacred body are upon it still."

"I did not know that," he replied, rebuked.

We were all silent. The woman jangled her keys. I felt the cobbler's cross-eyes upon me, and grew restless.

"Thank you," I said to both. "I have seen enough."

I gave the woman two hundred lire, which she stowed away in her voluminous skirt, shook hands with the cobbler, and thanked him for his courtesy. Then I walked down the steps of Ognissanti, guessing they were staring after me. It was possible that I had reminded him of something, someone, yet there was nothing to connect me, a man from Turin, with a lad of ten.

I retraced my steps to the piazza della Vita and found a small restaurant in the via San Cipriano, a few yards from the church. I had lunch and smoked a cigarette, my head still empty of plans. The restaurant must have been popular—it was new since my time—for it filled rapidly and customers were obliged to share tables. Instinctive wariness made me bring out my newspaper and prop it against the carafe of wine in front of me.

Somebody said, "Excuse me, is this place free?"

I raised my eyes. "By all means, signorina," I said, making room, jarred by the sudden interruption to my thoughts.

"I believe I saw you in the ducal palace this morning," she said.

I stared, then swiftly begged her pardon. I recognised the woman lecturer who had been in charge of the crowd of students.

"You tried to escape us," she said. "I can't say I blame you."

She smiled, and the smile was pleasing, though her mouth was too large. Her hair was parted in the centre and drawn smoothly back, her age a possible thirty-two. She had a large mole close to her left eye. Some men find these marks attractive, enhancing sexual charm. To each his own taste. . . .

"I did not try to escape you," I said, "only your audience."

After mixing so much with nationalities other than my own, especially Americans and Anglo-Saxons, and being always in a subservient position, I had lost touch with the women of my own country, who demand flirtation as a common courtesy.

"If you had wanted to know about the pictures in the palace," she said, "you could have joined us."

"I am not a student," I said, "and I dislike to be one of many."

"A private guide would be more to your choice, perhaps," she murmured.

Gallantry, I saw, would be the order for the remainder of the meal. When I tired of it, I could always look at my watch and make the excuse of time.

"The choice of most men," I said. "Haven't you found it so?"

She smiled, a conspiratorial smile, and gave her order to the waiter. "You are probably right," she said, "but as a lecturer on the staff of the university I have a job to do. I must make myself agreeable to both boys and girls, and endeavour to put facts into their reluctant heads."

"Is that a hard task?"

"With the majority of them, yes," she answered.

Her hands were small. I like small hands in women. She wore no ring.

"What are your duties?" I asked.

"I'm attached to the Faculty of Arts," she said. "I lecture two or three times a week in class to the second- and third-year students, and escort the first-year batch to the palace, as I did this morning, and to other places of importance. It's quite interesting. I've been here two years now." The waiter served her, and after eating in silence for a few moments she glanced at me and smiled. "And you?" she asked. "Are you on a visit here? You don't look like a tourist."

"I'm a courier," I said. "I look after tourists, as you look after students."

She grimaced. "Have you your charges with you in Ruffano?"

"No. I wished the last god-speed this morning."

"And now?"

"You might say I'm open to offers."

She said nothing for a moment. She was busy eating. Then she pushed aside her plate and turned to her salad.

"What sort of offers?" she asked.

"You make them. I'll tell you," I answered.

She looked at me in speculation. "What are your languages?"

"English, German and French. But I've never given a lecture in my life," I told her.

"I didn't suppose you had. Any degree?"

"Degree in modern languages, Turin."

"Why, then, a courier?"

"One sees the country. The tips are good."

I ordered more coffee for myself. The conversation did not commit me.

"So you're on vacation?" she said.

"Self-imposed. I've not been sacked. I just wanted a few weeks off from my regular work. As I told you, I'm open to offers."

She had finished her salad. I offered her a cigarette, which she took.

"I might be able to help you," she said. "They're temporarily understaffed in the university library. Half our stuff is still housed in a room in the palace. Later it will be moved into new quarters between the university and the students' hostel, but our fine new building won't be opened until after Easter. For the time being chaos reigns. The librarian, a good friend of mine, could do with extra help. And with a degree in modern languages. . . ." She left her sentence unfinished, but her gesture implied that the rest was easy.

"It sounds interesting," I said.

"I don't know about the pay," she said quickly. "It wouldn't be much. And the job is only temporary, as I said, but that might suit you."

"It might indeed."

She summoned the waiter in her turn for coffee, brought out a card from her bag and gave it to me. I glanced at it and read the words, "Carla Raspa, 5, via San Michele, Ruffano."

I handed mine in return. "Armino Fabbio, Sunshine Tours, Turin."

She raised ironic eyebrows and put it in her bag. "Sunshine Tours," she murmured, "I could do with one. Ruffano can be very dead after working hours." She drank her coffee, watching me as she did so. "Think it over. I must leave you—I have a lecture at three. I'll be in the library myself after four, and if you want to take this up I can introduce you to the librarian, Giuseppe Fossi. He'll do anything for me. Eats out of my hand."

The look in her eye suggested that he did more than that. Gallantly I returned the look. For courtesy's sake we were conspirators.

"You have your credentials on you?" she asked as she rose from the table.

I patted my breast pocket. "I carry them everywhere," I said.

"Fine. Goodbye for now."

"Goodbye, signorina. And thank you."

She disappeared through the restaurant entrance to the street. I glanced at the card once more. Carla Raspa. The name suited her. Hard as nails, with a soft centre, like a Neapolitan ice. I pitied the librarian Giuseppe Fossi. It might be my answer, though, for the next two or three weeks. Not her—the job. Possibly the one went with the other, but I should have to take care of that when the moment came.

I paid the bill and went out into the street, carrying my grip, feeling like a snail with the world upon his back. I crossed the street and tried the door of San Cipriano once again. This time it was open. I pushed my way inside and went into the chancel.

The smell brought back the past, as it had done at the ducal palace. Here the memory, though less intense, was more sombre, muted, connected with Sundays, feastdays, the necessity of silence, and an inner restlessness that mirrored my longing to be outside. I did not connect the church of San Cipriano with devout feelings or with prayer, only with an intense awareness of being small and hemmed in by adults, with impersonal priestly intoning, the puff of incense, the touch of Aldo's hand, a desire to urinate.

The church was empty, save for a sacristan who seemed to be busy with candles at the high altar, and I made my way up the nave on the left-hand side, tiptoeing as if by instinct, and so up the single step to the chapel. Hollow sounds came from the high altar in the church, as the sacristan went about his business. I looked for a light in the chapel and switched it on. The light fell upon the altar-piece. Small wonder I had been frightened as a child at that figure in his shroud, the wrappings from the face hanging in streamers, the eyes of terror staring out upon his Lord. I realised now that the painting was no masterpiece. Executed in the days when tortured expression and exaggerated form had been the vogue, the risen Lazarus, to my maturer eyes, now seemed grotesque. Yet the bowed figure of the supplicating Mary in the foreground was still Marta, still the humped woman on the steps of the church in Rome.

I switched off the light and left the chapel. Two nights ago, dreaming, I had been a child still, imagination vivid. Now there was disenchantment; the risen Lazarus had lost his power.

As I turned into the nave the sacristan came pattering down to meet me. A sudden thought came to me. "Excuse me," I said, "are the baptismal records kept here in the church?"

"Yes, signore," he answered, "the records are in the sacristy. They go back a number of years, to approximately the beginning of the century. Earlier than that, they are kept in the presbytery."

"Would it be possible for me to look up an entry for the year 1933?"

He hesitated a moment, murmuring something about the priest in charge of the records not being available. I slipped a note into his hand and told him I was passing through Ruffano, unlikely to return, and wished to consult a baptismal entry for a relative. He protested no more, and led the way into the sacristy.

I hovered while he searched for the book. The odour of sanctity was all about me. Stoles and surplices hung from hooks. The faint scent of incense mingled with floor-polish pervaded all. The sacristan approached me with a book.

"We have the entries here from 1931 to 1935," he said. "If your relative was baptised in San Cipriano, his name should be here."

I took the book and opened it. It was like turning back the pages into the past. How many of my contemporaries must be here, children born and baptised in Ruffano, now adult, scattered, or perhaps living in the city still, shopkeepers, clerks, yet in this book only a few days old. . . .

I turned to July the 13th, the day of my birth. Here was my baptism, on a Sunday two weeks later. "Armino. Son of Aldo Donati and Francesca Rossi. Godparents, Aldo Donati, brother, Federico Ponenti, Edda Ponenti." I had forgotten that Aldo, not then nine years old, had been my sponsor. He had written his name in a round, childish hand, that yet already had more character to it than the uniform scrawl of the second cousins who shared the responsibility. They had lived, if I remembered rightly, at Ancona. Now it all came back. The first communion. Aldo's eyes upon me, hinting eternal punishment should I, through fear or clumsiness, let fall the Host out of my open mouth.

"Have you found the entry?" asked the sacristan.

"Yes," I said, "yes, it's there."

I shut the book and gave it into his hands. He took it, and replaced it in the cupboard amongst a row of similar volumes.

"Wait," I said. "Have you the entries for the 'twenties too?"

"The 'twenties, signore? Which year?"

"Let me see. It would be 1925, I suppose."

He took out another volume. "Here is '21 to '25."

I took the book and turned to November. November the 17th. The date had always held significance for me because it was Aldo's birthday. Even in Genoa, on autumn mornings, when I looked at the office calendar, the number 17 under the month of November was somehow dedicated.

Curious . . . Aldo must have been a sickly infant, for here he was, baptised within a day of his birth. "Aldo. Son of Aldo Donati and Francesca Rossi." No mention of godparents.

I turned the page, and to my surprise the entry was repeated a few days later. "Aldo. Son of Aldo Donati and Francesca Rossi. Godparents, Aldo Donati, father, Luigi Speca, Francesca Rossi."

Who was Luigi Speca? I had never heard of him. Nor, I felt sure, had Aldo. And why the double entry?

"Tell me," I said to the sacristan, "have you ever heard of an infant being baptised twice?"

He shook his head. "No, signore. Though if the child was ailing, and the parents feared it might die, it is just conceivable that it might be baptised on the day of birth and the ceremony repeated later, when the child was stronger. Has the signore finished with the book?"

"Yes," I said. "Take it."

I watched him replace the book amongst its fellows in the cupboard, and turn the key. Then I came out into the sunlight, crossed the piazza della Vita and walked up the via Rossini. It was strange that Aldo should have been baptised twice. It was the sort of story, had we known it, that he would have turned to good advantage. "I was doubly blessed," I could imagine him telling me.

Marta would have known about the baptism. . . . So thinking, I was reminded of the cross-eyed cobbler, and I looked about me for his shop, situated, to the best of my recollection, halfway up, on the left-hand side. There it was. . . . But larger, smartened, and with rows of shoes to sell. No longer shoes with tickets and upturned soles, advertising repairs. A different name, too, above the door. My cross-eyed Ghigi of the morning must have retired, to live beside the oratorio. He was the only likely link with Marta, or his sister if she lived, and short of admitting my identity I did not see how I could approach him.

The same held good for the Longhis, at the Hotel dei Duchi. It would be so easy to go back, to say, "I meant to tell you last night. I am the younger son of Aldo Donati. You remember my father, the Superintendent at the ducal palace?" Even the flabby face of the signora would have creased into a smile, the first shock over. And then, "You remember Marta? What happened to Marta?"

It was no good. It would not work. Anyone returning from the past, as I was doing, must remain anonymous. Otherwise it meant useless involvement. Alone, in secret, I could unravel the threads of the past, but not with identity known.

I passed the ducal palace once again and then turned left, coming, after a moment, into the via dei Sogni. I wanted to look at my old home by day. The snow had melted, as it had done elsewhere in Ruffano, and the sun must have filled the house all morning, for behind the tree I could see the windows of the first floor, opened. This had been my parents' bedroom, in early days a sort of sanctum in my eyes, but later shunned.

Someone was playing the piano. There had never been a piano in our time.

The player had the touch of a professional. A torrent of sound rippled from the keys. It was something I knew, heard probably on the radio, or more likely still from the music-rooms in the university at Turin when I used to hurry past to lectures. My lips framed a silent echo to the sound as it rose and fell, half gay, half sad, a timeless melody. Debussy. Yes, Debussy. The well-worn "Arabesque", but with a master touch.

I stood beneath the wall and listened. The music ebbed and flowed, changed mood and entered the more solemn phrases, and then again that first light-hearted ripple, higher, ever higher, confident and gay, but at last with a descending scale, dissolving, vanishing. It seemed to say: All over, never-more. The innocence of youth, the joy of childhood, leaping from bed to welcome a new day . . . all gone, the fervour spent. The repetition of the phrase was only a reminder, an echo of what had been. So swift to go, impossible to hold.

The music ceased before the closing bars. I could hear the telephone. Whoever played must have gone to answer it. The window was closed, then all was still.

The telephone used to stand in the hall, and if my mother was upstairs she had to run to answer it, arriving breathless. I wondered if the player did the same. I looked up at the tree that shrouded the small garden like a canopy. Somewhere in the branches should be a rubber ball that I had much prized, kicked aloft one day in an idle mood and never recovered. I wondered if it lay there still, and with the wonder came resentment, a strange antagonism to the present owner of my home. Theirs the right to wander through the rooms, open and shut the windows, answer the telephone. I was just a stranger, staring at the wall.

The playing was resumed. This time a Chopin Prelude, mournful, passionate. The pianist's mood had changed with the telephone call, nerves were unleashed to sombre melancholy. And none of it my business.

I went on walking up the via dei Sogni, and so out into the via dell'8 Settembre, in front of the university. It was like walking into another age. The young were everywhere, pouring out of lecture rooms, laughing, talking, getting on to vespas. The old building which had always been known as the House of Studies boasted new wings, the windows glowing not only with fresh paint but with vitality. There were new buildings too across the way, and yet another in construction—the new library, possibly—topping the hill. This university was not the crumbling, rather faded seat of learning I remembered from childhood days. Austerity was banished. The young, with all their fine contempt for dusty ways, had taken over. Transistor radios blared.

I stood, clutching my grip, a wanderer between two worlds. The one the via dei Sogni of my past, with all its memories, but no longer mine; and this other, active, noisy, equally indifferent. The dead should not return. Lazarus was right to feel foreboding. Caught, as he must have been betwixt past and present, he evaded both in horror, seeking the anonymity of the tomb—but in vain.

"Hullo," said a voice in my ear, "have you made up your mind?"

I turned, and saw Carla Raspa. She looked cool, confident and self-possessed. No doubts for her.

"Yes, signorina. Thank you for your trouble. But I have decided to leave Ruffano." This was my intention, but the words were left unsaid. A youth, straddling a vespa, swerved past us, laughing. He had a small flag fixed to his machine which fluttered in the breeze, just as, years back, the staff car of my mother's Commandant carried his hated emblem. The student's flag was tourist junk, perhaps, bought for a few hundred lire in the piazza Maggiore, but it had for design the Malebranche Falcon and so was, to my nostalgic eye, a symbol.

Adopting my habitual mask of courier, of courtier, I bowed to the signorina, sweeping her from head to foot in a caressing glance that she knew, and I knew, meant precisely nothing.

"I was on my way to the ducal palace," I told her. "If you are free, perhaps we could go together?"

I had reached the point of no return.

CHAPTER SIX

THE UNIVERSITY LIBRARY was housed on the ground floor of the ducal palace, in what had been the banqueting-hall of long ago. It had been used for manuscripts and documents when my father was Superintendent, and I gathered was so still, on shelves separate from those temporarily loaned to the university. My new acquaintance led the way, with all the assurance of someone on home ground, while I followed, assuming a stranger's ignorance.

The room was vast, larger even than I remembered, with the musty smell inseparable from books, many of which were stacked high upon the floor. A certain confusion prevailed. One clerk knelt upon the floor, inserting printed slips into some of the volumes. A second was halfway up a ladder, busy among the higher shelves. A third, a harassed female, was taking notes, dictated by the individual whom I gathered, correctly, to be the librarian, Giuseppe Fossi. He was short, stout, with an olive-green complexion and the wandering, bulging eye I associate with clandestine appointments. He hurried forward at the sight of my companion, leaving his minion in mid-note.

"I've found you an assistant, Giuseppe," said Carla Raspa. "Signor Fabbio has a degree in modern languages, and would be grateful for temporary work."

The bulging eye of Giuseppe Fossi appraised me with some hostility—was I perhaps a rival?—then, stalling for time, he turned back to the object of his admiration.

"Signor Fabbio is a friend of yours?"

"A friend of a friend," she answered promptly. "Signor Fabbio has been working in Genoa for a touring agency. I know the manager."

The lie was unexpected, but it served. The librarian turned back to me.

"I certainly need help," he admitted, "and anyone with languages, who could catalogue the foreign books, would be invaluable. You see for yourself the mess we are in." He waved an apologetic gesture about the room, and went on, "I warn you, the remuneration is small, and I shall have to press a point with the university Registrar if I take you on."

I gestured a willingness to accept whatever was offered, and he looked from me to Carla Raspa. The response she gave him with her eyes was similar to that already given me in the restaurant in the via San Cipriano, but more compelling. Excitement filled him.

"Well, now . . . I will see what I can do with the Registrar. It would naturally leave me freer if I had your help. As it is, the evenings . . ."

The same conspiratorial glance passed between them. He turned to the telephone. I had understood what she meant when she told me that Ruffano could be dead by night; nevertheless, she must be easily pleased.

We feigned deafness while Giuseppe Fossi carried on a rapid conversation on the telephone. The receiver clamped. "All fixed," he said. "It's the same throughout the university at the moment. Nobody has any time to spare for other people's problems—we must all make our own decisions."

I expressed my thanks, with a certain wonder that even a temporary increase in staff could be such an easy matter to arrange.

"The Rector is away sick," explained Giuseppe Fossi. "Without him, authority is non-existent. He *is* the university."

"Our beloved Rector," murmured the signorina, and I thought I detected irony in her voice, "suffered a thrombosis, alas, after attending an assembly in Rome, and has been in hospital there ever since. We are all lost without him. He has been ill for weeks."

"Does nobody take over?" I asked.

"Professor Rizzio, the Deputy-Rector," she answered, shrugging, "who happens to be the Head of the Department of Education, and spends his time arguing with Professor Elia, the Head of the Department of Economics and Commerce."

The librarian expostulated reprovingly. "Come, Carla," he said, "gossip, like smoking, is forbidden in the library. You should know better." He patted her on the arm indulgently and looked at me, shaking his head. The head-shake suggested dissociation from her views, the pat on the arm possession. I smiled, remaining silent.

"I must leave you," she said, and which of us she addressed remained in doubt. "I have another lecture at five."

She raised her hand to me, saying "Be seeing you," and was on her way to the door. Signor Fossi hurried after her, calling, "One moment, Carla . . ." I waited for instructions, while one of the clerks glanced up at me and winked. After a murmured consultation with the signorina, Giuseppe Fossi returned and said briskly, "If you care to start work right away it will help us all."

I spent the next two hours learning my work under his direction. Special care had to be taken because certain of the volumes which were part of the university library had become mixed up with others which, belonging to the ducal palace proper, were in the care of the Arts Council of Ruffano.

"Gross inefficiency," said Signor Fossi. "It happened before my time. But there will be an end to these troubles when we have all our own stuff in the new university library. You have seen the building? It's almost finished. All due to the Rector, Professor Butali. He has achieved wonders for the university"—he lowered his tone, with an eye on the clerk within earshot—"against much opposition. The usual thing, in a small centre such as ours. There is rivalry amongst the Departments, and jealousy too between the university and the Arts Council. Some want one thing, some another. The Rector has the thankless task of keeping the peace between them all."

"Was that the reason for his heart attack?" I asked.

"I would think so," he said, and then, with a knowing look flickering an instant in his bulging eye, "he also has a beautiful wife. Signora Butali is several years younger than her husband."

I continued sorting books until, at a little after six, Giuseppe Fossi gave an exclamation and looked at his watch. "I have an appointment at seven," he said. "Do you mind remaining here for another hour? And when you leave, will you please go to the Registrar's office to sign in? They will, if you wish, give you a list of addresses where you can find lodgings—the university has first call on a number of rooms and small pensioni in the city. Signorina Catti will assist you if there is anything else you wish to know."

The female clerk, some fifty odd, peered at me dourly through her spectacles as Giuseppe Fossi bustled off, bidding us all goodnight. Then she continued to make notes, her sour expression unchanged, and the younger of the two clerks—I had already heard him addressed as Toni—moved across the room to help me.

"He'll lose some weight this evening," he murmured.

"With the lady who went out earlier?"

"They say she's tireless. I've never tried my luck."

Signorina Catti called him sharply to remove some books from the desk in front of her. I hid my face in an enormous ledger. The hour ticked by. At seven precisely I approached her desk and, after obtaining her grudging admission that there was nothing more I could do, made my way towards the Registrar's office. The young clerk, Toni, followed me, and we walked through the silent quadrangle towards the outer entrance.

I paused by the great stairway leading to the ducal apartments on the first floor. The lights were on, and I could hear the sound of voices.

"What's happening above? Don't they close at four o'clock out of season?"

"To the public, yes," said Toni, "but the Director of the Arts Council comes and goes as he pleases. Besides, he's particularly involved just now with all the arrangements for the Festival."

There was an attendant on duty by the side door. We bade him goodnight and went out into the piazza Maggiore.

"The Festival?" I enquired.

"Why, yes, don't you know about it? It's our great day. Inaugurated by the Rector, Professor Butali, really to put the university on the map, but now the whole of Ruffano takes a pride in it and the people flock in from miles around. The students give a fine display. Last year the performance took place here in the ducal palace." He walked to a vespa leaning against the wall and wound a scarf about his throat. "Got a date?" he asked. "If you haven't, my Didi will fix you up. She works in ceramics, down in the town, but she knows a lot of the C and E students, and their girls are a lively bunch."

"C and E?"

"Commerce and Economics. It only started three years ago, but soon it'll outnumber the other Faculties. The C and E students mostly live in the town, or come in by day, hence the fun! They aren't stuck away in the students' hostels like the rest."

He grinned, and started up his machine. I shouted above the din that I had to go to the Registrar and sign in, as well as find somewhere to sleep. He waved his hand, and was off. I watched him swerve away, feeling about a hundred. Anyone over thirty appears a dotard to the young.

I walked up to the university building. There was a door on the left marked "Registrar, Private", and beside it a sliding window-panel, with a clerk on duty behind it.

"The name is Fabbio," I said, pushing through my credentials. "The librarian, Signor Fossi, told me to call."

"Yes, yes. . . ."

He seemed to know about me, and scribbled something in a book. He handed me out a pass and a form to sign. Also a list of addresses.

"You ought to be able to find a room from one of these," he said. "They make a special price for us."

I thanked him and turned to go, but paused a moment. "By the way," I asked, "can you tell me who lives at No. 8, via dei Sogni?"

"No. 8?" he repeated.

"Yes," I said, "the house with the high wall, and the single tree in the small garden."

"That is the Rector's house," he said, staring, "Professor Butali. But he's away sick. He's in hospital in Rome."

"I knew that," I said, "but I had not realised that he lives in the via dei Sogni."

"Oh, yes," he replied. "The Rector and Signora Butali have been there for some years."

"Who plays the piano there?"

"The signora. She teaches music. But I doubt if she is at home. She's been in Rome with the Rector during the past weeks."

"I thought I heard music," I said, "when I passed the house this afternoon."

"She must be back, then," he answered. "I wouldn't necessarily know."

I wished him good evening and left. So . . . My home was honoured by being the residence of the Rector himself. In old days the head of the university had lived next door to the students' hostel. There had obviously been many changes, as the fellow selling postcards and flags had told me, and what with the boys and girls studying Commerce and Economics, many of them coming in by day, my quiet city of Ruffano would soon begin to rival Perugia or Turin.

I walked back downhill past the ducal palace and stood for a moment under the street lamp to study my list of addresses. Via Rossini, via dell'8 Settembre, via Lambetta . . . no, too close to the students. Via San Cipriano . . . perhaps. Via San Michele . . . I smiled. Wasn't that where Signorina Carla Raspa had her niche? I took out her card. Her address was No. 5; the address given me at the Registrar's office was 24. It was worth looking at. I picked up my grip once more and walked down to the piazza della Vita.

It must have been the snow of the preceding night that had driven the world indoors. This evening it was cold, but the stars glittered, the piazza was full, and unlike the midday session, when from long custom the middle-aged males took over, youth predominated. Girls, chattering and with arms interlocked, paraded before the colonnade, while the boys, hands in pockets, laughing, whistling, some of them straddling vespas, hung about in groups. The cinema, beneath the colonnade, was due to start. The lurid poster gave promise of passion under Caribbean skies. Across the way the Hotel dei Duchi looked forlorn and out of date.

I crossed the piazza, ignoring the glance of a little red-haired beauty—Commerce and Economics, I wondered?—and, turning right, found myself in the via San Michele. I looked for No. 5. Discreet enough, with a small car parked outside. Giuseppe Fossi's? There were chinks of light coming from the shutters on the first floor. Ah, well. . . . Good luck to him. I continued down the street, looking for No. 24. It was on the opposite side, but from the windows one would have a fair view of No. 5. Seized with sudden amusement, coupled with schoolboy malice, I decided to inspect the house. The door was open. Light flooded the hallway. I looked at the name on the list . . . Signora Silvani. I walked in and looked about me. It was clean, newly decorated, and an enticing smell of fégato alla salvia came from a hidden kitchen. Someone ran down the stairs, calling over her shoulder to the floor above. It was a girl of about twenty, with small elfin features and enormous eyes.

"Are you looking for Signora Silvani?" she asked. "She's in the kitchen—I'll tell her."

"No, wait a moment." I liked the atmosphere, I liked the girl. She might tell me what I wanted to know. "They gave me this address at the university," I said. "I'm a temporary assistant at the library, and I want a room for a week or two. Anything going?"

"There's one vacant on the top floor," she answered, "but it may be booked. You'll have to ask Signora Silvani. I'm only a student."

"Commerce and Economics?" I asked.

"Why yes, how did you know?"

"I'm told they enroll the best-looking girls."

She laughed, and arrived in the hall beside me. It is always a gratification to me when a girl is smaller than myself. This one could have been a child.

"I don't know about that," she said. "At least we're alive, and let the others know it. Isn't that true, Paolo?" A boy, equally handsome, had followed her down the stairs. "This is my brother," she said. "We're both C and E students. We come from San Marino."

I held out my hand to each of them. "Armino Fabbio," I said, "from Turin, though I work in Genoa usually."

They answered in one breath, "Caterina and Paolo Pasquale."

"Look," I said, "would you advise me to try for a room here?"

"Certainly," answered the boy. "It's clean, comfortable, she feeds you well," he jerked his head towards the kitchen, "and she doesn't bother you about time. We come and go as we like."

"We're an easy crowd," said the girl. "Whoever wants to work can work. Whoever wants to play can play. Paolo and I do a bit of both. Yes, you try for that room."

Her smile was comradely, inviting. So was his. Without waiting for my answer she went off down the hallway, calling for the signora. The door of the kitchen opened and Signora Silvani emerged. She was a broad, middle-aged woman with a high bosom and enormous hips, good-looking in an engaging, friendly way.

"You want a room?" she said. "Come and look at it."

She pushed past the boy Paolo and myself and began to climb the stairs.

"You see?" laughed Caterina. "It's all so simple. Well, I hope you take it. Paolo and I are off to the cinema. Be seeing you."

They left the house together, chatting and laughing, and I followed Signora Silvani up the stairs.

We reached the top floor and she threw open the door of a room, the windows of which looked out on the street below. She switched on the light and I crossed the room to throw back the shutters. I like to know where I am, what I can see. I looked up the street, and saw the small car still parked before No. 5. Then I glanced round the room. It was not large, but it had the essentials.

"I'll take it," I said.

"Good. Make yourself at home. Board is optional. Give warning in the morning if you want to eat out, but I'm not particular if you forget. We're serving dinner now, if you want a meal tonight."

The casual greeting, the informal atmosphere with no questions asked, this suited me exactly. I unpacked my small grip, washed, shaved, and went downstairs. Voices led me to the dining-room. Signora Silvani had already installed herself at the head of the table, and was ladling out the soup. There were four others present, a middle-aged man whom she immediately presented as her husband, as ample and well-fed as herself, and three students, all of them male, harmless in appearance, none of them as striking as young Paolo.

"Our new boarder, Signor Fabbio," called my hostess, "and these are Gino, Mario and Gerardo. Sit down, now, and make yourself at home."

"No formality, please," I said. "My name is Armino. It is not so very long ago that I was studying for my own degree in Turin."

"Arts?"

"Foreign languages. Do I look like Arts?"

There was an immediate chorus of "Yes" at this, and general laughter, while Gino, next to me, explained that it was a joke of the household—anyone new was immediately accused of being Arts.

"Well, I'm a courier in the tourist business usually," I told them, "but being temporarily attached to the university library I suppose I come under Arts?"

There was a universal shout of disapproval, all of it good-natured.

"Take no notice of them," smiled my host. "Just because these lads study Commerce and Economics they think they own Ruffano."

"But we do, signore," protested one of them—Gerardo, I think it was. "We're the new life-blood of the university. None of the others count."

"So you say," said Signora Silvani as she served my soup, "but I've heard differently. The Arts students, and most of the others too, for that matter, look upon your lot as a pack of hooligans."

She winked at me mischievously as another howl greeted her remark, and the whole table plunged into university politics, all of it over my head. I ate, and was amused. This was a Ruffano I had never known.

Gino, my neighbour, explained to me that the new Faculty of Commerce and Economics was already a thriving concern. Because of the additional fees which the students brought in the university had more money to spend than ever before in its long history—hence the additions to the various buildings, and the new library.

"They couldn't have afforded any of it but for us," he said passionately, "and then the rival Faculties, the Education saps, and the Arts, look down their noses and treat us like dirt, or try to do so. But we've nearly outnumbered them already, and in another year we'll flood them out."

"I tell you," said Mario, "one of these days it will come to a fight, and I know who'll win."

My friend Toni in the library had called the C and E students a lively crowd. He was certainly right.

"You know what it is," observed Signor Silvani, when the students were arguing amongst themselves, "these lads have never known war. They have to let off steam. Inter-Faculty rivalry is one way of doing it."

"Perhaps," I said, "but doesn't it suggest a want of tact amongst the professors?"

He shook his head. "The Rector is a fine man," he said. "There is no one more respected in Ruffano than Professor Butali. But you know he's sick."

"Yes, they told me so at the library."

"They say he nearly died, but he's on the mend. Signora Butali, too, is a very gracious lady. Highly respected, both of them. This silly rivalry has grown much worse while he's been away—once he's back it will soon be squashed, I can tell you. I agree with you, though. I blame much of it on the older professors, or so the chat goes where I work, at the prefettura. The Head of the Department of Education, Professor Rizzio, and his sister, who is in charge of the hostel for women students—they're both narrow and set in their ways, and perhaps naturally resentful of the Head of C and E, Professor Elia, who is what we call a thruster—rather too sure of himself, he comes from Milan."

I thought, as I did justice to Signora Silvani's excellent cooking, that to be in charge of a coach-load of tourists, all of them strangers, must be an easier matter than keeping the peace amongst a group of students like these. I had no recollection of such intensity of feeling at Turin.

Dinner over, our small party dispersed, the students to the piazza della Vita while I excused myself from joining the Silvanis in their parlour for coffee and cigarettes. They were affable and kindly, but I had had enough chatter for the evening.

I went up to my room to fetch my coat, and then left the house. The car had not moved from No. 5.

The young people of Ruffano were still parading in the piazza della Vita, but with numbers thinned. Many must have gone into the cinema to watch the Caribbean film, and the rest had wandered home to their lodgings, or to convenient dark corners. I passed the Hotel dei Duchi and walked down into the piazza del Mercato. High above me, on my left, loomed the western façade of the ducal palace, the twin towers thrusting to the sky. As a child I had always been in bed at this hour. I had never seen the towers so late at night, or understood their beauty and their grace. The silhouette might be that of some fantastic backdrop at a theatre, revealed suddenly to an amazed audience when the curtains parted. Fragile, ethereal at first view, the true impact came later. These walls were real, forbidding, with all the ingenuity of a fortress, concealing the strength within. The twin turrets above their encircling balustrades pierced the darkness like sharpened blades. Beauty was paramount, menace lurked within.

The via delle Mura surrounding the whole city of Ruffano stretched before me, curving gently, while immediately to my left were the steps leading up to the palace and to the city above. I decided to climb them. My foot was on the first step when I heard the sound of running. Someone was coming down the steps towards me, but in headlong flight. The descent was steep, and to run at speed was to court disaster.

"Watch out," I called, "you'll fall."

The running figure emerged from the darkness, stumbled, and I put out an arm to break the fall. The runner was a lad, a student possibly, and as he struggled in my hold, trying to break away, his startled eyes stared up at me in terror.

"No . . ." he said. "No. . . . Let me go."

Surprised, I relaxed my grip. He ran from me, sobbing, down the last of the steps. The hollow ring of his clattering feet rose to me where I stood.

Watchful, listening, I continued my climb. The steps were all in shadow, lighted only by one solitary lamp above. I saw a figure move back into the shadows.

"Anyone there?" I called.

There was no answer. I went warily, and when I reached the top paused and looked about me. The precincts of the ducal palace were to the right of me, the nearest of the twin towers darkly ominous. I noticed then that the small door close to the ever-barred portico between the towers was open. Someone was standing there. As I moved forward the figure vanished, the door was softly shut.

I continued up the rise, past the silent, shrouded palace, until I came out into the alley-way leading to the Duomo and the piazza Maggiore. The sight of the frightened boy had been disturbing. He might have broken his neck. The open door, the motionless figure, were somehow sinister. I walked on across the piazza. Everything was still. I took the side street leading into the via dei Sogni as I had the night before, seized with the same desire to look at my old home.

There was no one about. I stood for a moment under the wall staring up at the house. Light came from the chinks in the shutters of the room on the first floor, but I could hear no music. Then I heard footsteps coming down the street, following as it were in my wake, from the direction of the ducal palace. Some instinct made me hide myself behind an angle of the wall, and wait. The footsteps came on, purposeful and clear. No furtiveness about this pursuit, if pursuit it were.

Behind me the sombre bell of the campanile sounded ten, echoed a moment later by the other, more distant churches. The footsteps ceased. They had come to a halt by the door in the wall leading to the garden and to the house beyond. I leant forward and saw the figure of a man. He looked up at the house as I had done, and then moved forward and turned the handle of the door. The Rector's lady, like her predecessor in my home some twenty years before, perhaps sought consolation.

As the man paused a moment, opening the door, the street lamp by the side of the wall shone fully upon his face. He passed through, and closed the door behind him. I stood motionless, drained of all energy, all feeling. The man was surely no stranger, but my brother Aldo.

CHAPTER SEVEN

I BRUSHED PAST the group of students who were hovering, chatting, before No. 24, via San Michele, the Pasquale brother and sister amongst them, and went straight upstairs to my room. I sat down on the bed, staring in front of me. It was an illusion, of course, a trick of the light. Unconscious association with our home. Aldo had been shot down in flames in '43, my mother had received the telegram. I remembered it coming, and when it arrived she stared down at the envelope—for it must contain bad news of some kind—and then she went into the kitchen and called Marta, and they stayed in there together, the door closed.

Children have an instinct for knowing when news is bad. I sat on the stair and waited. Presently my mother came out again. She was not crying; she had the bruised, stunned look that adults wear when deeply moved or shocked. She said, "Aldo's dead. Killed flying. The Allies shot him down," and went upstairs to her room. I crept into the kitchen and Marta was sitting there, her hands in her lap. Unlike my mother she was not mute in her grief; the tears were flowing freely down her cheeks, and she held out her arms. I burst into tears instantly and ran to her, and the pair of us rocked together, crying, mourning our dead.

"My little Beato," she said, "my lamb, my Beato. You loved him so, you loved your brother."

"It isn't true," I kept saying between sobs, "it isn't true. They can't kill Aldo. Nobody can kill Aldo."

"Yes, it is true," she said, holding me close, "he has gone as he would have wished. He had to fly, he had to fall. Aldo, your Aldo."

Memory is merciful. There came a blank in time after that first day, and I had no further feeling. The weeks must have passed, and I must have gone daily to school with my companions, and worn a mourning armband, and have said to them, even with pride, "Yes, my brother's dead. Shot down in flames," as though to go thus added to his glory. I played. I ran up and down the stairs. It was around then that I kicked the ball into the tree. Incidents, isolated at the time, merged into others of wider implication: the surrender, the Armistice, which I did not understand, the arrival in Ruffano of the Germans, and the Commandant. Life, as I had known it, had come to an end.

Now, sitting on the bed in the Pensione Silvani, I lived those first moments once again, and told myself that he whom I had just seen was indeed a living person, but wrongly identified with a man long dead. This was hallucination. This was what had happened to the disciples when they looked, as they thought, upon their Lord, the risen Christ. . . .

There was a sudden knocking on the door. Startled, I called out, "Who's there?" I don't know what I expected. Perhaps the phantom stranger. My shout was taken for permission to enter the room. The door opened and the Pasquale brother and sister stood there, their faces concerned.

"Excuse us," said the girl, Caterina, "but you looked so ill when you came in just now. We wondered if anything was wrong."

I sat up on the bed. Made the supreme effort to appear at ease.

"It's nothing," I said, "absolutely nothing. I walked rather fast, that's all."

My poor reply was met by silence. I could see curiosity struggle with courtesy in their expressions.

"Why did you walk so fast?" asked Paolo.

I thought his question odd. It was as if he guessed . . . but how could he guess? I was a stranger. We were all strangers.

"I happened to do so," I said. "I made a tour round the ducal palace and the neighbouring streets and so back here. It turned out to be further than I had thought."

They exchanged glances. Again, it was as though they guessed, they knew.

"Don't think we want to pry," said Paolo, "but were you by any chance followed?"

"Followed?" I echoed. "Why . . . no. Who would follow me?"

I felt as if I were on the defensive. What could these children know about the past, about my home? What could they know of my dead brother Aldo?

"It's like this," said Caterina, and she spoke softly, shutting the door. "People do get followed, from time to time, if they prowl round the palace at night. There are all sorts of rumours. It never happens if you go in a group. Only to individuals."

I remembered then the running boy. The figure at the top of the steps. The softly closing door.

"It could have been," I said, half to myself and half to them, "it could have been that I was followed."

"Why, what happened?" asked Caterina quickly.

I told them about the boy and his headlong, breathless flight. I told them about the shadowed figure, and the withdrawal inside the palace door. I did not tell them about my return down the via dei Sogni, and how I stood outside my home. Once more they looked at each other, nodding.

"That's it," said Paolo decisively, "they were out."

"Who?" I asked.

"You're new to Ruffano, you wouldn't know," said Caterina. "It's a secret society within the university. We none of us know who the members are. They could be Arts, Education, C and E, Law, or a mixture of them all, but it's part of the oath they take, never to split on one another."

I handed them cigarettes. Already I was feeling more at ease. The past receded, and I was back in the world of university pranks.

"Don't smile," said Paolo. "It isn't amusing. We thought as you did, at first, that it was just ragging. It isn't so. Students have been hurt, and not only students but kids from the town. Seized and blindfolded . . . and, so rumour has it, even tortured. But nobody knows, that's the point. The victims don't tell. Something will slip out days later, a student will say he's sick, not turn up at lectures, and then the rumour spreads, *they've* got at him."

Brother and sister sat down on the bed on either side of me, their faces serious, yet eager. I felt it a compliment that they trusted me.

"Can't the authorities do something?" I asked. "Surely it's up to the university to stamp it out?"

"They can't," said Caterina. "You don't understand the power of these people. It's not like an ordinary society within the university, with its members known. This thing is secret. And it's evil too."

"For all we know," broke in Paolo, "it may include professors as well as students. And although all of us C and E students feel it's directed against us, we can't be sure—we have heard there are members of our own group acting as spies for the society."

"So you see," said Caterina, "that's why we were worried, when you came in. I said to Paolo—it's them."

I patted each upon the shoulder and got up from the bed. "No," I said, "if they were out, they weren't after me." I crossed to the window and opened the shutters. The car had gone from No. 5. "Sometimes," I said, addressing both brother and sister, "one can suffer from hallucinations. I've done so myself. You think you see something which is, frankly, out of this world, and then, later, it has an ordinary explanation. Your society may exist, it obviously does, but its importance could have been worked up in your minds, so that it appears more threatening than it is."

"Exactly," said Paolo, also rising to his feet. "That's what all the scoffers say. But it isn't so. You wait and see. Come on, Caterina."

His sister shrugged, and followed her brother to the door. "I know it sounds foolish," she said to me, "like a trick to scare children. But I'm sure of one thing. I would never walk about Ruffano by night without at least half-a-dozen others. It's all right round here, and in the piazza della Vita. Not up the hill, not by the palace."

"Thank you," I said. "I accept the warning."

I finished my cigarette, undressed, and went to bed. The tale of the "secret society" had proved an antidote to shock. Common sense told me that the encounter on the steps, the withdrawal of the figure to the open door of the ducal palace, had stimulated imagination already tensed because of the past, and when I came to my old home the natural consequence of this was to conjure, out of darkness into light, a living Aldo. The experience was, I now believed, the second of two. The first had been to confuse the murdered woman in the via Sicilia in Rome with Marta. No proof, hallucination. The second experience, the vision of my brother. Appeased, and in a strange way self-absolved, I fell asleep.

When I awoke in the morning, clear-headed, hungry, full of energy for the day ahead, I told myself that it was time to kill all phantoms, and put a final end to the shadows that had haunted me. I would search out the cross-eyed cobbler and ask him if Marta lived. I would even boldly ring the bell of my old home in the via dei Sogni and ask the Rector's lady, Signora Butali, the identity of her late-night caller. This last would, in all probability, produce a well-deserved rebuff, a complaint to the university Registrar, and an end to my temporary job. No matter if it did. My ghosts would then be truly laid, and I at liberty.

My young friends the Pasquales and the other students had dispersed to their various lectures before I left the house at a quarter to nine and walked up the via Rossini to the ducal palace. Ruffano wore her shining morning face, and the noise and bustle of the day were all about me. No shadowy figures now to lurk in doorways and scare the passers-by. I wondered how much truth there was in the students' story, whether the half of it was not a myth born of mass hysteria. Rumour, like infection, spreads rapidly.

I checked in at the palace library as the Duomo struck the hour, and so beat my superior by about three minutes. Giuseppe Fossi looked, I thought, subdued, and it could be that his activities of the preceding night had, in more ways than one, deflated him. He wished me and the others a brief good morning, and I was put at once to sorting and separating those volumes written in German and belonging to the university which had, by error, become mixed up with the palace possessions. The task, because it was so different from checking itineraries and figures, absorbed me, particularly so as one work in four volumes called *The History of the Dukes of Ruffano*, written in the early part of the nineteenth century by a German scholar, was, according to Giuseppe Fossi, extremely rare.

"There is a dispute between the Arts Council and ourselves as to its ownership," he told me. "Better put the books aside for the time being and not pack them with the rest. I shall have to check with the Rector."

I decided to stack the volumes carefully on a shelf by themselves. The leaves stuck together when I opened them. I doubt if they had ever been read. The Archbishop of Ruffano, who must have possessed them before the Risorgimento, either spoke no German or was too shocked by their contents to turn the pages.

"Claudio Malebranche, first Duke of Ruffano, was known as the Falcon," I read. "His brief life is shrouded in mystery, for contemporary authorities do not enable us to pronounce with certainty on the enormous vices wherewith tradition and innuendo have blackened his memory. A youth of outstanding promise, he became intoxicated by good fortune, and casting off his early discipline he surrounded himself by a small band of dissolute disciples, and dismayed the good citizens of Ruffano by licentious outrages and revolting cruelties. No one could walk by night for fear of the Falcon's sudden descent into the city, when, aided by his followers, he would seize and ravage. . . ."

"Signor Fabbio, a hand with these entries, if you please." My superior's voice, a little tired, a little testy, summoned me from the fascinating disclosures promised by the German scholar. "If you want to read the books in the library," he said, "you must do so in your own time, not in ours."

I apologised. He brushed the matter aside, and we concentrated upon the ledgers. Either the signorina's cooking, or her demands, had proved excessive. I ignored the by-play of Toni, who, behind our superior's back, cradled his head upon his hands in mock exhaustion, but I was not surprised when Giuseppe Fossi, shortly before noon, pronounced himself unwell.

"I must have eaten something last night," he said, "that disagreed with me. I shall have to go home and lie down. I'll return later in the afternoon if I feel better. In the meantime, I should be extremely obliged if you would carry on."

He left hurriedly, his handkerchief to his mouth. Signorina Catti remarked that it was well known that Signor Fossi suffered from his stomach. Also he was overworked. He never spared himself. Once again the irrepressible Toni gestured, once again I ignored the pantomime, this time more obvious, of an athlete at play. The telephone rang, and being closest to it I answered. A woman's voice, soft and pleasing, asked for Signor Fossi.

"I'm sorry," I replied, "Signor Fossi is not here. Can I help you?"

She asked how long he would be absent, and I said I was not sure. He had felt unwell, and had gone home. The enquirer was not Carla Raspa—the voice was pitched too low.

"Who am I speaking to?" came next.

"Armino Fabbio, temporary assistant to Signor Fossi," I replied. "May I ask who it is enquiring after him?"

"Signora Butali," she answered. "I have a message for him from the Rector about some books."

My interest quickened. The Rector's lady in person, speaking from my home. My courier's well-trained courtesy took over.

"If there is anything I can do, signora, you have only to ask," I said smoothly. "Signor Fossi left the library in the charge of Signorina Catti and myself. Would you perhaps entrust your message to me?"

There was a moment's hesitation before she replied. "The Rector is in hospital in Rome, as you know," she said, "and during a conversation on the telephone I had with him this morning he asked me to request Signor Fossi for the loan of some rather valuable books about which there is a trifling dispute between the university and the Arts Council. He would like to examine these books himself, with Signor Fossi's approval, and I could take them with me to Rome on my next visit."

"Of course, signora," I said. "I am quite certain Signor Fossi would raise no objection. What books are they?"

"*The History of the Dukes of Ruffano*, in German," she answered.

The secretary was making signs to me. I explained, my hand over the mouthpiece, that I was speaking to the Rector's lady. Her sour disapproval vanished. She rushed forward and snatched the receiver from me.

"Good morning, signora," she exclaimed, her voice all sugar. "I had no idea you were back from Rome. How is the Rector?" She smiled and nodded, hushing me to silence. "Naturally anything the Rector asks for he shall be given," she continued. "I will see that the books are delivered to you at the house today. Either I, or one of our assistants, will hand them to you personally."

Further assurances followed, with an added explanation that Signor Fossi was, as usual, overworked. More smiles. More nods. Then, apparently thanked and dismissed, she replaced the receiver.

Quickly I said, "I'll deliver the books to Signora Butali this afternoon."

Signorina Catti stared, her sourness returned. "There is no need to go yourself," she said. "If you will wrap the books for me I can take them. It won't be out of my way, and the signora knows me."

"Signor Fossi gave me instructions," I said, "not to let these books out of my sight. Also, I am more easily spared from the library than you."

Furious, but acknowledging defeat, she returned to her desk. A falsetto cough from the high ladder told me that Toni had been listening. I smiled, and went on with my work. Entry had been secured to my home in the via dei Sogni. For the moment this was all that mattered.

I did not return to the pensione for lunch. I found a small restaurant in the via Rossini which, though filled with students, sufficed for my hasty meal. I went back to the library while the other assistants were still lunching, and packed up the books for the Rector's lady. It intrigued me that the very volumes that had caught my fancy should be those demanded by the Rector from his sick bed. There was no time to linger over the life history of the Falcon. This I regretted. His madness I remembered, and his death. The intervening details had been glossed over by my father. Certainly they were not mentioned in the Ruffano guide-books, nor in the printed pamphlets issued to tourists in the ducal palace.

". . . The excesses were of so singular a nature that only the Devil could have inspired them. When accusations were made against him by the outraged citizens of Ruffano, Duke Claudio retaliated by declaring that he had been divinely appointed to mete out to his subjects the punishment they deserved. The proud would be stripped, the haughty violated, the slanderer silenced, the viper die in his own venom. The scales of heavenly justice would thus be balanced."

And so on for several pages. The picture of "The Temptation" in the ducal bedchamber above the library took on a new meaning for me.

"Duke Claudio was undoubtedly insane. Excuses were thus made for him, after his appalling death, by the good and gentle brother who succeeded him, the great Duke Carlo. No such consideration can be afforded to the Falcon's followers. This small band of debauchees did not believe themselves to hold divine appointment. Their mission was to sully and destroy. So great was the hatred and fear which they inspired amongst the populace of Ruffano that when the final massacre took place, and the Falcon and his band were slaughtered, it is said that the corridors and state rooms of the ducal palace ran with blood, and that atrocities, impossible to name, were committed upon the fallen victims."

These pages would certainly while away the Rector's hours of leisure in a hospital bed.

I packed the books and left the library as soon as the second assistant returned from lunch. Then I set forth for the via dei Sogni. My excitement increased as I approached the garden wall. No hovering in the shadows today. I was going home. As I drew near I could hear, as yesterday, the sound of piano-playing. It was a Chopin Impromptu. The notes rang out, up and down the scale, with almost savage intensity. It was like an argument, passionate and fierce, that would brook no interference but must sweep everything before it, then rippled, suddenly, to melting protestation. No music for a sick bed. But, of course, the Rector was some hundred and fifty miles away in Rome.

I put my hand on the garden door and entered. Nothing had changed. The single tree dominated the small enclosure as it had always done, though the grass was closer trimmed than in our day. I walked the short flagged pathway to the door and rang the bell. The music ceased. A sense of schoolboy panic came upon me. I nearly dropped the books before the door and fled. I heard, as I had heard a hundred, a thousand times before, footsteps descending the stairs. The door opened.

"Signora Butali?"

"Yes."

"Forgive me for disturbing you, signora. I have brought you the books you asked for from the palace library."

There is a picture in the audience room of the ducal palace known officially as the "Portrait of a Gentlewoman", though my father called her the Silent One. The face is grave, withdrawn, the dark eyes look out upon the man who painted her with indifference, some say disapproval. Aldo had it otherwise. I remember him arguing with my father that the Silent One had hidden fires, and that the mouth, supposedly so pursed, deceived the watcher. Signora Butali might have posed for that same gentlewoman. Her beauty was of the sixteenth century, not ours.

"Was it you I spoke to on the telephone?" she asked, and, taking the answer for granted, added, "It's good of you to come so soon."

She put out her hand for the books, but I was looking past her to the hall. The four walls were the same, but that was all. The alien shapes of chairs, not ours, and a tall mirror seemed to alter the perspective. My father, fond of reproductions of his favourite pictures at the palace, used to display them in abundance, doubtless a dated fashion, but because of this we came to know them well. Today there was but one picture hanging in the hall, and that contemporary—glazed fruit, too large, splurging beside a sheet of music. The staircase wall leading to the floor above, white in our time, was now dove grey. These things I perceived in a single flash, and with it came unreasoning resentment that anyone should dare to walk into our home and so despoil it to suit their taste, disturbing, as it were, the layer of habit underneath. Had the walls and ceilings that knew us no feeling in the matter? Must they stay dumb?

"Excuse me, signora," I said, "I did not come only at your request, but because I felt myself drawn to the house. I passed here yesterday and heard the piano. Being fond of music I stayed to listen. At that time I did not even know that this was the Rector's house—they told me later at the library. When you asked for the books this morning. . . ."

Like the gentlewoman in the portrait, the mouth remained unsmiling, but the eyes softened. "You decided that this was your chance," she interrupted.

"Frankly, yes," I said.

I put the books into her hands. Once again my eyes travelled up the stairs. The last time I descended them I was running. My mother was calling from the garden, holding her travelling-case, which she handed to the Commandant's orderly. The staff-car was waiting in the via dei Sogni.

"Do you play yourself?" asked the signora.

"No. No, I never had the gift. But yesterday . . . yesterday you were playing, I believe, the 'Arabesque' of Debussy, which God knows can be heard often enough from any radio station, but somehow it sounded different. It brought back memories of childhood and old forgotten things, why, I can't say . . . nobody played the piano in our family."

She looked at me gravely, as though considering a prospective pupil, and then she said, "If you can spare the time, come upstairs to the music-room and I'll play the 'Arabesque' for you."

"Spare the time?" I repeated. "It doesn't concern me whether I can spare the time or not. Can you?"

Once again the eyes softened. Even the mouth relaxed. "I would not invite you in if I could not," she answered. "It's early anyway. I don't expect my next pupil until three."

She closed the door, and leaving the books on a chair in the hall led the way upstairs, and so directly into my mother's bedroom. This was transformed. I recognised nothing. It was just as well, because as I entered I expected to see the tumbled double bed with all the sheets overturned, as they had been on the day we left, the wardrobe with its doors opened and the shelves awry, discarded clothes, unwanted by my mother, left to hang, tissue paper on the floor, the breakfast-tray with the cold dregs of coffee.

"I love this room," said the signora. "I find it peaceful. As soon as we came here I told my husband, 'This is where I shall have the piano'."

The walls were green. The chairs, stiff-backed, were padded in some striped material. The floor had a high polish. Another contemporary picture hung upon the wall, this time of monstrous sunflowers. The signora wandered to the piano, which stood on the exact site of my mother's double bed.

"Smoke if you wish," she said. "It doesn't worry me. Now, the 'Arabesque'."

I went and stood by the window, looking down through the branches of the tree to the garden below. The tree had spread. The branches stretched like wings, and nearly touched the walls. The ball, if it was still there, was deeply hidden.

The ripple of the music started, the rapture and the pathos and the pain. The hot July sun baked the flagstone path, and the orderly's feet rang out as he marched backwards and forwards for the luggage. Marta was at Mass in San Donato. "Hurry . . . hurry . . ." called my mother, "the Commandant won't wait." I had to find the snapshot of Aldo. Aldo, before he was shot down. Aldo in his uniform, wearing his pilot's wings.

"Come without it. Marta can send it on."

"No. I have it. It will go in my pocket."

And so running down the stairs. And so also the signora, higher, higher up the scale, and down, repeating the phrase, once more, again, carelessly, gaily. There was nothing emotional in an "Arabesque". Unless, like the listener, you were a courier, a charioteer, on and on and endlessly on, flying from the present to the past.

She said, "I was playing Chopin when you rang the bell."

It could be that we get the death we deserve. That my mother, with her cancerous womb, paid for the doubtful pleasure of that double bed, and that the Commandant, yes, and my father too, surfeited with what they had once had, doomed themselves to ultimate starvation, the one in a Russian, the other in an Allied prison camp. But why the knife for Marta?

I sat down in a chair and stared at Signora Butali. Her piano playing brought her to life, colour had come into her too pale face. Here, I supposed, she found release, and was able to forget her sick husband. I studied her dispassionately. My own age, or a few years older. Thirty-five to thirty-six. The age for regret, for sudden love, for drama. The age for opening the door to callers after ten.

The music was interrupted, as yesterday, by the shrill summons of the telephone. She rose from the piano and went to answer it, excusing herself with a glance. I noticed that it was in this room now and that she did not have to run downstairs, as my mother had done.

"Yes," she said, down the mouth-piece, "yes, I have them."

Something told me that she was referring to the books. The Rector must be anxious. He also, I surmised, asked his wife if she were alone, for she replied, in the voice one uses when others are present, "No, no, not just now. Call me later." She replaced the receiver rather quickly.

Following my train of thought, and foolishly, I asked her if the Rector was better. She looked confused, then instantly recovered.

"Ah, yes," she said, "very much better. I had many things to see to here at home, otherwise I should never have left Rome."

Did she think I was accusing her of neglect? Perhaps. In any event, I suspected that the brief telephone call, just ended, had not come from Rome.

The spell was broken, and she made no move back to the piano. I had stood up when the telephone rang. Now I glanced at my watch.

"You've been very kind, signora," I said. "You've given me much pleasure. Now I must not take up any more of your valuable time."

"Nor I yours," she answered. "You must come again. What did you say your name was?"

"Fabbio," I told her, "Armino Fabbio. I'm working at the library on a temporary basis."

"I feel sure they are very glad to have you," she said. "I hope Signor Fossi will soon recover. Please give my regards to him, and to Signorina Catti."

Already she was walking to the door. The telephone call had destroyed all magic. I followed her out to the landing. She must use for bedroom the room that we reserved for the occasional guest. It looked south-east beyond the via dei Sogni to the precincts of the old monastic buildings, used now as the city hospital. My room had lain beyond.

"Thank you again, signora," I said.

The smile she gave me was gracious but mechanical.

"It's nothing," she answered. "I like to play to anyone who is fond of music."

I followed her downstairs. When we reached the hall she picked up the books, the action suggesting that she would take them back upstairs with her after I had gone.

"You will find them interesting," I observed. "That is, if you can read German."

"I don't," she said, leaving it at that.

There was no further excuse for delay. I was a stranger, she had had enough of me. The house, my house, was equally indifferent. I smiled, bowed over her outstretched hand, and left. The door closed. I walked down the flagged path to the garden gate, and so into the street. An old, bent woman walking in the distance, the vanishing skirts of a priest, a dog sniffing at the wall, even the bright day, all of these belonged to the present time, to the Ruffano that was not mine.

They say, in English, that you should kill two birds with one stone. I might as well lay my second ghost hard upon the first. Instead of returning immediately to the ducal palace and the library, I walked downhill towards the oratorio of Ognissanti. The cross-eyed cobbler must be braved in his own domain. Before I reached the corner of the street I saw that a small crowd had collected there. People were leaning out of windows, amongst them the dour guardian of the oratorio. A car was drawn up short of the steps. A police car. A man and a woman were being bundled inside it. I drew back and waited for it to turn and pass. My view of the car and of the couple within became blocked by the chattering crowd in front of me. The crowd broke up, still talking, gesturing. I turned to one of them nearby, a round-eyed woman carrying a crying child.

"Were they arresting someone?" I asked.

She turned to me eagerly, desirous, like all women in a crowd, of imparting information to a passer-by.

"It's Signor Ghigi and his sister," she said. "No, they are not being arrested, mercifully for them, but the police have come for them all the same, to identify a body. They say it's the body of that woman murdered in Rome, it was in the newspapers, and it may be the body of the Ghigis' lodger, that's what they say, a woman who had been lodging with them for some months. She used to drink, and she disappeared days ago, saying nothing to either of them, and now they wonder, the police wonder, everybody in the quarter is wondering, can it be the same, can it be poor Marta Zampini?"

She was still talking, the child was still crying, as I turned away and walked back along the street, my heart pounding.

CHAPTER EIGHT

I BOUGHT A newspaper in the piazza della Vita and stood a moment under the colonnade, searching the pages. There was no mention of the murder. The police had obviously been working on information about missing persons in the provinces, and now they were taking the Ghigis to Rome to identify the body. Or perhaps not even that. Perhaps the police in Rome had sent items of clothing to be recognised, the shawls, the baskets. These would probably be enough.

And then? No nearer to a solution of the crime. No motive for robbery. The police would never find out that someone, just after midnight, had put a note for ten thousand lire into the victim's hand. By now it was spent, by now it had passed from the thief and murderer to a dozen other hands. The thief and murderer would not be caught. Nor the planter of the note. Both were guilty. Both must carry the burden of that guilt.

When I entered the library the secretary and the clerks had all long returned from lunch. It was mid-afternoon. Everyone stared at me. It was as though they must know I had come from the oratorio of Ognissanti, and my purpose in going there.

Taking no notice, I walked to the bookshelves and busied myself with sorting the remaining German books, but this time without interest. The face of the dead Marta, allowed to lapse into darkness during the past three days, revealed itself once more. It could no longer be denied. The Marta of the past would never torment me, only the huddled drunken figure she had become. Why the sour, stale smell? She who had been clean, fastidious, forever washing, pressing, folding clothes and fresh linen and laying them away in closets? Only two people could give me the answer now—the cobbler and his sister, our ex-cook. They would know. They could recount for me, interminably, with every sordid detail, the disintegration through the years.

It was our fault, of course. My mother's first, then mine. Living at Turin we could have written. I could have written. Enquiries could have been made. Or later, from the agency in Genoa, I could have contacted Ruffano by telephone, demanded information. I did not do so. Twenty years had passed. Marta had had to disintegrate through twenty years.

Later in the afternoon the telephone rang. Signorina Catti answered it. She spoke for a few moments in a honeyed voice, then put the receiver down.

"Signor Fossi is still unwell," she announced to the rest of us abruptly. "He will not be back today. He has asked us to carry on until seven o'clock."

Expostulation came from Toni. "It's Saturday," he protested. "Signor Fossi always lets us go by six on Saturday."

"Perhaps," replied the secretary, "but that is when he is here himself. Today is different. Signor Fossi is at this moment in bed."

She turned again to her ledger, and Toni clasped his hands to his belly in mock anguish. "When a man is past forty," he murmured, "he should restrain his appetite for bodily pleasure."

"When a man is under twenty-three," said the secretary, "he should have some respect for his superiors."

Her ears were sharper than I thought, perhaps her wits too. We returned to our business, but I think all four of us were surprised when shortly before seven the cause of Giuseppe Fossi's ills walked through the library door. She was wearing a red suit that became her well. Small gold earrings pierced her ears. A dark coat swung from her shoulders. Nodding casually to the secretary, ignoring the two clerks, Carla Raspa strolled across the room and made for me.

"Hullo," she said.

"Hullo," I answered.

"How are you doing?"

"I'm doing well."

"Like the work?"

"It's a change from tourists."

"That's what I thought. You can't have everything." She glanced up at the bookshelves, humming under her breath. The secretary, bending over the desk, might have been made of alabaster. "What are you doing this evening?" asked Carla Raspa.

"What am I doing?"

"That's what I said."

The eyes, like bitter almonds, appraised my person. I tried to remember what it was, whether bird or reptile, whose love-making ended always in the female devouring the male. It was an insect—the praying mantis.

"I have a date with a couple of students from the pensione where I am staying," I invented promptly. "We're all eating and then going to the cinema."

"Which pensione is that?"

I hesitated. "Signora Silvani's," I said.

"At 24, via San Michele?" she exclaimed. "Why then, we're neighbours!"

"I believe we are."

She smiled. The smile suggested that we were both of us engaged in some conspiratorial game. "Are you comfortable?" she asked.

"Very comfortable. The students are a pleasant bunch. All C and E."

"C and E! I'm sorry for you, then. You won't be able to sleep for the noise. They're a rackety crowd."

"They were quiet enough last night," I told her.

She continued to appraise me. I could see Toni listening from his ladder. "Where are you going to eat?" she asked.

"At the house," I said. "The food's very good." And, to make my alibi the more convincing, I added, "My young friends are called Pasquale, Paolo and Caterina Pasquale."

She shrugged her shoulders. "I never came in contact with the C and E students."

It was Toni who let me down. "Did you say the Pasquales?" he asked, zealous to show camaraderie.

"Yes."

"Then you must have got your date mixed up. They always go home to San Marino on Saturdays. In fact, I saw them depart this afternoon when I was returning from lunch. Bad luck!" He grinned, and crossed the library to fetch his coat, believing he had done me a service.

"Good," said my pursuer, "that means you're free."

I had a momentary vision of Giuseppe Fossi on his bed of sickness, then remembered, with relief, that he was my senior by several years. And it could have been the cooking. I flashed my courier's smile.

"Yes, I'm free," I murmured. "We'll eat at the Hotel dei Duchi."

She raised her eyebrows. "Why waste your money?" she said. "Anyway, they'll be closed down for the night by the time we're ready to eat."

The remark was ominous. It suggested an exhausting session without even an aperitivo to give appetite. I was not sure I should be equal to the strain. But if the remark was a pleasantry—well, I like to choose my moment for such things, and this was not one of them.

"So?" I questioned.

She allowed her eyes to drift towards the departing clerks and the retreating Signorina Catti, who still hovered by the door.

"I have plans," she said, her voice guarded.

We moved together towards the entrance. Signorina Catti, eyes averted, closed the door of the library behind us and wished us a cold good evening. She disappeared along the quadrangle, her heels tap-tapping on the stone floor. My companion waited until the last sound died away. Then she turned to me, smiling, and I became aware of a certain tense excitement that exuded not from her eyes and her mouth alone, but from her whole person.

"We're in luck," she said. "I've got two passes admitting us to the ducal apartments. I begged them from the Director of the Arts Council himself. It's an honour. He's very particular."

I stared at her. This was a strange volte-face. Or perhaps I had taken her choice of an evening pastime too much for granted.

"The ducal apartments?" I repeated. "But you can see them any time you like. You take parties of students there every day."

She laughed, and motioned me to give her a cigarette. I obliged, and lighted it for her.

"The evenings are different," she said. "No general public, no outside students, nobody from the town or from the university whom the Director does not personally invite. I tell you, we're honoured."

I smiled. It suited me. What must seem to her a great occasion was something my father had done in the past week after week. I was gratified that one at least of the forgotten customs should be continued. As a child I had, now and then, accompanied Aldo or my mother, and watched my father display to his friends the notable features of a room or a picture.

"What happens?" I asked. "Do we stand about hushed, in groups, while the Director expounds some theory?"

"I could not tell you," she answered. "This is what I am intrigued to find out. I imagine that this evening he will give us a pre-view of the Festival."

She glanced down at the two passes in her hand. "It says seven-thirty," she said, "but I think we might go up. We can always wait in the gallery if the doors are not open."

It amused me that an invitation from the Director of the Arts Council of Ruffano should produce such an impression upon a lecturer at the university, and so sophisticated a one as Signorina Carla Raspa. She must be lower in the ranks of the hierarchy than I had thought. She reminded me of those tourists who obtain tickets to a papal audience at the Vatican. Only the veil was missing. We mounted the stairs to the gallery above.

"What exactly is this Festival?" I asked.

"The Rector initiated it a few years ago," she answered. "The Department of Arts in the university here is small and with no titular head, and he keeps it under his own jurisdiction. He runs the Festival in conjunction with the

Director of the Arts Council. It has been a terrific success. Each year they choose an historical subject and the students act it out in the ducal apartments, or in the quadrangle, or in the former theatre below the palace. This year, because of the Rector's illness, the Festival is entirely the responsibility of the Director of the Arts Council."

We had arrived at the head of the stairs. There was already a small group of people waiting outside the closed door leading to the throne room. They were all young—students, doubtless, mostly male. They were chatting amongst themselves quietly, even soberly, with none of the hilarious, rather forced jocularity that I associated with a student body. Carla Raspa moved forward and shook hands with two or three. She introduced me and explained their status to me.

"All third- and fourth-year students," she said. "Nobody gets an invitation before the third year. How many of you will be performing in the Festival?"

"We've all volunteered," replied one of them, a shock-headed lad with the side-whiskers that my friends the Pasquales would undoubtedly have dubbed Arts, "but the Director has the final choice. If you don't measure up to standard you're out."

"What's the standard?" I enquired.

The shock-headed student looked at his companions. They all smiled.

"Tough," he answered. "You have to be physically fit, for one thing, and able to fence. Why? Search me! It's a new regulation."

Carla Raspa intervened. "Last Festival, when the Rector was in charge, it was really beautiful. They enacted the visit of Pope Clement to Ruffano, and Professor Butali himself played the Pope. They had the main door opened to the quadrangle and the students, dressed as the Papal guard, had to bear the Rector in, where he was received by the Duke and Duchess. Signora Butali played the Duchess, and Professor Rizzio, Director of the Department of Education, the Duke. Then they went in procession through the apartments. The costumes were magnificent."

We all moved towards the door of the throne room at the sound of the key turning in the lock. The double doors were flung wide open. A student—I supposed he was a student—stood at the entrance to scrutinise our passes. He must have passed the physical fitness test. He was lean, hard-looking, and reminded me of one of our professional football players from Turin. Perhaps, if we did not behave ourselves, he would be employed by the Arts Director as chucker-out.

We passed into the throne room, and across it to the Room of the Cherubs, whence came a murmur of voices. Others were before us. The atmosphere became more like that of a papal audience than ever, and at the entrance to the Room of the Cherubs there stood a second scrutineer, who this time took our passes from us. I felt bereft, for the passes were like badges, giving status. Then, a little startled, I saw that the electric lights in the Room of the Cherubs had been extinguished. The room was illuminated by flares and torches, which, throwing monstrous shadows upon the fluted ceiling and saffron walls, gave to the whole an eerie, sombre flavour, mediaeval and at the same time strange, exciting. A huge log-fire was burning on the open hearth beneath the priceless chimney-piece, sacrosanct in my father's time. The leaping flames of the fire drew all eyes like a magnet.

The torchlight and the flames, reflecting shadows on the ceiling, threw little light upon our neighbours, and which of them were fellow-guests and which were the hosts it was impossible to tell. All seemed to be young, and nearly all were male. The sprinkling of young women present would appear to be of the company on sufferance.

Slowly the great room filled, yet never for one moment becoming crowded, and as my eyes grew accustomed to the torchlight I saw that we, and some of the rest of the company who must also be newly admitted, stood about in groups, a little uncertain what to do, whereas others, moving more freely and with an air of authority, crossed and recrossed the vast room, now and then turning to stare at the rest of us with the indifferent, slightly contemptuous amusement of the habituated.

Suddenly the scrutineer at the entrance closed the door. He stood against it, his arms folded, his face expressionless. There was an instant silence. One of the women, nerves on edge, broke into a half-laugh, which was immediately hushed by her male companions. I glanced at Carla Raspa. She put out her hand to mine and held it, her fingers tense. The muted atmosphere communicated itself from one to the other, and I felt trapped. Escape, for anyone with a tendency to claustrophobia, would be impossible.

The door leading to the Duke's bedroom, closed hitherto, was flung open. A man entered, followed by six companions, who ranged themselves about him like a bodyguard. He advanced into the room, and putting out his hand immediately began to greet his guests, who, tension breaking, pressed forward eagerly to be amongst the first. Carla Raspa, her eyes shining, forgetting me, jostled in the queue.

"Who is it?" I asked.

She did not hear me. She had passed on. But a young man near to me, throwing me an astonished look, said, "Why, Professor Donati, of course, the Director of the Arts Council."

I stepped back out of the torchlight into the shadows. The figure with his bodyguard came on. A word to one, a laugh to another, a pat on the shoulder to a third—and there was no way of breaking from the line, no possible escape, the movement of those behind me urged me forward. Somehow I had caught up with my companion, and I heard her say, "This is Signor Fabbio. He is helping Signor Fossi in the library." I held out my hand and he shook it, saying, "Good, good. I am very pleased to see you," then, barely looking at me, passed on. Carla Raspa began talking excitedly to the neighbour on her left and not, thank God, to me. For me the tomb had opened. The heavens roared. Christ had come again in all his majesty. The stranger in the via dei Sogni the night before had been no phantom after all, and, if I still dared to doubt it, the name alone was now conclusive.

The Director of the Arts Council. Professor Donati. Professor Aldo Donati. Twenty-two years had brought maturity to the broadened figure, the assured step, the arrogant angle of the head, but the high forehead, the full dark eyes, the mouth with the imperceptible droop at the right corner, and the voice, deeper now but casual, always casual—these things belonged to my brother.

Aldo lived again. Aldo had risen from the dead, and my world was rocking.

I turned my face to the wall and began staring at a tapestry. I saw nothing, heard nothing. People moved about the room and talked, a thousand aircraft could have hummed about me in the air, it would not have signified. One aircraft two-and-twenty years ago had never crashed, this was all that mattered. Or if it crashed it had not burnt, or if it burnt the pilot had come out of it unscathed. My brother lived. My brother had not died.

Someone touched my arm. It was Carla Raspa. She said to me, "What do you think of him?"

I said, "I think he's God."

She smiled, and putting up her hand she whispered, "So do they all."

I drew back against the wall. I did not want her to see that I was shaking. My dread was that I might collapse, fall, draw attention to myself and Aldo discover me here, before all these people. Later, of course, later. . . . But not now. It was impossible to think, to plan. I must not give myself away. I must stop shaking.

"Inspection over," murmured Carla Raspa. "He's going to speak."

There was one chair in the room, the fifteenth century stool with the narrow back that usually stood before the fireplace. One of the bodyguard stepped forward and placed it in the centre of the room. Aldo smiled, and gestured with his hand. Everyone sat down upon the floor, some of us with our backs to the wall, others huddled close together, nearer to the speaker. The torchlight still threw shadows on the ceiling, now more grotesque than ever because of the massed heads. How many of us there were I could not tell—eighty, perhaps a hundred, perhaps more. Aldo sat down in the chair, the firelight flickered, and with a supreme effort I tried to still my shaking hands.

"Five hundred and twenty-five years ago this spring, the people of Ruffano killed their Duke," he said. "You won't find how they drove him to his death in the guide-books or in the official history of the times; the censors, you see, even then, stepped in to hide the truth. I am referring, of course, to Claudio, first Duke of Ruffano, known as the Falcon, despised and rejected of men because they feared him. Why did they fear him? Because he had the ability to read their souls. Their petty lies, their small deceits, their competition one with another in the commerce of the day—for all the Ruffanesi ever thought about was to enrich themselves at the expense of the starving peasantry—were condemned by the Falcon, and rightly so. They understood nothing of art, nothing of culture, and this at a time when a new age was dawning, the age of the Renaissance. The bishop and his priests allied themselves with the nobles and the merchants to keep the people ignorant, little better than beasts, and to obstruct the Duke by every possible means within their power.

"It was his intention to gather around him at his Court young men of distinction—birth did not matter, if they had intelligence and wit—who by their personal courage, force of arms, and single-minded devotion to Art in all its branches should form themselves, as it were, into an élite—call them fanatics if you will—who by their example would act as a torch, a fire to every dukedom in the country. Art would reign supreme, galleries filled with beautiful things be of more account than banking houses, a bronzed statuette of greater price than bales of cloth. He raised for this purpose taxes, which the merchants refused to pay. He held tournaments and knightly exercises at the Court, thereby to train his young courtiers, and the people vilified him as a debauchee.

"Five hundred and twenty-five years have passed, and I believe the time has come to reinstate the Duke. Or rather, to do honour to his memory. That is why, since it has fallen to me, in the absence of the Rector of the university, Professor Butali, whom we all revere and honour, to arrange this year's Festival, I have decided to enact the uprising of the city of Ruffano against their much misunderstood lord and master, Claudio, first duke, and called by all—the Falcon."

He paused. I knew this pause. He had employed it in the past when we were lying beside one another in the bedroom that we shared and he was telling me a story.

"Some of you," he continued, "know about this already. We have had our rehearsals. You must remember that the flight of the Falcon, which will be the name of this season's celebration—for such was the manner of Claudio's passing—has never before been acted, and probably never will be again. I want it so to live in all your minds, and in the memories of everyone who sees it, that it will endure for all time. What has been enacted up to the present in our Festival plays will be as nothing compared to this. I want to stage the greatest production that this city has ever seen. Because of this, I am going to ask for even more volunteers than we have had in previous years."

A murmur rose from the seated ranks below him on the floor. Every hand shot up into the air. The faces, pale in the flickering light, were turned to his.

"Wait," he said. "Not all will be chosen. I shall choose later those whom I think fit. The point is this. . . ." Once again he paused. He leant forward in his chair, watching their faces. "You know my methods," he said. "We used them last year, and the year before. It is essential that every volunteer should believe in the part he plays, should think himself into his creation. This year you will be the courtiers at the Falcon's palace. You will be that small body of dedicated men. You, the Arts students of the university, will, by your very nature, become the élite. You are so already. For this you are here in Ruffano, for this you have your reason for living. Yet you are a minority in the university, your ranks are small, the immense numbers swamping the other Faculties are barbarians and Goths and Vandals who, like the merchants of five hundred years ago, understand nothing of art, nothing of beauty. They would, if they had the power, destroy all the treasures we possess in the apartments here, perhaps even pull down the palace itself, and put in its stead . . . what? Factories, offices, banks, commercial houses, not to give employment and an easier life to the peasant who lives no better now than he did five centuries ago, but to enrich themselves, to better themselves, to own more cars, more television sets, more biscuit-box villas on the Adriatic, thus breeding ever greater discontent, poverty and misery."

Suddenly he rose. He held up his hand to silence the burst of applause that echoed to the fluted ceiling.

"That's enough," he said, "no more from me tonight. What we are going to do now is to give you a short display of the sort of training we have already carried out with volunteers. Keep back from the square, or you may get hurt!"

The applause, checked, turned to instant silence. The crowd leaned forward, intent on what was to follow. Two of the bodyguard came and took away the chair. Four more advanced, holding flares in either hand, and formed a square in the centre of the room, lit by the flames alone.

Aldo took his place beside one of the flares. As he did so two figures leapt into the square. They wore white shirts, the sleeves rolled to the elbow, and black jeans. Their faces were masked, not for protection but to conceal their features. Each carried a naked sword. They fought as duellists fought in days gone by, in earnest, not in play. There was no feint in parry or thrust, no pretence in the crouching stance of the competitors. The steel blades rang as they clashed and struck and dived, and when one of the duellists soon proved himself to have a longer reach than his adversary and in pursuit drove him to his knee, pointing the blade at his throat, a gasp rose from the huddled ranks as the half-fallen man, panting, stared through the narrow slits of his mask and the sharpened tip drew blood. A scratch, no more, perhaps, than a razor's slip might do, but the sword had done it, the drops of blood ran down his throat and stained the white shirt below.

"Enough!" cried Aldo. "You have shown what you can do. Well fought, and thank you."

He threw his handkerchief to the fallen man who, rising to his feet, staunched the wound. Both men left the lighted square and disappeared through the door to the Duke's bedchamber.

The spectators, stunned by the realism of the display, were too shaken to applaud. They waited, breathless, for Aldo to speak again. Once more I was reminded of my boyhood days and the effect he had had upon me then. This was the same power, but maturer, dangerous.

"You have seen," said Aldo, "that mock battles are not for us. Now, will the few women amongst us leave the room, and any of the rest who do not wish to volunteer? It will not be held against them. Those who care to offer themselves as volunteers, remain."

One girl pushed forward, protesting, but he shook his head. "I'm sorry," he said, "no women. Not for this. Go home and learn how to bandage, yes, but fighting is for us."

The door leading to the throne room was flung open. Slowly, reluctantly, the few women passed through it, followed by some dozen men, no more. I was amongst them. The scrutineer in the throne room waved us on. We walked silently to the gallery outside, and the door was closed behind us. We were, I suppose, about eighteen to twenty all told. The girls, contemptuous, did not even wait for escorts. Those who knew each other well linked arms and clattered down the stairs. The men, shamefaced, defensive, offered each other cigarettes.

"I can't swallow that stuff," said one. "It's fascism all over again, that's what he's driving at."

"You're crazy," said another. "Didn't you realise he was pitching into the industrialists? He's a Communist, it's obvious. They say he's a member of the Communist Party."

"I don't think he cares one hell for politics," said a third. "He's just a magnificent hoaxer, that's all, and that's the way he gets his Festival company to work. He did the same last year, when he dressed up the Papal Guard. I was ready to volunteer until I saw that fight. No Arts Director is going to hack me to pieces."

Nobody raised his voice. They argued, but in fierce whispers. We all tramped down the stairs in the wake of the girls.

"One thing's certain," observed somebody. "If this leaks out to the C and E crowd there'll be murder."

"Whose murder?"

"After the show we've just seen? Why, theirs. The C and E."

"Then I shall volunteer. Anything to have a go at that lot!"

"Same here. Up with the barricades!"

Loss of face had been recovered. They stood in the piazza, still arguing, discussing, and it was plain that bitterness ran dangerously high between the C and E students and the other Faculties. Then they drifted uphill towards the university and the students' hostel. I waited until the figure I had noticed standing on the Duomo steps came to join me.

"Well?" said Carla Raspa.

"Well?" I answered.

"I never wanted to be a man until tonight," she said. "Like the American song, I thought 'Anything they can do I can do better'. Except, so it seems—fight."

"Perhaps there will be parts for women, too," I said. "He'll recruit you later. There are always women in a crowd, to scream and throw stones."

"I don't want to scream," she said, "I want to fight." Then, looking at me with no less contempt than the student girls, she said, "Why didn't you volunteer?"

"Because," I answered, "I'm a bird of passage."

"That's no reason," she answered. "So am I, if it comes to that. I can leave at any time, take my lectures elsewhere. Get a transfer. Not now, though. Not after what I've heard tonight. It could be . . . ." she paused, while I lighted her cigarette, "it could be that this is what I'm looking for. A purpose. A cause."

We started walking down the via Rossini.

"Would acting in a Festival play give you a purpose?" I asked.

"He wasn't talking about acting," she said.

It was still early, and because it was Saturday evening the people were strolling up and down the street, in couples or family parties. Not many students, or so I judged. They had gone home until Sunday evening. The young who strolled the streets came from the shops, the banks, the offices. These were the native Ruffanesi.

"How long has he been here?" I asked.

"Professor Donati? Oh, some years. He was born here, fought in the war as a fighter-pilot, was given up for dead, then returned and took a post-graduate course. He stayed on as lecturer and finally became adopted by the Ruffano Arts Council as their bright boy, until a few years ago they voted him Director. He's the darling of some of the powers that be, and bitterly resented by others. Not by the Rector. Professor Butali believes in him."

"And the Rector's lady?"

"Livia Butali? I wouldn't know. She's a snob. Keeps herself to herself and thinks of nothing but music. She comes of an old Florentine family and won't let you forget it. I hardly think Professor Donati would have much time for her."

We had come to the piazza della Vita. I had forgotten, until that moment, my promise to take my companion out to dinner. I wondered if she had forgotten it too. We crossed over in the direction of the via San Michele, and stopped outside the door of No. 5.

Then abruptly she held out her hand. "Don't think I'm unfriendly," she said. "The truth is, I want to be alone. I want to think about what we saw tonight. I shall heat myself some soup and go to bed. Have I let you down?"

"No," I said, "I feel exactly as you do."

"Another time, then," she nodded. "Perhaps tomorrow, it all depends. . . . Anyway, you're a neighbour, you're just down the street. We can always find each other."

"Naturally," I said. "Goodnight. And thank you."

She let herself in at the door of No. 5, and I continued down the street to 24. I entered cautiously. No one was about. I could hear the sound of television coming from the Silvanis' living-room.

I took up the telephone directory lying on a table in the hall beside the telephone, and searched the pages. Donati. Professor Aldo Donati. The address, 2, via dei Sogni.

I went out again into the street.

CHAPTER NINE

MY WALK TOOK me past our old home and nearly to the top of the via dei Sogni, before it curved to the right into the via dell'8 Settembre above the university. No. 2 was a tall, narrow house standing on its own, looking down towards the church of San Donato and the long via delle Mura that encircled the city. In former days this had been our doctor's house, good Dr Mauri, who came and visited me whenever I coughed and wheezed—I was said to suffer from a weak chest—and I remember that he never used a stethoscope for the purpose of listening to my breathing but always laid his ear flat against my naked chest, gripping my small shoulders as he did so, a sudden proximity which I found distasteful. He was middle-aged even then, and must now be dead, or long past practising his medicine.

I came close to the house and saw the name-plate—Donati—on the right-hand door beneath the double entrance. This double entrance gave access both to the via dei Sogni and, through a half-passage, to the grassy slope beyond and the stone steps descending to the church of San Donato. To the left was the porter's domain, used in the old days by Dr Mauri's cook.

I stared at the name-plate. We had had a similar plate at No. 8. It had been Marta's pride to keep it polished, and it could, with a little imagination, be the same. There was a bell beside it. I put my finger on the button and pressed. I could hear the summons within. No one answered. Aldo must live alone, or, if not alone, whoever lived with him was now in the Room of the Cherubs at the ducal palace in his company.

I rang once again to make sure, but there was nothing. I turned and looked opposite at the porter's door. I hesitated a moment, and then rang that instead. After a moment the door opened, and a man asked my business. The bushy eyebrows, the hair en brosse, though grizzled, were familiar. Then I remembered. He had been a comrade-in-arms of my brother's, one of the ground-crew at the aircraft base. He had attached himself to Aldo, and once my brother had brought him home on leave. Save for turning grey, he had not changed. I had. Nobody, looking upon a man of thirty-two, would remember the boy of ten.

"Professor Donati," he told me, "is not at home. You will find him at the ducal palace."

"I know that," I answered. "I've already seen him there, but not in private. My business is personal."

"I'm sorry," he said, "I cannot tell you when the professor will be back. He hasn't ordered dinner. If you care to leave your name you could always telephone him for an appointment."

"The name is Fabbio," I said, "but he would not know it." I was not sure whether I cursed the anonymity of my step-father's heritage or blessed it.

"Signor Fabbio," answered the man. "I will remember. If I do not see Professor Donati tonight I will tell him in the morning."

"Thank you," I said, "thank you. Goodnight."

"Goodnight, signore."

He closed the door. I stood by the double entrance looking on to the via dei Sogni. I had remembered his name. Jacopo. He had been ill-at-ease when my brother brought him home on leave, believing himself out of place. Marta had seized the situation at a glance and taken him into the kitchen with herself and Maria Ghigi.

I wondered whether it would be any use going back to the ducal palace and looking for my brother there. No sooner thought than instantly dismissed. He would be attended by his bodyguard, perhaps by the whole crowd of adulating students.

I was about to step out of the porched entrance when I heard footsteps approaching. I looked and saw that it was a woman, and the woman Carla Raspa. I withdrew through the double entrance and stood behind the open doorway on the eastern side. She could not see me, but I could see her. When she came to Aldo's door she did as I had done and rang the bell. She waited a moment, glancing over her shoulder at Jacopo's entrance, but made no attempt to ring his bell. Then she felt in her bag, and bringing out an envelope pushed it through the letter-box to the floor within. I could sense the disappointment in her drooping shoulders. She went out once more into the via dei Sogni and I heard the patter of her high heels die away. Getting rid of me had been an excuse. No bowl of soup and bed for Carla Raspa. She must have had this in mind as soon as we left the ducal palace. Now, frustrated, she would find the soup more welcome, but she would have to drink it alone.

I waited until I judged her well ahead and out of sight and then I, in turn, returned to the via San Michele. This time I penetrated to the Silvani sanctum and explained to the signora that I had not eaten. Anything would do. Switching off the television she got up, protesting hospitality, and pushed me into the dining-room, her husband following to keep me company. I told them I had been to the ducal palace by invitation. They seemed impressed.

"Are you going to take part in the Festival?" enquired the signora.

"No," I answered, "no, I think not."

"You should do so," she insisted. "It's a great thing for Ruffano, this Festival. People come for miles to see it. Last year many had to be turned away. We were lucky. My husband managed to get seats in the piazza Maggiore and we watched the procession of the Papal Guard. It was so realistic that I said afterwards we might have been living in those times. When the Rector blessed me, in his guise as Pope Clement, I felt I had been blessed by the Holy Father himself."

She bustled around, helping me to food and drink.

"Yes," agreed her husband, "it was magnificent. They say this year it will be even better, despite the Rector's illness. Professor Donati is a great artist. Some feel he has missed his vocation. He ought to be a film director, instead of giving up his time to the Arts Council here. After all, Ruffano is only a small city."

I ate, more from emptiness than hunger. Excitement and emotion were still at fever-point.

"What sort of a fellow is he, this Professor Donati?" I asked.

The signora smiled and rolled her eyes. "You saw him tonight, didn't you?" she said. "Well, you can judge for yourself what a woman thinks of him. If I were half my age, I wouldn't let him alone."

Her husband laughed. "It's his dark eyes," he said. "He has a way with him, not only with the women, but with the municipality too. Whatever he asks for, he gets. Seriously, though, he and the Rector between them have done great things for Ruffano. Of course, he's a native. His father, Signor Donati, was Superintendent at the palace for many years, so he knew what was wanted. Do you know that he came back here, after the liberation, to find that his father had died in a prison camp, and his mother had run off with a German general, taking the younger brother with her—his whole family, you may say, wiped out? It takes guts to accept that. He stayed. Gave himself to Ruffano, has never looked elsewhere. Now, you can't help admiring the man for that."

Signora Silvani pushed fruit upon me. I shook my head.

"No more," I said. "Coffee only." I took one of the signore's cigarettes. "Then he never married?"

"No. You know what it is," said the signora. "When a young man comes home in a state of shock—he was a pilot, and he was shot down and joined the Resistance—and hopes to rejoin his family, it doesn't make him love the opposite sex better to learn that his mother has decamped with a German. My opinion is that it sickened him with women for good."

"Ah, no," said her husband, "he's recovered. After all, he was only a boy at the time. Professor Donati must be forty now. Give him time. He'll find himself a wife when he's ready for marriage."

I drank my coffee and stood up.

"You look tired," said Signora Silvani with sympathy. "They are working you too hard at the library. Never mind, it's Sunday tomorrow. You can stay in bed all day if you feel like it."

I thanked them and went upstairs. I flung my things off, my head still bursting, and lay down on the bed. But not to sleep. Only to see Aldo's face in the flickering firelight of the Room of the Cherubs, that pale, unforgettable face, and to hear again the loved, the feared, the well-remembered voice.

After tossing for two hours I got out of bed, opened the window and stood there, smoking a cigarette. The last loiterer had gone home, and all was still. I looked up the street and saw that the shutters on the first floor of No. 5 were open, as mine were. A woman was leaning out, also wakeful, also smoking a cigarette. If I could not sleep, neither could Carla Raspa. We were wakeful for the same cause.

The church bells roused me next morning from the fitful sleep into which I had eventually fallen. First at seven, then at eight. The Duomo, San Cipriano, then the others. Not the chimes for the hours, but the summons to Mass. I lay in bed and thought how we used to go, the four of us, my father, my mother, Aldo and myself, to High Mass in San Cipriano. Those were the early days before the war. We would set forth, dressed for Sundays, Aldo resplendent in his uniform of the Fascist Youth organisation. The girls had an eye for him even then. We would walk down the hill to San Cipriano, and my martyrdom near the altar-piece of Lazarus would begin.

I got up and threw wide the shutters I had closed last night. It was raining. Rivulets of water ran in the gutters. A few people hurried by bent under umbrellas. Down the street the shutters on the first floor of No. 5 were tightly closed. I had not been to Mass since my schooldays in Turin. At least, not by intention. Sometimes I would escort a flock of tourists bent on sight-seeing, and, pausing near the high altar in whichever church we were visiting, be obliged to stand and stare. Now I would go of my own volition.

I was half-dressed when a knock on the door announced Signora Silvani's arrival with rolls and coffee. "Don't move," she said. "Look at the weather. There's nothing to get up for."

I had said the same thing to myself over the years when chance brought me a free Sunday, wet or fine. Nothing to get up for in Turin or in Genoa. Now the world had changed.

"I'm going to Mass in San Cipriano," I said.

She nearly dropped the tray. Then she put it carefully on the bed. "Amazing," she said. "I thought nobody went to Mass any more, except old people and the very young. I'm glad to hear it. Do you always go?"

"No," I said, "but this is a special occasion."

"It's Lent," she said. "I suppose all of us should go in Lent."

"My Lent is over," I said. "I'm going to celebrate the Resurrection."

"You'd do better to stay in bed and wait for Easter," she told me.

I drank the coffee and finished dressing. My head no longer reeled. Even my hands were still. The rain did not matter, poor Marta's death did not matter despite the manner of it. Later in the day I would see Aldo. For the first time in my life I held the cards; I was prepared for it and he was not.

I went out of the house into the rain, the collar of my light overcoat that had to do duty for a raincoat turned high up to my ears. The shutters were still closed at No. 5. Crossing the piazza were a few stragglers, bent on the same mission as myself. Others stood huddled under the colonnades waiting for the bus that brought the Sunday papers, or waiting for another bus to take them out of Ruffano. A few young people, braving the weather, were setting forth on vespas.

"It won't last," somebody shouted above the roar of his machine. "They say the sun is shining on the coast."

The summons from San Cipriano rang forth. Not so deep as the Duomo, but for me more solemn, more compelling, with a sudden urgency before the hour struck as though to hurry laggards to their knees.

Once inside, moved by the familiar sombre smell, I was struck by the paucity of people. In childhood days we had arrived early because my father wished to take his accustomed place. The church had been full, with the people standing in the side aisles. Not so today. The numbers were halved. Mostly family parties, women and young children. I went and stood near the side-chapel, feeling that I was fulfilling some age-long rite. The gates of the chapel were open, but no light above the altar-piece shone upon the face of Lazarus. The picture was veiled by the dimness. So were the other pictures in the church, and the statues, and the crucifixes. Then I remembered that it must be Passion Sunday.

I heard the sung Mass through, letting the thin voices of the boy choristers seep through me without pain. My mind was empty. Or perhaps I dreamed. A middle-aged priest I did not recognise gave a twenty-minute sermon warning us of perils past, of perils still to come, that the Lord, the Christ, still suffered for our sins. A child close to me yawned, his small face white with fatigue, and a woman who might have been my mother nudged him to attention. Later, the few communicants shuffled to the rails. They were mostly women. One woman, well-dressed, her head covered with a black lace veil, had knelt throughout the Mass. She did not go to the rails. Her head was bowed in her hands. When it was all over, when the priests and the choristers had gone, the people dispersing with their faces solemn still yet somehow eased, their duty done, she rose to her feet and turned, and I saw that it was Signora Butali. I walked ahead, and waited for her outside the church. The boy on the vespa had been right. The rain had stopped. The sun that had been shining on the coast had broken through to Ruffano.

"Signora?" I said.

She looked at me with the blank eyes of someone far away brought back unwillingly to a less pleasant world. "Yes?" she answered.

I saw that I meant nothing. I had left no trace. "Armino Fabbio," I said. "I called at your house yesterday with some books."

Recognition dawned. I could read the thought passing through her mind. Ah, yes, the assistant librarian.

"Excuse me, of course," she said. "Forgive me. Good morning, Signor Fabbio."

"You were in front of me at Mass," I said. "At least, I thought it was you. I was not sure."

She walked down the steps at my side. She looked up at the sky and saw that the umbrella she carried was not necessary.

"I like to go to San Cipriano," she said. "It has more atmosphere than the Duomo. Is it going to be fine?"

Absently, she looked about her, and I felt a momentary hurt that she should feel so little interest in the man who stood by her side. A beautiful woman is usually aware of admiration, whatever the source. Effort is made. There is implicit understanding that homage is being paid. Signora Butali seemed unaware of these things.

"You have a car?" I asked.

"No," she said. "They're working on it at the garage over the weekend. I had trouble with it coming back from Rome."

"Would you object, then, if I walked with you up the hill? That is, if you are going home?"

"Not at all. Please do."

We crossed the piazza della Vita and began walking up the via Rossini as far as the prefettura, when she turned left and took the steps leading up to the via dei Sogni. Here we paused for breath, and for the first time she looked at me and smiled.

"The Ruffano hills," she said. "It takes time to get accustomed to them. Especially if, like me, you are a Florentine."

It made all the difference when she smiled. The mouth that seemed taut, disapproving, the mouth of the gentlewoman in the portrait my father loved, relaxed to femininity. There was even humour behind the eyes.

"Are you homesick?" I asked.

"Sometimes," she replied, "but what's the use? I knew what I was in for when I came here. My husband warned me."

She turned abruptly, and we set ourselves to climb the steps.

"It's not an easy life then, signora," I said, "to be wife of the Rector of a university?"

"Far from easy," she answered. "There are so many jealousies, factions, to which I have to shut my eyes. I am less patient than my husband. He has given his life, literally, to his work here. If it were not so he would not be in hospital now."

She bowed and wished good morning to a couple descending the steps, and from the gracious inclination of her head, without a smile, I understood why Carla Raspa had spoken in feminine spite. Signora Butali, consciously or not, exuded breeding. I wondered what effect she had upon the professors' wives.

"Last night," I said, "I was lucky enough to get a pass to the ducal palace for a session given by the Director of the Arts Council."

"Indeed?" she replied in sudden animation. "Do tell me about it. Did it impress you?"

"It impressed me very much," I answered, aware that she had turned now to look at me. "Not only the setting, lit with flares and torches for the occasion, but the duelling display that followed, and above all Professor Donati's address to the students."

A spot of colour had come into her cheeks, due, I felt, not so much to her exertion in climbing the steps as to the turn in the conversation.

"I must go to one of the sessions," she said, "I really must. Something always seems to prevent me."

"Last year," I said, "they were telling me you performed at the Festival. Are you going to do the same this year?"

"No, impossible," she answered, "with my husband in hospital in Rome. In any event, I doubt if there would be a part for me."

"You know the subject?"

"Poor Duke Claudio, isn't it? I'm afraid I'm a little vague. I just know there was an insurrection, and he was murdered."

We had reached the via dei Sogni, and in the distance I could see the garden wall. Imperceptibly I slackened my steps.

"Professor Donati seems to be a very remarkable man," I said. "They told me at the pensione where I am lodging that he is himself a Ruffanese."

"Very much so," she said. "His father was Superintendent at the ducal palace, and in fact he was born and spent all his boyhood at the house we live in now. It's one of his ambitions to have it back from us. That is not very likely, unless my husband's health forces us to retire. Professor Donati loves every room in the house, as you can imagine. I gather he was immensely proud of his father, and his father of him. The family history is quite a tragedy."

"Yes," I said, "yes, so I heard."

"He used to speak about it," she said, "but not any longer. I hope he's beginning to forget. After all, twenty years is a long time."

"What became of his mother?" I asked.

"He never discovered. She disappeared with the German forces which occupied Ruffano in '44, and since there was fighting in the north shortly afterwards it is almost certain that she must have been killed in the bombing, she and the little brother."

"There was a brother?"

"Yes, a small boy of ten or eleven. They were very devoted. I sometimes think that it is because of him that Professor Donati gives so much thought to the students."

We had reached the garden wall. I glanced furtively at my watch. It was about twenty-five minutes after eleven.

"Thank you, signora," I said, "it was very good of you to let me walk home with you."

"No," she said, "it is for me to thank you." She paused, with her hand on the garden door. "Would you like to meet Professor Donati personally?" she said. "If so, I should be delighted to introduce you."

Panic seized me. "Thank you, signora," I said, "but I wouldn't in any way wish . . ."

The smile returned. "No trouble." She cut me short. "It's a custom of the Rector's to ask a few of his colleagues to the house on Sunday mornings, and in his absence I do the same. Two or three people may call this morning, and Professor Donati is sure to be one of them."

I had not planned it thus. I had planned to go alone to his house in the via dei Sogni. Signora Butali took my panic for embarrassment, an assistant librarian at the palace library feeling himself out of place.

"Don't be shy," she said, smiling. "It will be something to tell the other assistants about tomorrow!"

I followed her into the garden and to the house door, still thinking of an excuse to get away.

"Anna will be busy preparing lunch," she said. "You can help me set out the glasses."

She opened the door. We entered the hall, and passed through to the dining-room on the left. It was no longer a dining-room. It was lined with books from floor to ceiling, and there was a large desk near the window.

"This is my husband's library," she said. "When he is at home he likes to entertain here, and when we are many we fling open the double doors to the small dining-room beyond."

The small dining-room beyond had been my playroom. She opened the double doors and I saw, astonished, how the table was set there in the centre, stiff and formal, laid for one. I thought of the mess I had left the room in, with my fleet of small cars scattered over the floor and two tins, upturned, for the garage.

"The vermouth is on the sideboard," said Signora Butali, "and the Campari. The glasses are on the trolley. Wheel the trolley into the library, will you?"

She had arranged things to her satisfaction and put out the cigarettes when the bell rang.

"Probably the Rizzios," she said. "I'm glad to have you here, she's so very formal. Professor Rizzio is Head of the Department of Education, and his sister is in charge of the hostel where the women students live."

She looked suddenly vulnerable, and younger than her age. Perhaps when her husband was at home he shouldered the burden of social responsibility.

I slipped into my courier guise and waited by the trolley, ready to pour vermouth at her command. She went to the door to greet the callers, and I heard the murmur of the usual compliments. Then she ushered her guests into the room. They were middle-aged, grey-haired and angular. He had the worn and harassed appearance of one perpetually up to the eyes in work, with intrays piled upon a desk that never cleared. I could picture him baying ineffectual commands to streams of tired subordinates. His sister had more authority, holding herself like a matron of old Rome. I pitied the luckless students who lived under her rule. I was introduced as Signor Fabbio, temporary assistant at the library. The signorina bowed, turning immediately to her hostess to enquire after the Rector.

Professor Rizzio peered at me with a puzzled air. "Forgive me," he asked, "but I don't recollect your name. How long have you been working at the library?"

"Since Friday," I told him. "I was engaged by Signor Fossi."

"Then your appointment went through him?" he said.

"Yes, professor," I answered. "I applied to Signor Fossi and he spoke to the Registrar."

"Really!" he commented. "I am surprised he did not consult me."

"I imagine he did not want to burden you with such a small matter," I murmured.

"Any appointment, however small, is of interest to the Deputy Rector," he said. "Where are you from?"

"I have been working in Genoa, professor," I replied, "but my home is in Turin. I graduated at the university there. I hold a degree in modern languages."

"That, at least, is fortunate," he said. "It is more than the other temporary assistants possess."

I asked him what he would have to drink, and he said a small glass of vermouth. I poured it for him and he moved away. His sister said she would take nothing, but when Signora Butali protested Signorina Rizzio was pleased to accept a glass of mineral water.

"So you are working at the library?" she said, dwarfing me with her presence.

Tall women bring out the worst in me, as they do in most men of less than average height. "I pass the time there, signorina," I said. "I am taking a vacation, and the job happens to suit me."

"You are fortunate," she replied, staring. "Many students in their third or fourth year would be glad to avail themselves of such an opportunity."

"Possibly, signorina," I said in smoothly courteous tones, "but I am not a student. I am a courier who speaks several languages, and I am accustomed to conducting parties of international repute through the more important cities of our country—Florence, Rome, Naples. . . ."

Dislike of my impertinence formed upon her features. She sipped at the mineral water, and her throat quivered as the liquid passed. Another ring at the front door spared her from further distress. My hostess, ears only for the bell, turned towards me, a tell-tale spot of colour in her cheeks.

"Answer it for me, will you?" she said. "It's probably Professor Donati."

She continued her rapid conversation with Professor Rizzio, her unwonted animation covering inward stress. A courier seldom drinks. He dares not. Now, however, I quickly swallowed a glass of vermouth under the disapproving eyes of Signorina Rizzio and, excusing myself, made for the front door. Aldo had opened it already, being, no doubt, persona grata in the house, and was frowning at the sight of Professor Rizzio's raincoat thrown down upon a chair. Then his eyes fell upon me. Without recognition. Without even a flicker of interest.

"Signora Butali is expecting you," I stammered.

"So I believe," he said. "Who are you?"

"My name is Fabbio," I said. "I had the honour of meeting you last night at the ducal palace. I was with Signorina Raspa."

"Oh, yes," he said, "yes, I remember. I hope you enjoyed yourself."

He did not remember. It mattered not at all what I thought of the evening. He moved forward into the dining-room, or rather the library, and at once the room became alive. Signora Butali called "Hullo", and he retorted with "Good morning", the morning a little emphasised. He bent over her hand and kissed it, then turned immediately to Signorina Rizzio. Signora Butali, without asking him what he wanted, filled a glass half-full of Campari and gave it to him.

"Thank you," he said, taking it from her, not looking at her.

The front-door bell rang once more, and questioning my hostess with a glance I went to open it. These menial duties kept me occupied, and served to steady the threatening tremor of my hands. Signor Fossi stood before me on the doorstep, accompanied by a lady. He looked taken aback at the sight of me, and immediately presented the lady as his wife. Somehow I had not thought of him as married.

"Signor Fabbio is helping us temporarily in the library," he explained to her, and, on my asking how he did, told me quickly that he had quite recovered.

I took up my stance once more behind the trolley, and poured them drinks. The conversation turned to health, our hostess touching upon her distress at the reason for Signor Fossi's absence from the library the day before.

"Luckily," she said, "Signor Fabbio was able to oblige me with the books I asked for."

The librarian, anxious to turn discussion away from his own past indisposition, did not dwell upon the loan of books, but immediately enquired after the Rector. Talk about Professor Butali became general, everyone hoping that he would be able to leave hospital in time for the Festival.

Behind me I could hear Signorina Rizzio complaining to Aldo about the rowdy behaviour of the C and E students, who had taken to circling the city in the evenings on their vespas.

"They even have the insolence to roar their machines beneath the women students' hostel," she said, "as late sometimes as ten o'clock at night. I have asked my brother to speak to Professor Elia, and he assures me he has done so, but the Professor takes no action. If it continues I shall bring the matter up before the university Council."

"Perhaps," suggested Aldo, "your young women encourage the vespa enthusiasts from their windows?"

"I assure you they do not," retorted Signorina Rizzio. "My young women, as you call them, are either engaged in reading up their notes for the next lecture or they are safely tucked up in bed with the shutters closed."

I poured myself out another glass of vermouth. Then, looking up, I perceived Aldo's eye upon me, puzzled. I moved away from the trolley and stood by the window, staring down into the garden. The voices hummed. The bell rang. Somebody else went to answer it. This time I did not bother to come forward to be introduced, and I think my hostess had forgotten me.

Presently, while I was still staring into the garden, I felt a hand on my shoulder. "You're an odd fellow," said Aldo. "I keep asking myself what you are doing here. Have I seen you before somewhere?"

"It's possible," I said, "that if I disguised myself in a winding-sheet and hid in the linen closet upstairs you might recognise me. My name is Lazarus."

I turned and looked at him. His smile vanished. His features dissolved. I was aware of nothing but two enormous eyes blazing from a pale face. It was my supreme moment. For the one and only time in his life the disciple had shocked his master.

"Beo . . ." he said. "Oh, my God . . . Beo."

He did not move. The grip on my shoulder tightened. It seemed to me that his eyes engulfed his whole person. Then, with a terrible effort, he controlled himself. His hand fell away.

"Make some excuse and go," he said. "Wait for me outside. I'll follow you. There's a car there, an Alfa-Romeo; get into it."

Like a sleepwalker I crossed the room and, murmuring an apology to my hostess, thanked her for her kindness and said goodbye. I bowed to the rest of the company who might have noticed me. I left the house, and passed through the garden to the street outside. There were three cars parked by the garden wall. I got into the Alfa-Romeo as he had bidden me. I sat there, smoking a cigarette, and later watched the Rizzios depart, then the Fossis, and others that I had not met. Aldo came last. He got into the car without saying a word and slammed the door. We drove away. Not to his own house, but downhill and so out of the city by the Porta Malebranche. Still he said nothing, and it was not until Ruffano lay behind us, and he had driven the car into the hills, that he pulled up suddenly, switched off the engine, and turned and looked at me.

CHAPTER TEN

Hɪs ᴇʏᴇs ɴᴇᴠᴇʀ left my face. It was the old inspection I remembered. He used to do this when he took me out, to see if my hair was brushed, my shoes were clean. Sometimes he sent me back to change my shirt.

"I always said you wouldn't grow," he said.

"I'm five foot five," I told him.

"As much as that? I don't believe it."

He gave me a cigarette and lit it for me. His hands were steady, mine were not.

"Your curls have gone. I'd have known you otherwise," he said.

He tugged at my hair, a savage gesture that invariably hurt me in old days. It hurt me still. I shook my head.

"It was the Frankfurt barber," I said. "He started the rot, and it grew straight ever after. I wanted to look like the brigadier, and succeeded for a time."

"The brigadier?"

"A Yankee. We lived with him two years."

"I thought it was a German."

"The German came first. He only lasted six months after we left Ruffano."

I unwound the car window and looked out at the blue hump of the mountain that lay ahead. It was Monte Cappello. We could see it from the house at home.

"Is she alive?" he asked.

"No. She died three years ago of cancer."

"I'm glad," he said.

A bird, a hawk of some sort, came into my line of vision and poised, hovering, against the sky-line. I thought he was going to dive but he soared higher, in a widening circle, and hovered once again.

"What set it off?" said Aldo.

He might have meant, how did the disease take her, but knowing my brother I understood him to be referring back to '44.

"I've often wondered," I said. "I don't think it was father's death or the news of yours. She accepted both as fate like anyone else. Perhaps she was lonely. Perhaps she just liked men."

"No," said Aldo, "I'd have known that. I can always tell." He did not smoke. He sat with his arm along the seat behind me. "The spoils of victory," he said, after a moment, "that's what she felt herself to be. For a woman of her sort, basically conventional and submissive to her husband, it would act like an aphrodisiac. First the German Commandant, in her home town, then the

Yankee after the German myth exploded. Yes . . . yes . . . I see the pattern. Very interesting."

I supposed it was, to him. Like reading history. Not if, like myself, one had been involved.

"Why Fabbio?" he asked.

"I was going to tell you. That was later, in Turin, when the Yankee brigadier left Frankfurt for the States. We met Enrico Fabbio in the train. He was polite and helpful with our baggage. In three months—he was a bank employee—she had married him. He couldn't have been kinder. And it was all part of the break with the past that I should take his name. After all, he paid."

"That's right. He paid."

I glanced at my brother. Did he resent the advent of our step-father? The inflection in his voice was strange.

"I'm grateful to him still," I said. "I continue to look him up if I'm in Turin."

"And that's as deep as it goes?"

"Why, yes. What else? He never took the place of father or of you. He was just a kind little man with a sense of family."

Aldo laughed. I wondered why my description struck him as funny.

"Anyway," I said, "we had nothing in common beyond sharing a roof and eating the same food, and after I took my degree at Turin I cut loose. I didn't fancy a job in the bank, which he suggested, so with my languages I entered the tourist trade."

"What as?"

"Junior clerk, clerk, guide, and finally courier."

"Tout," he said.

Well, yes. . . . Put bluntly, I was a tout. A superior tout. One degree higher than the fellow in the piazza Maggiore who hawked his picture-postcards.

"What firm employs you?" he asked.

"Sunshine Tours, Genoa," I replied.

"Good God!" he said.

He moved his arm from the back of the seat and started up the car. It was as though my admission had brought his interrogation to an end. No further questions needed. Case dismissed.

"They pay well," I protested in self-defence, "and I meet all sorts of people. It's experience, I'm travelling all the time. . . ."

"Where to?" he asked.

I did not answer. Where to, indeed. . . . He let in the clutch and the car roared ahead, climbing the surrounding heights, the road twisting and turning upon itself like a serpent's coils. The country spread out below us, the soil a patchwork quilt of dun and olive, and away westward the city of Ruffano, poised on her two hills, gleamed, a narrow circlet under the sun.

"And you?" I asked.

He smiled. Used as I was to Beppo's handling of the coach in Tuscany and the Umbrian undulations, where speed, of necessity, was second choice to safety, my brother's disrespect for his native Marches seemed to me profound. He courted death at every hairpin bend.

"You saw last night," he said. "I'm a puppeteer. I pull the strings, the puppets dance. It requires great skill."

"I believe you. But I don't see why. All that training, and that propaganda, for one day in the year, for a students' Festival?"

"Their day," he said, "this Festival. It's a world in miniature."

He had not replied to my question, but I let it go. Then abruptly he put to me the enquiry for which I had no answer. "Why didn't you come home before?"

Attack is the best method of defence. I forget who first coined the phrase. The German Commandant used to quote it.

"What was the use of my coming when I thought you were dead?" I said.

"Thank you, Beo," he replied. He seemed surprised. "Anyway," he added, "now you've come home I can make use of you."

He might have put it differently, after two-and-twenty years. I wondered if this was the moment to tell him about Marta. I decided not.

"Hungry?" he asked.

"Yes."

"Then we'll go back. To my house, 2, via dei Sogni."

"I know it. I called on you last night, but you were still out."

"Probably." He was not interested. He was thinking of something else.

"Aldo," I asked, "what are we going to say? Do we tell everyone the truth?"

"What truth?"

"Why, that we're brothers."

"I haven't yet decided," he replied. "It might be better not. How long are you here for anyway? Did Sunshine Tours give you the sack?"

"No," I said, "not the sack. I've taken a vacation."

"That's easy, then. We'll think of something."

The car turned from the hills to the valley below, and sped like an arrow towards Ruffano. We entered the city from the south, and climbed steeply to the via dell'8 Settembre, past the students' hostel, and then right. He drew up before the double entrance to his house.

"Out," he said.

I glanced about me, half hoping we might be seen, but the street was empty. Everyone was within doors having lunch.

"I saw Jacopo last night," I said as we entered the doorway together, "but he didn't recognise me."

"Why should he?" asked Aldo.

He turned the key and pushed me through into the hall. I went back twenty years. The furnishing, the decor, even the pictures on the wall, were those we had had at home. This was what I had sought for and had not found at No. 8. I looked up at Aldo, smiling.

"Yes," he said, "it's all here. What was left of it."

He stooped to pick up an envelope that was lying on the floor. The envelope that Carla Raspa must have pushed through the slit the night before. He glanced at the handwriting and threw the envelope on a table, unopened.

"Go on in," he said. "I'll call Jacopo."

I passed through to what must be his living-room. The chairs, the desk, the stiff-backed divan on which my mother used to sit, I recognised them all. Our father's portrait hung upon the wall, next to the bookcase. He seemed to have grown younger, to have shrunk in stature, but his air of benign authority was still there to humble me. I sat down and looked about me, my hands on my knees. The only concessions to a later age were pictures of aircraft on another wall. Aircraft in battle. Climbing, diving, smoke pouring from the tail.

"Jacopo will bring lunch directly," said Aldo, coming into the room. "It will be a few minutes. Have a drink."

He went to a table in the corner—I recognised that also—and poured out two Campari into glasses that were ours as well.

"I never knew, Aldo," I said, gesturing to the room, "that all this meant so much to you?"

He downed his Campari in a draught. "More, evidently," he replied, "than the surroundings of Signor Fabbio meant to you."

Cryptic, but what of it? It did not worry me. Nothing worried me. I was realising to the full the warmth of Easter-tide. Our own.

"I've told Jacopo who you are," said Aldo. "I think it's best."

"Just as you like," I answered.

"Where are you lodging?"

"In the via San Michele. No. 24, with Signora Silvani. She has a houseful of students, but not, I'm afraid, of your persuasion. All Commerce and Economics, very bigoted."

He smiled. "That's good," he said, "in fact, it's very good."

I shrugged. The rivalry between the two factions was still beyond me.

"You can be a go-between," he added.

I considered this, staring into my glass of Campari. I seemed to remember similar errands in the past, not always successful, when he was a scholar at the Ruffano liceo. Messages smuggled into schoolmates' pockets that sometimes went astray. The role had disadvantages.

"I don't know about that," I said.

"I do," said Aldo.

Jacopo came in to set the lunch. I called "Hullo," and he put down his tray and stood to attention like an orderly.

"I apologise for not having recognised you yesterday, Signor Armino," he said. "I am very glad to see you."

"Don't be pompous," said my brother. "Beo is only five foot five. Still small enough to put across your knee."

Which he had done, in '43. Egged on by Aldo. I had forgotten that. Marta had protested, and shut the kitchen door. Marta. . . .

Jacopo produced our meal, and a large carafe of wine made from the local grapes. Later I asked my brother if Jacopo did everything for him.

"He manages," said Aldo. "A woman comes to clean. I employed Marta until she took to drink. Then it was hopeless. I had to send her packing."

The time had come. I had finished. Aldo was busy eating.

"I've something to tell you," I said. "I'd better tell you now because I'm involved. I believe Marta's dead. I believe she was murdered."

He put down his fork and stared at me across the table. "What the hell do you mean by that?" he said harshly.

His eyes, accusing, never left my face. I wiped my mouth, pushed back my chair and began walking up and down the room.

"I could still be wrong," I said, "but I think not. I'm afraid not. And if it's true, then it's my fault. It's because of what I did."

I told him the whole story. From start to finish. The English tourists, the lone barbarian and his ten thousand lire tip, my nightmare in the small hours and its connection with the altarpiece in San Cipriano. The newspaper item the following day, the visit to the police, my recognition, as I thought, of the body, and the impulse that drove me to Ruffano. Finally, the sight of the cobbler Ghigi and his sister Maria disappearing yesterday in the custody of the local police.

Aldo heard me through to the end without a single interruption. I did not look at him as I told my tale, I just walked up and down the room, speaking much too fast. I could hear myself stammering as I might stammer to a judge, and I kept correcting myself in small particulars that did not matter.

When I had finished I sat down again in the chair. I thought his accusing eyes must be upon me still. But he was peeling an orange, unperturbed.

"You see?" I said, exhausted. "You understand?"

He put a large segment of the orange into his mouth and swallowed it. "Yes, I see," he said. "It's easy enough to check. I'm on very good terms with the Ruffano police. All I have to do is to lift the telephone and ask them if it's true that the dead woman is Marta."

"And if it is?"

"Well, it's just too bad," he said, reaching for another segment. "She'd have died anyway, in the state she was in. The Ghigis couldn't control her. Nobody could. You ask Jacopo. She was a drunk."

He had not understood. He had not seen that, if it was Marta who had been murdered, she had been murdered because I had put ten thousand lire into her hand. I explained this to him for the second time. He finished his orange. He dipped his fingers in the bowl of water beside the plate. "So what?" he said.

"Isn't it something I ought to have told the police in Rome? Wouldn't it explain the motive for murder?" I repeated.

Aldo stood up. He went to the door and shouted to Jacopo to bring coffee. After it had been brought and the door was closed, he poured out coffee for us both and began stirring his slowly, thoughtfully.

"A motive for murder," he said. "It's something we all have, at some time or other. You as much as anyone else. Run along to the police if you like, and tell them what you've just told me. You saw an old woman lying on the doorstep of a church, and it reminded you of an altar-piece that was your peculiar horror as a child. Fine. So what do you do? You bend over the woman and she lifts her head. She recognises you, the child who fled with the German army twenty years before. You recognise her, and something cracks in your brain. You kill her, a blind impulse to kill a nightmare memory that haunts you, and then, to stifle conscience, you put a note for ten thousand lire in her hand."

He swallowed his coffee and went across the room. He picked up the telephone. "I'll get on to the Commissioner," he said. "He'll be at home on a Sunday, very probably. At least he'll be able to give me the latest news."

"No, wait, Aldo . . . wait," I burst out, in sudden panic.

"What for? You want to know, don't you? So do I." He asked for a number. It was out of my hands. It was no longer my secret, my inner turmoil. Aldo now shared it, but in sharing it he made my confusion worse. I could have committed the murder as he described it. I had no witnesses to prove an alibi. The very motive he suggested made a desperate sense. Protestations of innocence would be in vain. The police would not believe me—why should they? I might never be able to prove that I was guiltless.

"You're not going to involve me, are you?" I asked.

He raised his eyes to heaven in mock despair, and spoke into the mouthpiece. "Is it you, Commissioner?" he said. "I hope I haven't dragged you from your lunch. It's Donati here, Aldo Donati. Very well, thank you. Commissioner, I've been very disturbed by a rumour going round Ruffano, brought me by my servant Jacopo, that my old family nurse Marta Zampini, who has apparently been missing for some days, may turn out to be this woman who was murdered in Rome. . . . Yes . . . yes. . . . No, I'm a very busy man, as you know. I rarely read a newspaper, and in any event I saw nothing about it. . . . The Ghigis, yes. She had lodged with them for some months. . . . I see. . . . Yes. . . ." He looked across at me, nodding his head. My heart sank. It was going to be true, and I was still further enmeshed. "So there's no doubt about it, then? I'm very sorry. She had completely gone to pieces, you know. I used to employ her until it became impossible. The Ghigis can't tell you anything, I suppose? Why Rome? Yes, some impulse, perhaps. . . . And you hope to make an arrest soon. Good. Good. Thank you, Commissioner. Yes, I shall be extremely obliged if you would contact me as soon as you have more news. Meanwhile, confidential, naturally. Thank you . . . thank you."

He replaced the receiver. He took an unopened packet of cigarettes from a box and threw them across to me.

"Calm down," he said, "you'll soon be out of the red. They expect to make an arrest within twenty-four hours."

His assumption that fear for my own skin was at the root of my distress was so reminiscent of his attitude to me of old that it was not worth denying. Guilty, yes. Guilty of putting the money into her hands and not turning back. Guilty of passing by on the other side.

Conscience, tortured, drove me to attack. "Why did she drink?" I asked. "Didn't you look after her?"

His passionate reply startled me. "I fed her, clothed her, cherished her, and she collapsed within," he said. "Why? Don't ask me why. A reversion to type, to her drunken peasant ancestry. When someone is bent on suicide you can't prevent them." Once again he shouted for Jacopo. The man entered and removed the coffee tray. "I'm in to nobody," Aldo said. "Beo and I are missing twenty-two years. It will take more than a few hours to wipe them out."

He looked at me, then smiled. The room, familiar now and personal because of its possessions, closed in upon me. Responsibility for the world and all its ills was mine no longer. Aldo would take charge.

CHAPTER ELEVEN

WE SAT THERE talking, letting the day go by. Sometimes Jacopo entered with a fresh brew of coffee, and went out again without a word. The room filled with the smoke from my cigarettes, mine, not Aldo's. He had given it up, he said, he had long ago lost the urge. I drew from him, indirectly, sparked off by questions fired at random, the story of his immediate post-war years. How, after the Armistice, he joined the partisans. Even then he knew nothing of the fateful telegram that had told us of his death, and he assumed that we believed him to be a prisoner of war. It was not until he found his way back to Ruffano, some months after we ourselves had fled from it with the Commandant, that he learnt the truth from Marta. They, in their turn, heard the rumour that while travelling north to the Austrian border our convoy had been bombed, and our mother and I killed. So, in our separate ways, our worlds had disintegrated.

He a young man of twenty, I a child of twelve, each had to face a new existence. Mine was to look, week after week, upon a woman without roots who daily, nightly became more superficial, more lacking in discrimination, faded, stale; his to remember her as she had bidden him goodbye when last he came on leave, warm-hearted, loving, full of plans for future meetings—and then to have this image crack when not only Marta but all who knew her in Ruffano told him of her end. The gossip there had been, the shame, the scandal. One or two had even seen her drive away, laughing, beside her Commandant, while I waved a swastika flag from the window of the car.

"That was the final thrust," said Aldo, "you, with your flag."

I began to live it once again, and through his eyes her shame became my shame and I suffered for her. I made excuses. He would have none of them.

"No use, Beo," he said, "I don't want to listen. Whatever she did in Frankfurt or Turin, what life she made for the man Fabbio whom you call your stepfather, whether she was ill or unhappy or in pain, does not count. She died for me the day she left Ruffano."

I asked him if he had seen our father's grave. He had. He had been to the prison-camp where he lay buried. Once. Never again. He did not want to discuss that either.

"He hangs there on the wall," said Aldo, gesturing towards the portrait, "that's all I needed of him. That and his possessions, here in this room. Besides the legacy of all he had achieved at the ducal palace. I made it my business to carry on where he left off, but, as you see, with more authority than he ever had. That was my goal."

He spoke with a strange bitterness throughout as though, despite his standing in Ruffano and his swift rise to his present position, the years were wasted. Something eluded him still. Not the satisfaction of personal ambition, nor money, nor fame. He spoke of himself continually in the past tense. "I wanted this. I wanted that. I determined to carry out such-and-such an undertaking." Never once did he talk in the present, or in the future. Later, in one of the pauses in conversation, I said to him, "Don't you plan one day to marry? To start a family? So that you too will leave something behind you when you go?" He laughed. He was standing by the window at the time, looking out on the distant hills. From the window one could see Monte Cappello, beneath which we had driven in the morning. Now, with the approach of evening, it stood humped and clear against the sky, blue like a mandarin's coat.

"Remember?" he said. "When you were very small, I sometimes took infinite pains constructing a house of cards on the dining-room table, the table we've been eating at today. I would have the whole space covered—I must have used half-a-dozen packs. Then came the moment of triumph. When, with one breath, I blew the whole edifice flat."

I remembered it well. The fragile cards tremblingly balanced like a giant pagoda, the effect, with the last card poised, strangely awe-inspiring and beautiful to a staring child.

"Yes," I said. "What's that to do with my question?"

"Everything," he answered.

He crossed the room, took down one of the sketches of aircraft that were hanging on the wall, and brought it over to me. The sketch was of a fighter plane falling to the ground in flames.

"This wasn't mine, but it could have been," he said. "That's how I saw others go. Comrades, whom I'd flown beside. Mine wasn't a true flamer, I baled out before she flared, then she scorched to earth like a sizzling kite. The point was that at the moment of impact, when she was hit—I was climbing at the time, and I knew what it was—the explosion and my release in the sky happened almost simultaneously, and the moment of triumph, of ecstasy, was indescribable. It was death and it was power. Creation and destruction all in one. I had lived and I had died."

He replaced the picture on the wall. I still did not see what it had to do with marriage or with founding a family, unless it was that the experience he had undergone, which I tried to imagine and into which I followed him in vain, still staring at the picture on the wall, made all things valueless. To have known and rejoiced in death belittled life.

Aldo glanced at the clock. It was a quarter to seven. "I must leave you," he said. "I have a meeting at the ducal palace. It may not take more than an hour. Further discussions about the Festival."

We had not touched on the Festival all day. Nor any of his present activities. The past had been with us all the time.

"Have you a date later?" he asked.

I smiled, and shook my head. What should I want with a date now we were together?

"Good," he said. "Then I'll take you to dinner with Livia Butali."

He went to the telephone and called a number. Instantly I stood in fancy outside our old home further down the via dei Sogni. I heard the sound of the piano, Chopin again, and the music suddenly stopping, and I saw the player cross the room to answer the telephone, the ring of which she had been waiting for all day.

Aldo spoke into the mouthpiece. "Two of us," he said. "Say a quarter-past eight."

He cut short her query and hung up. I could imagine her standing there, frustrated, wondering, then returning to the piano to burst into a passionate Etude.

"Did you say you had a knowledge of German," he asked me suddenly, "amongst your other superficial expertise?"

"Yes," I said, "the legacy of the Commandant."

He ignored the thrust, and going to a chair behind the divan picked up the volumes I had brought Signora Butali from the library the day before.

"Take a look at these, then, while I'm away," he said. "I was going to give them to one of my boys, a German scholar, but you'll do even better. Translate for me anything you consider especially appropriate, and write it down." He threw the books on the table beside my chair.

"I think I should warn you," I said, "that what I've read in them already—only a rough glance, I admit—suggests that the Falcon was not the misunderstood genius you described to your élite last night but something very different. If Signora Butali is really going to take them to Rome for her husband to read he'll have another heart attack."

"Don't worry," said Aldo, "he won't read them. She got the books for me, because I asked for them."

I shrugged. As Director of the Arts Council of Ruffano he evidently had the right.

"That German writer was prejudiced, of course," Aldo continued. "Those nineteenth century scholars always were. The early Italian manuscripts I read in Rome last week gave a somewhat different angle to certain aspects of his life. Jacopo?" He opened the door and shouted across the hall. Jacopo appeared. "I'll be gone for an hour," said Aldo. "Let no one in. Beo and I will be dining later at No. 8."

"Yes, signore," said Jacopo, and then he added, "A lady called twice during the afternoon. She gave her name. Signorina Raspa."

"What did she want?"

Jacopo's poker face flickered to a smile. "Evidently the signorina wanted you," he replied.

I pointed to the envelope still lying unopened on the hall table. "That came last night," I said. "I watched her put it through the door. I was standing beyond the double entrance."

Aldo picked up the envelope and threw it at me. "You read it," he said. "She's as much your friend as mine."

He went out of the house, slamming the door behind him. I heard him start up the Alfa-Romeo. It was not more than four minutes' walk to the ducal palace, but he had to use the car.

"A pilot still?" I asked Jacopo.

"Never anything else," he replied emphatically. "Arts Council?" He snapped his fingers in the air in a superb gesture of contempt, then, pouring out a glass of vermouth, set it before me with a flourish. "May you dine well," he said, and left me.

I opened Carla Raspa's letter without compunction. It began formally, thanking Professor Donati for his extreme kindness in allowing her and her companion passes for the evening session at the ducal palace. The experience had affected her profoundly. She wanted to discuss the many implications of his address to the students with the speaker himself. She would be in all evening should he return before midnight, and she was free all Sunday, should he have an hour to spare at any time throughout the day. She would be delighted to call upon him, or conversely, if he had nothing better to do, she would be honoured to offer him a drink or a meal at her apartment at No. 5, via San Michele. It ended with the same formality, offering salutations. The signature, Carla Raspa, looped its way across the page, the letters intertwined like amorous limbs. I replaced the letter in the envelope, wondering if the writer was waiting still, and turned, not without relief, to the Falcon's ploys.

"Duke Claudio's precocious gallantry," I read, "was a scandal to the more staid of Ruffano's citizens, and proved ruinous to his own constitution. His follies and his vices attained a dangerous height, so alarming the older members of the Court that they feared greater excesses would threaten their ruler's life. The Duke's evil genius brought him into the company of strolling players, and, delighting in their loose manners, he threw himself among them without reserve, appointing the younger of them to high places in his Court."

Well, Aldo had asked for it. I found a piece of paper and a pencil, and, sipping my vermouth, scribbled a translation of the more forceful passages.

"The Falcon's casual acquaintance with the comedians ripened into intimacy, gradually monopolising his time and thoughts. These persons, belonging to the vilest classes, became the Duke's associates in public and in private. Conforming his morals to theirs, he defied decency, advancing from one extravagance to another, and producing spectacles of so shameless a nature before his subjects that . . ."

The German writer, shuddering, turned to Greek. My Turin degree had not covered the classics. Perhaps, from the point of view of the Festival, it was just as well, but I felt frustrated. I flipped back over the pages to those I had read in the library the day before. Someone, Aldo's young student doubtless, had forestalled me. My brother must have called for the books soon after I left them with Signora Butali, and brought them back for his translator to skim through. A slip had been inserted to mark the passage I remembered.

". . . When accusations were made against him by the outraged citizens of Ruffano, Duke Claudio retaliated by declaring that he had been divinely appointed to mete out to his subjects the punishment they deserved. The proud would be stripped, the haughty violated, the slanderer silenced, the viper die in his own venom. The scales of heavenly justice would thus be balanced. On one occasion a page neglected to provide lights for the Duke's evening repast. He was seized by the Falcon's bodyguard, who enveloped the wretched lad in cere-cloth coated with combustibles, and after setting fire to his head drove him through the rooms of the ducal palace to die in agony."

A pretty tale. A little rough for heavenly justice. I read on.

"The citizens, indignant at the dishonour which nightly violated their domestic circles, finally rose at the instigation of the leading citizen, whose handsome wife had been profaned by the Falcon himself. It was in the riot that followed that the unhappy Duke met his end. The buffoonery he had learnt upon the stage with his low followers decided him to execute a feat, hitherto unattempted, of driving eighteen horses from the fort on the northern hill of Ruffano through the centre of the city and up the further hill to the ducal palace. He was set upon and pursued by almost the entire populace, after having trampled many of them to death beneath his horses' hooves. This last ride, known to the Ruffanesi in after years as the Flight of the Falcon, ended in the Duke's massacre."

I poured myself another glass of vermouth. I thought the Duke had flung himself from the topmost pinnacle of the tower, declaring that he was the bird whose name he bore. The German scholar said none of this. Perhaps the Italian manuscripts were more explicit. Laboriously I copied down the details for my brother. Somebody else would have to decipher the Greek.

When he returned a few minutes before eight, in excellent spirits, having cast aside the more sombre mood of early afternoon when together we revived the past, I handed him my notes and left him reading them while I washed my hands. I came back after a few minutes to find him smiling.

"This is good," he said, "very good indeed. It tallies with what I had read earlier."

I told him, in American fashion, that he was welcome. He stuffed the notes into his pocket. Then he called goodbye to Jacopo and we left the house. This time, I noticed, he did not use the car. We walked down the via dei Sogni to our former home.

"How do you explain me to Signora Butali?" I asked.

"I told her," he answered, "before I left this morning. She's as safe as Jacopo."

He led the way into the garden, and up the pathway to the house. The door was open for us. We might have been the pair of us, returning from some foray in the past, with our parents awaiting dinner, he to make the excuses, myself to be sent immediately to bed.

Our hostess had changed for the occasion. She looked, so I thought, more beautiful by evening light, the dark blue dress becoming her. She came towards me first, smiling and holding out her hand.

"I should have known," she said. "It wasn't Chopin or Debussy that drew you here. You wanted to see your home."

"It was all three," I said, kissing her hand. "If I seemed very rude and abrupt I ask forgiveness now."

I was no longer the assistant librarian who had walked home with her from church. I belonged, because of Aldo.

"It is fantastic," she said, "and very wonderful. I still can't believe it's true. This is going to make such a difference to both your lives. I'm so happy for you." She looked from one to the other of us, and tears, that possibly had been near the surface all day, rose to her eyes.

"Emotion," said my brother, "is wasted. Where's my Campari? Beo prefers vermouth."

She shook her head at him, protesting at his lack of feeling, and handed us the waiting glasses, filling one for herself.

"To you both," she said. "Long life and every happiness," and then to me, "I've always loved your name. 'Il Beato'. I think you fill it well."

Aldo shouted with laughter. "You know what he is?" he said. "He's nothing but a tourist tout. He scrambles around the country in a loaded coach showing the Anglo-Saxons Rome by night."

"Why shouldn't he?" she answered. "I'm sure he does it well and the tourists adore him."

"He does it for tips," said Aldo. "He dives into the Trevi fountain with his trousers off."

"Nonsense," she smiled, and to me, "Take no notice of him, Beo. He's jealous because you see the world and he is stuck in a small university city."

Beo came well from her. I liked it. And the teasing exchange between them put me at my ease. All the same . . . I glanced at my brother. He was walking about the room flipping at books, picking up objects and putting them down again, his restless manner, which I remembered from the past, suggesting suppressed excitement. Something brewed.

The double doors opened into what was now the dining-room, revealing the table set for three, lighted by candles. The girl who had put the food on the sideboard withdrew for us to help ourselves. My old playroom, subtly transformed with the curtains drawn and the candlelight playing upon the polished table and our three faces, had lost its morning strangeness. It was mine again, but warmer, intimate, and I had the impression that I was my boyhood self, promoted out of due time to join in one of Aldo's adult games.

It was my fortune often in the past to play the third, the aider and abetter of my brother's whims, whether to foster some budding friendship at the liceo where he spent his days, or to damp one down. He would prepare phrases for me first, and at a given sign I must out with them, to cause confusion, perhaps a furious argument, even a battle. His methods had not changed. Only the fish he wanted to play was now a woman, and to watch her rise to the flies he cast afforded him a double satisfaction with me as witness. I wondered how far he had gone; whether the banter that passed between them—myself frequently a butt for her to defend—was a ritual flight before the final act or if, already lovers, their secret increased in intensity and excitement by being flaunted before a supposedly innocent third.

There was no talk of Signora Butali's husband. The sick man in his hospital bed in Rome was no absent skeleton at the feast; he might not have existed. I wondered, had he been present, how it would have altered the behaviour of all three of us; our hostess withdrawing into her shell and becoming simply the doyenne of her dinner-table, whilst Aldo, flattering his host in a way that only I might possibly discern—he had done it as a boy with our father—would lead him on to self-disclosure, no matter whether interesting or tedious, as long as the undercurrent of intrigue remained unseen.

Dinner over, Signora Butali led the way upstairs to the music-room, and while we drank coffee and liqueurs the conversation turned upon the Festival.

"How are rehearsals?" she asked my brother. "Or is the whole thing to be as secret as last year to those who don't take part?"

"More so," he said, "but to the first part of your question, the rehearsals are going well. Some of us have been at it for months."

She turned to me. "You know, Beo," she said, "last year I played the Duchess Emilia, who received Pope Clement. Professor Rizzio, whom you met this morning, was the Duke. So lifelike were the rehearsals, and the coaxing methods of your brother who directed us, that I truly believe Professor Rizzio has imagined himself a Duke of Ruffano ever since."

"His manner to me this morning was certainly royal," I said. "I did not connect it with the Festival of a year ago. I thought perhaps that as Deputy Rector of the university and Head of the Department of Education he was simply aware of the great gulf between us."

"That's his trouble too," she agreed, and to Aldo, "but isn't it his sister's even more? I often feel sorry for the resident women students. They might be in a convent, shut up in that hostel with Signorina Rizzio."

My brother laughed, pouring himself cognac.

"Convents in old days were easier of access," he said. "An underground passage between the men's and women's hostels has yet to be constructed. Perhaps we might consider it."

He pulled the notes I had translated for him out of his pocket and, throwing himself in a chair, began to study them.

"There are many problems," I said to my hostess, "that have to be surmounted before the launching of this year's Festival."

"Such as?" she asked.

"Whether Duke Claudio was a moralist or a monster," I answered. "According to the historians he was a monster, and mad at that. Aldo thinks otherwise."

"He would," she said. "He likes to be different from everyone else."

Her voice was mocking, but the look she gave in his direction stimulating. My hostess was ready poised for another movement of the ritual flight. I thought of the dead expression on her face when I had walked with her from church, and the comparison was not flattering to me, the third.

"Anyway," I said, "the people of Ruffano believed him a monster and rose in a bloody insurrection against him and his Court."

"And are we to have this in the Festival?" she demanded.

"Don't ask me, ask Aldo," I replied.

She strolled over to his chair, her liqueur glass in her hand, humming beneath her breath, and the way she moved, the way she bent above him sitting there in the chair, was, to me, somehow evident of desire. Only my presence there stopped her from touching him.

"Well," she said, "do we have an insurrection, and if so who's to lead it?"

"Easy," he answered, without looking up. "The C and E students. They're ripe for rebellion anyway."

She raised her eyebrows at me and set her liqueur glass on the piano. "An innovation," she said, throwing back the piano lid. "I thought the acting in the Festival was meant for the Arts students alone."

"Not this year," he said. "There aren't enough of them."

She took a final sip of her liqueur, nectar to the queen before the flight, and sat down on the piano stool. "What shall I play for you?" she asked. The question was for me, the smile for me. The intonation in the voice, the whole poise of her person, hands ready above the keys, were for my brother.

"The 'Arabesque'," I said. "It's sexless."

It had been the day before, with me, a stranger, an alien in my own home, ghosts around me. Then the rise and fall, the ripple of descent, had spelt nostalgia, the shrugging reminder of the fleeting moment. Now it was night, and Aldo was in the house. The pianist, who yesterday had played from courtesy, now sought to woo my brother in the way instinctive to her. The "Arabesque", played throughout the country by a thousand pupils, became a dance of love, suggestive, shameless. I wondered that she should give herself away in this fashion, and sitting upright in my chair stared at the ceiling. From where she sat behind the raised lid of the piano she could not see the man she hoped to charm. I could. He had found a pencil and was adding to my translated notes, oblivious of the music. Debussy, Ravel, Chopin failed to rouse him. Music had never been one of Aldo's obsessions. If his hostess played, to him it was background sound, hardly more personal than traffic.

I could hardly bear it that her efforts should be so wasted, and lighting a cigarette began to weave a fantasy that I was in his shoes, and when the playing ceased I would get up from my chair, and cross the room, and put my hands over her eyes and she reach up to me. The fantasy intensified as the tempo of the music quickened. It became unendurable that I should sit there, dumbly, and endure her message, which, alas, was not for me. That Aldo, though indifferent to the music, was aware of its message I never for a moment doubted, and I wished him joy and her fulfilment; but to share their intimacy thus was at best doubtful pleasure.

Perhaps she sensed my discomfort, for suddenly she slammed the lid and rose. "Well," she asked, "is the insurrection over and done with? Can we all now relax?"

The irony, if intended as such, was as much wasted upon my brother as her music. He glanced at her, observed that she had ceased playing and was addressing him, and laid aside his notes.

"What's the time? Is it late?" he questioned.

"Ten o'clock," she answered.

"I thought we had only just finished dinner," he said.

He yawned, stretched, and put his notes into his pocket.

"I hope," she said, "that you've completed your opening scene, if indeed that is what you have been working on all evening."

She offered me more liqueur. I shook my head, and murmured something about getting back to the via San Michele. Aldo smiled, whether at my discretion, or Signora Butali's lightly-spoken gibe, I could not tell.

"My opening scene," he said, "which in fact was devised weeks ago, takes place off-stage, or should do, if we wish to be discreet."

"The thunder of horses' hooves?" I asked. "The Jehu act?"

"No, no," he frowned, "that won't be until the end. We must have the excitement first."

"Meaning just what?" enquired our hostess.

"The seduction of the lady," he replied, "what my German translator calls 'the profanation of the leading citizen's wife'."

Silence was prolonged. Aldo's quotation from my hastily scribbled notes was embarrassingly ill-timed. I leapt to my feet, my courier's smile too evident, and told Signora Butali that I had to be at the library next morning at nine. It was, so I thought, the only way to break the pause that threatened to turn oppressive, but after I had spoken I realised that my sudden departure was in itself a reflection on what had just been said.

"Don't let Signor Fossi work you, or himself, too hard," said my hostess, offering me her hand. "And come again whenever you feel like music. I don't need reminding, you know, that this house used to be your home. I'd like you to feel about it in the same way as your brother."

I thanked her for her graciousness, assuring her that if there were any books she wanted from the library at any time, either for herself or for her husband, she had only to reach for the telephone.

"It's very good of you," she said. "Later in the week I shall be in Rome. I'll let you know."

"I'll see you down," said Aldo.

See me down. Not leave, as I was doing. As we walked downstairs, with the door into the music-room still open, I chatted gaily and inanely about the many times he had chased me to the floor above. I did not want Signora Butali to think . . . exactly what she must be thinking. That I, the little brother, had my cue. The party was over.

Aldo came with me across the garden and opened the gate. The lamp above cast shadows down the street. The stars were brilliant.

"How beautiful she is," I said, "so sympathetic in every way, so restrained and calm. I don't wonder that you . . ."

"Look," he said, touching my arm, "here they come. See their lights?"

He pointed across the valley far below, where the main roads, entering Ruffano from east and north, were dotted with moving lights. The spluttering burst of vespas filled the air.

"What are they?" I asked.

"The C and E students returning from their weekend break," he said. "In a moment you'll hear them roaring up the via delle Mura like a herd of runts. They'll keep it up for another hour at least."

The city's peace was shattered. The Sunday quiet that in old days closed in upon Ruffano like a pall was interrupted.

"You have authority here," I said. "You could put a stop to it if it worries you so much."

Aldo smiled, and patted me on the shoulder. "It doesn't worry me," he said. "They can fart away all night for all I care. You're going straight back, aren't you?"

"Yes," I said.

"Don't hang about," he said. "Go there direct. Be seeing you, Beo, and thank you for today."

He went back into the garden and closed the gate. A moment later I heard him shut the door of the house. I walked off down the hill to my pensione, wondering what sort of reception he would get when he had climbed the stairs to the music-room once more. I wondered also if the girl who had brought in the dinner slept on the premises.

As I descended the hill the returning students were already converging upon the piazza della Vita. Small cars as well as vespas hummed and throbbed. Two coaches choked to a standstill by the colonnade. I caught a glimpse of my young friends the Pasquales laughing and chattering with a score of others. Tomorrow, possibly, but not tonight. Tonight I wanted to digest the day. I walked fast, so as not to be overtaken, and slipping through the open doorway of No. 24 ran upstairs and entered my own room. As I undressed I kept seeing Aldo standing in our mother's old bedroom with Signora Butali. I wondered if, being so used to the change in the room by now, the piano, the other furnishings, he no longer saw it as we had known it once, and as I saw it still.

The students were laughing and singing in the street outside, and at the far end, near the city centre, the gasp and splutter of the homing vespas warned the native Ruffanesi that the philistines had returned.

CHAPTER TWELVE

W HEN I WENT down for breakfast the next morning I was given a rousing reception by the students. They were standing round the table drinking coffee and exchanging gossip about the preceding day. At sight of me there was a general uproar and Mario, whom I remembered from that first evening as being the most obstreperous, waved his roll of bread in the air and demanded how the Arts graduate had spent the weekend break.

"First," I said, "we librarians don't get a half-day on Saturday. I was kept sorting books until after seven."

A groan, half-ironic, half-sympathetic, greeted my remark. "Slaves, all slaves," said Gino, "tied to an out-worn system. It's typical of the way they run things up the hill. Now our chief, Elia, has some sense. He knows we put all we've got into a five-day week, and sets us free for forty-eight hours to do what we please. Most of us go home. He does the same. He has a villa on the coast and shakes the dead dust of Ruffano off his feet."

Signora Silvani, attending to the coffee-pot, handed me a cup with a morning smile. "Did you get to Mass?" she asked. "When you didn't come back for lunch my husband and I wondered what had happened to you."

"I met a friend," I said, "and was invited home to lunch and to spend the day."

"That reminds me," she added, "a lady called during the late afternoon. A Signorina Raspa. She said, if you returned, to look her up at No. 5."

Poor Carla Raspa! Having failed twice with Aldo she had turned in exasperation back to me.

"Did someone mention Mass?" asked Gino. "Did I hear aright, or were my ears deceiving me?"

"I went to Mass," I said. "The bells of San Cipriano summoned me, and I obeyed."

"It's all superstition, you know," said Gino. "The priests get fat on it, but no one else."

"In old days," said Caterina Pasquale, coming to join the group, "there was nothing else to do but go to Mass. It was the morning's entertainment. You met your friends. Now there is so much more. Guess what we did, Paolo and I?" She smiled at me with her enormous eyes, biting a chunk out of her roll as she did so.

"You tell me," I said, smiling back.

"Borrowed our brother's car and drove to Venice," she said. "We went like stink and made it in four and a quarter hours. That's living, isn't it?"

"It could be dying too," I answered.

"Ah well, that's half the fun, taking the risk," she said.

Mario mimicked the action of Caterina at the wheel, banking, swerving, roaring the engine before a sudden crash. "You should do as I do," he said to me. "Run a vespa with a hotted-up engine."

"Yes," retorted Signora Silvani, "and wake us all with your noise. No one can sleep any longer on a Sunday night."

"Did you hear us?" laughed the student. "A whole crowd of us were coming back from Fano. Zup . . . zup . . . zup. . . . We hoped we'd enliven you all with our orchestration. Frankly, it's what you Ruffanesi need, a touch of exhaust music to melt the wax in your ears."

"You should have seen us," said Gerardo, "circling the city, up and round the via delle Mura, flashing our lights at the women's hostel to make them open their shutters."

"And did they?" asked Caterina.

"Not they. They were all tied down to their mattresses by nine o'clock."

Laughing, arguing, they scrambled off, but not before young Caterina, looking back over her shoulder, called, "See you this evening. The three of us might make a date."

Signora Silvani smiled after them, shaking an indulgent head. "What children!" she said. "No more sense of responsibility than babes in arms. And brilliant, every one of them. You'll see, in a year they'll all take Honours degrees, and then end up in some out-of-the-way provincial bank."

I left the house en route for the ducal palace, and saw that somebody was waiting for me higher up the street in the entrance of No. 5.

"Good morning, stranger," said Carla Raspa.

"Good morning, signorina," I replied.

"I thought," she said, turning with me towards the piazza della Vita, "that we had discussed the possibility of a Sunday date?"

"We did," I said. "What became of it?"

"I was in all day," she shrugged. "You had only to come for me."

"I was out," I said. "An impulse drove me to Mass at San Cipriano, where I bumped into no less a person than the Rector's lady, to whom I had taken some books the day before. I walked home with her and she invited me in for a drink."

Carla Raspa stopped and stared. "Which of course you accepted," she exclaimed, "and I don't blame you for it. One gracious nod from Livia Butali and you're there. No wonder you didn't bother to call on me after being given the entrée to her house. Who was there?"

"A flurry of professors," I said, "and amongst them my superior, Signor Fossi, with his wife."

I emphasised the wife. She laughed, and resumed walking.

"Poor Giuseppe," she said. "I can imagine him on his dignity, puffed up like a pigeon because of the invitation. What did you think of our Livia?"

"I found her beautiful. And charming. Very much more so than Signorina Rizzio."

"Heavens above! Was she there too?"

"Yes, with her brother. Both a little formal for my taste."

"Too formal for us all! You've done well for a newcomer, Armino Fabbio. There'll be no stopping you now. Congratulations. I haven't achieved as much in a couple of years."

We turned up the via Rossini. The pavement was crowded with morning shoppers and belated students hurrying to early lectures.

"I suppose," she said, "the Director of the Arts Council wasn't there by any chance?"

I had cut a good enough figure in her eyes without adding to my stature. Besides, it was better to be discreet. "He looked in for a moment, yes," I said. "I left before he did. I had a word with him while he drank Campari. He seemed amicable, and less imposing without his bodyguard."

Once again she paused and stared. "Incredible!" she exclaimed. "Only three days in Ruffano, and you have this sort of luck. You must be charmed. Did he mention me?"

"No," I said, "there was hardly time. I don't think he realised who I was."

"What an opportunity missed," she said. "If only I had known. You could have given him a message."

"Don't forget," I reminded her, "the whole morning was a fluke. If I hadn't gone to Mass. . . ."

"It's your baby face," she said. "Don't tell me that if I had gone to Mass and met Livia Butali she'd have bothered to invite me to an aperitivo. I suppose she likes to act the hostess amongst the university staff with her husband safe in hospital in Rome. Was Aldo Donati paying court to her?"

"Not that I noticed," I answered. "She seemed to have more to say to Professor Rizzio."

We parted, I to enter the ducal palace, she to continue up the hill to the university. A future date between us had not been mentioned. I felt, however, that it would come.

My easy Sunday had made me slow on schedule. When I arrived at the library I found that the others had arrived before me, including my boss, Giuseppe Fossi. They were standing in a group, talking excitedly. For some reason Signorina Catti was the centre of attention.

"There's no doubt about it," she was saying. "I had it from one of the students themselves, Maria Cavallini—she was locked in her room with four companions. It wasn't until the janitor came this morning to attend to the central heating that they, or any of the others, were released."

"It's outrageous, fantastic. There'll be a colossal row," said Giuseppe Fossi. "Have they informed the police?"

"No one could tell me that. I couldn't stay talking, I should have been late here."

Toni, his eyes on sticks, rushed across the room at sight of me. "You haven't heard the news?" he asked.

"No," I replied. "What news?"

"The women's hostel broken into last night," he said, "and the students locked in their rooms. No one knows what happened or who it was. The men were masked. How many of them, signorina?" He turned in excitement to the pallid secretary, who found herself so unexpectedly the bearer of strange tidings.

"A dozen or more, they say," she answered. "How they broke in nobody knows. It happened suddenly, just as all the C and E students were returning home. You know the appalling noise they create with their machines? They served as cover, of course, to let their fellows in. Well, you may call it a rag. I call it an outrage."

"Come now," said Giuseppe Fossi, his eyes still bulging with excitement, "as far as we know none of the girls was hurt. To be locked in their rooms is no great hardship—I'm told it happens all the time. But if the place was burgled . . . well, that's another matter. They'll have to call in the police. In any event, Professor Elia will have to answer for it. Now, shall we get to work?"

He bustled towards the desk, with a nod to his secretary. She followed with notebook and pencil, her chin held high.

"Why blame Professor Elia?" murmured Toni. "It's not his fault if his C and E students enjoy a rag. I shall get the truth from my girl-friend later today. She'll know what really happened from her chums."

We settled to the morning's labours with lack of concentration. Whenever the telephone rang we lifted our heads and listened, but Signor Fossi's "Yes" and "No" revealed no secrets. Invasion of the women's hostel was not the library's business.

Halfway through the morning he sent Toni and me up to the new library with several crates of books. We took them in the small van which was used for the purpose. It was my first visit to the new library beyond the university, standing at the summit of the hill, close to the other recent buildings, the commercial schools and the physics lab. They had not the grace of the old House of Studies, but their lines were not unpleasing, and the big windows gave light and air to the students who would work within their walls.

"All thanks to Professor Butali," said Toni, "and the younger members of the university Council. Old Rizzio fought it tooth and nail."

"Why so?" I asked.

"Degrading the scholastic atmosphere," grinned Toni, "turning his scholars into factory hands. According to him the University of Ruffano was intended as a teaching university, pure and simple, where serious-minded young men and women would go out into the world after graduation to impart their classical learning to the boys and girls at school."

"They can do so still."

"They can, but what a grind! Why, a fellow with an economics degree can get a job in a big firm overnight, and make in three months what a teacher earns in a year. No future there!"

We heaved the crates out of the van and bore them into the new library. The decorators, Toni told me, had only been out of the place a week. High, light, with a raised gallery above lined with shelves throughout and a reading-room beyond, the building would offer many more facilities than the old banqueting-hall in the ducal palace.

"Where did they raise the money?" I asked.

"The C and E intake. Where else?" Toni replied.

We dumped the crates, which were to be unpacked by the assistant staff under the supervision of one of Giuseppe Fossi's colleagues, but not before the irrepressible Toni had gleaned further news of the women's hostel break-in.

"They say Rizzio's going to resign unless Professor Elia makes a public apology in the name of the C and E students," he said eagerly, following me from the building. "This will be a fight to a finish, I warn you. I don't think Elia will stand for it for a moment."

"I was told I'd come to a dead city," I replied. "Do you have this sort of excitement every day?"

"No such luck," he said, "but I tell you what it is. With the Rector away Rizzio and Elia will seize the opportunity to cut each other's throats. They detest one another, and this is their chance."

As we were parking the van outside the ducal palace, at about a quarter to one, I saw Carla Raspa come out of the side entrance with a bevy of Arts students. She saw me and waved her hand. I waved back. She sent the students ahead and waited for me to join her.

"Doing anything for lunch?" she asked.

"No," I said.

"Go down to the restaurant where we first met," she said quickly. "Book a table for two. I can't stop now, I have to get my party home. No loitering allowed after what happened last night. You heard the news?"

"The break-in? Yes," I answered.

"I'll tell you more," she said. "It's unbelievable!"

She hurried after her flock, and I strolled off down the via Rossini. The restaurant, as before, was crowded, but I managed to get a table. There were no students. The place seemed to be the favourite rendezvous of those business-men of Ruffano who did not go home to lunch. Carla Raspa arrived soon after. She snapped her fingers at the waiter and we ordered lunch, then she looked at me and smiled.

"Out with it," I said. "I'm good at keeping secrets."

"No secret this," she answered, glancing, despite her words, over her shoulder. "It will be right through the university by now. Signorina Rizzio has been raped."

I stared in disbelief.

"It's true," she insisted, leaning forward. "I had it from one of her staff. These lads, whoever they were, didn't touch the girls. They locked the whole bunch in their rooms and set to work on the high and mighty one herself. Isn't it glorious?"

She was choking with laughter. I was not so much amused. The plateful of pasta placed in front of me by the waiter turned the edge off appetite. It looked like entrails.

"That's common assault," I said abruptly. "A matter for the police. Whoever did it will get ten years."

"No," she said, "that's it. They say the signorina's in a state of high hysteria and wants it all hushed up."

"Can't be done," I said, "the law won't allow it."

She attacked her own full plate with relish, covering the mashed-up brew with grated cheese. "The law can't take any action if nobody complains," she said. "The lads must have risked it, and guessed the reaction. Of course there'll be a row about the break-in, a terrific row. But what happened to Signorina Rizzio is her own affair. If she refuses to bring in a charge of assault, and her brother supports her, there's nothing anyone can do. Have you ordered wine?"

I had. I poured it out for her. She swallowed it down as though her throat was parched.

"It's not as though she had been knocked about," she continued. "I understand there was no question of that. No beating up. Just gently and persuasively shown what's what."

"How do you know?" I asked.

"Well, that's the tale. What the girls say at the hostel. Now that they have recovered from the fright of the masked men, and are themselves intact—those that were already, anyway—they can hardly contain themselves. That it should happen to her, the signorina! You have to hand it to those C and E boys. Imagine the nerve!"

"I still don't credit it," I said.

"I do," she answered, "and if the police are *not* summoned, and we're told the signorina is indisposed, you can bet your life it's true. Do you suppose she enjoyed it?"

Her eyes were gleaming. I felt slightly sick. Brutality in any form revolts me, and to commit violence upon the old or the very young was something I have never understood. I did not answer.

"She asked for it, you know," Carla Raspa continued, "treating her women students like novices taking their vows. No visits, even in the common room, from boys in the students' hostel, doors locked by ten. I know, because so many of the girls attend my lectures. They'd reached a breaking-point of exasperation. Of course one of the girls must have let the boys in, that's obvious. Then listened at the keyhole and spread the tale!"

I thought of the stately, formidable figure I had met the day before, sipping with mild distaste her mineral water. Imagination baulked.

Carla Raspa, facing the door of the restaurant, bent forward, touching my hand. "Don't turn now," he said. "Professor Elia has just come in. The Head of C and E himself. With a bunch of colleagues. What I ask myself is, will he have to resign?"

"Resign? Why should he?" I enquired. "How can anyone pin the break-in on his boys?"

"Because it's obvious," she said. "Signorina Rizzio has complained about the behaviour of the C and E students time after time. It was reported in the university journal. Last night was their answer."

I waited a moment for the party to settle at a table to the left of me, then half-turned in my seat to glance at them.

"The big man," murmured my companion, "with the shock of hair. More pleased with himself than anyone in Ruffano, and more self-opinionated, but he gets things done. He's a Milanese. He would be."

Professor Elia, eyes screened by thick-rimmed spectacles, black hair en brosse, had the large frame of one who can never fit into any sort of suit. Creases abounded in the impeccable cloth. He was talking rapidly, hunched over the table, allowing no one else to interrupt. Suddenly he threw back his undoubtedly fine head and uttered a thunderclap of laughter.

"Five of them," he said, "one after the other. That's what I'm told. And not a squeak in protest. Not a whimper.'

The table rocked. His laughter filled the restaurant. Other people eating turned to stare. One of Professor Elia's companions motioned him to silence. The big man looked about him with contempt and caught my eye.

"Nobody here," he said. "They don't know what I'm discussing. But I tell you this. If anything's said officially against our crowd I'll not only make the lady the laughing stock of Ruffano but . . ." he lowered his voice, and we could hear no more.

"You see," murmured Carla Raspa, "the poor old Rizzios won't get much change out of him. They'd be well advised to let it go, or, better still, clear out. Anyway, after this shock the signorina can never show her face again. If she does, she'll only be greeted with the sort of guffaw we've heard at the next table." She accepted a cigarette, finished her wine, and summoned the waiter. "My treat," she said. "We both of us work for our living. You've still to take me out to dinner. When?"

"Not tonight," I answered, remembering the Pasquales. "Perhaps tomorrow?"

"Tomorrow it is."

We rose from the table and left the restaurant, resuming our walk together up the hill.

"Heard the latest?" whispered Toni from his ladder as I entered the library.

"What?" I asked guardedly.

"There's talk of the women's hostel being closed down and the students sent home," he said. "They'll have to take their examinations by post. They're saying there was another break-in three months ago and all the girls are pregnant."

Giuseppe Fossi, dictating letters to his secretary, looked up at the offender from his desk. "Would you please observe the rules?" he said icily, pointing to the notice SILENCE that hung upon the library walls.

Twice during the afternoon we drove to the new building with further crates. Each time we ran into fresh rumours. Students gossiped in droves, and Toni knew a dozen of them. The break-in was the subject of the day, the assault upon Signorina Rizzio common knowledge. Some said it had nothing to do with the C and E crowd at all, that there was, unknown to all save a favoured few, a passage between the men's and women's hostels which had been in use for years. The signorina had entertained nights without number every professor in the university, with preference given to the more muscular. Others, defending the lady's honour, declared that Professor Elia in person had led the masked band of marauders into her sanctum, and that he had in his possession a captured nightdress belonging to the signorina which would bear witness to his feat.

Laughter was paramount then, but later in the day the mood changed. Word spread that the Authorities—whoever they might be—definitely put the blame for the break-in upon the C and E students, who, it was said, had returned from Sunday leave upon their vespas in a state of riot, and, circling beneath the windows of the women's hostel with songs and cat-calls, had fired the bolder amongst them to invasion.

Toni, looking over his shoulder, pointed out the first batch of angry C and E boys and girls emerging from the lecture-rooms allotted to them across the via dell'8 Settembre, not far from where we stood.

"Watch out," he called to me, "there's going to be trouble."

Somebody threw a stone. It shattered the windscreen of our van and the glass splintered. Another stone caught Toni on the side of the head. A shout went up from the small group of Arts students and others who were walking up the hill from the university proper. Some of them started running towards their supposed antagonists. In a moment there was shouting, yelling, more stones, more running, and two more boys, riding vespas, swerved into the midst of all of them, scattering students right and left.

"Come on," I said to Toni, "out of it. It's not our battle."

I pulled him into the van and started the engine. He did not say anything. He was mopping the side of his head, the blood flowing. We roared across the street, and avoiding the skirmish which students were running to join from all directions drove downhill past the university to the ducal palace.

I parked in our usual place and switched off the engine. "So much for university politics." I said.

Toni looked very white. I examined the cut. Not deep, but deep enough.

"Got a doctor you know?" I asked. He nodded. "Well, get along and see him. I'll make your excuses."

We climbed together from the van. He walked slowly to his vespa and straddled it, one hand still dabbing at his wound.

"You saw that fellow who threw the stone?" he said. "No ragging there, he did it deliberately, to start a fight. I'll get him later. Or my pals will."

He coasted slowly down the hill. I went into the library and reported the incident briefly to Giuseppe Fossi. He went off like a rocket.

"You had no business, either of you, to hang about the university buildings when the students are coming out of the lecture rooms," he exploded. "On a day like this, with rumours flying, it is asking for trouble. Now I shall have to put in a claim for the van, the matter will be reported back at the Registrar's office, Professor Rizzio may himself see the report. . . ."

"Of a bust wind-screen?" I interrupted. "Look, Signor Fossi, I'll get it seen to at some garage down the hill."

"There will be talk," he flustered. "Everyone knows the van, someone will have seen the incident. Trust Toni to tell all Ruffano."

I let him exhaust himself, then, when he quietened down, resumed my work. This was his problem, not mine. I had something else to think about. The feeling of disquiet that had nagged at me all day increased. If students cared to break in at the women's hostel it was their affair, and what they did there too. They would be either rounded up and punished, or permitted to go free. It was none of my business. But the timing bothered me. And my own translation from the German volumes.

". . . The citizens . . . finally rose at the instigation of the leading citizen, whose . . . wife had been profaned."

I was not the only one to handle the books and to read German. Aldo had shown them to one of his Arts students, a German scholar. The pages had been marked. Once again I heard my brother say, "We must have the excitement first. The profanation of the leading citizen's wife."

In retrospect I left the Butalis' house again, looked down from the street to the valley roads below, heard the throb of the returning vespas. Was it coincidence? Had the attack been planned?

It was difficult to keep my mind on sorting the more tedious works of German and English philosophers, and when the time came to close up for the evening I was the first to leave. Outside, I found the piazza Maggiore full of students. They were parading up and down in groups, some of them linking arms and all belligerent. What Faculties they represented I neither knew nor cared, but I realised they were stopping and challenging the casual passers-by. I hoped to escape notice, and had reached the steps of the Duomo when one big fellow happened to turn his head in my direction and swooped upon me.

"Hold on, shrimp," he cried, twisting my arm behind me. "Where are you sneaking off to?"

"Via San Michele," I said. "I lodge there."

"You lodge there, do you? And where do you work?"

"I'm an employee in the library."

"An employee in the library!" He mimicked my tone. "Well, that's a pretty dirty job, isn't it? Hands and face smothered in dust all day." He shouted down to others below the steps. "Here's a little Arts boy needs a wash. Shall we give him the water-treatment? What about dousing him in the fountain?"

A roar of laughter greeted the remark, some of it good-natured, but not all. "Hand him over! Clean him up!"

The fountain in the centre of the piazza was surrounded. Some of the students had already climbed the basin and were balancing, laughing and singing, upon the edge. There were many of them, fifty, a hundred. I felt very small, and very much alone. Suddenly a car, hooting high and long, swung into view from the direction of the university. The students fell back on either side of the piazza to let it pass. One fellow, losing his balance, stumbled into the fountain basin. There was a yell of laughter from the crowd, and as my captor, joining in the mirth, loosened his hold on me I ducked and slipped out of his hands. The car moved slowly on. It was the Alfa-Romeo, with Aldo at the wheel. Sitting beside him, waving his hand and smiling to the scattering students, who shouted and cheered at sight of him, was the Head of the Department of Commerce and Economics, Professor Elia.

I cut through the crowd of students to the passage leading from the via Rossini to the via dei Sogni. Here all was quiet. It might have been another world. No one roamed the street except for one lone cat that leapt on to the garden wall at sight of me. I opened the gate, walked up the pathway to the house and rang the bell. It was opened, after a while, by the girl who had brought in the dinner the night before.

"Signora Butali?" I enquired.

"I'm sorry, signore," she said, "the signora isn't at home. She left for Rome early this morning."

I stared at her blankly. "Left for Rome? I didn't think she was going until later in the week?"

"No, signore, nor did I. I found her gone when I came first thing this morning. She left a note for me, saying she had decided to go suddenly. She must have been away by seven."

"Is Professor Butali worse, then?"

"I know nothing about that, signore. She didn't say."

I looked past her to the empty house. Already, because of the signora's absence, it lacked warmth and charm.

"Thank you," I said, "there is no message."

I walked the long way down to the pensione, avoiding the piazza della Vita. This way the streets were free of students, and the people I met were ordinary citizens going about their business. When I came to the via San Michele I saw that the entrance to No. 24 was blocked by Gino, Mario, and one or two others, and with them Paolo Pasquale and his sister. At sight of me she ran forward and, glancing up to me, took hold of me by the hand.

"Have you heard the news?" she asked.

I sighed. It was with me once again. There was no escaping it. "I've heard nothing else all day," I said, "even the books on the library shelves were full of it. There's been a break-in at the women's hostel. All the girls are pregnant."

"Oh, that," she said impatiently. "Who cares about that? I hope Signorina Rizzio has twins . . . No, the Director of the Arts Council has invited as many of the C and E students as care to do so to take part in the Festival, as a gesture to show his faith in all of us and that we were not responsible for last night's affair. Professor Elia has accepted on our behalf, and there's to be a meeting this evening, held in the old theatre above the piazza del Mercato. We're all going from here, and you must come with us."

She looked at me, smiling. Her brother joined her. "Do come," he said. "Nobody knows who you are. It's an experience nobody should miss. We're all mad to know what Professor Donati is going to say."

I had an intuition that I already knew.

CHAPTER THIRTEEN

THE DOORS OF the theatre were to be opened at nine. We had dinner first with the Silvanis, and set out at a quarter to the hour. The piazza della Vita was already crammed with students, converging upon the square from their various lodgings up and down the city, and now turning in a body down the narrow via del Teatro to the theatre itself. I soon lost sight of Gino and his companions, but the Pasquales held on to me firmly, one on either side, and I felt like a puppet, almost swung from my feet. The theatre in my father's day had never been much used. Concerts and oratorios were given at certain times, and occasionally there was a recitation by a visiting literary celebrity; otherwise it remained an edifice of architectural splendour, little known to the passing tourist or indeed to the citizens of Ruffano themselves. Today, so the Pasquales told me, all was changed. Thanks to the Rector of the university and the Director of the Arts Council, the theatre was in use throughout the year. Lectures, plays, concerts, films, exhibitions, even dances, all took place within its august walls.

We arrived to find a solid block of students waiting to pass in. Paolo, with a determined face, pushed and squeezed his way amongst them, Caterina and I hanging on behind. They were a good-natured crowd, laughing and chattering, pushing us in turn, and I wondered why the ugly mood of earlier on had changed, until I remembered that here there were no opponents—the students in this milling crowd were all C and E.

A great shout went up as the doors were opened, and Paolo, tightening his grip upon my arm, dragged little Caterina and me bodily through the entrance. "First come, first served," called some fellow at the door. "Those who are in first seize a seat and cling to it."

The auditorium was already filling rapidly, the crashing of seats as the flaps went down ricocheting to the roof, but this was drowned in turn by a group of students on the stage. Equipped with guitars, drums, and every conceivable form of rattle, they were singing the hit songs of the day, to tremendous applause from the surprised and delighted audience.

"What's on?" Paolo enquired of a student who was jiving in the aisle beside us. "Isn't anyone going to speak?"

"Don't ask me," replied the youth, shaking happily. "We're invited, that's all I know."

"Who cares? Let's make the most of it," laughed Caterina, and, taking up her stance in front of me, tapped and twisted with unexpected grace.

I should be thirty-two next birthday and I felt my age. As a student in Turin I had samba'd to perfection, but that was over eleven years ago. A courier gets no practice in the finer arts. I swayed to and fro, not to lose face before the present company, but I knew the figure that I cut was tame. The uproar was tremendous. Nobody seemed to care. I thought, with amusement, that Carla Raspa would have enjoyed it too, for all her scorn of the C and E students, but I could see no one in the auditorium who could even remotely come from the staff. All were students, all were impossibly young.

"Look," said Paolo suddenly, "that's surely Donati himself? There, taking over the drums."

I had my back to the stage, in an endeavour to follow the whirling of his sister, but at Paolo's exclamation I turned. It was as he said. Aldo, apparently unnoticed, had come on to the stage and taken the place of the student at the drums, and was now executing a fine performance on his own. The guitarists and the rattlers turned towards him, the singing and shouting grew louder still, the sound was deafening, and the audience, realising his identity with delighted clapping, pressed nearer to the stage. Nothing could have been more in contrast to the entry at the ducal palace which I had witnessed on Saturday. Tonight no flares, no silence, no bodyguard, no element of mystery. Aldo, with a total disregard for status, had chosen to identify himself with the student throng. The gesture and timing were superb. I wondered when and how he had planned it.

"You know," said Caterina, "we've all misjudged him. I thought he was high and mighty like the rest of the professors. But look at him, just look! He might be one of us."

"I knew he wasn't really old," objected Paolo. "After all, he's barely forty yet. It's just that we've never had any contact with him, he doesn't belong to our crowd."

"He belongs now," said Caterina. "I don't care what anyone says."

The tempo increased. The whole audience swayed and shook to the throbbing of the guitars and the beating of the drums. Then suddenly, when exhaustion pitch was reached, came the final flourish. The sound went dead. Aldo came to the front of the stage and a student, one of the guitarists, pushed forward a chair from nowhere.

"Come on, all of you," said Aldo. "I'm through. Let's talk."

He collapsed into the chair, wiping his forehead. There was a burst of laughter and sympathy from the audience. He smiled and lifted his head, then beckoned those who were standing, or sitting in the front rows, to come nearer and gather round him. I noticed that the auditorium lights had dimmed, and an unseen light to the side of the stage threw his face and the group nearest to him into relief. Aldo had no microphone. He spoke clearly and distinctly, but in no sense did he declaim. It was as though he was chatting casually to the students closest to him.

"We ought to do that more often," he said, still mopping his forehead. "The trouble is that I don't get time. It's all right for you, you can work off steam any evening you care to, or at weekends—I'm not referring to last night, I'll discuss that later—but for an ulcer-ridden person like myself, spending half his days arguing with professors twenty years his senior, who steadfastly refuse to make one move that would bring Ruffano and the university up to date, it's just not on. Somebody has to wage war in this dust-ridden academy, and I'll continue to do so until I'm sacked."

A gulf of laughter greeted this remark, at which he stared about him, supposedly astonished.

"No, no, I'm serious," he said. "If they could get rid of me they would. Just as they would get rid of you, the whole fifteen hundred of you, if that's what you muster—I haven't the figures before me, but it's near enough. Why do they want to get rid of you? Because they're frightened. The old are always frightened of the young, but you represent a threat to their whole way of life. Any one of you who passes out of this university with a degree in Commerce and Economics is a potential millionaire, and, more than that, he will have a chance of helping to run the economy not only of this country but of Europe, possibly the world. You are the masters, my young friends, and everyone knows it. That's why you're hated. Hatred is bred of fear, and your contemporaries who haven't your brains and your technical knowledge and your enthusiasm for life as it will and must be lived tomorrow are frightened of you. Frightened blue! No schoolteacher, no grubby lawyer, no chicken-livered so-called poet or painter—and that's what the students of the other faculties are trying to become—will stand a chance beside you. The future's yours, and don't let any half-baked set of decaying professors and their pathetic dwindling band of followers stand in your way. Ruffano is for the living. Not the dead."

Tumultuous applause followed the gesture of contempt with which he dismissed all, apparently, but his present audience. He waited for it to cease, then leant forward in his chair.

"I've no business to talk to you like this. As Director of the city Arts Council I don't mix myself up with university politics. My job is to look after the possessions in the ducal palace, which belong to all of you, and not to a minority, as some people choose to think. The reason I've got you here is because a clique—I'm naming no names—wants to destroy you. They want to make your Faculty, and all you stand for, so stink in the nostrils of the authorities that you will be chucked out, you, the Head of your Department, Professor Elia, the whole bag of tricks. Then, so they think, patrician rule will be resumed, and Ruffano fall asleep once more. The budding schoolteachers, lawyers, poets, will have it their own way."

I flicked my eyes to Paolo on my right. He was watching Aldo attentively, his chin on his clenched fist. Caterina, on my left, was equally impressed. The mass of students with their upturned faces listened to him with as much intensity as the small élite in the ducal palace had done two nights before. But to a very different speech.

"Last night's break-in, and the outrage that followed," said Aldo softly, "if it was an outrage and not merely a trumped-up story, was a deliberate attempt to discredit you. This is the sort of game unscrupulous guerrillas play in wartime. Commit an atrocity on your own people, and blame it on the enemy. Fine. Even admirable. It starts the bullets flying. Now, the university of

Ruffano isn't geared to war at the present time, but, as you know, I run something called the Festival, which—if we like to make it so—can be used as your opportunity to take your revenge and show the enemy that you're as powerful and determined as they are. The display this year will be the insurrection of the lively up-and-coming young citizens of Ruffano against the decadent Duke Claudio and his band of sycophants five hundred years ago. The merchants and the working people of the city outnumbered the courtiers by thousands, but the Duke had the law behind him, and the weapons. He destroyed by night, stealing into the streets in disguise and maltreating harmless individuals, just as—so they tell me—a certain nameless clique sometimes does today."

Caterina, gripping my hand, whispered under her breath, "The secret society!"

"Now," said Aldo, standing up, "I want you, the life-blood of the university, to play the citizens of Ruffano in the coming Festival. You won't need elaborate rehearsals, but I warn you it may be dangerous. The lads playing the courtiers will be armed—it's got to be authentic. I want you to get out into the streets with sticks and stones and any home-made weapon you can find. There'll be fighting in the streets and fighting up the hill and fighting in the ducal palace. Anyone who's scared can stay at home, and I for one won't blame him. But whoever is itching for a chance to get his own back upon the high and mighty, the snobbish inner circle who think they run the university and all Ruffano too—here's your chance. Come up and volunteer. I'll guarantee your victory."

He beckoned, laughing, and someone behind him on the stage started beating a tattoo upon the drum. The combination of this sound and the cheers from the audience and the crashing of seats as the students scrambled forward towards the stage where Aldo, still laughing, waited for them rang in my ears like the discords of hell.

I left Caterina and Paolo cheering and shouting amongst the others, and turned through the pushing crowd to the nearest exit. I was the only one amongst the packed and cheering students to attempt to leave. The guard at the door—I thought I recognised one of the scrutineers who had examined the passes on the Saturday evening at the ducal palace—put out a hand to stop me, but I managed to slip by. I walked up the street to the piazza della Vita, which by now was practically deserted save for the few city folk who promenaded still, and so back to my room.

It was no use doing anything tonight. The session in the theatre might continue until midnight, for all I knew, or even later. There might be more pop music, more dancing, more talking, intermingled with another performance upon the drums. Aldo would gather in his volunteers. Tomorrow I would go to his house and get at the truth. My brother had not changed in two-and-twenty years. His technique was the same now as then. The only difference was that, where he had once played upon the imagination of a sibling and devoted ally, he was now playing upon the raw and feverish emotions of fifteen hundred students. To train actors for a Festival did not necessitate whipping them into rival factions with all the risk of precipitating a real catastrophe. Or did it? Was it Aldo's intention to launch his opposing teams into conflagration so that the air should finally be cleansed? This had been the theory of warlords of the past. It had not worked. Spilt blood, like compost, fertilises the soil, brewing further strife. I wished Signora Butali had not gone to Rome. I could have talked to her. I could have warned her about Aldo and his multitudinous schemes, his magnetic power over the unsuspecting, the vulnerable, the young. She might have reasoned with him, or laughed him out of it.

When the students returned to the pensione, shortly after midnight, I turned out my light. I heard the light step of Caterina climb the stairs, and she opened my door, calling softly. I did not reply. After a moment she went away. I was in no mood to listen to the converted, or give an explanation of my own behaviour.

The next morning, purposely, I waited until I had heard the whole batch leave the house before I descended to the dining-room. Signora Silvani was sitting at the table reading the newspaper.

"Here you are," she said. "I wondered if you had gone out early, but the children thought not. Here's your coffee. Were you as much impressed by the Director of the Arts Council as they were?"

"He has a way with him," I said. "He's very persuasive."

"So I believe," she answered. "He's certainly persuaded our lot, and I imagine most of the others. They're all to become citizens of Ruffano for the Festival." She pushed the paper towards me as I drank my coffee. "Here's the local paper," she said. "There's a small piece about the break-in at the women's hostel, but they say nothing was taken, and it was a simple student rag. Signorina Rizzio has an attack of asthma—nothing to do with the break-in—and has gone away for a fortnight for some mountain air."

I buttered my roll in silence and read the passage. Carla Raspa had been right. Poor Signorina Rizzio was unable to face her mocking world. True or untrue, to carry the stigma of an old maid deflowered brought the finger of scorn.

"Ruffano is in the headlines," went on Signora Silvani. "See at the top there, about the woman murdered in Rome? She came from Ruffano all the time, and the body's to be brought back for burial. They've caught the lad that did it. One of the underworld."

My eyes ran swiftly to the large type at the top.

"Last night the Rome police arrested Giovanni Stampi, a day-labourer, at present without employment, who has already served nine months for theft. He admitted stealing a note for ten thousand lire from the dead woman, but denies the murder."

I finished my coffee and pushed the newspaper aside. "He says he's innocent."

"Wouldn't you?" retaliated Signora Silvani.

I left the house and walked to work up the via Rossini. It was a week ago today that I had driven into Rome with my coach-party and that night had seen the woman, now proved to be Marta, sleeping in the doorway of the church. Only a week. A moment's impulse on my part had brought about her murder, my own flight home, and the encounter with my living brother. Chance or predestination? The scientists could not tell us. Nor could the psychologists, or the priests. But for that stroll into the street I should now be on the homeward route from Naples to Genoa, the shepherd of my flock. As it was, I had probably lost my courier's status for ever, exchanging it for what? A temporary job as an assistant librarian which I could not, dared not quit because of Aldo. He, returned from the dead, was my reason for living. We, my mother and I, had deserted him once, contributing, doubtless, to his present ambivalent mood. Never again. Whatever my brother chose to do, I must stand by him. Poor Marta's murder was no longer my concern, with the murderer caught; Aldo was my problem.

As yesterday, I found my fellow assistants in the library buzzing with rumour. The secretary, Signorina Catti, was busy denying the story spread by Toni that the unfortunate Signorina Rizzio had, after an X-ray at the local hospital, left Ruffano for an operation elsewhere.

"The story is malicious and entirely unfounded," she declared. "Signorina Rizzio was suffering from a bad cold anyway, and is asthmatic. She has gone with friends to Cortina."

Giuseppe Fossi dismissed the tale as students' gossip. "In any case," he said, "the whole unfortunate event will die a natural death, thanks to Professor Donati, who has brought about a reconciliation between Professor Rizzio and Professor Elia. He is giving a big dinner tonight at the Hotel Panorama for both of them. My wife and I have been invited, and all the professors. It will be an important affair, as you may imagine. Now, shall we stop all this nonsense and get to work?"

As I plodded away under his direction I felt easier in mind. A reconciliation between the Heads of the opposing Departments could do nothing but good. If this was Aldo's move, then I had misjudged him. Perhaps his address to the C and E students at the theatre had only been what it seemed to be on the surface—a wily bid for Festival volunteers and nothing more. Sensitive and intuitive to his every word and gesture I certainly was, but ignorant as to his achievements for the Festival up to date. Both Signora Silvani and Carla Raspa had been enthusiastic about the realism of previous occasions. The Butalis had taken part in last year's production, along with Professor Rizzio. Would this year's display be so very different after all?

I went back to the pensione for lunch, and was at once set upon by my companions of last night.

"Deserter . . . coward . . . traitor!" shouted Gino and his friends, until Signor Silvani, holding up his hand for silence, protested that he and his wife would put the whole lot out of the house.

"Shout yourselves hoarse at the Festival if you like," he said, "but not under my roof. Here I am master. Sit down and take no notice of them," he added for my benefit, and to his wife, "Serve Signor Fabbio first."

"If you want the truth," I said, addressing the table at large, "I came back early last night because I had a stomach ache." This was received with groans of disbelief. "Nor can I do the twist," I said, "or possibly it was that trying to do so made me ill."

"Forgiven," called Caterina, "and shut up, everybody. After all, we forget he isn't a student. Why should he commit himself?"

"Because who isn't for us is against us," put in Gerardo.

"No," said Paolo, "that doesn't go for strangers. And Armino is a stranger to Ruffano."

He turned to me, his young face serious. "We won't let them bully you," he said, "but, all the same, you do see what a fine thing Professor Donati is doing by including every one of us in the Festival?"

"He wants performers," I answered, "that's all there is to it."

"No," said Paolo, "that isn't all. He wants to show in public that he's on our side. It amounts to a vote of confidence in every C and E student in the university, and from a disinterested observer like the Director of the Arts Council of Ruffano that puts us on top."

A chorus of approval rose from the whole table. Signor Silvani wiped his mouth and pushed back his chair.

"You know what they are saying at the prefettura?" he observed. "That the whole university is getting too big for its boots. A plague on all your Faculties, and we'd do better to be shot of the lot of you and turn the city into a nice big tourist centre with spas and swimming-pools on either hill."

This put an end to the argument. I was permitted to finish my lunch without drawing further fire. Before returning to the library I found that a note had been left for me in the entrance of No. 24, and I recognised the looped handwriting of Carla Raspa.

"I have not forgotten our date this evening," I read, "and I suggest that instead of your taking me to the Hotel dei Duchi we pool our resources and try out the magnificence of the Hotel Panorama. A big dinner is being given there by the Director of the Arts Council, and we can tuck ourselves away in a corner and watch the splendour. Call for me at seven."

Her persistence was untiring, but I doubted if it would win her admission to No. 2, via dei Sogni. The nearest she could get to Aldo was in the public restaurant of a hotel. I scribbled a note in answer, accepting the challenge, and left it in the doorway of her house.

The afternoon at the library passed without incident, and strangely enough without gossip either. The C and E bully who had sought to douse me in the fountain the day before had been right about the dust in the library. The shelves that Toni and I were now engaged upon were coated with it, and the books we removed could not have been taken out for years. One collection, right at the top, bore a name upon it that struck a chord in memory. Luigi Speca. Where had I lately heard or seen the name Luigi Speca? . . . I paused, and shrugged my shoulders. I could not remember. Anyway, the collection proved uninteresting. Uniform editions of Dante's *Divina Commedia*, Poems of Leopardi, Sonnets of Petrarca, all lumped together with other miscellaneous works. "Donated to the University of Ruffano by Luigi Speca." This proved possession, and they could go to the new university library. I packed them in one of the crates and left the box of papers for another time. Giuseppe Fossi was already becoming restive, with one eye on the clock.

"I can't afford to be late," he said shortly after six. "The dinner at the Panorama is at eight-fifteen for a quarter to nine. Dinner-jacket optional, but I shall dress, of course."

I doubt whether, if he could have exchanged his date with mine, he would have done so. He stalked from the library with all the bombast of a minor cleric bidden to partake of a papal feast. I followed him about twenty minutes later. Since I had no tuxedo with which to impress Carla Raspa, my one and only dark suit must suffice.

"Going to watch the fun at the Panorama?" asked Toni. "All Ruffano will turn out, so the boys are saying down in the town."

"I might do just that," I answered. "Look out for me."

Washed, changed and sleek, I arrived at No. 5 as the campanile struck seven. I climbed the stairs to the first floor and, seeing the card "Carla Raspa" inserted neatly in a slot beside the door, knocked upon it. It was opened immediately and my date for the evening stood there, immaculate in black and white—white top, low-cut, contrasting with the stiff black skirt—hair shining, drawn smoothly back behind her ears, lips bloodless. A vampire, before swooping to feed upon its victim, could not have looked more dangerous.

"I'm overwhelmed," I said, bowing. "The trouble is, if you set foot in the streets you'll be mobbed. We'll never get as far as the Hotel Panorama."

"Don't worry," she answered, drawing me inside the apartment. "I've looked after that. Did you see the car outside?"

I had noticed a Fiat 600 parked by the kerbside as I entered the building. "Yes," I said. "Is it yours?"

"Mine for the evening," she smiled, "borrowed from an obliging neighbour on the floor above. Have a drink. Cinzano from your home-town of Turin."

She handed me a glass and took one for herself. I glanced about me. The furnishings, which I supposed were standard, the apartment being let furnished, had been embellished with accessories of the tenant's choice. Bright and enormous cushions splayed upon the divan-bed. A wrought-iron lamp-stand—made in Ruffano?—stood beside it, the light subdued by a deep parchment shade. The small kitchenette beyond had a scarlet floor, and a corner of the room was set for dining, with a table and two chairs, all black. This was where Giuseppe Fossi must indulge himself before seeking satiation on the divan-bed.

"You seem very well installed," I said. "My congratulations, signorina."

"I like my comforts," she replied, "and so do the few friends who visit me. If you count yourself one, call me Carla."

I lifted my glass and drank to this distinction. She lit a cigarette and moved about the room, the aromatic perfume that exuded from her person too pungent for my taste. No doubt it was intended to whet the appetite and heat the blood. My vitals remained unmoved. She caught sight of herself in the mirror on the wall and pouted. It was a reflex action, signifying pleasure.

"What's the excitement," I asked, "of watching a formal party of professors and their wives?"

"You don't realise," she said. "It will be a sight in a million. They say Professor Rizzio and Professor Elia haven't spoken for a year. I want to see the impact. Besides, any party given by Aldo Donati is worth watching. Just to hover on the fringe will be a stimulant."

Her nostrils quivered in anticipation like a brood mare prior to stud. I expected her at any moment to paw the ground.

"You know," I told her, "that Giuseppe Fossi and his wife have been invited. What if he sees us? Will it spoil your delightful friendship?"

She laughed, shrugging her shoulders. "He must take what's offered," she said. "Besides, he'll be so blown-up with pride that he won't have eyes for us. Shall we be going?"

It was barely a quarter-past seven. Giuseppe Fossi had said something in the library about the party assembling at a quarter-past eight. I told this to Carla Raspa.

"I know," she said, "but my idea is this. That we ourselves should feed early, and then, when Donati's party assembles in the hall for drinks, slip out of the restaurant and join them. No one will realise we aren't amongst the invited until afterwards, when they go in to dinner."

It had been my function before now to arrange similar small deceptions for the pleasure of my touring clients. It made their entire evening if they could stand about in the proximity of film-actors or diplomats and indulge, even for five minutes, the fantasy of belonging to another stratum.

"Anything you wish," I said to my companion. "My only stipulation is that we do *not* follow the invited into the restaurant and then endure the humiliation of being turned from the big table."

"I promise to behave," she said. "But you never know. The numbers might be wrong, and if there should be vacant places I'd seize one without a qualm."

I doubted Aldo's party being so disorganised, but left her hope unchallenged. We descended to the street, and at Carla Raspa's suggestion I took the wheel of the borrowed car. We shot away down the street, and passing the church of San Cipriano climbed the northern hill towards the piazza del Duca Carlo, drawing up some two hundred yards short of it before the imposing Hotel Panorama.

We were too early for the city sightseers promised by Toni, but our arrival did not pass unnoticed. A doorman in uniform rushed to help us out of the car. Another, equally resplendent, swung the revolving doors. I thought with compassion of my old friend Signor Longhi at the Hotel dei Duchi.

The vestibule was large, stone-floored and pillared, set about with orange-trees in tubs and dripping fountains. Windows in the rear gave on to a terrace where during the hot weather, so my companion told me, the clientèle would lounge and also dine. The hotel, now in its second season, was run by a syndicate. Professor Elia, Director of Commerce and Economics, was said to be a member. I was not surprised.

"Don't worry," murmured Carla Raspa, "about the bill. I've plenty if you run short. The charges are staggering. It's intended, of course, for American and German tourists. No one else can afford it, except the Milanese."

We passed through to the restaurant, empty at the moment except for ourselves. The enormous table in the centre, ready for the dinner-party later, reminded me of the set-up so frequently ordered by myself for Sunshine Tours. Only the flags were missing. The head waiter, with minions at his elbow, bowed us to the table which Carla Raspa had reserved beforehand, and handed us menus the size of proclamations. I studied mine in silence, thinking of my pocket. Carla Raspa, showing bravado, ordered for us both; the dish, a marriage-after-death of eel and octopus, presaged insomnia. Perhaps this was her intention.

"I should like," she said, "to live like this always. It won't happen as long as I remain a lecturer on the staff here."

I asked her the alternative. She shrugged her shoulders.

"A rich man somewhere," she answered, "preferably with a wife at home. Unmarried men tire sooner. They have so large a choice."

"You won't find one in Ruffano," I told her.

"I don't know," she said, "I live in hopes. Professor Elia has a wife who never emerges from Ancona. She won't be here tonight."

"I thought," I said, nodding at her ensemble, "all this was to attract Donati?"

"What's wrong with catching both?" she answered. "Donati is the more elusive. But they tell me Elia has a larger appetite."

Her frankness was disarming, and I felt myself secure. The table for two in the kitchenette and the divan-bed were not for me.

"Of course," she continued, "if a shrimp came along and offered marriage I'd accept him. But only if his bank balance were considerable." I got the message and affected a deep sigh. She patted my hand kindly. "As an escort you couldn't be better," she said. "Should I catch my fish and you stay on in Ruffano, you can share the pickings."

I professed myself obliged. We both of us became a little lit with a bottle of Verdicchio to smooth the passage of the eel and octopus. I found myself smiling for no reason. The walls of the Hotel Panorama receded. The head waiter became less attentive, and kept peering out of the door towards the pillared vestibule.

"Have you had enough?" asked Carla Raspa. "If so, I think we'd better move. They're beginning to arrive—I can tell from the noise outside. Ask for the bill."

The bill was ready, folded upon a plate. We had eaten the one dish only, but from the figures I could tell we needed the support of that bank balance already discussed. I drew out my pocket-book, while my companion slipped assistance on to my knee beneath the cover of the tablecloth.

Haughtily, like a god who has eaten his fill before the arrival of lesser mortals, I paid, and escorted my companion from the restaurant. We entered the vestibule to find it already filling with the invited guests. Waiters were buzzing about proffering trays laden with glasses. The men, as Giuseppe had warned me, were in dinner-jackets, the women in every variety of evening dress. The hairdressers of Ruffano had been working overtime.

Carla Raspa unblushingly seized a glass from the tray that the nearest waiter offered her. I did the same.

"There he is," said my companion in dishonour. "He looks even more alluring in a tuxedo. I'd like to eat him!"

Aldo was standing with his back to us, but despite the babble of voices the rather clear tone of Carla Raspa, pitched in a key more suitable to the lecture-rooms she was used to than this formal gathering, reached his ears. He turned, and saw us both. For a moment he looked nonplussed, a rare thing for my brother. I imagined his lightning thought—had two of the invitations gone astray? My look of embarrassment must have reassured him, and my attempt to back away. He cut me dead, but nodded civilly enough to my companion. Then he moved forward to greet another arrival, Professor Rizzio, alone, without his sister. The Deputy Rector of the university looked weary and very strained. He shook hands with Aldo, and murmured something I could not catch in answer to my brother's solicitous enquiry as to his sister's health. His haggard appearance troubled me, and I could barely look at him. Discreetly I moved out of earshot and watched the other new arrivals, none of them known to me. Only Giuseppe Fossi, bursting out of his over-tight dinner-jacket, was recognisable amidst a hub of strangers, with his wife, more like an eager hen than ever, pecking and clucking at his side.

I squinted through the entrance to the line of cars outside, and beyond them to the chattering, gaping crowd. Not all Ruffano, certainly, but a fair proportion strolling to take the air, both city folk and students. I turned back to the hall. Giuseppe Fossi had noticed Carla Raspa, and was busy directing his wife in the opposite direction. Aldo, still engaged with Professor Rizzio, glanced frowning at his watch. My companion edged towards me.

"The other guest of honour is late," she said. "It's almost ten to nine. He's done it on purpose, naturally. To make a greater stir than Rizzio."

I had forgotten Professor Elia. The purpose of the party, of course, was to effect a public reconciliation. Aldo's triumph was to bring the two men together.

The voices rose deafeningly. Glasses clinked. I shook my head when offered a third martini.

"Can't we go?" I whispered to Carla Raspa.

"And miss the meeting of the giants? Not on your life," she answered.

The minutes dragged like hours. The hands of the hotel clock stood at three minutes to nine. Aldo had ceased talking to Professor Rizzio and was tapping an impatient foot.

"Does he have far to come?" I asked my companion.

"Three minutes in a car," she said. "You know the big house at the corner of the piazza del Duca Carlo? Oh no, it's obvious. This is his method of making the rest look small."

The telephone rang at the reception desk. I happened to hear it because I stood between it and the guests. I saw the reception clerk answer, listen, then reach for a memo pad and scribble a message. He looked bewildered. Waving aside the page who stood beside him, he hurried from the desk across the crowded floor towards my brother, and handed him the message. I watched Aldo's face. He read the message, then turned rapidly to the receptionist and questioned him. The man, troubled, obviously repeated what he had just heard on the telephone. Aldo raised both his hands and called for silence. There was an immediate hush. Faces swung towards him.

"I'm afraid something has happened to Professor Elia," he said. "A message had just come over the telephone from an anonymous caller suggesting that I should go to the Professor's house immediately. It could be a hoax, but very possibly not. If you'll all excuse me I'll drive there instantly. If all is well, I'll report back at once."

A gasp of consternation came from the assembled guests. Professor Rizzio, looking more drawn than ever, plucked Aldo by the sleeve. He was evidently asking to go with him. Aldo nodded, already moving swiftly through the crowded room. Professor Rizzio followed. Others also broke away from their wives and turned towards the entrance. Carla Raspa, taking my hand, pulled me after them.

"Come on," she said. "It may be serious, it may be nothing. But whatever it is, we're not going to miss it."

I followed her through the swing-doors of the hotel. Already I could hear the roar of Aldo's Alfa-Romeo as it turned and spun away uphill towards the piazza del Duca Carlo.

CHAPTER FOURTEEN

WE FOLLOWED CLOSELY in our borrowed car, but others had the same idea. Those guests whose cars, like ours and Aldo's, had been parked in the space reserved for the hotel were soonest off. The crowd of watching students and city-folk, realising from the confusion that something was wrong, started running up the hill in their turn. Horns hooted wildly and there was a grinding and clashing of gears and much excited jabbering.

"That's Elia's house, there at the corner," pointed Carla Raspa. "The lights are on."

The Alfa-Romeo had already drawn up beside the house, which stood in its own garden on the right of the piazza del Duca Carlo. I saw Aldo spring from the car and dash inside, followed more slowly by Professor Rizzio. I slowed down, wondering what to do. We could not very well draw up behind Aldo's car. Cars hooted impatiently behind me.

"I'll circle the piazza," I said, "and come round again."

I shot ahead, but Carla Raspa, craning to look out of the window, said, "They're coming out again. He can't be there."

Chaos was piling up in my immediate rear, close to the house. I could see the lights of cars flashing in my mirror. People shouted.

"Donati's getting back into his car," said Carla Raspa. "No, he's not. Wait, Armino, wait. Park across to the right there, by the public gardens."

The piazza del Duca Carlo terminated in the formal municipal gardens laid out with gravel paths and trees and shrubs, with the statue of Duke Carlo dominating the scene. I parked the car close to some trees and we got out.

"Why the floodlights?" I asked.

"They are always switched on for the week of the Festival," said my companion. "Didn't you notice them last night? My God . . ."

She clutched my arm and pointed to the statue of Duke Carlo, who, serene and magnificent on his marble pedestal, gazed benignly down upon the gravel path below. Flood-lit, he was an imposing figure, but not so imposing was the man who sat immediately beneath him on the stone steps leading to the base. Sat, or rather straddled, for his hands and widely separated feet were bound to heavy weights, preventing movement. He was stark naked. Even from the distance where I stood, about twenty-five yards, I had no difficulty in recognising the powerful build, the shock of black hair, of Professor Elia.

As we stared, my companion choking back a cry half-frightened, half-hysterical, we saw Aldo, followed by some half-dozen men, run across the piazza towards the statue. In a moment the wretched victim was surrounded, masked from view by those who bent over him to set him free. I saw Aldo break away and wave his hand, shouting for a car. Another figure darted back across the piazza. Meanwhile more cars were approaching, drawing up, parking. The first of the running students swarmed up the hill. Everywhere people were calling, "What is it? Who is it? What's happened?"

We moved closer, drawn by the terrible instinct that pervades all humanity when witness to disaster. The instinct to be there. The desire to know. Being first upon the scene we had the advantage over our equally curious neighbours, although Aldo and the guests from the hotel who had followed hard upon him partially screened the unfortunate professor from our view.

Someone cut the thongs, the arms and legs sagged forward. The whole body drooped as though about to fall. The victim raised his head. He was not gagged. He could, had he so desired, have shouted for help before, and been freed the sooner. Why had he not done so? His eyes, without spectacles, searching the faces of those who in sympathy and consternation sought to screen him from the public gaze, gave me the answer. Professor Elia had not called for help because of shame. Shame at the lamentable, shocking and ridiculous figure he would cut before the inevitable strangers who must set eyes upon him first. As it happened, the man who stood before him, who looked down upon him with pity, even with anguish, and was the first to hand down the car rug that an eager helper thrust forward to envelop the naked frame, was his rival, the Deputy Rector of the university, Professor Rizzio, whose sister had been maltreated some forty-eight hours before.

"Help him to the car," called Aldo. "Screen him completely. And get all that rabble out of the way."

He and Professor Rizzio helped the victim to his feet. For a moment we caught a glimpse of him in all his drab disorder, his ugly white limbs contrasting with his coarse hair; then the merciful rug cloaked him, the protecting arms enveloped him. His friends led him to the shelter of the car, and the bewildered watchers fell back on either side. I left Carla Raspa staring after the rescue party. I went behind one of the newly-planted municipal trees and vomited. When I returned, my companion was standing by the car.

"Come on," she called impatiently. "We'll go after them."

I looked across the piazza. The summoned car, pushing through the assembling crowd, had stopped once more before Professor Elia's entrance.

"We can't go to his house," I said, "we've no business there."

"Not after him," she said, swiftly getting into the car, "after the gang. The thugs who did it. They can't be far away. Hurry . . . hurry . . ."

Once again, those who had cars shared her idea. The victim could safely be left to the ministrations of his friends and a hastily summoned doctor; but for the perpetrators of the outrage the hunt was on.

Four roads led from the piazza del Duca Carlo, so the choice of route was varied. Those running left swung west and out of the city. To turn to the right would bring us downhill to the Porta Malebranche and the via delle Mura. Another street, running south from the gate, would take us uphill once more to the piazza della Vita and the city centre. I chose the route to the right, and heard a second car behind me. We cruised downhill to the gate and then I let the other car pass. It shot east along the via delle Mura. Two students, straddling a vespa, followed it. I had no doubt that other pursuers had gone westward from the piazza del Duca Carlo, and all would eventually meet up on the southern hill beyond the students' hostels.

I halted the car on one of the ramparts in the via delle Mura overlooking the valley below, and turned to my companion. "It's a useless chase," I said. "Whoever did it has gone to ground. They had only to dive into the side streets and get lost, then saunter out into the piazza della Vita like anybody else."

"How would they have taken Elia from the house and to the statue if they hadn't a car?" she asked.

"Covered him with rugs and carried him," I answered. "Everybody was so busy watching the guests arrive at the Hotel Panorama that the piazza del Duca Carlo at the top of the hill was deserted. The culprits knew this, and took a chance. Then they telephoned the hotel from Professor Elia's house and scampered." I reached for a packet of cigarettes and lighted one for her and for myself. "Anyway," I said, "they'll find them in the end. Donati will have to send for the police."

"Don't be too sure," said Carla Raspa.

"Why not?"

"He'll have to get Professor Elia's authority first," she replied, "and he won't want his nudity blazoned in the press and everywhere else any more than Rizzio wanted the world to know about the assault upon his sister. I'm willing to bet you a thousand lire that this second rag is hushed up like the first."

"Impossible! Too many people saw."

"A lot of people saw nothing at all. Only a group of men huddled round a figure covered with rugs. If the powers-that-be want to hush it up, they will. You realise that Friday is Festival day, when the students' relatives and outsiders come to Ruffano? What a moment to announce a scandal!"

I was silent. The incident had been well-timed. Short of expelling the students en masse, there was little the authorities could do.

"It could be one of two things," continued Carla Raspa. "Either a pay-back from the Arts and Education lads for the insult to the Rizzios, or a double-bluff from the boys in C and E to throw the blame on their opponents. I don't know that it matters much either way. As a rag, it was superlative."

"You think so?" I said.

"Yes," she said, "don't you?"

I was not sure which had distressed me most—the strained face of Professor Rizzio burying his pride and shaking hands with my brother at the Hotel Panorama, or the tortured, haunted eyes of Professor Elia when his nakedness had been revealed. Both were pathetic figures, shorn of lustre.

"No," I answered. "I'm a stranger in Ruffano. Both incidents revolt me."

She opened the window of the car, laughing, and threw out her cigarette. She seized mine from my lips and threw it out as well. Then she turned and, taking my face in her hands, kissed my mouth.

"The trouble with you is that you need firm handling," she said.

The sudden display of passion caught me off-guard. The thrusting lips, the entwining legs, the fumbling hands, were unexpected. The approach that doubtless delighted Giuseppe Fossi repelled me. If this was her moment it wasn't mine. I pushed her back against the handle of the door and slapped her face. She looked surprised.

"Why so violent?" she asked, not in the least annoyed.

"Love-making in a car offends my taste," I told her.

"Very well, then. Let's go home," she answered.

I started up the car once more, and we drove along the via delle Mura and into the city, and so by a side-street to the via San Michele. At any other time I might have been amused, even willing, to follow her lead. Not so tonight. Her advances sprang, not from our casual acquaintance and the light-hearted intimacy of an evening spent in each other's company, but from another cause—the scene we had just witnessed. I drew the car up with a jerk in front of No. 5. She got out and went into the house, leaving the door open for me. But I did not follow. Instead I got out of the car and made my way uphill to the via dei Sogni.

I wondered how long she would wait for me. Whether she would go to the window and look down at the parked car, and then, possibly unbelieving still, descend the stairs once more and peer in to see if I were still there. She might even cross the street to No. 24 and enquire of the Silvanis if by any chance Signor Fabbio had entered and gone to his room.

Then I dismissed her from my mind. I walked past my old home, darkly shuttered, and arrived at my brother's house. I rang the bell of the porter's entrance on the left, and after a moment or two Jacopo emerged. He broke into a smile at the sight of me.

"Could you let me in to wait for Aldo?" I asked. "He's out, I know, but I want to see him when he returns."

"Of course, Signor Beo," he said, and then, possibly guessing something from my heated appearance, for I had walked fast, he added, "Is anything wrong?"

"There was a disturbance," I said, "up in the piazza del Duca Carlo. It broke up the party at the hotel. Aldo's dealing with it."

He looked concerned, and leading the way across the passage opened Aldo's door. He switched on the lights. "The students, I suppose," he said. "They are always excited this week, with the Festival. And then the break-in on the Sunday night. Was it something similar?"

"Yes," I said. "Aldo will explain."

He opened the door to the living-room and asked if I would like something to drink. I told him no. I could pour myself a drink if I needed one. He waited a moment, uncertain whether I was going to gossip with him or not, then, with the tact induced through long years with my brother, decided that I wished to be alone. He withdrew, and I heard him close the front door and return to his own domain.

I prowled about the room. Looked out of the window. Stared at the portrait of my father. Flung myself in a chair. The peace and the familiarity of home possessions were all about me, but I felt uneasy, sick. I got up again, and crossing to a table picked up the German volume of the *Lives of the Dukes of Ruffano*. It opened at the marked page, and I ran my eyes over it until I came upon the passage I remembered.

". . . When accusations were made against him by the outraged citizens of Ruffano, Duke Claudio retaliated by declaring that he had been divinely appointed to mete out to his subjects the punishment they deserved. The proud would be stripped, the haughty violated, the slanderer silenced, the viper die in his venom. The scales of heavenly justice would thus be balanced."

I closed the book and sat down again in another chair. Two faces were before me. That of Signorina Rizzio, haughty, unbending, hardly deigning to speak to me over her mineral water; and that of Professor Elia, lunching with his friends in the small restaurant off the via San Cipriano, guffawing at the rumour of assault, delighted, self-opinionated, proud. I had not seen Signorina Rizzio since Sunday morning. Whether she was with friends in Cortina or elsewhere hardly mattered. She had carried her shame with her. Professor Elia I had seen less than an hour ago. His shame was with him still.

The telephone started ringing. I stared at it, doing nothing. The persistent sound continued, and I got up and lifted the receiver. The operator said, "Will you take a call from Rome?" I answered, "Yes," mechanically. After a moment I heard a woman say, "Aldo, is it you?"

It was Signora Butali. I recognised her voice. I was about to tell her that my brother was out but she went on speaking, taking my silence for assent, or perhaps indifference. She sounded desperate.

"I've been trying to get you all the evening," she said. "Gaspare is adamant. He insists on coming home. Ever since Professor Rizzio telephoned him yesterday and told him what happened, he hasn't rested. The doctors say it would be better for him to return than to lie there, in hospital, working himself into a fever. Dearest . . . for God's sake, tell me what to do. Aldo, are you there?"

I put down the receiver. In about five minutes it rang again. I did not answer. I just went on sitting in Aldo's chair.

It was after midnight when I heard the key turn in the lock and the front-door slam. Jacopo may have heard the car arrive and gone to warn my brother that I was waiting for him, and then withdrawn to his own quarters, for there was no sound of voices. Soon Aldo came into the room. He looked at me, saying nothing, then went across to the tray of glasses and poured himself a drink.

"Were you up at the piazza del Duca Carlo too?" he asked.

"Yes," I said.

"How much did you see?"

"The same as you. Professor Elia naked."

He carried his glass to a chair and sprawled across it, one leg over the arm. "He wasn't even bruised," he said. "I called a doctor to examine him. Luckily the night was mild. He won't have caught pneumonia. Besides, he's as strong as an ox."

I did not comment. Aldo drank, then set down his glass and sprang to his feet. "I'm hungry," he said. "I haven't had any dinner. I wonder if Jacopo has left sandwiches. Be back in a minute."

He was gone about five minutes, and returned with a tray of prosciutto, salad and fruit, which he placed on the table beside the chair.

"I don't know what they did at the Panorama," he said, attacking the food. "I telephoned the manager to say that Professor Elia was unwell, that Professor Rizzio and I were staying with him, and would the others carry on without us? No doubt they did, or some of them. Most of the professors don't get a chance to eat up there on their salary, nor their wives. What in the world were you doing?"

"Watching the guests arrive," I said.

"Not your idea, I imagine?"

"No."

"Ah, well, she got her bellyful—that ought to keep her quiet for a couple of nights. Did she molest you?"

I ignored the question. He smiled, and continued eating.

"My little Beo," he said, "your homecoming hasn't been that easy. Who would think Ruffano could turn out to be so lively? You'd have a smoother passage in one of your touring coaches. Here, keep me company." He picked up an orange from his tray and threw it at me.

"I was at the theatre yesterday," I said, slowly peeling the orange. "You are quite a performer upon the drums."

He had not expected this. I could tell by the hardly imperceptible pause between his cutting a slice of ham and forking it to his mouth.

"You get around," he said. "Who took you there?"

"The C and E students from my lodgings," I answered, "who, like the mass of your audience, appeared as impressed by all you said as the élite on Saturday night at the ducal palace."

He waited a moment before answering. Then, pushing aside his plate and reaching for his salad, he observed, "The young are pliable."

I finished peeling the orange and offered him half. We ate in silence. I saw his eye fall upon the volume of the *Lives of the Dukes of Ruffano* lying on the further table where I had placed it. Then he looked at me. "'The proud would be stripped, the haughty violated'," I quoted. "What exactly are you trying to do? Mete out heavenly justice like Duke Claudio?"

Appetite satisfied, he got up, removed the tray to a table in the corner, poured himself half a glass of wine, and stood with it beneath our father's portrait.

"My immediate job is to train actors," he said. "If they choose to identify themselves with the parts allotted to them, so much the better. We shall get an even finer performance on the day of the Festival."

The smile, disarming to the world, did not deceive me. I knew it of old. Too often in days gone by he had employed it to get his way.

"There have been two incidents," I said, "both highly organised. Don't tell me a bunch of students could, or did, plan either of them."

"You underestimate this generation," he replied. "They have great powers of organisation, if they care to develop them. Besides, they are hungry for ideas. Give them a suggestion, and they're away."

He neither admitted nor denied association with what had happened on Sunday evening and tonight. I had no doubt that he had instigated both events.

"It doesn't disturb you," I asked, "to humiliate two people—three, counting Professor Rizzio—to such an extent that they are bound to lose authority forever?"

"Authority is bogus," he said, "unless it comes from within. Then it is inspiration and comes from God."

I stared. Aldo had never been religious. Our boyhood attendance at Mass on Sundays and feast days had been a routine affair, commanded by our parents, though frequently employed by my brother as a means to frighten me; the altar-piece in San Cipriano being an example of his powers to distort imagination to breaking point.

"Keep that for your students," I said. "It's the sort of thing the Falcon told his élite."

"And they believed him," he answered.

The smile, the tongue-in-cheek, were suddenly absent. The eyes, blazing in the pale face, were disturbing. I moved in my chair restlessly, and reached for a cigarette. When I glanced at him again the tension was over. He was finishing his glass of wine.

"You know the one thing that nobody in our country can endure?" he asked lightly, holding his glass against the light. "Not only our country but throughout the world, and right through history? Loss of face. We create an image of ourselves, and someone destroys the image. We are made to look ridiculous. You talked just now about humiliation, which is the same thing. The man, or the nation, who loses face either never recovers and so disintegrates, or learns humility, which is a very different thing from humiliation. Time will show how the Rizzios develop, and Elia, with the rest of the fry that make up this miniature Ruffano world."

I thought of someone who must have been losing face for the past three hours, and that was my companion of the evening, Carla Raspa. Perhaps she was too thick-skinned to admit it. Failure to come up to scratch would be blamed on me, not her. I did not care. She was welcome to whatever inference she chose to put upon my lack of gallantry.

"By the way," I said, "you had a telephone call from Rome at about ten-thirty."

"Oh?" said Aldo.

"Signora Butali, and she sounded anxious. The Rector insists on coming home, in connection, so I gathered, with Sunday night's incident."

"When?" asked Aldo.

"She didn't say. To tell you the truth, I hung up when she was still talking. She thought I was you, and I left it at that."

"Which was stupid of you," said Aldo. "I thought you had more intelligence."

"I'm sorry."

The information had disturbed him. I saw him eye the telephone. I took the hint and rose.

"Anyway," I said, "when Professor Butali hears about tonight . . ."

"He won't," interrupted Aldo. "What do you suppose Rizzio and Elia and I were discussing until midnight?"

"He may not hear officially," I said, "but don't tell me someone won't pass the word."

My brother shrugged. "That's a risk we have to take," he said.

I moved towards the door. I had achieved precisely nothing by coming to the via dei Sogni and waiting for Aldo, except confirmation of the suspicion nagging me. And to let him know I knew.

"If the Rector does come back," I asked, "what will he do?"

"He won't do anything," said Aldo, "there isn't time."

"Time?"

Aldo smiled. "Rectors are also vulnerable," he said, "they can lose face like other mortals. Beo . . ."

"Yes?"

He picked up a newspaper that was lying on the chair by the door. "Did you see this?"

He showed me the passage I had read at breakfast. The events of the day had put it completely from my mind.

"They've caught the murderer," I said. "Thank God for that."

"They've caught the thief," he interposed, "which apparently isn't the same thing. I had a call from the commissioner of police this morning. The fellow who took the ten thousand lire sticks to his story. He insists that Marta was already dead when he took the note from her, and the police have a hunch he's telling the truth."

"Already dead?" I exclaimed. "But then . . ."

"They're still looking for the murderer," he said, "which, for anyone hanging about the via Sicilia between midnight and the small hours last Tuesday night, might be unhealthy, or at least inconvenient." He put his hand on my head and rumpled my hair. "Don't worry, my Beato," he said, "they won't catch you. And if they did they'd soon acquit you. Innocence shines from your eyes."

What he had just told me knocked my composure sideways. The whole sick horror of the murder was with me still. I had thought it buried.

"What shall I do?" I asked desperately. "Shall I go to the police?"

"No," he said, "forget the whole thing. Come to my meeting tomorrow night and become one of the élite. Here's your pass." He felt in his pocket and brought out a small disk, bearing upon its face a falcon's head. "The boys will let you in with this," he said. "Entrance to the throne room at nine o'clock. And come alone. I don't propose entertaining Signorina Raspa or your playmates from 24, via San Michele. Sleep well."

He pushed me from the door and out into the street. It was after one, and everywhere was dark and still. I met no one between Aldo's house and the via San Michele. No. 24 was as quiet as the other shuttered houses. The door was unlocked and I went to my room without disturbing anyone, but judging from the sound of voices from Paolo Pasquale's room the whole company of students had gathered there, and were engaged in furious discussion. Tomorrow I might hear if they had been near the piazza del Duca Carlo.

I awoke about 5 a.m., not with any dream or nightmare, not with the vivid picture of the Head of the Department of Commerce and Economics seated in ignominious nudity beneath the marble pedestal bearing the bronze statue of Duke Carlo, but with the sudden recollection of where it was that I had read the name Luigi Speca—the problem which had puzzled me in the library during the afternoon. Luigi Speca had signed his name alongside my father's at Aldo's baptism. I had seen it written in the book of records kept at the sacristy of San Cipriano.

CHAPTER FIFTEEN

AT EIGHT O'CLOCK there was a knock on my door, and before I could answer Paolo burst in, closely followed by Caterina.

"I'm sorry," he said, seeing I was in the midst of shaving, "but we want to know if you're coming with us. The whole of C and E are cutting lectures, and we're going to demonstrate outside the house of Professor Elia."

"What about?" I asked.

"You know. We saw you," broke in Caterina. "You were in a car, with the Raspa woman. We saw you leave the hotel and drive up to the piazza del Duca Carlo. You were in the thick of it."

"That's right," chimed in Gino, whose head appeared over Caterina's, "and later we saw the same car parked by the municipal gardens. You must have seen what happened. You were much nearer than any of us."

I laid down my razor and reached for a towel. "I saw nothing," I said, "except a crowd of professors around the statue. There was a lot of movement and excited talk, and then they carried someone, or something, away. Perhaps it was a bomb."

"A bomb!" everyone shouted.

"That's the best yet," said Caterina, "and do you know, he could be right. They could have tied Elia to a bomb timed to explode within a certain number of minutes."

"Well, what happened to it?"

"What sort of bomb?"

"The point is, was he wounded or cut about? No one will tell us."

The passionate discussion that must have been going on half the night promised resumption once again, and in my bedroom.

"Look here," I said, "clear out, the lot of you. Go and demonstrate if you want to. I'm not a student. I'm an employee."

"A spy?" suggested Gino. "You haven't been here a week, and look what's happened!"

The laughter from the rest was not spontaneous. It held an element of doubt. Caterina turned impatiently, pushing the others from the room.

"Ah, leave him alone," she said. "What's the use? He doesn't care." Then, to give me a final chance, she said to me over her shoulder, "The idea is to demonstrate in a body outside Professor Elia's house and get him to appear. If we're satisfied he's all right, and unhurt, that's good enough, we'll turn up for the morning sessions."

A few minutes later I heard them leave the house. The inevitable splutter of vespas followed, belonging, I thought, to Gino and Gerardo. I stood by the window and watched them disappear down the street. Then I looked across at the first floor of No. 5. The shutters were thrown back, the windows open. Carla Raspa had begun her day.

Signor Silvani was finishing breakfast when I descended for coffee, and he immediately asked me if I knew anything of the events of the night before. I told him I had been near the piazza del Duca Carlo and had seen the crowd.

"We only know what our young people here told us," he said, "but I don't like the sound of it. We've had ragging before, you get it in every university, but this sounds vicious. Is it true they tarred and feathered Professor Elia?"

"I don't know," I said. "I didn't see."

"I shall hear the truth at the prefettura," he said. "If anything serious was done last night, it will mean drafting extra police into Ruffano for the next few days. It's chaotic enough anyway on Festival day, without adding demonstrations to all our problems."

I looked about for a morning paper, but saw none. Perhaps it was in the kitchen, or had not arrived. I finished my coffee and walked up to the piazza della Vita to buy one. Unrest stirred in the air. The piazza was crowded with morning shoppers, and with the inevitable group of workless individuals who, idle not from choice but from necessity, came to the city centre to stand and stare. Students were everywhere, arguing, loquacious, most of them streaming out of the piazza up the northern hill to the piazza del Duca Carlo. Rumour, floating from one hill to the other, and then converging from all corners to the piazza della Vita, emerged in the small space like smoke from a steaming cauldron.

There was a Communist plot to blow up the university. . . . There was a Fascist plot to take over the municipality. . . . Guests at the dinner-party at the Hotel Panorama had been poisoned. . . . The private residences of the Heads of Departments had been burgled. . . . A maniac from Rome, having murdered one of Ruffano's inhabitants, poor Marta Zampini, in the capital, was now loose in Ruffano itself, and had made an attempt on the life of Professor Elia. . . .

I bought a paper. There was nothing in it about last night's event, and only a brief statement about the murder. The police still held the thief in Rome pending further enquiries elsewhere. Elsewhere. Did this mean Ruffano?

There was a sudden movement in the crowd from the direction of the via dei Martiri. People fell back on either side to allow the passage of a priest and acolyte, and behind them four men bearing a coffin covered with a pall. In the rear came the mourners, a man with cross-eyes and a woman, heavily veiled, upon his arm. They made their way across the piazza to the church of San Cipriano. The gaping crowd closed in upon them. I followed, as in a dream, and stood within the precincts of the church in the midst of staring townsfolk, who participated out of curiosity. I listened for the opening words: "Requiem aeternam dona eis Domine: et lux perpetua luceat eis." Then I turned, and left the church.

As I pushed through the door I saw a man standing near the table where they sold candles. He was watching the crowd, and his eyes fell upon me. I thought I recognised him, and, from the momentary question in his eye, that he knew me too. It was one of the police agents who had been in the room taking notes when the English tourists made their statement at the police station in Rome. Today he wore plain clothes.

I ran down the steps and plunged into the piazza della Vita. Then darted along the via del Teatro and climbed the long ascending slope under the walls of the ducal palace. Instinct had made me run. Instinct had told me to take this devious way. If the agent had recognised me as the courier in Rome who had volunteered the statement about the murdered woman, he would remember that this same courier had been en route for Naples with his touring party, and he would ask himself, what was the courier doing in Ruffano? A word on the telephone to Sunshine Tours, a quick check-up with either the Rome or the Genoa office, would tell the agent that Armino Fabbio had asked to be released from the Naples tour and had gone north with a Herr Turtmann and his wife. Little doubt that further news would be elicited that the courier had deserted Herr Turtmann in Ruffano, and nothing had been heard of him since.

I looked about me. The agent could not have followed me. Or, if he had, I had thrown him off. Strollers, shoppers, students, were walking past the piazza Maggiore on their lawful business. I went into the Duomo by the side-entrance, crossed the chancel and emerged at the further side, immediately opposite the ducal palace. In a moment I was inside the walls, and crossing the quadrangle to the library. It was only then, as I paused a moment to recover my breath, that I realised I had acted in foolish panic. It might not have been the police agent. If it had, there was no reason to suppose he had recognised me. My action, in fact, had been a classic example of the behaviour of a guilty man. I stood mopping my forehead, and at that moment the library doors opened and Toni and the other assistant staggered forth, bearing a crate of books.

"Hullo! Who's been chasing you?" asked Toni.

The question was apt. Stung by his enquiry, I thrust my handkerchief into my pocket.

"No one," I said. "I got held up in the town."

"What's happening, then? Have they gone on strike? Are they demonstrating?" they asked simultaneously.

I was so preoccupied with my own endeavours in eluding the possible police agent that I was slow to seize their meaning.

"On strike? Who?" I said.

Toni raised despairing eyes to heaven. "Do you live in this world?" he enquired. "Don't you know that all Ruffano is in a ferment because of what happened last night in the piazza del Duca Carlo?"

"They say the Communists got hold of Professor Elia," said his companion, "and tried to bash his head in. Fossi's given orders to shift everything we can from here to the new building in case an attempt is made to set fire to the ducal palace."

They staggered off along the quadrangle with the crate. I went into the library to find chaos. Books were piled high upon the floor, and Giuseppe Fossi, with Signorina Catti at his side, was lumping volume after volume pell-mell into another groaning crate. He raised his perspiring face at sight of me and burst into a torrent of reproaches. Then, sending the secretary off to the other end of the library with a pile of books, he whispered in my ear, "You have heard what they did to Professor Elia?"

"No," I replied.

"Emasculated!" he hissed. "I had it first-hand from one of the guests at last night's dinner. They say the doctors were with him throughout the night to save his life. There may be other victims."

"Signor Fossi," I began, "I'm sure nothing of the sort . . ."

He frowned me to silence, jerking his head towards the secretary. "They'll stop at nothing, nothing," he said. "Anyone in a position of authority may be threatened."

I murmured something about police protection.

"Police?" he almost screamed. "Useless! They'll be looking after the senior members of the staff. The backbone of the university, the men who do all the work, will have to fend for themselves."

Attempts to calm him were wasted. Green with fatigue after his sleepless night, he sat on one of the empty crates and watched me pack the books into another. I wondered which of us was the greater coward—he, who had turned to jelly through false rumour, or myself, because of the encounter in San Cipriano.

We did not break for lunch. Toni brought us sandwiches and coffee from the university canteen. The news was reassuring. The C and E students had called off the strike and attended the late morning sessions. Professor Elia had admitted a deputation to his house and received them in his dressing-gown. He had assured them that all was well. He had not been hurt. He refused to make any other comment, but implored the students, for his sake, to attend their lectures as usual. They must not think of taking revenge upon other students in the university.

"The lads agreed," murmured Toni in my ear, "just to keep him quiet. But it's not blown over. They're seething, every one of them."

Giuseppe Fossi left during the afternoon to attend a meeting of the university Council called for three o'clock, and I went up with Toni to the new building to help supervise the unpacking of the crates at that end.

It was as well for Giuseppe Fossi's reputation that I did so. The books had been stowed into the boxes with a total disregard for order, which meant double work not only for ourselves but for the clerks in the new library. I put Toni in charge of the van (in action again with a new windscreen), and stayed myself in the new library directing operations. One of the clerks, more thorough than the rest, soon had every volume dusted, sorted, and put in its allotted place in the bookshelves, while I busied myself with the catalogue.

The blowing and shaking of the dust by the energetic clerk brought various items to light which, after consultation with me, he disposed of in the waste-paper bin. Faded flowers, loose nameplates, forgotten letters, bills. It was almost time to knock off, and still no sign of Giuseppe Fossi, when the clerk brought me another letter to dispose of.

"Found this in a book of poems," he said, "but as it's signed by the Director of Arts, Professor Donati, perhaps it shouldn't be thrown away?"

He handed me the letter. I glanced at the signature. Aldo Donati. It was not my brother's handwriting, but my father's.

"All right," I said, "I'll take care of it."

As the clerk went back to his sorting I called, "Where did you say you found the letter?"

"In a collected edition of Leopardi," he replied, "belonging to someone called Luigi Speca. Or that at least was the name on the book-plate."

The letter was brief. The heading at the top of the page said 8, via dei Sogni, Ruffano. The date, November 30th, 1925. The faded black ink, the grey writing-paper, and my father's handwriting moved me strangely. The letter must have lain between the pages of Leopardi's poems for nearly forty years.

"Dear Speca,

"All is well. We are remarkably proud of our young fellow. He is putting on weight fast and has a terrific appetite. He also promises to be extremely handsome! My wife and I can never thank you enough for your great kindness, sympathy and friendship in our moment of trouble, now happily behind us. We both of us look to the future with confidence. Please drop in on us and see the boy when you can spare the time.

"Your sincere friend,
"Aldo Donati.

"PS.—Marta proves to be not only a devoted nurse but an excellent cook. She sends her respects."

I read the letter three times, then put it in my pocket. The handwriting might be faded, but the message was as fresh as if it had been written yesterday. I could hear my father's voice, strong and clear, full of pride in his young son, now apparently restored to health after a dangerous illness. The baptismal entry was now plain. Luigi Speca must have been the doctor who attended him, a predecessor of our Dr Mauri. Even the postscript about Marta was somehow poignant. She had entered our parents' service at this time and remained faithful to the end. The end . . . I had seen this morning in the church of San Cipriano. Requiem aeternam dona eis Domine.

The doors of the new library opened and Giuseppe Fossi entered, followed by Toni looking sullen. My superior had lost his haunted look, he was assured once more, and rubbing his hands briskly.

"All in order? Everything sorted?" he demanded. "What are those crates doing there? Ah, I see, all empty. Good." He cleared his throat, drew himself up, and bustled to the desk I had just quitted. "There will be no further trouble tonight," he announced. "The university Council has ordered a nine o'clock curfew for all the students. Any of them seen on the streets after that time will be reported and automatically expelled. This applies equally to employees on the university staff who may live in lodgings. Instead of expulsion they will lose their jobs." He looked pointedly at Toni, the other assistants and myself. "Special passes for those engaged on essential business can be obtained from the Registrar on application," he added, "and it will be easy enough for the authorities to check up, should they be abused. In any event, it will hurt nobody to spend an evening within doors. Naturally, the regulations will be relaxed tomorrow, the eve of the Festival."

I understood the reason for Toni's despondency. No encounter with his girl-friend in the piazza della Vita, or a trip round the via delle Mura on the vespa.

"What about the cinema?" asked Toni sullenly.

"The cinema by all means," answered Giuseppe Fossi, "provided you are back home by nine o'clock."

Toni shrugged, and muttering under his breath lifted one of the empty crates to bear it back to the van. Should I say anything to my superior about Aldo's invitation to the meeting at the ducal palace? I waited for the other assistants to move out of earshot, and then approached him.

"Professor Donati was good enough to give me a pass this evening for the ducal palace," I said. "There is to be a meeting to discuss the Festival."

He looked surprised. "Then that is the responsibility of Professor Donati," he replied. "As Director of the Arts Council of Ruffano he will be well aware of tonight's regulations. If he chooses to issue invitations to comparative strangers to the community it is his own affair."

He turned his back on me, obviously grudging the supposed honour done to me. I felt for the disk my brother had given me. It was safe in my pocket, alongside the forty-year-old letter from my father to Luigi Speca. I looked forward to showing this to Aldo. Meanwhile, I supposed that I too must obtain the late pass from the Registrar if I wanted to go to the ducal palace. It would not matter to my brother if I turned up or not, but my own curiosity was strong.

We closed down at the new building at seven o'clock and I walked across to the Registrar's office, which was already besieged by students applying for late passes. Most of them, accompanied by anxious relatives, had made plans for dinner which were now threatened with cancellation. The pre-celebration of the Festival would go by the board if the passes were not forthcoming, and the relatives would be left to languish in their lodgings and hotels. "It is completely childish," was the comment of one angry father. "My son is in his fourth year, and the authorities take it into their heads to treat him as an infant."

The patient clerk repeated for the second time that these were the orders of the university Council. The students had brought it upon themselves by disorderly behaviour.

The disgusted parent snorted in contempt. "Disorderly behaviour?" he said. "A little healthy fun! Haven't we all done the same in our time?"

He looked about him for approval, finding it. The parents and relatives queuing for passes were unanimous in blaming the authorities for being some twenty-five years behind the times.

"Take your son to dinner, signore," said the harassed clerk, "but have him back at the students' hostel by nine o'clock. Or in his lodgings, if he is quartered in the town. You will have all the opportunity you require for celebrations tomorrow and the day after."

One by one they turned away rejected, followed by their disgruntled and protesting young. I put my head in at the window of the Registrar with small hope of success.

"The name is Fabbio," I said, "Armino Fabbio. I'm an assistant at the library, and have an invitation from Professor Donati for a meeting at the ducal palace this evening at nine o'clock."

To my surprise, instead of instantly rejecting me the clerk consulted a list at his side.

"Armino Fabbio," he said. "That's quite in order. We have your name on the list." He handed me a slip of paper. "Signed by the Director of the Arts Council himself." The clerk even had the courtesy to smile.

I took the slip and edged out of the queue before the parent behind me had time to protest. Next problem, where to eat? I had no intention of pushing my way into the already crowded restaurants in the town—what few there were—or of joining the Silvani dining-table. I decided to try my luck at the university canteen. Here there was standing-room only, but I did not mind. A bowl of soup and a plate of salami, a pleasant contrast to the octopus of the night before, soon took the edge off appetite. The mass of students were so busy eating and declaiming at the same time against the detested curfew that I passed unnoticed, or at any rate was taken for granted as a lesser member of the university staff.

The general intention, so I gathered, both ears alert, was to make up for this evening's treatment by painting the town red on the Thursday and the Friday nights. All hell would be let loose.

"They can't stop us!"

"We can't all be expelled."

"I've got my degree anyway, so shit to the lot of them."

One of the big-mouthed students was standing at the far end of the counter with his back to me. This was lucky, because it was the fellow who had wanted to douse me in the fountain on the Monday afternoon.

"I'm just not standing for it," he said. "My father can pull strings, and if there's any trouble he'll get some of these professors on the university Council sacked. I'm twenty-one, and they can't treat me like a child of ten. I shall ignore the curfew and stay on the streets until midnight if I feel like it. Anyway, the curfew isn't intended for the C and E students. It's for all these little teachers who study Latin and Greek and go bye-byes at the students' hostel."

He looked about him, hoping for trouble. I had caught his eye on Monday and had no desire to catch it again. I slipped out of the canteen and made my way downhill to the ducal palace. The piazza Maggiore already wore an air of festival. Although it was barely dusk the palace was floodlit, and the Duomo too. The rose walls of the first had an incandescent quality and the great windows of the eastern façade, luminous and marble white, came suddenly alive. The palace was no longer a museum, a gallery hung with tapestries and pictures round which the tourist would prowl his indifferent way, but a living entity. Thus the link-boys saw it five hundred years ago, under moonlight and with flares and torches. Horses' hooves rang on the cobbled stones, mingling with the clink of spurs. Harnesses jingled as saddles and trappings were removed, grooms and servants scattered, and through the great carved portico walked or rode the returning scion of the Malebranche, his gloved left hand upon his sword.

Tonight the students, with some twenty minutes or so still to spare before curfew, strolled up and down, arm-in-arm with visiting relatives. A group by the fountain began to whistle and call at two girls who pattered by, feigning the inevitable disdain. Somewhere a vespa spluttered, somewhere there was a shout of raucous laughter. I went to the side-entrance and pressed the bell, feeling like a wanderer between two worlds. Behind me lay the present, slick, proficient, uniform, the young the same the globe over, mass-produced like eggs; and before me stood the past, that sinister and unknown world of poison and rapine, of power and beauty, luxury and filth, when a painting could be carried through the streets and worshipped by the rich and by the rabble alike; when God was feared; when men and women sickened of the plague and died like dogs.

The door was opened, not by the night-guardian, but by a boy dressed as a page. He asked for my pass. I handed him the disk Aldo had given me and he took it, saying nothing, and lifting the flare from the stand beside him preceded me across the quadrangle. There were no lights. I had not thought how dark the palace would be without electricity. I had seen the torch-lit apartments above on Saturday, but here below, and on the stairs, the normal lighting had been switched on. Not so tonight. As we mounted the great stairs the torchlight turned our shadows into giants. The page who climbed before me, in his belted doublet and hose, did not seem to be in fancy-dress. I was the interloper. The gallery surrounding the quadrangle was black as pitch. One single flare, stuck in a bracket, cast a baleful stream of light upon the door of the throne room. The page knocked twice upon it. We were admitted.

The throne room was empty, lighted in similar fashion to the gallery outside, with two flares set in brackets, and we went across it to the Room of the Cherubs at the further end, where the session had been held on Saturday. This too was empty, and lit by torches. The doors leading to the Duke's bedroom, and to the audience room, were shut. The page knocked twice upon the door of the first. It was opened by a young man whose face I recognised as one of those guitarists who had made so merry upon the stage at the theatre on Monday. I recognised nothing else. He wore a jerkin of bottle green, the sleeves slashed with purple, and his hose were black. On his heart he wore the emblem of a falcon's head.

"Is it Armino Donati?" he asked.

My second name, unused for at least seventeen years, surprised me.

"Yes," I said cautiously, "sometimes known as Armino Fabbio."

"Here we prefer Donati," he replied.

He jerked his head for me to enter. I did so and the door was closed, the attendant page remaining in the Room of the Cherubs. I looked about me. The Duke's bedroom was half the size of the preceding room, and it was lighted, like the others, by flares in brackets, these flares placed on either side of the one great portrait on the wall to throw it into relief so that it dominated the room. It was the portrait of the "Temptation of Christ", Christ bearing the likeness to Duke Claudio.

There were twelve men in the room, including the guitarist who had admitted me. They were all dressed as courtiers of the early sixteenth century, and wore the insignia of the Falcon. The scrutineers who had examined our passes on the Saturday were amongst them, and the two duellists, and others I had seen on the stage on Monday evening. I felt, and no doubt looked, an idiot in my modern garb, and to give myself assurance strolled over to the picture to examine it. No one took any notice of me. All were aware of my presence, but they chose, perhaps from delicacy, to ignore it.

The Christ Duke Claudio, lit by flares, stared out with greater power from his frame than he did by day. The crudity of the modelling did not show, and the rather awkward stance, the hand upon the girdle, the inelegant feet, were now subdued. The eyes, deep-lidded, distant, stared into a troubled future that might have seemed imminent to the painter's mind, threatening his world, or else quiescent, not to erupt till centuries later. The tempter, Satan, was the same Christ in profile, suggesting, not a lack of models, but a rash attempt at truth. The portrait might have lost its power to terrify, but not to cause unease. I wondered that it had survived five centuries, to confound the vandals and to mock the Church. Today the tourist, with his eye upon his watch, the message missed, would pass it by unquestioning.

I felt a hand upon my shoulder. My brother stood behind me. He must have entered the room from the small dressing-room and chapel beyond.

"What do you make of it?" he asked.

"You knew once," I said. "I used to act him, as I acted Lazarus. But never willingly."

"You might do so again," he said.

He swung me round, showing me to his twelve companions. Like them, he was wearing the same period dress, but for the colour. Like the tempter, he was all in black.

"Here is our Falcon," he said. "He can play Duke Claudio at our Festival."

The twelve men looked at me and smiled. One of them seized a saffron-coloured robe that was lying on a stool near the chapel entrance and belted it around me. Another picked up a golden-curled wig and clapped it on my head. A third brought me a mirror. Time was no longer with me. Neither this time, nor the time of centuries past. I had gone back to childhood, to my bedroom in the via dei Sogni, and stood still to obey my brother's commands. The men who surrounded me were his companions of the liceo long ago. As then, protesting that I did not want to play, I stammered now, in what I hoped were adult words, "Aldo, I'd rather not. I came here to watch the rest of you. Not to take part."

"One and the same thing," said Aldo. "We are all equally involved. I'm offering you a choice. The part of the Falcon, one short hour of glory and adventure in your life which will never come again; or to be turned loose tonight in the streets of Ruffano without a pass, when you will be picked up and, your identity established, given a grilling by the local police, who, so I was told earlier today, have been continually in touch with the police in Rome."

None of the young faces crowded round me was hostile. They were friendly; they were also ruthless. They stood there, waiting for my answer.

"Here you are safe," said Aldo, "whether with me or with them. All these twelve lads have sworn to defend you whatever happens. If you go out of the palace alone who knows what may happen to you?"

Somewhere, either in the city centre, or parading in plain clothes up and down the via Rossini, or watching by the porta del Sangue or the porta Malebranche, could be my police agent from Rome, waiting to question me. Useless to tell myself that they could not prove me guilty. The question was—should I be able to establish my innocence? Both Aldo's alternatives appalled me, but the second frightened me the more. The voice that came from me was not my adult voice, but sounded to my ears like the ghostly echo of a child of seven, who, wearing the blanket robes of Lazarus, was thrust into his living tomb.

"What do you want me to do?" I asked my brother.

CHAPTER SIXTEEN

We WENT THROUGH to the audience room. It was here that the tapestry on the western wall concealed the door leading to the second of the twin towers, where the guardian had ejected me on my first visit nearly a week ago. Tonight there was no guardian, only Aldo and his bodyguard, and the tapestry hung as usual, with no suggestion that behind it lay the hidden door and the narrow twisting stairway beyond.

The audience room was lit by flares also, and to the left, upon its easel, stood the portrait of the gentlewoman which my father so much loved, and which put me in mind of Signora Butali. Someone had placed a long wooden table in the centre of the room, and upon it glasses and a carafe of wine. Aldo went forward and poured wine into a glass for each of us.

"You don't have to do anything," he said, answering at last the question which I had put to him in the other room, "except do as I tell you, when the time comes. Acting won't be required of you. As a courier you will play your part to perfection, because it will come naturally." He laughed, and raising his glass said, "Drink to my brother!"

One and all lifted their glasses, crying "Armino!", their faces turned to me.

Then Aldo introduced them one by one, walking the whole length of the table, tapping each one upon the shoulder as he called his name.

"Giorgio, born near Monte Cassino, parents killed in the bombardment, brought up by relatives . . . Domenico, born in Naples, parents died of tuberculosis, brought up ditto . . . Romano, found abandoned in the hills after the German retreat, brought up by partisans . . . Antonio, ditto . . . Roberto, ditto . . . Guido, Sicilian, father killed by the Mafia, ran away from home, brought up by Sisters of the Poor . . . Pietro, parents drowned in floods in the Po valley, brought up by neighbours . . . Sergio, born in a concentration camp, mother living . . . Federico, ditto, but no surviving parents, brought up by an uncle . . . Giovanni, born in Rome, abandoned in a church, brought up by foster-parents . . . Lorenzo, born in Milan, father died, mother married again and stepfather a pervert, ran away from home, worked in a factory to save enough to enter university . . . Cesare, born in Pesaro, father drowned at sea, mother died giving birth to him, brought up in an orphanage."

Aldo came to the far end of the table and put his hand upon my shoulder. "Armino, known in the family circle as Beo, or Il Beato, because of his curls and his cherubic disposition. Born in Ruffano, father died in an Allied prison-camp, mother fled to Germany with retreating German officer, taking the boy with her, later married in Turin. And now you all know each other—or shall I say recognise one another?—for what you are. The lost and the abandoned. The despised and the rejected. Kicked along in the world to date by relatives and others who did what they had to but little else besides. I drink to you." He raised his glass and nodding to the twelve, and finally to me, drank his toast. "And now to business," he said, setting down his glass.

The lad nearest to him, Giorgio, brought forward a map, which Aldo spread upon the table in front of him. It was a large-scale map of the city of Ruffano. I drew near, with the others. The introductions, totally unexpected and fantastic, had the effect, temporary, perhaps, of making me lose my identity. I was not Armino, a lone courier without aim or mission, hunted possibly by the police, but another Giorgio, another Lorenzo.

"The course will run, as you know, from the piazza del Duca Carlo to the piazza Maggiore," Aldo said. "In other words, from the northern hill down to the city centre at the piazza della Vita, and uphill by the via Rossini to the ducal palace. The course will be clear until the piazza della Vita, and then the fun will begin. The citizens, represented by the C and E students, will converge upon the piazza from all five roads, with the exception of the via Rossini, which will be held by the Court, in other words by the Arts and Education students. The fighting will start immediately the cortège of the Falcon has passed the piazza della Vita and has begun to ascend the hill. You, and the courtiers on guard here at the palace, will keep the citizens back until the Falcon has passed safely through your ranks and has crossed the quadrangle and ascended the stairs to the ducal apartments. Is that clear?"

"Perfectly," agreed Giorgio, who seemed to be spokesman for the rest.

"Good," said Aldo. "Then all we have to do is to assign a given spot on the via Rossini to every courtier, which you can arrange with the volunteers, and hand over the plan of the side-streets to the C and E leaders. We shall be outnumbered by about three to one, but that's the glory of it."

He folded up the map. I hesitated before speaking. The query was so obvious as to seem absurd.

"What about the general public? Who will clear the streets?" I asked.

"The police," said Aldo. "They do it every year. But this year their instructions will be more explicit. No one but performers allowed in the area after a stated time."

"And where will the public watch from?" I persisted.

"From every available window," answered Aldo, smiling, "beginning with the piazza del Duca Carlo and so down to the piazza della Vita, and up the via Rossini to the palace."

I bit my thumbnail, a childhood habit long discarded. Aldo reached forward, and my hand fell instinctively to my side.

"Last year," I said, "or so I was told, the university staff took part and a large audience watched from inside the palace."

"This year," replied Aldo, "only a few privileged people will have seats in the palace. Most of the university staff will be in the piazza del Mercato."

"But that's below the palace," I protested. "How can they see anything from there?"

"They'll hear plenty," replied Aldo, "and be on hand for the final act, which will be the most outstanding."

Someone knocked on the door leading from the audience room to the gallery outside.

"See what it is," said Aldo.

One of the students—Sergio, I think it was—went to the door and talked briefly with the page who had admitted me inside the palace. After a moment he returned.

"The sentries have brought in a fellow prowling round under the western portico," he said. "He had no late pass, and when questioned was abusive. They want to know whether to let him go."

"City man or student?" Aldo asked.

"Student. C and E. A big lout, wanted a scrap."

"If he wants a scrap he shall have it," said my brother. He told Sergio to have the intruder brought in.

"It could be my bully," I said, "a fellow who wanted to douse me in the fountain after the uproar on Monday. I saw him in the canteen tonight, and he was boasting he hadn't got a pass and didn't care."

Aldo laughed. "So much the better," he said. "He might entertain us. Masks, everyone. And one for Armino."

Giorgio came over to where I stood and gave me a small black mask with slits for eyes, similar to those worn by the two duellists on Saturday. Self-consciously I put it on, as did Aldo and the twelve. When we were all masked and I looked around me and saw how we were lighted only by the flares, the rest of the room in shadow, I realised that to an outsider the effect would be far from reassuring, even startling.

The sentries, masked as we were, entered, bearing the prisoner between them. They had bandaged his eyes, but I recognised instantly the bully from the canteen. Aldo glanced towards me and I nodded.

"Loose him," said my brother.

The sentries threw off the bandage. The student blinked and looked about him, rubbing his arms. All he could see was a dark room lit by torches, and fourteen men disguised and wearing masks.

"No late pass?" enquired Aldo gently.

The bully stared. It was possible, I thought, that he had never entered the ducal palace in his life. If so, the surroundings would seem forbidding.

"What's it to do with you?" he countered. "If this is one of the Arts rags I'd better warn you you'll be sorry for it."

"No rag," said Aldo. "I have authority here."

Nobody moved. The student shifted on his feet. He rearranged his collar and tie, which had become dishevelled during his struggle to avoid arrest.

"What authority?" he asked aggressively. "Do you think by putting on fancy dress you can frighten me? My name is Marelli, Stefano Marelli, and my father owns a chain of restaurants and hotels along the coast."

"We are not interested in your father," said Aldo. "Tell us about yourself."

The question, smoothly asked, deceived the bully into greater confidence. He looked at the rest of us with condescension. "Commerce and Economics, third year," he said, "and it couldn't matter to me less if I'm expelled. I don't need a degree to get a job—I shall take over one of my father's restaurants. He also happens to be a member of the syndicate owning the Panorama, and anyone who sacks me on a flimsy excuse will find himself unpopular with a fair number of influential people."

"Unfortunate," murmured Aldo. He turned to Giorgio. "Is he on the list of volunteers?" he asked.

Giorgio, who had been consulting a list while the questioning took place, shook his head.

The student Marelli laughed. "If you mean the Communist do at the theatre on Monday night, I was not there," he said. "I had something better to do. I have a girl in Rimini, and a fast car. Draw your own conclusions."

Despite my strong dislike of everything about him, from his personal appearance to his attempt to douse me in the fountain, I felt some stirring of compassion. Every word he uttered made his fate more certain.

"In that case, you won't be taking part in the Festival?" asked Aldo.

"The Festival?" echoed the student. "That charade? Not likely! I shall slip home for the weekend. My father's throwing a big party for me."

"A pity," said Aldo. "We could have given you some excitement here. However, there's no reason why you shouldn't have a foretaste of it tonight. Federico?"

One of the bodyguard approached. In their masks they all looked alike, but the lithe build of this one, and the light hair above his mask, suggested to me that he was one of Saturday's duellists.

"Have we anything in the book that would suit Stefano?" asked Aldo.

Federico looked at me. "We had better consult Armino," he replied. "He's the expert."

"Federico's my translator," explained Aldo. "He marked the various passages for us from the German history. Born in a concentration camp, he has a facility for languages."

The unease that had come upon me since the arrival of the captured student grew stronger. I shook my head. "I remember nothing," I said.

Aldo turned once more to Federico, who, drawing a sheaf of papers from his doublet, consulted them. He read them through in silence while we waited. "The page," he said at last, "the incident of the page would suit Stefano well."

"Ah, yes, the page," murmured Aldo, "the punishment for the page who forgot the lights. To heap coals of fire upon the head of one who would douse in a fountain those smaller than himself would be a fitting climax to a braggart's career. See to it, will you?"

The student, Marelli, drew back at the approach of the two sentries and of Federico. "Now, look here," he said, "if you try any trick on me I warn you that . . ."

But he was interrupted. The sentries seized either arm. Federico, stroking his chin, gave the appearance of one plunged into thought.

"The old brazier," he said, "stored with the iron-work in one of the rooms on the upper floor. It would fit him like a crown. First, shall I read to him the passage from the book?" He pulled out the papers once again. They were copies of the notes I had given Aldo on Sunday. "On one occasion," he read, "a page, who had neglected to provide lights for the Duke's evening repast, was seized by the Falcon's bodyguard. They enveloped the wretched lad in cere-cloth coated with combustibles, and after setting fire to his head drove him through the rooms of the ducal palace to die in agony." He replaced the paper inside his doublet and signalled to the sentries. "Let's to it," he said.

The student Marelli, who not two minutes before had boasted wealth and influence, crumpled between his guards. His face went suddenly grey and he began to scream. The screams continued as he was dragged out into the passage, and they echoed along the gallery and up the stairs to the floor above. Nobody spoke.

"Aldo . . ." I said, "Aldo . . ."

My brother looked at me. The screams died down and there was silence.

"Renaissance man had no compassion, why should we?" he asked.

A sudden horror seized me. My mouth went dry. I couldn't swallow. Aldo removed his mask, and so did the others. Their young faces bore a fearful gravity.

"Renaissance man tortured and killed without compunction," continued Aldo, "but usually he had a motive. Someone had done him a wrong, and he acted from revenge. A mistaken motive, possibly, but that is open to argument. In our time men have killed and tortured for their own amusement and for experiment. Those screams you have just heard, caused solely by cowardice and not by pain, were uttered with just cause day after day, month after month, in Auschwitz and in other prison-camps. In the prison-camp, for instance, where Federico and Sergio were born. Romano heard them in the hills when the enemy caught and tortured his friends the partisans; so did Antonio and Roberto. If you had been abandoned, Beo, you might have heard them too. But you were lucky. You were preserved by conquerors, and led a sheltered life."

I tore off my mask. I searched each one of their grave, unsmiling faces, listening at the same time for some sound from the upper floor, but there was none.

"It doesn't work out like that," I said. "You can't torture that student above because of what happened in the past."

"He won't be tortured," Aldo said. "The most that Federico will do to him will be to set a fire-cracker on his head and drive him out. Unpleasant, but salutary. Marelli will benefit from the experience and think twice in future about soaking smaller men in fountains." He beckoned Giorgio to his side. "Tell Beo the true story of the assault on Signorina Rizzio," he said.

Giorgio was one of the bodyguard whom I recognised from Saturday. It was he who had been born near Monte Cassino, his parents killed during the bombing. He was a big, broad-shouldered lad with a shock of unruly hair, and when he had been masked just now had looked strangely formidable.

"The break-in was easy," he said, "and the girls we locked in their rooms were disappointed, so we thought, because we did nothing to them. Five of us went to Signorina Rizzio's room and knocked on the door. She opened it in her dressing-gown, thinking one of the girls had knocked. Then she saw us, all masked and doubtless dangerous, and told us quickly that she had no valuables, she kept nothing of any worth in the hostel. I said to her, 'Signorina Rizzio, the most valuable thing in the hostel is yourself. We have come for you.' She might have thought, from my words, that I meant to kidnap her, but her mind jumped to the obvious. She told us instantly that if it was that we were after we must go to the girls. The girls would be willing. We could do whatever we cared to do to them if we left her alone. I repeated my warning. 'Signorina Rizzio,' I said, 'we have come for you.' Then, luckily—at least, for us—she fainted. We carried her to her bed and waited for her to come round. When she did so, about ten minutes later, the five of us were standing at the door. We thanked her for her generosity, and left. That, Armino, is how the rape of Signorina Rizzio was accomplished. The sequel was what she made of it herself."

Giorgio's face had lost its gravity and he was laughing. So were the others. I understood the laughter, I could appreciate the hoax, and yet . . .

"Professor Elia," I asked. "Was that part of the pantomime as well?"
Giorgio looked at Aldo. Aldo nodded.
"Not my sortie," answered Giorgio. "Lorenzo was in charge."
Lorenzo, a Milanese like the Head of the Department of Commerce and Economics, was half the size of the man he had helped to strip. His manner was evasive, diffident, and he had the veiled eyes of an innocent child.
"Some of my friends amongst the C and E students," he murmured, "have suffered from the attentions of the Professor from time to time. Both male and

female. Therefore, after consulting with Aldo we worked out our plan of campaign. Entrance to the house was easy—Professor Elia thought at first that students wearing masks were the prelude to an intriguing game before dining at the Panorama. He soon learnt otherwise."

So I was right. My brother had been behind both incidents. I saw that in his view, and in that of these boys, justice had been done. The scales were balanced, according to the strange laws of Duke Claudio the Falcon over five hundred years ago.

"Aldo," I said, "I asked you this last night and you didn't answer me. What is it you are trying to do?"

My brother looked at his eleven companions and back to me. "Ask them," he said, "what they hope to achieve in life. They'll each give you a different answer according to his temperament. They are none of them totalitarians, you know, or ideologists. And they have their personal ambitions."

I looked at Giorgio, who was nearest to me. "Rid the world of hypocrisy," he said, "starting with the old men of Ruffano, and the women too. They came into the world naked like the rest of us."

"Scum settles at the top of a pool," said Domenico. "If you skim it off you find clear water underneath, and all the living things. Clear away the scum."

"Live dangerously," said Romano. "It doesn't matter where or how, but with your friends."

"Find hidden treasure," said Antonio. "It could be at the bottom of a test-tube in the lab. I'm a physics student, so I'm prejudiced."

"I agree with Antonio," said Roberto, "but no test-tubes for me. There's an answer somewhere in the universe when we explore further. And I don't mean heaven."

"Feed the hungry," said Guido. "Not with bread only but with ideas."

"Build something lasting that won't be swept away," said Pietro, "as the men of the Renaissance did, who built this palace."

"Tear down the barriers that exist everywhere," said Sergio, "the fence between one man and another. Leaders, yes, to show the way. But no masters and no slaves. That goes for Federico too—we've often discussed it."

"Teach the young never to grow old," said Giovanni, "even when their bones are cracking."

"Teach the old what it felt like to be young," said Lorenzo, "and by young I mean pint-sized, helpless, and inarticulate."

The answers came swift and sharp from every lad like successive rifle shots. The last, Cesare, was the only one to hesitate. Finally, glancing across at Aldo, he said, "I think what we have to do is to make the men and women of our generation care. It doesn't matter what they care about, whether it's football or painting, people or great causes, but they have to care, and to care passionately, and if necessary forget about their precious skins and die."

Aldo looked at me and shrugged his shoulders. "What did I tell you?" he said. "They've all given different answers. Meanwhile, on the floor above us, Stefano Marelli has only one thought in mind, and that is to save himself."

The screaming had started once again, and with it the sound of rushing feet.

Giorgio opened the door. The rushing, blundering footsteps descended the stairs and ran along the gallery, seeking an exit. We passed through the Room of the Cherubs and stood at the entrance to the gallery, peering into the darkness. A figure came towards us, his hands bound behind his back, wearing upon his head a broken bucket, the bottom of it punched with holes. Squibs had been stuck in the holes, and they were spitting and sparking as he ran. Sobbing, he tripped, and fell upon his face at Aldo's feet. The bucket rolled from his head. The squibs, with a final splutter, died. Aldo bent forward, and with a swift flick of a knife I had not seen cut the cord that bound the student's hands. Then he jerked him on his feet.

"There are your coals of fire," he said, kicking the bucket and the extinguished fire-crackers. "Children could play with them."

The student, still sobbing, stared. The bucket rolled along the gallery and settled. The acrid smoke filled the air.

"I have seen men," said Aldo, "run from their flaming aircraft like living torches. Be thankful, Stefano, you were not one of them. Now, get out."

The student turned and blundered along the gallery to the stairs. The shadow of his loping figure cast by the flare-light on the walls loomed shapeless and distorted, like a gigantic bat. The sentries followed, turning him across the quadrangle below, for he had lost all sense of direction, to let him loose through the great door between the towers. We heard the sound of his shuffling, frightened feet no more. The night enveloped him.

"He won't forget," I said, "neither will he forgive. He'll go back and rouse a hundred others like him. He'll magnify the story out of all recognition. Do you really want to set the whole city against you?"

I looked at Aldo. He was the only one amongst us who had not answered my earlier question.

"That," he said, "is inevitable. Whether Stefano tells his friends or not. Don't imagine I'm here to bring peace to this city or to the university. I'm here to bring trouble and discord, to set one man against the other, to bring all the violence and hypocrisy and envy and lust out into the open, on to the surface, like the scum on Domenico's pool. Only then, when it bubbles and seethes and stinks, can we clear it away."

It was then that the conviction took hold upon me, which I had rejected before through loyalty and love, that Aldo was insane. The seed of insanity had laid dormant in him through childhood and adolescence, and now, ripened doubtless through all he had seen and suffered in war and afterwards, the shock of our father's death, the disappearance and supposed death of our mother and myself, it was strangling his intellectual powers like a cancerous growth. The scum rising to the surface was his own madness. The symbol he took as the world's ills was his own disease. And there was nothing I could do, no way in which I could prevent him from setting alight a conflagration on the day of the Festival which might, figuratively speaking, burn the entire city. His band of devoted students, themselves warped by the legacy of their childhood, would stand by him and question nothing. One person only might have influence, Signora Butali, and she, as far as I knew, was still in Rome.

Aldo led the way back into the audience room. He discussed for some little while further plans for the Festival, the route points, timing, and other technical matters. I barely listened. One thing seemed imperative, and that was to get the Festival cancelled. Only the Rector could achieve it, no one else.

Some time around ten-thirty Aldo rose to his feet. The half-hour had just chimed from the campanile. "Now, Beo, if you're ready, I'll drop you back at the via San Michele. So long, my braves. See you tomorrow."

He went through to the Duke's bedroom and thence to the dressing-room. There he threw off his jerkin and hose, and dressed himself once more in his usual clothes. "Off with the masquerade," he said. "You do the same. Here, in the suitcase. Giorgio will see to it."

I had forgotten—for over an hour I had been wearing the golden wig and the saffron robe. He saw my sudden realisation, and laughed.

"It's easy, isn't it," he said, "to go back five hundred years. Sometimes I lose all sense of time. That's half the fun of it." Now, in his own suit, the disguise discarded, he looked as normal as any other man.

We walked through the Room of the Cherubs and the throne room, and so to the gallery. The page was waiting for us, to light us with his flare down the stairs and across the quadrangle to the side entrance. It was the page who now seemed out of place, a mummer dressed for a pageant, and the walls of the ducal palace, the silent quadrangle, held no more menace than a darkened, dead museum. We went out into the paved way and to the flood-lit piazza Maggiore. The Alfa-Romeo was parked outside the centre door, and beside it, as though to watch for loiterers, stood two carabinieri. I hesitated, but Aldo walked straight on. The men recognised him and saluted. One of them opened the door of the car. Only then did I follow Aldo.

"All quiet?" asked my brother.

"All quiet, Professor Donati," said the man who had opened the door. "A handful of students without late passes, but we've dealt with them. The great majority were sensible. They want to enjoy themselves during the next two days."

"They'll do that," laughed Aldo. "Goodnight, good hunting."

"Goodnight, professor."

I got in the car beside him and we drove off down the via Rossini. The street was as quiet as it had been the first night of my arrival almost a week ago. But tonight no snow, no freak reminder of past winter. The air was warm, with a soft humidity about it coming from the Adriatic across the chain of hills.

"What did you think of my boys?" asked Aldo.

"They do you credit," I said. "I wish I had had their chance. No one watched over me when I was a student in Turin and groomed me to act bodyguard to a fanatic."

He paused by the entrance to the piazza della Vita. "A fanatic," he repeated. "Is that really what you think of me?"

"Aren't you?" I asked.

The city was truly dead. The cinema had closed. The city stragglers had all gone home.

"I was," he said, "when I first sought out those boys, and picked them for their birth and background. In each one of them I saw you. A child abandoned on some bloody hill, torn by bullets or a bomb. It's different now. One becomes inured, if never reconciled. Besides, my emotion was wasted, as it turned out. You survived." He swerved into the via San Michele and drew up at 24. "Nurtured by Teutons, Yanks and Torinesi," he said, "to flower finally as a courier to Sunshine Tours. Those whom the gods love live long."

Doubt was with me once again. Doubt and dismay. Doubt that anyone who mocked with so much justice could be mad. Dismay that whatever he had done for those orphaned boys was done for me.

"What happens now?" I said.

"Now?" he echoed. "The immediate now or the hereafter? Tonight you fall asleep and dream, if you care to do so, of Signorina Raspa across the way. Tomorrow you can wander at will about Ruffano watching the preparations for the Festival. You dine with me. After that, we shall see."

He pushed me from the car. As I climbed out I suddenly remembered the letter in my pocket. I pulled it out.

"You must read this," I said. "I found it quite by chance this afternoon. Tucked between the pages of a book amongst the volumes we were sorting in the new library. It's all about you."

"About me?" he asked. "What about me?"

"Your prowess as an infant," I said. "Listen, I'll read it to you, and then you shall keep it as a memento of your lively past."

I leant across the open window of the car and read aloud the letter. When I had finished I looked up at him and smiled, throwing the letter on his knee.

"It's touching, isn't it," I said, "how proud they were of you."

He did not answer. He sat motionless, his hands upon the wheel, staring straight ahead, his face expressionless and very pale.

"Goodnight," he said abruptly, and before I could answer the car shot away down the via San Michele and round the corner out of sight. I stood there, staring after it.

CHAPTER SEVENTEEN

WHY HAD THE letter produced that effect upon Aldo? I could think of nothing else, either as I went to bed or when I awoke the following morning. I could not remember the letter line for line, but it spoke of "our young fellow's" progress and his promise of good looks, and thanked Luigi Speca for his great kindness during a period of trouble which was happily over. As Luigi Speca had also signed the baptismal register in San Cipriano I judged him to be both godfather and the doctor who had attended Aldo's birth—which, from the double entry, must have been difficult, with Aldo nearly losing his life, and perhaps our mother hers. This would be the "time of trouble" referred to in the letter. But why should Aldo mind? The letter had moved me, but not as deeply as all that. I had expected him to laugh, and even make some quip about having passed for dead. Instead, the hard immobile face, the swift departure.

I did not rush the next morning to arrive at the library on time. We should all be kept there until late, for in the afternoon students and their relatives were to be permitted to view the new library premises, due to be officially opened after the short Easter vacation. I breakfasted alone, my fellow-lodgers having already left.

Just as I had finished the telephone rang. Signora Silvani answered it, and came to tell me that it was for me.

"Someone of the name of Jacopo," she said. "He wouldn't give a message. He said you would know who it was."

I went into the hall, my heart pounding. Something had happened to Aldo. Something had happened because of last night's letter. I lifted the receiver.

"Yes?" I said.

"Signor Beo?"

Jacopo's voice was steady, without anxiety. "I have a message for you from the Capitano," he said. "The plans for the evening have been changed. The Rector, Professor Butali, and Signora Butali have returned from Rome."

"I understand," I said.

"The Capitano would like to see you here some time this morning," he went on.

"Thank you," I replied, and before he rang off I said to him "Jacopo . . ."

"Signore?"

"Is Aldo all right? Is anything worrying him?"

There was a second's pause. Then Jacopo said, "I think the Capitano did not expect Professor Butali back so soon. They arrived late last night. The luggage was being taken in when he passed the house on his return home just before eleven o'clock."

"Thank you, Jacopo."

I hung up. A letter written some forty years ago was now the least of my brother's problems. The sick man had got his own way with the doctors and had returned, if not to take active charge at least to be on hand for consultation.

I heard Signora Silvani moving in the dining-room, and left the house quickly before she could start a conversation. I must somehow see Signora Butali before Aldo did. I must urge her to use her influence to try to stop the Festival, how and with what excuse God only knew.

It was half-past nine. After the Butalis' long journey yesterday the signora would probably be at home this morning—ten o'clock might be a good moment to call. I turned into the via San Martino and started walking uphill to the via dei Sogni. The sun was already hot, the sky cloudless. The day promised to be one of those I remembered well from childhood, when the distant slopes and valleys shimmered in a blue haze of heat and the city of Ruffano, set proudly on its two hills, dominated the world below.

I came to the gate set in the wall of our old garden, passed through it to the front door of the house and rang the bell. The door was opened by the girl I already knew, and she recognised me too.

"Is it possible to see the signora?" I asked.

The girl looked doubtful, and said something about the signora being engaged—she and Professor Butali had only returned from Rome late last night.

"I know," I said, "but it is urgent."

She disappeared upstairs, and as I stood there waiting I noticed that once more the atmosphere of the house had changed. The dull vacuum of Monday morning was no more. She was home. Not only were her gloves lying on the table, a coat flung loosely on a chair, but an indefinable scent clung to the hall, a reminder of her presence. Only this time she was not alone. The house, instead of containing her only, and by so doing becoming the more mysterious, the more tempting, so that anyone calling like myself on my first mission, and afterwards on the Sunday, was secretly disturbed and furtively attracted—the house now held her husband too. It was his home, and he was master. That stick placed in its stand was like a totem-pole to tell the world. The overcoat, the hat, a suitcase still unpacked, parcels of books—there was a male smell about the house that had not been before.

The girl came running down the stairs and I heard, in her wake, the sound of voices, the sound of closing doors. "The signora will be down in a moment," she said, "if you would please come in here."

She showed me into the room on the left, the study that had been our dining-room. Evidence of the husband's presence was here too. A briefcase on the desk, more books, letters. And a faint but distinctive odour of cigar, smoked last night on arrival, not yet faded in the morning air.

I must have waited there ten minutes or more, biting my knuckles, before I heard her footsteps on the stairs. Then panic seized me. I did not know what I was going to say. She came into the room. At sight of me her face, though ravaged, tired—for she seemed in some way to have aged within four days— but also expectant and alive, fell in disappointment and surprise.

"Beo!" she exclaimed. "I thought Anna said Aldo. . . ." Then, swiftly recovering, she crossed the room and gave me her hand. "You must forgive me," she said, "I don't know what I'm doing. The silly girl said, 'The signore who was here for dinner on Sunday night,' and in my stupidity and rush. . . ." She did not bother to finish her sentence. I understood. In her stupidity and rush the signore who came to dinner on Sunday could signify one man only. And it was not me.

"There's nothing to forgive, signora," I said. "I have to apologise to you. I heard, through Jacopo, that you and your husband were home, that you arrived late last night, and I would not dream of disturbing you so early and on your first morning home if I didn't think the matter was urgent."

"Urgent?" she repeated.

The telephone rang in the music-room above. She exclaimed in annoyance, and was turning to leave the room with a murmured, "Excuse me," when we heard slow footsteps overhead. Then the ringing stopped and a male voice murmured indistinctly.

"Exactly what I didn't want to happen," she said to me. "If my husband once starts answering the telephone, and talking first to this one, then the other. . . ." She broke off, straining her ears to listen, but the murmur was too faint. "It's no use," she said, shrugging. "He's answered it, and there's nothing I can do about it."

I was wretchedly aware of the trouble I was causing. I could not have called at a worse time. There were hollows under her eyes that told of fatigue and strain. They had not been there on the Sunday night. On Sunday night the world about her could have died.

"How is the Rector?" I asked.

She sighed. "As well as he could be, under the circumstances," she said. "What happened earlier in the week was a great shock to him. But you know already. . . ." She flushed, the colour appearing on her naturally pale face like a sudden stain. "I believe it was you I spoke to on Tuesday night," she said. "Aldo told me. He telephoned me later."

"I have to apologise for that as well," I said, "I mean, for hanging up. I did not want to embarrass you."

She moved the letters on the desk, so that her back was turned to me. The gesture was one of withdrawal, a warning that to probe would be unwelcome. My mission became more difficult than ever.

"You were saying," she said, "that you had something urgent to tell me?" Even as she spoke, the voice overhead grew louder. We could distinguish nothing, but prolonged discussion had obviously begun.

"Perhaps I should go up," she said, anxiously. "So much seems to have gone wrong these last few days. Professor Elia. . . ."

"So you've heard?" I asked.

She gestured, her hands outspread, and began to pace quickly up and down the room.

"The first telephone call this morning was to give my husband an exaggerated account of something that happened on Tuesday night," she answered. "Not from Professor Elia himself, or from Professor Rizzio, but from one of the busybodies in whom this place abounds. In any event, the damage has been done. My husband is greatly distressed. Your brother is to come here later to explain things and to soothe him down."

"Signora," I said, "it is about Aldo that I've come to see you."

She stiffened, and her face became a mask. Only the eyes betrayed awareness. "What about him?" she asked.

"The Festival," I began. "I've heard him speak to the students about the Festival. It's become as real to them as it has to him, and therefore dangerous. I think it should be cancelled."

The anxiety behind her eyes vanished. She broke into a smile. "But that is the whole idea," she said. "It is always the same. Your brother makes the story—whatever it is they act—so vivid and so real that everybody taking part feels himself a character out of history. I know we all did last year. And the result was magnificent. Anyone will tell you."

"I wasn't here last year," I said. "All I know is that this year will be different. It won't take place in the ducal palace, for one thing, but in the streets. The students will be fighting in the streets."

She looked at me, still smiling. Her relief that I had not touched upon her relationship with Aldo was manifest.

"We went in procession in the streets last year as well," she told me, "or rather my husband did, as Pope Clement, with his very lifelike entourage. I was with the ladies and gentlemen of the Court, awaiting his arrival in the palace quadrangle. I promise you there will be nothing to fear, the police are used to it, it will be most orderly."

"How can an insurrection be orderly?" I asked. "How can students, told to be armed with any sort of weapon, keep themselves in check?"

She gestured with her hands. "They were armed last year," she replied, "and surely if any of the students get out of hand it will be easy enough to stop them? Don't think me unsympathetic, Beo, but we have been running these Festivals in Ruffano for the past three years. Or rather my husband has, with your brother to help him. They know how to handle these affairs."

It was useless. My mission had been in vain. Nothing I was likely to say would convince her, unless I betrayed Aldo direct. Told her what I had heard from his lips the night before. And this loyalty forbade.

"I find Aldo changed," I said, trying a different line, "more moody, cynical. He will switch from laughter and chaffing to sudden silence."

"You had not seen him for twenty-two years," she reminded me. "You must make allowances."

"Take last night," I pursued, "take last night in particular. I showed him an old letter of our father's that I'd discovered by accident in one of the library books. A letter to Aldo's godfather, a doctor, I believe, saying what a fine fellow was his son. I thought Aldo would be amused. I read it to him. He didn't say a word, but drove away."

Her patient, rather pitying smile was maddening. "Perhaps he was too much touched," she said, "and didn't want you to know it. He was devoted to your father, wasn't he, and your father very proud of him? Or so I've always understood. Yes, I think I can understand why he forgot to say goodnight. He may seem cynical to you, Beo, but it's on the surface only. In reality . . ."

She broke off, emotion suddenly breaking to the surface, giving the lie to frigidity, to reserve. That was how she must have looked, I thought, on Sunday night, in the music room above, when Aldo returned to her after bidding me goodnight, and the vespas spluttered and roared, encircling the city, and the masked students broke into the women's hostel to fake their assault on Signorina Rizzio. "The wife of the leading citizen had been profaned." The question was, which one? I had no doubt about the answer.

"I'm sorry," I said, "I've taken up too much of your time. Please say nothing to Aldo about my visit when he sees you. But warn him to be careful."

"I'll do that certainly," she replied, "and anyway my husband will want to hear all the details of the Festival programme, though he may not be well enough to attend himself. Listen . . ."

The conversation above had ceased. The footsteps moved across the floor to the door and on to the landing. They began to descend the stairs.

"He's coming down," she said quickly. "He's not supposed to walk up and down the stairs." She went swiftly to the door, then turned. "He doesn't know who you are," she said, the telltale spot of colour in her cheeks, "I mean, your relationship to Aldo. I told him someone had called on business, that I was not sure who it was."

Her guilt communicated itself to me. I followed her to the door. "I'll go," I said.

"No," she answered, "there isn't time."

We went into the hall. The Rector was already halfway down the stairs. He was a man who might have been any age between fifty-five and sixty-five, broad-shouldered, of medium height, grey-haired, with the fine eyes and regular features of one who had been handsome in his youth and was so still, though the grey texture of his skin gave proof of his recent illness. He had the air of authority and distinction of one who must immediately command liking and respect, even affection. My guilt increased.

"This is Signor Fabbio," said his wife as he paused at sight of me. "He came with a message about the library, where he is working as assistant. He was just going."

I realised that she was anxious for me to disappear. I bowed. The Rector inclined his head, wishing me good morning.

"Please don't let me rush you away, Signor Fabbio," he said. "I should like to hear about the new library, if you can spare a few minutes for me too."

I bowed again, the instinctive courier manner talking hold. Signora Butali shook her head.

"The doctors said you were not to come downstairs, Gaspare," she remonstrated. "I heard you answer the telephone. You should have called me."

He descended the stairs and stood between us in the hall. He shook my hand, his fine eyes searching me, then turned to his wife. "I should have had to take the call anyway," he said. "I'm afraid it was bad news."

I tried to efface myself, but he put out his hand. "Don't go," he said. "It is not personal. An unfortunate and very unhappy accident to one of the students, who was found dead this morning at the bottom of the theatre steps."

Signora Butali exclaimed in horror.

"It was the Commissioner of Police on the telephone," he continued. "He has only just heard of my return, and very properly informed me what had happened. It seems," he turned to me, "there was a curfew last night, because of certain incidents earlier this week, and all students, except those with late passes, were warned to be in their hostels or lodgings by nine o'clock. This lad, and possibly others, defied the order. He must have taken fright, hearing a patrol, and run, taking the shortest route, which happened to be those infernal steps. He stumbled and fell the whole length, breaking his neck. His body was found early this morning." The Rector put out his hand for his stick, which Signora Butali gave him. He made his way slowly into the room we had just left. We followed him.

"This is terrible," she said, "at this moment of all moments, just before the Festival. Has the news been given out?"

"It will have been by mid-morning," her husband answered. "You can't hush up these things. The Commissioner will be here directly to discuss it."

Signora Butali pulled forward the chair by the desk. He sat down. The grey pallor of his face seemed to have increased.

"I shall have to summon a meeting of the university Council," he said. "I'm sorry, Livia. You will have to do a lot of telephoning." He patted his wife's hand, which was upon his shoulder.

"Of course," she said, and gestured hopelessly at me.

"I can't believe the curfew was necessary," said the Rector. "I'm afraid the Council acted out of panic, with the inevitable result that certain students rebelled, and so came this fatality. Was there much disturbance?"

He looked at me. I did not know how best to answer him.

"The various groups were lively," I said. "There seemed to be much rivalry amongst them, especially between the C and E students and the Arts and Education. The sudden curfew caused a lot of dissatisfaction. There was talk of nothing else in the canteen last night."

"Exactly," said the Rector, "and the more high-spirited amongst them were determined to send authority to blazes. I should have done the same when I was a student myself." He turned to his wife. "It was Marelli's boy who died," he said. "You remember Marelli, we stayed at one of his hotels a year or two ago. I don't know much about the boy, a third-year student, but Elia will tell me. What a tragedy for the parents. An only son."

My throat was dry. Whatever Signora Butali said in sympathy I echoed huskily. She was no longer so anxious for me to go. Perhaps my presence made some sort of a diversion for her husband.

"What time is the doctor coming?" he asked.

"He said half-past ten," she answered. "He might be here at any moment now."

"If the Commissioner of Police arrives first the doctor must wait," her husband said. "See if you can reach him, dear, at his home. If he's not at home he'll probably be at the hospital, and he can walk down from there. It's only two minutes away."

She paused a moment before leaving the room, flashing me a look of warning. It could have meant that I was not to tire him. It could have meant that I was not to talk of Aldo. All I wanted was to leave the house before the Commissioner arrived. But first I would have my say.

"This accident, professor," I said, "will it mean a cancellation of the Festival?"

He had taken up a small cigar and was busy lighting it. It was a moment or two before he answered. "Hardly that," he said. "There are something like five thousand students in the university of Ruffano, and to cancel one of their great days of the year because of a regrettable and unhappy accident to one of them would verge on hysteria. It would not be a good thing to do." He drew on his cigar and frowned. "No," he repeated, "you can rest assured that we shan't cancel the Festival. Why, are you taking part?"

The question took me by surprise. The gimlet eyes pierced me. "I'm not sure," I said. "Professor Donati might want me for some minor role."

"Good," he replied, "the more who take part the better. He is due here presently. I shall hear all about it. His choice of this year's subject rather surprised me, but he is sure to handle it superbly. He always does. Where are you from?"

"Where am I from?" I repeated.

"Your home, your university. I take it you are with us on a temporary basis?"

"Yes," I said, my throat tightening again. "I come from Turin. I needed a job to fill in time. I have a degree in modern languages."

"Good. And what do you think of our new library?"

"I've been very much impressed."

"And how long have you been working here?"

"A week."

"A week only?" He removed his cigar and stared. He looked surprised. "Forgive me," he said. "I happened to hear the maid say to my wife that the gentleman who had been to dinner on Sunday wanted to see her. I had not realised she had been giving a large party for the members of the university staff."

I swallowed. "Quite a small party," I said. "It was my good fortune to bring some books from the library for Signora Butali, and she was kind enough to play for me. The invitation to dinner came about after that."

"I see," he said.

He looked at me again. The look was somehow different. Appraising. The look of a husband who suddenly wonders why his beautiful wife should take it into her head to play the piano to a stranger and then invite him to dinner. It was evidently not a usual thing for her to do.

"You are fond of music?" he asked.

"Passionately," I answered, hoping to assuage his interest.

"Good," he said again. Then, abruptly, he fired another question. "How many were there at this party?" he asked.

I felt myself trapped. If I answered half-a-dozen it would be a lie, easily detected later when he might come to question her, and the answer would trap her too.

"You misunderstand me, professor," I said rapidly. "The party was on the Sunday morning."

"Then you didn't come to dinner?"

"I came to dinner too," I said. "I was brought by Professor Donati."

"Ah," he said.

I began to sweat. There was nothing else I could say. He could always question the maid, if not his wife.

"It was a musical evening," I explained. "The idea in coming was to listen to Signora Butali playing. She played to us until we left. It was a memorable evening."

"I am sure it was," he said.

Somehow I must have made a gaffe. Signora Butali, when she arrived at the hospital in Rome the following day, could have told a very different story. She could have said that she had dined alone on the Sunday night, and then, seized with anxiety about her husband, had left early the next morning for Rome to be at his bedside. I did not know.

"In Rome," he said, following a line of thought, "I became very out of touch with life in Ruffano."

"Yes," I said, "that's understandable."

"Although," he continued, "well-meaning friends did their best to keep me informed of everything that went on. Some of them perhaps not so well-meaning."

I smiled. A forced smile. The direct eyes were searching me again.

"You say you have only been here a week?" he reiterated.

"A week today," I said. "That's correct. I arrived last Thursday."

"From Turin?"

"No, from Rome." I could feel the sweat beginning to break out on my forehead.

"Had you been working in one of the libraries in Rome?"

"No, professor. I was passing through. It just happened that I took it into my head to visit Ruffano. I needed a holiday."

My story, even to my own ears, sounded false. It must have sounded doubly false to him. My nervousness was all too obvious. For a moment he said nothing; his ears were cocked to the sound of Signora Butali's voice on the telephone overhead, just as ours had been to the sound of his some minutes earlier.

"I apologise, Signor Fabbio," he said, after the pause, "for asking you such a string of questions. It's only that while I was in Rome I was bothered with anonymous telephone calls with certain allusions to Professor Donati. I tried to have the calls traced, but could only discover that they were made locally. The strange thing was that the caller—who was a woman, for I heard her whispering instructions—did not speak to me direct but through a third person, a man. It just occurred to me—and forgive me if I am wrong—that you might have been the man, and could tell me something about these calls."

This time my look of profound astonishment must have reassured him.

"I know nothing about any calls, Professor," I said. "I think it is best to tell you at once that I am a travel agent. I work with a firm in Genoa, and I was travelling for this firm with a coach-party from Genoa to Naples, via Rome. I certainly made no calls to you. I had never heard your name until after I arrived in Ruffano."

He put out his hand to me. "That's enough," he said. "Please think no more of it. Put it right from your mind. And don't mention the matter to anyone, above all my wife. The calls, like anonymous letters, were unpleasant, but there have been none now for more than a week."

The front-door bell sounded its alarming peal. "That will be the Commissioner of Police," he said, "or the doctor. I apologise again, Signor Fabbio."

"Please, professor," I murmured.

I bowed, and turned to the door. I could hear the girl going to answer the bell and Signora Butali descending the stairs at the same time. I went out into the hall and effaced myself as the front-door opened. The sight of the Commissioner in his uniform made me retreat still further towards the kitchen regions. Signora Butali's figure hid me from view as she showed him into the study. Then she turned to say goodbye to me. The girl who had opened the door still hovered within earshot; I could not warn Signora Butali of the conversation that had taken place between her husband and myself.

"We shall be seeing you again, I hope," she said, reverting to the formal manner of a hostess speeding the departing guest.

"I hope so too, signora," I replied, and then her husband called her into the room and she waved her hand at me and vanished.

I walked down the paved path and into the street, where the Commissioner's car was waiting, a uniformed police driver at the wheel. I turned left, so as not to pass him, and walked rapidly downhill. It did not matter where I went as long as I put some distance between myself and the police car. I decided to return to my room, stay there awhile, and then walk back to my brother's house. The news of Stefano Marelli's death had profoundly shocked me, but I was equally disturbed by what the Rector had said about anonymous telephone calls.

When I reached the via San Michele and started to walk towards the Pensione Silvani I saw that a man was standing before the door, talking to the signora. The figure, the bared head, the face in profile, were instantly recognisable. It was the police agent from Rome, the agent in plain clothes whom I had seen in church on Tuesday.

I was opposite No. 5, and instinctively I ducked inside the open door and climbed to the first floor. I knocked at the door of Carla Raspa's apartment. There was no answer. I turned the handle and found it open. I went in, and closed the door behind me.

CHAPTER EIGHTEEN

I THOUGHT THE room was empty, but the sound of the closing door disturbed someone in the bathroom. A woman came through wearing an apron, a floor-cloth in her hands. She stared at me suspiciously.

"What do you want?" she asked.

"I have an appointment with Signorina Raspa," I lied. "She told me she might be late and asked me to wait for her."

"Very well," said the woman. "This room is ready, but I haven't yet finished in the bathroom and kitchen. Make yourself comfortable."

She turned back to the bathroom and I heard the sound of running water. I crossed to the window and looked down the street to No. 24. The man was still there. Signora Silvani, waxing expansive, was doing most of the talking, and I could see her gesturing. She must be talking about me. She must be telling the agent that I worked every day in the library, that I would probably be there now, that I had been a guest under her roof for a week exactly, that I was a stranger to Ruffano. If he had explained who he was and given proof of his identity, surely he would demand to see my room? Surely he would go upstairs and open the drawers, search the cupboards and my suitcase? He would find nothing of any use to him. I carried my papers on me. But so far Signora Silvani had made no attempt to ask the man inside. They were still talking. Then the cleaning woman came back into the room and I drew away from the window.

"Would you like some coffee?" she asked.

"Please don't trouble yourself," I answered.

"No trouble," she said. "The signorina would wish it."

There was something familiar in the woman's face. She was young and not ill-looking, but with dishevelled hair suggesting an abortive attempt to copy some film-star on a cinema poster.

"I've seen you before, haven't I?" she asked.

"I was thinking the same," I replied, "but Ruffano is not a big city. Perhaps it was in the street."

"Perhaps," she said with a smile and a shrug.

She went into the kitchen and I returned to the window. In the interval the man had disappeared, but whether into the house or further down the street there was no way of telling. I stationed myself by the window, and picking up a magazine flicked the pages idly, keeping the house in view. In a moment the woman returned with the coffee.

"Here you are, signore," she said, "and I've remembered where it was I saw you. You were watching the crowd, near the Ognissanti. You asked me what it was about and why the police car was there. I had my baby in my arms, she was crying. Remember?"

I did. Ruffano was small indeed. There was no escape.

"You're right," I said. "I do remember now. Two people were getting into the car."

"The Ghigis," she said, "and it was just as I told you, they had to identify poor Marta Zampini's clothes. The police took them all the way to Rome—just imagine driving all that distance in a police car! If it hadn't been for such a wretched cause they would have enjoyed it. Neither of them had visited Rome before in their lives. And then the body was brought back and they buried her yesterday. What a crime, though! All for ten thousand lire. The wretch who did it still refuses to confess. The theft, yes, he acknowledges, according to what my husband read out to me from the paper, but not the murder. I suppose he hopes to save his skin by lying."

"Probably," I said. I drank the coffee, one eye still on the pensione further up the street.

"They'll force him to confess," she added. "The police have their methods; we all know that." She stood watching me drink the coffee, conversation making an interlude in the morning's work.

"Did you know the murdered woman?" I asked.

"Know Marta Zampini?" she repeated. "Everyone who lived near the Ognissanti knew Marta. She and Maria Ghigi used to work for Professor Donati's father in the old days. You know Professor Donati of the Arts Council?"

"Yes, I know him."

"They were saying yesterday that it was he who arranged for the police to bring back the body, and he paid for the burial. He's a wonderful man, he's done so much for Ruffano, like his father before him. If old Marta had continued to work for him she would have been alive today."

"Why did she leave?"

The woman shrugged. "Too much of this." She made a gesture of drinking. "She had gone to pieces during the past few months, so the Ghigis said. Always brooding. No one knows what she had to brood about, they took good care of her. Maria Ghigi said she was never the same after the war, when her life with the Donati family broke up. She missed the little boy. She was forever talking about the little boy, the professor's brother, who disappeared with the German troops. Well, that's life, isn't it? There's always something to go wrong."

I finished my coffee and pushed away the tray. "Thank you," I said.

"Let's hope Signorina Raspa won't be long," she said, and then with a sly, long glance at me she added, "She's handsome isn't she?"

"Very handsome," I agreed.

"The signorina has many admirers," she said. "I know, because I often have to clear up after they have been to dinner."

I smiled, but did not comment.

"Ah, well," she said, "I must be going. I have to do my own shopping before my husband comes home for his midday meal. Luckily my mother looks after the baby while I'm here working for the signorina."

There was still no sign of life from No. 24. The agent would have had time to search my room and come downstairs again. Perhaps he was having coffee too, with Signora Silvani. I pretended interest in the magazine. Some five minutes later the woman returned from the kitchen. She had put a cardigan over her dress and was carrying a string bag.

"Well, I'm off," she said. "I hope you spend a pleasant day with the signorina."

"Thank you," I said.

She wished me good morning and went out of the apartment. I heard her go downstairs and watched her walk up the via San Michele. I stayed there, my eyes fixed on No. 24, but no one entered or came out. The agent must have gone. He must have gone some while ago, when the cleaning woman first came in and suggested coffee. Now he could be anywhere, up at the university, perhaps, making enquiries at the Registrar's office or the library. Because of this the library was now barred to me. The Silvani pensione too. There was no refuge left but the apartment in which I sat, and my brother's house in the via dei Sogni. And if I left the apartment and walked up the hill to Aldo's house I might meet the agent on the way. He could even be watching for me to return to the Silvani pensione.

I pulled out a packet of cigarettes and began to smoke. I thought about the student Marelli breaking his neck at the bottom of the theatre steps. It was on those same steps that I had met the frightened boy on Friday of last week. Obviously he had been a student too. There had been no curfew then, but Aldo's sentries must have questioned him, as part of their fantastic, mediaeval game. This time the game had ended in a student's death. Were the scales of heavenly justice finally balanced? Could the game now end?

Aldo, in his capacity as Director of the Arts Council of Ruffano, was a member of the university board. He would thus attend the meeting called by the Rector for later in the day. Like everyone else, he would accept the reason which had been given for Marelli's death—that the student, taking fright, had run from a patrol—but in his heart he must surely acknowledge the true cause.

I looked at my watch. It was twenty-five minutes past eleven. I began to walk up and down the room. I looked out of the window. All was still quiet at No. 24. When Carla Raspa returned, what would be my excuse for being there? I had not seen her since the Tuesday night when I had, so ungallantly and deliberately, walked out on her. It was a strange moment to apologise.

I went through into the bathroom. Jars and bottles were on the shelves, and a dressing-gown had been flung on a stool. A nightgown, hastily rinsed through, hung limply on a hanger above the bath. The bidet was full of soapy water in which a pile of stockings had been left to soak. The sight made me sick. I went back into the kitchen, retching. The disorder, the intimacy, reminded me of hotel bedrooms long ago, in Frankfurt and other cities, when side by side with my mother's underwear, similarly washed and rinsed, would be male socks and handkerchiefs, tooth-brushes and hair-lotion. Streaky hairs would be lying in the bath. As a boy of eleven, or twelve, my stomach had heaved. The stench of lust pursued me across Germany to Turin. It followed me still.

I went and sat by the open window once again and lit another cigarette. I wondered what woman was it who, inspired by jealousy, had put through the anonymous telephone calls to the Rector in his hospital bed in Rome. A discarded mistress of my brother's, perhaps, or someone who had aspired to that position and failed. The woman, whoever she was, must have guessed the relationship between Aldo and the Rector's wife. The calls might have ceased, but Aldo must be warned before he himself spoke to the Rector. I might telephone Jacopo asking him to tell Aldo, as soon as he returned home, to put through a call to me here in Carla Raspa's apartment.

I fingered through the directory and found the number. I asked for it and waited. There was no answer. Jacopo was either out or in his own domain. I put down the telephone and went again to the window. A bunch of students was coming up the street, shouting and whistling, dressed for a masquerade in their coloured hats donned for the occasion, one of them carrying a bag on a stick which he thrust into the faces of passers-by.

"Help the poor scholars' fund," he called out. "Contributions welcome, however small. Every cent given will help some poor scholar to complete his education. Thank you, signore, thank you, signorina."

A man, shrugging, put something in the bag. A girl, pursued with hoots and whistles, did likewise, and laughingly escaped. The students spread out fan-wise across the street. A car coming downhill was stopped and the bag was poked through the window. The student bowed his thanks, flourishing his mediaeval hat.

"Thank you, signore, long life to you, signore."

They continued up the street, still singing, shouting, and turned in the direction of the piazza della Vita. The campanile beside the Duomo sounded twelve, echoed, before the last strokes finished, by the bells from San Cipriano. Noon sounded from every quarter of Ruffano, and I thought how in centuries gone by a fugitive like myself sought sanctuary within a church by the high altar. I wondered, if I did the same today, whether I should find protection, or whether the sacristan in San Cipriano would look at me aghast and straightway run blabbing to the police.

Then I heard footsteps coming up the stairs. The door opened. It was Carla Raspa. She stared at me, dumbfounded.

"I was just deciding," I said truthfully, "whether to remain here in your apartment or seek sanctuary in church."

"It depends on your crime," she said, closing the door behind her. "Perhaps you should confess it first."

She laid her bag and a parcel of books on the table. Then she looked me up and down. "You're about thirty-six hours late for our appointment," she said. "I don't mind waiting one hour for a date, or possibly two, but after that I prefer to find a substitute."

She reached in her bag for cigarettes and lit one. Then she passed into the kitchen and returned with a bottle of Cinzano and two glasses on a tray. "I suppose," she said, "the reason you ratted was that you funked the issue. It's happened before to bigger boys than you. I've usually managed to overcome it, though. There are ways and means." She poured the Cinzano into the glasses. "Courage!" she said. "You never know how good a thing can be until you try it."

She lifted her glass to me and smiled. I had never known anyone more magnanimous. I took the other glass. As I drank the Cinzano I came to a decision.

"I'm not here to apologise for Tuesday night," I said, "or to make good a reputation lost. I'm here because I believe the police are tailing me."

"The police?" she echoed, setting down her glass. "Then you have committed a crime—or are you joking?"

"I've committed no crime," I said. "I happened to be on the site of a murder ten days ago, and I suspect the police want to question me."

She saw from my face that I was not joking. She handed me one of her cigarettes. "You don't mean the murder of that old woman in Rome?" she asked.

"I do," I answered. "I gave her ten thousand lire the night she was killed. My reason for doing so doesn't matter. Next morning I learnt that she had been murdered. No need to tell you I didn't do that, but I gave her the money within minutes, possibly, of the crime. Clearly, therefore, I'm someone the police would be interested in."

"Why?" she asked. "They've caught the man, haven't they? It was reported in the newspapers."

"They've caught him, yes," I told her. "He admits the theft of the ten thousand lire but denies the murder."

She shrugged her shoulders. "So would I," she said. "That's up to the police. Why should you worry?"

I saw that I must explain further. I told her about the English tourists and how I had taken them to the police, but had said nothing about my gift of money, and had left for Ruffano the next day.

"Why did you do that?" she asked.

"Because I recognised the woman," I said, "and to be doubly sure I came to Ruffano to find out."

She finished her drink, and seeing that I had finished mine poured me another. Her manner was still casual, but more guarded than before. "I read in the paper that the woman came from Ruffano," she said. "How was it you happened to know her?"

"I was born here," I said. "I lived in Ruffano until I was eleven years old."

She shot a look at me across the table, then refilling her glass moved to the divan, propping the cushions behind her back. "You've been living quite a lie here for the past week, haven't you?" she said.

"You might call it that."

"And now the lie is catching up with you?"

"Not so much the lie as my omission to tell the truth to the police in Rome," I said, "and the fact that I believe one of their plain-clothes agents recognised me at Marta's burial service on Tuesday. He could hardly have regarded it as a coincidence. An hour ago this same agent was making enquiries at No. 24. I saw him from across the street and came in here."

She lay back against the cushions blowing smoke-rings in the air. "Coincidence or not," she said, "he would certainly think it suspicious. But if they've caught their man in Rome what are they doing here bothering about you?"

"I've already told you," I said. "The man denies he did it. It could be that they believe him, and the search for the murderer goes on."

She considered a moment, then looked across at me. "It could be that I believe him too," she said.

I shrugged my shoulders and moved towards the door. "In that case," I said, "I may as well clear out. You can report me to the police over the telephone."

At that moment the telephone rang. I felt it must be fate—the game was finished. She held up her hand to me to stay, then lifted the receiver. "Yes," she answered, "yes, Giuseppe . . . Lunch?" She paused, looked at me, shaking her head. "No, it's impossible, I've people coming. A student and her mother, due any minute now. I didn't know last night—they only telephoned this morning. I don't know, Giuseppe, I can't make plans . . . If it's possible I'll telephone you this afternoon at the library. So long." She hung up, smiling. "That's settled him for a few hours," she said. "You're in luck he telephoned and didn't walk right in. We had a tentative engagement for lunch which, as you see and I hope appreciate, I've turned down for you. Oh, don't worry. We won't go out. I'll make an omelette." She swung her legs down from the divan and smoothed her hair.

"Then you don't think I'm a murderer?" I asked her.

"No," she said. "Frankly, I doubt if you'd have the nerve to kill a wasp, let alone a woman."

She went into the kitchen and I followed her. She started doing things with pans at the stove and moving dishes from the rack. I sat down on one of the chairs and watched her. My confession had acted like a purge. Our relationship seemed suddenly easier.

"I suppose you want me to get you out of Ruffano?" she asked. "It shouldn't be difficult. I can borrow the car again."

"Not out of Ruffano," I told her, "just up the hill to a house in the via dei Sogni."

"Then you have a friend who knows all about you?"

"Yes," I said.

She hummed under her breath as she broke eggs into a basin and forked them briskly. "Do you mind telling me who it is?" she asked.

I hesitated. I had already committed my immediate fortunes to her hands, and I saw no reason to commit my brother.

"You don't have to tell me—I've already guessed," she said. "You forget, Ruffano is a small city. My daily cleaner lives near the Ognissanti, and I heard all about the murdered woman from her days ago. Old Marta lived for years with the Donati family, and looked after Aldo Donati when he was a boy. Did you visit his home when you were a child, and is that why you remembered her?"

Her guess was ingenious. It was also not quite the truth, but it served my purpose.

"As a matter of fact, yes," I answered her.

The smoke was rising from the pan and she poured in the eggs. "So you went and told your story to Donati?" she said. "And instead of advising you to scamper he suggested you stayed put?"

"That's about it."

"Was this last Sunday?"

"Yes," I said.

"Then it was you who was with Donati all Sunday afternoon and evening?"

"Yes," I said again.

The omelette was done. She slid it on to the dish and brought it to the table. "Eat it while it's hot," she said, drawing in a chair for herself.

I did as she told me, wondering what she would ask me next. She said nothing while we ate, rising from the table merely to fetch a bowl of salad and a bottle of wine. Her smile was enigmatic. I grew curious.

"Why are you smiling?" I asked.

"The truth has dawned on me," she said. "I should have guessed before, when your noble friend didn't take the trouble to answer my letter. He's not interested in women. A playmate from the past has more allure. Especially a baby-face like you."

This was a curious conjecture which no one would appreciate more than Aldo. I wondered whether to demur or let it go.

"Ah well," she said, "life is full of shocks. I'd never have believed it, though, of him. It only goes to show how wrong one can be. Still, it's a challenge. These escapades can pall." She forked her salad thoughtfully, and stared beyond me. "There's been some curious talk amongst the students," she mused. "Those rehearsals at the ducal palace behind closed doors—they could have been a cover for something else. If they were, Donati had me fooled on Saturday. I'd have followed him to the grave."

Still I said nothing. To comment either way might prove disastrous.

"Did you know a student broke his neck last night?" she asked.

"I heard a rumour."

"It's not official yet, but it soon will be. Defied the curfew, and ran from the patrols. At least, that's the story. A C and E lad in his third year. One wonders what their crowd will make of it. It may be the final straw."

She got up from the table once more and returned with fruit. She chose a pear and began to munch it, holding it unskinned between her hands, the juice running down her chin.

"What do you mean, the final straw?" I asked.

"The breaking-point between their crowd and ours," she said. "If so, God help us all tomorrow when Donati gets his performers into the streets. That concession of his to invite the C and E students to take part in the Festival won't conciliate the rival factions, as he believes—it will have the opposite effect."

She laughed, and sucking the pear-core dry threw the remains into the refuse pail below the sink. "Your Arts Director wasn't going to arm his women," she said, "but I can tell you this. Most of the girls I've lectured to the last few days are determined not to miss the battle, and if the C and E crowd attack their boy-friends we'll see all hell let loose. I pity the police."

She rose and stood by the stove, warming the coffee. "Anyway," she said, "they'll be too busy to look for you. You'll be safe and snug in Aldo Donati's hide-out. What's his house like? Monkish or affluent? Deep-carpeted or bare?"

"If you borrow that car and drive me there you might get a chance to see," I told her.

No sooner spoken than regretted. Aldo would have enough to contend with without adding Carla Raspa to the number. Yet I saw no way of getting to the via dei Sogni without her help.

"That's true," she answered smiling. "If I deliver his little playmate to him in person the least the Professor can do is to invite me in."

The telephone rang again. She went through to the living-room to answer it. I stood and listened. Like every fugitive, I expected any telephone call to refer to me.

"No, no, I'm still waiting for them," she said impatiently, shaking her head. "Something must have held them up, you know what the crowds are like already in the streets."

She held her hand over the mouthpiece and whispered across the room at me, "Giuseppe again. He thinks I'm expecting guests." She uncovered the mouthpiece. "You have a meeting. At a quarter to two. I understand. At the Rector's house. Is he back?" She looked at me, excited. "About the accident, naturally. I wonder what he'll have to say. Tell me, will Professor Donati be there? I see . . . Well, you'd better telephone me here when it's over. So long." She came back into the kitchen, smiling. "Butali's back," she said. "He's called a meeting of the university Council for a quarter to two. When he finds out what's been happening this past week he'll have another thrombosis."

She went over to the stove and returned with the coffee. I looked at my watch. It was just after one. I crossed the room and glanced out of the window. The car we had borrowed on the Tuesday evening was parked below.

"Giuseppe didn't know whether Donati was to be at this meeting or not," said Carla Raspa. "I see no point in dropping you at his house if we can't do it in style with the host there."

"To hell with style," I said. "The important thing is to get me there. Then your responsibility ends."

"Ah, but I don't want it to end," she said.

There was sound of movement from the apartment overhead. Heavy footsteps shook the ceiling.

"My neighbour with the car," said Carla Raspa. She went to the door and out on to the landing. Halfway up the stairs she shouted, "Walter?" The neighbour shouted back.

"Can I borrow the car for half-an-hour?" she called. "I've an important errand that can't be managed on foot."

The neighbour overhead called something in return that I couldn't catch.

"Oh, yes," she cried, "you shall have it back by half-past two."

She returned to the room, smiling. "He's very obliging," she told me, "but naturally I keep him that way. See how it pays. Let's drink our coffee and we'll be off. We may catch your illustrious boy-friend at his lunch."

"Shall I telephone him first?" I suggested.

She hesitated, then shook her head. "No," she said firmly, "he might put you off. I'm not going to lose my one and only opportunity of setting foot in his house."

There was nothing for it but to acquiesce. My hope was that my brother would not be there, and that Jacopo would admit me. We drank our coffee and she went into the bathroom. When she came back the whiff of scent was stronger, the mascara on her lashes deeper.

"War-paint," she said briefly. "Not that I have much hope, but you never know."

I looked out of the window and into the street. There was no one about.

"Come on, I'm ready," I told her.

I followed her downstairs and out of the house. I opened the door of the car for her and she settled herself in the driving-seat.

"I'll be chauffeur," she said, "and you can sit well back. If the streets are lined with police and agents in plain clothes they won't look at you with me at the wheel."

Her good humour was infectious. I felt like laughing for the first time that day. She started the car and we headed for the via dei Sogni. Our progress was erratic, her driving unprofessional but fast. Twice we nearly hit pedestrians endeavouring to cross street corners.

"Watch out," I said, "or the police will want you too."

She took the long way round by the via delle Mura, so as to avoid coming into the via dei Sogni near to the Rector's house. There was no Alfa-Romeo outside the entrance to No. 2, and I breathed a sigh of relief. My companion got out and looked about her. I glanced at my watch. It was nearly half-past one.

"Lead the way," she said, "and don't think you can throw me off. I'm here to stay."

We passed together through the entrance. I rang the bell of Aldo's front door, praying that Jacopo would answer it himself. He did. But he looked embarrassed when he saw me, and more so when he realised that I was not alone.

"The Professor isn't at home," he said promptly.

"It doesn't matter," I told him. "I'll come in and wait. This lady is Signorina Raspa. I've promised her I would show her the portrait in the living-room—the signorina is interested in pictures."

Jacopo looked more uncomfortable than ever. "Professor Donati already has one visitor waiting for him," he began, but Carla Raspa, determined not to be outdone, brushed past him smiling gaily.

"Then that makes three of us," she said.

I followed her to the door of the living-room, trying to prevent her entry. It was too late. She had already opened the door. A woman was sitting on the settee who, as she saw us, half rose in protest, then, seeing we were upon her, stood silent, saying nothing.

It was Signora Butali.

CHAPTER NINETEEN

I DON'T KNOW which of the two women looked the more surprised, or indeed discomfited. The onus was on me.

"I beg your pardon, signora," I said. "Professor Donati asked me to call, and I'm afraid I'm before my time. May I present Signorina Raspa, who was kind enough to bring me?"

The frigid smile hovered for an instant on her face and vanished. The eyes were distant, looking beyond us to Jacopo with a mute reproach. "Good afternoon, signorina," she said.

Carla Raspa, being the less embarrassed, recovered the quicker. She advanced with a certain brash assurance, holding out her hand. "We've never met, signora," she said, "but then, why should we? Although we share the university life we live in different worlds. I am a humble member of the Arts faculty, and spend most of my time conducting parties of students round the ducal palace. I hope the Rector is better?"

"Thank you," replied Signora Butali, "he is better but still very tired. We only arrived late last night."

"To find all Ruffano in an uproar and the sudden death of a student the climax," said Carla Raspa. "What a homecoming! I'm very sorry for you both."

Her plunge into the burning topic of the hour was ill-timed. Signora Butali stiffened. "The accident was tragic indeed," she said. "I know nothing of any uproar, nor does my husband."

Carla Raspa turned to me with a smile. "Professor and Signora Butali are lucky," she observed. "You and I were witnesses to one riotous event at least. But perhaps they will discuss it at the meeting." She turned again to the Rector's lady. "The librarian, Signor Fossi, is a good friend of mine," she explained. "He told me they were meeting at your house at a quarter to two."

The signora bowed. Comment must have seemed to her unnecessary. An awkward silence followed. Jacopo, who had lingered by the door, now disappeared, leaving the initiative to me. I looked at my watch.

"Don't forget," I reminded Carla Raspa, "your neighbour needs his car."

"It's early yet," she said. "I promised I'd have it back by half-past two. What a charming room!" She advanced further and looked about her, sizing up the décor and the furniture with a rapacious eye. She wandered to the portrait of my father hanging on the wall. "I suppose that's Donati the elder?" she remarked. "Not so handsome as his son, and lacking the Professor's devastating charm. These things must all have come from his old home. Wasn't it the house where you live now, signora?"

She flashed a look at Signora Butali, who, resembling more than ever the gentlewoman in the ducal palace portrait, bowed yet again with Florentine hauteur.

"That is true," she answered. "We are very fortunate in our surroundings."

"I wonder if Professor Donati grudges it?" smiled Carla Raspa.

"He has never said so," came the reply.

The atmosphere, chilly, threatened to become glacial. The signora, who had been first in the room and was the older of the ladies, continued to stand. But my companion ignored protocol and perched herself on the side of the settee.

"If he did, he'd put it deviously," she said, lighting a cigarette and offering one to Signora Butali, who shook her head. "But he'd charm the house out of you in the end by magic means. He has hypnotic eyes. Don't you agree, Armino?"

The smile she gave me was deliberate, the puff of smoke provocative. Remembering what she imagined to be the relationship between Aldo and myself, doubtless she found the present situation intriguing, even enjoyable.

"His eyes are dark," I said. "I don't know about hypnotic."

"His actors find them so, both male and female," she continued, one eye on Signora Butali. "They're dedicated, every one. I suppose, like the rest of us humble members of the university staff, they hope that he will take notice of each of them individually."

There was another pause, then, turning to the Rector's wife, she said, "You're not taking part this year, signora—such a pity. You made a beautiful Duchess of Ruffano last Festival under Professor Donati's superb direction."

Acknowledgement came from the signora, but no more. I felt the expression of agreeable attention already on my features become fixed.

"The rehearsals this year have been so secret," pursued Carla Raspa, now mistress of the scene. "Conferences behind locked doors to all hours of the night. No women taking part. Admission by ticket only to the open meetings, to which I was lucky enough to obtain two tickets from the Director himself, and took Armino. It was a revelation, I can tell you. But then you must have attended one or two of the rehearsals, surely?"

Signora Butali, assured in her own house when she played hostess, looked vulnerable under this roof that was not hers. Even her stance, her hands clasped in front of her, holding neither gloves nor bag—she must have hurried up here on an impulse to waylay my brother before he saw her husband— seemed one of evasion, even of self-defence.

"I'm afraid not," she said, "it wasn't possible. I've spent so much of my time just latterly in Rome."

I saw her furtively consult her watch in a downward glance, easy enough because of her clasped hands, and then with mournful eyes she looked at me, the message one of entreaty. There was nothing I could do. The only hope was for Aldo to return and himself take charge. I had no authority to turn Carla Raspa out of the house, nor had Signora Butali. The interloper, conscious of her power and caring not a jot for her intrusion into what was very obviously a private visit, intercepted the signora's glance and misinterpreted it as being hostile to me.

"Professor Donati must have been held up," she said. "It doesn't really matter to Armino, he can wait here for the rest of the afternoon if he feels inclined. Can't you, Armino?"

"I'm at his disposal," I said shortly.

"Such a pleasant corner of Ruffano this," Carla Raspa went on, lighting yet another cigarette from the butt of the first. "No traffic, no endless parading students, no peering neighbours to gossip about who goes out or who comes in. Your house is only just down the street, signora?"

"Yes."

"Convenient for Professor Donati when he wants to consult the Rector about anything. But of course, as you said, you've been so much in Rome."

The inflection in Carla Raspa's voice was now ironic. One allusion more to Aldo's proximity as neighbour to No. 8, and she might overstep into the realm of direct insult. If she did, I wondered whether Signora Butali would counter with a crushing retort or offer the other cheek.

"Luckily for your music pupils you were able to return to Ruffano at the weekends," the voice continued. "One or two of them attend my lectures, and they spoke of you most gratefully. I don't think many of them had to miss a single lesson through your absence."

"Signora Butali puts the interests of everybody else before her own," I commented. "She even found a moment to play to me last week."

The interruption did no good. Indeed, it whetted Carla Raspa's appetite.

"The psychologists tell us that piano-playing is therapeutic," she observed, "allowing full reign to the emotions. Do you agree, signora?"

The muscles of the victim's face tautened. "It helps one to relax," she answered.

"It wouldn't work for me," sighed Carla, "though I can see the point of a duet. There'd be stimulation there. Have you tried duets, signora?"

This time the intonation was unmistakable. Had it been last Sunday night and the three of us, Aldo, Signora Butali and myself, at the dinner-table under candle-light, a remark like this would have been accepted as a challenge in the sex-play we were all engaged in. The signora would have smiled, parrying the question with another equally light-hearted. Not so today. This was a thrust, seeking to probe her weak defences.

"No, signorina," she replied. "I leave that sort of thing to children. My pupils study for diplomas, to equip themselves as teachers."

Carla smiled. She was, I felt, gathering her forces for the kill. It was time for me to intervene. But before I could do so the slam of the front door signalled an

arrival. There was a hurried murmur from Jacopo in the hall, an expostulation—my brother's—then an ominous silence. Signora Butali turned pale.
Carla Raspa intuitively extinguished her cigarette. The door opened and Aldo
came into the room.

"I'm extremely honoured," he said, the inflection in his voice warning his
visitors that he had expected none of them. "I hope Jacopo has been looking
after you, or have you all already lunched?" He did not wait for a reply, but
crossed the room and kissed the signora's hand. "Signora," he said, "I was just
on my way to your house, and seeing a car here outside which I did not
recognise looked in to investigate."

"The car is mine," announced Carla Raspa, "or rather, borrowed for the
occasion. Armino lunched with me, and I dropped him here."

"How thoughtful of you, signorina," replied Aldo. "The hills of Ruffano
must be hard on a courier's legs." He turned to the Rector's wife with a manner
equally detached. "What can I do for you, signora?" he asked. "The meeting
called by the Rector hasn't been cancelled, has it?"

The long wait, and the conversation that succeeded it, seemed to have
drained Signora Butali of energy, of resource. It occurred to me that she had
been unable to reach Aldo by telephone since her arrival home, unless it had
been in her husband's presence, and that this was, in fact, their first encounter
since they last saw one another on Sunday night. Her eyes searched his to
convey a message. The anguish was very evident.

"No," she said, "it has not been cancelled." She struggled bravely to find
words that could not be turned by the listening Carla Raspa into food for gossip
through the university. "I merely wished to consult you, Professor, on a small
matter. It's really of no importance. Some other time, perhaps."

The lie was pitiful. Had the matter been so small she would never have
waited for him so long. Aldo looked at me. He must have wondered why I had
not gone discreetly, taking my companion with me, the instant I knew Signora
Butali was under his roof.

"You'll excuse us, signorina, I feel sure," he said, looking past me to the
cause of all the embarrassment. "Liqueurs, Beo, cigarettes, see to it, will you?
Signora, I'm so sorry . . . Would you come this way?"

He gestured to the hall and the dining-room beyond. Signora Butali passed
through, and Aldo closed the door behind him. I went to the tray of drinks and
poured Carla Raspa a liqueur which she did not deserve.

"You behaved disgracefully," I told her. "You'll never receive an invitation
to the Butalis' now."

She downed her liqueur and held out the glass for more. "*What* did Donati
call you?" she asked, her eyes curious.

"Beo," I said, "short for Il Beato, the blessed."

The eyes grew wider still. "How touching," she murmured. Then motion-
ing towards the dining-room, where supposedly they had gone, she added,
"Does the noble lady know?"

"Know what?" I asked.

"About you and Donati?"

The devil entered me. Things had reached such a pass that I did not care. "Oh, yes," I said, "we're quite open about it. But only to her."

"You amaze me," said Carla Raspa. She was so excited that she got up, spilling her drink. I mopped it up with my handkerchief. "But she's mad about him," she exclaimed, "a child could see it. It shrieks to the heavens. Doesn't she mind?"

"No," I said. "Why should she?"

"A woman like that? Avid to be the one and only? My dear Armino! Unless . . ." A world of possibilities filled her mind. Images floated before her. "Livia Butali, Donati, and you. It isn't possible . . ."

Her mind reeled. I took away her glass and put it on the tray.

"Now will you go?" I pleaded.

"No," she said, "not after that piece of information. Donati will have to kick me out. Where have they gone, into his bedroom?"

I looked at my watch. "Hardly," I said. "It's ten to two now. He's five minutes late at the Rector's meeting."

"You'll be telling me in a minute that the Rector's in this too," she said.

I shrugged. "He may be, for all I know," I answered.

Voices came from the hall and passed to the entrance outside. Then after a moment or two Aldo came back into the room.

"Who's next?" he asked. "I like to see my clients one at a time."

I spoke before she had a chance to get in first. "The police have been to 24, via San Michele," I said. "I thought it best to take refuge in Carla's apartment. I told her why."

"They've been to the library too," Aldo replied. "Fossi telephoned me. That was what held me up." Then, turning to Carla Raspa, he added, "Thank you for what you did. This fellow could be in trouble. I've stalled them for the time being, and he's safe enough here with me."

The signorina, having gained her ends and confronted her host face to face, was ready to call it quits.

"I was only too glad to help," she admitted frankly, "especially since it gave me a chance to enter your house at last. I've tried often enough. I've called about three times."

"How unfortunate," murmured Aldo. "I must have been engaged."

"You were," she said, looking at me, "with him."

She picked up her bag, and, wishing to show herself aware of the situation which she imagined between us, observed with emphasis, "I had no idea, Professor, that you and Armino were such close friends."

The parting shot fell wide of its target.

"We should be," said Aldo briefly. "He's my brother. We believed each other dead, and hadn't met for twenty-two years until last Sunday."

The effect was startling. Carla Raspa, who had taken my possible status as a suspected murderer without flinching, flushed a deep crimson. Aldo might have struck her.

"I didn't know," she said. "I hadn't realised . . . Armino said nothing." She looked from one to the other of us, overcome, and then, to my consternation, burst into tears. "I lost both brothers in the war," she said. "Much older than me, but I loved them dearly . . . I'm very sorry. Please forgive me."

She blundered towards the door, but Aldo stepped forward and, seizing her by the arm, swung her round and stared into her face.

"Just how lonely are you?" he asked.

"Lonely?" she echoed, the tears blotching her mascara, her skin, now the flush had died, sallow under her make-up. "I haven't said I'm lonely."

"You don't have to," he retorted brutally. "You proclaim it in your body each time you wrap yourself round a different man."

I stared aghast at this sudden violence on the part of my brother. Carla Raspa, by breaking down, had shown herself as vulnerable in her fashion as Signora Butali in hers. Why couldn't Aldo let her go in peace? She stared back at him, and, miraculously, everything collapsed. All pretence and all bravado.

"It's all I have," she said, "there's nothing else to give."

"What about your life?" he demanded. "Can't you lose that too?"

He dropped her arm. She continued staring at him. The running mascara had now smudged both eyes.

"I'd lose it for you," she said, "if you asked me for it."

Aldo smiled and, stooping, picked up the bag that had slipped from her shaking hands.

"That's all that matters then," he said.

He gave her the bag and patted her on the shoulder. He put his finger on her cheek, showed her the smudge of black and laughed. She smiled in answer, and dabbed at it with her handkerchief.

"I may ask for your life tomorrow, at the Festival," he told her, "so remember that you've promised it to me. I may need you at the ducal palace. You will get your instructions some time this evening on the telephone."

"I'll do whatever you want, now, and forever," she said.

He pushed her towards the door. "One thing's very certain," he said, "if you want to die, you won't have to die alone."

As she went into the hall she looked back over her shoulder at me. "Shall I see you again, Armino?" she asked.

"I don't know," I answered, "but thank you for giving me sanctuary."

She glanced enquiringly at Aldo. He gave her no indication of my future, and she passed out through the front door to the double entrance and the street. Through the open window of the room where we were standing came the thin high sound of San Donato striking two.

"I must go," said Aldo, "I'm already fifteen minutes late. I've just telephoned Cesare telling him you are here. He and Giorgio have been looking for you all the morning."

His manner was abrupt, evasive. Whether because of the trouble I had caused him or for some other reason I could not tell. It was as though he did not care to be alone with me.

"When Cesare comes, I want you to do whatever he tells you," he said. "Do you understand?"

"No," I replied, "not immediately. But perhaps I shall when Cesare appears." Then, hesitant, I added, "I don't know if the signora told you. I called at her house this morning."

"No," he said, "she didn't tell me."

"I met her husband," I went on, "and when she was out of the room we had a few minutes' conversation. During the course of it he mentioned—I won't bother with the details now—that he had been receiving anonymous telephone calls while he was in hospital in Rome. The caller was a woman, the allusions to you."

"Thank you," said Aldo. His voice remained unaltered. His expression did not change.

"I thought," I said awkwardly, "it was best to warn you."

"Thank you," he said again, and turned towards the door.

"Aldo," I said, "I apologise for what happened just now—the unfortunate clash between Signora Butali and Carla Raspa."

"Why unfortunate?" he asked, pausing, his hand on the door.

I gestured. "They're so different," I said, "no common ground between them."

He looked at me. The eyes were cryptic, hard. "That's where you are wrong," he said. "They both wanted one thing only. Carla Raspa happened to be more honest about it."

He left the room. I heard the front door slam. The uncertainty of what was yet to come closed in upon me with his presence gone.

CHAPTER TWENTY

I DID NOT want to be alone. I sought out Jacopo, who was about to leave for his own quarters across the double entrance.

"May I come with you?" I asked him diffidently.

He looked surprised, then pleased, and waved me on. "By all means, Signor Beo," he said. "I'm cleaning the silver. Come and keep me company."

We passed through to his domain. He led me to his own kitchen—kitchen and living-room in one, the window facing the via dei Sogni. It was cheerful, snug, a canary in its cage singing to the strains of a transistor radio which Jacopo, out of possible deference to me, switched off. The walls were covered with pictures of aircraft, torn from the pages of magazines and framed. Pieces of silver, knives and forks and spoons, dishes and jugs, stood on the centre of the kitchen table in various stages of his cleaning process, some covered with a pink paste, others already polished.

I recognised most of them. I picked up a small round porringer and smiled.

"That's mine," I said, "it was a christening present. Marta never would let me use it. She said it was too good."

"The Capitano keeps it for sugar," said Jacopo, "he always uses it with his morning coffee. His own is too big."

He showed me a larger bowl that he had not yet cleaned.

"I remember that too," I told Jacopo. "It stood in the dining-room, and my mother put flowers in it."

Both bowls, Aldo's and mine, were inscribed with our initials, A.D.

"The Capitano is very particular about all the family things," said Jacopo. "If any of the china gets broken, which isn't often, he is very upset, or if anything is lost. He will throw away nothing that belongs to the old days, and to his father."

I put the porringer back. Jacopo took it from me and began to clean it.

"It's strange," I said, "that he should be like that, and respect tradition."

"Strange?" repeated Jacopo, astonished. "I assure you it is not, Signor Beo. He's been that way as long as I've known him."

"Perhaps," I answered, "but he was a rebel as a boy."

"Ah, boys," shrugged Jacopo, "we are all of us different when we are boys. The Capitano will be forty in November."

"Yes," I said.

The canary started singing again. The song was artless, happy.

"I'm concerned about my brother, Jacopo," I said.

"No need," answered Jacopo shortly. "The Capitano always knows what he's about."

I picked up a leather and began polishing my own small porringer. "Has he not changed at all during the past years?" I asked.

Jacopo considered, frowning a little, as he warmed to his task. "He's more thoughtful, perhaps," he said, after a moment. "He has his moods, as I have mine. It doesn't do to disturb him when he's alone across the way, thinking."

"What does he think about?"

"If I knew that," replied Jacopo, "I wouldn't be here in my kitchen polishing the silver. I'd be like him, a member of the Arts Council, telling other people what to do."

I laughed and let it go. Jacopo had a certain rugged wisdom.

"We suit each other very well, the Capitano and I," he said. "We understand one another. I have never pried into his concerns, as Marta did."

"Marta?" I asked, surprised.

"It wasn't just the drinking, Signor Beo. She became possessive through the years. Her age, no doubt. She wanted to know everything. What the Capitano was doing, where he was going, who were his friends, what were his intentions. Oh yes, that, and a lot else besides. I told your brother, 'If I ever become like that, fire me immediately, I'll know the reason why.' He promised to do so. But he needn't worry. I shan't."

My porringer was clean. My initials shone with brilliance. Jacopo handed me Aldo's porringer and I started to polish that in turn.

"What happened finally?" I asked. "Did he turn her out of the house?"

"It was last November," said Jacopo, "just after his birthday. He had a small celebration for some of the students from the university, and one lady to act as hostess, Signora Butali." He paused a moment, then added, thinking perhaps to explain something that might seem surprising, even shocking, "Professor Butali was at a conference in Padua at the time. And no doubt it would seem to the signora that, as the guests were all students at her husband's university, there would be nothing improper about her acting as hostess to them. Marta cooked the dinner and I served. The evening was a great success. The students brought their guitars and there was singing, and later the Capitano took the signora home. Marta had been drinking and she wouldn't go to bed—she insisted on staying up until he returned. What happened I don't know, but there was some violent discussion between them, and next morning she packed her things and left and went to live with the Ghigis."

"And Aldo?" I asked.

"It upset him very much," admitted Jacopo. "He took the car and went off alone for about five days. He said he went to the sea. When he came back he told me briefly that he didn't want to discuss Marta or what had happened, and that was that. He continued to keep her, though—he paid for her board and lodging, the Ghigis told me. Marta never told them what had happened either. Even when she was drinking, and that was most of the time after she left here, she told them nothing. She did not as much as mention the Capitano's name. But you know, Signor Beo, it was jealousy, nothing more nor less than common jealousy. That's women for you." He whistled up at the canary, who, swaying on its perch, feathers rumpled, was nearly bursting its small heart in song. "They're all the same," he said, "whether they're women of quality like the signora or peasants like Marta. They try to squeeze a man dry. They come between a man and his work."

I held Aldo's porringer to the light. Through the scrolled initials my own face was reflected back at me. I wondered what they were discussing at 8, via dei Sogni, and whether, when the Heads of the Departments left, the Rector would speak to my brother alone, and if he would mention, deliberately or casually, the anonymous telephone calls.

Then suddenly I knew. The woman who had made the anonymous telephone calls had been Marta. That was why Marta had gone to Rome. Marta, dismissed by Aldo after the birthday dinner in November, had pondered and brooded during the ensuing weeks and months, had guessed perhaps that when Professor Butali fell ill in Rome after Christmas Aldo had grown closer to the signora, seen her more often, perhaps become her lover. Marta, her love and loyalty spurned, her mind disintegrating through drink and despair, had sought revenge upon Aldo by betraying him to the Rector.

I put down the silver porringer and went and stood by the window under the canary's cage. The calls had ceased now for more than a week, the Rector had told me. They had ceased for one good reason: the caller was dead. Now, for the first time in the ten days since it had happened, I was glad that she was dead. The Marta who had died was not the Marta I remembered. Alcohol, like poison, had turned her warm blood sour. Her last act, like that of a sick animal, had been to bite her master's hand, and in taking that final journey she had found death waiting for her at the end of it.

In a sense, it was retribution. The slanderer had been silenced, the serpent had died in its own venom . . . Why did I suddenly remember the crazy maxims of the Falcon, quoted by the German scholar in his lives of the Dukes of Ruffano? "The proud shall be stripped . . . the haughty violated . . . the slanderer silenced, the serpent die in its own venom . . ."

The canary's song finished in one last passionate trill. I looked up at it. The small throat quivered and was still.

"Jacopo," I said slowly, "when was my brother last in Rome?"

Jacopo was setting the silver he had cleaned and polished upon a tray to take it across the way to Aldo's house.

"In Rome, Signor Beo?" he replied. "Let me see, it was the Sunday before last—it will be two weeks this coming Sunday, Palm Sunday. He went to Rome on the Friday to consult some manuscripts in the Biblioteca Nazionale, and then he drove back to Ruffano through the Tuesday night. He likes to drive through the night. He was here for breakfast on Wednesday morning."

Jacopo went through into Aldo's house, carrying the tray, leaving the doors open. I sat down on one of his kitchen chairs, staring in front of me. Aldo could have killed Marta. Aldo could have driven past the church even as the touring coach had done and recognised the humped figure lying inside the porch. He could have got out of the car and gone to speak to her. She could have told him then, drunk and in despair, what she had been trying to do. He could have killed her. I remembered the knife that had slipped so suddenly from his sleeve last night at the ducal palace when he cut the bonds that bound Marelli's hands. Aldo could have carried the knife in Rome. Aldo could have murdered Marta.

I heard footsteps passing the window outside the kitchen. They paused by the double entrance, then turned in at Jacopo's door. A young voice said, "Armino?"

It was the student Cesare. He was wearing my light overcoat and hat and carried my suitcase.

"I've brought your things from the via San Michele," he said. "Giorgio and Domenico kept Signora Silvani engaged in the sitting-room, pestering her for a contribution for the university funds. She did not know that I went upstairs and packed for you. I was there less than five minutes. I've come to take you out of Ruffano."

I looked at him dully. His words were meaningless. Why should I have to leave Ruffano now? My thoughts of the last few minutes had left me numb.

"I'm sorry," he said, "those are Aldo's orders. He arranged everything this morning. If we could have found you we should have got you away sooner."

"I thought," I said, "I was supposed to play the Falcon in the Festival?"

"Not now," he answered. "I'm to drive you to Fano and put you on board a fishing-boat. It's all been fixed. Aldo gave no reason."

My brother had worked quickly. Whether he had taken his decision last night when we parted so abruptly, or later, I could not tell, nor apparently did

Cesare know. Perhaps it did not matter. Perhaps nothing mattered. Except that Aldo wanted to be rid of me.

"Very well," I said, "I'm ready."

I stood up, and he gave me my coat and hat. I followed him out of the kitchen. Jacopo came through to the double entrance carrying the empty tray. He nodded when he saw Cesare, and said good day.

"I have to leave, Jacopo," I told him. "I've had my orders."

His face remained inscrutable. "We shall miss you, Signor Beo," he said.

I shook hands with him, and he disappeared back into his own domain. The Alfa-Romeo was parked outside. Cesare opened the door and threw my suitcase into the back. I climbed into the passenger seat, and drove out of the city and on to the Fano road.

I was quitting, for the second time in twenty years, my birth-place and my home. Not, as then, waving an enemy flag, but still a fugitive, flying from a crime I had not committed, acting, perhaps—God knows—as my brother's surrogate. Hence my banishment, hence the flight to Fano. I was laying a false trail, away from Ruffano, away from Aldo.

I watched the road ahead, Ruffano behind us now for ever, hidden by the encircling hills, and the brown earth to the left, stubbled with the fast-growing shoots of corn, was saffron-coloured like the Falcon's robe. The road turned and twisted, and later the river ran to keep us company, soon to empty itself, blue-green and limpid, on to the Adriatic shores, already burning under the April sun. The nearer we drew to Fano the more despairing I became, the more angry, the more lost.

"Cesare," I said, "why do you follow Aldo? What makes you believe in him?"

"We have no one else we can follow," said Cesare, "Giorgio, Romano, Domenico, and the rest. He speaks in a language we understand. Nobody ever has before. We were orphans, and he found us."

"How did he find you?"

"By enquiries, through his old comrades who were partisans. Then he arranged for grants for us with the university Council. There are others who have graduated and left—they owe everything to him."

My brother had done this for me. He had done it because he thought me dead. Now, knowing that I lived, he was sending me away.

"But if he has worked all these years for the university and for students like yourselves who can't afford the fees," I persisted, "why does he want to destroy it now, setting one group of students against another, staging these elaborate hoaxes, the last of which ended in Marelli's death?"

"Do you call them hoaxes?" asked Cesare. "We don't. Nor would Rizzio and Elia. They've learnt humility. As for Marelli, he died because he ran. Didn't the priests teach you as a child? He that seeks to save his life shall lose it?"

"Yes," I replied, "but that's different."

"Is it?" said Cesare. "We don't think so. Nor does Aldo."

We were approaching the outskirts of Fano, the houses bleak and impersonal like biscuit tins splayed out upon the landscape. I was filled with a terrible despair.

"Where are you taking me?" I asked.

"To the port," he answered, "to a fisherman, an ex-partisan called Marco. You're to go on board his boat and he'll land you, in a day or so, further up the coast, perhaps at Venice. You don't have to think of anything. He'll wait for further instructions from Aldo."

Depending, I supposed, on what transpired with the police, and whether or not the trail was lost. Whether an absent courier, Armino Fabbio, had disappeared without a trace, successfully.

The rounded bay lay blue and still and the great beach, white like an inverted oyster-shell, was already dotted with the black figures of early tourists. Line upon line of bathing-sheds was being painted for the season. Easter was only another week away. The soft air stank of the humid sea. To the right lay the canal.

"Here we are," said Cesare.

He had drawn up before a café in the via Squero at the canal's edge, near where the fishing-boats were moored. A man in faded jeans, his skin burnt black by sea and sun, was sitting at a table smoking a cigarette, a drink in front of him. At sight of the Alfa-Romeo he sprang to his feet and came over to us. Cesare and I got out, and Cesare handed me my suitcase and my hat and coat.

"This is Armino," he said. "The Capitano sends his regards." The fisherman Marco put out a great hand and shook mine. "You are very welcome," he said. "I shall be pleased to have you on board my boat. Let me take your case and your coat. We will embark very shortly. I was only waiting for you and for my engineer. In the meantime, have a drink."

Never, not even as a child, had I felt more completely in the hands of a fate that was not mine to command. I was like a package dumped upon a quayside before being swung by a crane into a ship's hold. I think Cesare pitied me.

"You'll be all right," he said, "once you're at sea. Have you a message to send Aldo?"

What message could I send beyond what he must already know—that what I was doing now I did for him?

"Tell him," I said, "that before the proud were stripped and the haughty violated, the slanderer was silenced and the viper died in its own venom."

The words meant nothing to Cesare. It was his comrade Federico who had translated the German history. The manuscripts my brother had consulted in Rome would have borne Duke Claudio's maxims too.

"Goodbye," he said, "and good luck."

He climbed back into the car, and in a moment he had gone. The fisherman Marco was watching me with curiosity. He asked me what would I drink, and I told him a beer.

"So you're the Capitano's young brother?" he asked me. "You're not a scrap like him."

"Unfortunately," I replied.

"He's a fine man," he went on. "We fought in the hills side by side, we escaped from the same enemy. Now, when he needs a change from all his activities, he gets in touch with me and comes to sea." He smiled, and handed me a cigarette. "The sea blows away the dust," he said, "and all the cares and troubles of city life. You'll find it does the same to you. Your brother looked a sick man when he came here last November. Five days afloat—it was winter, mind you—and he had recovered."

The attendant brought my beer. I raised the glass and wished my companion fortune.

"Was that after his birthday?" I asked.

"Birthday? He said nothing about a birthday. It was somewhere around the third week of the month. 'I've had a shock, Marco,' he told me when he arrived. 'Don't ask me any questions. I'm with you to forget it.' Anyway, there was nothing wrong with him physically. He was as tough as in the old days, and worked like one of the crew. Something else had been worrying him, no doubt. Perhaps a woman." He raised his glass in answer to my toast. "Good health to you," he said, "and may you lose your troubles at sea also."

I drank my beer and thought of what Marco had said. It was evident that Aldo had sought him out after the birthday dinner and the quarrel with Marta. She must have railed at him, drunk, as Jacopo said, and outraged, like all peasants who are deeply religious and bound by a moral code. She must have taxed him with starting an affair with a married woman, and that woman the Rector's wife. The quarrel would have angered my brother, which was the reason he sent Marta from the house. But why did he talk of a shock?

Footsteps approached and another man stood before the table. Short and grizzled, he was burnt even blacker by the sun than Marco.

"This is Franco," said Marco, "my mate and engineer."

Franco stuck out a hand hairy as a monkey's paw, and covered with grease.

"Two hours' work still to do," he said to his skipper. "I thought it best to warn you, as it means delay in sailing."

Marco cursed and spat, then turned to me with a shrug of his shoulder.

"I promised your brother we would be at sea by noon," he said. "That was when he telephoned early this morning. Next, it seemed, there was difficulty in finding you. And now our engine has to give trouble. We shall be lucky if we are away by five." He stood up and pointed along the canal to where the vessels were moored. "See the blue boat there, with the yellow mast and the centre dog-house?" he said. "That's our craft, the 'Garibaldi'. Franco and I will take your case and coat aboard and you can follow us later, within the hour. Will that suit you, or would you prefer to come with us right away?"

"No," I said, "no, I'll stay here and finish my drink."

They walked off along the side of the canal and I sat outside the café, watching until they had climbed aboard. My quarters for the next few days did not tempt me. Marco was right when he told me I did not look like my brother. I was a seasoned traveller on land, but not on water. As a courier I had disgraced myself by being seasick in the Bay of Naples before my clients. The flat oily swell of the Adriatic looked equally repellent.

I sat there, finishing my beer. It was the dead hour of the day. I wondered if the meeting in the via dei Sogni was over. Presently I got up and wandered aimlessly along the side of the canal, but instead of going directly to the boat turned left and strolled on to the beach. Already the sun-worshippers were stripped and lying with torsos naked to the sky. Children screamed ·and paddled at the water's edge. The bathing-sheds, sticky with new paint, stood in rows, one behind the other, and in front of them, orange and brilliant red, the sun umbrellas spread canopies above the glaring sand. Despondency was heavy within me. I could not shake it off.

A group of children in grey uniforms with hair cropped short, escorted by a nun, came clumping down the beach towards the sea. They pointed to the water, their small faces alight with stupendous surprise, and turning to the nun ran to her, begging permission to take off their shoes. She gave it, her eyes kindly behind her gold-rimmed spectacles.

"Quietly now, children, quietly," she said, and as she bent to gather together their shoes her skirts and wimple billowed about her like a balloon. The children, suddenly released and free, ran with uplifted arms towards the sea.

"They're happy, anyway," I said.

"Their first visit to the sea," answered the nun. "They all come from orphanages inland, and at Easter we have a camp for them here at Fano. There is another camp at Ancona."

The children were knee deep in the water, shouting and splashing one another. "I shouldn't let them do that," said the nun, "but I ask myself, what does it matter? They have so little joy."

One little fellow, having stubbed his toe, burst into tears and came running up the beach towards her. She took him in her arms and comforted him, found a plaster from within her ample robes and placed it on his toe, sending him back again to join the others.

"This is the part of the work I like best," she confided, "bringing the children to the sea. The Sisters of the various organisations take it in turns. I have not far to come. I'm from Ruffano."

The world was small. I thought of the bleak building near to the now resplendent Hotel Panorama.

"The foundling hospital," I said. "I know it. I'm from Ruffano too, but long ago. I never went inside the hospital."

"The building needs replanning," she said, "and we may have to move. There is talk of building us new quarters at Ancona, where the former Superintendent of our hospital died."

We stood together, watching the children splashing in the sea.

"Are they all orphans?" I asked, thinking of Cesare.

"Yes, all," she said, "either orphaned, or left on the hospital doorsteps within a few hours of their birth. Sometimes the mother is too weak to move far, and we find her, and look after her and her baby. Then she goes to work, leaving the baby with us. Sometimes, but very rarely, it is possible to find a home where both are taken in." She raised her hand, and waved to the children not to venture in too far. "That is the happiest answer," she said, "both for the mother and the child. But there are not many people who will offer their home to a foundling these days. Occasionally a young married couple will have lost their first child at birth and come to us to seek another to replace it quickly, so bringing the child up as their own." She turned to me, smiling once more behind her spectacles. "But that," she said, "requires great confidence between the bereaved parents and the superintendent of the foundling hospital. The record remains a secret for ever afterwards. It's better for everyone concerned."

"Yes," I said, "yes, I suppose so."

She took a whistle from some capacious pocket within her skirt and blew it twice. The children turned their heads and stared, then rushed from the water up the beach towards her, scampering like little dogs.

"You see?" she said, laughing. "I have them very well trained."

I looked at my watch. I was well-trained as well. It would soon be four. Perhaps I should go and find my way on board the "Garibaldi" and settle in.

"If you come from Ruffano too," said the nun, "you should call in some time and see the children there. Not these, of course, but those I look after at the foundling hospital."

"Thank you," I lied politely, "perhaps I will," and then, more from courtesy than from curiosity, I said, "Will you move to the new orphanage at Ancona if they decide to build there?"

"Oh, yes," she said, "my life is with the children. Some fifty years ago I was a foundling too."

A kind of pity seized me. The plain, contented face had known no other existence, no other world. She, and hundreds like her, had been dumped upon a doorstep to find mercy.

"At Ruffano?" I asked.

"Yes," she said, "but it was harder for us in those days. The rules were strict, the life was spartan. No seaside holidays for orphans then, despite the kindness of our Superintendent, Luigi Speca."

The children had arrived and she gathered them round her in a semicircle and produced oranges and apples from a carrier bag.

"Luigi Speca?" I repeated.

"Yes," she answered, "but he died many years ago, in 1929. He was buried in Ancona, as I told you."

I said goodbye to her and thanked her. I don't know what I thanked her for. Perhaps it was for illumination from God. Perhaps the shaft of sunlight that fell upon my face as I turned west and walked up the beach beyond the bathing huts was like the blinding stroke that hit Saul upon the Damascus road. Suddenly I perceived. Suddenly I knew. My father's letter and the double baptismal entry were made plain. Aldo had been a foundling too. Their son had died, Luigi Speca had given them Aldo. The secret, held for nearly forty years, had been betrayed by Marta last November. Aldo, proud of his lineage, proud of his heritage, proud of all he held most dear, had learnt the truth and kept it to himself these past five months. It was Aldo who had been stripped and violated, Aldo who had lost face, not to the friends who did not know, but in his own eyes. The hoaxer had been hoaxed. He who had wanted to unmask hypocrisy had been himself unmasked.

I walked along the canal side in the opposite direction from the boat, and so into the town. My few belongings were on board the "Garibaldi", but they meant nothing. I had only one thought in mind, and that was to go to Aldo. Somewhere in Fano there must be a train, a bus, that would take me back to Ruffano. Tomorrow was the Festival, and I had to be with Aldo when the Falcon fell.

CHAPTER TWENTY-ONE

W HEN I REACHED the bus station I realised that I only had two thousand lire in my pocket-book. I was to have gone to the Registrar's office at the university that morning to receive my salary, but owing to my visit to Signora Butali, and because of hiding in Carla Raspa's apartment, I had never gone. I remembered too that I owed Signora Silvani for my lodging. Perhaps Aldo would have thought of that.

A car to Ruffano would cost more than two thousand lire. I enquired at the bus depot and was told that the last bus for Ruffano had left at half-past three. One was about to leave for Pesaro along the coast, and since Pesaro was some ten kilometres nearer to my destination than Fano I boarded it at once. As the road traversed the canal I looked right, towards the port, and thought of the partisan Marco and his mate Franco working on the engine, waiting for me to join them. When I did not turn up they would go into the town and look for me, enquire in the bars and cafés. Then Marco would telephone Aldo and tell him that I had vanished.

I looked out of the window, trying to make plans. If Aldo had killed Marta he had done so, not because she threatened to betray his possible liaison with Signora Butali, but because she intended to expose the secret of his birth. The Director of the Arts Council was not Donati's son but a foundling, the least of Ruffano's citizens, and this to Aldo meant unendurable humility and shame. What I wanted to do was to tell Aldo that I understood. That I did not care. That he was as much my brother now as always, that everything of mine was his. As a boy he had cherished and tormented me in turn, as a man he did so still. But I knew now what I had never known before, that he was vulnerable. Because of this, at long last, we should meet on equal terms.

The twelve kilometres to Pesaro were soon covered. I got down from the bus and studied the time-table to Ruffano. There was a bus at half-past five. I had just an hour to wait. I began to wander down the street, full of pedestrians, many of them tourists as aimless as myself, staring in shop windows or bound for the attractions of the beach beyond the town. Prolonged hooting sounded in my ear, two vespas swerved close to the pavement beside me and a girl's voice called, "Armino!" There were whistles and shouts. I turned, and there were Caterina and Paolo Pasquale on a vespa, she riding pillion, and behind them the two students Gino and Mario from the Silvani pensione.

"Caught you," called Caterina. "You can't escape. We know all about you, and how you sneaked upstairs and fetched your things, and went off without paying Signora Silvani what you owed her."

They all four dismounted and surrounded me. Passers-by turned to stare.

"Listen," I said, "I can explain . . ."

"You'd better explain," interrupted Paolo. "You can't treat the Silvanis that way; we won't allow it. Hand over the money now, or we'll turn you in to the police."

"I haven't got the money," I said. "I've got less than two thousand lire on me."

We were blocking the route. Someone in a passing car shouted at the students. Paolo jerked his head at Caterina.

"Follow us to the café Rossini," he said. "Armino shall ride behind me on the vespa. We'll get some sense out of him there. Gino and Mario, follow along behind; see he doesn't try any tricks."

There was nothing for it but to do as he said. To have argued further would have meant more trouble. Shrugging, I climbed behind him on the vespa and we shot off in the midst of the traffic to the piazza del Popolo, coming to a stop beside the colonnade beneath Pesaro's ducal palace. Here both vespas were parked, and with Paolo leading the way, and Gino and Mario on either side of me, I was marched to a small café-bar a few yards off. We went in, and Paolo pointed to a table near the window.

"This will do," he said. "Caterina will join us directly."

He ordered beer for all, including me, and when the waiter had disappeared he turned and faced me, his arms folded on the table.

"Now then," he asked, "what have you got to say?"

"I'm wanted by the police," I said. "I had to run."

The three students exchanged glances. "That's what Signora Silvani thought," Gino burst in. "Someone was enquiring for you this morning, but he didn't say why. He looked like a police agent in plain clothes."

"I know," I said, "I spotted him. That's why I ran. That's why I didn't pick up what was due to me from the Registrar's office, and why I couldn't pay Signora Silvani. If you were in my shoes you'd have done the same."

The three of them stared at me. The waiter arrived with our drinks, set them down and went away.

"What have you done?" asked Paolo.

"Nothing," I replied, "but the evidence is strong against me. In point of fact I believe I'm taking the rap for somebody else. If that's the case, I'll go on doing so. The other fellow happens to be my brother."

Caterina arrived, dishevelled and out of breath. She dragged forward a chair and sat between Paolo and me.

"What's happened?" she asked.

Paolo explained briefly. Caterina looked at me in turn.

"I believe him," she said, after a moment. "We've known him for a week. He's not the sort to run without good reason. Is it something to do with the tourist agency where you worked before coming to Ruffano?"

"Yes," I said. Which in a back-handed way was true.

Mario, who had remained silent up to now, leant forward. "Why Pesaro?" he asked. "With only two thousand lire. How do you plan to get away from here?"

They were no longer truculent or mistrustful. Gino handed me a cigarette. I looked at them, and thought how they were of the same generation as Cesare, Giorgio and Domenico. They were all young. They were all untried. However much they differed in their outlook, in their aims, fundamentally they were all eager for adventure and for life.

I said, "I've had time to think, the past few hours. I realise now it was a mistake to leave Ruffano. I want to go back. I was going to take the bus at half-past five."

They watched me silently, drinking their beer. I think they were puzzled.

"Why go back?" asked Paolo. "Won't the police get you?"

"Perhaps," I said. "But I'm no longer afraid. Don't ask me why."

They did not laugh or mock. They treated my admission seriously, just as Cesare or Domenico would have done.

"This isn't a thing that I can discuss with you in detail," I told them, "but my brother is in Ruffano, using another name. What's happened between us, if he's done what I think he's done, is because of family pride. I've got to straighten it out. I've got to talk to him."

This they understood. They pressed no questions. A live interest showed in all four faces. Caterina, impulsive, touched my arm.

"That makes sense," she said, "at any rate to me. If I was suspected of something I believed Paolo had done, even though I might take the blame for it I should want to know his reason. There must be honesty between people tied by blood. Paolo and I are twins. Perhaps that makes us closer."

"It's not just ties of family," said Gino, "it's ties of friendship too. I might take the blame for something Mario did, but first I should have to know why."

"Is that how you feel about your brother?" asked Caterina.

"Yes," I said, "it is."

They drank their beer and then Paolo said, "We'll see Signora Silvani gets her money. That's a small point now. The immediate thing is to get you to Ruffano, and at the same time dodge the police. We'll help you. But we've got to make a plan."

Their generosity moved me. Why did they have faith in me? There was no reason for it. Any more than there had been reason for Carla Raspa to let me hide in her apartment. I might have been a murderer, yet she believed in me. I could be a common swindler, yet the students trusted me.

"But of course," said Caterina suddenly, "the Festival. We just disguise Armino as one of us in the insurrection, and I defy any police agent to pick him out from amongst two thousand others."

"Disguise him how?" asked Gino. "You know Donati told our crowd to turn up just as we are."

"That's it," said Caterina, "in shirts, jeans, sweaters, anything. Look at Armino. That city suit, that shirt, those shoes. He even dresses like a courier! Give him a different hair-cut, and a coloured shirt inside a pair of jeans, and he won't even recognise himself."

"Caterina's right," said Paolo. "Let's take him to the nearest barber and get him crew-cut. Then we'll find him something to wear in the market-place. We'll share the cost all round. All right, Armino, keep your two thousand lire; you may need them."

I became a lay-figure in their hands. We left the café, Paolo paying for the drinks, and I was taken to a barber who transformed me from what I had hitherto believed myself to be, an elegant representative of Sunshine Tours, Genoa, into an undistinguished back-street hipster. This transformation became even more pronounced when they escorted me later to a cut-price store, and there, behind a row of bargain goods, I divested myself of my one good suit—the other was in the suitcase on board the "Garibaldi"—and donned a pair of black jeans, with a leather belt, a jade green shirt, an ersatz leather jerkin and a pair of sneakers. My own clothes were put in a parcel and handed to Caterina, who told me they were terrible, and she would do her best to lose them. They stood me in front of a mirror in the store, and—I suppose it was chiefly the hair-cut—I doubted if even Aldo would recognise me. I might have been an immigrant just landed on American shores, a semi-barbarian already, with only the flick-knife missing.

"You look terrific," said Caterina, squeezing my hand, "much better than before."

"You have style now," said Gino. "Before you had nothing."

Their admiration both baffled and discouraged me. If the object I now was pleased their aesthetic taste, what point in common had we? Or were they merely being kind?

"We'll live it up a little longer yet," said Paolo. "No need to return to Ruffano before dark. Caterina shall catch a later bus, and Armino ride with me. We'll escort the bus on our motorbikes. Let's go and see if the Sports Palace is open. Caterina, you meet us there."

Once again I mounted behind Paolo, and for the next few hours I enjoyed the doubtful pleasure of a student's holiday. We careered backwards and forwards by the beach, by the hotels, up and down the viale Trieste, sometimes racing in company with Gino and Mario, sometimes chasing tourist cars. We patronised the cafés with the loudest radios and the most crowded bars, ending up at a restaurant where we consumed bowlfuls of brodetto, the fish soup flavoured with saffron, garlic and tomato that Marta used to make me as a child. Finally, when it was nearing nine, we took Caterina, still carrying my discarded clothes, to catch her bus, and escorting it on either side, much to the disgust and fury of both driver and conductor, we rode back to Ruffano. What fate awaited me no longer mattered. I had ceased to care, while standing on the beach at Fano some five hours before. I clung to Paolo's belt, and like outriders to the bus we scorched and swerved over the intervening hills.

Ruffano, a celestial city, rose in front of us with a thousand winking lights, the flood-lit Duomo and campanile seeming to shine with a white radiance between either summit. Here from the east the ducal palace was screened by other buildings, but the pale glow in the sky revealed its presence and that of the university beyond, while staring across the slopes directly facing us as we rode towards the encircling wall below would be the lights from my old home in the via dei Sogni, where the Butalis must now be dining.

From one of those windows, impossible to discern amongst its neighbours, Aldo and I had looked across the valley here as boys, feeling ourselves superior to those who lived in the farmsteads beneath, and as I remembered this, clinging tight to Paolo's belt as we approached the porta Malebranche, I glanced up instinctively to the row of lights, uniform and straight, that came from the foundling hospital on the northern hill. There, in that cold building, forlorn, unclaimed, Aldo would have spent his childhood but for my father and for Luigi Speca. There, clad in a grey overall, with close-cropped head, he would have been a foundling boy, and matured, adult, he would have borne another name. I, the only son of my parents' later years, would have been christened Aldo in his stead.

The thought was sobering, even chastening. I should have been different too. Instead of growing up in Aldo's shadow, fearful, overawed, docile to his command, the whole course of my life must have been otherwise. We passed under the porta Malebranche and I knew I would not have it changed. He might not be my brother, he might not be my parents' son, but from the beginning he had possessed me, body, heart and soul, and he possessed me still. He was my god, he was my devil too. Through all the years I had believed him dead my world had been empty, without meaning.

The bus ground to a halt inside the city gate. Paolo and I, with our companion vespa, shot away to the northern summit and the piazza del Duca Carlo. Here, the scene of Tuesday's episode, Duke Carlo, floodlit as he had been then, gazed down benignly on the crowd beneath him. Students and Ruffanesi milled backwards and forwards across the piazza and around the gardens under the statue. The Honours graduates paraded wearing medallions strung on chains, as was the custom, so Paolo informed me, applauded and followed by strings of admiring fellow-students. Extempore music filled the air—mouth-organs, whistles and guitars. Proud parents watched and strolled with indulgent eyes. The inevitable collecting-boxes rattled. Crackers burst and dogs fled howling. Those who possessed cars drove slowly along the piazza, while the vespas, ours amongst them, roared and spluttered in an ever-widening circle.

"What did I tell you?" said Paolo as two carabinieri wandered sedately past us, immaculate in uniform. "Neither those fellows, nor a dozen others in plain clothes, would look at you. Tonight you're one of us."

The largest crowd of students had formed themselves into a group some hundreds strong outside Professor Elia's house, and were shouting and calling for him.

"Elia . . . Elia . . ." they chanted, and then, as for one brief moment he appeared and waved to them from the front door of his house, a burst of cheering came from the assembled students. Grouped behind him were his associates and members of his Department, and it seemed to me as he stood there, smiling and waving, that something of self-confidence and bravura had returned, yet not quite all. A momentary hesitation when, on the fringe of the crowd, an unseen student shouted, "Where are your bathing briefs?", followed immediately by an explosive burst from a cracker and a gulf of involuntary laughter, suggested, as the professor gave a final wave and then withdrew, that the memory of Tuesday night was with him still.

"Who said that?" cried Gino angrily, turning, with many others, to the back of the crowd from where the disturbance came, and at once the murmur rose from all about us, "It's an Arts man from the other hill. Get him, murder him . . ." In a moment all was confusion, heads turned, the crowd broke up, people began to run.

"A foretaste of what's to come," said Paolo in my ear. "Why worry about him now? We'll get the lot tomorrow."

Once more he set the vespa in motion, and Caterina, appearing suddenly from the midst of the crowd, dashed forward and climbed on to the narrow space between the handle bars.

"Come on," she said breathlessly, "it will take the three of us. Let's see what's doing on the other hill."

We swerved out of the piazza del Duca Carlo, followed by Gino and Mario, and so on to the encircling road on the south-west side of Ruffano, beneath the city walls. Now the façade of the ducal palace shone in splendour, the twin towers paramount, and it was as if the whole edifice was suspended there between heaven and earth, carved out in silhouette against a canopy of stars. We roared down into the valley and up on to the southern hill, but as we topped the rise beneath the students' hostel and the new university buildings we saw at once that the intermediate roads were blocked. A group of students was there, and not only in force but armed.

"What is it? Are the Arts crowd rehearsing?" shouted Gino as we caught the flash of steel. But they were running down the hill towards us, silently, not shouting, and as Gino braked with his foot and swerved a spear came hurtling through the air and struck the ground in front of us. "Come on at your risk!" a voice called. "My God," cried Paolo, "that's no rehearsal!", and braking, like Gino, he turned, before a second spear could follow the first.

We plunged back the way we had come, down into the valley beneath the city walls, braking to a halt on the further side, where we dismounted, staring at one another, while in the distance the floodlit ducal palace shone unheeding and serene. All four faces were white. Caterina was trembling, but with excitement, not with fear.

"Now we know," said Gino, breathing quickly. "That's what they have in store for us tomorrow."

"We were warned," said Paolo quietly. "Donati warned us at the theatre on Monday night. It's a question of striking first, that's all. If we get their forward lines with stones and break them up we can rush them and fight close before they have time to launch those spears or use their swords."

"All the same," said Mario, "we ought to tell our leaders what we've seen. Aren't they meeting tonight in the via dei Martiri?"

"Yes," said Gino.

Paolo turned to me. "This may not be your fight, but you're part of it now," he said. "What about your brother? Is he connected with the university?"

"Indirectly," I said.

"Then you had better warn him what he'll be in for if he goes on the streets tomorrow."

"I think he knows," I answered.

Caterina stamped her foot impatiently. "Why waste time talking?" she asked. "Shouldn't we spread the word round amongst all our crowd?" Her small face, passionate and white, looked suddenly distorted under her cloud of hair. "None of us should go to bed tonight," she said. "We ought to bring the others out here into the countryside and dig for stones. We'll never find stones inside the city. They should be jagged, this size," she formed a circle with her hands, "and bound with rope, so that we can swing them with greater force."

"Catte's right," said Gino. "Let's get moving. First to the via dei Martiri to tell the leaders—they may want to issue new instructions. Come on, Mario."

He swung himself on to his machine, Mario behind him, and took the road towards the porta dei Martiri.

Paolo looked at me. "Well," he asked, "what now? Do you want us to take you to your brother?"

"No," I said.

I had made up my mind. To return to the pensione would achieve nothing. Aldo might even hand me over to his students with orders to drive me straight to Fano again. Whereas tomorrow . . . Tomorrow the cortège of the Falcon would leave the piazza del Duca Carlo at 10 a.m. What it would consist of I did not know. Nobody seemed to know. But Aldo would be with it, that I felt certain.

The night was warm. The leather jerkin bought at Pesaro was protection enough. I would spend the night in the open on one of the benches in the public gardens behind the piazza del Duca Carlo.

When I told Paolo this he shrugged his shoulders. "If that's how you want it, we won't prevent you," he said, "but you'll join us in the morning, remember. We shall be on the steps of San Cipriano. If you're not in your place by nine you may be stopped. Here, take this." He handed me a knife. "I'll get another out of Gino," he said. "After what we've seen tonight you're going to need it."

Caterina and I climbed once more on to his machine, and we scorched our way up the northern hill again. The crowds had thinned. Townsfolk and students, relatives and visiting tourists, were wending their way downhill to the city centre. I should have the public gardens to myself.

"Don't forget," said Caterina, "to fill your pockets with stones. You'll find plenty there, under the trees. And take your parcel. It will do as a pillow. We'll look out for you tomorrow, and good luck."

I watched them swerve down the hill and out of sight, and as they disappeared suddenly, without warning, the floodlights were extinguished everywhere. The statue of Duke Carlo became a shadow. The campanile by the Duomo struck eleven. The city churches followed, one by one. And when the last note sounded I stretched myself out on a bench in the gardens, the parcel as a pillow, and with folded arms stared up at the darkening sky.

CHAPTER TWENTY-TWO

I DON'T REMEMBER sleeping. There were just gaps in time between periods of cold. There was a moment when I stamped up and down blowing on my hands, so stiff and numb that I nearly crept for shelter within the comparative warmth of Professor Elia's portico, but did not do so because my vigil in the open was, in its strange way, a sort of test. Aldo had done this in the past, night after night, amongst his partisans. Romano, Antonio, Roberto . . . the boys brought up in the hills during the Resistance years, they had lived thus as children, but not I. The sleazy furnishing of second-rate hotels, not mountains, formed my background. My ceiling was an apartment room, cramped, confining, not the sky. The adults who spoilt and petted me to win favour from my mother spoke an alien tongue. Their uniforms stank, not of sweat and the clean earth as the torn clothes of the partisans would have done, but of yesterday's spilt wine, of perspiration dribbled out in lust instead of in war. Aldo and his comrades, the orphaned boys and theirs, had the hard ground for bed, or at most a sleeping-bag, while I lay stifled with eiderdowns and coverlets in a small room next my mother's, the partition thin; and the night-cries of the hills were never mine, nor the sound of mountain streams, nor the echo of storms, only the sighs of pleasure's aftermath.

Therefore tonight, at least, I would share in fantasy the beauty and the hardship of a reality I had not known. However cold I became, however numb, these sensations made me a partner in what had been. The stiffness of my limbs became an offering, my body's chill belated sacrifice.

As I have said, there was a gap in time between sleeping and waking, and then when the temperature was lowest I awoke and went and stood close to the orphanage gate, and watched the dawn break on Ruffano. First light was grey and cold, a phantom day, a temporary shifting of night's shadows, and then the sky hardened, becoming white, and the shrouded city turned to rose. The sun came up over the sleeping hills. Arrows of gold broke up the patterned valleys, then struck the shuttered windows of the city. The trees in the municipal gardens rustled, and the hesitant birds, waking to another day, stirred and murmured, then, as the light strengthened and the sunlight touched them, sang.

Day after day I had awakened as a child to Aldo's voice, or to Marta calling from the kitchen, but not to this. Then there had seemed security and certainty, morning promised an eternity. Now as the sun turned the city's spires to swords and the rounded Duomo to a ball of fire, I knew there was no promise and no eternity, or if eternity only a repetition of a million ages gone with none to care and all the dead extinguished. The men who had built Ruffano lived in memory alone. This was their epitaph. They had created beauty, and it was enough. They lived for a brief span to burn and die.

I wondered then why we should desire more, why we should yearn to perpetuate ourselves in some everlasting paradise. Man was Prometheus, bound to his symbol rock the earth and all the other undiscovered stars that shamed the dark. The challenge was to dare. To brave extinction.

I went on standing there, watching the sun bring warmth and life to my city of Ruffano. I thought, not only of Aldo but of all those students, now asleep, who in a few hours would be fighting in the streets. This Festival was neither play nor pageant, nor a mock representation of mediaeval splendour, but a summons to destroy. I could no more stop it than any single man could stop a war. Even if the order came at the last moment to cancel the Festival display, the students would disregard it. They wanted to fight. They wanted to kill. Just as their forebears had done through centuries in the same haunted, bloody streets. This time I should not escape, I should be one of them.

It was nearing seven when I heard the horses first. The steady clopping sound came from the piazza behind me, and turning I walked back to the statue and I saw the leading string climb the summit of the hill. They came in pairs, each rider leading a second horse, and they were approaching from the long road leading up to Ruffano from the valley below.

Then I remembered how last night, when we were circling the city on our vespas, I had seen lights in the sports stadium to the right of us, which in the excitement of our ride I had soon forgotten. The horses and their escort must have camped there before sundown, and were now arriving in the piazza to take part in the display. This was the cortège mentioned by Aldo in the ducal palace on Wednesday night.

The riders dismounted, leading their horses to the shelter of the trees. The sun was drawing the moisture from the ground, and it rose like steam from the soaking grass about Duke Carlo's statue, filling the morning air with scent like hay.

I drew nearer and counted the horses. There were eighteen of them, sleek and beautiful, their proud heads lifted curiously to stare about them. None of them was saddled. Their coats shone as though polished, and their tails, whisking at the first flies of the day, were like the proud plumes of conquerors. I went up and spoke to one of the men.

"Where do they come from?" I enquired.

"From Senigallia," he said.

I stared at him, disbelieving. "You mean these are race-horses?" I asked.

"Yes," he answered, smiling, "every one of them. Lent for the Festival, each horse specially trained for this display. They've been training in the hills all winter."

"Training for what?" I asked.

This time it was he who stared. "Why, for this morning's run, what else?" he said. "Don't they tell you what's to happen in your own city?"

"No," I said, "no. All we've been told is that a cortège leaves here at ten for the ducal palace."

"A cortège?" he repeated. "Well, you can call it that, but it's a poor description of what you are going to see." He laughed, and called to one of his companions. "Here's a student from Ruffano," he said, "wants to know what's going to happen. Break it gently."

"Keep out of the way," said the second man, "that's all. The horses are insured, that's what matters to their owners." And then he added, "It was tried out, so they told us, some five hundred years ago, and never since. They must breed madmen in your city. But if he breaks his neck it's his affair, not ours. Here, look at this."

A van had now drawn up by the side of the piazza, and the man beside the driver jumped out and opened the rear doors. They let down a ramp and then, with great care, two men to the shaft and two to the wheels, they lowered a small vehicle painted red and gold. It was a perfect replica of a Roman chariot, and bore upon the front and above each wheel the insignia of the Malebranche, the Falcon with spread wings.

So it was true. The crazy, fantastic feat attempted by Duke Claudio more than five centuries ago was to be repeated now. The pages I had quoted mockingly from the German history to Aldo last Sunday as Jehu's feat, never for one moment thinking that any representation of the event would be other than a staged affair with perhaps two horses—and he himself on Wednesday had spoken of it simply as a cortège—would be translated into fact. Duke Claudio had driven eighteen horses from the northern to the southern hill. There were eighteen horses before me now. It was not possible. It could not be. I tried to remember what the history said. "He was set upon and pursued by almost the entire populace, after having trampled many of them to death beneath his horses' hooves."

Now a second van drew into the piazza, smaller than the first, and from this they lowered harness, traces, collars, ornamented with studs bearing the Falcon's head, and carried these things to the shelter of the trees where the horses stood, and the smell of the leather, polished and bitter-sweet like spice, mingled with the warm horse flesh and the scent of trees.

The grooms in attendance upon the horses began to sort the harness and the other appurtenances, quietly, methodically, chatting amongst themselves. The very orderliness of the sight, the absence of fuss, as if what they did was just part of a regular morning routine, made it the more fantastic, and as the sun rose higher and the horror of what was to happen became more imminent, I felt a sort of terror invade my whole being. It started in my guts and seized my heart, at the same time paralysing thought. Hearing was keener. Every sound was magnified. The church bells had sounded for first Mass at six, then once more at seven, then at eight. They seemed, to my imagination now in turmoil, to be the summons to a city's doom, until I remembered that it was Passion week, and this the Friday dedicated to the Mother of God. When we were young Marta had escorted us to San Cipriano and we had laid bunches of wild flowers before the statuette, which, its painted prettiness veiled, symbolised the seven sorrows that pierced the heart. It seemed to me then, kneeling in bewilderment, that the Mother played a sorry part in her Son's story, first goading Him to change the water into wine, and later standing with relatives on the crowd's fringe, calling to Him in vain, receiving no answer. Perhaps this was the seventh sorrow that struck her down, which the priests in Ruffano's churches were now commemorating. If so, they would do better to forget one woman's pain and go out into the streets and prevent mass murder.

Now a cordon was being formed around the piazza by uniformed police to keep away the traffic and the early crowd. They smiled and joked, good-natured for this day of Festival, and now and again called out laughing instructions to the grooms, busy with their dressing of the horses.

The nightmare scene became more vivid, more appalling. None of them knew, none of them understood. I went up to one of the policemen and touched him on the shoulder.

"Can't it be stopped?" I said. "Can't it be prevented? It's not too late, even now."

He looked down at me, a big cheerful fellow, wiping the sweat from his brow. "If you've got a seat in a window along the route get to it," he said. "There'll be no one on the streets after nine, except performers."

He had not heard what I said. He was not interested. His job was to see that the piazza was kept clear for the horses and the chariot. He moved away. Panic enveloped me. I did not know where to go, what to do. This must be the fear that comes upon men before a battle when only discipline and training saves them. I had no such discipline, no such training. The desire of a child to flee, to hide himself, to stifle sight and sound, was paramount. I began to run towards the trees in the municipal gardens, thinking that if I flung myself head downward amongst the shrubs and grass the world would be blotted out. Then, as I blundered forward into the splurge of colour made up by the horses and the jingling harness, the gaily-painted chariot and the heedless grooms, I saw the Alfa-Romeo come up into the piazza. The driver must have seen me too, for the car braked suddenly and stopped, and I altered my useless panic course and ran towards it. The door opened, and Aldo sprang out and caught me as I fell.

He jerked me to my feet and I clung to him, stammering, incoherent. "Don't let it happen," I heard myself saying. "Don't let it happen, please, God, no . . ."

He hit me, and the oblivion I had sought for came. Pain brought darkness and release. When I opened my eyes, dizzy and sick, my head swimming, I found myself propped against a tree. Aldo was squatting by me, pouring steaming coffee from a thermos jug.

"Drink this," he said, "then eat."

He gave me the cup and I drank. Then he broke a roll in half and forced it into my mouth. Mechanically I did what I was told.

"You disobeyed orders," he said. "If a partisan did that we shot him instantly. That is, if we found him. Otherwise he was left to rot alone up in the hills."

The coffee warmed me. The dry bread tasted crisp and good. I snatched at a second roll, and then a third.

"Orders disobeyed put other men to inconvenience," he continued. "Time is wasted. Plans are disrupted. Go on, drink some more."

The preparations went on about us, the horses stamped, the harness jingled.

"Cesare gave me your message," he said. "When I got it I telephoned the café at Fano and asked them to fetch Marco to speak to me. When he told me you hadn't turned up at the boat I guessed something of this sort might happen. But I didn't think you would come here."

The panic had gone, whether because of the blow he had struck me, or because the food and drink he had given me filled my craving belly, I did not know.

"Where else should I go?" I asked him.

"To the police, possibly," he shrugged, "thinking by accusing me to clear yourself. It wouldn't have worked, you know. They would never have believed you." He got up, and crossing to one of the grooms picked up a wash-leather, soaked it in a pail of water and came back. "Wash your face with this," he said. "There's blood on your mouth."

I cleaned myself after a fashion, then ate another roll and had a second drink of coffee.

"I know why you killed Marta," I said. "I came back, not with any idea of going to the police—they can arrest me if they want to—but to tell you that I understand."

I stood up, throwing the soaking leather back to him and brushing the earth off my clothes. I had forgotten until then how insignificant I must look, scruffy and unshaven in my black jeans with the jade green shirt, my hair with the new cut shaped like a convict. Aldo, dressed as I had seen him at the ducal palace on Wednesday night in doublet and hose, with a short cape slung from his shoulders, resplendent, elegant, looked part of the background, just as the horses did, parading now beneath Duke Carlo's statue.

"There are two baptismal entries in the San Cipriano records," I said. "One for a son that died, the second for you. The double entries made no sense to me when I read them for the first time last week, nor your sponsor's name, Luigi Speca, nor even the letter I gave you on Wednesday night. It was only yesterday on the beach at Fano that I guessed the truth. There was a nun there, with a little group of orphan boys. She told me the Superintendent of Ruffano foundling hospital, some forty years ago, was called Luigi Speca."

Aldo stared down at me, unsmiling. Then, abruptly, he turned on his heel and left me. He walked over to the horses and began giving orders to the grooms. I watched and waited. The long preliminaries of harnessing began. Each horse was fitted with its own decorated collar, scarlet with golden flanges, and the bridles they had been wearing up to now were changed to others, decorated as the collars were, bearing across the headstrap a medallion of a Falcon's head. Two of the horses were fitted with small saddles close to their collars, fastened by broad bands of scarlet round their chests. The chariot was then drawn up to them and the pole attached to the saddles by golden chains. These yoked horses were the centre pair, bearing the chariot between them, but then I saw that two more horses were being coupled to the centre pair on either side, making six in all, their traces fastened to the chariot front. The twelve remaining horses in groups of four were harnessed in their turn, some distance ahead of the chariot bearers and their fellows, their reins leading back to the arched chariot top. The chariot itself, a featherweight above the rubber mounted wheels, had a semicircular guard around the front and sides and a floor to stand upon. There was space upon the floor for two, no more, and the rear was open without rail or step. Chains, fastened to the front and side like aircraft safety-straps, would bind the riders to the chariot sides. Once fastened and in motion the riders could not fall unless the chariot itself upturned, when the galloping horses would drag vehicle and passengers in their wake, and so to instant death.

Now that the horses were harnessed, and the chariot in place, all movement ceased. The grooms, standing at the horses' heads, were silent, as were the police cordonning off the piazza. Then Aldo moved from the chariot and came towards me. His face was pale, inscrutable, as it had been in the car on Wednesday night.

"I sent you to Fano believing it best for both of us," he said, "but since you are here you may as well play your part. The role of the Falcon is still yours. That is, if you have nerve enough to accept it."

The voice took me back to boyhood days. It was the old challenge, given with the same contemptuous grace, the same tacit suggestion of my own inferiority. Yet, strangely, the mocking tone no longer stung.

"Who would have played the Falcon if I had sailed with Marco?" I asked.

"I intended to drive alone," he said. "There were no couriers five centuries ago. The Falcon was his own charioteer."

"Very well," I said, "then today you can be mine."

My retort, as surprising to myself as it was to him, caught him momentarily off guard. He must have expected my boyhood plea to be spared participation in his adventures. Then he smiled.

"You'll find Duke Claudio's robe in the car," he said, "and the flaxen wig. Jacopo's there. He'll give them to you."

I was no longer conscious of feeling, or of fear. I was predestined to what must be. The decision had been taken. I walked over to the car, and Jacopo was standing there. I had not noticed him earlier when the car arrived, but he must have been beside Aldo all the time.

"I'm going with him," I said.

"Yes, Signor Beo," he replied.

There was an expression in his eyes I had not seen before. Surprise, yes, but it was also respect, even admiration.

"I'm to be Duke Claudio," I said, "and Aldo the charioteer."

He did not comment, but opened the door of the car and handed out the robe. He helped me into it and tied the girdle round my waist. Then he gave me the wig, and I put it over my cropped hair and stared at myself in the mirror.

There was a cut on my mouth where Aldo had struck me, and the blood had dried. The blonde wig framed my white, unshaven face, and my eyes confronted me, pale and staring, like the eyes of Claudio in the ducal palace picture. They were also the eyes of Lazarus in the church of San Cipriano.

I turned to Jacopo. "How do I look?" I said.

He considered me gravely, his head a little on one side. "You look just like your mother, Signora Donati," he replied.

He meant it kindly, but it was the final insult. The humiliation of the years returned. The foolish figure that pattered in bare feet back to the chariot and mounted beside Aldo was not Duke Claudio, not the Falcon it was supposed to represent, but a scarecrow effigy of the woman I had rejected and despised for twenty years.

I stood motionless, allowing Aldo to bind me to the chariot with the safety chains. Then he shackled himself. The guide reins of the centre horses, the guide reins of the leaders, were passed up to him by the attendants across the chariot front. The attendants released their hold upon the bridles as Aldo gathered the myriad reins in his two hands. The horses, feeling the strain, moved forward. The distant campanile by the Duomo sounded ten, echoed by all the churches of Ruffano. The flight of the Falcon had begun.

CHAPTER TWENTY-THREE

WE CIRCLED THE piazza first, proudly, sedately, processing like the triumphant entry of the Emperor Trajan into Rome. The twelve leaders wheeled to the right, obedient to the rein, and then the six in line abreast wheeled likewise, the turning movement like the slow unfolding of a gigantic fan, bearing our painted chariot behind them.

The roads were empty, as the policeman had said they would be, but every window was flung open, black with spectators, and as we paraded slowly before them the gasp of astonishment, of wonder, became magnified into a single cry. The cry rose in the air from multitudinous throats, turning from wonder to acclaim, and then the applause began, with upraised hands sounding as they clapped like the fluttering of innumerable wings. The eighteen horses, indifferent to the thunder, circled and moved on, the burnished metal on their trappings glittering in the morning sun, the jingle of the harness making its own defiant music in opposition to the tumult from the crowds. There was no clatter from the horses' hooves, for all were specially shod, and as they stepped the sound was muffled, dull, an oddly muted note, silent like our chariot wheels.

Twice we circled the piazza, twice the eighteen horses and their charioteer wheeled and straightened in deference to the applauding crowd, and then the attendants approached the horses' heads once more, leading them and us to the far end of the piazza where it was broadest. We turned again, and now we were directly facing the via del Duca Carlo leading downhill to the city. Adjustments were made to the guide reins and the traces, and to the girths of the centre horses. The attendants examined every horse in turn, reporting to Aldo. It took about four minutes, and it seemed to me in those last brief moments, when Aldo gathered the reins and the attendants fell back on either side, that I had reached the peak of fear; nothing, not the final holocaust nor the ultimate crash, could exceed this second.

I looked at Aldo. He was pale, as always, but now with a tense excitement I had never seen in him before, and the smile at the corner of his mouth was a grimace.

I said to him, "Shall I pray?"

"If it stops the panic in your guts I should," he answered. "The only permissible prayer is a prayer for courage."

None of my childhood prayers was appropriate, neither the Pater Noster nor the Ave Maria. I thought of all the millions upon millions who had prayed to God and died—even Christ Himself upon the Cross.

"It's too late," I told him. "I never had any courage anyway. I depend on yours."

He laughed, and called to his horses. They broke into a trot and then a gallop, gathering speed, the muffled hoof-beats thudding the hard ground.

"Your German Commandant should have quoted Nietzsche to you," he said. "He who no longer finds what is great in God will find it nowhere; he must either deny it or create it."

We came to the front of the piazza and the last of the level ground, and the crowds, seeing the galloping horses, broke once more into a tornado of applause. The cries from the piazza now behind us were echoed by the waiting masses at each window, and for a single moment, here on the summit of the northern hill, I saw the full compass of the city spread below, roof-tops, churches, spires, and away yonder, crowning the southern slope, the Duomo and the ducal palace. Then the via del Duca Carlo opened up beneath us like the descent to hell, and as the street narrowed and curved, and the leading horses wheeled to the guiding reins, never pausing in their headlong flight, their muffled hooves stabbing the cobbles with their muted thunderous note, the houses closed in upon us, leaning precariously from the hill like cardboard shapes with windows all agape, each window spilling out a face, a scream, a terrible tumultuous roar.

There were no cordons here, no uniformed police, the street was ours alone, and when it narrowed before descending to the piazza della Vita in the city's heart the six horses spanning the chariot like a fan behind the leaders reached to the via del Duca Carlo's limits on either side. One check, one startled shy from any of the twelve leading horses, and he would bring his fellows down; they would collapse one upon the other in a sickening, plunging mass, ourselves and the chariot upturned and buried in the midst of them.

The street curved and narrowed further yet, the flanking horses must surely brush the lintels of the doors, and as we plunged deeper towards the city's heart I was not conscious of speed, nor of Aldo's voice cheering and calling to the horses, nor of the lurching, swaying cradle in which I stood; but only of the massed and terrified faces at all the windows, of the mounting screams as our headlong pace increased, and in my nostrils the smell of horseflesh and under my clenched hands the burning chariot rail. The church of San Cipriano swam into my line of vision on the left, the steps thronged with students, yelling, shouting, and there were students massing on the converging streets, and down we thundered into the piazza della Vita, every window of every building alight, aflame, with hands gesticulating, mouths that shouted, screamed. The horses, finding level ground again, tore on, the leaders heading for the via Rossini on the far side of the piazza, and so up the ascending hill towards the ducal palace, spurred by their own impetus, maddened and excited by the crescendo of terror and applause.

Looking back, I saw the students break from the streets into the piazza, burst from windows, doors, pour on to the square and cover it in a sudden movement like a massive tidal wave. But instead of the roar of anger I expected, the volleys of stones, the clash of steel, the outburst of pent-up hatred as the opposing factions met and mingled, they started swarming up the hill behind us, shouting, cheering, waving, and they were calling as they ran, "Donati . . . Donati . . . viva Donati . . ."

Now as we mounted the southern hill, up the via Rossini, our painted chariot lurching, trembling behind the galloping horses, the students spilt out of the buildings on either side to join their fellows. The screaming stopped, and the terror too, and the violence that came from all of them was the violence of excitement, of acclaim. All the city shouted, and there was no other sound but this, the roar "Donati . . . Donati . . ." Aldo yelled into my ear "Are they fighting yet?" and I yelled back at him, "They're not going to fight; they're coming after us. Don't you hear them calling you?"

Intent upon the horses he only smiled, and now as the street narrowed and became steeper yet the leaders, feeling the upward strain, strove to mount the hill before losing impetus, before the steeply rising street, curving to the right, defeated their attempt to master gravity.

"Arri! Arri!" yelled Aldo, and the cry, spurring the leaders to greater effort, with the thunder of the six abreast behind them, brought them in sight of the piazza Maggiore before the ducal palace and gallantly, superbly, they breasted the last incline. As they faltered, staggered, the students waiting beyond the fountain ran towards them, seizing their bridles. Our curving fan of six abreast, bearing us with them, dared the final slope, and sobbing, with heaving flanks, they felt the check of rein at last, and trembled to a halt where the piazza broadened before the palace doors.

Still the multitudinous cries rang out, and as I stared about me, dizzy, one hand still clutching the chariot rail, I saw that the windows of the ducal palace were black with faces too, as were the houses opposite. People were standing on the steps of the Duomo, they were clinging to the fountain, and now the mass of students who had followed us up the hill from the piazza della Vita came swarming into the square. In a moment we should be surrounded, overwhelmed, but the armed students waiting by the palace doors formed an immediate circle round us, while each of the eighteen horses had a student on either side to hold his bridle. The cavalcade, ourselves amongst it, was now protected by a single cordon bearing swords, each student dressed as Aldo was, in doublet and hose, and I recognised his friends, Cesare, Giorgio, Federico, Domenico, Sergio, and others of his bodyguard. The picture that they made, the splash of colour beside the painted chariot and the eighteen horses, still panting, heaving, from their victorious course, checked the body of emerging students as they advanced, shouting and yelling, on to the square. Once again the cry went up, "Donati . . . viva Donati . . .", echoed from the palace windows, from the houses opposite, from the Duomo steps. I looked at Aldo. He had the reins still in his hands and he was gazing down at the eighteen horses, unmindful of the cheers. Then he turned to me.

"We've done it," he said. "We've done it . . ." and he started laughing, he threw back his head and laughed, the laughter taken up with cheers by the waiting crowds of students and Ruffanesi. Then he unshackled me from the chains binding me to the chariot front, unshackled himself as well, and shouted to the students beyond the cordon, "Here is the Falcon! Here is your Duke!"

I saw nothing but waving arms and tossing heads, and the shouting never ceased but grew ever louder. The students guarding the chariot shouted too, and I stood there bewildered, helpless, a foolish figure in my golden wig and saffron robe, acknowledging the cheers that were not meant for me.

Something hit me on the cheek and fell upon the chariot floor. It was not the stone that I expected but a flower, and the girl who threw the flower was Caterina.

"Armino," she cried, "Armino!" her enormous eyes wide with laughter, and I saw that my saffron robe had come adrift, showing the jade shirt beneath and the black jeans, and wave upon wave of laughter, happy, friendly, rippled above the cheers.

I said to Aldo, "It's not me they want, it's you," but he did not answer, and looking behind me I saw that he had leapt from the chariot, and, diving under the surrounding cordon, was racing to the side door of the ducal palace. I cried to Giorgio, "Stop him . . . stop him . . ." but Giorgio, laughing, shook his head.

"It's part of the plan," he said, "it's all in the book. He's going to show himself to the crowds in the Piazza del Mercato from the palace."

I tore off my robe and the wig, and flung them down, and leapt out of the chariot after Aldo. The laughter and the cheers pursued me—I heard them as I ran. I shook off the restraining hand of Domenico, who tried to stop me, and ran through the side door, along the passage and across the quadrangle in chase of Aldo. I heard him race up the stairs to the gallery above, and I went after him. He burst through the great door to the throne room, and he was laughing as he ran. I was close upon his heels but he slammed the door, and when I opened it he had fled through the throne room to the Room of the Cherubs and beyond.

"Aldo . . ." I shouted, "Aldo . . ."

There was no one there. The Room of the Cherubs was empty. So was the Duke's bedroom, and the dressing-room, and the small temple beneath the right-hand tower. Hearing voices I went to the balcony between the towers, and Signora Butali was there, with the Rector, both of them staring at the piazza del Mercato far below. They turned in astonishment as I burst upon them, staring at me blankly, the signora in sudden fear.

"What is it, what's happened?" she asked. "We heard them cheering in the city. Is it all over?"

"How can it be over?" said the Rector. "Donati told us himself the finale followed the chariot flight. We've seen nothing yet."

He seemed perplexed, disappointed, cheated of the magnificence he had not witnessed. I went from the balcony through the study to the audience room. It was empty, like the others. Then, as I called Aldo once again, Carla Raspa came through from the gallery beyond. She put out her hands to me, laughing, crying.

"I saw you from the window," she said. "It was wonderful, superb. I watched you both driving behind the horses on to the piazza Maggiore. Where has he gone?"

There were no guardians here today, no guides. The portrait of the gentlewoman stood on its easel unattended, the tapestry was in its place upon the wall. I ran across the room and jerked it back, revealing the closed door. I opened it, and putting one hand before the other on the narrow twisting steps began to climb. As I climbed I shouted, "Aldo!" The sickness and the vertigo I had suffered as a child enveloped me. I could not see, I could only feel the twisting spiral of the steps above. Up, up, forever up, with bursting heart and retching belly, and the creeping dust of years on my fumbling hands. I heard myself sobbing as I crawled, and the tower was forever out of reach, like the pit below. Time was suspended, reason with it. There was nothing left within me but the urge to climb, and sliding, stumbling, I swung between heaven and hell. Then, raising my head, I felt the air upon it, and the door above was open to the balustrade. Once more I shouted "Aldo!", opening my eyes for the first time since I had begun to crawl the twisting stair. The patch of sky, brilliant with the sun, distorted vision. I thought I saw the spread wings of a bird, its body darkening the open door, and crawling blindly on, dizzy with nausea, I gripped the topmost stair and peered about me, recognising nothing.

The door was half the size of the one I dimly recollected from childhood days, and the narrow ledge beyond it, in the open, was not the balustrade we used to climb. The shape was not rounded but octagonal. Suddenly I understood. I had climbed beyond the balustrade. This was the smaller parapet beneath the minaret. The pinnacle rose above me to the sky.

I felt his hands upon me. He dragged me from the stairway to the ledge.

"Lie still," said Aldo. "The ledge reaches between hip and thigh, no more. If you look down, you'll fall."

It seemed to me that the turret rocked. Perhaps it was the sky. My hands fastened upon his. Mine were slippery with sweat, but his were cold.

"How did you find the way?" he asked.

"The door," I said, "the hidden door behind the tapestry. I remembered."

The eyes, astonished, searching, turned to laughter. "You win," he said. "I reckoned without that. Poor Beato . . ."

Then frowning, steadying me with his arm, he said, "You'd have done better to go with Marco on the boat. That's why I sent you to him. This isn't your battle. I realised that on Wednesday night."

They were still cheering and shouting in the piazza Maggiore by the entrance to the ducal palace, and now the cry had been taken up from the piazza del Mercato below the towers. Lying against Aldo I could see nothing but the sky. The shouting, coming from beneath us, rose on every side. The students must be swarming downhill from the Maggiore to the Mercato some hundreds of feet lower, beyond the Porta del Sangue and the city wall.

"There's been no battle," I said. "You miscalculated. Your firebrand speeches were just wasted effort. Hark at those cheers."

"That's what I meant," he said. "It could have gone the other way. If we and the horses had crashed, if we had failed, they'd have been murdering each other now, each faction screaming sabotage. It was a gamble."

I stared at him, uncomprehending. "You did it deliberately?" I asked. "You roused them to that pitch of frenzy, dicing with hundreds of lives, your own as well, on the incredibly long odds that Claudio's feat might temporarily unite them?"

He looked at me and smiled. "Not so temporary," he said. "You'll see. They've smelt blood, that's what they wanted. And the city too. Everyone who watched us ride today participated. It's the first and last lesson someone directing any spectacle has to learn: make your audience one."

Still holding me, he brought me closer to the narrow balustrade, and clutching his arm I stared down to the piazza del Mercato below the city walls. The great market-place was black with people, so were the converging streets, and immediately beneath us, on the sloping palace precincts, massed groups of students stood, their heads upturned.

"If by the remotest chance," he said, "my second exploit fails, I've left everything to you. It's yours by right. I made my will on Wednesday night after you gave me that letter, and had it witnessed by Livia Butali and her husband. The will says that we are brothers—my vanity forbade me to admit otherwise."

The cry "Donati" came now from the piazza del Mercato, as the students from above the palace went to swell those in the crowds below. They must have seen us move on our narrow ledge beneath the minaret, for the cries grew louder, and the cheers, and all the heads were tilted to the sky.

"You were right to suspect my determination not to lose face," said Aldo, "but wrong to accuse me of silencing the slanderer. The thief in Rome confessed. He stole and also murdered. The Commissioner telephoned to tell me late last night. The police weren't after you—they simply wanted to find out whether you knew more than you had told them."

"You didn't kill Marta?" I stammered, astonished and ashamed.

"Yes, I killed her," he said, "but not with a knife—the knife was merciful. I killed her by despising her, by being too proud to accept the fact I was her son. Wouldn't you say that counts as murder?"

Aldo was Marta's *son*. Then it all swung into focus. The pieces fitted. The foundling boy, with his mother to care for him as nurse, came to live under my parents' roof. The foundling took the place of the boy they had lost. The mother stayed, devoting herself to Aldo, then to me. She kept her secret until that birthday evening in November, when on a sudden lonely, drunken impulse she revealed the truth.

"Well," repeated Aldo, "it was murder, wasn't it?"

I thought no more of his relationship to Marta, but of my own mother who had died of cancer in Turin. When she had scribbled me a line from hospital, I had not answered.

"Yes," I said, "it was murder. But we're both guilty, and for the same cause."

Together we looked down at the cheering crowds. The cry "Donati . . . viva Donati!" was for neither of us; it was for a legendary figure which the university students and the Ruffanesi had created in their minds, born of all men's desire to worship something greater than themselves.

"The flight's over," I said. "Tell them it's finished."

"It isn't finished," he said. "The true flight's yet to come. Tested in the hills, just like the chariot drive."

He propped me against the ledge, and groping his way round the narrow balustrade reached down into the parapet for something long and slender, silver-coloured, made up of a million feathers that as he touched them shivered in the wind. The feathers were sewn upon silk, the silk of a parachute, and beneath the material were fibre struts, interwoven and interlaced. Cords hung from the centre, forming a harness. Aldo lifted them up, standing the whole contrivance on the parapet floor, and he unfolded them, and I saw that they were wings.

"No deception," said Aldo. "We've been working on these all winter. When I say we, I mean my ex-partisan friends who fly glider 'planes today. These wings are designed to a specific formula, identical with the real wings of a falcon. We tried them out in the hills, just as we did the horses, and I can promise you they frighten me far less."

He stood there laughing at me. "On my last flight I was airborne for ten minutes," he said, "on the western slopes of Monte Cappello. I tell you, Beo, there's nothing to it. The mechanism can't fail. The only thing that can fail is the human element. And after what I've just achieved that isn't likely."

He was no longer white and tense as he had been before the race. The smile on his face was joyous, no grimace. He raised one hand in salutation to the cheering crowds below.

"The landing may be ungainly, not the flight," he said. "I aim to clear the piazza itself, and strike the softer ground where the valley slopes. The parachute behind the wings will open when I release the cords, and become my brake. They told me, when I did it in the hills, that the actual drop looked like a crumpled kite. But you never know. I might soar further this time."

His confidence was arrogant, supreme. He looked out to the distant hills and smiled.

"Aldo, don't go," I said. "It's madness. Suicide."

He was not listening. He did not care. His faith was a fanatic's faith, proved through centuries to bring believers to destruction. Like Claudio before him, he could only die.

Standing on the ledge he began to strap the harness about his waist, buckle the bindings to his shoulders, step into the slots which would enclose his feet. He put both arms into the fibre webbing beneath the wings, raising them aloft. Spread-eagled thus, he appeared to me helpless, even grotesque. He would never free himself from the lashings that encompassed him. The fibre, black beneath the silver, looked like nails.

The crowd, three hundred feet or more below us in the piazza del Mercato, became suddenly silent. The massed heads, upturned, no longer cried "Donati!" They watched and waited while the figure, self-imprisoned, stood motionless on the parapet edge, outlined against the sky.

I crawled closer and put my arms about him, clasping his legs. "No," I said, "no . . ."

I must have shouted, for my voice came back to me in echo, mocking me, and travelling downwards was caught by the crowd immediately beneath, so breeding fear. A sigh arose, swelling to protestation and alarm.

"Listen to them," I cried. "They don't want it. They're afraid. You've proved yourself once. Why in the name of God again?"

He looked down at me and smiled. "Because that's it," he said. "Once is never enough. That's what they have to learn. You, Cesare, all those waiting students, all Ruffano—once is no good. You must always risk a second time, a third, a fourth, no matter what it is you want to achieve. Get out of my way!"

He thrust backwards with his foot and sent me sprawling against the door. I slumped sideways, striking the step with my chest, and, momentarily winded, knelt there an instant, gasping for breath, my eyes closed. When I opened them again he was standing with the wings spread poised for flight. He no longer looked grotesque, but beautiful. As he launched himself into the air the wind current filled the lining of the wings and they bellied out, then tautened, like the sudden jerking of a child's toy. His body was horizontal between the wings, his arms and feet within the slots were part of the structure. Buoyant, effortless, he soared above the crowd, drifting with the wind as he had foretold. The feathers, silver in the sunlight, turned to gold. Gliding south, he would touch down in the valley beyond the market-place.

I watched for him to pull the rip-cord of the braking parachute, as he had described. He did not do so. Instead, he must have kicked his body free, letting the apparatus which he had helped to build drift on without him. He threw himself clear, spreading his arms wide like the wings he had discarded, then, bringing them to his side, he plummeted to earth and fell, his body, small and fragile, a black streak against the sky.

PROFESSOR ALDO DONATI, Director of the Arts Council and a leading citizen of our beloved city, who lost his life in a tragic accident on the day of the Festival, will be mourned, not only by his surviving brother and his friends, but by every student within the university, by his colleagues and associates, and by all the inhabitants of the Ruffano he loved so well. The eldest son of Aldo Donati, who for many years was Superintendent of the Ducal Palace, he was born and educated in the city. During the war he served in the Air Force and won his pilot's wings. Shot down in 1943 he managed to escape, and during the German Occupation he formed a group of irregulars in the mountains and fought amongst his fellow-partisans until the Liberation.

Returning to Ruffano, he learnt of his father's death some time previously in an Allied prison camp, and his mother's and younger brother's presumed death by enemy bombing. Undaunted though bereaved, Aldo Donati studied at the university of Ruffano, and obtained an Honours Degree in Arts. He joined the Arts Council and devoted the remainder of his life to his work for the Council, for the preservation of the ducal palace and its treasures, and, last but not least, for the welfare of orphaned students. It was my privilege, as Rector of the university, to work with him on Festival productions, and I can only state, without any qualification whatsoever, that his ability in this field surpassed anything I had hitherto seen. He was brilliant, and his enthusiasm so inspired his actors and all who took part in Festival productions that they came to believe—and I speak from experience, my wife and I being amongst the participants until this year—that what they enacted was not fiction but reality.

Whether his choice for this year's Festival production was wise or not need not be discussed here. The unhappy Duke Claudio is not one whose memory we wish to recall; the Ruffanesi of both yesterday and today prefer to forget him. He was an evil man with evil intentions, ill-disposed to all his people, admired only by a narrow circle of friends as ignoble as himself. He left behind him a legacy of hate. However this may be, Aldo Donati decided that he had a claim to fame, if only because of his Jehu feat of driving eighteen horses through the city of Ruffano, from the northern to the southern hill. Whether Duke Claudio actually achieved this feat is still uncertain. Aldo Donati did. The people who watched him do so on Friday morning will never forget the experience.

Had he stopped there, it would have sufficed. What he had achieved was fantastic, even sublime. But he aimed higher still, and lost his life in so aiming. The mechanism was not at fault. Experts have examined the apparatus. Aldo Donati seems to have ignored the elementary rule learnt by every student parachutist—to pull the ripcord. Why he ignored it, we shall never know. His brother Armino Donati, who returned to Ruffano last week after an absence of over twenty years and who will, we hope, remain with us to carry on the work with orphaned students, told me he believed that his brother, in mid-air, had a sudden vision, some sort of ecstasy blinding him to danger.

It may be true. Like Icarus, he flew too near the sun. Like Lucifer, he fell. We, the Ruffanesi who remain, salute the courage of a man who dared.

GASPARE BUTALI,
Rector, University of Ruffano.

Ruffano. Easter Week.

THE HOUSE ON THE STRAND

For
my predecessors
at Kilmarth

Acknowledgements

I WISH TO thank Miss Hawkridge, Senior Assistant Archivist of the County Record Office, Truro; Mr H. L. Douch, M.A., Curator of the County Museum, Truro; Mr R. Blewett, M.A., of St Day; Mrs St George Saunders; and the Public Record Office, to all of whom I am indebted for information and original documents. Most especially I should like to express my gratitude to Mr J. R. Thomas of the Tywardreath Old Cornwall Society, whose unfailing kindness and generosity in lending me his own notes on the history of the Manor and Priory of Tywardreath first awakened my interest, and set me on the road to blending fact and fiction in this tale of the House on the Strand.

DAPHNE DU MAURIER

Note

A map and a family tree will be found on pages 665 and 667.

CHAPTER ONE

THE FIRST THING I noticed was the clarity of the air, and then the sharp green colour of the land. There was no softness anywhere. The distant hills did not blend into the sky but stood out like rocks, so close that I could almost touch them, their proximity giving me that shock of surprise and wonder which a child feels looking for the first time through a telescope. Nearer to me, too, each object had the same hard quality, the very grass turning to single blades, springing from a younger, harsher soil than the soil I knew.

I had expected—if I expected anything—a transformation of another kind: a tranquil sense of well-being, the blurred intoxication of a dream, with everything about me misty, ill-defined; not this tremendous impact, a reality more vivid than anything hitherto experienced, sleeping or awake. Now every impression was heightened, every part of me singularly aware: eyesight, hearing, sense of smell, all had been in some way sharpened.

All but the sense of touch: I could not feel the ground beneath my feet. Magnus had warned me of this. He had told me, "You won't be aware of your body coming into contact with inanimate objects. You will walk, stand, sit, brush against them, but will feel nothing. Don't worry. The very fact that you can move without sensation is half the wonder."

This, of course, I had taken as a joke, one of the many bribes to goad me to experiment. Now he was proved right. I started to go forward, and the sensation was exhilarating, for I seemed to move without effort, feeling no contact with the ground.

I was walking downhill towards the sea, across those fields of sharp-edged silver grass that glistened under the sun, for the sky—dull, a moment ago, to my ordinary eyes—was now cloudless, a blazing ecstatic blue. I remembered that the tide had been out, the stretches of flat sand exposed, the row of bathing-huts, lined like dentures in an open mouth, forming a solid background to the golden expanse. Now they had gone, and with them the rows of houses fronting the road, the docks, all of Par—chimneys, roof-tops, buildings—and the sprawling tentacles of St Austell enveloping the countryside beyond the bay. There was nothing left but grass and scrub, and the high distant hills that seemed so near; while before me the sea rolled into the bay, covering the whole stretch of sand as if a tidal wave had swept over the land, swallowing it in one rapacious draught. To the north-west the cliffs came down to meet the sea, which, narrowing gradually, formed a wide estuary, the waters sweeping inward, following the curve of the land and so vanishing out of sight.

When I came to the edge of the cliff and looked beneath me, where the road should be, the inn, the café, the almshouses at the base of Polmear hill, I realised that the sea swept inland here as well, forming a creek that cut to the east, into the valley. Road and houses had gone, leaving only a dip between the land which rose on either side of the creek. Here the channel ran narrowly between banks of mud and sand, so that at low tide the water would surely seep away, leaving a marshy track that could be forded, if not on foot, at least by a horseman. I descended the hill and stood beside the creek, trying to pin-point in my mind the exact course of the road I knew, but already the old sense of orientation had gone: there was nothing to serve as guide except the ground itself, the valley and the hills.

The waters of the narrow channel rippled swift and blue over the sand, leaving on either side a frothy scum. Bubbles formed, expanded and vanished, and all the ordinary timeless waste came drifting with the tide, tresses of dark seaweed, feathers, twigs, the aftermath of some autumnal gale. I knew, in my own time, it was high summer, however dull and overcast the day, but all about me now was the clearer light of approaching winter, surely an early afternoon when the bright sun, already flaming in the west, would turn the sky dark crimson before the night clouds came.

The first live things swam into vision, gulls following the tide, small waders skimming the surface of the stream, while high on the opposite hill, sharply defined against the sky-line, a team of oxen ploughed their steady course. I closed my eyes, then opened them again. The team had vanished behind the rise of the field they worked, but the cloud of gulls, screaming in their wake, told me they had been a living presence, no figment of a dream.

I drank deep of the cold air, filling my lungs. Just to breathe was a joy never yet experienced for its own sake, having some quality of magic that I had not sensed before. Impossible to analyse thought, impossible to let my reason play on what I saw: in this new world of perception and delight there was nothing but intensity of feeling to serve as guide.

I might have stood for ever, entranced, content to hover between earth and sky, remote from any life I knew or cared to know; but then I turned my head and saw that I was not alone. The hooves had made no sound—the pony must have travelled as I had done, across the fields—and now that it trod upon the shingle the clink of stone against metal came to my ears with a sudden shock, and I could smell the warm horse-flesh, sweaty and strong.

Instinct made me back away, startled, for the rider came straight towards me, unconscious of my presence. He checked his pony at the water's edge and looked seaward, measuring the tide. Now, for the first time, I experienced not only excitement but fear as well, for this was no phantom figure but solid, real, the shape of foot in stirrup, hand on rein, all too perilously close for my comfort. I did not fear being ridden down: what jolted me to a sudden sense of panic was the encounter itself, this bridging of centuries between his time and mine. He shifted his gaze from the sea and looked straight at me. Surely he saw me, surely I read, in those deep-set eyes, a signal of recognition? He smiled, patted his pony's neck, then, with a swift kick of heel to flank, urged the beast across the ford, straight through the narrow channel, and so to the other side.

He had not seen me, he could not see me; he lived in another time. Why, then, the sudden shift in the saddle, the swing round to look back over his shoulder to where I stood? It was a challenge. "Follow if you dare!"— compelling, strange. I measured the depth of water across the ford, and, though it had reached the pony's hocks, plunged after him, careless of a wetting, realising when I reached the other side that I had walked dry-shod, without sensation.

The horseman rode uphill, I following, the track he took muddied and very steep, swinging abruptly to the left when it traversed the higher ground. This, I remembered, pleased with the recognition, was the same course that the lane took today—I had driven up it only that morning. Here resemblance ended, for no hedges banked the track as they did in my own time. Plough-lands lay to right and left, bare to the winds, and patches of scrubby moor with clumps of furze. We came abreast the team of oxen, and for the first time I could see the man who drove them, a small, hooded figure humped over a heavy wooden plough. He raised a hand in greeting to my horseman, shouted something, then plodded on, the gulls crying and wheeling above his head.

This greeting of one man to another seemed natural, and the sense of shock that had been part of me since I first saw the horseman at the ford gave place to wonder, then acceptance. I was reminded of my first journey as a child in France, travelling by sleeper overnight, throwing open the carriage window in the morning to see foreign fields fly by, villages, towns, figures labouring the land humped like the ploughman now, and thinking, with childish wonder, "Are they alive like me, or just pretending?"

My excuse for wonder was greater now than then. I looked at my horseman and his pony, and moved within touching, smelling distance. Both exhaled a pungency so strong that they seemed of the essence of life itself. The sweat-streaks on the pony's flanks, the shaggy mane, the fleck of froth at the bit's edge; and that broad knee in the stockinged leg, the leather jerkin laced across the tunic, that movement in the saddle, those hands upon the reins, that face itself, lantern-jawed and ruddy, framed in black hair which fell below his ears—this was reality, I the alien presence.

I longed to stretch out my hand and lay it on the pony's flank, but I remembered Magnus's warning. "If you meet a figure from the past, don't for heaven's sake touch him. Inanimate objects don't matter, but if you try to make contact with living flesh the link breaks, and you'll come to with a very unpleasant jerk. I tried it: I know."

The track led across the plough-lands and then dipped, and now the whole altered landscape spread itself before my eyes. The village of Tywardreath, as I had seen it a few hours earlier, had utterly changed. The cottages and houses that had formed a jigsaw pattern, spreading north and west from the church, had vanished: there was a hamlet here now, boxed together by a child, like the toy farm I used to play with on my bedroom floor. Small dwellings, thatch-roofed, squat, clustered round a sprawling green on which were pigs, geese, chickens, two or three hobbled ponies, and the inevitable prowling dogs.

Smoke rose from these humble dwellings, but not from any chimneys, from some hole in the thatch. Then grace and symmetry took charge again, for below the cluster was the church. But not the church that I had known a few hours earlier. This one was smaller and had no tower, and forming part of it, or so it seemed, ran a long, low building of stone, the whole encompassed by stone walls. Within this enclosure were orchards, gardens, outbuildings, a wooded copse, and beneath the copse the land sloped to a valley, and up that valley came the long arm of the sea.

I would have stood and stared, the setting had such beauty and simplicity, but my horseman travelled on, and compulsion to follow sent me after him. The track descended to the green, and now the village life was all about me; there were women by the well at the near corner of the green, their long skirts caught up round the waist, their heads bound with cloth covering them to the chin, so that nothing showed but eyes and nose. The arrival of my horseman created disturbance. Dogs started barking, more women appeared from the dwellings that now, on closer inspection, proved to be little more than hovels, and there was a calling to and fro across the green, the voices, despite the uncouth clash of consonants, ringing with the unmistakable Cornish burr.

The rider turned left, dismounted before the walled enclosure, flung his reins over a staple in the ground, and entered through a broad, brass-studded doorway. Above the arch there was a carving showing the robed figure of a saint, holding in his right hand the cross of St Andrew. My Catholic training, long forgotten, even mocked, made me cross myself before the door, and as I did so a bell sounded from within, striking so profound a chord in my memory that I hesitated before entering, dreading the old power that might turn me back into the childhood mould.

I need not have worried. The scene that met my eyes was not that of orderly paths and quadrangles, quiet cloisters, the odour of sanctity, the silence born of prayer. The gate opened upon a muddied yard, round which two men were chasing a frightened boy, flicking at his bare thighs with flails. Both, from their dress and tonsure, were monks, and the boy a novice, his skirt secured above his waist to make their sport more piquant.

The horseman watched the pantomime unmoved, but when the boy at last fell, his habit about his ears, his skinny limbs and bare backside exposed, he called, "Don't bleed him yet. The Prior likes sucking-pig served without sauce. The garnish will come later when the piglet turns tough." Meanwhile the bell for prayer continued, without effect upon the sportsmen in the yard.

My horseman, his sally applauded, crossed the yard and entered the building that lay before us, turning into a passage-way which seemed to divide kitchen from refectory, judging by the smell of rancid fowl, only partly sweetened by turf smoke from the fire. Ignoring the warmth and savour of the kitchen to the right, and the colder comfort of the refectory with its bare benches on his left, he pushed through a centre door and up a flight of steps to a higher level, where the passage was barred by yet another door. He knocked upon it, and without waiting for an answer walked inside.

The room, with timbered roof and plastered walls, had some semblance of comfort, but the scrubbed and polished austerity, a vivid memory of my own childhood, was totally absent. This rush-strewn floor was littered with discarded bones half-chewed by dogs, and the bed in the far corner, with its musty hangings, appeared to serve as a general depository for dumped goods—a rug made from a sheep's coat, a pair of sandals, a rounded cheese on a tin plate, a fishing-rod, with a greyhound scratching itself in the midst of all.

"Greetings, Father Prior," said my horseman.

Something rose to a sitting posture in the bed, disturbing the greyhound, which leapt to the floor, and the something was an elderly, pink-cheeked monk, startled from his sleep.

"I left orders I was not to be disturbed," he said.

My horseman shrugged. "Not even for the Office?" he asked, and put out his hand to the dog, which crept beside him, wagging a bitten tail.

The sarcasm brought no reply. The Prior dragged his coverings closer, humping his knees beneath him. "I need rest," he said, "all the rest possible, to be in a fit state to receive the Bishop. You have heard the news?"

"There are always rumours," answered the horseman.

"This was not rumour. Sir John sent the message yesterday. The Bishop has already set out from Exeter and will be here on Monday, expecting hospitality and shelter for the night with us, after leaving Launceston."

The horseman smiled. "The Bishop times his visit well. Martinmas, and fresh meat killed for his dinner. He'll sleep with his belly full, you've no cause for worry."

"No cause for worry?" The Prior's petulant voice touched a higher key. "You think I can control my unruly mob? What kind of impression will they make upon that new broom of a Bishop, primed as he is to sweep the whole Diocese clean?"

"They'll come to heel if you promise them reward for seemly behaviour. Keep in the good graces of Sir John Carminowe, that's all that matters."

The Prior moved restlessly beneath his covers. "Sir John is not easily fooled, and he has his own way to make, with a foot in every camp. Our patron he may be, but he won't stand by me if it doesn't suit his ends."

The horseman picked up a bone from the rushes, and gave it to the dog. "Sir Henry, as lord of the manor, will take precedence over Sir John on this occasion," he said. "He'll not disgrace you, garbed like a penitent. I warrant he is on his knees in the chapel now."

The Prior was not amused. "As the lord's steward you should show more respect for him," he observed, then added thoughtfully, "Henry de Champernoune is a more faithful man of God than I."

The horseman laughed. "The spirit is willing, Father Prior, but the flesh?" He fondled the greyhound's ear. "Best not talk about the flesh before the Bishop's visit." Then he straightened himself and walked towards the bed. "The French ship is lying off Kylmerth. She'll be there for two more tides if you want to give me letters for her."

The Prior thrust off his covers and scrambled from the bed. "Why in the name of blessed Antony did you not say so at once?" he cried, and began to rummage amongst the litter of assorted papers on the bench beside him. He presented a sorry sight in his shift, with spindle legs mottled with varicose veins, and hammer-toed, singularly dirty feet. "I can find nothing in this jumble," he complained. "Why are my papers never in order? Why is Brother Jean never here when I require him?"

He seized a bell from the bench and rang it, exclaiming in protest at the horseman, who was laughing again. Almost at once a monk entered: from his prompt response he must have been listening at the door. He was young and dark, and possessed a pair of remarkably brilliant eyes.

"At your service, Father," he said in French, and before he crossed the room to the Prior's side exchanged a wink with the horseman.

"Come, then, don't dally," fretted the Prior, turning back to the bench.

As the monk passed the horseman he murmured in his ear, "I'll bring the letters later tonight, and instruct you further in the arts you wish to learn."

The horseman bowed in mock acknowledgement, and moved towards the door. "Goodnight, Father Prior. Lose no sleep over the Bishop's visit."

"Goodnight, Roger, goodnight. God be with you."

As we left the room together the horseman sniffed the air with a grimace. The mustiness of the Prior's chamber had now an additional spice, a whiff of perfume from the French monk's habit.

We descended the stairs, but before returning through the passage-way the horseman paused a moment, then opened another door and glanced inside. The door gave entrance to the chapel, and the monks who had been playing pantomime with the novice were now at prayer. Or, to describe it more justly, making motion of prayer. Their eyes were downcast, and their lips moved. There were four others present whom I had not seen in the yard, and of these two were fast asleep in their stalls. The novice himself was huddled on his knees, crying silently but bitterly. The only figure with any dignity was that of a middle-aged man, dressed in a long mantle, his grey locks framing a kindly, gracious face. With hands clasped reverently before him, he kept his eyes steadfast on the altar. This, I thought, must be Sir Henry de Champernoune, lord of the manor and my horseman's master, of whose piety the Prior had spoken.

The horseman closed the door and went out into the passage, and so from the building and across the now empty yard to the gate. The green was deserted, for the women had left the well, and there were clouds in the sky, a sense of fading day. The horseman mounted his pony and turned for the track through the upper plough-lands.

I had no idea of time, his time or mine. I was still without sense of touch, and could move beside him without effort. We descended the track to the ford, which he traversed now without wetting his pony's hocks, for the tide had ebbed, and struck upward across the further fields.

When we reached the top of the hill and the fields took on their familiar shape I realised, with growing excitement and surprise, that he was leading me home, for Kilmarth, the house which Magnus had lent me for the summer holidays, lay beyond the little wood ahead of us. Some six or seven ponies were grazing close by, and at sight of the horseman one of them lifted his head and whinnied; then with one accord they swerved, kicked up their heels, and scampered away. He rode on through a clearing in the wood, the track dipped, and there immediately below us in the hollow lay a dwelling, stone-built, thatched, encircled by a yard deep in mud. Piggery and byre formed part of the dwelling, and through a single aperture in the thatch the blue smoke curled. I recognised one thing only, the scoop of land in which the dwelling lay.

The horseman rode down into the yard, dismounted and called, and a boy came out of the adjoining cow-house to take the pony. He was younger, slighter than my horseman, but had the same deep-set eyes, and must have been his brother. He led the pony off, and the horseman passed through the open doorway into the house, which seemed at first sight to consist of one room only. Following close behind, I could distinguish little through the smoke, except that the walls were built of the mixture of clay and straw that they call cob, and the floor was plain earth, without even rushes upon it.

A ladder at the far end led to a loft, only a few feet above the living-space, and looking up I could see straw pallets laid upon the planking. The fire, stacked with turf and furze, lay in a recess let into the wall, and a stew-pot simmered above the smoke, slung between iron bars fixed to the earthen floor. A girl, her lank hair falling below her shoulders, was kneeling by the fire, and as the horseman called a greeting she looked up at him and smiled.

I was close upon his heels, and suddenly he turned, staring straight at me, shoulder to shoulder. I could feel his breath upon my cheek, and I put out one hand, instinctively, to fend him off. I felt a sudden sharp pain on my knuckles and saw that they were bleeding, and at the same time I heard a splintering of glass. He was not there any longer, neither he, nor the girl, nor the smoking fire, and I had driven my right hand through one of the windows of the disused kitchen in Kilmarth's basement, and was standing in the old sunken courtyard beyond.

I stumbled through the open door of the boiler-room, retching violently, not at the sight of blood but because I was seized with an intolerable nausea, rocking me from head to foot. Throbbing in every limb, I leant against the stone wall of the boiler-room, the trickle of blood from my cut hand running down to my wrist.

In the library overhead the telephone began to ring, sounding, in its insistency, like a summons from a lost, unwanted world. I let it ring.

CHAPTER TWO

Iᴛ ᴍᴜsᴛ ʜᴀᴠᴇ taken the best part of ten minutes for the nausea to pass. I sat on a pile of logs in the boiler-room waiting. The worst thing about it was the vertigo: I dared not trust myself to stand. My hand was not badly cut, and I soon staunched the blood with my handkerchief. I could see the splintered window from where I sat, and the fragments of glass on the patio beyond. Later on I might be able to reconstruct the scene, judge where my horseman had been standing, measure the space of that long vanished house where there were now patio and basement: but not now. Now I was too exhausted.

I wondered what sort of figure I must have cut, if anyone had seen me walking over the fields and across the road at the bottom of the hill, and climbing the lane to Tywardreath. That I had been there I was certain. The state of my shoes, the torn cloth of one trouser leg, and my shirt clammy cold with sweat—this had not come about from a lazy amble on the cliffs.

Presently, the nausea and vertigo having passed, I walked very slowly up the back stairs to the hall above. I went into the lobby where Magnus kept his oilskins and boots and all the rest of his junk, and stared at myself in the looking-glass above the wash-basin. I looked normal enough. A bit white about the gills, nothing worse. I needed a stiff drink more than anything. Then I remembered that Magnus had said: "Don't touch alcohol for at least three hours after taking the drug, and then go slow." Tea would be a poor second-best, but it might help, and I went into the kitchen to make myself a cup.

This kitchen had been the family dining-room when Magnus was a boy; he had converted it during recent years. While I waited for the kettle to boil I looked out of the window at the courtyard below. It was a paved enclosure, surrounded by old, moss-encrusted walls. Magnus, in a burst of enthusiasm at some time, had attempted to turn it into a patio, as he called it, where he could flop about nude if a heat-wave ever materialised. His mother, he told me, had never done anything about the enclosure because it led out from what were then the kitchen quarters.

I looked upon it now with different eyes. Impossible to recapture what I had so lately seen—that muddied yard, with the cow-house adjoining, and the track leading to the wooded grove above. Myself following the horseman through the trees. Was the whole thing hallucination engendered by that hell-brew of a drug? As I wandered, mug in hand, through to the library, the telephone started to ring again. I suspected it might be Magnus, and it was. His voice, clipped and decisive as always, stood me in greater stead than the drink I could not have, or the mug of tea. I flung myself down in a chair and prepared for a session.

"I've been ringing you for hours," he said. "Had you forgotten you promised to put through a call at half-past three?"

"I had not forgotten," I told him. "The fact is, I was otherwise engaged."

"So I imagined. Well?"

The moment was one to savour. I wished I could keep him guessing. The thought gave me a pleasing sensation of power, but it was no use, I knew I had to tell him.

"It worked," I said. "Success one hundred per cent."

I realised, from the silence at the other end of the line, that this piece of information was totally unexpected. He had visualised failure. His voice, when it came, was pitched in a lower key, almost as though he were talking to himself.

"I can hardly believe it," he said. "How absolutely splendid . . ." And then, taking charge, as always, "You did exactly as I told you, followed the instructions? Tell me everything, from the beginning . . . Wait, though, are you all right?"

"Yes," I said, "I think so, except that I feel bloody tired, and I've cut my hand, and I was nearly sick in the boiler-room."

"Minor matters, dear boy, minor matters. There's often a feeling of nausea afterwards, it soon passes. Go on."

His impatience fed my own excitement, and I wished he had been in the room beside me instead of three hundred miles away.

"First of all," I said, enjoying myself, "I've seldom seen anything more macabre than your so-called lab. Bluebeard's chamber would be an apter description for it. All those embryos in jars, and that revolting monkey's head . . ."

"Perfectly good specimens and extremely valuable," he interrupted, "but don't get side-tracked. I know what they are for: you don't. Tell me what happened."

I took a sip of my rapidly cooling tea, and put down the mug.

"I found the row of bottles," I continued, "all in the locked cupboard. Neatly labelled, A, B, C. I poured exactly three measures from A into the medicine-glass, and that was that. I swallowed it, replaced the bottle and glass, locked the cupboard, locked the lab, and waited for something to happen. Well, nothing did."

I paused, to let this information sink in. No comment from Magnus.

"So," I went on, "I went into the garden. Still no reaction. You told me the time factor varied, that it could be three minutes, five, ten, before anything happened. I expected to feel drowsy, although you hadn't specifically mentioned drowsiness, but as nothing seemed to be happening I thought I would go for a stroll. So I climbed over the wall by the summer-house into the field, and began to walk in the direction of the cliffs."

"You damn fool," he said. "I told you to stay in the house, at any rate for the first experiment."

"I know you did. But, frankly, I wasn't expecting it to work. I planned to sit down, if it did, and drift off into some delightful dream."

"Damn fool," he said again. "It doesn't happen that way."

"I know it doesn't, now," I said.

Then I described my whole experience, from the moment the drug took effect to the smashing of the glass in the basement kitchen. He did not interrupt me at all except to murmur, when I paused for breath and a sip of tea, "Go on . . . go on . . ."

When I had finished, including the aftermath in the boiler-room, there was complete silence, and I thought we had been cut off. "Magnus," I said, "are you there?"

His voice came back to me, clear and strong, repeating the same words that he had used at the start of our telephone session.

"How splendid," he said. "How absolutely splendid."

Perhaps. . . . The truth was that I was completely drained, exhausted, having been through the whole process twice.

He began to talk rapidly, and I could just imagine him sitting at that desk of his in London, one hand holding the receiver, the other reaching out for his inevitable doodling-pad and pencil.

"You realise," he said, "that this is the most important thing that has happened since the chemical boys got hold of teonanacatl and ololiuqui? These only push the brain around in different directions—quite chaotic. This is controlled, specific. I knew I was on to something potentially tremendous, but I couldn't be sure, having only tried it on myself, that it wasn't hallucinogenic. If this was so, you and I would have had similar physical reactions—loss of touch, greater intensity of vision, and so on—but not the same experience of altered time. This is the important thing. The tremendously exciting thing."

"You mean," I said, "that when you tried it on yourself you also went back in time? You saw what I did?"

"Precisely. I didn't expect it any more than you did. No, that's not true, because an experiment I was working on then made it remotely possible. It has to do with DNA, enzyme catalysts, molecular equilibria and the like—above your head, dear boy, I won't elaborate—but the point that interests me at the moment is that you and I apparently went into an identical period of time. Thirteenth or fourteenth century, wouldn't you say, judging from their clothes? I too saw the chap you describe as your horseman—Roger, didn't the Prior call him?—the rather slatternly girl by the fire, and someone else as well, a monk, which immediately suggested a tie-up with the mediaeval priory that was once part of Tywardreath. The point is this: does the drug reverse some chemical change in the memory systems of the brain, throwing it back to a particular thermodynamic situation which existed in the past, so that the sensations elsewhere in the brain are repeated? If it does, why does the molecular brew return to that particular moment in time? Why not yesterday, five years ago, or a hundred and twenty years? It could be—and this is the thing that excites me—it could be that there is some very potent link connecting the taker of the drug with the first human image recorded in the brain, while under the drug's influence. In both our cases we saw the horseman. The compulsion to follow him was particularly urgent. You felt it, so did I. What I don't yet know is why he plays Virgil to our Dante in this particular Inferno, but he does, there's no escaping him. I've made the 'trip'—to use the students' phraseology—a number of times, and he's invariably there. You'll find the same thing happens on your next adventure. He always takes charge."

The assumption that I was to continue acting as guinea-pig for Magnus did not surprise me. It was typical of our many years of friendship, both at Cambridge and afterwards. He called the tune, and I danced, in God only knew how many disreputable escapades in our undergraduate life together, and later when we went our separate ways, he to his career as a biophysicist and thence to a professorship at London University, I to the tamer routine of a publisher's office. My marriage to Vita three years ago had made the first break between us, possibly a salutary one for us both. The sudden offer of his house for the summer holidays, which I had accepted gratefully, being between jobs—Vita was urging me to accept a directorship in a flourishing New York publishing firm run by her brother, and I needed time to decide—now appeared to have strings attached. The long, lazy days with which he had baited me, lying about in the garden, sailing across the bay, were beginning to take on another aspect.

"Now look here, Magnus," I said, "I did this for you today because I was curious, and also because I was on my own, and whether the drug had any effect or not didn't matter one way or the other. It's quite out of the question to go on. When Vita and her children arrive I shall be tied up with them."

"When do they come?"

"The boys break up in about a week. Vita's flying back from New York to fetch them from school and bring them down here."

"That's all right. You can achieve a lot in a week. Look, I must go. I'll ring you at the same time tomorrow. Goodbye."

He had gone. I was left holding the receiver, with a hundred questions to ask and nothing resolved. How damnably typical of Magnus. He had not even told me if I must expect some side-effect from his hell-brew of synthetic fungus and monkeys' brain-cells, or whatever the solution was that he had extracted from his range of loathsome bottles. The vertigo might seize me again, and the nausea too. I might suddenly go blind, or mad, or both. To hell with Magnus and his freak experiment. . . .

I decided to go upstairs and take a bath. It would be a relief to strip off my sweaty shirt, torn trousers, the lot, and relax in a tub of steaming water primed with bath-oil—Magnus was nothing if not fastidious in his tastes. Vita would approve of the bedroom suite he had put at our disposal, his own, in point of fact, bedroom, bathroom, dressing-room, the bedroom with a stunning view across the bay.

I lay back in the bath, letting the water run until it reached my chin, and thought of our last evening in London, when his dubious experiment had been proposed. Previously he had merely suggested that, if I wanted somewhere to go during the boys' school holidays, Kilmarth was mine for the taking. I had telephoned Vita in New York, pressing the offer. Vita, not altogether enthusiastic, being a hot-house plant like many American women, and usually preferring to take a vacation under a Mediterranean sky with a casino handy, demurred that it always rained in Cornwall, didn't it, and would the house be warm enough, and what should we do about food? I reassured her on all these points, even to the daily woman who came up every morning from the village, and finally she agreed, chiefly, I think, because I had explained there was a dish-washer and an outsize fridge in the lately converted kitchen. Magnus was much amused when I told him.

"Three years of marriage," he said, "and the dish-washer means more to your conjugal life than the double bed I'm throwing in for good measure. I warned you it wouldn't last. The marriage, I mean, not the bed."

I skated over the somewhat thorny topic of my marriage, which was going through a period of reaction after the first impulsive, passionate twelve months, for if it was thorny this was largely because I wanted to remain in England and Vita wanted me to settle in the States. In any event, neither my marriage nor my future job concerned Magnus, and he passed on to talk about the house, the various changes he had made since his parents had died—I had stayed there several times when we were at Cambridge—and how he had converted the old laundry in the basement to a laboratory, just for the fun of it, so that he could amuse himself with experiments that would have no connection with his work in London.

On this last occasion he had prepared the ground well with an excellent dinner, and I was under the usual spell of his personality, when he suddenly said, "I've had what I think is a success with one particular piece of research. A combination of plant and chemical into a drug which has an extraordinary effect upon the brain."

His manner was casual, but Magnus was always casual when he was making some statement that was important to him.

"I thought all the so-called hard drugs had that effect," I said. "The people who take them, mescalin, LSD, or whatever, pass into a world of fantasy filled with exotic blooms and imagine they're in Paradise."

He poured more brandy into my glass. "There was no fantasy about the world I entered," he said. "It was very real indeed."

This piqued my curiosity. A world other than his own egotistical centre would have to possess some special attraction to draw him into it.

"What sort of world?" I asked.

"The past," he answered.

I remember laughing as I cupped the brandy glass in my hand. "All your sins, do you mean? The evil deeds of a misspent youth?"

"No, no," he shook his head impatiently, "nothing personal at all. I was merely an observer. No, the fact was . . ." he broke off, and shrugged his shoulders. "I won't tell you what I saw: it would spoil the experiment for you."

"Spoil the experiment for me?"

"Yes. I want you to try the drug yourself, and see if it produces the same effect."

I shook my head. "Oh, no," I told him, "we're not at Cambridge any more.

Twenty years ago I might have swallowed one of your concoctions and risked death. Not any longer."

"I'm not asking you to risk death," he said impatiently. "I'm asking you to give up twenty minutes, possibly an hour, of an idle afternoon, before Vita and the children arrive, by trying an experiment on yourself that may change the whole conception of time as we know it at present."

There was no doubt that he meant every word he said. He was no longer the flippant Magnus of Cambridge days: he was a professor of biophysics, already famous in his particular field, and, although I understood little if anything of his life's work, I realised that if he really had hit upon some remarkable drug he might be mistaken in its importance, but he was not lying about his own evaluation of it.

"Why me?" I asked. "Why not try it on your disciples in London University under proper conditions?"

"Because it would be premature," he said, "and because I'm not prepared to risk telling anyone, not even my disciples, as you choose to call them. You are the only one to know that I'm even thinking along these particular lines, which is way outside the stuff I usually do. I stumbled on this thing by chance, and I've got to find out more about it before I'm even remotely satisfied that it has possibilities. I intend to work on it when I come down to Kilmarth in September. Meanwhile, you're going to be alone in the house. You could at least try it once, and report back. I may be entirely wrong about it. It may have no effect upon you except to turn your hands and feet temporarily numb and make your brain, such as you possess, dear boy, rather more alert than it is at present."

Of course in the end, after another glass of brandy, he had talked me into it. He gave me detailed instructions about the lab, he gave me the keys to the lab itself and to the cupboard where he kept the drug, and described the sudden effect it might have—no intervening stage, but direct transition from one state to another—and he said something about the after-effects, the possibility of nausea. It was only when I asked him directly what I was likely to see that he became evasive.

"No," he said, "it might predispose you, unconsciously, to see what I saw. You've got to make this experiment with an open mind, unprejudiced."

A few days later I left London and drove to Cornwall. The house was aired and ready—Magnus had briefed Mrs Collins from Polkerris, the small village below Kilmarth—and I found vases filled with flowers, food in the fridge, and fires in the music-room and the library, although it was mid-July; Vita could not have done better herself. I spent the first couple of days enjoying the peace of the place, and the comfort, too, which, if I remembered rightly, had been lacking in former times when Magnus's delightful and somewhat eccentric parents were in command. The father, Commander Lane, had been a retired naval man with a passion for sailing a ten-ton yacht in which we were invariably sea-sick, the mother a vague, haphazard creature of great charm who pottered about in an enormous broad-brimmed hat whatever the weather, indoors and out, and spent her time snipping the dead heads off roses, which she grew with

passion but with singular lack of real success. I laughed at them and loved
them, and when they died within twelve months of one another I was almost
more distressed than Magnus was himself.

It all seemed a long time ago now. The house was a good deal changed and
modernised, yet somehow their engaging presence lingered still, or so I had
thought, those first few days. Now, after the experiment, I was not so sure.
Unless, having seldom penetrated the basement in those early holidays, I had
been unaware that it held other memories.

I got out of the bath and dried myself, put on a change of clothes, lit a
cigarette, and went downstairs to the music-room, so called in lieu of the more
conventional "drawing-room" because Magnus's parents excelled at playing
and singing duets. I wondered if it was still too soon to pour myself the drink I
badly needed. Better be safe than sorry—I would wait another hour.

I switched on the radiogram and picked a record at random from the top of
the stack. Bach's Brandenburg Concerto No. 3 might restore my poise and
equanimity. Magnus must have mixed up his records the last time he was
down, however, for it was not the measured strains of Bach that fell upon my
ears, as I lay stretched on the sofa before the log fire, but the insidious,
disquieting murmur of Debussy's *La Mer*. Odd choice for Magnus when he
had been down at Easter. I thought he eschewed the romantic composers. I
must have been mistaken, unless his taste had changed through the years. Or
had his dabbling in the unknown awakened a liking for more mystical sounds,
the magical conjuring of sea upon the shore? Had Magnus seen the estuary
sweeping deep into the land, as I had done this afternoon? Had he seen the
green fields sharp and clear, the blue water prodding the valley, the stone walls
of the Priory graven against the hill? I did not know: he had not told me. So
much unasked on that abortive telephone conversation. So much unsaid.

I let the record play to the end, but far from calming me it had the opposite
effect. The house was strangely silent now the music had stopped, and with the
rise and fall of *La Mer* still lingering in my head I walked through the hall to the
library and looked out of the wide window to the sea. It was slatey grey,
whipped darker in places by a westerly wind, yet calm, with little swell.
Different from the more turbulent blue sea of afternoon glimpsed in that other
world.

There are two staircases descending to the basement at Kilmarth. The first,
leading from the hall, goes direct to the cellars and the boiler-room, and thence
to the door into the patio. The second is reached by passing through the
kitchen, and so down to the back entrance, the old kitchen, scullery, larder and
laundry. It was the laundry, reached by the second staircase, that Magnus had
converted to a laboratory.

I went down these stairs, turned the key of the door, and entered the
laboratory once again. There was nothing clinical about it. The old sink still
stood upon the stone flagged floor beneath a small barred window. Beside it
was an open fireplace, with a cloam oven, used in old days for baking bread, cut
into the thickness of the wall. In the cobwebbed ceiling were rusty hooks, from
which in former times salted meat and hams must have hung.

Magnus had ranged his curious exhibits along the slatted shelves fixed to the walls. Some of them were skeletons, but others were still intact, preserved in a chemical solution, their flesh bleached pale. Most were hard to distinguish— for all I knew they could have been kittens in embryo form, or even rats. The two specimens I recognised were the monkey's head, the smooth skull perfectly preserved, like the bald pate of a tiny unborn child, with eyes closed, and, next to it, a second monkey's head from which the brain had been removed, and which now lay in a jar near by, pickled and brown. There were other jars and other bottles that held fungi, plants and grasses, grotesquely shaped, with spreading tentacles and curling leaves.

I had mocked him, over the telephone, calling the laboratory Bluebeard's chamber. Now, as I looked round it again, the memory of my afternoon still vivid in my mind, the small room seemed to hold a different quality. I was reminded not so much of the bearded potentate in the Eastern fairy-tale as of an engraving, long forgotten, that had scared me as a child. It was called "The Alchemist". A figure, naked save for a loin-cloth, was crouching by a walled oven like the one here in the laundry, kindling a fire with bellows, and to his left stood a hooded monk and an abbot, carrying a cross. A fourth man, in mediaeval hat and cloak, leant upon a stick conferring with them. There had been bottles, too, upon a table, and open jars containing egg-shells, hairs and thread-like worms, and in the centre of the room a tripod with a rounded flask balanced upon it, and in the flask a minute lizard with a dragon's head.

Why only now, after some five-and-thirty years, did the memory of that dread engraving return to haunt me? I turned away, locking the door of Magnus's laboratory, and went upstairs. I could not wait any longer for that much-needed drink.

CHAPTER THREE

IT RAINED THE following day, one of those steady mizzles that accompany a drifting fog from the sea, preventing any enjoyment out of doors. I awoke feeling perfectly normal, having slept surprisingly well, but when I drew back the curtains and saw the state of the weather I went back to bed again, despondent, wondering what I was going to do with myself all day.

This was the Cornish climate about which Vita had expressed her doubts, and I could imagine her reproaches if it happened when the holidays were in full swing, my young stepsons staring aimlessly out of the window, then forced into wellingtons and macs and sent, protesting, to walk along the sands at Par. Vita would wander from music-room to library altering the position of the furniture, saying how much better she could arrange the rooms if they were hers, and when this palled she would telephone one of her many friends from the American Embassy crowd in London, themselves outward bound for Sardinia or Greece. These symptoms of discontent I was spared for a while longer, and the days ahead of me, wet or fine, were at least free, my own time for my own movements.

The obliging Mrs Collins brought me up my breakfast and the morning paper, commiserated with me about the weather, saying that the Professor always found plenty to do in that funny little old room of his down under, and informed me that she would roast one of her own chickens for my lunch. I had no intention of going "down under", and opened the morning paper and drank my coffee. But the doubtful interest of the sports page soon palled, and my attention wandered back to the all-absorbing question of exactly what had happened to me the previous afternoon.

Had there been some telepathic communication between Magnus and myself? We had tried this at Cambridge, with cards and numbers, but it had never worked, except once or twice by pure coincidence. And we had been more intimate in those days than we were now. I could think of no means, telepathic or otherwise, by which Magnus and I could have undergone the same experience, separated by an interval of some three months—it was Easter, apparently, when he had tried the drug himself—unless that experience was directly connected with previous happenings at Kilmarth. Part of the brain, Magnus had suggested, was susceptible to reversal, restoring conditions, when under the influence of the drug, to an earlier period in its chemical history. Yet why that particular time? Had the horseman planted so indelible a stamp on his surroundings that any previous or later period was blotted out?

I thought back to the days when I had stayed at Kilmarth as an undergraduate. The atmosphere was casual, happy-go-lucky. I remembered asking Mrs Lane once whether the house was haunted. My question was an idle one, for certainly it did not have an haunted atmosphere—I asked simply because it was old.

"Good heavens, no!" she exclaimed. "We're far too wrapped up in ourselves to encourage ghosts. Poor things, they'd wither away from tedium, unable to draw attention to themselves. Why do you ask?"

"No reason," I assured her, afraid I might have given offence. "Only that most old houses like to boast a spook."

"Well, if there is one at Kilmarth we've never heard it," she said. "The house has always seemed such a happy one to us. There's nothing particularly interesting about its history, you know. It belonged to a family called Baker in sixteen hundred and something, and they had it until the Rashleighs rebuilt the place in the eighteenth century. I can't tell you about its origins, but someone told us once that it has fourteenth-century foundations."

That was the end of the matter, but now her remarks about early fourteenth-century foundations returned to me. I thought about the basement rooms and the courtyard leading out of them, and Magnus's curious choice of the old laundry for his laboratory. Doubtless he had his reasons. It was well away from the lived-in part of the house, and he would not be disturbed by callers or Mrs Collins.

I got up rather late and wrote letters in the library, did justice to Mrs Collins' roast chicken, and tried to keep my thoughts on the future and what I was going to decide about that offer of a New York partnership. It was no use. The whole thing seemed remote. Time enough when Vita arrived and we could discuss it together.

I looked out of the music-room window and watched Mrs Collins walk up the drive on her way home. It was still drizzling, and a long, uninviting afternoon lay ahead. I don't know when it was that the idea came to me. Perhaps I had been harbouring it unconsciously since I awoke. I wanted to prove that there had been no telepathic communication between Magnus and myself when I had taken the drug the day before in the laboratory. He had told me he had made his first experiment there, and so had I. Perhaps some thought process had passed between us at the moment when I actually swallowed the stuff, so influencing my train of ideas and what I saw, or imagined I saw, during the course of the afternoon. If the drug was taken elsewhere, not in that baleful laboratory with its suggestive likeness to an alchemist's cell, might not the effect be different? I should never know unless I tried it out.

There was a small pocket-flask in the pantry cupboard—I had noticed it the evening before—and I got it out now, and rinsed it under the cold tap. This did not commit me to anything one way or another. Then I went downstairs to the basement, and, feeling like the shadow of my boyhood self when I had sneaked a bar of forbidden chocolate during Lent, I turned the key in the door of the laboratory.

It was a simple matter to disregard the specimens in their jars and reach for the neat little row of labelled bottles. As yesterday, I measured the drops from bottle A, but into the pocket flask this time. Then I locked the laboratory door behind me, went across the yard to the stable block, and fetched the car.

I drove slowly up the drive, turned left out of the lane to the main road, and went down Polmear hill, pausing when I reached the bottom to survey the scene. Here, where the almshouses and the inn stood now, had been yesterday's ford. The lie of the land had not altered, despite the modern road, but the valley where the tide had swept inward was now marsh. I took the lane to Tywardreath, thinking, with some misgiving, that if I had in fact taken this same route yesterday, under the influence of the drug, I could have been knocked down by a passing car without hearing it.

I drove down the steep, narrow lane to the village and parked the car a little above the church. There was still a light rain falling, and nobody was about. A van drove up the main Par road and disappeared. A woman came out of the grocer's shop and walked uphill in the same direction. No one else appeared. I got out of the car, opened the iron gates into the churchyard, and stood in the church porch to shelter from the rain. The churchyard itself sloped away in a southerly direction until it terminated at the boundary wall, and beneath it were farm-buildings. Yesterday, in that other world, there were no buildings, only the blue waters of a creek filling the valley with the incoming tide, and the Priory buildings had covered the space the churchyard held today.

I knew the lie of the land better now. If the drug took effect I could leave the car where it was and walk home. There was no one around. Then, like a diver taking a plunge into some arctic pool, I took the flask and swallowed the contents. The instant I had done so panic seized me. This second dose might have a quite different effect. Make me sleep for hours. Should I stay where I was, or should I be better off in the car? The church porch gave me claustrophobia, so I went out and sat down on one of the tombstones, not far from the pathway but out of sight of the road. If I stayed quite still, without moving, perhaps nothing would happen. I began to pray, "Don't let anything happen. Don't let the drug have any effect."

I went on sitting for about five minutes, too apprehensive about the possible effects of the drug to mind the rain. Then I heard the church clock strike three, and glanced down at my watch to check the time. It was a few minutes slow, so I altered it, and almost immediately I heard shouting from the village, or cheering, perhaps—a curious mélange of the two—and a creaking sound like wheels. Oh God, what now, I thought, a travelling circus about to descend the village street? I shall have to move the car. I got up and started to walk along the path to the churchyard gate. I never arrived, because the gate had gone, and I was looking through a rounded window set in a stone wall, the window facing a cobbled quadrangle bounded by shingle paths.

The entrance gate at the far end of the quadrangle was open wide, and beyond it I could see a mass of people assembled on the green, men, women, children. The shouting was coming from them, and the creaking sounds were the wheels of an enormous covered wagon drawn by five horses, the second leader and the horse between the shafts carrying riders upon their backs. The wooden canopy surmounting the wagon was painted a rich purple and gold, and as I watched the heavy curtains concealing the front of the vehicle were drawn aside, the shouting and the applause from the crowd increased, and the figure which appeared in the aperture raised his hands in blessing. He was magnificently dressed in ecclesiastical robes, and I remembered that Roger and the Prior had spoken of an imminent visit by the Bishop of Exeter, and how apprehensive the Prior had been—doubtless with reason. This must be His Grace in person.

There was a sudden hush, and everyone went down upon their knees. The light was dazzling, the feeling had gone from my limbs, and nothing seemed to matter any more. I did not care—the drug could work on me as it wished; my only desire was to be part of the world about me.

I watched the bishop descend from his covered vehicle, and the crowd pressed forward. Then he entered the gate into the quadrangle, followed by his train. From some door beneath me I saw the Prior advance to meet him at the head of his flock of monks, and the entrance gates were closed against the crowd.

I looked over my shoulder and saw that I was standing in a vaulted chamber filled with a score or more of people, waiting to be presented, to judge by their hushed sense of expectancy. From their clothes they belonged to the gentry, and so presumably were permitted entrance to the Priory.

"Mark it well," said the voice in my ear, "she'll not wear paint on her face on this occasion."

My horseman, Roger, stood beside me, but his remarks were addressed to a companion, a man of about his own age or somewhat older, who put his hand before his mouth to stifle laughter.

"Painted or plain, Sir John will have her," he answered, "and what better moment than the eve of Martinmas, with his own lady safely brought to bed eight miles away at Bockenod?"

"It could be contrived," agreed the other, "but with some risk, for she cannot depend upon Sir Henry's absence. He will scarcely sleep at the Priory tonight, with the Bishop in the guest chamber. No, let them wait awhile longer, if only to whet appetite."

Scandal had not changed much through the centuries, then, and I wondered why this back-chat should intrigue me now, which, if it had been exchanged by my contemporaries at some social event, would have made me yawn. Perhaps, because I was eavesdropping in time and within monastic walls, the gossip held more spice. I followed the direction of their gaze to the small group near to the door, the favoured few, no doubt, to be presented. Which was the gallant Sir John—the same who liked a foot in both camps, if I remembered the Prior's comment rightly—and which the favoured lady of his choice, shorn of her paint?

There were four men, three women and two youths, and the fashion of the women's headgear made it difficult to distinguish their features from a distance, swathed as they were in coif and wimple. I recognised the lord of the manor, Henry de Champernoune, the dignified, elderly man who had been at his prayers in the chapel yesterday. He was dressed more soberly than his friends, who wore tunics of varying colours hanging to mid-calf, with belts slung low beneath the hip, and pouch and dagger in the centre. All of them were bearded and had their hair curled to a frizz, which must have been the prevailing fashion.

Roger and his companion had been joined by a newcomer in clerical dress, a rosary hanging from his belt. His red nose and slurred speech suggested a recent visit to the Prior's buttery.

"What is the order of precedence?" he mumbled. "As parish priest and chaplain to Sir Henry surely I should form part of his entourage?"

Roger laid a hand on his shoulder and swung him round to face the window. "Sir Henry can do without your breath, and his Grace the Bishop likewise, unless you wish to forfeit your position."

The newcomer protested, clinging nevertheless to the protection of the wall, then lowered himself on to the bench beside it. Roger shrugged his shoulder, turning to the companion at his side.

"It surprises me that Otto Bodrugan dares show his face," said his friend. "Not two years since he fought for Lancaster against the King. They say he was in London when the mob dragged Bishop Stapledon through the streets."

"He was not," replied Roger. "He was with many hundreds of the Queen's party up at Wallingford."

"Nevertheless, his position is delicate," said the other. "If I were the Bishop I should not look kindly upon the man reputed to have condoned the murder of my predecessor."

"His Grace has not the time to play politics," retorted Roger. "He will have his hands full with the diocese. Past causes are no concern of his. Bodrugan is here today by reason of the demesnes he shares with Champernoune, because his sister Joanna is Sir Henry's lady. Also, out of his obligation to Sir John. The two hundred marks he borrowed are still unpaid."

Commotion at the door made them move forward for a better view, small fry on the lower rungs of this particular ladder. The Bishop entered, the Prior beside him, sprucer and cleaner than when he had sat up in his tumbled bed with the scratching greyhound. The gentlemen made obeisance, the ladies curtseyed, and the Bishop extended his hand for each to kiss, while the Prior, flustered by the ceremonial, presented them in turn. Playing no part in their world I could move about at will, so long as I touched none of them, and I drew closer, curious to discover who was who in the company.

"Sir Henry de Champernoune, lord of the manor of Tywardreath," murmured the Prior, "lately returned from a pilgrimage to Campostella."

My elderly knight stepped forward, bending low with one knee on the ground, and I was struck once more by his air of dignity and grace, coupled with humility. When he had kissed the extended hand he rose, and turned to the woman at his side.

"My wife Joanna, your Grace," he said, and she sank to the ground in an endeavour to equal her husband in humility, bring off the gesture well. So this was the lady who would have painted her face but for the Bishop's visitation. I decided she had done well enough to let it alone. The wimple that framed her features was adornment enough, enhancing the charms of any woman, plain or beautiful. She was neither the one nor the other, but it did not surprise me that her fidelity to her conjugal vows had been in question. I had seen eyes like hers in women of my own world, full and sensual: one flick of the male head, and she'd be game.

"My son and heir, William," continued her husband, and one of the youths came forward to make obeisance.

"Sir Otto Bodrugan," continued Sir Henry, "and his lady, my sister Margaret."

It was evidently a closely knit world, for had not my horseman Roger remarked that Otto Bodrugan was brother to Joanna, Champernoune's wife, and so doubly connected with the lord of the manor? Margaret was small and pale, and evidently nervous, for she stumbled as she made her curtsey to His Grace, and would have fallen had not her husband caught her. I liked Bodrugan's looks: there was a panache about him, and he would, I thought, be a good ally in a duel or escapade. He must have had a sense of humour, too, for instead of colouring or looking vexed at his wife's gaffe he smiled and reassured her. His eyes, brown like those of his sister Joanna, were less prominent than hers, but I felt that he had his full share of her other qualities.

Bodrugan in his turn presented his eldest son Henry, and then stepped back to give way to the next man in the line. He had clearly been itching to put himself forward. Dressed more richly than either Bodrugan or Champernoune, he wore a self-confident smile on his lips.

This time it was the Prior who made the introduction. "Our loved and respected patron, Sir John Carminowe of Bockenod," he announced, "without whom we in this Priory would have found ourselves hard-pressed for money in these troublous times."

Here then was the knight with a foot in either camp, one lady in confinement eight miles away, the other present in this chamber but not yet bedded. I was disappointed, expecting a roisterous type with a roving eye. He was none of these, but small and stout, puffed up with self-importance like a turkey-cock. The lady Joanna must be easily pleased.

"Your Grace," he said in pompous tones, "we are deeply honoured to have you here amongst us," and bent over the proffered hand with so much affectation that had I been Otto Bodrugan, who owed him two hundred marks, I would have kicked him on the backside and compounded the debt.

The Bishop, keen-eyed, alert, was missing nothing. He reminded me of a general inspecting a new command and making mental notes about the officers: Champernoune past it, needs replacing; Bodrugan gallant in action but insubordinate, to judge from his recent part in the rebellion against the King; Carminowe ambitious and over-zealous—apt to make trouble. As for the Prior, was that a splash of gravy on his habit? I could swear the Bishop noticed it, as I did; and a moment later his eye travelled across the heads of the lesser fry and fell upon the almost recumbent figure of the parish priest. I hoped, for the sake of the Prior's charges, that the inspection would not be continued later in the Priory kitchen, or, worse still, in the Prior's own chamber.

Sir John had risen from his knees, and was making introductions in his turn.

"My brother, your Grace, Sir Oliver Carminowe, one of His Majesty's Commissioners, and Isolda his lady." He elbowed forward his brother, who, from his flushed appearance and hazy eye, looked as if he had been passing the hours of waiting in the buttery with the parish priest.

"Your Grace," he said, and was careful not to bend his knee too low for fear of swaying when he stood upright. He was a better-looking fellow than Sir John, despite the tippling; taller, broader, with a ruthless set about the jaw, not one to fall foul with in an argument.

"She's the one I'd pick if fortune favoured me."

The whisper in my ear was very near. Roger the horseman was at my side once more; but he was not addressing me but his companion. There was something uncanny in the way he led my thoughts, always at my elbow when I least supposed him there. He was right, though, in his choice, and I wondered if she too was aware of his attention, for she stared straight at us as she rose from her curtsey, and the kissing of the Bishop's hand.

Isolda, wife to Sir Oliver Carminowe, had no wimple to frame her features, but wore her golden hair in looped braids, with a jewelled fillet crowning the small veil upon her head. Nor did she wear a cloak over her dress like the other women, and the dress itself was less wide in the skirt, more closely fitting, the long, tight sleeves reaching beyond her wrist. Possibly, being younger than her companions, not more than twenty-five or twenty-six, fashion played a stronger part in her life; if so, she did not seem conscious of the fact, wearing her clothes with casual grace. I have never seen a face so beautiful or so bored, and as she swept us with her eyes—or rather, Roger and his companion—without the faintest show of interest, the slight movement of her mouth a moment later betrayed the fact that she was stifling a yawn.

It is the fate of every man, I suppose, at some time or other to glimpse a face in a crowd and not forget it, or perhaps, by a stroke of luck, to catch up with the owner at a later date, in a restaurant, at a party. To meet often breaks the spell and leads to disenchantment. This was not possible now. I looked across the centuries at what Shakespeare called "a lass unparalleled", who, alas, would never look at me.

"How long, I wonder," murmured Roger, "will she stay content within the walls of Carminowe and keep a guard upon her thoughts from straying?"

I wished I knew. Had I been living in his time I would have handed in my resignation as steward to Sir Henry Champernoune and offered my services to Sir Oliver and his lady.

"One mercy for her," replied the other, "she does not have to provide her husband with an heir, with three stout stepsons filling the breach. She can do as she pleases with her time, having produced two daughters whom Sir Oliver can trade and profit by when they reach marriageable age."

So much for woman's value in other days. Goods reared for purchase, then bought and sold in the market-place, or rather manor. Small wonder that, their duty done, they looked round for consolation, either by taking a lover or by playing an active part in the bargaining over their own daughters and sons.

"I tell you one thing," said Roger. "Bodrugan has an eye to her, but while he's under this obligation to Sir John he has to watch where he steps."

"I lay you five denarii to nought she will not look at him."

"Taken. And if she does I'll act as go-between. I play the role often enough between my lady and Sir John."

As eavesdropper in time my role was passive, without commitment or responsibility. I could move about in their world unwatched, knowing that whatever happened I could do nothing to prevent it—comedy, tragedy, or farce—whereas in my twentieth-century existence I must take my share in shaping my own future and that of my family.

The reception appeared over, but the visit was not yet through, for a bell summoned one and all to vespers and the company divided, the more favoured to the Priory chapel, the lesser ranks to the church, which was at the same time part of the chapel, an arched doorway, with a grille, dividing the one from the other.

I thought I might dispense with vespers, though by standing close to the grille I could have watched Isolda; but my inevitable guide, craning his neck with the same thought in mind, decided that he had been idle long enough, and, signalling to his companion with a quick jerk of the head, made his way out of the Priory building and across the quadrangle to the entrance gate. Someone had flung it open once again and a cluster of people, lay brothers and servants, were standing there, laughing, as they watched the Bishop's attendants struggle to turn the clumsy vehicle towards the Priory yard. The wheels were stuck between muddied road and village green, but this was by no means the only fun to be observed, for the green itself was crowded with men, women and children. Some sort of market seemed to be in progress, for there were little booths and stalls set up, some fellow was beating a drum and another squeaked on a fiddle, while a third nearly split my ears with two horns as long as himself, which he managed by sleight of hand to play simultaneously.

I followed Roger and his friend across the green. They paused every moment to greet acquaintances, and I realised that this was no sudden jollification put on for the Bishop's benefit but some butcher's paradise, for newly slaughtered sheep and pigs, still dripping blood, were hanging upon posts at every booth. The dwellings bordering the green boasted a like display. Each householder, a knife in hand, was hard at work stripping the pelt off some old ewe, or slitting a pig's throat, and one or two fellows, higher perhaps on the feudal ladder, brandished the heads of oxen, the wide-spread horns winning shouts of applause and laughter from the crowd. Torches flared as the light faded, slaughterers and strippers taking on a demonic aspect, working fast and furiously to have their task accomplished before night came, and because of it the excitement mounted, and the musician with the horn in either hand, wandering in and out amongst the crowd, lifted his instruments high to make a greater blast upon the air.

"God willing, they'll have their bellies lined this winter," observed Roger. I had forgotten him in all the tumult, but he was with me still.

"I take it you have every beast counted?" asked his friend.

"Not only counted but inspected before slaughter. Not that Sir Henry would know or care if he was lacking a hundred head of cattle, but my lady would. He's too deep in his prayers to watch his purse, or his belongings."

"She trusts you, then?"

My horseman laughed. "Faith! She's obliged to trust me, knowing what I do of her affairs. The more she leans upon my counsel, the sounder she sleeps at night."

He turned his head as a new commotion fell upon our ears, this time from the Priory stableyard, where the Bishop's equipage had finally been housed, taking the place of smaller vehicles, similarly furnished with wooded canopy and sides, and bearing coats-of-arms. Half-chariot, half-wagonette, they seemed a clumsy method of carrying ladies of rank about the countryside, but this was evidently their purpose, for three of them emerged from the rear premises, creaking and groaning with every turn of the wheel, and stood in line before the Priory entrance.

Vespers was over, and the faithful who had attended were emerging from the church, to mingle with the crowd upon the green. Roger made his way into the quadrangle, and so to the Priory building itself, where the Prior's guests were gathering before departure. Sir John Carminowe was in the forefront, and beside him Sir Henry's lady, Joanna de Champernoune. As we approached he murmured in her ear, "Will you be alone if I ride to you tomorrow?"

"Perhaps," she said. "Better still, wait until I send word."

He bent to kiss her hand, then mounted the horse which a groom was holding, and cantered off. Joanna watched him go, then turned to her steward.

"Sir Oliver and Lady Isolda lodge with us tonight," she said. "See if you can hasten their departure. And find Sir Henry too. I wish to be away."

She stood there in the doorway, foot tapping impatiently upon the ground, the full brown eyes surely brooding upon some scheme which would further her own ends. Sir John must be hard-pressed to keep her sweet. Roger entered the Priory, and I followed him. Voices came from the direction of the refectory, and, enquiring from a monk who was standing by, he was told that Sir Oliver Carminowe was taking refreshment with others of the company, but that his lady was in the chapel still.

Roger paused a moment, then turned towards the chapel. I thought at first that it was empty. The candles on the altar had been extinguished, and the light was dim. Two figures stood near to the grille, a man and a woman. As we came closer I saw that they were Otto Bodrugan and Isolda Carminowe. They were speaking low and I could not hear what they said, but the weariness had gone from her face, and the boredom too, and suddenly she looked up at him and smiled.

Roger tapped me on the shoulder. "It's much too dark to see. Shall I switch on the lights?"

It was not his voice. He had gone, and so had they. I was standing in the southern aisle of the church, and a man wearing a dog-collar under his tweed jacket was by my side.

"I saw you just now in the churchyard," he said, "looking as if you couldn't make up your mind whether to come in out of the rain. Well, now you have, let me show you round. I'm the vicar of St Andrew's. It's a fine old church, and we're very proud of it."

He put his hand on a switch and turned on all the lights. I glanced down at my watch, without nausea, without vertigo. It was exactly half-past three.

CHAPTER FOUR

———

THERE HAD BEEN no perceptible transition. I had passed from one world to the other instantaneously, without the physical side-effects of yesterday. The only difficulty was mental readjustment, requiring an almost intolerable degree of concentration. Luckily the vicar preceded me up the aisle, chatting as we went, and if there was anything strange in my expression he was too polite to comment.

"We get a fair number of visitors in the summer," he said, "people staying at Par, or they come over from Fowey. But you must be an enthusiast, hanging about the churchyard in the rain."

I made a supreme effort to pull myself together. "In point of fact," I said, surprised to find that I could even speak, "it was not really the church itself or the graves that interested me. Someone told me there had been a Priory here in former days."

"Ah, yes, the Priory," he said. "That's been gone a long time, no trace of it left, unfortunately. The buildings all fell in after the dissolution of the monasteries in 1539. Some say the site was where Newhouse Farm is now, just below us in the valley, and others that it occupied the present churchyard itself, south of the porch, but nobody really knows."

He led me to the north transept and showed me the tombstone of the last Prior, who had been buried before the altar in 1538, and pointed out the pulpit and some pew-ends, and all that was left of the original rood screen. Nothing of what I observed bore any resemblance to the small church I had so lately seen, with the grille in the wall dividing it from the Priory chapel; nor, as I stood here now beside the vicar, could I reconstruct from memory anything of an older transept, an older aisle.

"Everything's changed," I said.

"Changed?" he repeated, puzzled. "Oh, no doubt. The church was largely restored in 1880, possibly not altogether successfully. Are you disappointed?"

"No," I assured him hastily, "not at all. It's only that . . . Well, as I was saying, my interest goes back to very early days, long before the dissolution of the monasteries."

"I understand." He smiled in sympathy. "I've often wondered myself what it all looked like in former times, with the Priory close by. It was a French house, you know, attached to the Benedictine Abbey of St Sergius and Bacchus in Angers, and I believe most of the monks were French. I wish I could tell you more about it, but I've only been here a few years, and I'm afraid I'm no historian."

"Neither am I," I told him, and we retraced our steps towards the porch.

"Do you know anything," I asked, "about the lords of the manor in early times?"

He paused to switch off the lights. "Only what I have read in the *Parochial History*," he said. "The manor is mentioned in Domesday as Tiwardrai—the House on the Strand—and it belonged to the great family of Cardinham until the last heiress Isolda sold it to the Champernounes, in the thirteenth century, and when they died out it passed to other hands."

"Isolda?"

"Yes, Isolda de Cardinham. She married someone called William Ferrers of Bere in Devon, but I'm afraid I don't remember the details. You would find out more about it in the St Austell public library than from me." He smiled again, and we passed through the door to the churchyard. "Are you staying in the neighbourhood or passing through?" he asked.

"Staying. Professor Lane has lent me his house for the summer."

"Kilmarth? I know it, of course, but I've never been inside. I don't think Professor Lane gets down very often, and he doesn't come to church."

"No," I replied, "probably not."

"Well," he said, as we parted at the gate, "if you feel like coming, either to a service or just to wander around, it will be nice to see you."

We shook hands, and I walked up the road to where I had parked the car. I wondered whether I had been impossibly rude. I had not even thanked him for his courtesy, or introduced myself. Doubtless he considered me just another summer visitor, more boorish than usual, and a crank into the bargain. I got into the car, lit a cigarette, and sat there to collect my thoughts. The fact that there had been no physical reaction to the drug whatsoever was an astonishing relief. Not a suspicion of dizziness or nausea, and my limbs did not ache as they had done the day before, nor was I sweating.

I wound down the car window and looked up the street, then back again to the church. None of it fitted. The green where the people had so lately crowded must have covered all the present area, and beyond it too, where the modern road turned uphill. The Priory yard, where the bishop's equipage nearly came to grief, would have been in that hollow below the gents' hairdresser, boundering the east wall of the churchyard, and the Priory itself, according to one theory mentioned by the vicar, filled the entire space that the southern portion of the churchyard held today. I closed my eyes. I saw the entrance, the quadrangle, the long narrow building forming kitchens and refectory, monks' dormitory, chapter-house, where the reception had been held, and the Prior's chamber above. Then I opened them again, but the pieces did not fit, and the church tower threw my jigsaw puzzle out of balance. It was no good—nothing tallied save the lie of the land.

I threw away my cigarette, started the car, and took the road past the church. A curious feeling of elation came to me as I swept downhill past the valley stream, and so to the low-lying, straggling shops of Par. Not ten minutes since the whole of this had been under water, the sloping Priory lands lapped by the sea. Sand-banks had bordered the wide sweep of the estuary where those bungalows stood now, and houses and shops were all blue channel with a running tide. I stopped the car by the chemists' and bought some tooth-paste, the feeling of elation increasing as the girl wrapped it up. It seemed to me that she was without substance, the shop as well, and the two other people standing there, and I felt myself smiling furtively because of this, with an urge to say, "You none of you exist. All this is under water."

I stood outside the shop, and it had stopped raining. The heavy pall that had been overhead all day had broken at last into a patchwork sky, squares of blue alternating with wisps of smoky cloud. Too soon to go back home. Too early to ring Magnus. One thing I had proved, if nothing else: this time there had been no telepathy between us. He might have had some intuition of my movements the preceding afternoon, but not today. The laboratory in Kilmarth was not a bogey-hole conjuring up ghosts, any more than the porch in St Andrew's church had been filled with phantoms. Magnus must be right in his assumption that some primary chemical process was reversible, the drug inducing this change; and conditions were such that the senses, reacting to the situation as a secondary effect, swung into action, capturing the past.

I had not awakened from some nostalgic dream when the vicar tapped me on the shoulder, but had passed from one living reality to another. Could time be all-dimensional—yesterday, today, tomorrow running concurrently in cease-less repetition? Perhaps it needed only a change of ingredient, a different enzyme, to show the future, myself a bald-headed buffer in New York with the boys grown-up and married, and Vita dead. The thought was disconcerting. I would rather concern myself with the Champernounes, the Carminowes, and Isolda. No telepathic communication here: Magnus had mentioned none of them, but the vicar had, and only after I had seen them as living persons.

Then I decided what to do: I would drive to St Austell and see if there was some volume in the public library that would give proof of their identity.

The library was perched above the town, and I parked the car and went inside. The girl at the desk was helpful. She advised me to go upstairs to the reference library, and search for pedigrees in a book called *The Visitations of Cornwall*.

I took the fat volume from the shelves and settled myself at one of the tables. First glance in alphabetical order was disappointing. No Bodrugans and no Champernounes. No Carminowes either. And no Cardinhams. I turned to the beginning once again, and then, with quickening interest, realised that I must have muddled the pages the first time, for I came upon the Carminowes of Carminowe. I let my eye travel down the page, and there Sir John was, married to a Joanna into the bargain—he must have found the similarity of name of wife and mistress confusing. He had a great brood of children, and one of his grandsons, Miles, had inherited Boconnoc. Boconnoc . . . Bockenod . . . a change in the spelling, but this was my Sir John without a doubt.

On the succeeding page was his elder brother Sir Oliver Carminowe. By his first wife he had had several children. I glanced along the line and found Isould his second wife, daughter of one Reynold Ferrers of Bere in Devon, and below, at the bottom of the page, her daughters, Joanna and Margaret. I'd got her—not the vicar's Devon heiress, Isolda Cardinham, but a descendant.

I pushed the heavy volume aside, and found myself smiling fatuously into the face of a bespectacled man reading the *Daily Telegraph*, who stared at me suspiciously, then hid his face behind his paper. My lass unparalleled was no figure of the imagination, nor a telepathic process of thought between Magnus and myself. She had lived, though the dates were sketchy: it did not state when she was born or when she died.

I put the book back on the shelves and walked downstairs and out of the building, the feeling of elation increased by my discovery. Carminowes, Champernounes, Bodrugans, all dead for six hundred years, yet still alive in my other world of time.

I drove away from St Austell thinking how much I had accomplished in one afternoon, witnessing a ceremony in a Priory long since crumbled, coupled with Martinmas upon the village green. And all through some wizard's brew concocted by Magnus, leaving no side-effect or aftermath, only a sense of well-being and delight. It was as easy as falling off a cliff. I drove up Polmear hill doing a cool sixty, and it was not until I had turned down the drive to Kilmarth, put away the car and let myself into the house that I thought of the simile again. Falling off a cliff . . . Was this the side-effect? This sense of exhilaration, that nothing mattered? Yesterday the nausea, the vertigo, because I had broken the rules. Today, moving from one world to another without effort, I was cock-a-hoop.

I went upstairs to the library and dialled the number of Magnus's flat. He answered immediately.

"How was it?" he asked.

"What do you mean, how was it? How was what? It rained all day."

"Fine in London," he replied. "But forget the weather. How was the second trip?"

His certainty that I had made the experiment again irritated me. "What makes you think I took a second trip?"

"One always does."

"Well, you're right, as it happens. I didn't intend to, but I wanted to prove something."

"What did you want to prove?"

"That the experiment was nothing to do with any telepathic communication between us."

"I could have told you that," he said.

"Perhaps. But we had both experimented first in Bluebeard's chamber, which might have had an unconscious influence."

"So . . ."

"So, I poured the drops into your drinking-flask—forgive me for making myself at home—drove to the church, and swallowed them in the porch."

His snort of delight annoyed me even more.

"What's the matter?" I asked. "Don't tell me you did the same?"

"Precisely. But not in the porch, dear boy, in the churchyard after dark. The point is, what did you see?"

I told him, winding up with my encounter with the vicar, the visit to the public library, and the absence, or so I had thought, of any side-effects. He listened to my saga without interruption, as he had done the day before, and when I had concluded he told me to hang on, he was going to pour himself a drink, but he reminded me not to do likewise. The thought of his gin and tonic added fuel to my small flame of irritation.

"I think you came out of it all very well," he said, "and you seem to have met the flower of the county, which is more than I have ever done, in that time or this."

"You mean you did not have the same experience?"

"Quite the contrary. No chapter-house or village green for me. I found myself in the monks' dormitory, a very different kettle of fish."

"What went on?" I asked.

"Exactly what you might suppose when a bunch of mediaeval Frenchmen got together. Use your imagination."

Now it was my turn to snort. The thought of fastidious Magnus playing peeping Tom amongst the fusty crowd brought my good humour back again.

"You know what I think?" I said. "I think we found what we deserved. I got His Grace the Bishop and the County, awaking in me all the forgotten snob appeal of Stonyhurst, and you got the sexy deviations you have denied yourself for thirty years."

"How do you know I've denied them?"

"I don't. I give you credit for good behaviour."

"Thanks for the compliment. The point is, none of this can be put down to telepathic communication between us. Agreed?"

"Agreed."

"Therefore we saw what we saw through another channel—the horseman, Roger. He was in the chapter-house and on the green with you, and in the dormitory with me. His is the brain that channels the information to us."

"Yes, but why?"

"Why? You don't think we are going to discover that in a couple of trips? You have work to do."

"That's all very well, but it's a bit of a bore having to shadow this chap, or have him shadow me, every time I may decide to make the experiment I don't find him very sympathetic. Nor do I take to the lady of the manor."

"The lady of the manor?" He paused a moment, I supposed for reflection. "She's possibly the one I saw on my third trip. Auburn-haired, brown eyes, rather a bitch?"

"That sounds like her. Joanna Champernoune," I said.

We both laughed, struck by the folly and the fascination of discussing someone who had been dead for centuries as if we had met her at some party in our own time.

"She was arguing about manor lands," he said. "I did not follow it. Incidentally, have you noticed how one gets the sense of the conversation without conscious translation from the mediaeval French they seem to be speaking? That's the link again, between his brain and ours. If we saw it before us in print, old English or Norman-French or Cornish, we shouldn't understand a word."

"You're right," I said. "It hadn't struck me. Magnus . . ."

"Yes?"

"I'm still a bit bothered about side-effects. What I mean is, thank God I had no nausea or vertigo today, but on the contrary, a tremendous sense of elation, and I must have broken the speed-limit several times driving home."

He did not reply at once, and when he did his tone was guarded. "That's one of the things," he said, "one of the reasons we have to test the drug. It could be addictive."

"What do you mean exactly, addictive?"

"What I say. Not just the fascination of the experience itself, which we both know nobody else has tried, but the stimulation to the part of the brain affected. And I've warned you before of the possible physical dangers—being run over, that sort of thing. You must appreciate that part of the brain is shut off when you're under the influence of the drug. The functional part still controls your movements, rather as one can drive with a high percentage of alcohol in the blood and not have an accident, but the danger is always present, and there doesn't appear to be a warning system between one part of the brain and another. There may be. There may not. All this is part of what I have to find out."

"Yes," I said. "Yes, I see." I felt rather deflated. The sense of exhilaration which I had experienced while driving back had certainly been unusual. "I'd better lay off," I said, "give it a miss, unless the circumstances are absolutely right."

Again he paused before he answered. "That's up to you," he said. "You must judge for yourself. Any more questions? I'm dining out."

Any more questions . . . A dozen, twenty. But I should think of them all when he had rung off. "Yes," I said. "Did you know before you took your first trip that Roger had once lived here in this house?"

"Absolutely not," he replied. "Mother used to talk about the Bakers of the seventeenth century, and the Rashleighs who followed them. We knew nothing about their predecessors, although my father had a vague idea that the foundations went back to the fourteenth century; I don't know who told him."

"Is that why you converted the old laundry into Bluebeard's chamber?"

"No, it just seemed a suitable place, and the cloam oven is rather fun. It retains the heat if you light the fire, and I can keep liquids there at a high temperature while I'm working at something else alongside. Perfect atmosphere. Nothing sinister about it. Don't run away with the idea that this experiment is some sort of a ghost-hunt, dear boy. We're not conjuring spirits from the vasty deep."

"To reduce it to its lowest level, if you sit in an armchair watching some old movie on television, the characters don't pop out of the screen to haunt you, although many of the actors are dead. It's not so very different from what you were up to this afternoon. Our guide Roger and his friends were living once, but are well and truly laid today.''

I knew what he meant, but it was not as simple as that. The implications went deeper, and the impact too; the sensation was not so much that of witnessing their world as of taking part in it.

"I wish," I said, "we knew more about our guide. I daresay I can dig up the others in the St Austell library—I've found the Carminowes already, as I told you, John, and his brother Oliver, and Oliver's wife Isolda—but a steward called Roger is rather a long shot, and is hardly likely to figure in any pedigree."

"Probably not, but you can never tell. One of my students has a buddy who works in the Public Record Office and the British Museum, and I've got the business in hand. I haven't told him why I am interested, just that I want a list of tax-payers in the parish of Tywardreath in the fourteenth century. He should be able to find it, I gather, in the Lay Subsidy Roll for 1327, which must be pretty near the period we want. If something turns up I'll let you know. Any news of Vita?''

"None."

"Pity you didn't arrange to fly the boys over to her in New York," he said.

"Too damned expensive. Besides, that would have meant I had to go too."

"Well, keep them all at bay for as long as you can. Say something has gone wrong with the drains—that will daunt her.''

"Nothing daunts Vita," I told him. "She'd bring some plumbing expert down from the American Embassy.''

"Well, press on before she arrives. And while I think of it, you know the sample marked B in the lab, alongside the A solution you're using?''

"Yes."

"Pack it carefully and send it up to me. I want to put it under test."

"Then you *are* going to try it out in London?''

"Not on myself, on a healthy young monkey. He won't see his mediaeval forebears, but he might get the staggers. Goodbye."

Magnus had hung up on me again in his usual brusque fashion, leaving me with the inevitable sense of depletion. It was always so, whenever we met and talked, or spent an evening together. First the stimulation, sparks flying and the moments speeding by, then suddenly he would be gone, hailing a taxi and disappearing—not to be seen again for several weeks—while I wandered aimlessly back to my own flat.

"And how was your Professor?" Vita would ask in the ironic, rather mocking tone she assumed when I had passed an evening in Magnus's company, an emphasis on the "your" which never failed to sting.

"In the usual form," I would answer. "Full of wild ideas I find amusing."

"Glad you had fun," was the reaction, but with a biting edge that implied the reverse of pleasure. She told me once, after a somewhat longer session than usual, when I had come home rather high about 2 a.m., that Magnus sapped me, and that when I returned to her I looked like a pricked balloon.

It was one of our first rows, and I did not know how to deal with it. She wandered around the sitting-room punching cushions and emptying her own ash-trays, while I sat on the sofa looking aggrieved. We went to bed without speaking, but the next morning, to my surprise and relief, she behaved as if nothing had happened, and positively glowed with feminine warmth and charm. Magnus was not mentioned again, but I made a mental note not to dine with him again unless she had a date herself elsewhere.

Today I did not feel like a pricked balloon when he rang off—the expression was rather offensive, come to think of it, suggesting the fetid air of somebody's breath exploding—merely denuded of stimulation, and a little uneasy too, because why did he suddenly want a test done on the bottle marked B? Did he want to make certain of his findings on the unfortunate monkey before putting me, the human guinea-pig, to a possibly sharper test? There was still sufficient solution in bottle A to keep me going . . .

I was brought up sharply in my train of thought. Keep me going? It sounded like an alcoholic preparing for a spree, and I remembered what Magnus had said about the possibilities of the drug being addictive. Perhaps this was another reason for trying it out on the monkey. I had a vision of the creature, bleary-eyed, leaping about his cage and panting for the next injection.

I felt in my pocket for the flask, and rinsed it out very thoroughly. I did not replace it on the pantry shelf, however, for Mrs Collins might take it into her head to move it somewhere else, and then if I happened to want it I should have to ask her where it was, which would be a bore. It was too early for supper, but the tray she had laid with ham and salad, fruit and cheese looked tempting, and I decided to carry it into the music-room and have a long evening by the wood fire.

I took a stack of records at random and piled them one on top of the other on the turn-table. But, no matter what sounds filled the music-room, I kept returning to the scenes of this afternoon, the reception in the Priory chapter-house, the stripping of carcasses on the village green, the hooded musician with his double horn wandering amongst the children and the barking dogs, and above all that lass with braided hair and jewelled fillet who, one afternoon six hundred years ago, had looked so bored until, because of some remark which I could not catch, spoken by a man in another time, she had lifted her head and smiled.

CHAPTER FIVE

THERE WAS AN airmail letter from Vita on my breakfast tray next morning. It was written from her brother's house on Long Island. The heat was terrific, she said, they were in the pool all day, and Joe was taking his family to Newport on the yacht he had chartered mid-week. What a pity we had not known his plans earlier on. I could have flown the boys over and we could all have spent the summer vacation together. As things were, it was too late to change anything. She only hoped the Professor's house would turn out to be a success—and how was it, anyway? Did I want her to bring a lot of food down from London? She was flying from New York on Wednesday, and hoped there would be a letter for her at the flat in London.

Today was Wednesday. She was due in at London airport around ten o'clock this evening, and she would not find a letter in the flat because I had not expected her until the weekend.

The thought of Vita arriving in the country within a few hours came as a shock. The days I had thought my own, with complete freedom to plan as I wished, would be upset by telephone calls, demands, questions, the whole paraphernalia of life *en famille*. Somehow, before the first telephone call came through, I must be ready with a delaying device, some scheme to keep her and the boys in London for at least another few days.

Magnus had suggested drains. Drains it well might be, but the trouble was that when Vita finally arrived she would naturally start asking Mrs Collins about it, and Mrs Collins would stare at her in blank surprise. The rooms not ready? This would reflect on Mrs Collins, and bode ill for future relations between the two women. Electricity failure? But it hadn't any more than the drains. Nor could I pretend to be ill, for this would bring Vita down immediately to move me, wrapped in blankets, to hospital back in London; she was suspicious of all medical treatment unless it was top grade. Well, I must think of something, if only for Magnus's sake; it would be letting him down if the experiment was brought to an abrupt conclusion after only two attempts to prove success.

Today was Wednesday. Say experiment on Wednesday, give it a miss on Thursday, then experiment on Friday, a miss on Saturday, experiment on Sunday, and, if Vita was adamant about coming down on Monday, then Monday she must come. This plan allowed for three "trips" (the LSD phraseology was certainly apt) and, providing nothing went wrong and I chose my moment well, did nothing foolish, the side-effects would be nil, just as they had been yesterday, apart from the sense of exhilaration, which I should immediately recognise and accept as a warning. In any event I felt no exhilaration now; Vita's letter was doubtless the cause of the slight despondency that appeared to be my form today.

Breakfast over, I told Mrs Collins that my wife was arriving in London tonight, and would probably be coming down with her boys next week, on Monday or Tuesday. She immediately produced a list of groceries and other things which would be needed. This gave me an opportunity to drive down to Par to collect them, and at the same time think out the text of a letter to Vita which she would get the following morning.

The first person I saw in the grocer's was the vicar of St Andrew's, who crossed the shop to say good morning. I introduced myself, belatedly, as Richard Young, and told him that I had taken his advice and gone to the county library at St Austell after leaving the church.

"You must be a real enthusiast," he smiled. "Did you find what you wanted?"

"In part," I replied. "The heiress Isolda de Cardinham proved elusive in the book of pedigrees, although I found a descendant, Isolda Carminowe, whose father was a Reynold Ferrers of Bere in Devon."

"Reynold Ferrers rings a bell," he said. "The son, I believe I'm right in saying, of Sir William Ferrers who married the heiress. Therefore your Isolda would be their granddaughter. I know the heiress sold the manor of Tywardreath to one of the Champernounes in 1269, just before she married William Ferrers, for one hundred pounds. Quite a sum in those days."

I made a rapid calculation in my head. My Isolda could hardly have been born before 1300. She had not looked more than about twenty-eight at the bishop's reception, which would date that event around 1328.

I followed the vicar round the shop as he made his purchases. "Do you still celebrate Martinmas at Tywardreath?" I asked.

"Martinmas?" he echoed, looking bewildered—he was hesitating between a choice of biscuits. "Forgive me, I don't quite follow you. It was a well-known feast in the centuries before the Reformation. We keep St Andrew's Day, of course, and generally hold the church fête in the middle of June."

"Sorry," I murmured, "I've got my dates rather mixed. The truth is, I was brought up a Catholic, and went to school at Stonyhurst, and I seem to remember we used to attach a certain importance to St Martin's Eve . . ."

"You are perfectly right," he interrupted, smiling. "November 11th, Armistice Day, has rather taken its place, hasn't it? Or rather, Armistice Sunday. But now I understand your interest in the Priory, if you're a Catholic."

"Non-practising," I admitted, "but you have a point. Old customs cling. Do you ever have a fair on the village green?"

"I'm afraid not," he said, plainly puzzled, "and to the best of my knowledge there has never been a village green at Tywardreath. Excuse me . . ."

He leant forward to receive the purchases dropped in his basket, and the assistant turned his attention to me. I consulted the list given me by Mrs Collins, and the vicar, with a cheery good morning, went his way. I wondered if he thought me mad, or merely one of Professor Lane's more eccentric friends. I had forgotten St Martin's Eve was November 11th. An odd coincidence of dates. Slaughter of oxen, pigs and sheep, and in the world of today a commemoration of uncounted numbers slain in battle. I must remember to tell Magnus.

I carried my load of groceries outside, dumped them in the boot of the car, and drove out of Par by the church road to Tywardreath. But instead of parking outside the gents' hairdressers, as I had done the day before, I drove slowly up the hill through the centre of the village, trying to reconstruct that non-existent village green. It was hopeless. There were houses to right and left of me, and at the top of the hill the road branched right to Fowey, while to the left the sign-post said "To Treesmill". Somewhere, from the top of this hill, the Bishop and his cortège had driven yesterday, and the covered wagonettes of Carminowes, Champernounes and Bodrugans, their coats-of-arms emblazoned on the side. Sir John Carminowe would have taken the left-hand fork—if it existed—to Lostwithiel and his demesne of Bockenod, where his lady awaited her confinement. Today Bockenod was Boconnoc, a vast estate a few miles from Lostwithiel; I had passed one of the lodge gates on my drive down from London. Where, then, did the lord of the manor, Sir Henry de Champernoune, have his demesne? His wife Joanna had told her steward, my horseman Roger, "The Bodrugans lodge with us tonight". Where would the manor house have stood?

I stopped the car at the top of the hill and looked about me. There was no house of any great size in the village of Tywardreath itself; some of the cottages could be late eighteenth century, but none belonged to an earlier period. Reason told me that manor houses were seldom destroyed, unless by fire, and even if they were burnt to the ground, or the walls crumbled, the site would be put to another purpose within a few years, and a farmhouse erected on the spot to serve the one-time manor lands. Somewhere, within a radius of a mile or two of Priory and church, the Champernounes would have built their own dwelling, or the original manor-house would have awaited them when the first Isolda, the Cardinham heiress, sold them the manor lands in 1269. Somewhere—down that left-hand fork, perhaps, where the sign-post read "To Treesmill"—the foot-tapping Joanna, impatient to be home, had driven in her painted wagonette from the Priory reception, accompanied by her sad-faced lord Sir Henry, and their son William, and followed by her brother Otto Bodrugan and his wife Margaret.

I glanced at my watch. It was past twelve, and Mrs Collins would be waiting to put away the groceries and cook my lunch. Also I had to write to Vita.

I settled to the letter after lunch. It took an hour or so to compose, nor was I satisfied with the result, but it would have to serve.

"Darling," I said, "I had not realised, until your letter came this morning, that you were actually flying back today, so you won't get this before tomorrow. If I've muddled things, forgive me. The fact is there has been a tremendous amount to do here to get the place straight for you and the boys, and I've been hard at it ever since I arrived. Mrs Collins, Magnus's daily, has been wonderful, but you know what a bachelor household is, and Magnus himself has not been down since Easter, so things were bit sketchy. Also, and this is the real crux, Magnus asked me to go through a lot of his papers, and so on—he keeps a mass of scientific stuff in his laboratory which must not be touched—and all this has to be put away safely. He asked me to see to it as a personal favour, and I can't let him down, because after all we are getting the house rent-free, and it's some sort of return. I ought to be clear of this chore by Monday, but want the next few days free to get on with it, and the weekend too. Incidentally, the weather has been foul. It rained without ceasing all yesterday, so you aren't missing anything, but the locals say it will improve next week.

"Don't worry about food, Mrs C has everything under control, and she's a very good cook, so you won't have to worry on that score. Anyway, I'm sure you can occupy the boys until Monday, there must be museums and things they haven't seen, and you will want to meet people, so, darling, I suggest we plan for next week, and by then there should be no problems.

"I'm so glad you enjoyed yourself with Joe and family. Yes—perhaps, in retrospect, it might have been a good idea to have flown the boys out to New York, but it's easy to be wise after the event. I hope you're not too tired, darling, after the flight. Ring me when you get this.

"Your loving Dick."

I read the letter through twice. It seemed better the second time: it rang true. And I did have to sort things for Magnus. When I lie I like to base the lie on a foundation of fact, for it appeases not only conscience but a sense of justice. I stamped the envelope and put it in my pocket, and then I remembered that Magnus wanted bottle B from the laboratory sent up to him in London. I rummaged about, found a small box, paper and string, and went down to the lab. I compared bottle B with bottle A, but there seemed to be no difference between the two. I was still carrying the flask of yesterday in my jacket pocket, and it was a simple matter to measure a second dose from A into the flask. I could use my judgement when, and if, I decided to take it.

Then I locked the lab and went upstairs, and had a look at the weather through the library window. It was not raining, and the sky was clearing out to sea. I packed up bottle B with great care, then drove down to Par to register it and to drop Vita's letter in the box, wondering, not so much what she would say when she read it, as how the monkey would react to his first trip into the unknown. My mission accomplished, I drove up through Tywardreath and took the left-hand fork to Treesmill.

The narrow road, with fields on either side of it, ran steeply to a valley, and before the final descent sloped sharply to a humped-backed bridge beneath which the main railway line ran between Par and Plymouth. I braked by the bridge and heard the hoot of the diesel express as it emerged from the tunnel out of sight to my right, and in a few moments the train itself came rattling down the line, passed under the bridge, and curved its way through the valley down to Par. Memories of undergraduate days came back to me. Magnus and I had always travelled down by train, and directly the train came out of the tunnel between Lostwithiel and Par we used to reach for our suitcases. I had been aware, then, of steep fields to the left of the carriage window and a valley to the right, full of reeds and stumpy willows, and suddenly the train would be at the station, the large black board with the white lettering announcing "Par Change For Newquay", and we should have arrived.

Now, watching the express disappear round the bend in the valley, I observed the terrain from another angle, and realised how the coming of the railway over a hundred years ago must have altered the sloping fields, the line literally dug out of the hill-side. There had been other disturbers of the peace besides the railway. Quarries had scarred the opposite side of the valley on the high ground where the tin and copper mines had flourished a century ago—I remembered Commander Lane telling us once at dinner how hundreds of men had been employed in the mines in Victorian days, and when the slump came chimneys and engine-houses were left to crumble into decay, the miners emigrating, or seeking work in the newer industry of china-clay.

This afternoon, the train out of sight and the rattle spent, all was quiet once again, and nothing moved in the valley except a few cows grazing in the swampy meadow at the base of the hill. I let the car descend gently to the end of the road before it rose sharply again to climb the opposite hill out of the valley. A sluggish stream ran through the meadow where the cows were grazing, spanned by a low bridge, and above the stream, to the right of the road, were old farm-buildings. I lowered the window of the car and looked about me. A dog ran from the farm, barking, followed by a man carrying a pail. I leant out of the window and asked him if this was Treesmill.

"Yes," he said. "If you continue straight on you'll come to the main road from Lostwithiel to St Blazey."

"In point of fact," I answered, "I was looking for the mill itself."

"Nothing left of it," he said. "This building here was the old mill-house, and all that's left of the stream is what you see. The main stream was diverted many years ago, before my time. They tell me that before they built this bridge there was a ford here. The stream ran right across this road, and most of the valley was under water."

"Yes," I said, "yes, that's very possible."

He pointed to a cottage the other side of the bridge. "That used to be a pub in old days," he said, "when they were working the mines up at Lanescot and Carrogett. It would be full of miners on a Saturday night, so they tell me. Not many people alive who know much about the old days now."

"Do you know," I asked him, "if there is any farmhouse here in the valley that might have been a manor house in days gone by?"

He considered a moment before replying. "Well," he said, "there's Trevenna up back behind us, on the Stonybridge road, but I've never heard it was old, and Trenadlyn beyond that, and of course Treverran up the valley nearer the railway tunnel. That's an old house all right, fine old place, built hundreds of years ago."

"How long ago?" I enquired, interest rising.

He considered again. "There was a piece about Treverran in the paper once," he said. "Some gentleman from Oxford went to look at it. I believe it was 1705 they said it was built."

My interest ebbed. Queen Anne houses, tin and copper mines, the pub across the road, all these were centuries later than my time. I felt as an archaeologist must feel who discovers a late Roman villa instead of a Bronze Age camp.

"Well, thanks very much," I said, "good day to you," and turned the car and drove back up the hill. If the Champernounes had descended this road in 1328, their covered wagonettes would have been baulked by the mill-stream at the bottom, unless an older bridge than the one I had seen once forded it. Half-way up the hill I turned left into a side-lane, and presently saw the three farmsteads the man had mentioned. I reached for my road-map. This side-road that I was on would join the main road at the top of the hill—the long tunnel must run deep underground beneath the road, a fine feat of engineering—and yes, the farm on my right was Trevenna, the one in front of me Trenadlyn, and the third, near to the railway line itself, would be Treverran. So what, I asked myself? Drive to each in turn, knock upon the door, and say, "Do you mind if I sit down for half an hour, give myself what the drug-addicts call 'a fix' and see what happens?"

Archaeologists had the best of it. Someone to finance their digs, enthusiastic company, and no risk of a lunatic asylum at the end of the day. I turned, drove back along my side-road, and up the steep hill towards Tywardreath. A car, towing a caravan, was trying to edge its way into the entrance of a bungalow half-way up the hill, effectively blocking my passage. I braked, almost in the ditch, and let the driver proceed with his manoeuvres. He shouted his apologies, and finally succeeded in getting both car and caravan parked beside the bungalow.

He climbed out of his car and walked towards me, apologising once again. "I think you can get past now," he said. "I'm sorry for the hold-up."

"That's OK." I told him, "I'm in no hurry. You did a fine job getting your caravan clear of the road."

"Oh well, I'm used to it," he said. "I live here, and the caravan gives us extra room when we have summer visitors."

I glanced at the name on the gate. "Chapel Down," I said. "That's unusual."

He grinned. "That's what we thought when we built the bungalow," he said. "We decided to keep the name of the actual plot of ground. It's been Chapel Down for centuries, and the fields across the road are both called Chapel Park."

"Anything to do with the old Priory?" I asked.

He did not register. "There were a couple of cottages here once," he said, "some sort of a Methodist meeting-house, I believe. But the field names go back a lot further than that."

His wife came out of the bungalow with a couple of children, and I started up the car. "All clear ahead," he called, and I pulled away from the ditch and drove up the hill until the curve in the road hid the bungalow from sight. Then

I pulled across to a lay-by on the right, where there was a pile of stones and timber.

I had reached the summit of the hill, and beyond the lay-by the road curved down to Tywardreath, the first houses already in sight. Chapel Down . . . Chapel Park . . . Could there have been a chapel here in former days, long since demolished, either on the site of the caravan-owner's bungalow or near the lay-by, where a modern house fronted the road?

Below the house a gate led into a field, and I climbed over it, circuiting the field and keeping close to the hedge until the sloping ground hid me from sight. This was the field the caravan-owner said was Chapel Park. It had no distinctive feature that I could see. Cows were grazing at the far end. I scrambled through the hedge at the bottom, and found myself on the precipitous grassland a few hundred feet above the railway, looking straight into the valley.

I lit a cigarette and surveyed the scene. No chapels tucked away, but what a view, Treesmill Farm away to my right, the other farms beyond, all sheltered from prevailing wind and weather, immediately below me the railway, and beyond it the strange sweep of the valley, no pattern of fields, nothing but a tapestry of willow, birch and alder. A paradise, surely, for birds in spring, and a good place for boys to hide from the parental eye—but boys never went birds-nesting nowadays, at least my stepsons didn't.

I sat down against the hedge to finish my cigarette, and as I did so became aware of the flask in my breast pocket. I took it out and looked at it. It was a handy size, and I wondered if it had belonged to Magnus's father; it would have been just right for a nip of rum in his sailing days, when the breeze freshened. If only Vita had disliked flying and had chosen to come by sea it would have given me several more days. . . . A rattle beneath me made me look down to the valley. A solitary diesel engine was coming up the line, going hell for leather without its load of carriages, and I watched it worm its way, like a fat, swift-moving slug, above the willows and the birches, pass under the bridge above Treesmill, and disappear finally into the gaping jaws of the tunnel a mile distant. I unscrewed the flask and downed its contents.

All right, I told myself, so what? I'm bloody-minded. And Vita's still in mid-Atlantic. I closed my eyes.

CHAPTER SIX

THIS TIME, SITTING motionless with my back against the hedge and my eyes shut, I would try to pin-point the moment of transition. On the previous occasions I had been walking, the first time across fields, the second up the churchyard path, when the vision altered. Now it would surely happen otherwise, because I was concentrating on the moment of impact. The sense of well-being would come, like a burden being lifted, and with it the sensation of lightness as feeling went from my body. No panic today, and no dismal falling rain. It was even warm, and the sun must be breaking through the clouds—I could sense the brightness through my closed eyelids. I took a last pull at the fag-end of my cigarette and let it drop.

If this drowsy content lasted much longer I might even fall asleep. Even the birds were rejoicing in the burst of sunshine; I could hear a blackbird singing in the hedge somewhere behind me, and more delightfully still a cuckoo called from the valley, distant at first, then near at hand. I listened to the call, a favourite sound, connected in my mind with every sort of carefree boyhood ramble thirty years ago. There, he called again, immediately overhead.

I opened my eyes and watched him wing his strange, unsteady flight across the sky, and as he did so I remembered that it was late July. The cuckoo's brief English summer ceased in June, along with the blackbird's song, and the primroses that were blooming in the bank beside me would have withered by mid-May. This warmth and brightness belonged to another world, an earlier spring. It had happened, despite concentration, in a moment of time that had not registered in my brain. All the sharp green colour of that first day was spread about me on the sloping hill below, and the valley with its tapestry of birch and willow lay submerged beneath a sheet of water, part of a great winding estuary that cut into the land, bordered by sandbanks where the water shallowed. I stood up, and saw how the river narrowed to mingle with the tumbling mill-stream below Treesmill, the farmhouse altered in shape, narrow, thatched, the hills opposite thickly forested with oak, the foliage young and tender because of spring.

Immediately beneath me, where the field had shelved precipitously to the railway cutting, the ground took on a gentler slope, in the midst of which a broad track ran to the estuary, the track terminating in a quay beside which boats were anchored, the channel there being deep, forming a natural pool. A larger vessel was moored in mid-stream, her sail party stowed. I could hear the voices of the men aboard her singing, and as I watched a smaller boat alongside pushed off to ferry someone ashore, and the voices were suddenly hushed, as the passenger in the small boat lifted his hand for silence. Now I looked around me, and the hedge had gone, the hill behind me was thickly wooded like the hills opposite, and to my left, where there had been scrub and gorse, a long stone wall encircled a dwelling-house; I could see the roof-top above the surrounding trees. The path from the quay led straight uphill to the house.

I drew nearer, watching the man below descend from the boat at the quay, then proceed to climb the road towards me. As he did so the cuckoo called again, flying overhead, and the man looked up to watch it, pausing for breath as he climbed, his action so ordinary, so natural, that it endeared him to me for no reason except that he lived, and I was a ghost in time. A time, moreover, that was not constant, for yesterday it had been Martinmas, and now, by the cuckoo's call and the primroses in flower, it must be spring.

He came close, breasting the hill, and as I recognised him, though his expression was graver, more solemn than that of the preceding day, the analogy came to me that these faces were like the diamonds, hearts and spades in some well-thumbed pack of cards shuffled by a patience-player; however they were sorted, they still formed themselves into a combination that the player could not guess at. I did not know, nor they, how the game would go.

It was Otto Bodrugan climbing the hill, followed by his son Henry, and, when he raised his hand in greeting, so instinctive was the gesture that I raised mine in answer, and even smiled; but I should have known the futility of my action, for father and son brushed past me towards the entrance gate of the house, and Roger the steward came forward to greet them. He must have been standing there watching them approach, but I had not seen him. Gone was the festive air of yesterday, the mocking smile of the would-be go-between; he wore a dark tunic, as did Bodrugan and his son, and his manner was as grave as theirs.

"What news?" asked Bodrugan.

Roger shook his head. "He is sinking fast," he said. "There is little hope for him. My lady Joanna is within, and all the family. Sir William Ferrers is already come from Bere, accompanied by the lady Matilda. Sir Henry does not suffer, we have seen to that—or, to speak more plainly, Brother Jean has done so, for he has been at the bedside night and day."

"And the cause?"

"Nothing but the general weakness of which you know, and a sudden chill with that late frost we had. He wanders in his mind, speaking of his grievous faults and asking pardon. The parish priest heard his confession, but, not content with that, he begged to be shriven by Brother Jean as well, and has received the last rites."

Roger stood aside to let Bodrugan and his son pass through the entrance gates, and now the extent of the building came into view, stone-walled with tiled roof, fronting upon a court, an outside staircase leading to an upper chamber, the steps similar to those serving a farmhouse granary today. There were stables at the rear, and beyond the walls the track wound uphill towards Tywardreath the thatched cottages of the serfs who tilled the surrounding lands scattered on either side of it.

Dogs ran barking across the court at our approach, crouching low, ears flat, as Roger shouted at them, and a scared-faced servant emerged from a corner of the building to drive them off. Bodrugan and his son Henry crossed the threshold, with Roger in attendance, and I his shadow close behind. We had entered a long, narrow hall, extending the full width of the house, small casement windows giving upon the court on the eastern side and looking down to the estuary on the west. There was an open hearth at the far end, the banked turf barely smoking, and across the width of the room was a trestle table, with benches alongside. The hall was dark, partly because of the small windows and the smoke that lingered in the atmosphere, partly because the walls were plastered a deep vermilion, giving the whole a rich and sombre air.

There were three youngsters straddling the benches, two boys and a girl, their sprawling attitude of dejection suggesting a numb bewilderment at the approach of death rather than actual sorrow. I recognised the eldest, William Champernoune, who had been presented to the Bishop; he was the first to rise now and come forward to greet his uncle and cousin, while the younger two, after momentary hesitation, followed his example. Otto Bodrugan bent to embrace all three, and then, as children will at the sudden entrance of adults in a moment of stress, they seized the opportunity to escape from the room, taking their cousin Henry with them.

Now I had leisure to observe the other occupants of the room. Two of them I had not seen before—a man and a woman, the man light-haired, bearded, the woman stout, with a sharp expression which boded ill for those who crossed her. She was already dressed in black, ready for calamity when it came, her white coif contrasting with her dark gown. This must be Sir William Ferrers, who, so Roger had said, had come post-haste from Devon, and his wife Matilda. The third occupant of the room, who was sitting on a low stool, was no stranger; it was my girl Isolda. She had made her own gesture to impending mourning by wearing lilac; but the silver sheen of the dress glistened, and a lilac ribbon, looping her braided hair away from her face, had been placed there with care. The prevailing mood seemed to be one of tension, and Matilda Ferrers wore an expression of high dudgeon which spoke of trouble.

"We expected you long since," was her immediate reproof to the new arrival, Otto Bodrugan, as he advanced towards her chair. "Does it take so many hours to sail across the bay, or did you delay purposely that your men might amuse themselves fishing?"

He kissed her hand, ignoring the reproach, and exchanged a glance with the man behind her chair. "How are you, William?" he said. "One hour from my anchorage to this, which was fair going, with the wind abeam. It would have taken longer had we ridden."

William nodded, with an imperceptible shrug, used to his lady's temper. "I thought as much," he murmured. "You could not have come sooner, and in any event there is nothing you can do."

"Nothing he can do?" echoed Matilda. "Except support us all when the moment comes, and add his voice to ours. Dismiss the French monk from the bedside and that drunken parish priest from the kitchen. If he cannot use a brother's authority and persuade Joanna to listen to reason, nobody can."

Bodrugan turned to Isolda. He barely brushed her hand in greeting, nor did she look up at him and smile. The constraint between them surely was due to caution: one word of too great intimacy would draw comment.

November . . . May . . . Six months must have passed, in my leap through time, since the reception at the Priory for the Bishop's visitation.

"Where is Joanna?" asked Bodrugan.

"In the chamber above," replied William, and now I saw the family likeness to Isolda. This was William Ferrers, her brother, but at least ten, perhaps fifteen, years older, his face lined, his light hair turning grey. "You are aware of the trouble," he continued. "Henry will have no one near him but the French monk Jean, receives no treatment but from his hands, and refuses the surgeon

who came with us from Devon and stands in high repute. Now, the treatment
having failed, he is fallen into a coma and the end is near, probably within a few
hours."

"If such is Henry's wish and he is not suffering, what is there to complain
of?" asked Bodrugan.

"Because it is ill done!" exclaimed Matilda. "Henry has even expressed a
wish to be buried in the Priory chapel, which should be withstood on every
account. We all know the reputation of the Priory, the lax behaviour of the
Prior, the lack of discipline amongst the monks. Such a resting-place for
someone of Henry's standing would make fools of all of us in the eyes of the
world."

"Whose world?" asked Bodrugan. "Does yours embrace the whole of
England or only Devon?"

Matilda crimsoned. "We know well enough where your allegiance lay seven
years past," she said, "supporting an adulterous Queen against her son, the
lawful King. Doubtless all things French have your attachment, from invading
forces, should they cross the Channel, to dissolute monks serving a foreign
Order."

Her husband William laid a restraining hand upon her shoulder. "We gain
nothing by opening old wounds," he said. "Otto's part in that rebellion does
not concern us now. However . . ." he glanced at Bodrugan, "Matilda has a
point. It might not be politic for a Champernoune to be interred amongst
French monks. It would be more fitting if you would let him lie at Bodrugan,
seeing that Joanna holds much of your manor fee as her marriage portion. Or I
should be most happy for him to be buried at Bere, where we are rebuilding the
church at the present time. After all, Henry is my cousin: the connection is
almost as close as your own."

"Oh, for the love of God," Isolda broke in impatiently, "let Henry lie where
he will. Must we conduct ourselves like butchers haggling over a sheep's
carcase before the beast is slain?"

It was the first time I had heard her voice. She spoke in French, like the rest,
with the same nasal intonation, but perhaps because she was younger than
they, and I was prejudiced, I found the quality more musical, holding a ring of
clarity theirs did not possess. Matilda at once burst into tears, to the consternation of her husband, while Bodrugan strode over to the window and stared
moodily at the view beyond. As for Isolda, who had caused the commotion, she
tapped her foot impatiently, an expression of disdain upon her face.

I glanced at Roger standing beside me. He was making a supreme effort to
conceal a smile. Then he stepped forward, his attitude one of respect towards
all present, and observed to no one in particular, but I suspected to catch
Isolda's eye, "If you wish, I will tell my lady of Sir Otto's arrival."

Nobody answered, and Roger, taking silence for acquiescence, bowed and
withdrew. He climbed the stairway to the upper chamber, I following close
upon his heels as if some thread bound us together. He entered without
knocking, pushing aside the heavy hangings that masked the entrance to the
room, which was half the size of the hall beneath, most of the space taken up by

a dropped bed at the further end. The small, pane-less windows gave little light, the aperture tight closed by oiled parchment, while the lighted candles standing on the trestle table at the bed's foot threw monstrous shadows on ochre-coloured walls.

There were three people in the room, Joanna, a monk, and the dying man. Henry de Champernoune was propped up in the bed by a great bolster that thrust him forward, forcing his chin upon his breast, and a white cloth was bound round his head turban fashion, giving him an incongruous likeness to an Arab sheik. His eyes were closed, and judging by the pallor of his face he was on the point of death. The monk was bending to stir something in a bowl on the trestle table, and he lifted his head as we entered. It was the young man with the brilliant eyes who had served the Prior as secretary or clerk on my first visit to the Priory. He said nothing but continued stirring, and Roger turned to Joanna, who was seated at the other end of the room. She was perfectly composed, without a sign of grief on her face, and was engaged in drawing threads of coloured silk through a frame to form a pattern.

"Are they all here?" she asked, without turning her eyes from the frame.

"Those who were bidden," answered the steward, "and already at odds with one another. Lady Ferrers first scolded the children for speaking too loud, and has now fallen out with Sir Otto, while Lady Carminowe, by her looks, wishes herself elsewhere. Sir John has not yet come."

"Nor likely to," replied Joanna. "I left the matter to his discretion. If he is premature in condolence it might be thought over-zealous on his part, and his sister Lady Ferrers will be the first to make mischief out of it."

"She is making mischief already," replied the steward.

"I'm aware of it. The sooner the business is over the better for all of us."

Roger crossed to the foot of the bed and looked down upon the helpless occupant. "How long now?" he asked the monk.

"He will not wake again. You may touch him if you will, he cannot feel it. We are only waiting for the heart to cease, and then my lady can announce his death."

Roger shifted his gaze from the bed to the small bowls on the trestle table. "What did you give him?"

"The same as before, meconium, the juice of the whole plant, in equal parts with henbane to the strength of a dram."

Roger looked at Joanna. "It would be as well if I removed these, lest there should be discussion as to the treatment. Lady Ferrers spoke of her own surgeon. They hardly dare go against your wishes, but there could be trouble."

Joanna, still employing herself with her skeins of silk, shrugged her shoulders.

"Take the ingredients if you will," she said, "though we have disposed of the liquids down the drain. The vessels you may remove if you consider it safer, but I hardly think Brother Jean has anything to fear. His discretion has been absolute."

She smiled at the young monk, who responded with one glance from his expressive eyes, and I wondered if he too, like the absent Sir John, had found favour during the weeks of her husband's illness. Between them, Roger and the monk, they made a package of the bowls, wrapping them in sacking, and all the while I could hear the murmur of voices from the hall below, suggesting that Lady Ferrers had recovered from her fit of crying and was in full spate again.

"How is my brother Otto taking it?" asked Joanna.

"He made no comment when Sir William suggested that interment in Bodrugan chapel would be preferable to the Priory. I think he is hardly likely to interfere. Sir William proposed his own church at Bere as an alternative."

"To what purpose?"

"For self-aggrandisement, perhaps—who knows? I would not recommend it. Once they had Sir Henry's body in their hands there could be meddling. Whereas in the Priory chapel . . ."

"All would be well. Sir Henry's wishes observed, and ourselves at peace. I look to you to see there is no trouble with the tenants, Roger. The people have no great love of the Priory."

"There'll be no trouble if they are treated well at the funeral feast," he answered. "A promise of mitigation of fines at the next court and a pardon for all misdemeanours. That should content them."

"Let us hope so." She pushed aside her frame and, rising from her chair, went to the bed. "Is he living still?" she asked.

The monk took the lifeless wrist in his hand and felt the pulse, then lowered his head to listen to his patient's heart.

"Barely," he answered. "You may light the candles if you will, and by the time the family has been summoned he will have gone."

They might have been talking of some wornout piece of furniture that had lost its use, instead of a woman's husband on the point of death. Joanna returned to her chair, took up a piece of black veiling, and began to drape it round her head and shoulders. Then she seized a looking-glass made of silver from the table near at hand.

"Should I wear it thus," she asked the steward, "or covering my face?"

"More fitting to be covered," he told her, "unless you can weep at will."

"I have not wept since my wedding-day," she answered.

The monk Jean crossed the dying man's hands upon his breast and fastened a linen bandage about his jaw. He stood back to observe his work, and as a finishing touch placed a crucifix between the folded hands.

Meanwhile Roger was rearranging the trestle table. "How many candles do you require?" he asked.

"Five on the day of death," replied the monk, "in honour of the five wounds of Our Lord Jesus Christ. Have you a black coverlet for the bed?"

"In the chest yonder," said Joanna, and while monk and steward draped the bed with its black pall she looked in the mirror for the last time, before covering her face with the veil.

"If I may presume," murmured the monk, "it would make the better impression if my lady knelt beside the bed and I stationed myself at the foot. Then when the family comes into the chamber I can recite the Prayers for the Dead. Unless you prefer the parish priest to do so."

"He is too drunk to mount the stairs," said Roger. "If Lady Ferrers has one glimpse of him it will be his finish."

"Then leave him alone," said Joanna, "and let us proceed. Roger, will you descend and summon them? William first, for he is the heir."

She knelt beside the bed, head bowed in grief, but raised it before we left the room, saying over her shoulder to the steward, "It cost my brother Sir Otto near on fifty marks at Bodrugan when my father died, not counting the beasts that were slaughtered for the funeral feast. We must not be outdone. Spare no expense."

Roger drew aside the hangings by the door, and I followed him on to the steps outside. The contrast between the bright day without and the murky atmosphere within must have struck him as forcibly as it did me, for he paused at the top of the steps and looked down over the surrounding walls to the gleaming waters of the estuary below. The sails of Bodrugan's ship were furled loosely on the yard as she lay at anchor, and a fellow in a small boat astern skulled to and fro in search of fish. The youngsters from the house had wandered down the hillside to stare at their uncle's boat. Henry, Bodrugan's son, was pointing out something to his cousin William, and the dogs leapt about them, barking once again.

I realised at that moment, more strongly than hitherto, how fantastic, even macabre, was my presence amongst them, unseen, unborn, a freak in time, witness to events that had happened centuries past, unremembered, unrecorded; and I wondered how it was that standing here on the steps, watching yet invisible, I could so feel myself involved, trouble, by these loves and deaths. The man who was dying might have been a relative from my own lost world of youth—my father, even, who had died in spring when I was about the age of young William down there in the field. The cable from the Far East—he had been killed fighting the Japanese—arrived just as my mother and I had finished lunch, staying in an hotel in Wales for the Easter holidays. She went up to her bedroom and shut the door, and I hung about the hotel drive, aware of loss but unable to cry, dreading the sympathetic glance of the girl at the reception desk if I went indoors.

Roger, carrying the piece of sacking containing the bowls stained by herb-juices, descended to the court, and went through an archway at the further end leading to a stable-yard. What servants made up the household seemed to be gathered there, but at the steward's approach they broke up their gossip and scattered, all but one lad whom I had seen that first day and recognised, by his likeness to the horseman, as Roger's brother. Roger summoned him to his side with a jerk of his head.

"It is over," he said. "Ride to the Priory at once and inform the Prior, that he may give orders for tolling the bell. Work will cease when the men hear the summons, and they will start to come in from the fields, and assemble on the green. Directly you have delivered your message to the Prior ride on home and place this package in the cellar, then wait for my return. I have much to do, and may not be back tonight."

The boy nodded, and disappeared into the stables. Roger passed through the archway into the court once more. Otto Bodrugan was standing at the entrance to the house. Roger hesitated a moment, then crossed the court to him.

"My lady asks you to go to her," he said, "with Sir William and Lady Ferrers and the lady Isolda. I will call William and the children."

"Is Sir Henry worse?" asked Bodrugan.

"He is dead, Sir Otto. Not five minutes since, without recovering consciousness, peacefully, in his sleep."

"I am sorry," said Bodrugan, "but it is better so. I pray God we may both go as peacefully when our time comes, though undeservedly." Both men crossed themselves. Automatically I did the same. "I will tell the others," he continued. "Lady Ferrers may go into hysterics, but no matter. How is my sister?"

"Calm, Sir Otto."

"I expected it."

Bodrugan paused before turning into the house. "You are aware," he said, and there was something hesitant in his manner, "that William, being a minor, will forfeit his lands to the King until he attains his majority?"

"I am, Sir Otto."

"The confiscation would be little more than a formality in ordinary circumstances," Bodrugan went on. "As William's uncle by marriage, and therefore his legal guardian, I should be empowered to administer his estates, with the King as overlord. But the circumstances are not ordinary, owing to the part I took in the so-called rebellion." The steward maintained discreet silence, his face inscrutable. "Therefore," said Bodrugan, "the escheator acting for the minor and the King is likely to be one held in greater esteem than myself—his cousin Sir John Carminowe, in all probability. In that event, I don't doubt he will arrange matters smoothly for my sister."

The irony in his voice was unmistakable.

Roger inclined his head without replying, and Bodrugan went into the house. The steward's slow smile of satisfaction was instantly suppressed as the young Champernounes, with their cousin Henry, entered the court, laughing and chatting, having momentarily forgotten the imminence of death. Henry, the eldest of the party, was the first to sense, intuitively, what must have happened. He called the younger pair to silence, and motioned William to come forward. I saw the expression on the boy's face change from carefree laughter to apprehension, and I guessed how sudden dread must have turned his stomach sick.

"Is it my father?" he asked.

Roger nodded. "Take your brother and sister with you," he said, "and go to your mother. Remember, you are the eldest; she will look to you for support in the days to come."

The boy clutched at the steward's arm. "You will remain with us, will you not?" he asked. "And my uncle Otto too?"

"We shall see," answered Roger. "But you are the head of the family now."

William made a supreme effort at self-control. He turned and faced his younger brother and sister and said, "Our father is dead. Please follow me," and walked into the house, head erect, but very pale. The children, startled, did as they were told, taking their cousin Henry's hand, and glancing at Roger I saw, for the first time, something of compassion on his face, and pride as well; the boy he must have known from cradle days had not disgraced himself. He waited a few moments, then followed them.

The hall appeared deserted. A tapestry hanging at the far end near the hearth had been drawn aside, showing a small stairway to the upper room, by which Otto Bodrugan and the Ferrers must have ascended, and the children too. I could hear the shuffle of feet overhead, then silence, followed by the low murmur of the monk's voice, "Requiem aeternam dona eis, Domine, et lux perpetua luceat eis."

I said the hall appeared deserted, and so it was, but for the slender figure in lilac: Isolda was the only member of the group who had not gone to the room above. At sight of her Roger paused on the threshold, before moving forward with deference.

"Lady Carminowe does not wish to pay tribute with the rest of the family?" he asked.

Isolda had not noticed him standing there by the entrance, but now she turned her head and looked at him direct, and there was so much coldness in her eyes that standing where I was, beside the steward, they seemed to sweep me with the same contempt as they did him.

"It is not my practice to make a mockery of death," she said.

If Roger was surprised he gave no sign of it, but made the same deferential gesture as before. "Sir Henry would be grateful for your prayers," he said.

"He has had them with regularity for many years," she answered, "and with increasing fervour these past weeks."

The edge in her voice was evident to me, and must have been doubly so to the steward. "Sir Henry has ailed ever since making the pilgrimage to Campostella," he replied. "They say Sir Ralph de Beaupré suffers today from the same sickness. It is a wasting fever, there is no cure for it. Sir Henry had so little regard for his own person that it was hard to treat him. I can assure you that everything possible was done."

"I understand Sir Ralph Beaupré retains full possession of his faculties despite his fever," Isolda replied. "My cousin did not. He recognised none of us for a month or more, yet his brow was cool, the fever was not high."

"No two men are alike in sickness," Roger answered. "What will save the one will trouble the other. If Sir Henry wandered in his mind it was his misfortune."

"Made the more effective by the potions given him," she said. "My grandmother, Isolda de Cardinham, had a treatise on herbs, written by a learned doctor who went to the Crusades, and she bequeathed it to me when she died, because I was her namesake. I am no stranger to the seeds of the black poppy and the white, water hemlock, mandragora, and the sleep they can induce."

Roger, startled out of his attitude of deference, did not answer her at once. Then he said, "These herbs are used by all apothecaries for easing pain. The monk, Jean de Meral, was trained in the parent-house at Angers and is especially skilled. Sir Henry himself had implicit faith in him."

"I don't doubt Sir Henry's faith, the monk's skill, or his zeal in employing that skill, but a healing plant can turn malign if the dose is increased," replied Isolda.

She had made her challenge, and he knew it. I remembered that trestle table at the foot of the bed, and the bowls upon it, now carefully wrapped in sacking and carried away.

"This is a house of mourning," said Roger, "and will continue so for several days. I advise you to speak of this matter to my lady, not to me. It is none of my business."

"Nor mine either," replied Isolda. "I speak through attachment to my cousin, and because I am not easily fooled. You might remember it."

One of the children started crying overhead, and there was a sudden lull in the murmur of prayers, the sound of movement, and the scurrying of footsteps down the stairs. The daughter of the house—she could not have been more than ten—came running into the room, and flung herself into Isolda's arms.

"They say he is dead," she said, "yet he opened his eyes and looked at me, just once, before closing them again. No one else saw, they were too busy with their prayers. Did he mean that I must follow him to the grave?"

Isolda held the child to her protectively, staring over her shoulder at Roger all the while, and suddenly she said, "If anything evil has been done this day or yesterday, you will be held responsible, with others, when the time comes. Not in this world, where we lack proof, but in the next, before God."

Roger moved forward, with some impulse, I think, to silence her or take the child from her, and I stepped into his path to prevent him, but stumbled, catching my foot in a loose stone. And there was nothing about me but great mounds of earth and hillocks of grass, gorse-bushes and the root of a dead tree, and behind me a large pit, circular in shape like a quarry, full of old tins and fallen slate. I caught hold of a twisted stem of withered gorse, retching violently, and in the distance I could hear the hoot of a diesel engine as it rattled below me in the valley.

CHAPTER SEVEN

T HE QUARRY WAS steep, carved out of the hillside, spread about with holly and clumps of ivy, the debris of years scattered amongst the earth and stones, and the path leading out of it ran into a small pit, and then another, and yet a third, all heaped about with banks and ditches and knolls of tufted grass. The gorse was everywhere, masking the view, and because of my vertigo I could not see but kept stumbling against the banks, with one thought paramount in my mind—that I must get out of this waste land and find the car. It was imperative to find the car.

I caught hold of a thorn-tree and held on to it to steady myself, and there were more old cans at my feet, a broken bedstead, a tyre, and still more clumps of ivy and holly. Feeling had returned to my limbs, but as I staggered up the mound above me the dizziness increased, the nausea too, and I slithered down into another pit and lay there panting, my stomach heaving. I was violently sick, which gave momentary relief, and I got up again and climbed another mound. Now I saw that I was only a few hundred yards from the original hedge where I had smoked my cigarette—the mounds and the quarry beyond had been hidden from me then by a sloping bank and a broken gate. I looked down once more into the valley, and saw the tail-end of the train disappearing round the corner to Par station. Then I climbed through a gap in the hedge and began to walk uphill across the field and back to the car.

I reached the lay-by just as another violent attack of nausea came upon me. I staggered sideways amongst the heap of cement and planks and was violently sick again, while ground and sky revolved around me. The vertigo I had experienced that first day in the patio was nothing to this, and as I crouched on the heap of cement waiting for it to pass I kept saying to myself, "Never again . . . never again . . ." with all the fervour and weak anger of someone coming round from an anaesthetic, the revulsion beyond control.

Before I collapsed I had been aware, dimly, that there was another car in the lay-by besides my own, and after what seemed an eternity, when the nausea and the vertigo ceased, and I was coughing and blowing my nose, I heard the door of the other car slam, and realised that the owner had come across and was staring down at me.

"Are you all right now?" he asked.

"Yes," I said, "yes, I think so."

I rose unsteadily to my feet, and he put out a hand to help me. He was about my own age, early forties, with a pleasant face and a remarkably strong grip.

"Got your keys?"

"Keys . . ." I fumbled in my pocket for the car keys. Christ! What if I had dropped them in the quarry or amongst those mounds—I should never find them again. They were in my top pocket, with the flask; the relief was so tremendous that I felt steadier at once, and walked without assistance to the car. Another fumble, though: I could not fit the key into the lock.

"Give it to me, I'll do it," said my Samaritan.

"It's extremely kind of you. I do apologise," I said.

"All in a day's work," he answered. "I happen to be a doctor."

I felt my face stiffen, then quickly stretch into a smile intended to disarm. Casual courtesy from a passing motorist was one thing; professional attention from a medico another. As it was he was staring at me with interest, and small blame to him. I wondered what he was thinking.

"The fact is," I said, "I must have walked up the hill a bit too fast. I felt giddy when I reached the top, and then was sick. Couldn't stop myself."

"Oh, well," he said, "it's been done before. I suppose a lay-by is as good a place as any to throw up in. You'd be surprised what they find down here in the tourist season."

He was not fooled, though. His eyes were particularly penetrating. I wondered if he could see the shape of the flask bulging the top pocket of my jacket.

"Have you far to go?" he asked.

"No," I said, "a couple of miles or so, no more."

"In that case," he suggested, "wouldn't it be more sensible if you left your car here and let me drive you home? You could always send for it later."

"It's very kind of you," I said, "but I assure you I'm perfectly all right now. It was just one of those passing things."

"H'm," he said, "rather violent while it lasted."

"Honestly," I said, "there's nothing wrong. Perhaps it was something I had for lunch, and then walking uphill . . ."

"Look," he interrupted, "you're not a patient of mine, I'm not trying to prescribe. I'm only warning you that it might be dangerous to drive."

"Yes," I said, "it's very good of you and I'm grateful for your advice." The thing was, he could be right. Yesterday I had driven to St Austell and back home with the greatest ease. Today it might be different. The vertigo might seize me once again. He must have seen my hesitation, for he said, "If you like I'll follow you, just to see you're OK."

I could hardly refuse—to have done so would have made him the more suspicious. "That's very decent of you," I told him. "I only have to go to the top of Polmear hill."

"All on the way home," he smiled. "I live in Fowey."

I climbed rather gingerly into my car and turned out of the lay-by. He followed close behind, and I thought to myself that if I drove into the hedge I was done for. But I navigated the narrow lane without difficulty, and heaved a sigh of relief as I emerged on to the main road and shot up Polmear hill. When I turned right, to go to Kilmarth, I thought he might follow me to the house, but he waved his hand and continued along the road to Fowey. It showed discretion, at any rate. Perhaps he thought I was staying in Polkerris or one of the near-by farms. I passed through the gate and down the drive, put the car away in the garage, and let myself into the house. Then I was sick again.

The first thing I did when I recovered, still feeling pretty shaky, was to rinse out the flask. Then I went down to the laboratory and stood it in the sink to soak. It was safer there than in the pantry. It was not until I went upstairs once more, and flung myself into an armchair in the music-room, exhausted, that I remembered the bowls wrapped in sacking. Had I left them in the car?

I was about to get up and go down to the garage to look for them, because they must be cleansed even more thoroughly than the flask and put away under lock and key, when I realised with a sudden wave of apprehension, just as though something were being vomited from my brain as well as my stomach, that I had been on the point of confusing the present with the past. The bowls had been given to Roger's brother, not to me.

I sat very still, my heart thumping in my chest. There had been no confusion before. The two worlds had been distinct. Was it because the nausea and the vertigo had been so great that the past and the present had run together in my mind? Or had I miscounted the drops, making the draught more potent? No way of telling. I clutched the sides of the armchair. They were solid, real. Everything about me was real. The drive home, the doctor, the quarry full of old cans and crumbling stones, they were real. Not the house above the estuary, nor the people in it, nor the dying man, nor the monk, nor the bowls in sacking—they were all products of the drug, a drug that turned a clear brain sick.

I began to be angry, not so much with myself, the willing guinea-pig, as with Magnus. He was unsure of his findings. He did not know what he had done. No wonder he had asked me to send up bottle B to try out the contents on the laboratory monkey. He had suspected something was wrong, and now I could tell him what it was. Neither exhilaration nor depression, but confusion of thought. The merging of two worlds. Well, that was enough. I had had my lot. Magnus could make his experiments on a dozen monkeys, but not on me.

The telephone started ringing, and, startled out of my chair, I went across to the library to answer it. Damn his telepathic powers. He would tell me he knew where I had been, that the house above the estuary was familiar ground, there was no need to worry, it was all perfectly safe providing I touched no one; if I felt ill or confused it was a side-effect of no consequence. I would put him right.

I seized the telephone and someone said, "Hold on a moment, please, I have a call for you," and I heard the click as Magnus took over.

"Damn and blast you," I said. "This is the last time I behave like a performing seal."

There was a little gasp at the other end, and then a laugh. "Thanks for the welcome home, darling."

It was Vita. I stood stupefied, holding on to the receiver. Was her voice part of the confusion?

"Darling?" she repeated. "Are you there? Is something wrong?"

"No," I said, "nothing's wrong, but what's happened? Where are you speaking from?"

"London airport," she answered. "I caught an earlier 'plane, that's all. Bill and Diana are collecting me and taking me out to dinner. I thought you might call the flat later tonight and wonder why I didn't answer. Sorry if I took you by surprise."

"Well, you did," I said, "but forget it. How are you?"

"Fine," she said, "just fine. What about you? Who did you think I was when you answered me just now? You didn't sound too pleased."

"In point of fact," I told her, "I thought it was Magnus. I had to do a chore for him . . . I've written you all about it in my letter, which you won't get until tomorrow morning."

She laughed. I knew the sound, with the slight "I thought as much" inflection. "So your Professor has been putting you to work," she said. "That doesn't surprise me. What's he been making you do that has turned you into a performing seal?"

"Oh, endless things, sorting out junk, I'll explain when I see you. When do the boys get back?"

"Tomorrow," she said. "Their train arrives at a hideous hour in the morning. Then I thought I'd pack them in the car and come on down. How long will it take?"

"Wait," I said, "that's just it. I'm not ready for you. I've told you so in my letter. Leave it until after the weekend."

There was silence the other end. I had dropped the usual clanger.

"Not ready?" she repeated. "But you must have been there all of five days? I thought you'd fixed up with some woman to come in and cook and clean, make beds and so on. Has she let us down?"

"No, it's not that," I told her. "She's first-rate, couldn't be better. Look, darling, I can't explain over the telephone, it's all in my letter, but, frankly, we weren't expecting you until Monday at the earliest."

"We?" she said. "You don't mean the Professor is there too?"

"No, no . . ." I could feel irritation rising in both of us. "I meant Mrs Collins and myself. She only comes in the morning, she has to bicycle up from Polkerris, the little village at the bottom of the hill, and the beds aren't aired or anything. She'll be terribly put out if everything isn't absolutely straight, and you know what you are, you'll take a dislike to the place if it isn't shining."

"What absolute nonsense," she said. "I'm fully prepared to picnic, and so are the boys. We can bring food with us, if that's worrying you. And blankets too. Are there enough blankets?"

"Masses of blankets," I said, "masses of food. Oh, darling, don't be obstructive. If you come down right away it won't be convenient, and that's the plain truth of it. I'm sorry."

"OK." The lift in the "K" had the typical upward ring of Vita temporarily defeated in argument but determined to win the final battle. "You'd better find yourself an apron and a broom," she added as a parting shot. "I'll tell Bill and Diana you've turned domestic and are going to spend the evening on your hands and knees. They'll love it."

"It's not that I don't want to see you, darling," I began, but her "Bye", still with the upward inflection, told me I had done my worst, and she had hung up on me and was now making her way to the airport restaurant to order a Scotch on the rocks and smoke three cigarettes in quick succession before the arrival of her friends.

Well, that was that. . . . What now? My anger against Magnus had been deflected to Vita, but how could I know she was going to catch an earlier 'plane and ring me unexpectedly? Anyone in the same situation would have been caught on the wrong foot. But that was the rub. My situation was not the same as anyone else's: it was unique. Less than an hour ago I had been living in another world, another time, or had imagined myself to be doing so, through the effect of the drug.

I began to walk from the library through the small dining-room across the hall to the music-room and back again, like someone pacing the deck of a ship, and it seemed to me that I was not sure of anything any more. Neither of myself, nor of Magnus, nor of Vita, nor of my own immediate world, for who was to say where I belonged—here in this borrowed house, in the London flat, in the office I had left when quitting my job, or in that singularly vivid house of mourning which lay buried beneath centuries of rubble? Why, if I was determined not to see that house again, had I dissuaded Vita from coming down tomorrow? The excuses had been immediate, a reflex action. Nausea and vertigo had gone. Accepted. They might strike again. Accepted also. The drug was dangerous, its implications and its side-effects unknown. This, too, accepted. I loved Vita, but I did not want her with me. Why?

I seized the telephone once more and dialled Magnus. No answer. No answer, either, to my self-imposed question. That doctor with his intelligent eyes might have given me one. What would he have told me? That a hallucinatory drug could play curious tricks with the unconscious, bringing the suppressions of a lifetime to the surface, so let it alone? A practical answer, but it did not suffice. I had not been moving amongst childhood ghosts. The people I had seen were not shadows from my own past. Roger the steward was not my alter-ego, nor Isolda a dream-fantasy, a might-have-been. Or were they?

I tried Magnus two or three times later, but there was never a reply, and I spent a restless evening, unable to settle to newspapers, books, records or TV. Finally, fed up with myself and the whole problem, to which there seemed no solution, I went early to bed, and slept, to my astonishment when I awoke next morning, amazingly well.

The first thing I did was to ring the flat, and I caught Vita just as she was tearing off to meet the boys.

"Darling, I'm sorry about yesterday . . ." I began, but there was no time to go into it, she told me, she was late already.

"Well, when shall I ring you?" I asked.

"I can't give you a time," she answered. "It depends upon the boys, what they want to do, whether there'll be a mass of shopping. They'll probably need jeans, swimming-trunks, I don't know. Thanks for your letter, by the way. Your Professor certainly keeps you employed."

"Never mind Magnus . . . How was your dinner with Bill and Diana?"

"Fun. Lots of scandal. Now I must go, or I'll keep the boys hanging about at Waterloo Station."

"Give them my love," I shouted, but she had gone. Oh well, she sounded happy enough. The evening with her friends and a good night's rest must have changed her ideas, and my letter too, which she seemed to have accepted. What a relief. . . . Now I could relax once more. Mrs Collins knocked on the door and came in with my breakfast tray.

"You're spoiling me," I said. "I ought to have been up an hour ago."

"You're on holiday," she said. "There's nothing to get up for, is there?"

I thought about this as I drank my coffee. A revealing remark. Nothing to get up for. . . . No more hopping into the underground from West Kensington to Covent Garden, the familiar office window, the inevitable routine, discussions about publicity, jackets, new authors, old authors. All finished, through my resignation. Nothing to get up for. But Vita wanted it to start all over again on her side of the Atlantic. Darting down the subway, elbowing strangers on side-walks, an office building thirty stories high, the inevitable routine, discussions about publicity, jackets, new authors, old authors. Something to get up for. . . .

There were two letters on my breakfast-tray. One was from my mother in Shropshire saying how lovely it must be in Cornwall and she envied me, I must be getting so much sun. Her arthritis had been bad again and poor old Dobsie was getting very deaf. (Dobsie was my stepfather, and I didn't wonder he was deaf; it was probably a defence mechanism, for my mother never drew breath.) And so on and so on, her large looped handwriting covering about eight pages. Pangs of conscience, for I had not seen her for a year, but to give her her due she never reproached me, was delighted when I married Vita, and always remembered the boys at Christmas with what I considered an unnecessarily thumping tip.

The other envelope was long and slim, and contained a couple of typewritten documents and a note scribbled by Magnus.

"Dear Dick," it read, "my disciple's long-haired friend who spends his time browsing around the BM and the PRO had produced the enclosed when I arrived at my desk this morning. The copy of the Lay Subsidy Roll is quite informative, and the other, mentioning your lord of the manor, Champernoune, and the to-do about removing his body may amuse you.

"I shall think about you this afternoon and wonder if Virgil is leading Dante astray. Do remember not to *touch* him; reaction can be progressively unpleasant. Keep your distance and all will be well. I suggest you stay put on the premises for your next trip.

"Yours, Magnus."

I turned to the documents. The research student had scribbled at the top of the first, "From Bishop Grandisson of Exeter. Original in Latin. Excuse my translation." It read as follows:

"Grandisson. A.D. 1329. Tywardreath Priory.

"John, etc., to his beloved sons men of a religious order, the Lords, the Prior and Convent of Tywardreath, greetings, etc. By the laws of the sacred Canons it is known that we are warned that the bodies of the Faithful, once delivered for burial by the Church, may not be exhumed except by those same laws. It has lately come to our ears that the body of the Lord Henry of Champernoune, Knight, rests buried in your consecrated church. Certain men, however, directing their mind's eyes in worldly fashion upon the transitory pomps of this life rather than on the welfare of the said Knight's soul and the discharging of due rites, are busying themselves about the exhumation of the said body, in circumstances not permitted by our laws, and about removing it to another place without our licence. Wherefore strictly enjoining upon you the virtue of obedience we give orders that you, in resistance to such reckless daring, must not allow the exhumation of the said body or its removal to be undertaken in any way, when we have not been consulted, nor have the reasons for such exhumation or removal, if there were any, been examined, discussed, or approved; even as you wish to escape divine retribution or that of ourselves. While we for our part lay an inhibition on all and each of our subjects, and no less upon others through whom it is hoped apparently to perpetrate a crime of this kind, so that they should not, under pain of excommunication, afford any help, counsel or favour for such an exhumation or removal of this kind which is in question. Given at Paignton on the 27th of August."

Magnus had added a foot-note. "I like Bishop Grandisson's forthright style. But what is it all about? A family squabble, or something more sinister, of which the Bishop himself was ignorant?"

The second document was a list of names, headed "Lay Subsidy Roll, 1327, Paroch Tiwardrayd. Subsidy of a twentieth of all moveable goods . . . upon all the Commons who possess goods of the value of ten shillings or upwards." There were forty names in all, and Henry de Champernoune headed the list. I ran my eye down the rest. Number twenty-three was Roger Kylmerth. So it wasn't hallucination—he had really lived.

CHAPTER EIGHT

W HEN I HAD dressed I went to the garage and fetched the car, and skirting Tywardreath took the road to Treesmill. I purposely avoided the lay-by and drove down the hill into the valley, but not before the fellow at the bungalow Chapel Down, who was busy washing his caravan, waved a hand in greeting. The same thing happened when I stopped the car below the bridge near Treesmill Farm. The farmer of yesterday morning was driving his cows across the road, and paused to speak to me. I thanked my stars neither of them had been at the lay-by later in the day.

"Found your manor house yet?" he asked.

"I'm not sure," I told him. "I thought I'd take another look round. That's a curious sort of place half-way up the field there, covered in gorse-bushes. Has it got a name?"

I could not see the site from the bridge, but pointed roughly in the direction of the quarry where yesterday, in another century, I had followed Roger into the house where Sir Henry Champernoune lay dying.

"You mean up Gratten?" he said. "I don't think you'll find anything up there except old slate and rubble. Fine place for slate, or was. Mostly rubbish now. They say when the houses were built in Tywardreath in the last century they took most of the stones and slates from that place. It may be true."

"Why Gratten?" I asked.

"I don't know exactly. The ploughed field at the back is the Gratten, part of Mount Bennett farm. The name has something to do with burning, I believe. There's a path opposite the turning to Stonybridge will lead you to it. But you'll find nothing to interest you."

"I don't suppose I shall," I answered, "except the view."

"Mostly trains," he laughed, "and not so many of them these days."

I parked the car half-way up the hill, opposite the lane, as he suggested, then struck across the field towards the Gratten. The railway and the valley were beneath me, to my right, the ground descending very steeply to a high embankment beside the railway, then sloping away more gradually to swamp and thicket. Yesterday, in that other world, there had been a quayside midway between the two, and in the centre of the wooded valley, where trees and bush were thickest, Otto Bodrugan had anchored his craft mid-channel, the bows of the boat swinging to meet the tide.

I passed the spot below the hedge where I had sat and smoked my cigarette. Then I went through the broken gate, and stood once more amongst the hillocks and the mounds. Today, without vertigo or nausea, I could see more clearly that these knolls were not the natural formation of uneven ground, but must have been walls that had been covered for centuries by vegetation, and the hollows which I had thought, in my dizziness, to be pits were simply the enclosures that long ago had been rooms within a house.

The people who had come to gather slates and stones for their cottages had done so for good reason. Digging into the soil that must have covered the foundations of a building long vanished would have given them much of the material they needed for their own use, and the quarry at the back was part of this same excavation. Now, the quest ended, the quarry remained a tip for useless junk, the discarded tins rusted with age and winter rains.

Their quest had ended, while mine had just begun, but, as the farmer down at Treesmill had warned me, I should find nothing. I knew only that yesterday, in another time, I had stood in the vaulted hall that formed the central feature of this long-buried house, had mounted the outer stairway to the room above, had seen the owner of the dwelling die. No courtyard now, no walls, no hall, no stable-quarters in the rear; nothing but grassy banks and a little muddy path running between them.

There was a patch of even ground, smooth and green, fronting the site, that might have been part of the courtyard once, and I sat down there looking into the valley below as Bodrugan had done from the small window in the hall. Tiwardrai, the House on the Strand. . . . I thought how, when the tide ebbed in early centuries, the twisting channel would stay blue, revealing sandy flats on either side of it, these flats a burnished gold under the sun. If the channel was deep enough, Bodrugan could have raised anchor and made for sea later that night; if not, he would have returned on board to sleep amongst his men, and at daybreak, perhaps, come out on deck to stretch himself and stare up at the house of mourning.

I had put the documents that had come by post this morning into my pocket, and now I drew them out and read them through again.

Bishop Grandisson's order to the Prior was dated August, 1329. Sir Henry Champernoune had died in late April or early May. The Ferrers pair were doubtless behind the attempt to remove him from his Priory tomb, with Matilda Ferrers the more pressing of the two. I wondered who had carried the rumour to the Bishop's ears, so playing on ecclesiastical pride, and ensuring that the body would escape investigation? Sir John Carminowe, in all probability, acting hand in glove with Joanna—whom he had, no doubt, long since successfully taken to bed.

I turned to the Lay Subsidy Roll, and glanced once again through the list of names, ticking off those that corresponded to the place-names on the road map I had brought from the car. Ric Trevynor, Ric Trewiryan, Ric Trenathelon, Julian Polpey, John Polorman, Geoffrey Lampetho . . . all, with slight variations in the spelling, were farms marked on the road-map beside me. The men who dwelt in them then, dead for over six hundred years, had bequeathed their names to posterity; only Henry Champernoune, lord of the manor, had left a heap of mounds as legacy, to be stumbled upon by myself, a trespasser in time. All dead for nearly seven centuries, Roger Kylmerth and Isolda Carminowe amongst them. What they had dreamt of, schemed for, accomplished, no longer mattered, it was all forgotten.

I got up and tried to find, amongst the mounds, the hall where Isolda had sat yesterday, accusing Roger of complicity in crime. Nothing fitted. Nature had done her work too well, here on the hillside and below me in the valley, where the estuary once ran. The sea had withdrawn from the land, the grass had covered the walls, the men and women who had walked here once, looking down upon blue water, had long since crumbled into dust.

I turned away, retracing my steps across the field, low-spirited, reason telling me that this was the end of the adventure. Emotion was in conflict with reason, however, destroying peace of mind, and for better, for worse, I knew myself involved. I could not forget that I had only to turn the key of that laboratory door for it to happen once again. The choice, perhaps, put to Man from the beginning, whether or not to eat of the Tree of Knowledge. I got into the car and drove back to Kilmarth.

I spent the afternoon writing a full account of yesterday to Magnus, and told him also that Vita was in London. Then I drove to Fowey to post the letter, and arranged to hire a sailing-boat after the weekend, when Vita and the boys were down. She would not experience the flat calm of Long Island sound, or the luxury of her brother Joe's chartered yacht, but the gesture showed my will to please, and the boys would enjoy it.

I rang nobody that evening, and nobody rang me, with the result that I slept badly, continually waking and listening to silence. I kept thinking of Roger Kylmerth in his sleeping quarters over the kitchen of the original farmstead, and wondering whether his brother had thoroughly scoured out the bowls six hundred and forty years ago. He must have done so, for Henry Champernoune to lie undisturbed in the Priory chapel until that chapel had crumbled into dust as well.

No breakfast in bed the following morning, for I was too restless. I was drinking my coffee on the steps outside the french window of the library when the telephone rang. It was Magnus.

"How are you feeling?" he asked at once.

"Jaded," I told him. "I slept badly."

"You can make up for it later. You can sleep all afternoon in the patio. There are several lilos in the boiler-room, and I envy you. London is sweltering in a heat-wave."

"Cornwall isn't," I replied, "and the patio gives me claustrophobia. Did you get my letter?"

"I did," he said. "That's why I rang. Congratulations on your third trip. Don't worry about the aftermath. It was your own fault, after all."

"It may have been," I said, "but the confusion was not."

"I know," he agreed. "The confusion fascinated me. Also the jump in time. Six months or more between the second and third trips. You know what? I've a good mind to get away in a week or so and join you so that we can go on a trip together."

My first reaction was one of excitement. The second, a zoom to earth. "It's out of the question. Vita will be here with the boys."

"We can get rid of them. Pack them off to the Scillies, or for a long day at the Land's End, scattering banana skins. That'll give us time."

"I don't think so," I said. "I don't think so at all." He did not know Vita well. I could imagine the complications.

"Well, it's not urgent," he said, "but it could be a lot of fun. Besides, I'd like to take a look at Isolda Carminowe."

His flippant voice restored my jagged nerves. I even smiled. "She's Bodrugan's girl, not ours," I told him.

"Yes, but for how long?" he queried. "They were always changing partners in those days. I still don't see where she fits in amongst the rest."

"She and William Ferrers seem to be cousins to the Champernounes," I explained.

"And Isolda's husband Oliver Carminowe, absent at yesterday's death-bed, is brother to Matilda and Sir John?"

"Apparently."

"I must write all this down and get my slave to check for further details. I say, I was right about Joanna being a bitch." Then, abruptly changing his tone, "So you're satisfied now that the drug works, and what you saw was not hallucination?"

"Almost," I replied, with caution.

"Almost? Don't the documents prove it, if nothing else?"

"The documents help to prove it," I countered, "but don't forget you read them before I did. So there is still the possibility that you were exercising some kind of telepathic influence. Anyway, how's the monkey?"

"The monkey." He paused a moment. "The monkey's dead."

"Thanks very much," I said.

"Oh, don't worry—it wasn't the drug. I killed him on purpose; I have work to do on his brain cells. It will take some time, so don't get impatient."

"I'm not in the least impatient," I replied, "merely appalled at the risk you appear to be taking with *my* brain."

"Your brain's different," he said. "You can take a lot more punishment yet. Besides, think of Isolda. Such a splendid antidote to Vita. You might even find that . . ."

I cut him short. I knew exactly what he had been going to say. "Leave my love life out of this," I said. "It doesn't concern you."

"I was only about to suggest, dear boy, that moving between two worlds can act as a stimulant. It happens every day, without drugs, when a man keeps a mistress round the corner and a wife at home. . . . That was a major find on your part, by the way, landing on the quarry above Treesmill valley. I'll put my archaeological friends on to digging the site when you and I have finished with it."

It struck me, as he spoke, how our attitude to the experiment differed. His was scientific, unemotional, it did not really concern him who was broken in the process so long as what he was attempting to prove was proved successfully; whereas I was already caught up in the mesh of history: the people who to him were puppets of a bygone age were alive for me. I had a sudden vision of that long-buried house reconstructed on concrete blocks, admission two shillings, car park at Chapel Down. . . .

"Then Roger never led you there?" I asked.

"To Treesmill valley? No," he answered. "I strayed from Kilmarth once only, and that was to the Priory, as I told you. I preferred to remain on my own ground. I'll tell you all about it when I come down. I'm off to Cambridge for the weekend, but remember you have all Saturday and Sunday for self-indulgence. Increase the dose a little—it won't hurt you."

He rang off before I could ask him for his telephone number, should I want it over the weekend. I had hardly put down the receiver before the telephone rang again. This time it was Vita.

"You were engaged a long while," she said. "I suppose it was your Professor?"

"As a matter of fact it was," I told her.

"Loading you up with weekend chores? Don't exhaust yourself, darling." Acidity, then, was the morning mood. She must blow it off on the boys, I could not cope.

"What are you planning for today?" I asked, ignoring her previous remark.

"Well, the boys are going swimming at Bill's club. That's a must. We've a heatwave here in London. How's it with you?"

"Overcast," I said without glancing at the window. "A trough of low pressure crossing the Atlantic will reach Cornwall by midnight."

"It sounds delightful. I hope your Mrs Collins is getting on with airing the beds."

"Everything's under control," I told her, "and I've hired a sailing-boat for next week, quite a big one, with a chap in charge. The boys will love it."

"What about Mom?"

"Mom will love it too, if she takes enough seasick pills. There's also a beach below the cliffs here, only a couple of fields to cross. No bulls."

"Darling,"—the acidity had turned sweet, or at any rate mellow—"I believe you are looking forward to our coming after all."

"Of course I am," I said. "Why should you think otherwise?"

"I never know what to think when your Professor's been at you. There's some sort of hoodoo between us when he's around. . . . Here are the boys," she went on, her voice changing. "They want to say hullo."

My stepsons' voices, like their appearance, were identical, though Teddy was twelve and Micky ten. They were said to resemble their father, killed in an air crash a couple of years before I met Vita. Judging by the photograph they carried round with them, this was true. He had, they had, the typical Teuton head, hair cropped close, of many American young. Blue eyes, innocent, set in a broad face. They were nice kids. But I could have done without them.

"Hi, Dick," they said, one after the other.

"Hi," I repeated, the phrase as alien to my tongue as if I had been speaking Tongalese.

"How are you both?" I asked.

"We're fine," they said.

There was a long pause. They couldn't think of anything more to say. Neither could I. "Looking forward to seeing you next week," I told them.

I heard a lot of whispering, and then Vita was back on the line again. "They're raging to swim. I shall have to go. Take care of yourself, darling, and don't overdo it with your pail and broom."

I went and sat in the little summer-house that Magnus's mother had erected years ago, and looked down across the bay. It was a happy spot, peaceful, sheltered from all winds except a south-westerly blow. I could see myself spending a lot of time here during the holidays, if only to get out of bowling to the boys; they were sure to bring cricket stumps with them, and a bat, and a ball which they would continually hit over the wall into the field beyond.

"Your turn to get it!"

"No, it's not, it's yours!"

Then Vita's voice chiming in from behind the hydrangea bushes. "Now, now, if you're going to quarrel there won't be any cricket at all, and I mean it," with a final appeal to me—"Do something, darling, you're the only adult male."

But at least today, in the summer-house, looking up the bay as a ray of sun touched the horizon, there was peace at Kylmerth. Kylmerth . . . I had pronounced the word in thought as originally spelt, and quite unconsciously. Confusion of thought becoming habit? Too tired for introspection, I got up again and wandered aimlessly about the grounds, clipping at hedges with an old hook I found in the boiler-house. Magnus had been right about the lilos. There were three of them, the kind you inflate with a pump. I'd set to work on them in the afternoon, if I had the energy.

"Lost your appetite?" asked Mrs Collins, when I had laboured through my lunch and asked for coffee.

"Sorry," I said, "no reflection on your cooking. I'm a bit out of sorts."

"I thought you looked tired. It's the weather. Turned very close."

It was not the weather. It was my own inability to settle, a sort of restlessness that drove me to physical action, however futile. I strolled down across the fields to the sea, but it looked exactly the same as it had from the summer-house, flat and grey, and then I had all the effort of walking up again. The day dragged on. I wrote a letter to my mother, describing the house in boring detail just to fill the pages, reminding me of the duty letters I used to write from school: "I'm in another dormitory this term. It holds fifteen." Finally, physically and mentally exhausted, I went upstairs at half-past seven, threw myself fully clothed upon the bed, and was asleep within minutes.

The rain awoke me. Nothing much, just a pattering sound on the open window, with the curtain blowing about. It was quite dark. I switched on the light; it was four-thirty. I had slept a solid nine hours. My exhaustion had vanished and I felt ravenous, having had no supper.

Here was the pay-off for living alone: I could eat and sleep entirely as and when I pleased. I went downstairs to the kitchen, cooked myself sausages, eggs and bacon, and brewed a pot of tea. I felt fighting fit to begin a new day, but what could I possibly do at five o'clock in this grey, cheerless dawn? One thing, and one thing only. Then take the weekend to recover, if recovery was needed. . . .

I went down the backstairs to the basement, switching on all the lights and whistling. It looked better lit up, much more cheerful. Even the laboratory had lost its alchemistic air, and measuring the drops into the medicine-glass was as simple as cleaning my teeth.

"Come on, Roger," I said, "show yourself. Let's make it a tête-à-tête."

I sat on the edge of the sink and waited. I waited a long time. The thing was, nothing happened. I just went on staring at the embryos in the bottles as it grew gradually lighter outside the barred window. I must have sat there for about half-an-hour. What a frightful swindle! Then I remembered that Magnus had suggested increasing the dose. I took the dropper, very cautiously let two or three more drops fall on to my tongue, and swallowed them. Was it imagination, or was there a taste to it this time—bitter, a little sour?

I locked the door of the laboratory behind me, and went down the passage into the old kitchen. I switched off the light, for it was already grey, with the first dawn in the patio outside. Then I heard the back door creak—it had a habit of grating on the stone flag beneath—and it blew wide open in the sudden draught. There was the sound of footsteps and a man's voice.

"God!" I thought. "Mrs Collins has turned up early—she said something about her husband coming to mow the grass."

The man pushed past the door, dragging a boy behind him, and it was not

Mrs Collins' husband, it was Roger Kylmerth, and he was followed by five other men, carrying flares, and there was no longer any dawn light coming from the patio, only the dark night.

CHAPTER NINE

I HAD BEEN standing against the old kitchen dresser, but there was no dresser behind me now, only the stone wall, and the kitchen itself had become the living quarters of the original house, with the hearth at one end and the ladder leading to the sleeping-room beside it. The girl I had seen kneeling by the hearth that first day came running down the ladder at the sound of the men's footsteps, and at sight of her Roger shouted, "Go back out of it! What we have to say and do does not concern you."

She hesitated, and the boy, the brother, was there too, looking over her shoulder. "Out of it," shouted Roger, "the pair of you," and they backed away again, up the ladder, but from where I stood I could see them crouching there, out of sight of the group of men, who entered the kitchen behind the steward.

Roger sat his flare upon a bench, lighting the room, and I recognised the boy he was holding—it was the young novice I had seen on my first visit to the Priory, the lad who had been forced to run round the stable yard to make sport for his fellow-monks, and later had wept at his prayers in the Priory chapel.

"I'll make him talk," said Roger, "if the rest of you cannot. It will loosen his tongue to have a taste of Purgatory to come."

Slowly he rolled up his sleeves, taking his time, his eyes upon the novice all the while, and the boy backed away from the bench, seeking shelter amongst the other men, who thrust him forward, laughing. He had grown taller since I had seen him last, but it was the same lad, there was no mistaking him, and the look of terror in his eyes suggested that the rough handling he dreaded this time was not sport.

Roger seized him by his habit and pushed him on to his knees beside the bench. "Tell us all you know," he said, "or I'll singe the hair off your head."

"I know nothing," cried the novice. "I swear by the Mother of God . . ."

"No blasphemy," said Roger, "or I'll set fire to your habit too. You've played spy long enough, and we want the truth."

He took hold of the flare and brought it within an inch or so of the boy's head. The boy crouched lower and began to scream. Roger hit him across the mouth. "Come on, out with it," he said.

The girl and her brother were staring from the ladder, fascinated, and the five men drew nearer to the bench, one of them touching the boy's ear with his knife. "Shall I prick him and draw blood," he suggested, "then singe his pate afterwards where the flesh is tender?"

The novice held up his hands for mercy. "I'll tell all I know," he cried, "but it's nothing, nothing . . . only what I overheard Master Bloyou, the Bishop's emissary, say to the Prior."

Roger withdrew the flare, and set it back upon the bench. "And what did he say?"

The terrified novice glanced first at Roger and then at his companions. "That the Bishop was displeased with the conduct of some of the brethren, Brother Jean in particular. That he, with others, acts against the Prior's will, and squanders the property of the monastery in dissolute living. That they are a scandal to the whole Order, and a pernicious example to many outside it. And that the Bishop cannot close his eyes to the situation any longer, and has given Master Bloyou all power to enforce the canon law, with the aid of Sir John Carminowe."

He paused for breath, seeking reassurance in their faces, and one of the men, not the fellow with the knife, moved away from the group.

"By the faith, it's true," he muttered, "and who are we to deny it? We know well enough that the Priory, and all within it, are a scandal. If the French monks went back where they belong, we'd be well rid of them."

A murmur of agreement rose from the others, and the man with the knife, a great hulking chap, losing interest in the novice, turned to Roger.

"Trefrengy has a point," he said sullenly. "It stands to reason we valley men this side of Tywardreath would stand to gain if the Priory closed its doors. We'd have a claim to the surrounding land, on which they grow fat, instead of being pushed to graze our cattle amongst reeds."

Roger folded his arms, spurning the still frightened novice with his foot. "Who speaks of closing the Priory doors?" he asked. "Not the Bishop up in Exeter, he speaks for the Diocese only, and can recommend the Prior to discipline the monks, but nothing further. The King is overlord, as you are perfectly aware, and every one of us who are tenants under Champernoune has had fair treatment, and received benefits from the Priory into the bargain. More than that. None of you have held back from trading with the French ships when they cast anchor in the bay. Is there anyone amongst you who has not had his cellars filled because of them?"

Nobody answered. The novice, believing himself safe, began to crawl away, but Roger caught at him once again and held him.

"Not so fast," he said, "I haven't finished with you. What else did Master Henry Bloyou tell the Prior?"

"No more than I have said," stammered the boy.

"Nothing concerning the safety of the realm itself?"

Roger made as though to seize the flare from the bench, and the novice, trembling, put up his hands in self-defence.

"He spoke of rumours from the north," he faltered, "that trouble is still brewing between the King and his mother Queen Isabella, and might break out into open strife before long. If so, he wondered who in the west would be loyal

to the young King, and who would declare for the Queen and her lover
Mortimer."

"I thought as much," said Roger. "Now crawl into a corner and stay mute. If
you blab a word of this outside these walls I'll slit your tongue for you."

He turned and faced the five men, who stared back at him uncertainly, this
latest information having shocked them into silence.

"Well?" asked Roger. "What do you make of it? Are you all dumb?"

The fellow called Trefrengy shook his head. "It's none of our business," he
said. "The King can quarrel with his mother if he wants. It does not concern
us."

"You think not?" queried Roger. "Not even if the Queen and Mortimer
should keep the power within their own hands still? I know of some in these
parts who would prefer it so, and would be recompensed for declaring for the
Queen when the battle was done. Yes, and pay liberally if others would do the
same."

"Not young Champernoune," said the man with the knife. "He's under-age
and tied to his mother's apron-strings. As for you, Roger, you'd never risk
rebellion against a crowned king—not holding your position."

He laughed derisively and the others joined in, but the steward, looking at
each in turn, remained unmoved.

"Victory is assured if action is swift and power seized overnight," he said.
"If that is what the Queen and Mortimer intend, we shall all of us be on the
winning side if we keep sweet with their friends. There could be some division
of manor lands, who knows? And instead of grazing your cattle amongst reeds,
Geoffrey Lampetho, you might have the advantage of the hills above."

The man with the knife shrugged his shoulders. "Easy said," he observed,
"but who are these friends, so ready with their promises? I know of none."

"Sir Otto Bodrugan, for one," said Roger quietly.

A murmur rose amongst the men, the name Bodrugan was repeated, and
Henry Trefrengy, who has spoken against the French monks, shook his head
once more.

"He's a fine man, none better," he said, "but the last time he rebelled against
the Crown, in 1322, he lost, and was fined a thousand marks for his pains."

"He was recompensed four years later when the Queen made him Governor
of Lundy island," replied Roger. "The lea of Lundy makes good anchorage for
vessels carrying arms, and men as well, who can lie in safety there until they're
needed on the mainland. Bodrugan is no fool. What is easier for him, holding
lands in Cornwall and in Devon, and Governor of Lundy into the bargain, than
to raise the men and ships that the Queen needs?"

His argument, smooth, persuasive, seemed to make impact, especially upon
Lampetho. "If there's profit in it for us I'd wish him well," he said, "and rally
to his side when the deed is done. But I won't cross the Tamar for any man,
Bodrugan or another, and you can tell him so."

"You may tell him yourself," said Roger. "His vessel lies below, and he
knows I await him here. I tell you, friends, Queen Isabella will show her
gratitude to him, and to others, who knew which side to favour."

He went to the foot of the ladder. "Come down, Robbie," he called. "Take a light across the field and see if Sir Otto is on his way," and turning to the others, "I'm ready to strike a blow for him if you are not."

His brother came down the ladder, and, seizing one of the flares, ran out into the yard beyond the kitchen.

Henry Trefrengy, more cautious than his companions, stroked his chin. "What lies in it for you, Roger, by siding with Bodrugan? Will the lady Joanna join forces with her brother against the King?"

"My lady has no part in any of it," replied Roger shortly. "She is away from home, at her other property of Trelawn, with her own children and Bodrugan's wife and family. None of them have any knowledge of what is at stake."

"She won't thank you when she hears of it," replied Trefrengy, "nor Sir John Carminowe either. It is common knowledge they only wait for Sir John's lady to die so that they can marry."

"Sir John's lady is healthy and likely to continue so," answered Roger, "and when the Queen makes Bodrugan Keeper of Restormel Castle and overseer of all the Duchy lands, my lady may lose her interest in Sir John and look upon her brother with more affection than she does now. I don't doubt I shall be recompensed by Bodrugan, and forgiven by my lady." He smiled, and scratched his ear.

"By the faith," said Lampetho, "we all know you lay your plans to suit yourself. Whoever wins the day will find you at his elbow. Bodrugan or Sir John at Restormel Castle, and you will be standing at the drawbridge, holding a well-lined purse."

"I don't deny it," said Roger, smiling still. "If you possessed the same ability for thought you would do like wise."

Footsteps sounded from the yard beyond, and he crossed to the door and flung it open. Otto Bodrugan stood on the threshold, with young Robbie behind him.

"Enter, sir, and welcome. We are all friends," said Roger, and Bodrugan came into the kitchen, looking sharply about him, surprised, I think, to see the little group of men who, embarrassed by his sudden arrival, drew back against the wall. His tunic was laced to the throat, with a padded leather jerkin over all, belted with purse and dagger, and a travelling cloak, fur-trimmed, hung from his shoulders. He made a contrast to the others in their homespun cloth and hoods, and it was evident from his air of confidence that he was used to commanding men.

"I am very glad to see you," he said at once, advancing to each in turn. "Henry Trefrengy, isn't it? And Martin Penhelek. John Beddyng I know too—your uncle rode north with me in '22. The others I have not met before."

"Geoffrey Lampetho, sir, and his brother Philip," said Roger. "They farm the valley adjoining Julian Polpey's land, beneath the Priory manor."

"Is Julian not here, then?"

"He awaits us at Polpey."

Bodrugan's eye fell upon the novice, still crouching beside the bench. "What is the monk doing here amongst you?"

"He brought us information, sir," said Roger. "There has been some trouble at the Priory, a matter of discipline in the house amongst the brothers, of no concern to us, but disturbing in that the Bishop has lately sent Master Bloyou from Exeter to enquire into the business."

"Henry Bloyou? A close friend to Sir John Carminowe and Sir William Ferrers. Is he still at the Priory?"

The novice, anxious to please, touched Bodrugan's knee. "No, sir, he has gone. He left yesterday for Exeter, but promised to return shortly."

"Well, get to your feet, lad, no harm shall come to you." Bodrugan turned to the steward. "Have you been threatening him?"

"Not a hair of his head," protested Roger. "He is only frightened that the Prior might learn of his presence here, despite my promise to the contrary."

Roger signalled to Robbie to take the novice to the upper room, and the pair of them disappeared up the ladder, the novice in as much hurry to be gone as a kicked dog. When the two had gone Bodrugan, standing before the hearth, his hands on his belt, looked keenly at each one of the men.

"What Roger has been telling you about our chances I do not know," he said, "but I can promise you a better life when the King is in custody." No one answered. "Has Roger informed you that most of the country will declare for Queen Isabella in a few days' time?" he asked them.

Henry Trefrengy, who seemed to be spokesman, was bold enough to speak. "He has told us so, yes," he said, "but little detail of it."

"It is a question of the timing," replied Bodrugan. "Parliament now sits at Nottingham, and it is planned to seize the King—with all care for his safety, naturally—until he comes of age. In the meantime Queen Isabella will continue as Regent, with Mortimer to aid her. He may lack popularity with some, but he is a strong man, and capable, and a very good friend of many Cornishmen. I am proud to count myself amongst them."

Silence again. Then Geoffrey Lampetho stepped forward. "What would you have us do?" he asked.

"Come north with me, if you will," answered Bodrugan, "but if not, and God knows I cannot make you, then promise to swear allegiance to Queen Isabella when word comes from Nottingham that we hold the King."

"That's spoken fairly," said Roger. "For my part I say yes, and gladly, and will ride with you."

"And so will I," said another, the man called Penhelek.

"And I too," cried the third, John Beddyng.

Only the Lampetho brothers and Trefrengy were reluctant.

"We'll swear allegiance when the moment comes," said Geoffrey Lampetho, "but we'll swear it at home, not across the Tamar."

"Also fairly spoken," said Bodrugan. "If the King had the power himself we should be at war with France within ten years, fighting across the Channel. By supporting the Queen now we strike a blow for peace. I have the promise of at least a hundred men from my own lands, from Bodrugan, from Tregrehan and further west, and from Devon too. Shall we go and see how Julian Polpey stands?"

There was a general stir amongst the men as they made towards the door.

"The tide is flooding across the ford," said Roger. "We must cross the valley by Trefrengy and Lampetho. I have a pony for you, sir. Robbie?" he called his brother from the room above. "Have you the pony saddled for Sir Otto? And mine as well? Make haste, then . . ." And as the boy came down the ladder he whispered in his ear, "Brother Jean will send for the novice later. Keep him until then. As for myself, I cannot say when I shall return."

We found ourselves in the stableyard, a huddle of ponies and men, and I knew I must go too, for Roger was mounting his pony beside Bodrugan, and wherever he went I was compelled to follow. The clouds were racing across the sky, and the wind was blowing, and the stamping of ponies and the jingle of harness rang in my ear. Never before, neither in my own world nor on the previous occasions when I had strayed into the other, had I felt such a sense of unity. I was one of them, and they did not know it. I belonged amongst them, and they did not know it. This, I think, was the essence of what it meant to me. To be bound, yet free; to be alone, yet in their company; to be born in my own time yet living, unknown, in theirs.

They rode up the track through the little copse bordering Kilmarth, and at the top of the hill, instead of following the route of the modern road I knew, they struck across the summit and then plunged steeply towards the valley. The track was rough, making the ponies stumble from time to time, and twisting too. The descent seemed almost as sharp as a cliff-face, but, disembodied as I felt myself to be, I was no judge of height or depth, and my only guides were the men upon their ponies. Then, through the darkness, I saw the gleam of water, and presently we plumbed the valley's depth and reached a wooden bridge bordering a stream, across which the ponies walked dry-shod in single file, and the path wound to the left, following the water's course, until the stream itself widened to a broad creek that opened out in the far distance to the sea itself. I knew I must be on the opposite side of the valley from Polmear hill, but because I was abroad in their world and it was night, the judging of distance was impossible; I could only follow the ponies, my eyes firmly fixed on Roger and Bodrugan.

The path led us past farm-buildings, where the Lampetho brothers dismounted, the elder, Geoffrey, shouting that he would follow later, and we went on again, the track rising to higher ground but still bordering the creek. There were further farm-buildings ahead above the sand-dunes where the river met the sea; even in the darkness I could see the gleam of the white rollers as they broke in the distance and then ran upon the shore. Someone came to meet us, there were barking dogs and flares, and we were in yet another stableyard, similar to the one at Kilmarth, with outbuildings surrounding it. As the men dismounted from their ponies the door of the main building opened, and I recognised the man who came forward to greet us. It was Roger's companion on the day of the Bishop's reception at the Priory, the same who had walked with him afterwards on the village green.

Roger, the first to dismount, was the first at his friend's side, and even in the dim light of the lantern by the house door I could see his expression change as the man whispered hurriedly in his ear, pointing to the further side of the farm-buildings.

Bodrugan saw this too, for jumping off his pony he called out, "What's amiss, Julian? Has your opinion changed since I saw you last?"

Roger turned swiftly. "Bad tidings, sir. For your ear only."

Bodrugan hesitated for a moment, then quickly said, "As you will," and put out his hand to the owner of the house. "I had hoped," he said, "we would muster arms and men at Polpey, Julian. My ship is anchored below Kylmerth, you must have seen her. There are several aboard, ready to disembark."

Julian Polpey shook his head. "I am sorry, Sir Otto, they will not be needed, nor yourself either. Word came not ten minutes ago that the whole scheme has been defeated before it took final shape. A very special messenger has brought you the news herself, disregarding, if I may say so, her own safety."

I could hear Roger, over my shoulder, telling the men to mount their ponies and ride back to Lampetho, where he would presently join them. Then, handing his pony's reins to the servant standing by, he joined Polpey and Bodrugan as they made their way past the outbuildings to the further side of the house.

"It is Lady Carminowe," said Bodrugan to Roger, his glad confidence vanished, his face sharp with anxiety. "She has brought bad news."

"Lady Carminowe?" exclaimed Roger, incredulous, then with sudden understanding, and lowering his voice, "you mean the lady Isolda?"

"She is on her way to Carminowe," said Bodrugan, "and, guessing my movements, has broken her journey here at Polpey."

We came to the other side of the house, which fronted upon the lane leading to Tywardreath. A covered vehicle was drawn up outside the gate, similar to the wagonettes I had seen at the Priory at Martinmas, but this was smaller, drawn by two horses only.

As we approached the curtain was held aside from the small window, and Isolda leant from it, the dark hood that covered her head falling back upon her shoulders.

"Thank God I am in time," she said. "I come straight from Bockenod. Both John and Oliver are there, and believe me half-way to Carminowe to rejoin the children. The worst has happened for your cause, and what I feared. News came before I left that the Queen and Mortimer have been seized at Nottingham Castle and are prisoners. The King is in full command, and Mortimer is to be taken to London for trial. Here is an end, Otto, to all your dreams."

Roger exchanged a glance with Julian Polpey, and as the latter, from discretion, moved away into the shadows I could see the conflict of emotion on Roger's face. I guessed what he was thinking. Ambition had led him astray, and he had backed a losing cause. It now remained for him to urge Bodrugan to return to his ship, disband his men and speed Isolda on her journey, while he himself, having explained his volte-face to Lampetho, Trefrengy and the rest as best he could, reinstated himself as Joanna Champernoune's trusted steward.

"You have risked discovery in coming here," said Bodrugan to Isolda. Nothing in his face betrayed how much he had lost.

"If I have done so," she replied, "you know the reason why."

I saw her look at him, and he at her. We were the only witnesses, Roger and I. Bodrugan bent forward to kiss her hand, and as he did so I heard the sound of wheels from the lane, and I thought, "She came too late to warn him after all. Oliver, the husband, and Sir John have followed her."

I wondered that neither of them heard the wheels, and then I saw they were not with me any longer. The wagonette had gone, and the mail van from Par had come up the lane and stopped beside the gate.

It was morning. I was standing inside the drive leading to a small house across the valley from Polmear hill. I tried to hide myself in the bushes bordering the drive, but the postman had already got out of his van and was opening the gate. His stare combined recognition and astonishment, and I followed the direction of his eyes down to my legs. I was soaking wet from crutch to foot: I must have waded through bog and marsh. My shoes were water-logged and both trouser legs were torn. I summoned a painful smile.

He looked embarrassed. "You're in a proper mess," he said. "It's the gentleman living up Kilmarth, isn't it?"

"Yes," I replied.

"Well, this is Polpey, Mr Graham's house. But I doubt if they're up yet, it's only just turned seven. Were you intending to call on Mr Graham?"

"Good heavens, no! I got up early, went for a walk, and somehow lost my way."

It was a thumping lie, and sounded like one. He seemed to accept it, though.

"I have to deliver these letters, and then I'll be going up the hill to your place," he said. "Would you care to get in the van? It would save you a walk."

"Thanks a lot," I said. "I'd be most grateful."

He disappeared down the drive and I climbed into his van. I looked at my watch. He was right, it was five past seven. Mrs Collins was not due for at least another hour and a half, and I should have plenty of time for a bath and a change.

I tried to think where I had been. I must have crossed the main road at the top of the hill, then walked downhill across country and through the marshy ground at the bottom of the valley. I had not even known that this house was called Polpey.

No nausea, though, thank God, no vertigo. As I sat there, waiting for him to return, I realised that the rest of me was wet as well, jacket, head, for it was raining—it had probably been raining when I left Kilmarth almost an hour and a half ago. I wondered whether I should enlarge upon my story to the postman or let it go. Better let it go . . .

He came back and climbed into the van. "Not much of a morning for your walk. It's been raining hard since midnight."

I remembered then that it had been the rain which woke me up originally, blowing the curtain at the bedroom window.

"I don't mind the rain," I told him. "I get short of exercise in London."

"Same as me," he said cheerfully, "driving this van. But I'd rather be snug in my bed this weather than take a walk across the marsh. Still, there it is, it wouldn't do if we were all the same."

He called at the Ship Inn at the bottom of the hill and at one of the cottages near by, and as the van raced up the main road I looked leftward over my shoulder to the valley, but the high hedge hid it from view. God only knew what swampy meadowland and marsh I must have traversed. My shoes were oozing water on the floor of the van.

We left the main road and turned right down the drive to Kilmarth.

"You're not the only early bird," he said as the sweep in front of the house came into sight. "Either Mrs Collins has had a lift up from Polkerris or you have visitors."

I saw the large open boot of the Buick packed tight with luggage. The horn was blowing continuously, and the two children, with macs held over their heads to protect them from the rain, were running up the steps through the front garden to the house.

The shock of disbelief turned to the dull certainty of impending doom.

"It's not Mrs Collins," I said, "it's my wife and family. They must have driven down from London through the night."

CHAPTER TEN

THERE WAS NO question of driving past the garage to the back entrance. The postman, grinning, stopped his van and opened the door for me to get out, and anyway the children had already seen me, and were waving.

"Thanks for the lift," I said to him, "but I could do without the reception," and I took the letter that he held out to me and advanced to meet my fate.

"Hi, Dick," called the boys, tearing back down the steps. "We rang and rang, but we couldn't make you hear. Mom's mad at you."

"I'm mad at her," I told them. "I didn't expect you."

"It's a surprise," said Teddy. "Mom thought it would be more fun. Micky slept at the back of the car, but I didn't. I read the map."

The blowing of the horn had ceased. Vita emerged from the Buick, immaculate as always, wearing just the right sort of clothes for Piping Rock on Long Island. She had a new hair-do, more wave in it, or something; it looked all right but it made her face too full.

Attack is the best form of defence, I thought. Let's get it over. "Well, for God's sake," I said, "you might have warned me."

"The boys gave me no peace," she said. "Blame it on them."

We kissed, then both stood back, eyeing each other warily like sparring partners before a shadow feint.

"How long have you been here?" I asked.

"About half an hour," she said. "We've been all round, but we couldn't get in. The boys even tried throwing earth at the windows, after they'd rung the bell. What's happened? You're soaked to the skin."

"I was up very early," I said. "I went for a walk."

"What, in all this rain? You must be crazy. Look, your trousers are torn, and there's a great rent in your jacket."

She seized hold of my arm and the boys crowded round me, gaping. Vita began to laugh. "Where on earth did you go to get in a state like this?" she asked.

I shook myself clear. "Look," I said, "we'd better unload. It's no good doing it here—the front door is locked. Hop in the car and we'll go round to the back."

I led the way with the boys, and she followed in the car. When we reached the back entrance I remembered that it was locked too from the inside—I had left the house by the patio.

"Wait here," I said, "I'll open the door for you," and with the boys in close attendance I went round to the patio. The boiler-house door was ajar—I must have passed through it when I followed Roger and the rest of the conspirators. I kept telling myself to keep calm, not to get confused; if confusion started in my mind it would be fatal.

"What a funny old place. What's it for?" asked Micky.

"To sit it," I said, "and sun-bathe. When there is any sun."

"If I were Professor Lane I'd turn it into a swimming-pool," said Teddy. They trooped after me into the house, and through the old kitchen to the back door. I unlocked it, and found Vita waiting impatiently outside.

"Get in out of the rain," I said, "while the boys and I fetch in the suit-cases."

"Show us round first," she said plaintively. "The luggage can wait. I want to see everything. Don't tell me *that* is the kitchen through there?"

"Of course it isn't," I said. "It's an old basement kitchen. We don't use any of this."

The thing was, I had never intended to show them the house from this angle. It was the wrong way round. If they had arrived on Monday I should have been waiting for them on the steps by the porch, with the curtains drawn back, the windows open, everything ready. The boys, excited, were already scampering up the stairs.

"Which is our room?" they shouted. "Where are we to sleep?"

Oh God, I thought, give me patience. I turned to Vita, who was watching me with a smile.

"I'm sorry, darling," I said, "but honestly . . ."

"Honestly what?" she said. "I'm as excited as they are. What are you fussing about?"

What indeed! I thought, with total inconsequence, how much better organised this would have been if Roger Kylmerth, as steward, had been showing Isolda Carminowe the lay-out of some manor house.

"Nothing," I said, "come on . . ."

The first thing Vita noticed when we reached the modern kitchen on the first floor was the debris of my supper on the table. The remains of fried eggs and sausages, the frying-pan not cleaned, standing on one corner of the table, the electric light still on.

"Heavens!" she exclaimed. "Did you have a cooked breakfast before your walk? That's new for you!"

"I was hungry," I said. "Ignore the mess, Mrs Collins will clear all that. Come through to the front."

I hurried past her to the music-room, drawing curtains, throwing back shutters, and then across the hall to the small dining-room and the library beyond. The *pièce de résistance*, the view from the end window, was blotted out by the mizzling rain.

"It looks different," I said, "on a fine day."

"It's lovely," said Vita. "I didn't think your Professor had such taste. It would be better with that divan against the wall and cushions on the window-seat, but that's easily done."

"Well, this completes the ground-floor," I said. "Come upstairs."

I felt like a house-agent trying to flog a difficult let, as the boys raced ahead up the stairs, calling to each other from the rooms, while Vita and I followed. Everything had already changed, the silence and the peace had gone, henceforth it would be only this, the take-over of something I had shared, as it were, in secret, not only with Magnus and his dead parents in the immediate past, but with Roger Kylmerth six hundred years ago.

The tour of the first floor finished, the sweat of unloading all the luggage began, and it was nearly half-past eight when the job was done, and Mrs Collins arrived on her bicycle to take charge of the situation, greeting Vita and the boys with genuine delight. Everyone disappeared into the kitchen. I went upstairs and ran the bath, wishing I could lie in it and drown.

It must have been half an hour later that Vita wandered into the bedroom. "Well, thank God for her," she said. "I shan't have to do a thing, she's extremely efficient. And must be sixty at least. I can relax."

"What do you mean, relax?" I called from the bathroom.

"I imagined something young and skittish, when you tried to put me off from coming down," she said. She came into the bathroom as I was rubbing myself with the towel. "I don't trust your Professor an inch, but at least I'm satisfied on that account. Now you're all cleaned up you can kiss me again, and then run me a bath. I've been driving for seven hours and I'm dead to the world."

So was I, but in another sense. I was dead to her world. I might move about in it, mechanically, listening with half an ear as she peeled off her clothes and flung them on the bed, put on a wrapper, spread her lotions and creams on the dressing-table, chatting all the while about the drive down, the day in London, happenings in New York, her brother's business affairs, a dozen things that formed the pattern of her life, our life; but none of them concerned me. It was like hearing background music on the radio. I wanted to recapture the lost night and the darkness, the wind blowing down the valley, the sound of the sea breaking on the shore below Polpey farm, and the expression in Isolda's eyes as she looked out of that painted wagon at Bodrugan.

". . . And if they do amalgamate it wouldn't be before the fall anyway, nor would it affect your job."

"No."

Response was automatic to the rise and fall of her voice, and suddenly she wheeled round, her face a mask of cream under the turban she always wore in the bath, and said, "You haven't been listening to a word I said!"

The change of tone shocked me to attention. "Yes, I have," I told her.

"What, then? What have I been talking about?" she challenged.

I was clearing my things out of the wardrobe in the bedroom, so that she could take over. "You were saying something about Joe's firm," I answered, "a merger of some sort. Sorry, darling, I'll be out of your way in a minute."

She seized the hanger bearing a flannel suit, my best, out of my hand, and hurled it on the floor.

"I don't want you out of the way," she said, her voice rising to a pitch I dreaded. "I want you here and now, giving me your full attention, instead of standing there like a tailor's dummy. What on earth's the matter with you? I might be talking to someone in another world."

She was so right. I knew it was no use counter-attacking; I must grovel, and let her tide of perfectly justifiable irritation pass over my head.

"Darling," I said, sitting down on the bed and pulling her beside me, "let's not start the day wrong. You're tired, I'm tired; if we start arguing we'll wear ourselves out and spoil things for the boys. If I am vague and inattentive, you must blame it on exhaustion. I took that walk in the rain because I couldn't sleep, and instead of pulling me together it seems to have slowed me up."

"Of all the idiotic things to do. . . . You might have known. . . . And anyway, why couldn't you sleep?"

"Forget it, forget it, forget it."

I rose from the bed, seized armfuls of clothes and bore them through to the dressing-room, kicking the door to with my foot. She did not follow me. I heard her turn the taps off and get into the bath, slopping the water so that some of it ran into the overflow.

The morning drifted on. Vita did not appear. I opened the bedroom door very softly just before one, and she was fast asleep on the bed, so I closed it again and lunched downstairs alone with the boys. They chatted away, perfectly content with a "yes" or "perhaps" from me, invariably undemanding when Vita was absent. It continued to rain steadily, and there was no question of cricket or the beach, so I drove them into Fowey and let them loose to buy ice-creams, peppermint rock, western paperbacks and jig-saw puzzles.

The rain petered out about four, giving place to a lustreless sky and a pallid, constipated sun, this was enough for the boys, who rushed on to the Town Quay and demanded to be water-born. Anything to please, and postpone the moment of return, so I hired a small boat, powered by an outboard engine, and we chug-chugged up and down the harbour, the boys snatching at passing flotsam as we bobbed about, all of us soaked to the skin.

We arrived home about six o'clock, and the children rushed to sit down to the enormous spread of tea that the thoughtful Mrs Collins had provided for them. I staggered into the library to pour myself a stiff whisky, only to find a revitalised Vita in possession, smiling, the furniture all moved around, the morning mood, thank heaven, a thing of the past.

"You know, darling," she said, "I think I'm going to like it here. Already it's beginning to look like home."

I collapsed into an armchair, drink in hand, and watched through half-closed eyes as she pottered about the room rearranging Mrs Collins' brave efforts with the hydrangeas. My strategy henceforth would be to applaud everything, or, when occasion demanded silence, to stay mute, play each moment as it came by ear.

I was on my second whisky, and off my guard, when the boys burst into the library.

"Hi, Dick," shouted Teddy, "what's this horrible thing?"

He had got the embryo monkey in its jar. I leapt to my feet. "Christ!" I said. "What the hell have you been up to?" I seized the jar from his hand and made for the door. I remembered only then that when I had gone out from the lab in the small hours, after taking my second dose, I hadn't pocketed the key but had left it in the lock.

"We weren't doing anything," said Teddy, aggrieved, "we were only looking through the empty rooms below." He turned to Vita. "There's a little dark room full of bottles, just like the stinks lab at school. Come and look, Mom, quick—there's something else in one of the jars like a dead kitten . . ."

I was out of the library in a flash, and down the small stairway in the hall leading to the basement. The door of the lab was wide open, and the light was on. I looked quickly around. Nothing had been touched except the jar holding the monkey. I switched off the light and stepped into the passage, locking the door behind me and pocketing the key. As I did so the boys came running through the old kitchen, Vita at their heels. She looked concerned.

"What did they do?" she asked. "Have they broken something?"

"Luckily, no," I said. "It was my fault for leaving the door unlocked."

She was peering over my shoulder down the passage. "What is through there anyway?" she asked. "That object Teddy brought up looked perfectly ghastly."

"I dare say," I answered. "It happens that this house belongs to a professor of biophysics, and he uses the small room behind there as a laboratory. If I ever catch either of the boys near that room again there'll be murder!"

They stalked off, muttering, and Vita turned to me. "I must say," she said, "I think it's rather extraordinary of the Professor to keep a room like that, with all sorts of scientific things in it, and not make certain it's kept properly locked."

"Now don't you start," I said. "I am responsible to Magnus, and I can assure you it won't happen again. If you had only come next week instead of turning up this morning at an unearthly hour, when nobody expected you, it would never have happened."

She stared at me, startled. "Why, you're shaking!" she said. "Anyone would think there were explosives in there."

"Perhaps there are," I said. "Anyway, let's hope those kids have learnt their lesson."

I switched off the basement lights and walked upstairs. I was shaking, and small wonder. A nightmare of possibilities crowded my mind. They might have opened the bottles containing the drug, they might have poured the contents into the medicine-glass, they might even have emptied the bottles into the sink. I must never again let that key of my sight. I kept touching it in my pocket. Perhaps I could get an impression made of it, and keep both; it would be safer. I went into the music-room and stood there, staring at nothing, thrusting my finger-tip into the little hole in the key.

Vita had gone upstairs to the bedroom. Presently, I heard the tell-tale click of the telephone from the bell in the hall. It meant she was speaking from the extension upstairs. I went and washed my hands in the downstairs lavatory, and then wandered into the library. I could still hear Vita talking from the bedroom overhead. Listening to conversations on the telephone is not a habit of mine, but now some furtive instinct made me cross to the instrument in the library and pick up the receiver.

". . . So I just don't know what to make of it," Vita was saying. "I've never heard him speak sharply to the boys before. They're quite upset. He doesn't look awfully well. Very hollow-eyed. He says he's been sleeping badly."

"High time you got down there," came the answer. I recognised the drawl; it was her friend Diana. "A husband on the loose is a husband on the prowl, I've told you so before. I've had experience with Bill."

"Oh, Bill," said Vita. "We all know Bill can't be trusted out of your sight. Well, I don't know. . . . Let's hope it will be fine and we can all be out a lot. I believe he's arranged to hire some boat."

"That sounds healthy enough."

"Yes. . . . Well, let's hope that Professor of his hasn't been putting Dick up to something. I don't trust that man. Never have, and never will. And I know he dislikes me."

"I can guess why that is," laughed Diana.

"Oh, don't be idiotic. He may be like that, but Dick certainly isn't. Very much the reverse."

"Maybe that's his attraction for the Professor," said Diana.

I replaced the receiver very gently. The trouble was, with women, they had one-track minds, and to their narrow view everything male, be it man, dog, fish or slug, pursued but a single course, and that the dreary road to copulation. I sometimes wondered if they ever thought of anything else.

Vita and her friend Diana nattered on for at least another fifteen minutes, and when she came downstairs, fortified by feminine advice, she made no reference to my scene in the basement, but, humming gaily and wearing an apron of bizarre design—it looked as if it had apples and serpents all over it—set about cooking us steaks for supper heaped about with parsley butter.

"Early bed for all," she announced as the boys, heavy-eyed and silent, yawned their way through the meal—the seven-hour journey in the car and the jaunt in the harbour was catching up with them. After supper she installed herself on the sofa in the library, and set about mending the rents in my trousers torn in the valley. I sat down at Magnus's desk murmuring something about unpaid bills, but in reality looking once again through the Lay Subsidy Roll for Tywardreath Parish for 1327. Julian Polpey was there, Henry Trefrengy, Geoffrey Lampetho. The names had meant nothing when I first read through the list, but they could have registered unconsciously in my mind. The figures might still be phantom figures that I had followed to the valley, passing the farms that still bore their names today.

I noticed an unopened letter on my desk. It was the one the postman had given me that morning; in my flurry at the family's arrival I had laid it down. It was just a scrap, typewritten, from the research student in London.

"Professor Lane thought you might like this note on Sir John Carminowe," it read. "He was the second son of Sir Roger Carminowe of Carminowe. Enrolled in the military 1323. Became a knight 1324. Summoned to attend Great Council at Westminster. Appointed Keeper of Tremerton and Restormel castles April 27th, 1331, and on October 12th of the same year keeper of the King's forests, parks, woods and warrens, etc., and of the King's game in the county of Cornwall, so that he had to answer yearly for the profit of the pannage and herbage within the said forests, parks and woods, by the hand of the steward there, and deputy keepers under him."

The student had written in brackets, "Copied from Calendar of Fine Rolls 5th year Edward III". He had added a further note beneath, "October 24th. Patent Rolls, for same year (1331), mentions a licence for Joanna, late wife of Henry de Champernoune, tenant-in-chief, to marry whomsoever she will of the King's allegiance. Pay fine of 10 marks."

So . . . Sir John had got what he wanted and Otto Bodrugan had lost, while Joanna, in anticipation of Sir John's wife dying, had a marriage licence handy in some bottom drawer. I filed the paper with the Lay Subsidy Roll, and getting up from the desk went to the bookshelves, where I remembered seeing the numerous volumes of the *Encyclopaedia Britannica*, legacy of Commander Lane. I pulled out Volume 8, and turned to Edward III.

Vita stretched herself on the sofa, yawning, her repeated sighs following one another in swift succession. "Well, I don't know about you," she said, "but I'm off to bed."

"I'll be up in a moment," I told her.

"Still hard at work for your Professor?" she asked. "Take that volume to the light, you'll ruin your eyes."

I did not answer.

"Edward III (1312-1377), king of England, eldest son of Edward II and Isabella of France, was born at Windsor on the 13th of November 1312. . . .

On the 13th of January 1327 parliament recognised him as king, and he was crowned on the 29th of the same month. For the next four years Isabella and her paramour Mortimer governed in his name, though nominally his guardian was Henry, Earl of Lancaster. In the summer of 1327 he took part in an abortive campaign against the Scots, and was married to Philippa at York on the 24th of January 1328. On the 15th of June 1330 his eldest child, Edward the Black Prince, was born."

Nothing there about a rebellion. But here was the clue.

"Soon after, Edward made a successful effort to throw off his degrading dependence on his mother and Mortimer. In October 1330 he entered Nottingham Castle by night, through a subterranean passage, and took Mortimer prisoner. On the 29th of November the execution of the favourite at Tyburn completed the young king's emancipation. Edward discreetly drew a veil over his mother's relations with Mortimer, and treated her with every respect. There is no truth in the stories that henceforth he kept her in honourable confinement, but her political influence was at an end."

Bodrugan's too, what he possessed in Cornwall. Sir John, only a year later appointed Keeper of Tremerton and Restormel castles, a good King's man, was in command, with Roger, playing it safe, imposing silence on his valley friends, the October night forgotten. I wondered what had happened after that meeting at Polpey's farm when Isolda risked so much to warn her lover; whether Bodrugan, brooding on what might-have-been, returned to his estates and thought about his love, and whether she, when her husband Oliver was absent, met him perhaps in secret. I had been standing beside them both less than twenty-four hours ago. Six centuries ago. . . .

I put the volume back on the shelf, switched off the lights and went upstairs. Vita was already in bed, the curtains pulled back so that when she sat up she could look through the wide windows to the sea.

"This room is heaven," she said. "Imagine what it will be like with a full moon. Darling, I'm going to love it here, I promise you, and it's so wonderful to be together again."

I stood for a moment at the window, staring out across the bay. Roger, from his sleeping-quarters above the original kitchen, had the same dark expanse of sea and sky for company, and as I turned away, towards the bed, I remembered Magnus's mocking remark on the telephone the day before, "I was only about to suggest, dear boy, that moving between two worlds can act as stimulant." It was not true—in fact, the contrary.

CHAPTER ELEVEN

———————————

THE NEXT DAY being Sunday, Vita announced her intention over breakfast of taking the boys to church. She did this sort of thing from time to time during the holidays. Two or three weeks would go by with never a mention of devotional duty, and then suddenly, without giving any reason, and generally when they were otherwise happily employed, she would burst into their room saying, "Come on, now, I'll give you just five minutes to get ready."

"Ready? What for?" they would query, looking up from fitting together a model aeroplane or something momentarily engrossing their attention.

"Church, of course," she would answer, sweeping from the room again, deaf to their wails of protestation. It was always a let-out for me. Pleading my Catholic upbringing, I would lie late in bed, reading the Sunday papers. Today, despite sunshine flooding our room as we awoke, and the beaming smile of Mrs Collins as she bore in our tray of toast and coffee, Vita looked preoccupied, and said she had had a restless night. I at once felt guilty, having slept like a log myself, and I thought how this thing of how well or how badly one had slept was really the great test of marital relationship; if one partner came off poorly during the night hours the other was immediately to blame, and the following day would come apart in consequence.

This particular Sunday was to be no exception to the rule, and when the boys came into the bedroom to say good morning dressed in jeans and tee-shirts, she immediately exploded.

"Off with those things at once and into your flannel suits!" she said. "Have you forgotten it's Sunday? We're going to church."

"Oh, Mom . . . No!"

I admit, I felt for them. Sunshine, blue sky, the sea below the fields. They must have had one thought in mind, to get down to it and swim.

"No arguing now," she said, getting out of bed. "Go off and do as I say." She turned to me. "I take it there is a church somewhere in the vicinity, and you can at least drive us there?"

"You have a choice of churches," I said, "either Fowey or Tywardreath. It would be easier to take you to Tywardreath." As I said the word I smiled, for the very name had a special significance, but to me alone, and continued casually, "As a matter of fact, it's quite interesting historically. There used to be a priory where the churchyard is today."

"You hear that, Teddy?" said Vita. "There used to be a priory where we are going to church. You always say you like history. Now hurry along."

I have seldom seen a sulkier pair of figures. Shoulders hunched, mouths drooping. "I'll take you swimming later," I shouted as they left the room.

It suited me to drive the party to Tywardreath. Morning service would be at least an hour, and I could drop them off at the church, and then park the car above Treesmill and stroll across the field to the Gratten. I did not know when I might get another chance to revisit the site, and the quarry with its surrounding grassy banks held a compulsive fascination.

As I drove Vita and the reluctant boys, dressed in their Sunday suits, down Polmear hill I glanced over to the right at Polpey, wondering what would have happened if the present owners had discovered me lurking in the bushes instead of the postman, or, worse, what might well have happened had Julian Polpey bidden Roger and his guests inside. Should I have been found attempting to break into the downstairs rooms? This struck me as amusing, and I laughed aloud.

"What's so funny?" asked Vita.

"Only the life I lead," I answered. "Driving you all to church today, and yesterday taking that early morning walk. You see the marsh down there? That's where I got so wet."

"I'm not surprised," she said. "What an extraordinary place to choose for walking. What did you think you were going to find?"

"Find?" I echoed. "Oh, I don't know. A damsel in distress, perhaps. You never know your luck."

I shot up the lane to Tywardreath elated, the very fact that she knew nothing of the truth filling me with a ridiculous sense of delight, like hoodwinking my mother in the past. It was a basic instinct fundamental to all males. The boys possessed it too, which was the reason I backed them up in those petty crimes of which Vita disapproved, eating snacks between meals, talking in bed after lights out.

I dropped them at the church gate, the boys still wearing their hard-done-by expressions.

"What are you going to do while we are in church?" Vita asked.

"Just walk around," I said.

She shrugged her shoulders, and turned through the gate into the church-yard. I knew that shrug; it implied that my easy-going morning mood was not in tune with hers. I hoped Matins would bring consolation.

I drove off to Treesmill, parked the car, and struck off across the field to the Gratten. The morning was superb. Warm sunshine filled the valley. A lark soared overhead bursting his heart in song. I wished I had brought sandwiches and could have had the whole long day ahead of me instead of one stolen hour.

I did not enter the quarry with its trailing ivy and old tin cans, but stretched myself full-length on a grassy bank in one of the small hollows, wondering how the place would look by night when the sky was full of stars, or rather how it had looked once, when water filled the valley below. Lorenzo's scene with Jessica came to my mind.

"In such a night,
Troilus methinks mounted the Trojan walls,

> And sighed his soul toward the Grecian tents,
> Where Cressid lay that night . . .

> "In such a night
> Stood Dido with a willow in her hand
> Upon the wild sea-banks, and wav'd her love
> To come again to Carthage.

> "In such a night,
> Medea gather'd the enchanted herbs
> That did renew old Aeson . . ."

Enchanted herbs was apt. The point was that, when Vita and the boys were getting ready for church, I had gone down to the lab and poured four measures into the flask. The flask was in my pocket. God knew when I should get the chance again . . .

It happened very quickly. But it was not night, it was day, and a day in summer, too, though late afternoon, judging from the western sky, which I could see from the casement window in the hall. I was leaning against a bench at the far end, with a view of the entrance court with its surrounding walls. I recognised it at once—I was in the manor-house. Two children were playing in the courtyard, girls, aged around eight and ten possibly—it was difficult to tell, with the close-fitting bodices and ankle-length skirts—but the long golden hair falling down their backs, and the small clear-cut features so much alike, proclaimed them miniature editions of their mother. No one but Isolda could have produced such a pair, and I remembered Roger saying to his companion Julian Polpey at the Bishop's reception that she had grown stepsons amongst the first wife's brood, but only two daughters of her own.

They were playing some chequer game upon the flags, on a square marked out for them, with pieces like ninepins dotted about, and as they moved the pieces shrill arguments broke out between them as to whose turn was next. The younger reached forward to seize a wooden pin and hide it in her skirt, and this in turn led to cries and slaps and the pulling of hair. Roger emerged into the court suddenly, from the hall where he had been standing watching them, and thrusting himself between them squatted on his haunches, taking the hand of each in turn.

"You know what comes about when women scold?" he said to them. "Their tongues turn black and curl into their throats, choking them. It happened to my sister once, and she would have died had I not reached her side in time to pluck it back. Open your mouths."

The children, startled, opened their mouths wide, thrusting out their tongues. Roger touched each in turn with his finger-tip, and waggled it.

"Pray God that does the trick," he said, "but it may not last unless you let your tempers cool. There now, shut your mouths, and only open them for your next meal, or to let kind words fly. Joanna, you're the elder, you should teach Margaret better manners than to hide a man under her skirt." He pulled out the ninepin from the younger girl's dress and set it down upon the flags. "Come now," he said, "proceed. I'll see that you play fair."

He stood up, legs wide apart, and let them move their pieces round him, which they did at first with some hesitation, then with greater confidence, and soon with peals of delighted laughter as he rocked sideways, stumbling, knocking the pieces down, so that all had to be set straight once more with Roger helping. Presently a woman—their nurse, I supposed—called them from a second doorway beyond the hall, and the pieces were taken up and given solemnly to Roger, who as he took them, promising to play again next day, winked at the nurse, advising her to examine both their tongues later, and let him know if they showed signs of turning black.

He put the pieces down near the entrance and came into the hall, while the children disappeared into the back regions with their nurse; and it seemed to me for the first time that he had showed some human quality. His steward's role, calculating, cool, very possibly corrupt, had been momentarily put aside, and with it the irony, the cruel detachment I associated with all his actions hitherto.

He stood in the hall, listening. There was no one there but our two selves, and looking about me I sensed that the place had somehow changed since that day in May when Henry Champernoune had died; it no longer had the feeling of permanent occupancy, but more of a house where the owners came and went, leaving it empty in their absence. There was no sound of barking dogs, no sign of servants, other than the children's nurse, and it came to me suddenly that the lady of the house herself, Joanna Champernoune, must be away from home with her own brood of sons and daughter, perhaps in that other manor of Trelawn, which the steward had mentioned to Lampetho and Trefrengy in the Kilmarth kitchen on the night of the abortive rebellion. Roger must be in charge, and Isolda's children and their nurse were here to break their journey between one house and another.

He crossed over to the window, through which the late sunlight came, and looked out. Almost at once he flattened himself against the wall as though someone from outside might catch sight of him, and he preferred to remain unseen. Intrigued, I also ventured to the window, and immediately guessed the reason for his manœuvre. There was a bench beneath the window, with two people sitting on it, Isolda and Otto Bodrugan, and because of the angle of the wall, which jutted outward, giving the bench shelter, anyone who sat there would have privacy unless he was spied upon from this one window.

The grass beneath the bench sloped to a low wall, and beyond the wall the fields descended to the river where Bodrugan's ship was anchored. I could see the mast-head, but not the deck. The tide was low, the channel narrow, and on either side of the blue ribbon of water were sand-flats, crowded with every sort of wading bird, dipping and bobbing around the pools where the tide had ebbed. Bodrugan held Isolda's hands in his, examining the fingers, and in a foolish sort of love-play bit each one of them in turn, or rather made pretence of biting them, grimacing as he did so as though they tasted sour.

I stood by the window watching them, oddly disturbed, not because I, like the steward, was playing spy, but because I sensed in some fashion that the relationship between these two, however passionate it might be at other times, was at this moment innocent, without guile and altogether blessed, and it was the kind of relationship that I myself would never know. Then suddenly he released both hands, letting them drop on to her lap.

"Let me stay another night and not sleep aboard," he said. "In any event the tide may serve me ill, and I may find myself hard aground if I make sail."

"Not if you choose your moment," she replied. "The longer you remain here the more dangerous for us both. You know how gossip travels. To come here anyway was madness, with the vessel well known."

"There's nothing to that," he said. "I come frequently to the bay and to this river, either on business or for my own pleasure, fishing between here and Chapel Point. It was pure chance that brought you here as well."

"It was not," she said, "and you know it very well. The steward brought you my letter telling you I should be here."

"Roger is a trusty messenger," he answered. "My wife and children are at Trelawn, and so is my sister Joanna. The risk was worth the taking."

"Worth taking, yes, this once, but not for two nights in succession. Nor do I trust the steward as you do, and you know my reasons."

"Henry's death, you mean?" He frowned. "I still think you judged unfairly there. Henry was a dying man. We all knew it. If those potions made him sleep the sooner, free from pain and with Joanna's knowledge, why should we shake our heads?"

"Too easy done," she said, "and with intent. I'm sorry for it, Otto, but I cannot forgive Joanna, even if she is your sister. As for the steward, doubtless she paid him well, and his monk accomplice."

I glanced at Roger. He had not moved from his shadowed corner by the window, but he could hear them as well as I did, and judging by the expression in his eyes he hardly relished what she said.

"As to the monk," added Isolda, "he is still at the Priory, and adds something to his influence every day. The Prior is wax in his hands, and his flock do as they are bidden by Brother Jean, who comes and goes as he pleases."

"If he does so," said Bodrugan, "it is no concern of mine."

"It could become so," she told him, "if Margaret comes to have as much faith in his herbal knowledge as Joanna. You know he has treated your family lately?"

"I know nothing of the sort," he answered. "I have been at Lundy, as you know, and Margaret finds both the island and Bodrugan too exposed, and prefers Trelawn." He rose from the bench and began pacing up and down the grass walk in front of her. Love-making was over, with the problems of domestic life upon them once again. They had my sympathy. "Margaret is too much a Champernoune, like poor Henry," he said. "A priest or a monk could persuade her to abstinence or perpetual prayer if he had the mind to do so. I shall look into it."

Isolda also rose from the bench, and standing close to Bodrugan looked up at him, with her hands upon his shoulders. I could have touched them both had I leant from the window. How small they were, inches below adult height today, yet he was broadly-built and strong, with a fine head and a most likable smile, and she as delicately formed as a porcelain shepherdess, hardly taller than her own daughters. They held each other, kissing, and once again I felt this strange disturbance, a sense of loss, utterly unlike anything I might experience in my own time, had I seen two lovers from a window. . . . Intense involvement, and intense compassion too. Yes, that was the word, compassion. And I had no way of explaining my sense of participation in all they did, unless it was that stepping backwards, out of my time to theirs, I felt them vulnerable, and more certainly doomed to die than I was myself, knowing indeed that they had both been dust for more than six centuries.

"Have a care for Joanna, too," said Isolda. "She is no nearer being married to John now than she was two years ago, and has altered for the worse in consequence. She might even serve his wife as she served her husband."

"She would not dare, nor John," answered Bodrugan.

"She would dare anything if it suited her. Harm you likewise, if you stood in her way. She has one thought in mind, to see John Keeper of Restormel and Sheriff of Cornwall, and herself his wife, queening it over all the crown lands as Lady Carminowe."

"If it should come about I can't prevent it," protested Bodrugan.

"As her brother you could try," said Isolda, "and at least prevent that monk from trailing at her heels with his poisonous draughts."

"Joanna was always headstrong," replied her lover. "She has always done as she pleased. I cannot be on watch continually. I might say a word to Roger."

"To the steward? He is as thick with the monk as she," said Isolda scornfully. "I warn you again, don't trust him, Otto. Neither on her account, nor on ours. He keeps our few meetings secret for the time because it pleases him."

Once again I glanced at Roger, and saw the shadow on his face. I wished someone would call him from the room so that he could no longer play eavesdropper. It would put him against her to hear his faults so plainly stated and with such dislike.

"He stood by me last October and will do so again," said Bodrugan.

"He stood by you then because he reckoned he had much to gain," replied Isolda. "Now you can do little for him, why should he risk losing his position? One word to Joanna, and thence to John, and thence to Oliver, and we'd be lost."

"Oliver is in London."

"London today, perhaps. But malice travels with every wind that blows. Tomorrow Bere or Bockenod. The next day Tregest or Carminowe. Oliver cares not a jot if I live or die, he has women wherever he goes, but his pride would never brook a faithless wife. And that I know."

A cloud had come between them, and in the sky too, gathering above the hills beyond the valley. All the brightness of the summer day had gone.

Innocence had vanished, and with it the serenity of their world. Mine too. Separated by centuries, I somehow shared their guilt.

"How late is it?" she asked.

"Near six, by the sun," he answered. "Does it matter?"

"The children should be away with Alice," she said. "They may come running to find me, and they must not see you here."

"Roger is with them," he told her, "he will take care they leave us alone."

"Nevertheless, I must bid them goodnight, or they will never mount their ponies."

She began to move away along the grass, and as she did so the steward also slipped from his dark corner and crossed the hall. I followed, puzzled. They could not be staying in the house after all but somewhere else, at Bockenod, perhaps. But the Boconnoc I knew was a longish ride for children on ponies in late afternoon; they would hardly reach it before dusk.

We went through the hallway to the open court beyond, and through the archway to the stables. Roger's brother Robbie was there, saddling the ponies, helping the little girls to mount, laughing and joking with the nurse who, propped high on her own steed, had some trouble in making it stand still.

"He'll go quietly enough with two of you on his back," called Roger. "Robbie shall sit on the pony with you and keep you warm. Before you or behind you, state your preference. It's all the same to him, isn't it, Robbie?"

The nurse, a country girl with flaming cheeks, gawked delightedly, protesting she could ride very well alone, and there was further giggling, instantly silenced with a frown from Roger as Isolda came into the stable yard. He moved to her side, head bent in deference.

"The children will be safe enough with Robbie," he said, "but I can escort them if you prefer it."

"I do prefer it," she said briefly. "Thank you."

He bowed, and she crossed the yard to the children, who were already mounted, managing their ponies with the greatest ease.

"I shall stay here awhile," she told them, kissing each in turn, "and return later. No whipping of the ponies on the road, mind, to make them go the faster. And do as Alice bids you."

"We'll do as *he* bids," said the youngest, pointing her small whip at Roger, "or he'll twist our tongues to see if they turn black."

"I don't doubt it," answered Isolda, "that, or some other method of enforcing silence."

The steward smiled in some confusion, but she did not look at him and he went forward, seizing the children's bridles in either hand, and began to lead the ponies towards the archway, jerking his head to Robbie to do likewise with the nurse's mount. Isolda came with us as far as the entrance gate, and then I was torn between compulsion and desire. Compulsion to follow the little party led by Roger, desire to look at Isolda as she stood alone, waving to her children, unconscious that I stood beside her.

I knew I must not touch her. I knew if I did it would have no more effect upon her than a draught of air—not even that, for in her world I never had existed, nor ever could exist, for she was living and I a ghost without shape or form. If I gave myself the sudden useless pleasure of brushing her cheek there would be no contact, she would instantly dissolve, and I should be left with all the agony of vertigo, nausea and inevitable remorse. Luckily I was spared the choice. She waved her hand once more, looking straight into my eyes and through me, then turned and crossed the court back to the house.

I followed the riding party down the field. Isolda and Bodrugan would be alone for a few more hours. Perhaps they would make love. I hoped, with a sort of desperate sympathy, that they would. I had the feeling time was running out for them, and for me as well.

The track led downwards to the ford where the mill-stream, coursing through the valley, met the salt-water from the creek. Now, the tide low, the ford was passable, and when the children came to it Roger released the bridles, and clapping his hand on the hindquarters of either pony set them to gallop through the splash, the children screaming with delight. He did the same to the third pony, bearing Robbie and the nurse, who let out a shriek that must have been heard on either side of the valley. The blacksmith from the forge across the stream—the fire's glow and the anvil beside it, and a couple of horses waiting to be shod showed that this must be the smithy—came out from his shed grinning, and seizing a pair of bellows from the lad at his side pointed them at the nurse, so that the blast caught her petticoats, already spattered with the mill-stream.

"Take the poker red from the fire to warm her up," shouted Roger, and the blacksmith made pretence of brandishing an iron bar, sparks flying in all directions, while Robbie, half-strangled by the hysterical nurse and doubled up with laughter, dug his heels into the pony's side to make him jump the more. The spectacle brought out the miller and his mate from the mill this side of the stream. I saw that they were monks, and there was a cart drawn up in the yard beside the building, tended by two others, who were filling it with grain. They paused in their work, grinning like the blacksmith, and one of them put his two hands to his mouth and hooted in imitation of an owl, while his companion flapped his arms rapidly above his head as wings.

"Make your choice, Alice," called Roger. "Fire and wind from Rob Rosgof in the forge, or shall the brothers tie you by your kirtle to the water-wheel?"

"The water-wheel, the water-wheel," screamed the children from the further side of the ford, believing, in their excitement, that Alice was to be dowsed. Then suddenly, as swiftly as it had started, the sport was over. Roger waded through the splash with the water mid-thigh, and, seizing the children's ponies once again, took the right-hand track up the valley, with Robbie and the nurse in close pursuit.

I was preparing to follow him across the ford when one of the labouring monks in the mill-yard let out another shout—at least, I took it to be the monk, and turned to see what he was about, but instead a small car, with an irate driver at the wheel, had braked sharply behind me.

"Why don't you buy yourself a deaf-aid?" he yelled, swerving past me, almost plunging into the ditch as he did so. I stood blinking after the car as it shot away, and the people in the back seat, three abreast, dolled for a Sunday outing, stared through the rear window in shocked surprise.

Time had done its trick, too swift, too soon. There was no running mill-stream and no water-splash, no forge the further side; I was standing in the middle of the Treesmill road at the bottom of the valley.

I leant against the low bridge spanning the marsh. A near-miss; it might have landed the whole party in the ditch, and myself as well. I couldn't apologise, for the car had already disappeared up the opposite hill. I sat still for a while waiting for any reaction, but none came. My heart was beating rather faster than usual, but that was natural, due to the shock of the car. I was lucky to escape. No blame to the driver, all my fault.

I began to walk up the hill to the turning where I had parked my own car, and sat in the driving seat for another short spell, fearing confusion. I must not turn up at the church unless my mind was perfectly clear. The image of Rôger escorting the children on their ponies up the track through the valley was still vivid, but I knew it for what it was, part of the other world already vanished. The house above the sand-flats had reverted to the Gratten quarry, grass-covered, empty, except for the gorse bushes and the tin cans. Bodrugan and Isolda were no longer making love. Present reality was with me once again.

I looked at my watch, and stared in disbelief. The hands showed half-past one. Matins at St Andrew's had been over for an hour and a half, possibly longer.

I started up the car, guilt-stricken. The drug had played me false, spinning out the time in some incredible way. I couldn't have been more than half an hour at most up at the house, with another ten minutes, possibly, following Roger and the children to the ford. The whole episode had passed swiftly and I had done nothing but listen at the window, watch the children mount their ponies, and so away. As I drove up the hill I was more bothered about the action of the drug than the prospect of meeting Vita with another trumped-up excuse about walking and losing my way. Why the time-lag, I asked myself? I remembered then that when I went into the past I never looked at my watch—the impulse to do so never came; therefore there was no means of knowing how time passed: their sun was not my sun, nor their sky mine. There was no check, no possibility of measuring the time limit of the drug. As always, when the thing went wrong, I blamed Magnus. He should have warned me.

I drew up at the church, but of course nobody was there. Vita must have waited with the boys, fuming with rage, then begged a lift home from someone, or else found a taxi.

I drove to Kilmarth trying to think of some better excuse than losing my way and my watch having stopped. Petrol. Could I have run out of petrol? A puncture. What about a puncture? Oh, bloody hell, I thought . . .

I rattled down the drive and swerved to a standstill before the house, then walked through the front garden, up the steps and into the hall. The dining-room door was closed. Mrs Collins, with an anxious face, emerged from the passage to the kitchen.

"I think they've finished," she said apologetically, "but I've kept yours hot. It won't be spoilt. Did you have a breakdown?"

"Yes," I said, with gratitude.

I opened the door of the dining-room. The boys were clearing away, but Vita was still seated at the table, drinking coffee.

"God damn that blasted car . . ." I began, and the boys turned round, staring, uncertain whether to giggle or slink away. Teddy showed sudden tact, and with a glance at Micky they hurriedly left the room, Teddy bearing out the laden tray.

"Darling," I went on, "I'm most frightfully sorry. I wouldn't have had this happen for the world. You've no idea . . ."

"I've a very good idea," she said. "I'm afraid we've rather spoilt your Sunday."

Her irony was lost on me. I hesitated, wondering whether to continue or not with my brilliant story of a breakdown on the road.

"The vicar was extremely kind," she went on. "His son drove us back in their car. And when we arrived Mrs Collins gave me this." She pointed to a telegram beside her plate. "It arrived just after we left for church, she said. Thinking it must be important, I opened it. From your Professor, naturally."

She handed me the telegram. It had been wired from Cambridge.

"Have a good trip this weekend," it read. "Hope your girl turns up. Shall be thinking of you. Greetings. Magnus."

I read it twice, then looked at Vita, but she had already turned towards the library, blowing clouds of cigarette smoke over her shoulder, as Mrs Collins came into the dining-room bringing me an enormous plate of hot roast beef.

CHAPTER TWELVE

IF MAGNUS HAD wanted to drop a deliberate brick it could not have been better timed, but I absolved him. He believed Vita to be in London and myself alone. Nevertheless, the wording was unfortunate, to say the least. Catastrophic would be more apt. It must have conjured an instant vision to Vita of my sneaking off with shaving-kit and toothbrush to meet some floozie in the Scilly Isles. My innocence would be difficult to prove. I followed her into the library.

"Now, listen," I said, firmly shutting the folding doors between the two rooms in case Mrs Collins overheard me, "that telegram is a complete joke—a leg-pull on the part of Magnus. Don't make an absolute idiot of yourself by taking it seriously."

She turned round and faced me, her posture the classical one of outraged wife, one hand on hip, the other brandishing her cigarette held at an angle, eyes narrowed in a frozen face.

"I'm not interested in the Professor or his jokes," she said. "You share so many of them, and keep me out, that I'm past caring. If that telegram was a joke good luck to you both. I repeat, I'm sorry I spoilt the weekend. Now you had better go and eat your lunch before it gets cold."

She picked up a Sunday paper and pretended to look at it. I snatched it away. "Oh no, you don't," I said, "you just pay attention to me." Taking her cigarette I squashed it in the ash-tray. Then I seized both her wrists and swung her round.

"You know perfectly well that Magnus is my oldest friend," I said. "What's more he's lent us this house rent free, and thrown Mrs Collins in for good measure. In return for this I've been doing bits and pieces of research for him in connection with his work. The telegram was just his way of wishing me luck."

My words made no impression. Her face was frozen stiff. "You're not a scientist," she said. "What sort of research can you possibly do? And where were you going?"

I dropped her wrists and sighed, as one whose patience is becoming rapidly exhausted by a wilfully misunderstanding child.

"I wasn't going anywhere," I insisted, emphasis on the anywhere. "I had vaguely planned to drive along the coast and visit one or two sites he happens to be interested in."

"How extremely plausible," she said. "I can't think why the Professor doesn't have a teach-in here, with you as his chief assistant. Why don't you suggest it? I'd be in the way, of course, and would make myself scarce. But he'd probably like to keep the boys."

"Oh, for God's sake," I said, opening the door to the dining-room, "you're behaving like every well-worn joke about wives I've ever heard. The simplest thing to do will be to ring up Magnus first thing tomorrow morning and tell him you're filing a divorce suit because you suspect me of wanting to meet-up with some scrubber at Land's End. He'll howl his head off."

I went into the dining-room and sat down at the table. The gravy was beginning to congeal, but no matter. I filled a tankard with beer to wash down the beef and two veg before tackling apple tart. Mrs Collins, tactfully silent, brought in coffee and stood it on the hot-plate, then disappeared. The boys, at a loose end, were kicking the gravel on the path in front of the house. I got up, and called to them from the window.

"I'll take you swimming later," I shouted. They brightened visibly, and came running up the steps to the porch. "Later," I said. "Let me have my coffee first, and see what Vita wants to do." Their faces fell. Mom would be a non-starter, and possibly throw cold water on the plan. "Don't worry," I said. "I promise I'll take you."

Then I went into the library. Vita was lying on the sofa, her eyes closed. I knelt beside her, and kissed her. "Stop being bloody-minded," I said. "There's only one girl in this world for me, and you know it. I'm not going to take you upstairs to prove it because I've told the boys I'd take them swimming, and you don't want to spoil their day for them, do you?"

She opened one eye. "You've succeeded in spoiling mine," she said.

"Balls!" I told her. "And what about my lost weekend with that floozie? Shall I tell you what I'd planned to do with her? A strip-tease show at Newquay. Now shut up." I kissed her again with vigour. Response was negligible, but she did not push me away.

"I wish I understood you," she said.

"Thank God you don't," I said. "Husbands loathe wives who understand them. It makes for monotony. Come and swim. There's a perfectly good empty beach below the cliffs. It's blazing hot, and it isn't going to rain."

She opened both eyes. "What were you actually doing this morning while we were in church?" she asked.

"Mooching about in a derelict quarry," I told her, "less than a mile from the village. It has connections with the old Priory, and Magnus and I happen to be interested in the site. Then I couldn't start the car, which I'd parked rather awkwardly in a ditch."

"It's news to me that your Professor is an historian as well as a scientist," she said.

"Good news, don't you think? Makes a change from all those embryos in bottles. I encourage it."

"You encourage him in everything," she said, "that's why he makes use of you."

"I'm adaptable by nature, always have been. Come on, those boys are itching to be off. Go and make yourself beautiful in a bikini, but put something over it, or you'll startle the cows."

"Cows?" she almost shrieked. "I'm not going in any field with cows, thank you very much."

"They're tame ones," I said, "fed on a certain sort of grass so that they can't move out of a slow amble. Cornwall's famous for them."

I think she believed me. Whether she believed my story about the quarry was another matter. She was pacified, for the moment. Let it rest . . .

We spent a long, lazy afternoon on the beach. Everybody swam, and afterwards, while the boys scrambled about in pools hunting for non-existent prawns, Vita and I stretched ourselves full-length on a spit of yellow sand, letting it trickle through our fingers. Peace reigned.

"Have you thought about the future at all?" she asked suddenly.

"The future?" I repeated. In point of fact, I was staring across the bay wondering if Bodrugan had made it that night with a rising tide, after he and Isolda had said goodbye. He had mentioned Chapel Point. In old days, Commander Lane had taken us sailing across the bay from Fowey to Mevagissey, and had pointed out Chapel Point jutting out on the port side before we entered Mevagissey harbour. Bodrugan's house must have lain somewhere close at hand. Perhaps the name existed still. I could find it on the road map if it was still there.

"Yes," I said, "I have. If it's fine tomorrow we'll go sailing. You couldn't possibly be seasick if it's as calm as it is today. We'll sail right across the bay and anchor off that headland over there. Take lunch, and go ashore."

"Very nice," she agreed, "but I didn't mean the immediate future. I meant the long-term one."

"Oh, that," I said. "No, darling, frankly I have not. So much to do getting settled in here. Don't let's be premature."

"That's all very well," she said, "but Joe can't wait for ever. I think he was hoping to hear from you fairly soon."

"I know that. But I've got to be absolutely sure. It's all right for you, it's your country. It isn't mine. Pulling up roots won't be easy."

"You've pulled them up already, chucking that London job. To be blunt, you have no roots. So there's no argument," she said.

She was right, for all practical purposes.

"You'll have to do something," she went on, "whether it's in England or the States. And to turn down Joe's offer when no one has offered you anything comparable in this country seems utterly crazy. I admit I'm prejudiced," she added, putting her hand in mine, "and would adore to settle back home. But only if you want it too."

I did not want it, that was the crux. Nor did I want a similar job, literary agency or publishing, in London. It was the end of the road, the end, temporarily, of a particular moment in time, my time. And I could not plan ahead, not yet.

"Don't go on about it now, darling," I said. "Let's take each moment as it comes. Today, tomorrow . . . I'll think constructively about the whole thing soon, I promise you."

She sighed, and let go of my hand, reaching in the pocket of her towelling wrap for a cigarette. "As you say," she said, the upward inflection on the "say" proclaiming her origins on the western Atlantic seaboard. "But don't blame me if you find yourself left high and dry by brother Joe."

The boys came running across the beach with various trophies to show us, star-fish, mussels, and an oversize, long-dead crab that stank to heaven. The moment of truth had passed. It was time to gather up our things and face the trek uphill back to Kilmarth. As I brought up the rear I looked over my shoulder across the bay. The coast was clearly defined, and the white houses on the edge of Chapel Point, some eight miles distant, were caught by the western sun.

> "In such a night
> Otto methinks mounted Bodrugan walls,
> And sighed his soul towards the Treesmill creek
> Where Isold lay that night . . ."

But did she? Surely she must have followed the children later, after Otto sailed. But where to? Bockenod, where her husband's brother, the self-important Sir John, lived? Too far. Something was missing. She had mentioned another name. Treg something. I must look on the map. The trouble was that every other farmhouse in Cornwall began with Tre. It had not been Trevenna, Treverran or Trenadlyn. So where was it that Isolda and her two children had lain their heads that night?

"I don't see myself doing this often," complained Vita. "My heaven, what a hill! It's like the ski slopes in Vermont. Let me take your arm."

The thing was, they had crossed the water-splash below the mill and taken a track to the right. And then I had not seen them any more, because of that car coming up behind me. They could have gone in any direction. And Roger was on foot. When the tide came in the ford would be fully covered. I tried to remember if there was a boat beneath the blacksmith's forge to ferry him back.

"After all this exercise and air I ought to sleep tonight," said Vita.

"Yes," I replied.

There had been a boat. High and dry on the edge of the creek. At high water this would be used for carrying passengers to and fro between the blacksmith's forge and Treesmill.

"You couldn't care less, could you," she asked, "what sort of a night I have, and whether I'm dead on my feet right now?"

I stopped and stared at her. "I'm sorry, darling," I said, "of course I care." Why revert suddenly to that business of a sleepless night?

"You were miles away in thought—I can always tell," she said.

"Four miles at the most," I told her. "If you really want to know, I was thinking about a couple of children riding ponies I saw this morning. I wondered where they were going."

"Ponies?" We continued walking, Vita a dead weight on my arm. "Well, that's the most sensible thought you've had yet," she said. "The boys love riding. Maybe the ponies were let out on hire?"

"I doubt it," I said. "I imagine they came from some farm."

"Well, you could always make enquiries. Nice-looking children?"

"Enchanting. Two little girls, and a youngish woman who looked as if she might be their nurse, and a couple of men."

"All riding ponies?"

"One man was walking, holding the children's bridles."

"Then it must be a riding-school," she said. "Do find out. It would make something for the boys to do other than swimming or sailing."

"Yes," I said.

How convenient it would be if I could summon Roger from the past and bid him saddle two of the Kilmarth ponies for Teddy and Micky, then send them off with Robbie for a gallop on Par sands! Roger would handle Vita to perfection. Her slightest whim obeyed. Juice of henbane whistled up from Brother Jean at the Priory to induce a restful night, and if that failed . . . I smiled.

"What's the joke?"

"No joke." I pointed to the fading foxgloves, a purple mass thrusting tall stems through the hedge encircling the paddocks below Kilmarth. "If you have a heart attack, no problem. Digitalis comes from foxgloves. You've only to say the word and I'll crush the seeds."

"Thanks a lot. No doubt your Professor's laboratory is full of them, along with other poisonous seeds and goodness knows what sinister mixtures."

How right she was. An error, though, to let her dwell on Magnus. "Here we are," I said. "Through that gate and into the garden. I'll mix you a long, cool drink, and the boys as well. Then I'll cope with the supper. Plenty of cold beef and salad."

Let cheerfulness prevail. Memories of my misspent morning fade into an urge to please. Attentive husband, smiling stepfather; keep the whole thing going to bedtime and beyond.

As it turned out, beyond took care of itself. The swim, the long climb and the soporific Cornish air had done their trick. Vita, yawning her head off at a television play, was in bed by ten, and fast asleep when I crept in stealthily beside her an hour later. Tomorrow would be fine, judging by the sky, and we would sail to Chapel Point. Bodrugan existed still. I had found it on the road-map after supper.

There was just enough breeze to take us out of Fowey harbour. Our skipper, Tom, a stalwart fellow with a ready smile, busied himself with the sails, aided or hindered by the boys, while I stationed myself at the tiller. I knew just enough about it not to bring the boat up into the wind and set the sails flapping, but neither Vita nor the boys knew this, and were suitably impressed by my air of efficiency. Soon we had mackerel lines astern, the boys hauling them in with shouts of excitement as soon as they felt the slightest tug, caused by the ripple of tide or a piece of weed, while Vita stretched herself at my side. Her jeans became her—like all Americans, she had a stunning figure—and so did her scarlet sweater.

"This is heaven," she said, snuggling close and leaning her head against my shoulder. "So clever of you to arrange it, I give you full marks for once. The water couldn't be smoother."

The trouble was, it didn't stay heaven for long. I remembered of old, after passing the Cannis buoy and the Gribbin Head, a westerly wind met the tide with a smacking force, increasing the boat's speed—always a joy to the helmsman with his heart in his job, like Commander Lane—but causing the craft to heel over, so that the passenger sitting on the leeward side found himself within a few inches of the sea. In this case the passenger was Vita.

"Hadn't you better let the man steer?" she said nervously, after the boat had curtseyed three times like a rocking-horse—my fault, too close to the wind—then lay firmly on her side with the lea rail awash.

"Not a bit of it," I said cheerfully. "Crawl under the boom and sit on the weather side."

She groped to her feet, and caught her head an almighty tonk on the boom. As I bent to help her unravel a rope from her ankle, which took my eye off my work as helmsman, I shipped a short sea across the bows, thus drenching the whole party, myself included.

"A drop of salt water hurts nobody," I shouted, but the boys, clinging to the weather rail, were not so sure, and with their mother made a dive for the shelter of the small cabin, which, lacking headroom, forced them to crouch like hunchbacks on the tiny locker seat, where they rose and fell with every curtsey of the over-lively craft.

"Nice fresh breeze," said our skipper Tom, grinning all over his face. "We'll be at Mevagissey in no time at all."

I bared my teeth in imitation of his confidence, but the three white faces upturned to me in the cockpit lacked enthusiasm, and I had the impression that none of them shared the skipper's opinion about the breeze.

He offered me a cigarette, but it proved an error after three puffs, and I let it fall over the side when he was not looking, while he proceeded to light up a particularly noxious pipe. Some of the smoke found its way down to the cabin and circled there in rings.

"The lady would feel the motion less if she sat in the cockpit," suggested Tom, "and the lads as well."

I looked at the boys. The boat was steady enough now, but penned in the dark cabin they felt every thump, and an ominous yawn appeared on Micky's face. Vita, her eyes glazed, appeared hypnotised by Tom's oilskin, which was hanging on a hook by the cabin door, swaying to and fro with the boat's motion like a hanging man.

Tom and I exchanged glances, seized by a sudden freemasonry, and while he took over the tiller and knocked out his pipe I pulled the family up into the cockpit, where Vita and her youngest were promptly sick. Teddy survived, possibly because he kept his head averted.

"We'll soon be under the lea of Black Head," said Tom. "They won't feel any motion in there."

His touch on the tiller was like magic. Or perhaps it was pure chance. The rocking-horse motion moved to a gentle lilt, the white faces lost their pallor, teeth ceased their chattering, and the pasties baked by Mrs Collins were torn from their napkins in the basket and fallen upon by all of us, even Vita, with the ferocity of carrion crows. We passed Mevagissey and came to anchor on the western side of Chapel Point. There was not a tremor in sea or sky, and the sun blazed down.

"Rather extraordinary," observed Vita, now stripped of her sweater, which she bunched under her head as a pillow, "that as soon as Tom took charge of the boat it scarcely moved at all and the wind dropped."

"Not really," I said. "We were coming closer to the land, that's all."

"I know one thing," she said, "and that is that he's going to steer the boat home."

Tom was helping the boys into the dinghy. They had bathing-shorts and towels under their arms. Tom had fishing-lines, baited with worm.

"If you want to stay aboard, sir, with the lady, I'll see the lads come to no harm," he said. "This beach is quite safe for bathing."

I did not want to stay aboard with the lady. I wanted to climb up through the fields and find Bodrugan.

Vita sat up, and removing her dark glasses looked around her. It was half-tide and the beach looked tempting, but I saw, with delight, that it was temporarily in the possession of half a dozen cows, who were mooning about aimlessly, spattering the sand in the evitable fashion.

"I'll stay aboard," said Vita firmly, "and if I want to swim I'll swim from the boat."

I yawned, my immediate reaction when feeling guilty. "I'll go ashore and stretch my legs," I said. "It's too early to swim anyway, after a pasty lunch."

"Do as you like," she said. "It's perfect here. Those white houses on the point look enchanting. We might be in Italy."

I let her think it, and climbed into the dinghy with the others. "Land me over there, in the left-hand corner," I said to Tom.

"What are you going to do?" asked Teddy.

"Walk," I said firmly.

"Can't we stay in the dinghy and fish for pollack?"

"Of course you can. Much the best plan," I told him.

I sprang ashore amongst the cows, free of encumbrance.

The boys were equally glad to be rid of me. I stood for a moment, watching them pull away. Vita waved a languid hand from the anchored boat. Then I turned, and struck uphill.

The path ran parallel with a stream and curved, passing a cottage on the right-hand side, and then the sea was out of sight. The track continued up the hill, leading to a gate between old walls, and on the left-hand side what appeared to be the ruins of a mill. I ventured through the gate, and Bodrugan farm was all about me, a big pond to my left that must have fed the mill-stream, and to my right the gracious, slate-hung farmhouse of today, early eighteenth century, perhaps, curiously like Magnus's Kilmarth, and beside it and beyond great stone-walled barns of a much earlier date that surely must have stood upon the site of Otto's fourteenth-century home. Two children were playing under the windows of the farmhouse, but they took no notice of me and I ventured on, crossing the wide sweep where cows were grazing, and stepped inside the high-roofed barn the further side.

This served as a granary today, and must have done for centuries, but six hundred years ago perhaps a dining-hall stood there, and other rooms, while the long, low barn across the way could have been the chapel. The whole demesne was vast, far larger than the space covered by those mounds and banks that once had formed the home of the Champernounes, below the Gratten; and I realised now why Joanna, born and bred a Bodrugan in this place, may have thought the house above the Treesmill creek a poor exchange when she married Henry Champernoune.

I came out of the barn and followed the low stone walls surrounding the entire farm, then, striking off to the hills on the opposite slope, came once more in sight of the sea. Here, on top of the high field, was a mound that must once have formed a keep or outpost, commanding the bay, and I wondered how often Otto rode here from his house, and looked out from the keep past Black Head to the cliffs in the far distance that gradually descended to Tywardreath bay and to the winding estuary with its narrow arms, the first running to the Lampetho valley, the second to the Priory walls, the third to Treesmill and the

Champernoune demesne. He would have seen all of this on a clear day, even perhaps the humped dwelling of Kylmerth, and the little straggling copse beyond.

This would have been the moment to have the flask in my pocket, and have seen Otto leaning from the round tower of his keep, and beneath him, in the sheltered cove where the boys fished today, his ship at anchor, ready to make sail. Or travel even further back in time and watch him ride away to that first rebellion against Edward the Second in 1322, younger and hot-headed, to be fined a thousand marks when the rebellion failed. Champion of lost causes, seeker after forbidden fruit; how often, I wondered, did he steal across that bay, leaving his dim-faced wife Margaret, Henry Champernoune's sister, snugly secure inside Bodrugan house, or in their other property of Trelawn, wherever that might be, in which the Champernounes also seemed to have rights?

I clumped back to the beach, hot and curiously tired. It was odd, but it seemed more of an effort to face the family now, without having swallowed the drug and moved in the other world, than it would had I actually taken a trip in time. I felt thwarted, drained of energy, and filled with a strange sense of apprehension. Imagination was not enough; I craved the living experience which had been denied me, and which I could have possessed had I taken a few drops from the flask safely locked away in the old laundry at Kilmarth. I might have witnessed scenes, on that old site above the cliff, or by the farmstead itself, that now I should never know; and the frustration was absolute.

The cows had gone from the beach. The boys had returned to the anchored boat and were sitting in the cockpit having tea, their swimming trunks strung up on the mast to dry. Vita was standing in the bows taking snapshots. A contented party, everybody happy, myself the odd man out.

I wore bathing trunks under my trousers, and stripping off my clothes I entered the water. It struck chill, after the walk, and seaweed floated on the surface like tresses from the drowned Ophelia's hair. I turned over on my back and stared at the sky, still filled with this strange feeling of despondency, almost of doom. It would need a tremendous effort to respond to the family greeting, join in the general chatter, smile and joke.

Tom had seen me, and was bringing the dinghy ashore to fetch my clothes. I swam out to the boat and managed somehow to clamber aboard, with the aid of a rope's end and the willing hands of Vita and the boys.

"Look, three pollack," shouted Micky. "Mom says she'll cook them for supper. And we've found a lot of shells."

Vita came forward with the remains of the tea from the thermos jug. "You look all in," she said. "Did you walk far?"

"No," I said, "only across the fields. There was a castle of sorts there once, but nothing's left of it."

"You should have stayed on the boat," she said. "The bathing was heaven. Here, rub yourself down with this towel, you're shivering. I hope you haven't taken a chill. Such a mistake to plunge into cold water when you've been perspiring."

Micky thrust a damp doughnut into my hand tasting of cotton wool, and I swallowed the lukewarm tea. Then Tom climbed aboard, bearing my clothes, and before long it was up anchor and away, with Tom at the tiller. I put on another jersey and went and sat up in the bows, where Vita presently joined me.

The little popple in mid-bay sent her back to the cockpit, to wrap herself in Tom's oilskin, and I stared ahead towards the distant prospect of Kilmarth, screened by its belt of trees. In old days, sailing nearer to the coast, Bodrugan would have had a closer view, as he steered his ship towards the estuary that covered Par sands then, and Roger, had he been watching from the fields, could have signalled to him that all was well. I wondered whose fever was the greater, Bodrugan's as he rounded the sloping headland to the channel, knowing she waited for him in that empty house behind the low stone walls, or Isolda's, when she sighted the masthead and saw the first flutter of the dark sail. Now, with the sun astern, we passed the Cannis buoy and made for Fowey, entering the harbour, to the great excitement of the boys, just as a large vessel, her decks white with china-clay and escorted by two tugs, left it outward bound.

"Can we come again tomorrow?" they clamoured, as I paid off Tom and thanked him for our sail.

"We'll see," I said, uttering the inevitable adult formula that must be so infuriating to the young. See what, they might have asked? If the mood suits and there is harmony in the grown-up world? The success or failure of their day depended upon the state of truce between their mother and myself.

My immediate problem, when we got back to Kilmarth, was to telephone Magnus before he telephoned me, which he was bound to do, now the weekend was over. I hung about the library furtively, waiting for a good moment, and then the boys came in and switched on the TV, so I had to go upstairs to the bedroom. Vita was downstairs in the kitchen seeing about supper: it was now or never. I dialled his number and he answered immediately.

"Look," I said quickly," "I can't talk long. The worst has happened. Vita and the boys arrived unexpectedly on Saturday morning. They caught me almost in *flagrant delit*. You understand? And your telegram was an equal calamity. Vita opened it. Since when the situation has been decidedly tricky, and that's putting it mildly."

"Oh, dear . . ." said Magnus, in the tone of an elderly maiden aunt confronted with a mild household problem.

"It's not 'Oh, dear' at all, it's hell and damnation," I exploded, "and the end of the road, as far as any more trips are concerned. You realise that, don't you?"

"Keep calm, dear boy, keep calm. You say she arrived and actually caught you en route?"

"No, I was returning from one. Seven in the morning. I won't go into it now."

"Was it valuable?" he asked.

"I don't know what you call valuable," I said. "It concerned a near rebellion against the Crown. Otto Bodrugan was there, and Roger, of course. I'll write you fully about it tomorrow, and Sunday's trip as well."

"So you *did* risk it again, despite the family? How splendid."

"Only because they went to church, and I was able to slip off to the Gratten. And there is a time problem, Magnus; I can't account for it. The trip seemed to last half an hour to forty minutes at the most, but in actual fact I was 'out' for about two and a half hours."

"How much did you take?"

"The same as Friday night—a few more drops than on the first two or three trips."

"Yes, I see."

He was silent a minute, considering what I had told him.

"Well?" I asked. "What's the significance?"

"I'm not sure," he said. "I'll have to work on it. Don't worry, it won't be serious, at this stage. How are you feeling in yourself?"

"Well . . . healthy enough physically, we've been sailing all day. But it's a hell of a strain, Magnus."

"I'll see how the week goes and then try to get down. I shall have some results from the lab up here in a few days and we can discuss them. Meanwhile, go easy on the trips."

"Magnus . . ."

He had rung off, which was as well. I thought I could hear Vita coming up the stairs. In a sense, I was relieved this time at the thought of seeing him, even if it meant difficulties with Vita. He would adopt his special brand of charm and smooth them away, and the responsibility would be his, not mine. Besides, I was worried about the drug. This sense of depression, of foreboding, might be a side-effect.

I looked in the shaving-mirror in the bathroom. There was something odd about my right eye, it looked bloodshot, and there was a faint red streak across the white. A blood-vessel burst, perhaps, which was nothing, but I did not remember it having happened before. I hoped Vita would not notice it.

Supper passed off all right, with the boys chatting happily about their day and enjoying the pollack they had caught (the most tasteless of all fish, to my mind, but I did not damp their ardour). Just as we were clearing away the telephone rang.

"I'll get it," said Vita quickly, "it could be for me."

At least it would not be Magnus. The boys and I loaded the dish-washer and had set it going when Vita came back into the kitchen. She had on a face I knew. Determined, rather defiant.

"That was Bill and Diana," she said.

"Oh, yes?"

The boys disappeared to the library to watch TV. I poured out coffee for us both.

"They're flying to Dublin from Exeter," she said. "They're in Exeter now." Then, before I could make some adequate reply, she said hurriedly, "They're just crazy to see the house, so I suggested they put off their flight for forty-eight hours or so, and came down to us for lunch tomorrow and to stay the night. They jumped at the idea."

I put down my cup of coffee untasted, and slumped in the kitchen chair. "Oh, my God!" I said.

CHAPTER THIRTEEN

THERE ARE FEW strains more intolerable in life than waiting for the arrival of unwelcome guests. I had said no more in protest after my first groan of despair, but we had spent the hours until bedtime in separate rooms, Vita in the library watching television with the boys, myself in the music-room listening to Sibelius.

Now, the next morning, Vita was sitting on what she liked to call the terrace, outside the french windows of the music-room, listening for the blare of their horn, while I paced up and down inside, primed with my first gin and tonic, my eye on the clock, wondering which state was the worse—this of anticipating the dire moment of a car coming down the drive, or the full flush of their having settled in, cardigans strewn on chairs, cameras clicking, voices loud and long, the smell of Bill's inevitable cigar. The second, perhaps, was better, the heat of battle rather than the bugle's call.

"Here they come," yelled the boys, tearing down the steps, and I advanced through the french window like one facing up to mortar-shells.

Vita, as a hostess, was magnificent: Kilmarth was transformed instantly into some American embassy overseas, lacking only a flagstaff bearing the Stars and Stripes. Food borne in by the willing and triumphant Mrs Collins graced the dining-room table. Liquor flowed, cigarette smoke filled the air, we lunched at two and rose at half-past three. The boys, fobbed off with the promise of swimming later, vanished to play cricket in the orchard. The girls, disguised in uniform dark glasses, dragged lilos out of earshot to indulge in gossip. Bill and I installed ourselves on the patio intending, or so I hoped, to sleep, but sleep was intermittent; like all diplomats, he enjoyed hearing his own voice. He held forth on world policy and policy nearer home, and then, with elaborate unconcern and obviously briefed by Diana, touched on my future plans.

"I hear you're going into partnership with Joe," he said. "That's wonderful."

"It's not settled," I replied. "There's a lot still to be discussed."

"Oh, naturally," he said. "You can't just decide on a flick of a coin, but what an opportunity! His firm is on the crest of the wave right now, and you'd never regret it. Especially as I gather you've nothing really to lose this side. No special ties." I did not answer. I was determined not to be led into a lengthy discussion. "Of course, Vita would make a home anywhere," he went on. "She has the knack. And with an apartment in New York and a weekend place in the country, you'd lead a very full life together, with plenty of opportunities for travel thrown in."

I grunted, and tilted an old panama hat of Commander Lane's over my right eye, which was still bloodshot. Unremarked, so far, by Vita.

"Don't think I'm butting in," he said, lowering his voice, "but you know how the girls talk. You've got Vita worried. She told Diana you've blown cool over the idea of coming to the States, and she can't figure out why. Women always think the worst." He then launched into a long, and to my mind loaded, story about a girl he had met in Madrid when Diana was in the Bahamas with her parents. "She was only nineteen," he said. "I was crazy about her. But of course we both knew it couldn't last. She had a job in the Embassy there, and Diana was due back in London when her vacation was over. I was so wild about that kid I felt like cutting my throat when we said good-bye. However, I survived and so did she, and I haven't seen her since."

I lit a cigarette to counteract the clouds of smoke from his blasted cigar. "If you think," I said, "that I've got a girl round the corner you couldn't be more wrong."

"Well, that's fine," he said, "just fine. I wouldn't blame you if you had, as long as you kept it quiet from Vita."

There was a long pause while he tried, I suppose, to think of another tactic, but he must have decided that discretion was the better part of valour, for he went on abruptly, "Didn't those boys say something about wanting to swim?"

We wandered off to find our wives. Their session was apparently still in full swing. Diana was one of those over-ripe blondes who are said to be grand fun at a party and a tigress in the home. I had no desire to try her out in either capacity. Vita told me she was the loyalest of friends, and I believed her. The session ceased immediately we appeared, and Diana changed down into second gear, her invariable custom at the approach of masculine company.

"You've got a tan, Dick," she said. "It suits you. Bill turns lobster red at the first touch of the sun."

"Sea air," I told her. "Not synthetic like your own."

She had a bottle of sun oil beside her with which she had been lubricating her lily-white legs.

"We're going down to the beach to swim," said Bill. "Rouse yourself, pug-face, it will take off some of that surplus fat."

The usual badinage ensued, the interplay of married couples before their kind. Lovers never did this, I thought; the game was played in silence, and was in consequence the more delightful.

Carrying towels and snorkels, we made the long trek to the beach. The tide was low, and to enter the water the intending swimmer had to pick his way over seaweed and uneven slabs of rock. It was an experience new to our guests, but they took it in good part, splashing about like dolphins in the shallows, proving my favourite maxim that it is always easier to entertain, albeit unwillingly, out-of-doors.

The evening to come would be the real test of hospitality, and so it proved. Bill had brought his own bottle of bourbon (a gift to the house), and I cleared the fridge of ice so that he could consume it on the rocks. The muscadet which we drank with supper, on top of the bourbon, made too rich a mixture, and with the dish-washer throbbing away in the kitchen we staggered into the music-room after dinner considerably the worse for wear. I did not have to worry about my bloodshot eye. Both Bill's looked as if he had been stung by bees, while our wives had the high flush of barmaids lounging in some disreputable sailor's joint.

I went over to the gramophone and put on a stack of records—the choice did not matter, so long as the sound served the purpose of keeping the party quiet. Vita was a moderate drinker as a general rule, but when she had had one too many I found her embarrassing. Her voice took on a strident tone, or alternatively turned silky sweet. Tonight the sweetness was for Bill, who, nothing loath, lolled beside her on one sofa, while Diana, patting the empty place next to her on the second, pulled me to it with a meaning smile.

I realised, with distaste, that these manœuvres had been worked out by the two women earlier on, and we were set for one of those frightful evenings of swapping partners, not for the ultimate act itself, but as a preliminary try-out, like a curtain-raiser before a two-act play. I could not have been more bored. The only thing I wanted to do was to go to bed, and, by God, to go alone.

"Talk to me, Dick," said Diana, so close that I had to turn my head sideways like a ventriloquist's doll. "I want to know all about your brilliant friend Professor Lane."

"A detailed account of his work?" I asked. "There was a very informative article about certain aspects of it in the *Biochemical Journal* a few years ago. I've probably got a copy in the flat in London. You must read it some time."

"Don't be idiotic. You know perfectly well I wouldn't understand a word. I want to know what he's like as a man. What are his hobbies, who are his friends?"

Hobbies . . . I considered the word. It conjured a vision of an absent-minded buffer chasing butterflies.

"I don't think he has any hobbies," I told her, "beyond his work. He's fond of music, particularly church music, Gregorian chants and plainsong."

"Is that what you have in common, a liking for music?"

"It started that way. We happened to meet in the same pew one evening at King's College when a carol service was in progress."

In point of fact we had not gone for the carols but to stare at one particular choir-boy with a golden aureole of hair like the infant Samuel. But though the meeting was accidental it was the first of many. Not that my tastes inclined to choir-boys, but the combination of holy innocence with adeste fideles and a halo of curls was so aesthetically pleasing to our twenty years that we were subsequently enraptured for several days.

"Teddy told me there was a room locked up in the basement here full of monkeys' heads," she said. "How deliciously creepy."

"One monkey's head, to be exact," I replied, "and a number of other specimens in jars. Highly toxic, and not to be disturbed."

"You hear that, Bill?" said Vita from the opposite sofa. I noticed, with aversion, that he had his arm round her and her head was on his shoulder. "This house is built on dynamite. One false movement, and we'd be blown skyhigh."

"Any movement?" queried Bill, with an offensive wink at me. "What happens if we get a little closer? If dynamite sends us both up to the floor above it's OK by me, but I'd best ask Dick's permission first."

"Dick's staying right here," said Diana, "and should the monkey's head explode you two can rise and Dick and I'll descend. That way we'll all be happy, but in different worlds. Isn't that so, Dick?"

"Oh, absolutely," I agreed. "And in any event I've had enough of this particular world. So if you three like to triple-up on one piece of furniture, go ahead and enjoy yourselves. There's a quarter of bourbon left in the bottle, and it's all yours. I'm for bed."

I got up and left the room. Now that I had broken up the foursome the petting party would automatically stop, and they would all three sit for another hour or more solemnly discussing the various facets of my character, how I had or had not changed, what could be done about me, what the future held.

I undressed, plunged my head into cold water, flung the curtains wide, climbed into bed and fell instantly asleep.

The moon awakened me. It came through a chink of the curtains, which Vita had drawn, and sent a shaft of light on to my pillow. She lay on her own side of the bed and was snoring, a thing she rarely did, and with her mouth wide open. It must have been that last quarter of bourbon. I glanced at my watch: it was half-past three. I got out of bed, went through to the dressing-room, and pulled on a pair of jeans and a sweater.

I stood at the head of the stairs and listened at the guest-room door. Not a sound. Silence, too, along the passage where the boys slept. I went downstairs, down the back way to the basement, and so to the lab. I was perfectly sober, cool and collected, neither elated nor depressed; I have never felt more normal in my life. I was determined to take a trip, and that was that. Pour four measures in the flask, get the car out of the garage, coast downhill to Treesmill valley, park the car, and walk to the Gratten. The moon was bright, and when it paled in the western sky the dawn would come. If time played tricks with me and the trip lasted until breakfast, what did it matter? I would return when I was ready to return. And Vita and her friends could lump it.

On such a night . . . a rendezvous with whom? The world of today asleep, and my world not awakened, or not as yet, until the drug possessed me. Tywardreath was a ghost village as I skirted it, but in my secret time I knew I traversed the green, and the Priory stood conspicuous though aloof behind stone walls. I crept down the Treesmill road and the moonlight flooded the valley, shining on the grey-lidded hutches of the mink-farm on the further side. I parked the car close to the ditch, and climbed the gate across the field.

Then I made my way to the pit near the quarry which I knew formed the site of part of the original hall, and in the darkness there, close to a tree-stump, in a square patch of moonlight, swallowed the contents of the flask. Nothing happened at first, except a humming in my ears which I had not experienced before. I leant against the bank and waited.

Something stirred, a rabbit, perhaps, in the hedge, and the humming in my ears increased. A piece of corrugated iron behind me in the quarry rattled and fell. The humming became universal, part of the world around me, changing from the sound in my own ears to the rattle of the casement in the great hall, and the roaring of the wind without. The rain was teeming down from a grey sky, falling slantwise across the parchment panes, and moving forward I looked out and saw that the water in the estuary below was turbulent and high, short-crested seas racing with the tide. What trees there were on the opposite slopes bent in unison, the autumn leaves scattering with the force of the wind, and a flock of starlings flying north formed into a clamouring mass and disappeared. I was not alone. Roger was by my side, peering down into the creek also, his face concerned, and when a greater draught of wind rattled the casement he fastened it tight, shaking his head and murmuring, "Pray God he does not venture here in this."

I glanced round, and saw that a curtain had been drawn across the hall, dividing it in two, and voices came from behind it. I followed Roger as he crossed the hall and drew the curtain aside. I thought for a moment that time had played another trick, taking me into a past I had witnessed already, for there was a pallet bed against one wall, with someone lying on it, while Joanna Champernoune was seated at the foot, and the monk Jean close to the pillow. But drawing closer I saw that the sick man was not her husband but his namesake, Henry Bodrugan, Otto's eldest son and her own nephew, and standing well withdrawn, with his handkerchief covering his mouth, was Sir John Carminowe. The young man, evidently in a high fever, kept trying to raise himself, calling for his father, as the monk wiped the sweat from his forehead and tried to ease him back on to his pillow.

"Impossible to leave him here, with the servants at Trelawn and no one to care for him," said Joanna. "And even if we tried to move him there we could not do so before nightfall, in such a gale. Whereas we could have him beneath your own roof, at Bockenod, within an hour."

"I dare not risk it," said Sir John. "If it should prove to be smallpox, as the monk fears, none of my family have had it. There is no other course but to leave him here in Roger's care."

He looked at the steward, his eyes apprehensive above the handkerchief, and I thought what a poor figure he must cut before Joanna, showing such fear that he might catch the disease himself. Gone was the cocksure bearing I had seen at the Bishop's reception. He had increased in weight, and his hair was turning grey. Roger, respectful as ever before his masters, inclined his head, but I noticed a look of scorn in his lowered eyes.

"I am willing to do whatever my lady commands me," he said. "I had smallpox as a child, my father died of it. My lady's nephew is young and strong, he should recover. Nor can we be certain yet of the disease. Many a fever starts in the same fashion. In twenty-four hours he could be himself once more."

Joanna rose from her chair and approached the bed. She still wore her widow's headdress, and I remembered the note scribbled by the student at the Public Record Office from the Patent Rolls dated October, 1331: "Licence for Joan late the wife of Henry de Champernoune to marry whomsoever she will of the King's allegiance." If Sir John was still her choice of suitor, then the marriage had not yet taken place. . . .

"We can only hope so," she said slowly, "but I am of the monk's opinion. I have seen smallpox before. I too had the disease as a child, and Otto with me. If it were possible to send word to Bodrugan, Otto himself would come and fetch him home." She turned to Roger. "How is the tide?" she asked. "Is the ford covered?"

"It has been covered for an hour or more, my lady," he replied, "and the tide is still flooding. There is no possibility of traversing the ford before the water ebbs, or I would ride to Bodrugan myself and tell Sir Otto."

"Then there is nothing for it but to leave Henry in your care," said Joanna, "despite the lack of servants in the house." She turned to Sir John. "I will come with you to Bockenod, and proceed to Trelawn at daybreak and warn Margaret. She is the one who should be at her son's bedside."

The monk, despite his preoccupation with young Henry, had been listening to every word. "There is another course open to us, my lady," he said. "The guest chamber at the Priory is vacant, and neither I nor my fellow brethren fear smallpox. Henry Bodrugan would fare better under our roof than here, and I would make it my business to watch him night and day."

I saw the expression of relief on Sir John's face, and on Joanna's too. Whatever happened they would be quit of responsibility.

"We should have decided upon this sooner," said Joanna, "then we could all have been on our way hours since, before this gale. What do you say, John? Is not this the only remedy?"

"It would seem so," he said hastily, "that is, if the steward can arrange for his removal to the priory. We dare not take him in your chariot for fear of infection."

"Infection for whom?" laughed Joanna. "You mean for yourself? You can ride as escort, surely, with your handkerchief over your face as you have it now? Come, we have delayed long enough."

The decision taken, she had no further thought for her nephew but went to the door of the great hall, escorted by Sir John, who flung it open, only to stagger back with the force of the wind.

"You'd be well advised," she said with irony, "to travel in comfort at my side, despite that sick boy, rather than feel the wind on your back when we reach high ground."

"I have no fear for myself," he began, and then, seeing the steward close behind him, added, "You understand, my wife is delicate, and my sons also. The risk would be too great."

"Too great indeed, Sir John. You show prudence."

Prudence my arse, I thought, and so did Roger, judging from his expression, and Joanna's too.

The lumbering chariot was drawn up outside the further gate, and crossing the court in the blustering wind we escorted the widow to it, whilst Sir John mounted his horse. Then we returned once more to the hall. The monk was piling covers about the half-conscious Henry.

"They are ready and waiting," said Roger. "We can bear the mattress between us. Now we are alone, what hope have you of his recovery?"

The monk shrugged. "As you said yourself, he is young and strong, but I have seen weaklings live and stalwarts die. Let him remain at the Priory under my care, and I will try certain remedies."

"Watch your skill on this occasion," said Roger. "If you should fail you would have to answer for it to his father, and in that event the Prior himself could not protect you."

The monk smiled. "From what I understand, Sir Otto Bodrugan will have trouble enough protecting himself," he answered. "You know Sir Oliver Carminowe lay at Bockenod last night and left at dawn, telling none of the servants of his destination? If he has ridden in secret along the coast it would be for one thing only, to seek out his lady's lover and destroy him."

"Let him try," scoffed Roger. "Bodrugan is the better swordsman."

Once again the monk shrugged. "Possibly," he said, "but Oliver Carminowe used other methods when he fought his enemies in Scotland. I would not give much for Bodrugan's chances should he be caught in ambush."

The steward signalled him to silence as young Henry opened his eyes. "Where is my father?" he asked. "Where are you taking me?"

"Your father is home, sir," said Roger. "We are sending for him, he will come to you in the morning. This night you are to rest at the Priory in the care of brother Jean. Then, if you feel stronger and as your father so decides, you can be moved either to Bodrugan or to Trelawn."

The young man looked from one to the other in bewilderment. "I have no wish to stay at the Priory," he said. "I would rather go home tonight."

"It is not possible, sir," replied Roger gently. "It is blowing a full gale and the horses cannot travel far. My lady is waiting for you in the chariot, and will take you to the Priory. You will be safely in bed in the guest-chamber there within half an hour."

They bore him on the mattress, still protesting weakly, through the hall and across the court to the waiting vehicle, stretching him full-length at his aunt's feet. Then the monk climbed in beside him. Joanna looked at her steward through the open window. The veil had blown back from her face, and I noticed how her features had coarsened since I saw her last. Her mouth was slacker, and there were pouches under her full eyes.

She leant close to the window, so that her nephew could not hear. "There have been rumours," she said softly, "of possible trouble between Sir Oliver and my brother. Whether Sir Oliver is in the neighbourhood or not I cannot say. But it is one of the reasons I want to be away, and quickly."

"As you will, my lady," answered the steward.

"Neither Sir John nor I wish to take part in the dispute," she said. "It is not our quarrel. If they come to blows my brother can take care of himself. My strict charge upon you is that you side with neither, but concern yourself solely with my affairs. Is that understood?"

"Perfectly, my lady."

She nodded briefly, then turned her attention to young Henry at her feet. Roger signalled to the driver, and the heavy vehicle pursued its course up the muddied road towards the Priory, followed by Sir John on horseback and an attendant servant, both riders bent low on their saddles, lashed by the wind and rain. As soon as they had topped the brow and disappeared, Roger walked swiftly through the archway into the stableyard and called for Robbie. His brother came at once, leading a pony, his mat of unruly hair falling over his face.

"Ride like the devil to Tregest," Roger said, "and warn Lady Isolda to stay within doors. Bodrugan was to have sailed here to the creek tonight, but he will never venture in this gale. Whether Sir Oliver is with her or not—and I doubt it—she must get my message without fail."

The boy leapt on to the pony's back and was away, streaking across the field, but in an easterly direction, our side of the valley, and I remembered that Roger had said the ford was impassable because of the tide. He would have to cross the stream higher up the valley, if the place called Tregest lay the other side. The name conveyed nothing. I knew there was no Tregest on the ordnance map today.

Roger made his way across the court and through the gate in the wall to the sloping hill above the creek. Here the strength of the wind nearly blew him off his feet, but he continued downhill towards the river, into the driving rain, taking the rough track that led to the quayside at the bottom. His expression was anxious, even haggard, quite different from his usual air of self-possession, and as he walked, or rather ran, he kept looking towards the river mouth where it entered the wide Par estuary. The sense of foreboding that had been mine when I returned from the expedition across the bay was with me once again, and I felt that it was with him too, that somehow we shared a common bond of anxiety and fear.

There was some shelter when we came to the quay because of the hill behind us, but the river itself was in turmoil, the wavelets short and steep, bearing upon their crests every sort of autumn debris, floating branches, logs and seaweed, which, as they were driven towards the quay or passed it in mid-channel, were skimmed by a flock of screaming gulls endeavouring with outstretched wings to stem the wind.

We must have seen the ship simultaneously, our eyes turned seaward, but not the brave craft I had admired at anchor on a summer's afternoon. She staggered like a drunken thing, her mast broken, the yards upon it hanging half-way to the deck, and the sails dropping around the yards like shrouds. The rudder must have gone too, for she was out of control, at the mercy of both wind and tide that bore her forward but broadside on, her bows turned towards the shallower sands where the seas broke shortest. I could not see how many were on board, but there were three at least, and they were endeavouring to launch from the deck a little boat that was caught up in the tangle of sail and fallen yards. Roger cupped his hands to his mouth and shouted, but they could not hear him, because of the wind. He sprang on to the quay wall and waved his arms, and one of those aboard—it must have been Otto Bodrugan—saw him and waved in answer, pointing to the opposite shore.

"This side the channel," shouted Roger, "this side the channel," but his voice was lost in the wind. They did not hear him, for they were still working hard to launch the boat from the ship's side.

Doubtless Bodrugan knew the channel well, and if they launched the smaller boat they would have little difficulty in getting ashore, despite the short seas breaking above the sand-flats on either side. It was not like open sea, rock-bound and dangerous, and, although the river was broadest where the craft drifted, she could at worst only run aground and wait for the falling tide.

Then I saw the reason for Roger's fear, and why he strove to attract Bodrugan and his sailors to the quay. A line of horsemen was riding on the opposite hill, some dozen of them, in single file. Because of the contours of the land the men aboard were not aware of their presence, the clump of trees masking them from the vessel.

Roger continued to shout and wave, but those on board took it as encouragement for the successful launching of the small boat, and replied in like fashion. Then, as the vessel drifted on up-channel, they managed to lower the boat over the side, all three men dropping into it a moment afterwards. They had a hawser fastened from the ship's bows to the stern of the small boat, and while two of the men bent to the oars and pulled towards the opposite shore the third, Bodrugan, crouched in the stern, holding fast to the hawser in an attempt to turn the vessel in the same direction as themselves.

They were too intent upon their task to pay further attention to Roger, and as they drew slowly nearer to the opposite shore I saw the horsemen on the hill dismount by the belt of trees. Taking advantage of the cover they crept down towards the creek, where the land dipped suddenly to the water's edge, forming a spit of sand. Roger shouted for the last time, waving his arms in desperation, and forgetting my phantom status I did the same, without sound, more powerless as an ally than any spectator at a football game cheering a losing side, and as the small boat drew nearer to the shore so their enemies, screened by the belt of trees, came closer to the spit of sand.

Suddenly the hawser parted as the larger vessel ran aground, and Bodrugan, flung off his feet, tumbled amongst his men and the small boat upset, throwing all three of them into the water. They were already so close to the opposite shore that the river had no great depth where they received their ducking, and Bodrugan was the first to stand, the water up to his chest, while the others floundered beside him, and Bodrugan answered Roger's final warning yell with a triumphant cry.

It was his last. The band of men were upon him and his companions before they had time to turn their heads or defend themselves, a dozen against three, and before the driving rain that burst upon us, heavier than ever, blotted them from view I saw, with sick revulsion, that instead of dragging their victims up the spit of sand to finish them there, by sword or dagger, they were thrusting them face-downwards in the water. One was already still, the other struggling, but it took eight men to hold Bodrugan down. Roger started to run along the river's edge towards the mill, cursing, gasping, and I knew it was useless, that we ran in vain, for long before he could summon help it would be over.

We came to the ford below the mill, and, just as he had told Joanna earlier, the water ran swiftly here, and deep, almost to the door of the forge itself. Once again Roger put his hands to his mouth.

"Rob Rosgof," he yelled, "Rob Rosgof," and the frightened figure of the blacksmith appeared at the door, with his wife beside him.

Roger pointed downstream, but the man gestured with both his hands in denial, shaking his head, then jerked his thumb up the hill behind him, this play without words suggesting he had known of the ambush and could do nothing, and he dragged his wife with him inside the forge and barred the door. Roger turned in despair to the mill, and the three monks I had seen there on the Sunday morning, when Isolda's children crossed the ford, came through the yard to meet him.

"Bodrugan and his men have been driven ashore," cried Roger. "His vessel's aground, and an ambush lay in wait to destroy them. They are dead men, all three, against a dozen fully armed."

I hardly know which showed the more strongly upon his face, his anger, or his grief, or his powerlessness to help.

"Where is Lady Champernoune?" asked one of the monks. "And Sir John Carminowe? We saw the carriage at the house all afternoon."

"Her nephew, Bodrugan's son, is sick," answered Roger. "They have taken him to the Priory, and they themselves are now on the road to Bockenod. I have sent Robbie to Tregest to warn the household there, and I pray God none of them ventures forth, or their lives could be in danger too."

We stood there, below the millyard, uncertain whether to go or stay, and all the time straining our eyes towards the river, where the curving banks above the creek hid the stranded vessel and the murderous scene on the spit of sand.

"Who led the ambush?" asked the monk. "Bodrugan had enemies once, but that is long past, with the King firmly established on the throne."

"Sir Oliver Carminowe, who else?" answered Roger. "They fought on opposing sides in the rebellion of '22, and today he does murder in another cause."

No sound but the wind, and the turmoil of the river as it coursed between the narrowing banks, with the gulls skimming the surface, screaming. Then one of the monks pointed to the bend in the creek and cried, "They've launched the boat, they're coming up with the tide!"

It was not a boat, at least not the whole of it, but what seemed in the distance to be part of the planking stripped from its side, and set afloat upstream as jetsam, circling slowly as it drifted with the current. Something was lashed to it that now and again bobbed to the surface, then disappeared, only to reappear again. Roger looked at the monks and I at him, and with one accord we ran down to the edge of the creek where the eddy carried the driftwood and the scum, and all the while, as we waited, the planking rose and fell with the force of the tide, and the thing that was lashed upon it rose as well. Then there was shouting from the opposite bank, and through the belt of trees rode the horsemen, their leader ahead. They cantered down to the road by the forge, and the shouting ceased, and they stood there watching in silence.

We plunged into the river to drag the plank ashore, the monks with us, and as we did so the leading horseman shouted, "A birthday package for my wife, Roger Kilmerth. See that she receives it with my compliments, and when she has done with it tell her that I await her at Carminowe."

He burst out laughing, and his men with him, and then they turned their horses up the hill and rode away.

Roger and the first monk drew the plank ashore. The others crossed themselves and began to pray, and one of them went down upon his knees at the water's edge. There was no knife wound upon Bodrugan, no sign of violence. The water streamed from his mouth and his eyes were open. They had drowned him before they lashed him to the plank.

Roger untied the hawser strands and bore him in his arms, with the water dripping from his hair, towards the mill. "Merciful God," he said, "how am I to tell her?"

There was no need. As we turned towards the mill we saw the ponies, Robbie upon his own, Isolda mounted on a second, her hair loose upon her shoulders, wet and lank, her cloak billowing out behind her like a cloud. Robbie at a glance saw what had happened, and put out his hand to seize her bridle and turn her pony back, but in a moment she had dismounted and came running down the hill towards us.

"Oh, my love," she said, "oh, no . . . oh, no . . . oh, no . . . ," her voice, that had started clear and strong, trailing off into a single cry.

Roger laid his burden on the ground and ran towards her, and so did I. As we took hold of her outstretched hands she slipped out of our grasp and fell, and instead of holding on to her cloak I was scrambling amongst bales of straw piled against a corrugated tin shed across the road from Treesmill farm.

CHAPTER FOURTEEN

I LAY THERE waiting for the nausea and the vertigo to pass. I knew it had to be endured, and the quieter I remained the quicker it would go. It was already light, and I had sense enough to glance at my watch. It was twenty-past five. If I gave myself a quarter of an hour, without moving, all should be well. Even if the people at Treesmill farm were already astir no one was likely to cross the road and come to the shed, which was hard against the wall of an old valley orchard, the stream a few yards away from where I lay, all that remained of the tidal creek.

My heart was thumping, but it gradually eased, and the dreaded vertigo was not as bad as that previous time when I had come to at the Gratten, and had the encounter with the doctor at the lay-by at the top of the hill.

Five minutes, ten, fifteen . . . then I struggled to my feet, and slipping from the orchard walked very slowly up the hill. So far so good. I climbed into the car and sat another five minutes, then started the engine and drove equally carefully back to Kilmarth. Plenty of time to put away the car and lock up the flask in the lab, then the wisest thing to do would be to go straight to bed and try to get some rest.

There was nothing more I could do, I told myself. Roger would take Isolda back to that Tregest place, wherever it was, and poor Bodrugan's body would be safe in the care of those monks. Someone would have to carry the news to Joanna at Bockenod. Roger would take care of that, I felt sure. I now had a regard, even an affection for him, he was so obviously moved by Bodrugan's appalling death, and we had shared the horror of it together. I was right to have had that sense of foreboding on the beach below Chapel Point before sailing back to Fowey with Vita and the boys. Vita and the boys . . .

I drove into the garage just as I remembered them, and with the memory came full understanding. I had driven home in one world with my brain still in the other. I had driven home, part of my brain completely sensible to the fact that I had the wheel in my hands and belonged to the present, while the rest of me was still in the past, believing Roger on the way to Tregest with Isolda.

I began to sweat all over. I sat quite still in the car, my hands trembling. It must not happen again. I must take a grip on myself. It was just on six o'clock in the morning. Vita and the boys, and those damned guests of ours, were all asleep upstairs, and Roger and Isolda and Bodrugan had been dead for more than six centuries. I was in my own time. . . .

I let myself in at the back door and put the flask away. It was fully light by now, but the house was silent still. I crept upstairs and into the kitchen, and put on the electric kettle to make myself a cup of tea. Tea was the answer, a steaming cup. The purr of the kettle was oddly comforting, and I sat down at the table, remembering suddenly how much we had all had to drink the night before. The kitchen still smelt of the lobster we had eaten, and I got up and opened the window.

I was in the middle of my second cup when I heard a creak on the stairs, and I was about to streak down to the basement and remain *perdu* when the door opened and Bill came into the room. He grinned sheepishly.

"Hullo," he said. "Two minds with but a single thought. I woke up, thought I heard a car, and suddenly had the most fearful thirst. Is that tea you're drinking?"

"Yes," I said. "Have a cup. Is Diana awake?"

"No," he replied, "and if I know my wife after a binge, not likely to, either. We were all pretty well stoned, weren't we? I say, no hard feelings?"

"No, none," I told him.

I poured him out a cup of tea, and he sat down at the table. He looked a mess, and his pyjamas, a livid pink, did not tone with his grey complexion.

"You're dressed," he said. "Have you been up long?"

"Yes," I said. "I've been out, as a matter of fact—I couldn't sleep."

"Then it was your car I heard coming down the drive?"

"It must have been," I said.

The tea was doing me good, but it was making me sweat as well. I could feel the sweat pouring down my face.

"You look a bit off," he said critically. "Are you all right?"

I took my handkerchief out of my coat pocket and wiped my forehead. My heart had started thumping again. Must be something to do with the tea.

"As a matter of fact," I said slowly, and I could hear myself slurring my words, as if the tea had been a strong dose of alcohol that had temporarily knocked me off balance, "I was an unseen witness to an appalling crime. I just can't forget it."

He put down his cup and stared at me. "What on earth?" he began.

"I felt I needed some air," I said, speaking very fast, "so I took the car down to a place I know, about three miles from here, near the estuary, and a boat went aground. It was blowing damned hard, and the chap aboard with his crew had to take to the dinghy. They made the opposite shore all right and then this appalling thing happened . . ." I poured myself another cup of tea, despite my trembling hands. "These thugs," I said, "these bloody thugs on the opposite shore—the chap from the boat didn't have a chance. They didn't knife him or anything, they forced his head under water and let him drown."

"My God!" said Bill. "My God, how terrible. Are you sure?"

"Yes," I said, "I saw it. I saw the poor devil drown . . ." I got up from the table and began walking up and down the kitchen.

"Well, what are you going to do?" he asked. "Hadn't you better ring the police?"

"Police?" I said. "It's not a job for the police. It's this chap's son I'm thinking of. He's ill, and someone will have to tell him, and the other relatives."

"But, good God, Dick, it's your duty to inform the police! I can see you don't want to be involved, but this is murder, surely? And you say you know the chap who was drowned, and his son?"

I stared at him. Then I pushed aside my cup of tea. It had happened, oh, sweet Christ, it had happened. The confusion. The confusion between worlds. . . . The sweat was running down the whole of my body.

"No," I said, "I don't know him personally. I've seen him about, he keeps a yacht the other side of the bay, I've heard people talk about the family. You're right, I *don't* want to be involved. And anyway I wasn't the only witness. There was another chap watching, and he saw the whole thing. I'm pretty sure he will report it—in fact, he's probably done so already."

"Did you speak to him?" asked Bill.

"No," I said, "no, he didn't see me."

"Well, I don't know," said Bill. "I still think you ought to telephone the police. Would you like me to do it for you?"

"No, on no account. And, Bill, not a word of this to Diana or Vita. Swear it."

He looked very troubled. "I understand that," he said. "It would upset them terribly. My God, you must have had one hell of a shock."

"I'm all right," I told him, "I'm all right." I sat down again at the kitchen table.

"Here, have some more tea?" he suggested.

"No," I said, "no, I don't want anything."

"It just goes to prove what I'm always saying, Dick. The crime figures are mounting steadily, in every civilised country in the world. The authorities have just got to take things in hand. I mean, who would believe it happening here, off the map, down in Cornwall? A set of thugs, you say? Any idea where they came from? Were they local men?"

I shook my head. "No," I said, "I don't think so. I've no idea who they were."

"And you're quite certain this other fellow saw, and was going to report to the police?"

"Yes, I saw him running. He was making straight for the nearest farmhouse. They'll have a telephone there."

"I hope to heaven you're right," he said.

We sat for a while in silence. He kept sighing, and shaking his head. "What an experience for you. What a damned awful experience."

I put my hands in my pockets so that he should not see them shaking. "Look, Bill," I said, "I think I'll go upstairs and lie down. I don't want Vita to know I've even been out. Or Diana either. I want this thing to remain absolutely private between ourselves. There's nothing you or I can do now. I want you to forget it."

"OK," he said, "about not saying anything. But I shan't forget what you've told me. And I'll listen for it on the news. By the way, we shall have to leave after breakfast if we're to catch that 'plane from Exeter. Is that all right by you?"

"Of course," I said. "I'm only sorry to have spoilt your morning."

"My dear Dick, I'm the one to be sorry, and for you. Yes, I should go upstairs, and try to get some sleep. And look here, don't bother to get up and say goodbye. You can always plead a hangover." He smiled, and held out his hand. "We loved yesterday," he said, "and a thousand thanks for everything. I only hope nothing else comes up to spoil your holiday. I'll write you from Ireland."

"Thanks, Bill," I said, "thanks a lot."

I went upstairs, undressed in the dressing-room, then retched violently for about five minutes down the lavatory. The sound must have woken Vita, for I heard her calling from the bedroom.

"Is that you?" she said. "What's the matter?"

"All that muscadet on top of bourbon," I said. "Sorry, I can hardly stand. I'm going to turn in on the divan here. It's still quite early—about half-past six."

I closed the dressing-room door and threw myself on the divan bed. I was back in the world of today, but God alone knew how long it would stay that way. One thing was certain. As soon as Bill and Diana had gone I should have to telephone Magnus.

The unconscious is a curious thing. I was deeply disturbed over this total confusion of thought that might have made me blab the truth to Bill about the experiment itself; but five minutes or so after I had lain down on the divan I was asleep and dreaming, not, strangely enough, about Bodrugan and his appalling fate, but of a cricket match at Stonyhurst when one of the team got hit on the head with a cricket-ball and died of haemorrhage of the brain twenty-four hours later. I had not thought about the incident for at least twenty-five years.

When I awoke just after nine I was perfectly lucid and clear in the head, apart from a hell of a genuine hangover, and my right eye was more bloodshot than ever. I bathed and shaved, and could hear sounds of movement from our guests in the room next door. I waited until I heard Bill and Diana go downstairs, then I put a call through to Magnus. No luck. He was not at the flat. So I left a message with his secretary at the University saying I wanted to speak to him very urgently, but it might be better if I put the call through to him rather than he to me. Then I stuck my head out of the dressing-room window overlooking the patio and shouted to Teddy to bring me up a cup of coffee. I would appear in the hall to bid our guests godspeed five minutes before departure, and not a moment before.

"What's wrong with your eye? You hit the floor or something?" asked my elder stepson as he brought coffee.

"No," I told him. "I think it's a back-lash from the wind on Monday."

"You were up early anyway," he said. "I heard you talking to Bill in the kitchen."

"I was making tea," I said. "We both of us had too much to drink at dinner."

"Guess that's what turned your eye all streaks and not the sea," he said, looking so like his mother in one of her more perceptive moods that I turned away, and then remembered that his room was above the kitchen and he could conceivably have overheard our conversation.

"Anyway," I asked before he left the dressing-room, "what were we talking about?"

"How should I know?" he replied. "Do you think I'd pull up the floorboards to listen?"

No, I reflected, but his mother might, if she heard a discussion going on between her husband and her guest at 6 a.m.

I finished dressing, drank down my coffee, and appeared at the top of the stairs just in time to help Bill down with the suitcases. He greeted me with a conspiratorial glance of enquiry—the girls were below us in the hall—and murmured, "Get any sleep?"

"Yes," I said, "yes, I'm fine," I saw him staring at my eye. "I know," I said, touching it, "no explanation for that. Must have been the bourbon. By the way," I added, "Teddy heard us talking this morning."

"I know," he said, "I heard him tell Vita. Everything's OK. Don't worry." He patted me on the shoulder, and we clumped downstairs.

"Heavens!" cried Vita. "What have you done to your eye?"

"Bourbon allergy," I said, "combined with shellfish. It happens to some people."

Both girls insisted on examining me, suggesting alternative remedies from penicillin ointment to TCP.

"It can't be the bourbon," said Diana. "I don't want to be personal, but I noticed it yesterday as soon as we arrived. I said to myself, 'Whatever's Dick done to his eye?'"

"You didn't say anything to me," said Vita.

Enough was enough. I put a hand on each of their shoulders and pushed them through the porch. "Neither one of you would win a beauty prize this morning," I said, "and it wasn't the bourbon that woke me at dawn, but Vita snoring. So shut up."

We had to install ourselves on the steps for the inevitable picture-taking by Bill, and it was nearly half-past ten before they were finally off. Once again Bill's hand-clasp was that of a conspirator.

"Hope we get this fine weather in Ireland," he said. "I'll watch the papers and listen to the radio forecasts to see what's happening here in Cornwall." He looked at me, nodding imperceptibly. He meant that his eyes and ears would be alert for the first mention of a dastardly crime.

"Send us postcards," said Vita. "Wish we were coming with you."

"You always can," I said, "when you get fed-up here."

It was not perhaps the most encouraging of remarks, and when we had finished waving and turned back towards the house Vita wore an abstracted air. "I really believe," she said, "you'd be glad if the boys and I had gone off with them. Then you'd have this place to yourself again."

"Don't talk nonsense," I said.

"Well, you made your feelings pretty clear last night, flinging off to bed directly we'd finished dinner."

"I flung off to bed, as you call it, because it bored me stiff to see you lolling about in Bill's arms and Diana waiting to do the same in mine. I'm just no good at party games, and you ought to know it by now."

"Party games!" she laughed. "What utter nonsense! Bill and Diana are my oldest friends. Where's your much-vaunted British sense of humour?"

"Not in tune with yours," I said. "I've a cruder sense of fun. If I pulled a mat from under your feet and you slipped up, I'd have hysterics."

We wandered back into the house, and just at that moment the telephone rang. I went into the library to answer it, and Vita followed me. I was afraid it might be Magnus, and it was.

"Yes?" I said guardedly.

"I got your message," he said, "but I've a very full day. Is it an awkward moment?"

"Yes," I said.

"You mean Vita is in the room?"

"Yes."

"I understand. You can answer yes or no. Anything turned up?"

"Well, we've had visitors. They arrived yesterday, and have just left."

Vita was lighting up a cigarette. "If it's your Professor—and I can't think who else it would be—give him my regards."

"I will. Vita sends her regards," I told Magnus.

"Return them. Ask her if it would be convenient for me to come for the weekend, arriving Friday evening."

My heart leapt. Whether with excitement or the reverse I couldn't say. In any case with relief. Magnus would take over.

"Magnus wants to know if he can come on Friday for the weekend," I said to her.

"Surely," she answered. "It's his house, after all. You'll have more fun entertaining your friend than you had putting up with mine."

"Vita says of course," I repeated to Magnus.

"Splendid. I'll let you know the train later. About your urgent call. Does it concern the other world?"

"Yes," I said.

"You went on a trip?"

"Yes."

"With ill-effect?"

I paused a moment, with a glance at Vita. She had made no attempt to leave the room. "As a matter of fact I'm feeling pretty lousy," I said. "Something I ate or drank disagreed with me. I've been violently sick and have a peculiar bloodshot eye. It may be due to drinking bourbon before lobster."

"Combined with taking a trip, you may well be right," he answered. "What about confusion?"

"That also. I could hardly think straight when I awoke."

"I see. Anyone notice?"

I took another glance at Vita. "Well, we were all pretty high last night," I said, "so the males of the party woke early. I had suffered a very vivid nightmare, and told Vita's friend Bill about it over a morning cup of tea."

"How much did you tell?"

"About the nightmare? Just that. It was very real, you know what nightmares are. I thought I saw someone set on by thugs and drowned."

"Serves you right," said Vita. "And it sounds more like the two helpings of lobster than the bourbon."

"Was it one of our friends?" asked Magnus.

"Yes," I answered. "You know that chap who used to keep a boat years ago over at Chapel Point, and was always sailing round to Par? Well, the nightmare was about him. I dreamt his ship was dismasted in a storm, and when he finally came ashore he was murdered by a jealous husband who thought he was after his wife."

Vita laughed. "If you ask me," she said, "a dream of that sort means an uneasy conscience. You thought I was getting off with Bill and your vivid nightmare resulted from that. Here, let me talk to your Professor." She crossed the room and seized the receiver from me. "How are you, Magnus?" she said, her voice full of calculated charm. "I shall be delighted to see you here in your own home next weekend. Maybe you'll put Dick in a better temper. He's very sour right now." She smiled, her eyes on me. "What's wrong with his eye?" she repeated. "I haven't the slightest idea. He looks as if he's lost a prize-fight. Yes, of course I'll do my best to keep him quiet until you arrive, but he's very stubborn. Oh, by the way, you'll be able to tell me. My boys adore riding, and Dick says he saw some children on ponies having a lot of fun on Sunday morning when we were in church. I wondered if there were riding-stables some-where the other side of the village there—what-do-you-call-it—Tywardreath. You don't know? Well, never mind, Mrs Collins might tell me. What? Hold on, I'll ask him . . ." She turned to me. "He says were the children the two little girls of someone called Oliver Carminowe and his wife? Old friends of his.

"Yes," I said. "I'm almost sure they were. But I don't know where they live."

She turned back to the telephone. "Dick thinks yes, though I don't see why he should know if he hasn't met them. Oh well, if the mother is attractive he's probably seen her around some place, and that's how he knows who they were." She pulled a face at me. "Yes, you do that," she added, "and if you get in touch with them next weekend we might ask them round for drinks, and Dick can get an introduction to her. See you Friday, then."

She handed the receiver back to me. Magnus was laughing at the other end of the line.

"What's this about getting in touch with the Carminowes?" I asked.

"I got out of that rather neatly, don't you think?" he countered. "In any event, it's what I intend to do, if we can get rid of Vita and the boys. In the meantime I'll get my lad in London to check up on Otto Bodrugan. So he came to a sticky end, and it upset you?"

"Yes," I said.

"Roger was there, of course? Did he have a hand in it?"

"No."

"Glad to hear it. Look, Dick, this is important. Absolutely no more trips unless we take one together. No matter how big the temptation. You must sweat it out. Is that agreed?"

"Yes," I said.

"As I told you before, I shall have the first results from the lab by the time I see you. In the meantime, abstention. Now I must go. Take care of yourself."

"I'll try," I said. "Goodbye."

It was like cutting off the only link between both worlds.

"Cheer up, darling," said Vita. "Less than three days and he'll be here. Won't that be wonderful? Now what about going upstairs to the bathroom and doing something about that eye?"

Later on, the eye bathed and Vita having disappeared into the kitchen to tell Mrs Collins about Magnus coming for the weekend, and doubtless to discuss his gastronomic tastes, I got out my road-map and had another look for Tregest. It just was not there. Treesmill was marked, as I knew, and Treverran, Trenadlyn, Trevenna—the last three on the Lay Subsidy Roll as well—but that was all. Perhaps Magnus would find the answer from his London student.

Presently Vita wandered back into the library. "I asked Mrs Collins about the Carminowes," she said, "but she'd never heard of them. Are they very great friends of Magnus's?"

It startled me for a moment to hear her speak the name. I knew I must be careful, or the confusion might start up again.

"I think he's rather lost sight of them," I replied. "I doubt if he's seen them for some time. He doesn't get down very often."

"They're not in the telephone directory—I've looked. What does Oliver Carminowe do?"

"Do?" I repeated. "I don't really know. I think he used to be in the army. Has some sort of government job. You'll have to ask Magnus."

"And his wife's very attractive?"

"Well, she was," I said. "I've never spoken to her."

"But you've seen her since you got down here?"

"Only in the distance," I said. "She wouldn't know me."

"Was she around in the old days when you used to stay here as an undergraduate?"

"She could have been," I said, "but I never met her, or the husband. I know very little about them."

"But you knew enough to recognise her children when you saw them the other day?"

I felt myself getting tied up in knots. "Darling," I said, "what is all this? Magnus occasionally mentions names of friends and acquaintances, and the Carminowes were amongst them. That's all there is to it. Oliver Carminowe was married before and Isolda is his second wife, and they have two daughters. Satisfied?"

"Isolda?" she said. "What a romantic name."

"No more romantic than Vita," I replied. "Can't we give her a rest?"

"It's funny," she said, "that Mrs Collins has never heard of them. She's such a mine of information on local affairs. But in any case there's a perfectly good stables up the road from here at Menabilly Barton, she tells me, so I'm going to fix something up with the people there."

"Thank God for that," I said. "Why not fix it right away?"

She stared at me a moment, then turned round and went out of the room. I surreptitiously got out my handkerchief and wiped my forehead, which was sweating again. It was a lucky thing the Carminowes were extinct, or she would have run them to earth somehow and invited a bewildered descendant to lunch next Sunday.

Two, nearly three days to go before Magnus came to my rescue. It was difficult to fob Vita off once her interest was aroused, and it was typical of his malicious sense of fun to have mentioned the name.

The rest of Wednesday passed without incident, and thank heaven I had no return of confusion. It was such a relief to be without our guests that little else mattered. The boys went riding and enjoyed themselves, and, although Vita may have suffered from anti-climax and a normal reaction from a hangover, she had the good sense not to say so, nor did she make any further reference to our party the preceding night. We went to bed early and slept like logs, awaking on Thursday to a day of steady rain. It did not worry me, but Vita and the boys were disappointed, having planned another expedition in the boat.

"I hope it's not going to be a wet weekend," said Vita. "What in the world shall I do with the boys if it is? You won't want them hanging about the house all day when the Professor is here."

"Don't worry about Magnus," I told her. "He'll be full of suggestions for them and for us. Anyway, he and I may have work to do."

"What sort of work? Surely not shutting yourselves up in that peculiar room in the basement?"

She was nearer the truth than she imagined. "I don't know exactly," I said vaguely. "He has a lot of papers tucked away, and he may want to go through them with me. Historical research, and so on. I've told you about this new hobby."

"Well, Teddy might be interested in that, and so should I," she said. "It would be fun if we all took a picnic to some historical site or other. What about Tintagel? Mrs Collins says everyone should see Tintagel."

"Not exactly Magnus's line of country, and anyway too full of tourists," I said. "We'll see what he wants to do when he arrives."

I wondered how the hell we should be shot of them if Magnus wanted to visit the Gratten. Anyway, it would be his problem, not mine.

Thursday dragged, and a dreary walk along Par sands did little to alleviate it. Magnus had told me to sweat it out, and by the evening I knew what he meant. Sweat was the operative word, and in the physical sense. I had seldom if ever been troubled by this common affliction of mankind. At school, yes, after violent exercise, but not to the extent suffered by some of my companions. Now, after any minor exertion, or even perhaps when sitting still, I would sweat from every pore, the perspiration having a peculiar acid tang to it that I fervently hoped nobody would be aware of but myself.

The first time it happened, after the walk along Par sands, I thought it was merely connected with the exercise I had taken, and I had a bath before dinner, but during the course of the evening, when Vita and the boys were watching television and I was sitting comfortably in the music-room listening to records, it started again. A clammy feeling of sudden chill, then the sweat pouring from my head, neck, armpits, trunk, lasting for perhaps five minutes before it passed, but my shirt was wringing wet by the time the attack was over. Laughable, like sea-sickness, when it happens to anyone but oneself, this side-effect, which was obviously a new reaction from the drug, threw me into sudden panic. I switched off the gramaphone and went upstairs to wash and change for the second time, wondering what on earth would happen if I suffered a further attack later when I was in bed with Vita.

Nervous apprehension did not make for an easy night, and Vita was in one of her conversational moods that lasted through undressing and continued until we were lying side by side. I could not have been more nervous had I been a bridegroom on the first night of honeymoon, and I found myself edging away to my side of the bed, giving vent to prodigious yawns as a sign that excessive fatigue had overtaken me. We turned out the bedside lights, and I went through a kind of pantomime of heavy breathing on the verge of sleep which may or may not have fooled Vita, but after one or two attempts to coil close—which I ignored—she turned over on her side and was soon asleep.

I lay awake thinking of the hell I would give Magnus when he arrived. Nausea, vertigo, confusion, a bloodshot eye, and now acid sweat, and all for what? A moment in time, long past, that had no bearing on the present, that served no purpose in his life or mine, and could as little benefit the world in which we lived as a scrapbook of forgotten memories lying idle in a dusty drawer. So I argued, up to midnight and beyond, but common sense has a habit of vanishing when the demon of insomnia rides us in the small hours, and as I lay there, counting first two, and then three, on the illuminated face of the travelling clock beside the bed, I remembered how I had walked about that other world with a dreamer's freedom but with a waking man's perception. Roger had been no faded snapshot in time's album; and even now, in this fourth dimension into which I had stumbled inadvertently but Magnus with intent, he lived and moved, ate and slept, beneath me in his house Kylmerth, enacting his living Now which ran side by side with my immediate Present, and so the two merged.

Am I my brother's keeper? Cain's cry of protest against God suddenly had new meaning for me as I watched the hands of the clock move towards ten past three. Roger was my keeper, I was his. There was no past, no present, no future. Everything living is part of the whole. We are all bound, one to the other, through time and eternity, and, our senses once opened, as mine had been opened by the drug, to a new understanding of his world and mine, fusion would take place, there would be no death. . . . This would be the ultimate meaning of the experiment, surely, that by moving about in time death was destroyed. This was what Magnus so far had not understood. To him, the drug released the complex brew within the brain that served up the savoured past. To me, it proved that the past was living still, that we were all participants, all witnesses. I was Roger, I was Bodrugan, I was Cain; and in being so was more truly myself.

I felt myself on the brink of some tremendous discovery when I fell asleep.

CHAPTER FIFTEEN

I DID NOT wake up until after ten, and when I did Vita was standing by the bed with the breakfast tray of toast and coffee.

"Hullo," I said. "I must have overslept."

"Yes," she said, and then, looking at me critically, "Are you feeling all right?"

I sat up in bed and took the tray from her. "Perfectly," I said. "Why?"

"You were restless during the night," she told me, "and perspired a great deal. Look, your pyjama top is quite damp."

It was, and I threw it off. "Extraordinary thing," I said. "Be an angel and get me a towel."

She brought me one from the bathroom, and I rubbed myself down before reaching for the coffee.

"Something to do with all that exercise on Par beach with the boys," I said.

"I wouldn't have thought so," she replied, staring at me, puzzled, "and anyway you took a bath afterwards. I've never known you perspire from exercise before."

"Well, it happens to people," I said. "It's my age-group. The male menopause, perhaps, striking me down in my prime."

"I hope not," she said. "How very unpleasant."

She wandered over to the dressing-table and surveyed herself in the mirror as if that might hold the answer to the problem. "It's odd," she went on, "but both Diana and I remarked on the fact that you weren't looking yourself despite that suntan from sailing." She wheeled round suddenly, facing me. "You must admit you're not a hundred per cent," she went on. "I don't know what it is, darling, but it worries me. You're moody, distrait, as if you had something on your mind all the time. Then that funny bloodshot eye . . ."

"Oh, for heaven's sake," I interrupted, "give it a miss, can't you? I admit I was foul-tempered when Bill and Diana were here, and I apologise. We all had too much to drink, and that was that. Must we do a post-mortem on every hour?"

"There you go again," she said. "Always on the defensive. I hope the arrival of your Professor straightens you out."

"It will," I answered, "providing this inquisition on our behaviour doesn't continue through the entire weekend."

She laughed, or rather her mouth twitched in the way wives' mouths are wont to twitch when they desire to inflict a wound upon the husband. "I would not dare presume to conduct an inquisition on the Professor. His state of health and his behaviour are no concern of mine, but yours are. I happen to be your wife, and I love you."

She left the room and went downstairs, and this, I thought, as I buttered my piece of toast, is a good beginning to the day—Vita offended, myself with the sweating sickness, and Magnus due to arrive some time in the evening.

There was a card on the breakfast tray from him, as it happened, hidden by the toast-rack. I wondered if Vita had obscured it deliberately. It said he would be catching the 4.30 from London, arriving at St Austell around ten. This was a relief. It meant that Vita and the boys could go to bed, or at any rate only stay up for the courtesy of greeting the new arrival, and then Magnus and I could talk in comfort on our own. Cheered, I got up, and bathed and dressed with a determination to improve upon the morning's mood and abase myself before Vita and the boys.

"Magnus won't be here until after ten," I shouted down the stairs, "so there's no food problem. He'll dine on the train. What does everybody want to do?"

"Go sailing," cried the boys, who were hanging about in the hall in the customary aimless fashion of all children who are incapable of organising their own day.

"No wind," I said, with a rapid glance out of the window on the stairs.

"Then hire a motor boat," said Vita, emerging from the direction of the kitchen.

I decided to appease them all, and we set forth from Fowey with a picnic lunch and our skipper Tom in charge, this time not in the sailing-boat but in an ex-lifeboat of his own conversion with an honest chug-chug engine that forged along at about five knots and not a centimetre faster. We went east, out of the harbour, and anchored off Lanlivet Bay, where we picnicked, swam, and took our ease, everybody happy. Half a dozen mackerel caught on the homeward journey proved a further delight for Teddy and Micky, and a sop to Vita's culinary plans for the evening meal. The expedition had proved an unqualified success.

"Oh, do say we can come again tomorrow," pleaded the boys, but Vita, with a glance at me, told them it would depend upon the Professor. I saw their faces fall, and guessed their feelings. What could be more boring than to have to adjust themselves to this possibly stuffy friend of their stepfather's whom instinct told them their mother did not care for anyway?

"You can go with Tom," I said, "even if Magnus and I have other plans." In any event, I thought, a let-out for us, and Vita would hardly allow them to go alone, even in Tom's charge.

We arrive back at Kilmarth about seven o'clock, Vita going immediately to the kitchen to see about the mackerel, while I had a bath and changed. It was not until about ten to eight that I wandered down the front stairs into the dining-room and saw the piece of paper in Mrs Collins' handwriting propped up against the place where I usually sat. It read: "Telegram came over the 'phone to say Professor Lane is catching the 2.30 train from London instead of the 4.30. Arriving St Austell 7.30."

God! Magnus must have been kicking his heels at St Austell station for the last twenty minutes. . . . I tore into the kitchen.

"Crisis!" I shouted. "Look at this! I've only just seen it. Magnus caught an earlier train. Why the hell didn't he telephone? What a bloody mess-up!"

Vita, distraught, looked at the half-fried mackerel. "He'll be here for dinner, then? Good heavens, I can't give him this! I must say it shows very little consideration for us. Surely . . ."

"Of course Magnus will eat mackerel," I shouted, already half-way down the back stairs. "Brought up on it, very probably. And we've cheese and fruit. What are you fussing about?"

I tore out to the car, in half-agreement with her immediate reaction that to change his time of arrival, knowing we could easily be out for the day, showed small consideration for his hosts. But that was Magnus. An earlier train had suited his plans and he had caught it. If I arrived late to meet him he would probably take a taxi and pass me en route with a callous wave of the hand.

Ill-luck dogged me to St Austell. Some fool had driven his car into the side of the road, and there was a long queue of traffic waiting to get past. It was a quarter to nine before I drew up at St Austell station. No sign of Magnus, and I did not blame him. The platform was empty, and everywhere seemed to be shut up. Finally I routed out a porter on the other side of the station. He looked vague, and told me that the seven-thirty had been on time.

"I dare say," I replied. "That's not the point. The point is I was meeting someone off it, and he isn't here."

"Well, sir," he grinned, "he probably got tired of waiting and took a taxi."

"If he'd done that," I said, "he would have telephoned, or left a message with the chap in the booking-office. Were you here when the train came in?"

"No," he said. "The booking-office will be open again in time for the next down train, due at a quarter to ten."

"That's no good to me," I told him, exasperated. Poor devil, it wasn't his fault.

"I tell you what, sir," he said, "I'll open it up and see if your friend left a message."

We went back to the station and laboriously, or so it seemed to me, he fitted a key in the lock and opened the office door. I followed close behind. The first thing I noticed was a suitcase standing against the wall with the initials M.A.L. upon it.

"That's it," I said, "that's his case. But why did he leave it here?"

The porter went to the desk and picked up a piece of paper. "Suitcase with initials M.A.L. handed in by guard on seven-thirty train," he read, "to be delivered to gentleman named Mr Richard Young. You Mr Young?"

"Yes," I said, "but where's Professor Lane?"

The porter studied the piece of paper. "Owner of suitcase, Professor Lane, gave message to guard that he had changed his mind and decided to get out at Par and walk from there. Told guard Mr Young would understand." He handed me the scrap of paper, and I read it for myself.

"I don't understand," I said, more exasperated than ever. "I didn't think the London trains stopped at Par these days."

"They don't," replied the porter. "They stop at Bodmin Road, and anyone wanting Par changes there, and gets the connection. That's what your friend must have done."

"What a bloody silly thing to do," I said.

The porter laughed. "Well, it's a fine evening for a walk," he said, "and there's no accounting for tastes."

I thanked him for his trouble and went back to the car, throwing the suitcase on the back seat. Why the hell Magnus should take it into his head to alter every one of our arrangements beat me. He must be at Kilmarth by this time, sitting down to his mackerel supper, making a joke of the affair to Vita and the boys. I drove back at breakneck speed and arrived home just after half-past nine, furiously angry. Vita, changed into a sleeveless frock and with fresh make-up on, appeared from the music-room as I ran up the steps.

"Whatever happened to you both?" she said, the hostess smile of welcome fading as she saw I was alone. "Where is he?"

"You mean to say he hasn't turned up yet?" I cried.

"Turned up?" she repeated, bewildered. "Of course he hasn't turned up. You met the train, didn't you?"

"Oh, Jesus! What the hell is going on? Look," I said wearily, "Magnus wasn't at St Austell, only his suitcase. He left a message with the guard on the 7.30 train that he'd be getting out at Par and walking here. Don't ask me why. One of his bloody silly ideas. But he should have been here by now."

I went into the music-room and poured myself a drink and Vita followed, the boys running down to the car to fetch the suitcase.

"Well really," she said, "I expected more consideration from your Professor, I must say. First he changes trains, then he changes connections, and finally he doesn't bother to turn up at all. I expect he found a taxi at Par and has gone off to have dinner somewhere."

"Maybe," I said, "but why not telephone to say so?"

"He's your friend, darling, not mine. You're supposed to know his ways. Well, I'm not going to wait any longer, I'm starving."

The uncooked mackerel was put aside for Magnus's breakfast, though I was pretty sure orange juice and black coffee would be his choice, and Vita and I sat down to a hasty snack of game pie, which she remembered she had brought down from London and had put at the back of the fridge. Meanwhile Teddy rang, or tried to ring, Par station, with no result. They did not answer.

"You know what," he said, "the Professor may have been kidnapped by some organisation in search of secret documents."

"Very likely," I said. "I'll give him half an hour longer and then ring Scotland Yard."

"Or had a heart attack," suggested Micky, "flogging up Polmear hill. Mrs Collins told me her grandfather died walking up it thirty years ago when he missed the bus."

I pushed aside my plate and swallowed the last drop of whisky.

"You're perspiring again, darling," said Vita. "I can't say I blame you. But don't you think it might be a good idea if you went up and changed your shirt?"

I took the hint and left the dining-room, pausing at the top of the stairs to glance into the spare-room. Why the hell hadn't Magnus telephoned to say what he was doing, or at least written a note instead of giving the guard a verbal message that had probably been garbled anyway? I drew the curtains and switched on the bedside light, which made the room look more snug. Magnus's suitcase was lying on the chair at the bottom of the bed, and I tried the hasps. To my surprise it opened.

Magnus, unlike myself, was a methodical packer. Sky-blue pyjamas and Paisley dressing-gown reposed beneath a top layer of tissue paper, with blue leather bedroom slippers in their own cellophane container alongside. A couple of suits, a change of underwear beneath. Well, it was not an hotel or a stately home; he could do his own unpacking. The only gesture from host to guest—or was it the other way round?—would be to place the pyjamas on the pillow and drape the dressing-gown over the chair.

I took both out of the case, and saw that there was a long, buff-coloured envelope immediately beneath them, and typed upon it the words:

"Otto Bodrugan. Writ and Inquisition. 10 Oct. 5 Edward III. (1331)"

The student must have been at work again. I sat down on the edge of the bed and opened the envelope. It was a copy of a document giving the names of the various manors and lands owned by Otto Bodrugan at the time of his death. The manor of Bodrugan was amongst them, but he apparently paid rent for it to Joanna, "Relict of Henry de Campo Arnulphi" (which must be Champernoune). A further paragraph followed: "Henry his son, aged twenty-one years and more, was his next heir, who died three weeks after his said father, so that he had no seisin in the inheritance aforesaid, nor did he know of his father's death. William son of the aforesaid Otto, and brother of the said Henry, aged twenty years on the morrow of the feast of St Giles last, is his next heir."

It was a strange sensation, sitting there on the bed, reading something I already knew. The monks had done their best, or perhaps their worst, for young Henry at the Priory, and he had not survived. I was glad he had never been told of his father's death.

There was another long list of properties which Henry, if he had lived, would have inherited from Otto, and then a further note, take from the Calendar of Fine Rolls.

"Oct 10. Westminster. 1331. Order to the escheator on this side Trent to take into the King's hand the lands late of Otto de Bodrugan, deceased, tenant-in-chief."

The student had scribbled PTO at the bottom of the page, and turning over I found a half-page attached, also taken from the Calendar of Fine Rolls, and dated Nov. 14th, 1331, from Windsor.

"Order to the escheator on this side Trent to take into the King's hand the lands late of John de Carminowe, deceased, tenant-in-chief. The like to the same touching the lands of Henry son of Otto de Bodrugan."

So Sir John must have caught the infection he had so greatly feared and died immediately, and Joanna had lost her choice of a second husband. . . .

I forgot the present, forgot the mix-up at the station, and sat there on the spare-room bed thinking about the other world, wondering what advice, if any, Roger had given to the disappointed Joanna Champernoune. The two Bodrugan deaths, with the successor her nephew and a minor, must have given her every hope of greater power over the Bodrugan lands, and just as the power was within her grasp she found the tables turned, and the Keeper of Restormel and Tremerton Castles gone as well. I felt almost sorry for her. And for Sir John, who, luckless fellow, had held his handkerchief to his mouth in vain. Who would take his place as keeper of castles, woods and parks in the county of Cornwall? Not his brother Oliver, I hoped, the bloody murderer. . . .

"What are you going to do?" Vita called up the stairs.

Do? What could I do? Oliver had ridden off with his gang of thugs leaving Roger to take care of Isolda. I still did not know what had happened to Isolda. . . .

I heard Vita coming up the stairs, and instinctively I put the papers back in the envelope and stuffed them in my pocket, closing the suitcase. I must switch myself back to the present. This was not the moment to become confused.

"I was just getting out Magnus's pyjamas and dressing-gown," I said as she came into the room. "He'll be pretty well fagged out when he does turn up."

"Why not run his bath for him as well?" she countered. "And lay a tray for early morning tea? I didn't notice you being so attentive a host to Bill and Diana."

I ignored the sarcasm and went along to my dressing-room. The murmur of the television came from the library below. "Time those boys went to bed," I said, without conviction.

"I promised them they could wait up for the Professor," said Vita, "but really I think you're right, there's not much point in their hanging about any longer. Don't you think you ought to drive down to Par? He might be in some pub getting blind to the world."

"Magnus isn't the type to hang about in pubs."

"Well then, he must have come across old friends and has been taking dinner off them instead of us."

"Very unlikely. And damn rude not to telephone," I replied. We went together down the stairs and into the hall, and I added, "Anyway, he doesn't have any local friends, to my knowledge."

Vita suddenly gave a little cry. "I know," she said, "he's met the Carminowes! They haven't got a telephone. That's what's happened. He must have run into them at Par, and they took him back to dine with them."

I stared at her, my brain confused. What on earth was she talking about? And suddenly I knew. Suddenly the message from the guard came clear and full of meaning. "Owner of suitcase, Professor Lane, gave message to guard that he had changed his mind and decided to get out at Par, and walk from there. Told guard Mr Young would understand."

Magnus had taken the local connection from Bodmin Road to Par because it would travel more slowly through the Treesmill valley than the express. He knew, from my description, that he had only to look left and up, after passing above Treesmill Farm, to see the Gratten. Then, because it was still light when the train arrived at Par, he would have walked up the Tywardreath road and cut across the fields to inspect the site.

"God!" I exclaimed. "What a fool I've been! It never entered my head. Of course that's it."

"You mean he's gone to see the Carminowes?" said Vita.

I suppose I was tired. I suppose I was excited. I suppose I was relieved. All three in one, and I could not bother to explain or think up some different lie. The most natural thing to say just tripped off my tongue.

"Yes," I replied. I ran down the steps and across the front path to the car.

"But you don't know where they live!" called Vita.

I did not answer. I waved my hand and leapt into the car, and in a moment I was tearing up the drive and out on to the road.

It was quite dark, with only a waning moon that did not help, but I took the short cut up the lane skirting the village, meeting no one on the way, and parked in the lay-by near the house called Hill Crest. If Magnus found the car before I found him he would recognise it, and wait for me. It was hard going across the field to the Gratten, stumbling about amongst the banks and mounds, and I shouted for him, once I was well out of earshot of the house, but he did not answer. I covered the site thoroughly, but there was no sign of him. I walked along the lower path to the valley itself, and down to Treesmill Farm, but he was not there either. Then I walked up the road to the top of the hill and back to the car. It was as I had left it, empty. I drove down into the village, and walked round the churchyard. The hands on the clock-face said after half-past eleven; I had been searching for Magnus for over an hour.

I went to the telephone-box near the hairdresser and dialled Kilmarth. Vita answered immediately. "Any luck?" she asked.

My heart sank. I had hoped he might have arrived home. "No, not a trace of him."

"What about the Carminowes? Did you find their house?"

"No," I said, "no, I think we were on the wrong track there. It was stupid of me. Actually, I've no idea where they live."

"Well, someone must know," she said. "Why don't you ask the police?"

"No," I said, "it wouldn't do any good. Look, I'll drive down the village to the station and then come slowly home. There's nothing more I can do."

But Par station appeared to be closed for the night, and though I circled Par itself twice there was no sign of Magnus.

I began to pray, "Oh, God, let me see him walking up Polmear hill!" I knew just how he would look, my headlights picking him up at the side of the road, the tall angular figure with a loping stride, and I would hoot loudly and he would stop, and I would say to him, "What the bloody hell . . ."

He was not there, though. There was no one there. I turned down the Kilmarth drive, and walked slowly up the steps into the house. Vita was waiting for me by the porch. She looked distressed.

"Something must have happened to him," she said. "I do think you ought to ring up the police."

I brushed past her and went upstairs. "I'll unpack his things," I said. "He may have left a note. I don't know . . ."

I took his clothes out of the suitcase and hung them in the wardrobe, and put his shaving tackle in the bathroom. I kept telling myself that any moment I should hear a car coming down the drive, a taxi, and Magnus would jump out of it, laughing, and Vita would call up the stairs to me, "He's here, he's arrived!"

There was no note. I felt in all the pockets. Nothing. Then I turned to the dressing-gown, which I had unpacked already. My hand closed upon something round in the left-hand pocket, and I drew it out. It was a small bottle, which I recognised at once. It bore a label: B. It was the bottle I had posted to him the week before, and it was empty.

CHAPTER SIXTEEN

I WENT ALONG to my dressing-room, found my own suitcase, put the bottle in one of the pockets and the documents about Bodrugan as well, locked the case and joined Vita downstairs.

"Did you find anything?" she asked.

I shook my head. She followed me into the music-room and I poured myself a whisky. "You'd better have one too," I said.

"I don't feel like it," she answered. She sat down on the sofa and lit a cigarette. "I'm quite certain we ought to ring the police."

"Because Magnus has taken it into his head to roam the countryside?" I queried. "Nonsense, he knows what he's doing. He must know every inch of the district for miles around."

The clock in the dining-room struck midnight. If Magnus had left the train at Par, he had been walking for four and a half hours . . .

"You go to bed," I said. "You look exhausted. I'll stay down here in case he comes. I can lie on the sofa if I feel like it. Then as soon as it's light, if I'm awake and he hasn't arrived, I'll go out in the car and have another search."

It was true, she looked all-in: I was not trying to get rid of her. She stood up uncertainly, and wandered towards the door. Then she looked back at me, over her shoulder.

"There's something odd about all this," she said slowly. "I have a feeling you know more than you say." I had no ready answer. "Well, try and get some sleep," she went on. "Something tells me you're going to need it."

I heard the bedroom door shut, and stretched myself out on the sofa with my hands behind my head, trying to think. There were only two solutions. The first, as I had originally imagined, that Magnus had decided to find the Gratten site, and had either lost his way or ricked his ankle, and so decided to wait where he was until daylight; or the second . . . and the second was the one I feared. Magnus had gone on a trip. He had poured the contents of bottle B into some container that could be carried in a coat pocket, and had got out of the train at Par and walked—to the Gratten, to the church, anywhere in the district, and then swallowed the drug and waited . . . waited for it to take effect. Once this had happened he would not be responsible for his actions. If time took him into that other world that we both knew he would not necessarily witness what I had witnessed, the scene could be different, the point in time earlier or later, but the penalty for touching anyone, as he well knew, would be the same for both of us; nausea, vertigo, confusion. Magnus had not, as far as I knew, touched the drug for at least three or four months; he, the inventor, was not prepared and might not have the stamina to endure it as I, the guinea-pig, could.

I closed my eyes and tried to picture him walking away from the station, up the hill and across the fields to the Gratten, and swallowing the drug, laughing to himself. "I've stolen a march on Dick!" Then the leap backwards in time, and the estuary below, the walls of the house about him, Roger close at hand—leading him where? To what strange encounter on the hills or beside the strand? To what month, what year? Would he see, as I had seen, the faltering ship, dismasted, enter the creek, the horsemen riding on the opposite hill? Would he see Bodrugan drowned? If so, his actions might not be the same as mine. Knowing his taste for the dramatic, he might have flung himself headlong into the river and struck out for that opposite shore—and there would have been no river, only the smothered valley, the scrub, the marsh, the trees. Magnus could be lying there now, in that impassable waste land, shouting for help, and none to hear. There was nothing I could do. Nothing until daylight came.

I did sleep, after a fashion, waking with a jerk from some distorted dream that instantly faded, to fall off again once more. A deeper sleep must have come with the first light, for I remember looking at my watch at half-past five and telling myself another twenty minutes would not hurt, and then when I opened my eyes again it was ten past seven.

I made a cup of tea, then crept upstairs and washed and shaved. Vita was already awake. She did not even question me. She knew Magnus had not come.

"I'm going to Par station," I said. "They'll know if he handed the ticket in. Then I'll try and trace his movements from there. Somebody must have seen him."

"It would be so much simpler," she insisted, "if you went direct to the police."

"I will go to them," I said, "if no one can tell me anything at the station."

"If you don't," she called as I left the room, "I shall ring them up myself."

I drew a blank at the station: a chap wandering about told me the booking-office would not be open for half an hour. I filled in the time by walking up to the bridge that spanned the railway-line and gave a view of the valley. Once this would have been wide estuary; Bodrugan's ship, dismasted by the gale, would have drifted past this very spot, driven by wind and tide, seeking shelter up the creek and finding death instead. Today, part reedy marsh, part scrub, it was still easy enough to trace the original course of the river from the winding valley itself. A man, sick or in some way hurt, might lie beneath those stubby, close-packed trees for days, for weeks, and no one know of it. Even the marsh ground on which the station stood, the wide, flat expanse between Par and neighbouring St Blazey, was still waste land to a large extent; even here there were large tracks where no one wandered. Except, perhaps, a traveller in time whose mind trod a vessel's deck upon blue water while his body stumbled amongst scrub and ditch.

I returned to the station and found the booking-office open, and for the first time proof that Magnus had arrived. The clerk had not only taken his ticket but remembered the holder of it. Tall, he said, going grey, hatless, wearing a sports jacket and dark trousers, with a pleasant smile, and carrying a stick. No, the clerk had not seen which way he had gone after leaving the station.

I got into the car and drove half-way up the hill, to where a footpath went off to the left. Magnus could have taken it, and I did the same, striking across country to the Gratten. It was warm and misty, foretelling a hot day. The farmer the land belonged to must have opened a gate somewhere since the preceding night, because cows wandered on the hillside now, amongst the gorse-bushes and the mounds, following me in curiosity to the entrance of the overgrown quarry itself.

I searched it thoroughly, every corner, every dip, but found nothing. I looked down into the valley below, across the intervening railway line, to the sweeping mass of trees and bushes covering the one-time river bed. They might have been woven tapestry, coloured with silken threads in every shade of golden green. If Magnus was there, nothing would ever find him but tracker dogs.

Then I knew I must do what I should have done earlier, what I should have done last night. I must go to the police. I must go, as any other man would go whose guest had failed to arrive over twelve hours earlier, though his ticket had been given up at the station at the correct time.

I remembered there was a police station at Tywardreath, and I wound my weary way back again and drove straight there. I felt inadequate, guilty, like all persons who have been lucky enough never to have found themselves involved with the police, beyond minor traffic offences, and my story, as I told it to the sergeant, sounded shamefaced, somehow, irresponsible.

"I want to report a missing person," I said, and instantly had a vision of a poster with the haunted face of a criminal staring from it, and the words "WANTED" in enormous letters underneath. I pulled myself together, and told the exact story of all that had happened the preceding day.

The sergeant was helpful, sympathetic and extremely kind. "I haven't had the pleasure of meeting Professor Lane personally," he said, "but we know all about him, of course. You must have had a very anxious night."

"Yes," I said.

"There's been no report to us of any accident," he said, "but of course I will check with Liskeard and St Austell. Would you like a cup of tea, Mr Young?"

I accepted the offer gratefully, while he got busy on the telephone. I had the sick feeling at the pit of my stomach that people get waiting outside a hospital ward during an emergency operation performed on someone they love. It was out of my hands. There was nothing I could do. Presently he came back.

"There's been no report of any accident," he said. "They're alerting the patrol cars in the district, and the other police stations. I think the best thing you can do, sir, is to go back to Kilmarth and wait there until you hear from us. It could be that Professor Lane twisted an ankle and spent the night at one of the farms, but they're mostly on the telephone these days, and it's strange he shouldn't have rung you up to let you know. No previous history of loss of memory, I suppose?"

"No," I told him, "never. And he was very fit when I dined with him in London a few weeks ago."

"Well, don't worry too much, sir," he said, "there'll probably be some simple explanation at the end of it."

I went back to the car, the sick feeling with me still, and drove down to the church. I could hear the organ—they must have been having choir practice. I went and sat on one of the graves near the wall above the orchard—Priory orchard once. Where I sat would have been the monks' dormitory, looking south over the Priory creek; and close at hand was the guest-chamber where young Henry Bodrugan had died of smallpox. In that other time he could be dying still. In that other time the monk, Jean, could be mixing some hell-brew that finished off the business, then sending word to Roger that he must carry the news to the mother and the aunt, Joanna Champernoune. Ill-tidings were all about me, in the other world and in my own. Roger, the monk, young Bodrugan, Magnus; we were all links in an inter-woven chain, bound one to the other through the centuries.

> "In such a night
> Medea gather'd the enchanted herbs
> That did renew old Aeson."

Magnus could have sat here and taken the drug. He could have gone to any of the places where I had been. I drove down to the farm where Julian Polpey had lived six centuries ago, and where the postman had found me a week ago, and walked down the farm-track to Lampetho. If I had traversed the marsh at night, my body in the present, my brain in the past, Magnus could have done the same. Even now, with no water and no tide filling the inlet, only meadow-marsh and reeds, the route was familiar, like some scene from a forgotten dream. The track petered out, though, into marsh, and I could see no way forward, no means of crossing the valley to the other side. How I had done it myself at night, following, in that earlier world, Otto and the other conspirators, God only knew. I retraced my footsteps past Lampetho Farm, and an old man came out of one of the buildings, calling to his dog, who ran towards me, barking. He asked if I had lost my way and I told him no, and apologised for trespassing.

"You didn't by any chance see anyone walking this way last night?" I asked. "A tall man, grey-haired, carrying a stick?"

He shook his head. "We don't get many visitors coming here," he said. "Doesn't lead anywhere, just to this farm. Visitors stay mostly on Par beach."

I thanked him and walked back to the car. I was not convinced, though. He could have been indoors between half-past eight and nine; Magnus could be lying in the marsh below his farm. . . . But surely someone would have seen him? The effect of the drug, if he had taken it, would have worn off hours ago; if he had taken it at half-past eight, or nine, he would have come to by ten, by eleven, by midnight.

There was a police car drawn up outside the house when I arrived, and as I entered the hall I heard Vita say, "Here's my husband now."

She was in the music-room with a police officer and a constable.

"I'm afraid we've no definite news for you, Mr Young," the Inspector said, "only a slight clue, which may lead us to something. A man answering to the description of Professor Lane was seen last evening between nine and half-past walking along the Stonybridge lane above Treesmill past Trenadlyn Farm."

"Trenadlyn Farm?" I repeated, and the surprise must have shown in my face, for he said quickly, "You know it, then?"

"Why, yes," I said, "it's much higher up the valley than Treesmill, it's the small farm right on the lane itself."

"That's right. Have you any idea why Professor Lane should have been walking in that particular direction, Mr Young?"

"No," I said with hesitation. "No. . . . There was nothing to take him there. I would have expected him to be walking lower down the valley, nearer to Treesmill."

"Well," the Inspector replied, "our information is that a gentleman was seen walking past Trenadlyn between nine and half-past. Mrs Richards, wife of Mr Richards who owns the farm, saw him from her window, but her brother, who farms Great Treverran, higher up the lane, saw no one. If Professor Lane was walking to Kilmarth it seems a long way round, even for someone who wanted exercise after sitting in a train."

"Yes, I agree. Inspector," I went on hesitantly, "Professor Lane is very interested in historical sites, and this may have been the reason for his walk. I think he was looking for an old manor house which he believes stood there once. But it couldn't have been either of the farms you mentioned, or he would have called at one of them."

I knew now why Magnus—and it must have been Magnus, from the woman's description—was walking past Trenadlyn on the Stonybridge lane. It was the route Isolda had taken on horseback with Robbie, when the two of them had come riding down to Treesmill to the creek, to find Bodrugan murdered, drowned. It was the only route to the unknown Tregest when the ford across Treesmill was impassable through flood or high tide. Magnus, when he passed Trenadlyn farm, was walking in time. He could have been following Roger, and Isolda too.

Vita, unable to contain herself, turned to me impulsively. "Darling, all this historical business is beside the point. Please don't be angry with me for butting in, but I feel it's essential." She turned to the Inspector. "I'm quite sure, and so was my husband last night, that the Professor was going to call on some old friends of his, people called Carminowe. Oliver Carminowe is not on the telephone, but he does live somewhere in that district, where the Professor was last seen. It's quite obvious to me that he was on his way to call on them, and the sooner somebody contacts them the better."

There was a momentary silence after her outburst. Then the Inspector glanced at me. His expression had changed from concern to surprise, even disapproval.

"Is that so, Mr Young? You said nothing about the possibility of Professor Lane visiting friends."

I felt my mouth flicker in a weak smile. "No, Inspector," I said, "of course not. There was no question of the Professor visiting anyone. I'm afraid my wife had her leg pulled over the telephone by the Professor, and I very foolishly did nothing to put her wise, but kept up the joke. There are no such people as Carminowe. They don't exist."

"Don't exist?" echoed Vita. "But you saw the children riding ponies on Sunday morning, two little girls with their nurse, you told me so."

"I know I did," I said, "but I can only repeat I was pulling your leg."

She stared at me in disbelief. I could tell, from the expression in her eyes, that she thought I was lying to get Magnus and myself out of an awkward situation. Then she shrugged her shoulders, flicked a rapid glance at the Inspector and lit a cigarette. "What a very stupid joke," she said, and added, "I beg your pardon, Inspector."

"Don't apologise, Mrs Young," he said, rather more stiffly, I thought, than before. "We all get our legs pulled from time to time, especially in the police force." He turned again to me. "You're quite certain about that, Mr Young? You know of no one whom Professor Lane might have been calling upon after he arrived at Par station?"

"Absolutely not," I said. "As far as I know we are his only friends here, and he was definitely coming to spend the weekend with us. The house belongs to him, as you know. He's lent it to us for the summer holidays. Quite frankly, Inspector, I was not really concerned about Professor Lane until this morning. He knows the district well, for his father, Commander Lane, had this house before him. I was sure he couldn't lose himself, and that he'd turn up with some plausible explanation of where he had been all night."

"I see," said the Inspector.

Nobody said anything for a moment, and I had the impression that he doubted my story, just as Vita did, and that they both thought Magnus had been bound on some doubtful assignation and I was covering up for him. Which, indeed, was true.

"I realise now," I said, "that I should have got in touch with you last night. Professor Lane must have twisted his ankle, probably shouted for help, and nobody heard. There wouldn't have been much traffic up that side road once it was dark."

"No," the Inspector agreed, "but the people from Trenadlyn and Treverran would have been astir early this morning, and should have seen or heard something of him by now, if he had had some mishap on the road. More likely he walked up to the main road, and then he could have taken either direction, on towards Lostwithiel or back to Fowey."

"The name Tregest doesn't convey anything to you?" I asked cautiously.

"Tregest?" The Inspector thought a moment, then shook his head. "No, I can't say it does. Is it the name of a place?"

"I believe there was a farm of that name once, somewhere in the district. Professor Lane could have been trying to find it, in connection with his historical research." Then I suddenly had another idea. "Trelawn," I said, "where exactly is Trelawn?"

"Trelawn?" repeated the Inspector, surprised. "That's an estate a few miles from Looe. Must be eighteen miles or more from here. Professor Lane would surely not start to try to walk there around nine o'clock at night?"

"No," I said, "no, of course not. It's just that I'm trying to think of old houses of historical interest."

"Yes, but, darling," interrrupted Vita, "as the Inspector says, Magnus would hardly start looking for something of that sort, miles away, without telephoning us first. That's what I can't understand, why he didn't attempt to telephone."

"He didn't telephone, Mrs Young," said the Inspector, "because he apparently thought Mr Young would know where he was going."

"Yes," I said, "and I didn't know. I don't know now. I only wish to God I did."

The telephone rang with startling suddenness, like an echo to all our thoughts. "I'll get it," said Vita, who was nearest to the door. She crossed the hall to the library, and we stood there in the music-room saying nothing, listening to her voice.

"Yes," she said briefly, "he is here. I'll get him."

She came back into the room and told the Inspector that the call was for him. We waited for what seemed an interminable three or four minutes, while he answered in monosyllables, his voice muffled. I looked at my watch. It was just on half-past twelve. I had not realised it was so late. When he returned he looked directly at me, and I saw from the expression on his face that something had happened.

"I'm very sorry, Mr Young," he said, "I'm afraid it's bad news."

"Yes," I said, "tell me."

One is never prepared. One always believes, in moments of acute stress, that things will turn out all right, that even now, with Magnus missing for so long, it would surely be to say that someone had picked him up with loss of memory and taken him to hospital.

Vita came and stood beside me, her hand in mine.

"That was a message from Liskeard police station," said the Inspector. "Word has come through that one of our patrols has found the body of a man resembling Professor Lane near the railway-line just this side of Treverran tunnel. He seems to have received a blow on the head from a passing train, unobserved by the driver or the guard. He managed, apparently, to crawl into a small disused hut just above the line, and then he collapsed. It looks as if he must have been dead for some hours."

I went on standing there, staring at the Inspector. Shock is a peculiar thing, numbing emotion. It was as though life itself had ebbed away, leaving me a shell, like Magnus. I was only aware of Vita holding my head.

"I understand," I said, but it was not my voice. "What do you want me to do?"

"They are on their way to the mortuary in Fowey now, Mr Young," he said. "I hate to trouble you at such a moment, but I think it would be best if we took you there right away to identify the body. I should like to think, for both your sakes, yours and Mrs Young's, that it is not Professor Lane, but in the circumstances I can't offer you much hope."

"No," I said, "no, of course not."

I let go of Vita's hand and walked towards the door and out of the house into the hot sunlight. Some Scouts were putting up tents in the field beyond the Kilmarth meadow. I could hear them shouting and laughing, and hammering the pegs into the ground.

CHAPTER SEVENTEEN

THE MORTUARY WAS a smallish, red-brick building not far from Fowey station. There was nobody there when we arrived: the second patrol car was still on its way. When I got out of the car the Inspector looked at me a moment, and then he said, "Mr Young, there may be some delay. I'd like to offer you a cup of coffee and a sandwich at the café just up the road."

"Thank you," I said, "but I'm all right."

"I can't insist," he continued, "but it really would be wise. You'll feel the better for it."

I gave in, and allowed him to lead me along to the café, and we each had some coffee, and I had a ham sandwich too. As we sat there I thought of the times in the past, as undergraduates, when Magnus and I had travelled down by train to Par to stay with his parents at Kilmarth. The rattle in the darkness and the echo of sound in the tunnel, and suddenly that welcome emergence into the light, with green fields on either side. Magnus must have made that journey every school holiday as a boy. Now he had met his death by the entrance to that same tunnel.

It would make sense to no one. Not to the police, or to his many friends, or to anyone but myself. I should be asked why a man of his intelligence had wandered close to a railway-line on a summer's evening at dusk, and I should have to say that I did not know. I did know. Magnus was walking in a time when no railway-line existed. He was walking in an age when the hillside was rough pasture, even scrub. There was no gaping tunnel mouth yawning from the hillside in that other world, no metal lines, no track, only the bare grassland, and perhaps a man astride a pony, leading him on. . . .

"Yes?" I said.

The Inspector was asking me if Professor Lane had any relatives.

"I'm sorry," I said, "I didn't hear what you said. No, Commander and Mrs Lane have been dead for a number of years, and there were no other children. I've never heard him mention cousins or anyone."

There must be a lawyer somewhere who dealt with his affairs, a bank which managed his finances: now I came to think of it I did not even know his secretary's name. Our relationship, binding, intimate, did not concern itself with day-to-day matters, with ordinary concerns. There must be someone other than myself who would know about all this.

Presently the constable came to tell the Inspector that the second patrol car had arrived, and the ambulance too, and we walked back to the mortuary. The constable murmured something which I did not hear, and the Inspector turned to me.

"Dr Powell from Fowey happened to be at Tywardreath police station when the message came through from our patrol," he said, "and he agreed to make a preliminary examination of the body. Then it will be up to the Coroner's pathologist to conduct the post mortem."

"Yes," I said. Post mortem . . . inquest . . . the whole paraphernalia of the law.

I went into the mortuary. The first person I saw was the doctor I had met at the lay-by, who had watched me recovering from my attack of vertigo over ten days ago. I saw the instant recognition in his eyes, but he did not let on when the Inspector introduced us.

"I'm sorry about this," he said, and then, abruptly, "If you haven't seen anyone before who's been badly smashed up in an accident, let alone a friend, it's not a pleasant sight. This man has had a great gash on the head."

He took me to the stretcher lying on the long table. It was Magnus, but he looked different—smaller, somehow. There was a sort of cavity caked with blood above his right eye. There was dried blood on his jacket, which was torn, and a tear in one of his trouser legs.

"Yes," I said, "yes, that is Professor Lane."

I turned away, because Magnus himself wasn't there. He was still walking in the fields above the Treesmill valley, or looking about him, in great wonder, in some other undiscovered world.

"If it's any consolation to you," said the doctor, "he couldn't have lived very long after receiving a blow like that. God knows how he managed to crawl the few yards to the hut—he wouldn't have been conscious of his movements, he would have died literally a few moments afterwards."

Nothing was a consolation, but I thanked him all the same. "You mean," I said, "he would not have lain there, wondering why nobody came?"

"No," he answered, "definitely not. But I'm sure the Inspector will let you have the full details, as soon as we know the extent of the injuries."

There was a walking-stick lying at the end of the table. The sergeant pointed it out to the Inspector. "The stick was lying half-way down the embankment, sir," he said, "a short distance from the hut."

The Inspector looked enquiringly at me, and I nodded. "Yes," I said, "it's one of many he had. His father collected walking-sticks; there are about a dozen in his flat in London."

"I think the best thing to do now is for us to run you straight back to Kilmarth, Mr Young," said the Inspector. "You'll be kept fully informed, of course. You realise that you will be required to give evidence at the inquest."

"Yes," I said. I wondered what would happen to Magnus's body after the post mortem. I wondered if it was going to lie there through the weekend. Not that it mattered. Not that anything mattered.

As the Inspector shook hands he said that they would probably come out on Monday and ask me a few more questions, in case I could add to my original statement. "You see, Mr Young," he explained, "there might be a question of amnesia, or even suicide."

"Amnesia," I repeated. "That's loss of memory, isn't it? Most unlikely. And suicide, definitely no. The Professor was the last man in the world to do such a thing, and he had no cause. He was looking forward to the weekend, and was in very good spirits when I spoke to him on the telephone."

"Quite so," said the Inspector. "Well, that's just the sort of statement the Coroner will want to have from you."

The constable dropped me at the house, and I walked very slowly through the garden and up the steps. I poured out the equivalent of a triple whisky, and flung myself on the divan bed in the dressing-room. I must have passed out shortly afterwards, for when I woke up it was late afternoon or early evening, and Vita was sitting on the chair near by with a book in her hands, the last of the sun coming through the western window that gave on to the patio.

"What's the time?" I asked.

"About half-after six," she said, and came and sat on the bed beside me.

"I thought it wisest to let you lie," she went on. "The doctor who saw you at the mortuary telephoned during the afternoon, and asked if you were all right, and I told him you were sleeping. He said to let you sleep as long as possible, it was the best thing that could happen." She put her hand in mine and it was comforting, like being a child again.

"What did you do with the boys?" I asked. "The house seems very quiet."

"Mrs Collins was wonderful," she said. "She took them down to Polkerris to spend the day with her. Her husband was going to take them fishing after lunch and bring them back about seven. They'll be home any moment now."

I was silent a moment, and then I said, "This mustn't spoil their holiday, Magnus would have hated that."

"Don't bother about them or me," she said. "We can take care of ourselves. What worries me is the shock it's been for you."

I was thankful she did not pursue the subject, go over the whole business again—why it had happened, what Magnus had been doing, why he did not notice the approaching train, why the driver had not seen him; it would have led us nowhere.

"I ought to get on the telephone," I said. "The people at the University should be told."

"The nice Inspector is taking care of all of that," she said. "He came back again, quite soon after you must have gone upstairs. He asked to see Magnus's suitcase. I told him you'd unpacked it last night and hadn't found anything. He didn't either. He left the clothes hanging in the closet."

I remembered the bottle in my own suitcase, and the papers about Bodrugan. "What else did he want?"

"Nothing. Just said to leave everything to them, and he'd be in touch with you on Monday."

I put out my arms and pulled her down to me. "Thanks for everything, darling," I said. "You're a great comfort. I can't really think straight yet."

"Don't try," she whispered. "I wish there was more I could say, or do."

We heard the boys talking together in their room. They must have come in by the back entrance. "I'll go to them," said Vita, "they'll want some supper. Would you like me to bring yours up here?"

"No, I'll come down. I'll have to face them some time."

I went on lying there awhile, watching the last of the sun filtering through the trees. Then I had a bath and changed. Despite the shock and the turmoil of the day my bloodshot eye was back to normal. The trouble may have been coincidental, nothing to do with the drug. In any event it was something, now, that I should never know.

Vita was giving the boys their supper in the kitchen. I could hear what they were saying as I hovered in the hall, bracing myself before I went in.

"Well, I bet you anything you like it turns out to be foul play." Teddy's rather high-pitched, nasal voice came clearly through the open kitchen door. "It stands to reason the Professor had some secret scientific information on him, probably to do with germ warfare, and he'd arranged to meet someone near that tunnel, and the man he met was a spy and knocked him on the head. The police down here won't think of that, and they'll have to bring in the Secret Service."

"Don't be idiotic, Teddy," said Vita sharply. "That's just the sort of frightful way rumours spread. It would upset Dick terribly to hear you say things like that. I hope you didn't suggest such a thing to Mr Collins."

"Mr Collins thought of it first," chimed in Mickey. "He said you never knew what scientists were up to these days, and the Professor might have been looking for a site for a hush-hush research station up the Treesmill valley."

This conversation had the instant effect of pulling me together. I thought how Magnus would have loved it, played up to it, too, encouraged every exaggeration. I coughed loudly and went towards the kitchen, hearing Vita say "Ssh . . ." as I passed through the door.

The boys looked up, their small faces taking on the expression of shy discomfort that children wear when suddenly confronted with what they fear to be an adult plunged in grief.

"Hullo," I said. "Had a good day?"

"Not bad," mumbled Teddy, turning red. "We went fishing."

"Catch anything?"

"A few whiting. Mom's cooking them now."

"Well, if you've any to spare, I'll stand in the queue. I had a cup of coffee and a sandwich in Fowey, and that's been my lot for the day."

They must have expected me to stand with bowed head and shaking shoulders, for they cheered visibly when I attacked a large wasp on the window with the fly-swatter, saying "Got him!" with enormous relish as I squashed it flat. Later, when we were eating, I said to them, "I may be a bit tied up next week because they'll have to hold an inquest on Magnus, and there'll be various things to attend to, but I'll see to it that you go out with Tom in one of his boats from Fowey, engine or sailing, whichever you like best."

"Oh, thanks awfully," said Teddy, and Micky, realising that the subject of Magnus was no longer taboo, paused, his mouth full of whiting, and enquired brightly, "Will the Professor's life story be on TV tonight?"

"I shouldn't think so," I replied. "It's not as if he were a pop-singer or a politician."

"Bad luck," he said. "Still, we'd better watch just in case."

There was nothing, much to the disappointment of both boys, and secretly, I suspected, of Vita too, but to my own considerable relief. I knew the next few days would bring more than enough in the way of publicity, once the press got hold of the story, and so it proved. The telephone started ringing first thing the following morning, although it was Sunday, and either Vita or I spent most of the day answering it. Finally we left it off the hook and installed ourselves on the patio, where reporters, if they rang the front-door bell, would never find us.

The next morning she took the boys into Par to do some shopping, leaving me to my mail, which I had not opened. The few letters I had were nothing to do with the disaster. Then I picked up the last of the small pile and saw, with a queer stab of the heart, that it was addressed to me in pencil, bore an Exeter postmark, and was in Magnus's handwriting. I tore it open.

"Dear Dick," I read, "I'm writing this in the train, and it will probably be illegible. If I find a post-box handy on Exeter station I'll drop it in. There is probably no need to write at all, and by the time you receive it on Saturday morning we shall have had, I trust, an uproarious evening together with many more to come, but I write as a safety-measure, in case I pass out in the carriage from sheer exuberance of spirits. My findings to date are pretty conclusive that we are on to something of prime importance regarding the brain. Briefly, and in layman's language, the chemistry within the brain cells concerned with memory, everything we have done from infancy onwards, is reproducible, returnable, for want of a better term, in these same cells, the exact contents of which depends upon our hereditary make-up, the legacy of parents, grandparents, remoter ancestors back to primeval times. The fact that I am a genius and you are a lay-about depends solely upon the messages transmitted to us from these cells and then distributed through the various other cells and throughout our body, but, our various characteristics apart, the particular cells I have been working upon—which I will call the memory-box—store not only our own memories but habits of the earlier brain pattern we inherit. These habits, if released to consciousness, would enable us to see, hear, become cognoscent of things that happened in the past, not because any particular ancestor witnessed any particular scene, but because with the use of a medium—in this case a drug—the inherited, older brain pattern takes over and becomes dominant. The implications from a historian's point of view don't concern me, but, biologically, the potential uses of the hitherto untapped ancestral brain are of enormous interest, and open immeasurable possibilities.

"As to the drug itself, yes, it's dangerous, and could be lethal if taken to excess, and should it fall into the hands of the unscrupulous it might bring even more havoc upon our already troubled world. So, dear boy, if anything happens to me, destroy what remains in Bluebeard's chamber. My staff— who, however, know nothing of the implications of my discovery, for I have been working on this on my own—have similar instructions here in London, and can be trusted implicitly. As to yourself, if I don't see you again, forget the whole business. If we meet this evening as arranged, and take a walk and perhaps a trip together, as I hope we shall, I intend to have a close look, if I have the luck, at the beautiful Isolda, who, from the evidence in the document at the top of my suitcase, appears to have lost her lover just as you said, and must be in dire need of consolation. Whether Roger Kylmerth can supply it we may discover at the same time. No time to say any more, we are drawing into Exeter. A bientôt, in this world, or the other, or hereafter.

                                                            "Magnus."

If we had not gone sailing on the Friday I should have found the telephone message about the earlier train in time . . . If I had made straight for the Gratten after leaving St Austell station, instead of going home. . . . Too many "ifs", and none of them working out. Even this letter, coming now like a message from the dead, should have reached me on Saturday morning instead of today, Monday. Not that it would have done any good. Nor did it say anything about Magnus's real intentions. Even then, as he posted it, he may not have made up his mind. The letter was a safety-measure, as he said, in case anything went wrong. I read it through again, once, twice, then put my lighter to it and watched it burn.

I went down to the basement and through the old kitchen to the lab. I had not entered it since early Wednesday morning, after returning from the Gratten, when Bill had come downstairs and found me making tea in the kitchen. The rows of jars and bottles, the monkey's head, the embryo kittens and the fungus plants held no menace for me now, nor had they done so since the first experiment. Now, with their magician gone, never to return, they had a wasted, almost a forlorn appearance, like puppets and props from a conjurer's bag of tricks. No ebony wand would bring these things to life, no cunning hand extract the juices, pick the bones and set them fermenting in some bubbling cauldron brew.

I took the jars which held various liquids and poured the contents down the sink. Then I washed the jars out and put them back on the shelf. They could have been used for preserving fruit or jam, for all anybody would ever know; there were no distinctive marks upon them—only labels which I stripped off and pocketed. Then I fetched an old sack which I remembered seeing in the boiler-house, and set about unscrewing the remaining jars and bottles that contained the embryos and the monkey's head. I put them all in the sack, having first poured down the sink the liquid that had preserved them, taking care that none of it touched my hands. I did the same with the various fungi, putting them also in the sack. Only two small bottles remained, bottle A, containing the remains of the drug I had been using myself to date, and bottle C, untouched. Bottle B I had sent to Magnus, and it was lying empty in my suitcase upstairs. I did not pour the contents of either down the sink. I put them in my pocket. Then I went to the door and listened. Mrs Collins was moving about between the kitchen and the pantry—I could hear her radio going.

I swung the sack over my shoulder and locked the door of the lab. Then I went out through the back door and climbed up to the kitchen garden behind the stable block, and into the wood at the top of the grounds. I went to where the undergrowth was thickest, straggling laurels, rhododendrons that had not bloomed for years, broken branches of dead trees, brambles, nettles, the fallen leaves of successive autumn gales, and I took one of the dead branches and scraped a pit in the wet, dank earth and emptied the sack into it, smashing the monkey's head with a jagged stone so that it no longer bore any resemblance to a living thing, only fragments, only jelly, and the embryos slithered amongst the fragments, unrecognisable, like the stringy entrails flung to a seagull when a fish is gutted. I covered them, and the sack, with the rotting leaves of years, and the brown earth, and a heap of nettles, and the sentence came into my mind, "Ashes to ashes, dust to dust", and in a sense it was as if I were burying Magnus and his work as well.

I went back into the house, through the basement, and up the little side-stairway to the front, thus avoiding Mrs Collins, but she must have heard me entering the hall, for she called, "Is that you, Mr Young?"

"Yes," I said.

"I looked for you everywhere—I couldn't find you. The Inspector from Liskeard was on the telephone."

"I was in the garden," I told her. "I'll ring him back."

I went upstairs to the dressing-room, and put bottles A and C in my suitcase along with the empty bottle B, locked it once again, put the key on my ring, washed, and went downstairs to the library. Then I put a call through to the police-station at St Austell.

"I'm sorry, Inspector," I said, when they got him on the line. "I was in the garden when you telephoned."

"That's all right, Mr Young," he said. "I thought you would like to know the news to date. Well, we've made some headway. It was a freight-train that caused the accident, that seems to be clearly established. It passed through Treverran tunnel, going up the line, at approximately ten minutes to ten. The driver saw no one near the line as he approached the tunnel, but these freight trains are sometimes of considerable length, and this one carried no guard in the rear, so that once the engine had entered the tunnel there would be no one to observe whether anybody came on to the line and was struck by one of the passing wagons."

"No," I said, "no, I appreciate that. And you think this is what happened?"

"Well, Mr Young, everything points to it. It would seem as though Professor Lane must have continued up the lane past Trenadlyn Farm, but before he got to the main road he turned off into a field they call Higher Gum, well above Treverran, and crossed it in a diagonal direction towards the railway. It is possible, by climbing through the wire and scrambling up a bank, to get on to the line, but anyone doing so could not have failed to notice the freight train. It was dark, of course, but there is a signal just outside the tunnel, and a freight train is far from silent, quite apart from the warning hoot of the diesel engine, which is routine procedure before entering the tunnel."

Yes, but six centuries ago there were no signals, no wire, no lines, no warning hoots sounding on the air. . . .

"You mean," I said, "that anyone would have to be blind or stone-deaf not to be aware of a train coming up that valley, even when it is some distance off?"

"Well yes, Mr Young. Of course, it is possible to stand at the side of the line as the train goes by—there is plenty of room on either side of the double tracks—and it would seem that this was what Professor Lane did. We have found marks on the ground where he slipped, and up the bank where he dragged himself to the hut."

I thought a moment, and then I said, "Inspector, would it be possible for me to go and see the exact spot myself?"

"As a matter of fact, Mr Young, it was what I was going to suggest, but I was not sure how you would feel about it. It could be helpful, not only to you but to us."

"Then I'm ready whenever you are."

"Shall we say eleven-thirty outside the police station at Tywardreath?"

It was already eleven. I was backing my car out of the garage when Vita came down the drive in the Buick with the boys. They scrambled out, clutching baskets filled with provisions.

"Where are you going?" asked Vita.

"The Inspector wants me to see the spot near the tunnel where they found Magnus," I told her. "They think they know what did it—a freight train that passed there around ten minutes to ten. The driver would already have been in the tunnel when Magnus walked, or slipped, into one of the rear wagons."

"Run along," said Vita sharply to both boys, who were hovering. "Take those things up to Mrs Collins," and when they were out of earshot, "But why should Magnus have been on the line? It makes no sense at all. You know what people are going to say? I heard it in one of the shops, and I felt dreadful. . . . That it must have been suicide."

"Complete and utter drivel," I said.

"Well, I know. . . . But when anyone is well known, and there is a disaster, there's always such talk. And scientists are supposed to be peculiar anyway, border-line cases."

"So are we all," I said, "ex-publishers, policemen, the lot. Don't wait lunch—I don't know when I'll be back."

The Inspector took me to the site he had described over the telephone on the lane above Treverran farm. On the way he told me that they had got in touch with the senior man on Magnus's staff, who had been unable to throw any light on the disaster.

"He was very upset, naturally," the Inspector went on. "He knew Professor Lane was intending to spend the weekend with you, and was looking forward to it. He concurred with you in stating that the Professor was in perfect health and excellent spirits. Incidentally, he did not seem to be aware of his interest in historical sites, but agreed that it could undoubtedly be a private hobby."

We took the Treesmill road out of Tywardreath and turned right at the Stonybridge lane, past Trenadlyn and Treverran, and drew up near the top of the lane, parking beside a gate leading into a field.

"What is difficult to understand," observed the Inspector, "is why, if Treverran Farm was the place that interested Professor Lane, he did not call there, instead of walking across these fields some distance above the farm."

I threw a quick glance around me. Treverran was to the left, above the valley but in a dip, with the railway running below it; and beyond the railway line itself the land sloped down again. Centuries ago the contour of the land would have been the same, but a broad stream would have run through the valley below Treverran Farm, more than a stream, a river, which in high autumn spate would flood the low-lying ground before it entered the waters of Treesmill creek.

"Is there a stream there still?" I asked, pointing to the valley base.

"Still?" repeated the Inspector, puzzled. "There is a ditch at the bottom of the hill, below the railway—you might call it a stream, rather sluggish—and the ground is marshy."

We walked down the field. The railway was already in sight, and just to the right of us was the ominous tunnel-mouth.

"There might have been a road here once," I said, "descending to the valley, and a ford across the stream to the other side."

"Possibly," the Inspector said. "Not much sign of one now, though."

Magnus wanted to ford the stream. Magnus was following someone on horseback who was going to ford the stream. Therefore he moved swiftly. And it was not a summer's evening at dusk on a clear night: it was autumn, and the wind was blowing, and the rain was coming in gusts across the hills. . . .

We descended the field to the railway embankment, close to the tunnel. A short distance to the left there was an archway under the line, forming a passage between one field and another. A number of cattle were standing here, under the arch, seeking shelter from the flies.

"You see," said the Inspector, "there's no need for the farmer or anyone to cross the line to get to the opposite field. They can go through the passage-way there, where those cattle are standing."

"Yes," I said, "but the Professor might not have noticed it, if he was walking higher up the field. It would be more direct to cross the line itself."

"What, climb the embankment, get through the wire, and scramble down the bank on to the line?" he said. "And in the darkness too? I shouldn't care to try it myself."

In point of fact, it was what we did right then, in broad daylight. He led the way, I followed, and once over the wire he pointed to the disused hut, covered with ivy, a few yards higher up the embankment, just above the line.

"The undergrowth is beaten down because we were here yesterday," he told me, "but Professor Lane's tracks were plain enough, where he dragged himself clear of the line and up to the hut; semi-conscious as he must have been, it showed almost superhuman strength and tremendous courage."

Which world had surrounded Magnus, the present or the past? Had the freight train rattled towards the tunnel unobserved, as he scrambled down the bank on to the line? With the engine already in the tunnel did he make to cross the line, which in his vision was grass-meadow still, sloping down to the stream below, and so was struck by the swinging wagon? In either world, it was the *coup de grâce*. He could not have known what hit him. The instinct for survival made him crawl towards the hut, and then, please God, merciful oblivion, no sudden loneliness, no knowledge of imminent death.

We stood there, staring into the empty hut, and the Inspector showed me the spot on the earthen floor where Magnus had died. The place was impersonal, without atmosphere, like some forgotten toolshed with the gardener long gone.

"It hasn't been used for years," he said. "The gangs working on the line used to brew tea here, and eat their pasties. They use the other hut lower down now, and that not often."

We turned away, retracing our footsteps along the overgrown bank to the strands of sagging wire through which we had climbed. I looked across to the opposite hills, some of them thickly wooded. There was a farm to the left, with a smaller building above it, and away to the north another cluster of buildings. I asked their names. The farm was Colwith, and the smaller building had been a schoolhouse once. The third, almost out of sight, was another farm, Strickstenton.

"We're on the borders of three parishes here," the Inspector said, "Tywardreath, St Sampsons or Golant, and Lanlivery. Mr Kendall of Pelyn is a big landowner hereabouts. Now that's a fine old manor house for you, Pelyn, just down the main road on the way to Lostwithiel. Been in the family for centuries."

"How many centuries?"

"Well, Mr Young, I'm no expert. Four, maybe?"

Pelyn could not turn itself into Tregest. None of the names fitted Tregest. Somewhere here, though, within walking distance, Magnus had been following Roger to Oliver Carminowe's dwelling, whether it was manor-house or farm.

"Inspector," I said, "even now, despite all you've shown me, I believe Professor Lane intended to find the head of the stream somewhere in the valley, and cross it to the other side."

"With what object, Mr Young?" He looked at me, not unsympathetic but frankly curious, trying to see my point of view.

"If you get bitten by the past," I said, "whether you're a historian, or an archaeologist, or even a surveyor, it's like a fever in the blood; you never rest content until you've solved the problem before you. I believe that Professor Lane had one object in mind, and that was why he decided to get off at Par rather than St Austell. He was determined to walk up this valley, for some reason which we shall probably never discover, despite the railway-line."

"And stood there, with the train passing, and then walked into the rear?"

"Inspector, I don't know. His hearing was good, his eyesight was good, he loved life. He didn't walk into the back of the train deliberately."

"I hope you'll convince the Coroner, Mr Young, for Professor Lane's sake. You almost convince me."

"Almost?" I asked.

"I'm a policeman, Mr Young, and there's a piece missing somewhere; but I agree with you, we shall probably never find it."

We retraced our steps up the long field to the gate at the top of the hill. As we drove back I asked him if he had any idea how long it would be before the inquest was held.

"I can't tell you exactly," he answered. "A number of factors are involved. The Coroner will do his best to expedite matters, but it may be ten days or a fortnight, especially as the Coroner is bound to sit with a jury, in view of the unusual circumstances of the death. By the way, the pathologist for the area is on holiday, and the Coroner asked Dr Powell if he would perform the autopsy, as he had already examined the body. The doctor agreed. We should have his report some time today."

I thought of the many times Magnus had dissected animals, birds, plants, bringing to his work a cool detachment which I admired. He suggested once that I should watch him remove the organs of a newly-slaughtered pig. I stood it for five minutes, and then my stomach turned. If anyone had to dissect Magnus now, I was glad it was Dr Powell.

We arrived at the police station just as the constable came down the steps. He said something to the Inspector, who turned to me.

"We've finished the examination of Professor Lane's clothes and effects," he said. "We are prepared to hand them over to you if you are willing to accept the responsibility."

"Certainly," I replied. "I doubt if anyone else will claim them. I'm hoping to hear from his lawyer, whoever he may be."

The constable returned in a few minutes with a brown paper parcel. The wallet was separate, lying on the top, and a paperback he must have bought to read in the train, *Some Experiences of an Irish RM* by Somerville and Ross. Anything less conductive to a sudden brainstorm or attempted suicide I could not imagine.

"I hope," I said to the Inspector, "you've noted down the title of the book for the Coroner's attention."

He assured me gravely that he had already done so. I knew I should never open the paper parcel, but I was glad to have the wallet and the stick.

I drove back to Kilmarth feeling tired, dispirited, no nearer to a conclusion. Before I turned off the main road I stopped on the crown of Polmear hill to let a car pass. I recognised the driver—it was Dr Powell. He pulled in at the side of the road by the grass verge, and I did the same. Then he got out and came to my window.

"Hullo," he said. "How are you feeling?"

"All right," I told him. "I've just been out to Treverran tunnel with the Inspector."

"Oh, yes," he said. "Did he tell you I'd done the post mortem?"

"Yes," I said.

"My report goes to the Coroner," he went on, "and you'll know about it in due course. But, unofficially, you would probably like to know that it was the blow on the head that killed Professor Lane, causing extensive haemorrhage to the brain. There were other injuries too, due to falling; there's no doubt he must have walked slap into one of the wagons on the freight train."

"Thank you," I said. "It's good of you to tell me personally."

"Well," he said, "you were his friend, and the most directly concerned. Just one other thing. I had to send the contents of the stomach away for analysis. A matter of routine, actually. Just to satisfy the Coroner and jury he wasn't loaded with whisky or anything else at the time."

"Yes," I said, "yes, of course."

"Well, that's about it," he said. "I'll see you in Court."

He returned to his own car, and I went slowly down the drive to Kilmarth. Magnus drank sparingly in the middle of the day. He could conceivably have had a gin-and-tonic on the train. Possibly a cup of tea during the afternoon. This much, I supposed, would show up in analysis. What else?

I found Vita and the boys already at lunch. There had been a series of telephone-calls throughout the morning, including one from Magnus's lawyer, a man called Dench, and Bill and Diana from Ireland, who had heard the news over the radio.

"It's going to be endless," said Vita. "Did the Inspector say anything about the inquest?"

"Probably not for ten days or a fortnight," I told her.

"Not much holiday for us," she sighed.

The boys went out of the room to collect their next course and she turned to me, her face anxious. "I didn't say anything in front of them," she said in a low voice, "but Bill was aghast at the news, not just because it was such a tragedy anyway, but because he wondered if there was anything awful behind it. He wasn't specific, but he said you'd know what he meant."

I laid down my knife and fork. "Bill said what?"

"He was rather mysterious," she said, "but is it true you told him about some gang of thugs in the neighbourhood who were going about attacking people? He hoped you had told the police."

It only needed that, and Bill's ham-fisted, misplaced efforts to help, to put us all in trouble.

"He's crazy," I said shortly. "I never told him anything of the sort."

"Oh," she said, "oh, well . . ." and then she added, her face still troubled, "I do hope you *have* told the Inspector everything you know."

The boys came back into the dining-room and we finished the meal in silence. Afterwards I took the paper-parcel, the wallet and the walking-stick up to the spare-room. Somehow they seemed to belong there, with the rest of the things hanging in the wardrobe. I would use the stick myself; it was the last thing that Magnus had ever held in his hands.

I remembered the collection at the flat. There had been a gun-stick and a sword-stick, a stick with a telescope at one end, and another with a bird's head on the handle. The one was comparatively simple, with the usual silver knob on top, engraved with Commander Lane's initials. He had been the originator of the craze for family walking-sticks, and vaguely I had a recollection of him showing me this particular example, long ago, when I was staying at Kilmarth. It contained some gadget, I had forgotten what, but by pressing the knob down a spring was released. I tried it; nothing happened. I tried it again and then twisted the knob, and something clicked. I unwound the knob and it came away in my hands, and revealed a minute silver-lined measure, just large enough to hold a half-dram of spirit or other liquid. The measure had been wiped clean, probably by a tissue thrown away or buried, when Magnus set off upon his last walk, but I knew now, with absolute certainty, what it must have contained.

CHAPTER EIGHTEEN

THE LAWYER, Herbert Dench, telephoned again during the afternoon, and expressed great shock at his client's sudden death. I told him that the inquest was not likely to be for ten days or a fortnight, and suggested that he should leave the funeral arrangements to me, coming down himself on the morning of the cremation. This suited him, greatly to my relief, for he sounded what Vita called a "stuffed shirt", and with luck would have the tact to return by an afternoon train, which meant that he wouldn't be on our hands for more than a couple of hours or so.

"I would not trespass upon your time at all, Mr Young," he said, "were it not out of respect for the late Professor Lane and the unhappy circumstances of his death, and for the fact that you are a beneficiary under his will."

"Oh," I said, rather taken aback, "I had not realised . . ." and hoped it would be the walking-sticks.

"It is something I would prefer not to discuss over the telephone," he added.

It was not until I had put down the receiver that I realised I was in a somewhat awkward position, living in Magnus's house rent-free by verbal agreement. It might be the lawyer's intention to kick us out in the shortest possible time, immediately after the inquest, perhaps. The thought stunned me. Surely he would not do such a thing? I would offer to pay rent, of course, but he might bring up some objection, and say the place must be shut up, or handed over to agents prior to a sale. I was depressed and shaken enough, without the prospect of a sudden move to make things worse.

I spent the rest of the afternoon on the telephone, arranging about the funeral, after checking with the police that it was in order to go ahead, and finally ringing back the lawyer to tell him what I had arranged. None of it seemed to have anything to do with Magnus. What the undertaker did, what happened in the meantime to his body, the whole paraphernalia of death before committal to the flames, did not concern the man who had been my friend. It was as though he had become part of that separate world I knew, the world of Roger, of Isolda.

Vita came into the library when I had finished telephoning. I was sitting at Magnus's desk by the window, staring out to sea.

"Darling," she said, "I've been thinking," and she came and stood behind me, putting her hands on my shoulders. "When the inquest is over, don't you think it would be best if we went away? It would be rather awkward for us to go on staying here, and sad for you, and in a way the whole point of it has gone, hasn't it?"

"What point?" I asked.

"Well, the loan of the house, now Magnus is dead. I can't help feeling an interloper, and that we've really no right to be here. Surely it would be much more sensible if we spent the rest of the holidays somewhere else? It's only the beginning of August. Bill was saying over the telephone how lovely Ireland is; they've found a delightful hotel in Connemara, some old castle or other, with its own private fishing."

"I bet he has," I said. "Twenty guineas a night, and full of your compatriots."

"Don't be unfair! He was just trying to be helpful. He took it for granted you would want to get away from here."

"Well, I don't," I said. "Not unless the lawyer kicks us out, and that's a different matter."

I told her that the cremation was fixed for Thursday, and that Dench would be coming down, and perhaps some of Magnus's staff as well. The prospect of guests for lunch or dinner, or even the night, took her mind off the longer-term suggestion of Ireland, but as it turned out we were spared the worst of it, Dench and Magnus's senior assistant, John Willis, elected to travel down together through the Wednesday night, attend the cremation, accept our hospitality for lunch, and return to London by a night-train. The boys were sent off for the whole of Thursday for a fishing expedition in charge of the obliging Tom.

I remember little of the cremation service, beyond thinking how Magnus might have devised a simpler method of disposing of the dead by chemicals instead of by fire. Our companions in mourning, Herbert Dench and John Willis, were quite unlike what I had imagined. The lawyer was big, hearty, un-pompous, ate an enormous lunch, and regaled us while we consumed our funeral meats with stories of Hindu widows committing suttee on their husbands' pyres. He had been born in India, and swore he had witnessed such a sacrifice as a babe in arms.

John Willis was a little mouse-like man, with intent eyes behind horn-rimmed spectacles, who would not have looked out of place behind a bank's grille; I could not picture him at Magnus's elbow, ministering to live monkeys or dissecting their brain cells. He barely uttered. Not that this signified, for the lawyer spoke enough for all.

Lunch over, we walked through to the library, and Herbert Dench bent to his dispatch-case for a formal reading of the will, in which apparently John Willis figured as well as I. Vita, tactfully, was about to withdraw, but the lawyer told her to stay.

"No necessity for that, Mrs Young," he said cheerfully. "It's very short and to the point."

He was right. Legal language apart, Magnus had left whatever financial assets he possessed at the time of his death to his own college for the advancement of biophysics. His flat in London and his personal effects there were to be sold, and the money given to the same cause, with the exception of his library, which he bequeathed to John Willis in gratitude for ten years of professional co-operation and personal friendship. Kilmarth, with all its contents, he left to me, for my own use or to dispose of, as I wished, in memory of years of friendship dating back to undergraduate days, and because the former occupants of the house would have wished it so. And that was all.

"I take it," said the lawyer, smiling, "that by the former occupants he is referring to his parents, Commander and Mrs Lane, whom I believe you knew?"

"Yes," I said, bewildered, "yes, I was very fond of them both."

"Well, there we are. It's a delightful house. I hope you will be very happy here."

I looked at Vita. She was lighting a cigarette, her usual defence in a moment of sudden shock. "How . . . how extraordinarily generous of the Professor," she said. "I really don't know what to say. Of course it's up to Dick whether he intends to keep it or not. Our future plans are in a state of flux at present."

There was a moment's awkward silence, as Herbert Dench looked from one to the other of us.

"Naturally," he said, "you will have a great deal to discuss together. You realise, of course, that the house and contents will have to be valued for probate. I would appreciate it if I could see over it, by the way, if it wouldn't be too much trouble?"

"Why, of course."

We all rose to our feet, and Vita said, "The Professor had a laboratory in the basement, a most alarming place—at least, so my small sons thought. I suppose the things there would hardly go with the house but should be returned to his laboratory in London? Perhaps Mr Willis would know what they are."

Her face was all innocence, but I had the impression that her mention of the laboratory was deliberate, and she wanted to know what was there.

"A laboratory?" queried the lawyer. "Did the Professor do any work down here?" He addressed himself to Willis.

The little mouse-like man blinked behind his horn-rimmed spectacles. "I very much doubt it," he said with diffidence, "and, if he did, it would be of little scientific importance, and have no connection with his work in London. He may have made a few experiments, just to amuse himself on a rainy day—certainly nothing more, or he would have mentioned it to me."

Good man. If he knew anything he was not going to commit himself. I could see that Vita was on the point of saying I had told her the contents of the laboratory were of inestimable value, so I suggested that we should inspect the laboratory before visiting the rest of the house.

"Come along," I said to Willis, "you're the expert. The room used to be an old laundry in Commander Lane's day, and Magnus kept a lot of bottles and jars in it."

He looked at me, but said nothing. We all trooped down to the basement, and I opened the door.

"There you are," I said. "Nothing very exciting. Just a lot of old jars, as I told you."

Vita's face was a study as she looked around her. Amazement, disbelief, and then a swift glance of enquiry at me. No monkey's head, no embryo kittens, only the empty rows of bottles. She had the supreme intelligence to remain silent.

"Well, well," said the lawyer, "the valuer might put a price of sixpence apiece on the jars. What do you say, Willis?"

The biophysicist ventured a smile. "I would think," he said, "that Professor Lane's mother may have preserved fruit here in former days."

"A still-room, didn't they call them?" laughed the lawyer. "The still-room maid would make preserves for the whole year. Look at the hooks in the ceiling! They probably hung the meat here too. Great sides of ham. Well, Mrs Young, this will be your province, not your husband's. I recommend an electric washing-machine in the corner to save your laundry bills. Expensive to install, but it will pay for itself in a couple of years, with a young family."

He turned, still laughing, back into the passage, and we followed. I locked the door behind me. Willis, who was hovering in the rear, bent to pick up something from the stone floor. It was a label from one of the jars. He gave it to me without a word, and I put it in my pocket. Then we tramped upstairs to inspect the remainder of the house, Herbert Dench making the remarkable suggestion that if we wanted to turn the property into an investment we might split the whole place up into flatlets for summer visitors, keeping for our own use the bedroom-suite with the view of the sea. He was still extolling the idea to Vita as we wandered round the garden. I saw Willis glance at his watch.

"You must have had about enough of us," he said. "I told Dench on the way down that we would call in at Divisional Headquarters at Liskeard and answer any questions the police might want to put to us. If you'd telephone for a taxi we could go there straight away, and have dinner in Liskeard later before catching the night train."

"I'll drive you myself," I said. "Hold on, there's something I want to show you." I went upstairs, and after a few minutes came back with the walking-stick. "This was near Magnus's body. It belongs with the others in the London flat. Do you think they will let me keep it?"

"Surely," he said, "and the other sticks too. I'm so glad you've got this house, by the way, and I hope you won't part with it."

"I don't intend to."

Vita and Dench were still a short distance off on the terrace.

"I think," said Willis quietly, "we had better tell more or less the same story at the inquest. Magnus was an enthusiastic walker, and if he wanted some exercise after hours in the train it was typical of him."

"Yes," I said.

"Incidentally, a young friend of mine, a student, has been looking up historical stuff for Magnus at the BM and the Public Record Office. Do you want him to continue?"

I hesitated. "It might be useful. Yes. . . . If he turns anything up ask him to send it to me here."

"I'll do that."

I noticed for the first time an expression of loss, of emptiness, behind the horn-rimmed spectacles.

"What are your own plans?" I asked.

"I shall go on just the same, I suppose," he said. "Try to carry on something of Magnus's work. But it will be tough going. As boss and colleague he will be irreplaceable. You probably realise that."

"I do."

The others came up, and nothing further was said between Willis and myself. After a cup of tea, which none of us wanted, but Vita insisted on getting, Willis suggested the move to Liskeard. I knew now why Magnus had chosen him as senior member of his staff. Professional competence apart, loyalty and discretion were the qualities behind that mouse-like appearance.

Once we were in the car, Dench asked if we might cover part of the route Magnus had taken on the Friday night. I drove them along the Stonybridge lane past Treverran farm and up to the gate near the top of the hill, and pointed across the fields down to the tunnel.

"Incredible," Dench murmured, "quite incredible. And dark, too, at the time. I don't like it, you know."

"How do you mean?" I asked.

"Well, if it doesn't make sense to me it won't to the Coroner, or to the jury. They're bound to see something behind it."

"What sort of thing?"

"Some sort of compulsion to get to that tunnel. And once he found it we know what happened."

"I don't agree," said Willis. "As you say, it was dark at the time or nearly dark. The tunnel wouldn't have shown up from here, or the line either. I believe he had the idea to go down into the valley, perhaps take a look at that farmhouse from the other side, and when he got to the bottom of the field the railway viaduct interfered with his view. He scrambled up the bank to find out the lie of the land, and the train hit him."

"It's possible. But what an extraordinary thing to do."

"Extraordinary to the legal mind," said Willis, "but not to Professor Lane. He was an explorer in every sense of the word."

After I had landed them safely at the police headquarters I turned back for home. Home. . . . The word had a new significance. It was my home now. The place belonged to me, as it had once belonged to Magnus. The strain that had been upon me through the day began to lift, and the weight of depression, too. Magnus was dead; I should never see him again, never hear his voice, rejoice in his company or be aware of his presence in the background of my life, but the link between us would never be broken because the home that had been his was mine. Therefore I could not lose him. Therefore I should not be alone.

I passed the entrance to Boconnoc, which in that other time had been Bockenod, before descending the hill to Lostwithiel, and thought of poor Sir John Carminowe, already infected with the dreaded smallpox, riding beside Joanna Champernoune's clumsy chariot on that windy October night in 1331, to die a month later, having enjoyed his position as Keeper of Restormel and

Tremerton Castles for barely seven months. On the other side of Lostwithiel I took the road to Treesmill, so that I could have a closer view of the farms situated on the opposite side of the valley from the railway. Strickstenton was on the left-hand side of the narrow road, and, from the brief glimpse I had from the car, of considerable age, and what a tourist brochure would describe as "picturesque". The pasture land belonging to it sloped downwards to a wood.

Once I was out of sight of the house I got out of the car and looked across to the railway on the other side of the valley. The tunnel showed up plainly, and even as I watched a train emerged like a straggling snake, yellow-headed, evil, and wound its way below Treverran Farm and disappeared down to the lower valley. The freight train that had killed Magnus had appeared from the opposite direction, climbing the rising ground and vanishing into the tunnel, a reptile seeking cover in the underworld, as Magnus, who had neither seen nor heard it, dragged himself, dying, to the hut above. I drove on down the twisting lane, noting on my left the turning which, I judged, led past Colwith Farm to the bottom of the valley and what remained of the original river stream. At some time, before the railway cut into the land, there would have been a track leading from Great Treverran across the valley to its smaller neighbour, Little Treverran. Either farm might be the Tregest of the Carminowes.

I went on down to Treesmill, and up the hill to the call-box in Tywardreath. I dialled the Kilmarth number, and Vita answered.

"Darling," I said, "it seems rather rude to leave Dench and Willis on their own in Liskeard, so I think I'll hang around until they have finished with the police, and then have dinner with them."

"Oh well," she said, "if you must. But don't be late. No need to wait for the train."

"Probably not," I told her. "It depends how much there is to discuss."

"All right. I'll expect you when I see you."

I rang off, and returned to the car. Then I drove back again to Treesmill and up the twisting lane, and this time took the turning that led to Colwith. The lane went on, past the farm, as I had thought it would, becoming steeper, and finally petered out in a small water-splash at the bottom of the hill. To the left, across a cattle-grid, was a narrow entrance to Little Treverran. The buildings themselves were out of sight, but a board with lettering on it said: "W. P. Kelly. Woodworker."

I risked the water-splash and parked the car, out of sight of the lane, in the field beyond, close to a line of trees and only a few hundred yards from the railway.

I looked at my watch. It was a little after five. I opened the boot of the car and took out the walking-stick, which I had primed, in the dressing-room, with the last of bottle A, before showing it to John Willis in the library.

CHAPTER NINETEEN

I was snowing. The soft flakes fell upon my head and my hands, and the world all about me was suddenly white, no lush green summer grass, no line of trees, and the snow fell steadily, blotting the hills from sight. There were no farm-buildings anywhere near me—nothing but the black river, about twenty foot broad where I was standing, and the snow, which had drifted high on either bank, only to slither into the water as the mass caved in from the weight, revealing the muddied earth beneath. It was bitter cold; not the swift, cutting blast that sweeps across high ground, but the dank chill of a valley where winter sunshine does not penetrate, nor cleansing wind. The silence was the more deadly, for the river rippled past me without sound, and the stunted willows and alder growing beside it looked like mutes with outstretched arms, grotesquely shapeless because of the burden of snow they bore upon their limbs. And all the while the soft flakes fell, descending from a pall of sky that merged with the white land beneath.

My mind, usually clear when I had taken the drug, was stupefied, baffled; I had expected something akin to the autumn day that I remembered from the previous time, when Bodrugan had been drowned, and Roger carried the dripping body in his arms towards Isolda. Now I was alone, without a guide; only the river at my feet told me I was in the valley.

I followed its course upstream, groping like a blind man, knowing by instinct that if I kept the river on my left I must be moving north, and that somewhere the strip of water would narrow, the banks would close, and I should find a bridge or ford to take me to the other side. I had never felt more helpless or lost. Time, in this other world, had hitherto been calculated by the height of the sun in the sky, or, as when I traversed the Lampetho valley at night, by the stars overhead; but now, in this silence and beneath the falling snow, there was no means of gauging whether it was morning or afternoon. I was lost, not in the present, with familiar landmarks close at hand, the reassuring presence of the car, but in the past.

The first sound broke the silence, a splash in the river ahead, and moving swiftly I saw an otter dive from the further bank and swim his way upstream. As he did so a dog followed him, and then a second, and immediately there were some half-dozen of them yelping and crying at the river's brink, splashing their way into the water in chase of the otter. Someone shouted, the shout taken up by another, and a group of men came running towards the river through the falling snow, shouting, laughing, encouraging the dogs, and I saw they were coming from a belt of trees just beyond me, where the river curved. Two of them scrambled down the bank into the water, thrashing it with their sticks, and a third, holding a long whip, cracked it in the air, stinging the ear of one of the dogs still crouching on the bank, which plunged after its companions.

I drew nearer, to watch them, and saw how the river narrowed a hundred yards or so beyond, while on the left, at the entrance to a copse of trees, the land fell away and the stream formed a sheet of water like a miniature lake, a film of ice upon its surface.

Somehow the men and the dogs, between them, drove the hunted otter into the gulley that fed the lake, and in a moment they were upon him, the dogs crying, the men thrashing with their sticks. The dogs floundered as the ice cracked, the surface crimsoned, and blood spattered the film of white above black water as the otter, seized between snapping jaws, was dragged from the hole he sought, and torn to pieces where the ice held firm.

The lake can have held little depth, for the men, hallooing and calling to the dogs, strode forward on to it, careless of the crack appearing suddenly from one end to the other. Foremost among them was the man with the long whip, who stood out from his fellows because of his height, and his dress as well, a padded surcoat buttoned to the throat and a high beaver hat upon his head, shaped like a cone.

"Drive them clear," he shouted, "to the bank on the further side. I'd as soon lose the lot of you as one of these," and bending suddenly, amongst the pack of yelping hounds, he lifted what remained of the otter from the midst of them and flung it across the lake to the snow-covered verge. The dogs, baulked of their prey, struggled and slid across the ice to retrieve it where it now lay, while the men, less nimble than the animals, and hampered by their clothing, floundered and splashed in the breaking ice, shouting, cursing, jerkins and hoods caked white with the falling snowflakes.

The scene was part brutal, part macabre, for the man with the conical hat, once he knew his hounds were safe, turned his attention, laughing, to his companions in misfortune. While he himself was wet now to the thigh, he at least had boots to protect his feet, while his attendants, as I supposed they were, had some of them lost their shoes when the ice broke, and were thrashing about with frozen hands in useless search of them. Their master, laughing still, regained the bank, and, lifting his conical hat a moment, shook the snowflakes clear before replacing it once more. I recognised the ruddy face and the long jaw, although he was some twenty feet away. It was Oliver Carminowe.

He was staring hard in my direction, and although reason told me he could not see me, and I had no part in his world, the way he stood there, motionless, his head turned towards me, disregarding his grumbling attendants, gave me a strange feeling of unease, almost of fear.

"If you want to have speech with me, come across and say so," he called suddenly. The shock of what I thought discovery sent me forward to the lake's edge, and then, with relief, I saw Roger standing beside me to become, as it were, my spokesman and my cover. How long he had been there I did not know. He must have walked behind me along the river bank.

"Greetings to you, Sir Oliver!" he cried. "The drifts are shoulder-high above Treesmill, and your side of the valley too, so Rob Rosgof's widow told me at the ferry. I wondered how you fared, and the lady Isolda too."

"We fare well enough," answered the other, "with food enough to last a siege of several weeks, which God forbid. The wind may change within a day or two and bring us rain. Then, if the road does not flood, we shall leave for Carminowe. As to my lady, she stays in her chamber half the day sulking, and gives me little of her company." He spoke contemptuously, watching Roger all the while, who moved nearer to the river bank. "Whether she follows me to Carminowe is her concern," he continued. "My daughters are obedient to my will, if she is not. Joanna is already promised to John Petyt of Ardeva, and, although a child still, prinks and preens before the glass as if she were already a bride of fourteen years and ripe for her strapping husband. You may tell her godmother Lady Champernoune so, with my respects. She may wish a like fortune for herself before many years have passed." He burst out laughing, and then, pointing to the hounds scavenging beneath the trees, said, "If you have no fear of fording the river where the plank has rotted, I will find an otter's paw which you may present to Lady Champernoune with my compliments. It may remind her of her brother Otto, being wet and bloody, and she can nail it on the walls of Trelawn as a memento to his name. The other paw I will deliver to my own lady for a similar purpose, unless the dogs have swallowed it."

He turned his back and walked towards the trees, calling to his hounds, while Roger, moving forward up the river bank, and I beside him, came to a rough bridge, made out of lengths of log bound together, the whole slippery with the fallen snow, and partly sagging in the water. Oliver Carminowe and his attendants stood watching as Roger set foot upon the rotting bridge, and when it collapsed beneath his weight and he slipped and fell, soaking himself above his thighs, they roared in unison, expecting to see him turn again and claw the bank. But he strode on, the water coming nearly to his waist, and reached the other side, while I, dry-shod, followed in his wake. He walked directly to the edge of the copse where Carminowe stood, whip in hand, and said, "I will deliver the otter's paw, if you will give it to me."

I thought he would receive a lash from the whip across his face, and I believe he expected the same himself, but Carminowe, smiling, his whip raised, lashed suddenly amongst the dogs instead, and whipping them from the torn body of the otter took the knife from his belt, and cut off two of the remaining paws.

"You have more stomach than my steward at Carminowe," he said. "I respect you for that, if for nothing else. Here, take the paw, and hang it in your kitchen at Kylmerth, amongst the silver pots and platters you have doubtless stolen from the Priory. But first walk up the hill with us and pay your respects to Lady Carminowe in person. She may prefer a man, once in a while, to the tame squirrel she occupies her days with."

Roger took the paw from him and put it in his pouch, saying nothing, and we entered the copse and began threading our way through the snow-laden trees, walking steadily uphill, but whether to right or left I had no idea, having lost all sense of direction, knowing only that the river was behind us and the snow was falling still.

A track packed high with snow on either side led to a stone-built house, tucked snugly against the hill; and, while Carminowe's attendants still straggled in our rear, he himself kicked open the door before us and we entered a square hall, to be greeted at once by the house-dogs, fawning upon him, and the two children, Joanna and Margaret, whom I had last seen riding their ponies across the Treesmill ford on a summer's afternoon. A third, somewhat older than the others, about sixteen, whom I took for one of Carminowe's daughters by his first marriage, stood smiling by the hearth, nor did she embrace him, but pouted with a sort of petulant grace when she saw he was not alone.

"My ward, Sybell, who seeks to teach my children better manners than their mother," Carminowe said.

The steward bowed and turned to the two children, who, after having kissed their father, came to welcome him. The elder, Joanna, had grown, and showed some sign of dawning self-consciousness, as her father had said, by blushing, and tossing her long hair out of her eyes, and giggling, but the younger, with still some years to go before she too ripened for the marriage-market, struck out her small hand to Roger and smote him on the knee.

"You promised me a new pony when last we met," she said, "and a whip like your brother Robbie's. I'll have no truck with a man who fails to keep his word."

"The pony awaits you, and the whip too," answered Roger gravely, "if Alice will bring you across the valley when the snow melts."

"Alice has left us," replied the child. "We have her to mind us now," and she pointed a disdainful finger at the ward Sybell, "and she's too grand to ride pillion behind you or Robbie."

She looked so much like her mother as she spoke that I loved her for it, and Roger must have seen the likeness too, for he smiled and touched her hair, but her father, irritated, told the child sharply to hold her tongue or he would send her supperless to bed.

"Here, dry yourself by the fire," he said abruptly, kicking the dogs out of the way, "and you, Joanna, warn your mother the steward has crossed the valley from Tywardreath and has a message from his mistress, if she cares to receive him."

He took the remaining otter's paw from his surcoat and dangled it in front of Sybell. "Shall we give it to Isolda, or will you wear it to keep you warm?" he teased. "It will soon dry, furry and soft, inside your kirtle, the nearest thing to a man's hand on a cold night."

She shrieked in affectation and backed away, while he pursued her, laughing, and I saw by the expression in Roger's eyes that he had fully grasped the relationship between guardian and ward. The snow might remain upon the hills for days or weeks; there was little at the moment to tempt the master of this establishment back to Carminowe.

"My mother will see you, Roger," said Joanna, returning to the hall, and we crossed a passage-way into the room beyond.

Isolda was standing by the window, watching the falling snow, while a small red squirrel, a bell around its neck, squatted upon its haunches at her feet, pawing at her gown. As we entered she turned and stared, and although to my prejudiced eyes she looked as beautiful as ever I realised, shocked, that she had become much thinner, paler, and there was a white streak in the front of her golden hair.

"I am glad to see you, Roger," she said. "There have been a few encounters between our households of late, and we are seldom here at Tregest these days, as you know well. How is my cousin? You have a message from her?"

Her voice that I remembered, clear and hard, defiant, almost, had become flat, toneless. Then, sensing that Roger wished to speak to her in private, she told her daughter Joanna to leave them alone.

"I bear no message, my lady," said Roger quietly. "The family are at Trelawn, or were, when I last had word. I came out of respect for you, Rob Rosgof's widow having told me you were here, and were not well."

"I'm as well as I ever shall be," she answered, "and whether here or at Carminowe the days are much the same."

"That's ill-spoken, my lady," said Roger. "You showed more spirit once."

"Once, yes," she replied, "but I was younger then . . . I came and went as I pleased, for Sir Oliver was more frequently at Westminster. Now, whether from malice through not obtaining Sir John's position as Keeper of the King's forests and parks in Cornwall, as he hoped, he wastes his days keeping women instead. The present fancy is hardly more than a child. You have seen Sybell?"

"I have, my lady."

"It's true she is his ward. If I should die it would be convenient to both of them, for he could marry her and install her at Carminowe in all legality."

She stooped to pick up the pet squirrel at her feet, and, smiling for the first time since we had come into the small room, which was as sparsely furnished as a nun's cell, she said, "This is my confidante now. He takes hazel nuts from my hand and regards me wisely all the while with his bright eyes." Then, serious once more, she added, "I am kept prisoner, you know, both here and when we are at Carminowe. I am prevented even from sending word to my brother Sir William Ferrers at Bere, who is told by his wife that I have gone out of my mind and am therefore dangerous. They all believe it. Sick in body, indeed, I have been, and in pain, but so far it has not sent me mad."

Roger moved silently to the door, opened it, and listened. There was still the sound of laughter from the hall: the otter's paw continued to cause diversion. He closed the door again.

"Whether Sir William believes it or not I cannot say," he said, "but talk of your illness there has been, and for some months. That is why I have come, my lady, to prove it a lie for myself, and now I know it to be so."

Isolda, with the squirrel in her arms, might have been her small daughter Margaret as she looked at the steward steadily, weighing in the balance his trustworthiness.

"I did not like you once," she said. "You had too shrewd an eye, casting about you for your own advantage, and, because it suited you to serve a woman rather than a man, you let my cousin Sir Henry Champernoune die."

"My lady," said Roger, "he was mortally sick. He would have died anyway within a few weeks."

"Perhaps, but the way he went showed undue haste. It taught me one thing—to beware of potions brewed by a French monk. Sir Oliver will seek to rid himself of me by other methods, a dagger's thrust or strangulation. He won't wait for nature to put an end to me." She dropped the squirrel on the floor and, moving to the window, looked out once more at the still falling snow. "Before he does," she said, "I'll rather take myself outdoors and perish. With the country covered as it is today I'd freeze the sooner. How about it, Roger? Carry me in a sack upon your back and cast me somewhere at the cliff's edge? I'd thank you for it."

She meant it as a joke, if somewhat twisted, but crossing to the window beside her he stared up at the pall of sky and pursed his lips in a soundless whistle.

"It could be done, my lady," he said, "if you had the courage."

"I have the courage if you have the means," she replied.

They stared at one another, an idea suddenly taking root in both their minds, and she said swiftly, "If I went from here, and thence to my brother's at Bere, Sir Oliver would not dare to follow me, for he could never sustain his lies about my sick mind. But in this weather the roads would be impassable. I could not reach Devon."

"Not immediately," he said, "but once the roads are fit it could be done."

"Where would you hide me?" she asked. "He has only to cross the valley to search the Champernoune demesne above Treesmill."

"Let him do so," answered Roger. "He would find it barred and empty, with my lady at Trelawn. There are other hiding-places, if you cared to trust yourself to me."

"Such as where?"

"My own house, Kylmerth. Robbie is there, and my sister Bess. It's nothing but a rough farm, but you are welcome to it, until the weather mends."

She said nothing for a moment, and I could see, by the expression in her eyes, that she still had some lingering doubt of his integrity.

"It's a question of choice," she said. "To stay here a prisoner, at the mercy of my husband's whim, who can hardly wait to rid himself of a wife who is a lasting reproach, and an encumbrance too, or throw myself on your hospitality, which you may deny when it pleases you to do so."

"It will not please me," he answered, "nor will it ever be denied, until you say the word yourself."

She looked out once again at the falling snow and the slowly darkening sky, which foretold not only worsening weather to come but the approach of evening and all the hazards of a winter's night.

"I am ready," she said, and throwing open a chest against the wall drew out a hooded cloak, a woollen kirtle, and a pair of leather shoes that must surely never have seen service out of doors except thrust into a covering bag when she rode side-saddle.

"My own daughter Joanna, who overtops me now, climbed from this same window a week ago," she said, "after a wager with Margaret that she had grown too fat. I am thin enough, in all conscience. What do you say? Do I lack spirit now?"

"You never lacked it, my lady," he answered, "only the spur to prick you to endeavour. You know the wood below your pasture-land?"

"I should," she said. "I rode in it most days when I was free to do so."

"Then lock your door, after I have left the room, climb from the window, and make your way to it. I will see that the track is deserted and the household all within, and will tell Sir Oliver that you dismissed me and wish to be alone."

"And the children? Joanna will be aping Sybell, as she has done continually these past weeks, but Margaret . . ." she paused, her courage ebbing. "Once I lose Margaret, there is nothing left."

"Only your will to live," he said. "If you keep that, you keep all things. And your children too."

"Go quickly," she said, "before I change my mind."

As we left the room I heard her lock the door, and looking at Roger I wondered if he knew what he had done, urging her to risk her life and her future in an escapade that must surely fail. The house had grown silent. We walked along the passage to the hall and found it empty, except for the two children and the dogs. Joanna was pirouetting before the looking-glass, her long hair dressed in braids with a ribbon threaded through it which had, a short time before, been on Sybell's head; while Margaret sat astride a bench, her father's conical hat upon her head and his long whip in her hand. She looked at Roger severely when he entered.

"Observe now," she said, "I am obliged to make do with a bench for a horse and borrowed plumage for equipment. I'll not remind you of your failings again, my master."

"Nor shall you have to," he told her. "I know my duty. Where is your father?"

"He's above," answered the child. "He cut his finger severing the otter's paw, and Sybell is dressing it for him."

"He'll not thank you to disturb him," said Joanna. "He likes to sleep before he dines, and Sybell sings to him. It makes him drop off the sooner and wake with better appetite. Or so he says."

"I do not doubt it," replied Roger. "In that event, please thank Sir Oliver for me and bid him goodnight. Your mother is tired and does not wish to see anyone. Perhaps you will tell him so?"

"I may," said Joanna, "if I remember."

"I'll tell him," said Margaret, "and wake him too, if he does not descend by six o'clock. Last night we dined at seven, and I can't abide late hours."

Roger wished them both goodnight and, opening the hall-door, stepped outside, closing it softly behind him. He stole round to the back of the house and listened. There were sounds coming from the kitchen quarters, but windows and doors were fastened tight, and the shutters barred. The hounds were yelping from outbuildings in the rear. It would be dark within half an hour or even less; already the copse below the field was dim, shrouded by the pall of snow, and the opposite hills were bleak and bare under the grey sky. The tracks we had made ascending to the house were almost blotted out by the fresh-fallen snow, but beside them were new prints, closer together, like those of a child who, hurrying for shelter, runs like a dancer upon her toes. Roger covered them with his own long stride, disturbing the ground, kicking the snow in front of him as he walked rapidly downhill towards the copse; and now if anyone should venture forth before darkness came they would see nothing but the tracks he had made himself, and those would be blotted too within the hour.

She was waiting for us by the entrance to the wood, carrying her pet squirrel, her cloak drawn close around her and her hood fastened under her chin. But her long gown, which she had tried to fasten up under the belted cloak, had slipped down again below her ankles and hung about her feet like a dripping valance. She was smiling, the smile her daughter Margaret would have worn had she too set forth on some adventure, with the promise of a pony at the end of it instead of a bleak unknown.

"I dressed my pillow in my night-attire," she said, "and heaped the covers over it. It may fool them for a while, should they break down the door."

"Give me your hand," he said. "Disregard your skirts and let them trail. Bess will find warm clothes for you at home."

She laughed and put her hand in his, and as she did so I felt as if it were in mine as well, and that the pair of us were lifting, dragging her through the fallen snow, and he was no longer a steward bound in the service of another woman and I a phantom from a later world, but both of us were men sharing a common purpose and a common love that neither of us, in his time or mine, would ever dare make plain.

When we came to the river and the rotten bridge that lay half-broken in mid-stream he said to her, "You must trust me once again and let me carry you across, as I would your daughter."

"But if you let me fall," she answered, "I will not clout you about the head, as Margaret would."

He laughed, and bore her safely to the other side, once more soaking himself nearly to the waist. We went on walking through the little line of stunted, shrouded trees, the silence all about us no longer ominous, as it had been when I walked alone, but hushed with a sort of magic, and a strange excitement too.

"The snow will be thicker in the valley around Treverran," he said, "and if Ric Treverran should see us he might not hold his tongue. Have you breath enough left to strike out into the open and climb the hill to the track above? Robbie awaits me there with the ponies. You shall choose which of us you please to ride behind. I am the more cautious."

"Then I choose Robbie," she said. "Tonight I bid farewell to caution, and for ever."

We turned left and began to climb the hill out of the valley, the river behind us, the snow reaching above the knees of my companions with every step, making progress laborious and slow.

"Wait," he said, letting go her hand, "there may be a drift ahead before we strike the path," and he plunged upwards, sweeping the snow aside with both his hands, so that for a moment, as he walked on alone to higher ground, I was left with her, and could stare for a brief instant at the small, pale, resolute face beneath the hood.

"All's well," he called. "The snow is firmer here. I'll come and fetch you."

I watched him turn and advance, half-sliding down the slope towards her, and it seemed to me suddenly that two men were moving there, not one, and both of them were holding out their hands to help her climb. It must be Robbie, having heard his brother's voice, who had come down from the track above.

Some instinct warned me not to move, not to climb, but to let her go alone and grasp their hands. She went from me and I lost sight of her, and of Roger, and of the third shadowy figure too, in a sudden great pall of snow that blotted all of them from sight. I stood there, shaking, the strands of wire between me and the line, and it was not snow that blanketed the opposite hills and the high bank, but the grey canvas hangings looped to the wagons of the freight-train as it rattled and lumbered through the tunnel.

CHAPTER TWENTY

SELF-PRESERVATION IS common to all living things, linked perhaps to that older brain which Magnus said forms part of our natural inheritance. Certainly in my own case instinct transmitted a danger signal: had it not done so I should have died as he did, through the same cause. I remember stumbling blindly away from the railway embankment to the protection of the passage-way where the cattle had sheltered, and I heard the wagons thunder over my head as they passed down the line into the valley. Then I crossed a hedge and found myself in a field behind Little Treverran, home of the wood-worker, and so on to the field where I had left the car.

There was no nausea, no vertigo, the instinct to "awake" had spared me this as well as my life, but as I sat huddled behind the wheel, still shaking all over, I wondered whether, had Magnus and I ventured forth together on that Friday night, there would have been what the reporters like to term a double tragedy. Or would both of us have survived? It would never now be proved; the opportunity for us to wander together in another time had gone for ever. One thing I knew, which no one else would ever know, and that was why he had died. He had stretched out his hand to help Isolda in the snow. If instinct had warned him otherwise he had disregarded it, unlike myself, and therefore showed the greater courage.

It was after half-past seven when I started the car, and as I drove over the water-splash I still did not know how far I had walked during the excursion to the other world, or which farm or former site had proved to be Tregest. Somehow it no longer mattered. Isolda had escaped, and on that winter's night of 1332, or '33, perhaps even later, had been bound for Kilmarth; whether she reached it or not I might discover. Not now, nor tomorrow, but one day. . . . My immediate purpose must be to conserve my strength and mental alertness for the inquest, and above all watch out for the after-effects of the drug. It would not do to appear in Court with a couple of bloodshot eyes and an inexplicable sweating sickness, especially with Dr Powell's experienced eye upon me.

I had no desire for food, and when I arrived home at about half-past eight, having parked the car at the top of the hill to while away the time, I called to Vita that we had all dined early at the hotel in Liskeard, and I was dead-beat and wanted to go to bed. She and the boys were eating in the kitchen, and I went straight upstairs without disturbing them, and put away the walking-stick in the dressing-room cupboard. I knew now, to the fullest extent, what it felt like to lead what is called a "double life". The walking-stick, the bottles locked in the suitcase, were like keys to some woman's flat, to be used when opportunity offered; but more tempting still, and more insidious, was the secret knowledge that the woman herself might be under my own roof, even now, tonight, in her own time.

I lay in bed, my hands behind my head, wondering how Robbie and the wild-haired sister Bess received their unexpected visitor. First warm clothes for Isolda, and food before the smoky hearth, the youngsters tongue-tied in her presence, Roger playing host; then groping her way to bed up that ladder to one of the straw-filled mattresses, hearing the cattle moving and stamping in the byre beneath her. Sleep might come early, through exhaustion, but it would more likely be late, because of the strangeness of everything about her, and because she would be thinking about her children, wondering whether she would see them again.

I shut my eyes, trying to picture that dark, cold loft. It would correspond in position, surely, to the small back bedroom above the basement, used in other days by Mrs Lane's unfortunate cook, and filled today with discarded trunks and cardboard boxes. How near to Roger in the kitchen below, how unattainable, both then and now!

"Darling . . ."

It was Vita bending over me, fantasy and confusion combining to make her other than she was, and when I pulled her down beside me it was not the living woman and my wife whom I held but the phantom one I sought and who I knew, in reality and the present, never could respond. Presently, when I opened my eyes—for I must have dozed off for a while—she was sitting on the stool before the dressing-table, smothering her face with cream.

"Well," she said smiling, looking at me in the glass, "if that's the way you celebrate your inheritance of this place I'm all for it." .

The towel, wrapped turban-fashion round her head, and the mask of cream gave her a clown-like appearance, and suddenly I felt revolted by the puppet world in which I found myself, and desired no part of it, neither now, nor tomorrow, nor at any time. I wanted to vomit. I got out of bed and said, "I'm going to sleep in the dressing-room."

She stared at me, her eyes like holes in the mask. "What on earth's the matter?" she said. "What have I done?"

"You've done nothing," I told her. "I want to sleep alone."

I went through the bathroom to the dressing-room and she followed me, the silly shift she wore in bed flouncing round her knees, grotesquely ill-suited to the turban; and it struck me for the first time that the varnish on her finger-nails made her hands like claws.

"I don't believe you've been with those men at all," she said. "You left them in Liskeard and have been drinking at some pub. That's it, isn't it?"

"No," I answered.

"Something's happened, all the same. You've been somewhere else, you're not telling me the truth; everything you say and do is one long lie. You lied about the laboratory to the lawyer and that Willis man, you lied to the police about the way the Professor died. For God's sake what's behind it? Did you have some secret pact between you both that he would kill himself, and you knew about it all the time?"

I put my hands on her shoulders and began to push her out of the room. "I've not been drinking. There was no suicide pact. Magnus died accidentally, walking into a freight-train as it was going into a tunnel. I stood by the line an hour ago and nearly did the same. That's the truth, and if you won't accept it it's just too bad. I can't make you."

She stumbled against the bathroom door, and as she turned to look at me I saw a new expression on her face, not anger, but amazement, and disgust as well.

"You went and stood there again," she said, "by the place where he was killed? You deliberately went and stood there and watched a train go by that might have killed you too?"

"Yes."

"Then I'll tell you what I think. I think it's unhealthy, morbid, crazy, and the worst thing about it is that you were capable, after such an experience, of coming here and making love to me. That I'll never forgive, or forget. So for heaven's sake sleep in the dressing-room. I prefer it that way."

She slammed the bathroom door, and I knew this time it was not another of her gestures, made on impulse, but something fundamental, springing from the core of innermost feeling shocked beyond measure. I understood, even honoured her for it, and was torn by a strange, inarticulate pity, but there was nothing I could say, nothing I could do.

We met next morning not as husband and wife on edge after yet one more marital tiff, but as strangers who, through force of circumstance, were obliged to share a common roof—dress, eat, walk from room to room, make plans for the day, exchange pleasantries with the children, who were bred of her body and not mine, thus making the division yet more complete. I sensed her profound unhappiness, was aware of every sigh, every dragging step, every weary inflection in her voice, and the boys, sharp like little animals to the atmospheric change of mood, watched both of us with gimlet eyes.

"Is it true," asked Teddy warily, catching me alone, "that the Professor has left the house to you?"

"It is," I answered. "Unexpected, but very kind of him."

"Will it mean we shall come here every holidays?"

"I don't know, it depends on Vita," I said.

He began fiddling with things on tables, picking them up and putting them back again, then kicking aimlessly at the backs of chairs.

"I don't believe Mom likes it here," he said.

"Do you?" I asked.

"It's all right," he shrugged.

Yesterday, because of fishing and the genial Tom, enthusiasm. Today, with the adult mood at odds, apathy and insecurity. My fault, of course. Whatever happened in this house had been, would be, my fault. I could not tell him so, or ask forgiveness.

"Don't worry," I said. "It will sort itself out. You'll probably spend the Christmas holidays in New York."

"Whew . . . How super!" he exclaimed, and ran out of the room on to the terrace, calling to Micky, who was outside, "Dick says we may spend next holidays back home."

The cheer that echoed from his young brother summed up their joint attitude to Cornwall, England, Europe, doubtless to their step-father as well.

We got through the weekend somehow, though the weather broke, making it the more difficult, and while the boys played a form of racquets in the basement—I could hear the balls thudding against the walls below—and Vita wrote a ten-page letter to Bill and Diana in Ireland, I made an inspection of all Magnus's books, from the nautical tales of Commander Lane's day to his own more personal choice, touching each one with possessive pride. The third volume of *The Parochial History of the County of Cornwall* (L to N—no sign of the other volumes) was tucked behind *The Story of the Windjammers*, and I pulled it out and ran my eye over the index of parishes. Lanlivery was there, and in the chapter allotted to it pride of place was given to Restormel Castle. Alas for Sir John; his seven months' tenure as Keeper was not mentioned. I was just about to replace the book, with the intention of reading it in full another time, when a line at the top of the page caught my attention.

"The manor of Steckstenton or Strickstenton, originally Tregesteynton, belonged to the Carminowes of Boconnoc, and passed from them to the Courtenays, and eventually to the representatives of the Pitt family. The estate of Strickstenton is the property of N. Kendall, Esq."

Tregesteynton . . . the Carminowes of Boconnoc. I had got it at last, but too late. Had I known ten days ago, had we both known, Magnus could have crossed the valley lower down, at Treesmill, and need not have died. As to the original manor-house, the site of it had surely been below the present farmhouse, or, trespassing there in time last Thursday evening, I must have been seen by the present owners.

Strickstenton . . . Tregesteynton. One thing was certain: I could bring the name up in Court if the Coroner questioned me.

The date of the inquest was fixed for Friday morning—earlier than had been expected. Dench and Willis would do as they had done before—travel down by a night train and return after it was over. I was congratulating myself, as I was shaving on the day of the inquest, that I had suffered no side-effects from the drug, no sweats, no bloodshot eyes, and despite the estrangement with Vita had passed the last few days in comparative peace, when suddenly, for no reason, the razor dropped from my hand into the wash-basin. I tried to pick it up, and my fingers would not co-ordinate; they were numb, with a sort of cramp. There was no feeling in them, no pain—they just did not function. I told myself it was nerves, due to the forthcoming ordeal, yet later at breakfast, as I reached for a cup of coffee without thinking, the cup slipped out of my hand, spilling the contents and smashing itself on the tray.

We were breakfasting in the dining-room to be on time for the inquest, and Vita was sitting opposite me.

"Sorry," I said. "What a bloody clumsy thing to do."

She stared at my hand, which had started to tremble, the tremor seeming to run up the wrist to the elbow. I could not control it. I thrust my hand into my jacket pocket and kept it close to my side, and the tremor eased.

"What's wrong?" she asked. "Your hand is all shaking."

"It's cramp," I said. "I must have lain on it during the night."

"Well, blow on it or something," she said. "Stretch the fingers, and bring the circulation back."

She began mopping up the tray, and poured me a fresh cup of coffee. I drank it with my left hand, but appetite had gone. I was wondering how I was going to drive the car, with one hand trembling or useless. I had told Vita that I preferred to attend the inquest alone, for there was no reason for her to come with me, but when the moment drew near to leave my hand was still useless, although the tremor had ceased.

"Look, I think you'll have to take me into St Austell," I said. "My right hand has still got this infernal cramp."

The warm sympathy which would have been hers a week ago was lacking. "I'll drive you, of course," she replied, "but it's rather odd, isn't it, suddenly to have cramp? You've never had it before. You had better keep your hand in your pocket, or the Coroner will think you have been drinking."

It was not a remark calculated to put me at my ease, and the very business of having to sit as passenger, humped beside Vita as she drove instead of being at the wheel myself, did something to my self-respect. I felt inadequate, frustrated, and began to lose the thread of the answers to the Coroner which I had so carefully rehearsed.

When we arrived at the White Hart and met Dench and Willis Vita, quite unnecessarily, apologised for her presence by saying, "Dick's disabled. I had to act as chauffeur," and the whole silly business was then explained. There was little time for talking, and I walked with the others to the building where the inquest was to be held, feeling a marked man, while the Coroner, doubtless a mild enough individual in private life, took on, in my eyes, the semblance of a judge of the Criminal Court, with the jury, one and all, adepts at finding a prisoner guilty.

The proceedings started with the police evidence about the finding of the body. It was straightforward enough, but as I listened to the story I thought how strangely it must fall on other ears, and how suggestive of someone who had temporarily lost his reason and been bent on his own destruction. Dr Powell was then called to give evidence. He read his statement in that clear, no-nonsense-about-it voice which suddenly reminded me of one of the younger Rugger-playing priests at Stonyhurst.

"This was the well-preserved body of a man of about forty-five years of age. When first examined at 1 p.m. on Saturday August 3rd death had occurred about fourteen hours previously. The autopsy, performed the following day, showed superficial bruises and abrasions of the knees and chest, deeper and more severe bruising of the upper arm and shoulder, and extensive laceration of the right side of the scalp. Underlying this was a depressed fracture of the right parietal region of the skull, accompanied by lacerations of the brain and bleeding from the right middle meningeal artery. The stomach was found to contain about one pint of mixed food and fluid, which on subsequent analysis contained nothing abnormal and no alcohol. Blood samples examined were also normal, and the heart, lungs, liver and kidneys were all normal and healthy. In my opinion, death was due to a cerebral haemorrhage following a severe crushing blow on the head."

I relaxed in my seat, tension momentarily lifted, wondering if John Willis did the same, or whether he had never had cause for concern.

The Coroner then asked Dr Powell if the brain injuries were consistent with what might be expected if the deceased had come into violent contact with a passing vehicle such as the wagon of a freight train.

"Yes, definitely," was the reply. "A point of some importance is that death was not instantaneous. He had strength enough to drag himself a few yards to the hut. The head blow was sufficient to cause severe concussion, but actual death from haemorrhage probably took place five or ten minutes afterwards."

"Thank you, Dr Powell," said the Coroner, and I heard him call my name. I stood up, wondering if the fact that my right hand was in my pocket gave me too casual an appearance, or whether, in point of fact, anyone noticed it at all.

"Mr Young," said the Coroner, "I have your statement here, and propose reading it to the jury. Stop me if there is anything you wish to correct."

The statement, as read by him, made me sound callous, as if I had been more preoccupied in missing my dinner than anxious for the safety of my guest. The jury would get the impression of a loafer, spinning away the small hours with a cushion behind his head and a bottle of whisky at his elbow.

"Mr Young," said the Coroner, when he had finished, "it did not occur to you to contact the police on the Friday night. Why?"

"I thought it unnecessary," I replied. "I kept expecting Professor Lane to turn up."

"You were not surprised at his getting off the train at Par and taking a walk instead of meeting you at St Austell as arranged?"

"I was surprised, yes, but it was quite in character. If he had some objective in view he followed it through. Time and punctuality meant nothing to him on these occasions."

"And what do you think was the particular objective Professor Lane had in view on the night in question?" asked the Coroner.

"Well, he had become interested in the historical associations of the district, and the sites of manor-houses. We had planned to visit some of them during the weekend. When he did not turn up I assumed he must have decided to take a walk to some particular site which he had not told me about. Since I made my statement to the police I believe I have located the site he had in mind."

I thought there might be a stir of interest amongst the jury but they remained unmoved.

"Perhaps you will tell us about it," said the Coroner.

"Yes, of course," I answered, self-confidence returning, and inwardly blessing the *Parochial History*. "I believe now, which I did not know at the time, that he was trying to locate the one-time manor of Strickstenton in Lanlivery parish. This manor belonged at one time to a family called Courtenay"—I was careful not to mention the Carminowes, because of Vita—"who also used to own Treverran too. The quickest way between these houses, as the crow flies, would be to cross the valley above the present Treverran farm, and walk through the wood to Strickstenton."

The Coroner asked for an ordnance map, which he examined carefully. "I see what you mean, Mr Young," he said. "But surely there is a passage-way under the railway which Professor Lane would have taken in preference to crossing the line itself?"

"Yes," I said, "but he had no map. He might not have known it was there."

"So he cut across the line, despite the fact that it was by then quite dark, and a freight-train was coming up the valley?"

"I don't think the darkness worried him. And obviously he didn't hear the train—he was so intent on his quest."

"So intent, Mr Young, that he deliberately climbed through the wire and walked down the steep embankment as the train was passing?"

"I don't think he walked down the bank. He slipped and fell. Don't forget it was snowing at the time."

I saw the Coroner staring at me, and the jury too. "I beg your pardon, Mr Young," said the Coroner, "did I hear you say it was snowing?"

I took a moment or two to recover, and I could feel the sweat breaking out on my forehead. "I'm sorry," I said. "That was misleading. The point was that Professor Lane had a particular interest in climatic conditions during the Middle Ages; his theory was that winters were much harder in those days than they are now. Before the railway cutting was built through the hillside above the Treesmill valley the ground would have sloped down continuously all the way to the bottom, and drifts would have lain there heavily, making communication between Treverran and Strickstenton virtually impossible. I believe, from a scientific rather than a historical point of view, he was thinking so much about this, and the general incline of the land about him, and how it would be affected by snowfall, that he became oblivious of everything else."

The incredulous faces went on staring at me, and I saw one man nudge his companion, signifying that either I was a raving lunatic or the Professor had been.

"Thank you, Mr Young, that is all," said the Coroner, and I sat down, pouring with sweat and a tremor shooting down my arm from elbow to wrist.

He called John Willis, who proceeded to give evidence that his late colleague had been in the best of health and spirits when he saw him before the weekend, that he was engaged in work of great importance to the country which he was not at liberty to speak about, but that naturally this work had no connection with his visit to Cornwall, which was in the nature of a private visit and in pursuance of a personal hobby, mainly historical.

"I must add," he said, "that I am in complete agreement with Mr Young as to his theory of how Professor Lane met his death. I am not an antiquarian, nor a historian, but certainly Professor Lane held theories about the extent of snowfall in previous centuries," and he proceeded, for about three minutes, to launch into jargon so incomprehensible and above my head and the heads of everybody present that Magnus himself could not have surpassed it had he been giving an imitation, after a thundering good dinner, of the sort of stuff published in the more obscure scientific journals.

"Thank you, Mr Willis," murmured the Coroner when he had finished. "Very interesting. I am sure we are all grateful for your information."

The evidence was concluded. The Coroner, summing up, directed that, although the circumstances were unusual, he found no reason to suppose that Professor Lane had deliberately walked on to the line as the train approached. The verdict was death by misadventure, with a rider to the effect that British Railways, Western Region, would do well to make a more thorough inspection of the wiring and danger notices along the line.

It was all over. Herbert Dench turned to me with a smile, as we left the building, and said, "Very satisfactory for all concerned. I suggest we celebrate at the White Hart. I don't mind telling you I was afraid of a very different verdict, and I think we might have had it but for your and Willis's account of Professor Lane's extraordinary preoccupation with winter conditions. I remember hearing of a similar case in the Himalayas . . ." and he proceeded to tell us, as we walked to the hotel, of a scientist who for three weeks lived at some phenomenal altitude in appalling conditions to study the atmospheric effect upon certain bacteria. I did not see the connection but was glad of the respite, and when we reached our destination went straight to the bar and got quietly and very inoffensively drunk. Nobody noticed, and what is more the tremor in my hand ceased immediately. Perhaps after all it had been nerves.

"Well, we mustn't keep you from enjoying your delightful new home," the lawyer said, when we had consumed a brief but hilarious lunch. "Willis and I can walk up to the station."

As we moved towards the door of the hotel I said to Willis, "I can't thank you enough for your evidence. What Magnus would have called a remarkable performance."

"It made its impact," he admitted, "though you had me somewhat shaken. I wasn't prepared for snow. Still, it goes to prove what my boss always said: the layman will accept anything if it is put forward in an authoritative enough fashion." He blinked at me behind his spectacles and added quietly, "You did make a clean sweep of all the jam-jars, I take it? Nothing left that could do you or anyone else any damage?"

"Buried," I replied, "under the debris of years."

"Good," he said. "We don't want any more disasters."

He hesitated, as if he might have been going to say something else, but the lawyer and Vita were waiting for us by the hotel entrance, and the opportunity was lost. Farewells were said, hands shaken, and we all dispersed. As we made our way to the car-park Vita remarked in wifely fashion, "I noticed your hand recovered as soon as you reached the bar. Be that as it may, I intend to drive."

"You're welcome," I said, borrowing her country's curious phraseology, and, tilting my hat over my eye as I got into the car, I prepared myself for sleep. My conscience pricked me, though. I had lied to Willis. Bottles A and B were empty, true enough, but the contents of bottle C were still intact, and lay in my suitcase in the dressing-room.

CHAPTER TWENTY-ONE

T HE EFFECTS OF conviviality in the White Hart subsided after a couple of hours, leaving me in a truculent mood and determined to be master in my own house. The inquest was over, and despite my gaffe about the snow, or perhaps because of it, Magnus's good name remained untarnished. The police were satisfied, local interest would die down, and there was nothing more I had to fear except interference from my own wife. This must be dealt with, and speedily. The boys had gone off riding and were not yet home. I went to look for Vita and found her eventually, tape-measure in hand, standing on the landing outside the boys' room.

"You know," she said, "that lawyer was perfectly right. You could get half a dozen small apartments into this place—more if you used the basement too. We could borrow the money from Joe." She flicked the tape-measure back into its case and smiled. "Have you any better ideas? The Professor didn't leave you the money to keep up his house, and you haven't a job, unless you cross the ocean and Joe gives you one. So . . . How about being realistic for a change?"

I turned and walked downstairs to the music-room. I expected her to follow me, and she did. I planted myself before the fireplace, the traditional spot sacrosanct from time immemorial to the master of the house, and said, "Get this straight. This is my house, and what I do with it is my affair. I don't want suggestions from you, lawyers, friends, or anyone else. I intend to live here, and if you don't care to live here with me you must make your own arrangements."

She lighted a cigarette and blew a great puff of smoke into the air. She had gone very white. "This is the showdown, is it?" she asked. "The ultimatum?"

"Call it what you like," I told her. "It's a statement of fact. Magnus has left me this house, and I propose to make a life for myself here, and for you and the boys if you want to share it. I can't speak plainer than that."

"You mean you have given up all idea of taking the directorship Joe offered you in New York?"

"I never had the idea. You had it for me."

"And how do you think we are going to live?"

"I haven't the slightest idea," I said, "and at the moment I don't care. Having worked in a publishing firm for over twenty years I know something about the game, and might even turn author myself. I could start by writing a history of this house."

"Good heavens!" She laughed, and extinguished her barely-lighted cigarette in the nearest ash-tray. "Well, it might keep you occupied if nothing else. And what would I do with myself in the meantime? Join the local sewing society or something?"

"You could do what other wives do, adapt."

"Darling, when I agreed to marry you and live in England you had a perfectly worth-while job in London. You've thrown it up for no reason at all, and now want to settle down here at the back of beyond, where neither of us knows a soul, hundreds of miles from all our friends. It's just not good enough."

We had reached an impasse; and I disliked being called darling when we were locked in argument instead of an embrace. Anyway, the situation bored me; I had said my say, and argument led nowhere. Besides, I had an intense desire to go up to the dressing-room and examine bottle C. If I remembered rightly, it looked slightly different from bottles A and B. Perhaps I ought to have given it to Willis to try out on his laboratory monkeys; but if I had taken him into my confidence he might never have sent it back.

"Why don't you take your tape-measure," I suggested, "and think up some bright ideas for curtains and carpets, and send them to Bill and Diana for their opinion in Ireland?"

I did not mean to be sarcastic. She could do what she liked, within reason, with Magnus's furnishings and bachelor taste. Rearranging rooms was one of her favourite things: it kept her happy for hours.

My effort to appease rebounded. Her eyes filled, and she said, "You know I'd live anywhere if only I thought you loved me still."

I can take anger any day and feel justified in returning blow for blow. Not unhappiness, not tears. I held out my arms and she came at once, clinging to me for comfort like a wounded child.

"You've changed so these last weeks," she told me. "I hardly recognise you."

"I haven't changed," I said. "I do love you. Of course I love you."

Truth is the hardest thing to put across, to other people, to oneself as well. I did love Vita, for moments shared during months and years, for all those ups and downs of married life that can be precious, exasperating, monotonous and dear. I had learnt to accept her faults, and she mine. Too often, wrangling, the insults hurled were never meant. Too frequently, used to each other's company, we had left the sweeter things unsaid. The trouble was, some inner core within had been untouched, lain dormant, waiting to be stirred. I could not share with her or anyone the secrets of my dangerous new world. Magnus, yes . . . but Magnus was a man, and dead. Vita was no Medea with whom I could gather the enchanted herbs.

"Darling," I said, "try and bear with me. It's a moment of transition for me, not a parting of the ways. I just can't see ahead. It's like standing on a spit of shore with an incoming tide, waiting to take the plunge. I can't explain."

"I'll take any plunge you want, if you'll take me with you," she answered.

"I know," I said, "I know . . ."

She wiped her eyes and blew her nose, the temporarily blotched features oddly touching, making me feel the more inadequate.

"What's the time? I shall have to pick up the boys," she said.

"No, we'll go together," I told her, glad of an excuse to prolong the *entente*, to justify myself not only in her eyes but in my own as well. Cheerfulness broke in; the atmosphere, that had been so heavy with resentment and unspoken bitterness, cleared and we were almost normal again. That night I returned from self-banishment in the dressing-room, not without regret, but I felt it politic; besides, the divan bed was hard.

The weather was fine, and the weekend passed with sailing, swimming, picnics with the boys, and as I resumed my role of husband, stepfather, master of the house, I planned in secret for the week ahead. I must have one day to myself alone. Vita herself, in all innocence, supplied the opportunity.

"Did you know Mrs Collins has a daughter in Bude?" she said on Monday morning. "I told her we'd take her over there one day this week, drop her off with the daughter, and pick her up again later in the afternoon. So how about it? The boys are keen to go, and so am I."

I pretended to damp the idea. "Awful lot of traffic," I said. "The roads will be jammed. And Bude packed with tourists."

"We don't mind that," said Vita. "We can make an early start, and it's only about 50 miles."

I assumed the look of a hard-pressed family man with a back-log of work on hand he was given no time to clear. "If you don't mind, I'd rather you left me out of it. Bude on a mid-August afternoon is not my idea of a perfect way of life."

"OK . . . OK . . . We'll have more fun without you."

We settled for Wednesday. No tradesmen called that day, so it suited me. If they left at half-past ten and picked up Mrs Collins again around five o'clock, they'd be home by seven at the latest.

Wednesday dawned fine, luckily, and I saw the party off in the Buick soon after half-past ten, knowing that I had at least eight hours ahead of me, hours for experiment and recovery too. I went up to the dressing-room and took bottle C out of my suitcase. It was the same stuff all right, or appeared to be, but there was a brownish sediment at the bottom, like cough-mixture put away after the winter and forgotten until the cold weather comes again. I took out the stopper and smelt the contents: they had no more colour and smell than stale water—less, in fact. I poured four measures into the top of the walking-stick, and then decided to screw it up for future use, and pour a fresh dose into the medicine-glass, which was still lying on a shelf with the jars in the old laundry.

It was an odd sensation, standing there once more, knowing that the basement all around me and the house above were empty of their present occupants, Vita, the boys, while waiting in the shadows were possibly the people of my secret world.

When I had swallowed the dose I went and sat in the old kitchen, expectant and alert as a theatre-goer who has just slipped into his stall before the curtain rises on the eagerly awaited third act of a play.

In this case either the players were on strike or the management at fault, for the curtain of my private theatre never rose, the scene remained unchanged. I sat down there in the basement for an hour, and nothing happened. I went out on to the patio, thinking the fresh air might do the trick, but time stayed obstinately at Wednesday morning in mid-August; I might have swallowed a draught from the kitchen tap for all the effect bottle C had upon mind or stomach.

At twelve o'clock I returned to the lab and poured a few more drops into the medicine-glass. This had done the trick once before, and without any ill-effect.

I returned to the patio and stayed until after one o'clock, but still nothing happened, so I went upstairs and had some lunch. It must mean that the contents of bottle C had lost their strength, or Magnus had somehow missed out on the special ingredients and bottle C was worthless. If this was so, I had made my last trip. The curtain had risen on my journey across the Treesmill stream in the snow, only to fall by the railway tunnel at the close of the third act. I had come to journey's end.

The realisation was so devastating that I felt stunned. I had lost not only Magnus but the other world. It lay here, all around me, but out of reach. The people of that world would travel on in time without me, and I must keep to my own course, fulfilling God only knew what monotonous day-by-day. The link between the centuries had gone.

I went down to the basement once more and out into the patio, thinking that by walking on the stone flags and touching the walls some force would come through to me, that Roger's face would look out at me from the hatch-door to the boiler-room, or Robbie would emerge from the stables under the loft leading his pony. I knew they must be there, and I could not see them. Isolda too, waiting for the snows to melt. The house was inhabited not by the dead but by the living, and I was the restless wanderer, I was the ghost.

This urge to see, to listen, to move amongst them was so intense that it became intolerable; it was as though my brain had been set alight by some tremendous fire. I could not rest. I could not set myself to any humdrum task in the house or garden; the whole day had gone to waste, and what had promised to be hours of magic were slipping by unused.

I got out the car and drove to Tywardreath, the sight of the solid parish church a mockery to my mood. It had no right to be there in its present form. I wanted to sweep it away, leaving only the south aisle and the Priory chapel, see the Priory walls enclosing the churchyard. I drove aimlessly to the lay-by at the top of the hill beyond the Treesmill turning and parked, thinking that, if I walked down the road and crossed the fields to the Gratten, memory of what I had once seen would fill the vacuum.

I stood by the car, reaching for a cigarette, but it had not touched my lips before a jolt shook me from head to foot, as though I had stepped on a live cable. There was no serene transition from present to past but a sensation of pain, with flashes before my eyes and thunder in my ears. "This is it," I thought. "I'm going to die." Then the flashes cleared, the thunder died away, and there was a mass of people lining the summit of the hill where I stood, crowding and pressing towards a building across the road. More people came from the direction of Tywardreath, men, women, children, some walking, some running. The building was the magnet, irregular in shape, with leaded windows, and what appeared to be a small chapel beside it. I had seen the village once before at Martinmas, but that was from the green beyond the Priory walls. Now there were no booths, no travelling musicians, no slaughtered beasts. The air was crisp and cold, the ditches banked with frozen snow that had turned grey and hard from lying during weeks. Small puddles in the road had turned to craters of sheeted ice, and the ploughlands across the ditches were black with frost. Men, women and children alike were wrapped and hooded against the cold, their features sharp like the beaks of birds, and the mood I sensed was neither jocular nor gay but somehow predatory, the mob mood of people bent upon a spectacle that might turn sour. I drew nearer to the building, and saw that a covered chariot was drawn up by the chapel entrance, with servants standing by the horses' heads. I recognised the Champernoune coat-of-arms, and the servants too, while Roger himself stood within the chapel porch, his arms folded.

The door of the main building was shut, but as I stood there watching it opened, and a man, better dressed than those lining the route, emerged with a companion. I knew them both, for I had seen them last on the night when Otto Bodrugan had urged them to join in his rebellion against the King: they were Julian Polpey and Henry Trefrengy. They came down the pathway, and threading their way through the crowd paused near to where I stood.

"God preserve me from a woman's spite," said Polpey. "Roger has held the office for ten years, and now to be dismissed without reason being given, and the stewardship handed to Phil Hornwynk . . ."

"Young William will reinstate him when he comes of age, no doubt of that," replied Trefrengy. "He has his father's sense of justice and fair play. But I could smell the change coming these past twelve months or more. The plain truth is that she lacks not only a husband but a man as well, and Roger has had his belly-full and will oblige no more."

"He finds his oats elsewhere."

The last speaker, Geoffrey Lampetho from the valley, had shouldered his way through the crowd to join them. "Rumour has it there's a woman under his roof. You should know, Trefrengy, being his neighbour."

"I know nothing," answered Trefrengy shortly. "Roger keeps his counsel, I keep mine. In hard weather such as this wouldn't any Christian give shelter to a stranger on the road?"

Lampetho laughed, digging him with his elbow. "Neatly said, but you can't deny it," he said. "Why else does my Lady Champernoune come here from Trelawn, disregarding the state of the roads, unless to snuff her out? I was in the geld-house here before you to pay my rents, and she sat in the inner room while Hornwynk collected. All the paint in the world couldn't hide the black look on her face: dismissing Roger from his stewardship won't see the end of it. Meantime, sport for the populace of another kind. Will you stay to watch the fun?"

Julian Polpey shook his head in disgust. "Not I," he answered. "Why should we in Tywardreath have some custom foisted upon us from elsewhere, making us barbarians? Lady Champernoune must be sick in mind to think of it. I'm for home."

He turned and disappeared into the crowd, which was now thick not only upon the summit of the hill where the house and chapel stood, but half-way down the track to Treesmill. One and all wore this curious air of expectancy upon their faces, half-resentful, half-eager, and Geoffrey Lampetho, pointing this out to his companion, laughed again.

"Sick in mind, maybe, but it salves her conscience to have another widow act as scapegoat, and sweetens Quadragessima for us. There's nothing a mob likes more than witnessing public penance."

He turned his head, like the rest, towards the valley, and Henry Trefrengy edged forward past the Champernoune servants to the chapel entrance where Roger stood, while I followed close behind.

"I'm sorry for what has happened," he said. "No gratitude, no recompense. Ten years of your life wasted, gone for nothing."

"Not wasted," answered Roger briefly. "William will come of age in June and marry. His mother will lose her influence, and the monk as well. You know the Bishop of Exeter has expelled him finally, and he must return to the Abbey at Angers, where he should have gone a year ago?"

"God be praised!" exclaimed Trefrengy. "The Priory stinks because of him, the parish too. Look at the people yonder. . . ."

Roger stared over Trefrengy's head at the gaping crowd. "I may have acted hard as steward, but to make sport of Rob Rosgof's widow was more than I could stomach," he said. "I stood against it, and this was another reason for my dismissal. The monk is responsible for all of this, to satisfy my lady's vanity and lust."

The entrance to the chapel darkened, and the small, slight figure of Jean de Meral appeared in the open doorway. He put his hand on Roger's shoulder.

"You used not to be so squeamish once," he said. "Have you forgotten those evenings in the Priory cellars, and in your own as well? I taught you more than philosophy, my friend, on those occasions."

"Take your hand off me," replied Roger curtly. "I parted company with you and your brethren when you let young Henry Bodrugan die under the Priory roof, and could have saved him."

The monk smiled. "And now, to show sympathy with the dead, you harbour an adulterous wife under your own?" he asked. "We are all hypocrites, my friend. I warn you, my lady knows your wayfarer's identity, and it is partly on her account that she is here in Tywardreath. She has certain proposals to put before the Lady Isolda when this business with Rosgof's widow has been settled."

"Which business, please God, will be struck from the manor records in years to come, and rebound upon your head instead, to your everlasting shame," said Trefrengy.

"You forget," murmured the monk, "I am a bird of passage, and in a few days' time shall have spread my wings for France."

There was a sudden stir amongst the crowd, and a man appeared at the door of the adjoining building, which Lampetho had named the geld-house. Stout, florid-faced, he held a document in his hand. Beside him, wrapped in a cloak from head to foot, was Joanna Champernoune.

The man, whom I took to be the new steward Hornwynk, advanced to address the crowd, unrolling the document in his hand.

"Good people of Tywardreath," he proclaimed, "whether freeman, customary tenant or serf, those of you who pay rent to the manor court have done so here today at the geld-house. And since this manor of Tywardreath was once held by the Lady Isolda Cardinham of Cardinham, who sold it to our late lord's grandfather, it has been decided to introduce here a practice established in the manor of Cardinham since the Conquest." He paused a moment, the better to impress his words upon his listeners. "The practice being," he continued, "that any widow of a customary tenant, holding lands through her late husband, who has deviated from the path of chastity, shall either forfeit her lands or make due penance for their recovery before the lord of the manor and the steward of the manor court. Today before the Lady Joanna Champernoune, representing the lord of the manor William, a minor, and myself, Philip Hornwynk, steward, Mary, widow of Robert Rosgof, must make such penance if she desires the restoration of her lands."

A murmur rose from the crowd, a strange blend of excitement and curiosity, and a sudden sound of shouting came from the road leading down to Treesmill.

"She'll never face them," said Trefrengy. "Mary Rosgof has a son at home who would rather surrender his farmland ten times over than have his mother shamed."

"You are mistaken," answered the monk. "He knows her shame will prove his gain in six months' time, when she is brought to bed of a bastard child, and he can turn both out of doors and keep the lands himself."

"Then you've persuaded him," said Roger, "and lined his purse in so doing."

The shouting and the cries increased, and as the people pressed forward I saw a procession ascend the hill from Treesmill, lumbering towards us at a jog-trot. Two lads raced ahead, brandishing whips, and behind them came five men escorting what at first sight I took to be a small moorland pony with a woman mounted on its back. They drew closer, and the laughter amongst the spectators turned to jeers, as the woman sagged upon her steed and would have fallen, had not one of the men escorting her held her fast, flourishing a hay-fork in his other hand. She was not mounted upon a pony at all but on a great black sheep, his horns be-ribboned with crepe, and the two fellows on either side had thrust a halter over his head to lead him, so that, startled and terrified of the crowd about him, he ducked and stumbled in a vain endeavour to throw his passenger from his back. The woman was draped in black to match her steed, with a black veil covering her face, her hands bound in front of her with leather thongs; I could see her fingers clutching at the thick dark wool on the sheep's neck.

The procession came stumbling and lurching to the geld-house, and as it drew to a standstill before Hornwynk and Joanna, the escort jerking the halter, the man with the hay-fork dragged off the woman's veil to disclose her features. She could not have been more than thirty-five, her eyes as terror-stricken as the sheep that bore her, while her dark hair, roughly scissored, stood out from her head like a cropped thatch. The jeering turned to silence as the woman, trembling, bowed her head before Joanna.

"Mary Rosgof, do you admit your fault?" called Hornwynk.

"I do in all humility," she answered, her voice low.

"Speak louder for all to hear, and state its nature," he cried.

The wretched woman, her pale face flushing, raised her head and looked towards Joanna.

"I lay with another man, my husband not six months dead, thus forfeiting the lands I held in trust for my son. I crave indulgence of my lady and the manor court, and beg for the restoration of my lands, confessing my incontinence. Should I give birth to a base-born child, my son will take possession of the lands and do with me as he pleases."

Joanna beckoned the new steward to her side, and he bent low as she whispered something in his ear. Then he turned once more and addressed the penitent.

"My gracious lady cannot condone your fault, which is of a nature abhorrent to all people, but since you have admitted it in person, and before the manor court and others of this parish, she will, in great clemency, restore the forfeited lands you rent from her."

The woman bowed her head and murmured gratitude, then asked with swimming eyes if there was further penance she must do.

"Aye," returned the steward. "Descend from the sheep that carried you in your shame, proceed to the chapel here, crawling on your knees, and confess your sin before the altar. Brother John will hear your confession."

The two men who held the sheep pulled the woman from its back, forcing her to her knees, and as she dragged herself along the path towards the chapel, hampered by her skirts, a groan arose from the watching crowd, as if this total degradation could in some way appease their own sense of shame. The monk waited until she had crawled to his feet, then turned into the chapel, where she followed him. Her escort, at a sign from Hornwynk, set the sheep free, whereupon it ran in terror amongst the crowd, scattering them to either side, and a great shout of hysterical laughter burst forth, as they drove it back along the road to Treesmill, pelting it with pieces of packed snow, sticks, anything they could find. With the sudden release from tension everyone was in a moment laughing, joking, running, seized by a holiday mood, what was happening making a break between winter and the Lenten season just begun. Soon they had all dispersed, and no one was left before the geld-house but Joanna herself, Hornwynk the steward, and Roger and Trefrengy standing to one side.

"So be it," said Joanna. "Tell my servants I am ready to leave. There is nothing further to keep me here in Tywardreath save a certain business which I can attend to on the road home."

The steward went down the path to prepare for her departure, the servants opening the carriage door in readiness, and Joanna, pausing, looked across the path at Roger.

"The people were well satisfied if you are not," she said, "and will pay their rents the sooner for it in the future. The custom has its merits if it inspires fear, and may well spread to other manors."

"God forbid," answered Roger.

Geoffrey Lampetho had been right about the paint on her face, or perhaps the atmosphere inside the geld-house had been close. It ran in streaks now on either cheek, which, with increasing weight, were a puffy puce. She seemed to have aged, since I saw her last, a good ten years. The splendour had gone from her brown eyes, turning them hard like agate.

She put out her hand now and touched Roger's arm. "Come," she said, "we have known one another too long for lies and subterfuge. I have a message for the Lady Isolda from her brother Sir William Ferrers, which I have promised to deliver to her in person. If you bar your door to me now I can summon fifty men from the manor to break it down."

"And I another fifty between here and Fowey to withstand them," answered Roger. "But you may follow me to Kylmerth if you wish, and beg an interview. Whether it will be granted or not I cannot say."

Joanna smiled. "It will," she said, "it will," and taking her skirts in her hands she swept down the path towards the carriage, followed by the monk. Once it would have been Roger who helped her mount the steps into the waiting vehicle; today it was the new steward Hornwynk, flushed with self-esteem and bowing low, while Roger, crossing to a gate behind the chapel, where his pony was tethered, leapt upon its back, and kicking his heels into its side rode out into the road. The lumbering chariot rumbled after him, Joanna and the monk inside it, and the few stragglers at the top of the hill stared to watch it pass down the icy road to the village green and the Priory walls beyond. A bell sounded from the Priory chapel and the vehicle began to draw away from me, and Roger too, and I started running, fearing to lose both. Then a pounding in my heart began, and a singing in my ears, and I saw the carriage lurch to a standstill; the window was lowered, and Joanna herself looked out of it, waving her hand and beckoning to me. I stumbled to the window, breathless, the singing increasing to a roar. Then it ceased, absolutely, and I was swaying on my feet, with the clock in St Andrew's church striking seven, and the Buick had drawn up on the road ahead of me, with Vita waving from the window, and the surprised faces of the boys and Mrs Collins looking out.

CHAPTER TWENTY-TWO

THEY WERE ALL talking at once, and the boys were laughing. I heard Micky say, "We saw you running down the hill, you looked so funny . . ." and Teddy chimed in, "Mom waved and called, but you didn't hear at first, you seemed to look the other way." Vita was staring at me from the open window by the driving seat. "You'd best get in," she said, "you can hardly stand," and Mrs Collins, red in the face and flustered, opened the door for me the other side. I obeyed mechanically, forgetting my own car parked in the lay-by, and squeezed in beside Mrs Collins, as we continued along the lane skirting the village towards Polmear.

"A good thing we drove this way," said Vita. "Mrs Collins said it was quicker than going down through St Blazey and Par."

I could not remember where they had been or what they were doing, and although the singing in my ears had stopped my heart was thumping still, and vertigo was not far away.

"Bude was super," said Teddy. "We had surf-boards, but Mom wouldn't let us go out of our depth. And the ocean was rolling in, huge great waves, much better than here. You ought to have come with us."

Bude, that was right. They had gone to spend the day at Bude, leaving me alone in the house. But what was I doing wandering in Tywardreath? As we passed the almshouses at the bottom of Polmear hill and I looked across to

Polpey and the Lampetho valley, I remembered how Julian Polpey had not waited for the loathsome spectacle outside the geld-house but had walked home, and Geoffrey Lampetho had been one of those amongst the crowd who had pelted the sheep with stones.

It was over and done with, finished. It was not happening any more. Mrs Collins was saying something to Vita about dropping her at the top of Polkerris hill, and the next thing I knew was that she had disappeared and Vita had drawn up outside Kilmarth.

"Run along in," she said sharply to the boys. "Put your swimming-trunks in the hot cupboard and start laying the supper," and when they had vanished up the steps into the house she turned to me and said, "Can you make it?"

"Make what?" I was still dazed, and could not follow her.

"Make the steps," she said. "You were rocking on your feet when we came on you just now. I felt terrible in front of Mrs Collins and the boys. However much have you had to drink?"

"Drink?" I repeated. "I haven't drunk a thing."

"Oh, for heaven's sake," she said, "don't start lying. It's been a long day, and I'm tired. Come on, I'll help you into the house."

Perhaps this was the answer. Perhaps it was best she should think I had been sitting in some pub. I got out of the car, and she was right—I was still rocking on my feet, and I was glad of her arm to steady me up the garden and into the house.

"I'll be all right," I said. "I'll go and sit in the library."

"I'd rather you went straight to bed," she said. "The boys have never seen you like this. They're bound to notice."

"I don't want to go to bed. I'll just sit in the library and shut the door. They needn't come in."

"Oh well, if you insist on being obstinate . . ." She shrugged in exasperation. "I'll tell them we'll eat in the kitchen. For heaven's sake don't join us—I'll bring you something later."

I heard her walk through the hall to the kitchen, and slam the door. I flopped on a chair in the library and closed my eyes. A strange lethargy crept over me; I wanted to sleep. Vita was right, I should have gone to bed, but I hadn't the energy even to get up out of the chair. If I stayed here quietly, in the stillness and the silence, the feeling of exhaustion, of being drained, would pass away. Tough luck on the boys, if there was some programme they hoped to watch on TV, but I would make it up to them tomorrow, take them sailing, go to Chapel Point. I must make up to Vita too; this business would set us back again, the sweat of reconciliation would have to start all over again.

I awoke with a sudden jerk, to find the room in darkness. I glanced at my watch, and it was almost half-past nine. I had slept for nearly two hours. I felt quite normal, hungry too. I went through the dining-room into the hall, and heard the sound of the gramophone coming from the music-room, but the door was shut. They must have finished eating ages ago, for the lights were turned out in the kitchen. I rummaged in the fridge to find eggs and bacon to fry, and I had just put the frying-pan on the stove when I heard someone moving about in the basement. I went to the top of the back stairs and called, thinking it was one of the boys, who might report to me on Vita's mood. Nobody answered.

"Teddy?" I shouted. "Micky?"

The footsteps were quite definite, passing across the old kitchen and then on towards the boiler-room. I went down the stairs, fumbling for the lights, but they were not in the right place, I couldn't find the switch, and I had to grope my way to the old kitchen by feeling for the walls. Whoever it was ahead of me had passed through the boiler-room on to the patio, for I could hear him stamping about there, and he was drawing water from the well that lay in the near corner and was covered up and never used. And now there were further footsteps, but not from the patio, from the stairs, and turning round I saw the stairs had gone and the footsteps were coming from the ladder leading to the floor above. It was no longer dark, but the murky grey of a winter afternoon, and a woman was coming down the ladder, bearing a lighted candle in her hands. The singing started in my ears, the bursting thunder-clap of sound, and the drug was taking effect all over again *without having been renewed*. I did not want it now, I was afraid, for it meant that past and present were merging, and Vita and the boys were with me, in my own time, in the front part of the house.

The woman brushed past me, shielding the candle's flame from the draught. It was Isolda. I flattened myself against the wall, holding my breath, for surely she must dissolve if I as much as moved, and what I was seeing was a figment of the imagination, an aftermath of what had been that afternoon. She set the candle down on a bench, lighting another that stood beside it, and began humming under her breath, an odd sweet snatch of song, and all the time I could hear the distant throbbing of the radiogram from the music-room on the ground floor of the house.

"Robbie," she called softly. "Robbie, are you there?"

The boy came in from the yard through the low arched doorway, setting his pail of water on the kitchen floor.

"Is it freezing still?" she asked.

"Aye," he said, "and will do until full moon is past. You must stay a few days yet, if you can bear with us."

"Bear with you?" she smiled. "Rejoice in you, rather, and willingly. I wish my daughters were as well-mannered as you and Bess, and minded what I tell them as you mind your brother Roger."

"If we do it's from respect for you," he answered. "We got hard words from him, and a belting too, before you came." He laughed, shaking the thick hair out of his eyes, and lifting the pail poured the water into a pitcher on the trestle table. "We eat well, too," he added. "Meat every day instead of salted fish, and the pig I slaughtered yesterday would have stayed in his sty until Quadragessima was done had you not graced our table. Bess and I would have you live with us forever and not leave us when the weather mends."

"Ah, I understand," said Isolda, mocking. "It isn't for myself you like me here but for the ease of living."

He frowned, uncertain what she meant, then his face cleared, and he smiled again. "Nay, that's untrue," he said. "We feared when you first came that you'd play the lady and we couldn't please you. It's not so now, you could be one of us. Bess loves you, and so do I. As for Roger, God knows he has sung your praises to us these past two years or more."

He flushed, suddenly awkward, as if he had said too much, and she put out her hand to him and touched his arm.

"Dear Robbie," she said gently, "I love you too, and Bess, and the warm welcome you have given me these past weeks. I shall never forget it."

The sound of footsteps made me raise my head to the loft above, but it was only the girl descending the ladder, certainly cleaner than when I saw her last, her long hair combed and smooth, her face well scrubbed.

"I can hear Roger riding through the copse," she called. "See to the pony, Robbie, when he comes, while I set the table."

The boy went out into the yard and his sister heaped fresh turf upon the hearth, and furze as well. The furze flickered and caught, throwing great tongues of flame upon the smoky walls, and as Bess looked over her shoulder, smiling at Isolda, I knew how it must have been here for the four of them, night after night, during the time of frost, seated at the trestle table with the candles set amongst the pewter plates.

"Here's your brother now," said Isolda, and she went and stood by the open door as he rode into the yard and flung himself off the pony, throwing the reins to Robbie. It was not yet dark, and the yard, so much wider than the patio I knew, stretched to the wall above the fields, so that through the open gate I could see the fields sloping to the sea beyond and the wide expanse of bay. The mud in the yard was frosted hard, the air was sharply cold, and the small trees in the copse stood black and naked against the sky. Robbie led the pony to his shed beside the byre, as Roger crossed the yard towards Isolda.

"You bring bad news," said Isolda. "I can tell it from your face."

"My lady knows you are here," said Roger. "She is on her way to see you, with a message from your brother. If you wish it I can turn the chariot back from the top of the hill. Robbie and I will have no trouble with her servants."

"No trouble now, perhaps," she answered, "but later she could do harm to you, to Robbie and Bess, to this whole place. I would not have that happen for the world."

"I would sooner she razed the house to the ground than cause you suffering," he said.

He stood there, looking down at her, and I knew instinctively that they had reached a point in their relationship, through proximity and sympathy during the past days, when his love for her could no longer smoulder and be contained, but must burn up and reach the sky, or else be quenched.

"I know you would, Roger," she said, "but any further suffering that may come my way I can bear alone. If I have brought dishonour on two houses, my husband's and Otto Bodrugan's, which doubtless will be said about me down the years, I'll not do the same to yours."

"Dishonour?" He spread out his hands and looked about him at the low walls encircling the yard, the narrow thatched dwelling where the ponies and the cows were housed. "This was my father's farm and will be Robbie's when I die, and had you sheltered here for one night only and not fifteen, you would have lent it grace enough to last through centuries."

She must have sensed the depth of feeling in his voice, and possibly the passion too, for a sudden shadow came across her face, a wariness, as if prompted by an inner voice that murmured, "Thus far, and no further." Moving to the open gate she put her hand upon it, and looked out over the fields to the bay beyond.

"Fifteen nights," she repeated, "and on each one of them, since I have been with you, and in the daytime too, I have stood looking out across the sea to Chapel Point, remembering that his ship would anchor there, below Bodrugan, and this was the bay he sailed when he came to find me in the Treesmill creek. Part of me died with him, Roger, the day they drowned him, and I think you know it."

I wondered what Roger's dream had been, and whether, as we all do, he had created a fantasy that their lives would somehow fuse; not in marriage, not as lovers, even, but in some sort of drifting intimacy, intuitive and silent, that no one else would ever share. Whether it were so or not, the dream was shattered; by speaking Bodrugan's name she had made this plain.

"Yes," he said, "I have always known it. If I have given you cause to believe otherwise, forgive me."

He lifted his head and listened. She did the same, and beyond the dark copse above the farm came the sound of voices and tramping of feet, and then the figures of three of the Champernoune servants emerged through the naked trees.

"Roger Kylmerth?" one of them called. "Your road is too rough to drive the chariot down to your dwelling, and my lady waits within it on the hill."

"Then she must stay there," answered Roger, "or come on foot, with your assistance. It's one and the same to us."

The men hesitated a moment, conferring under the trees, and Isolda, at a sign from Roger, turned quickly and passed across the yard into the house. Roger whistled, and Robbie came out of the door where the ponies were stabled.

"Lady Champernoune is above, and some of her servants," said Roger quietly. "She could have summoned others between here and Tywardreath, and we may have trouble. Stay within call should I need you."

Robbie nodded, and went back into the stables. It was growing darker every moment, colder too, the trees in the copse etched more sharply against the sky. Presently I saw the lights of the first flares on the crest of the hill; Joanna was descending, three of the servants with her, and the monk as well. They came slowly and in silence, Joanna's dark cloak and the monk's habit blending as though the two were one; and standing beside Roger, watching their progress, it seemed to me that the group had something sinister about it; the hooded figures could have been walking in procession through a churchyard to a waiting grave.

When they arrived at the open gate Joanna paused and looked about her, then she said to Roger, "In all the ten years you served my household you never thought to bid me welcome here."

"No, my lady," he replied, "you neither asked for refuge nor desired it. Consolation was ever ready for you under your own roof."

The irony did not touch her, or if it did she chose to ignore it, and Roger led the way towards the house.

"Where must my servants wait?" she asked. "Have the courtesy to direct them to your kitchen."

"We ourselves live in the kitchen," he told her, "and Lady Carminowe will receive you there. Your men will find it warm enough in the byre amongst the cows, or with the ponies, whichever they please."

He stood aside to let her pass with the monk, and followed after, and as we crossed the threshold I saw that the trestle table had been pulled close to the hearth, the tallow candles set upon it, and Isolda sat alone at the head of the table. Bess must have gone to the room above.

Joanna stared about her, at a loss, I think, to find herself in such surroundings. God knows what she had expected—some greater attempt at comfort, perhaps, with furnishings pilfered from her own abandoned manor house.

"So . . ." she said at last, "this is the retreat, and snug enough, no doubt, on a winter's night, apart from the smell of beasts across the yard. How do you do, Isolda?"

"I do very well, as you see," Isolda answered. "I have lived better here, and had more kindness, in two weeks than in as many months or years spent at Tregesteynton or Carminowe."

"I don't doubt it," said Joanna. "Contrast ever whetted appetite grown stale. You had a fancy for Bodrugan Castle once, but had Otto lived you would have become as weary there and of him as you have of other properties and other men, including your own husband. Well, this is a rich reward. Tell me, do both brothers share you here before the hearth?"

I heard Roger draw in his breath, and he moved forward, as though to place himself between the two women, but Isolda, her small face pale in the flickering light of two candles, only smiled.

"Not as yet," she said. "The elder is too proud, the younger too shy. My protestations of affection fall upon deaf ears. What do you want with me, Joanna? Have you brought a message from William? If so, speak plainly and have done with it."

The monk, who was still standing by the door, took a letter from his habit to give to Joanna, but she waved it aside.

"Read it to Lady Carminowe," she said. "I have no desire to strain my eyes in this dim light. And you may leave us," she added to Roger. "Family matters are no longer your concern. You meddled with them enough when you were my steward."

"This is his house, and he has the right to be here," said Isolda. "Besides, he is my friend, and I prefer him to stay."

Joanna shrugged, and sat down at the lower end of the table opposite Isolda.

"If Lady Carminowe permits," said the monk smoothly, "this is the letter from her brother, Sir William Ferrers, which came to Trelawn a few days since, Sir William thinking his messenger would find her there with Lady Champernoune. It reads thus:

"'Dearest Sister, the news of your flight from Tregesteynton has only reached us here at Bere within the past week, because of the hard weather and the state of the roads. I am at a loss to understand either your action or your great imprudence. You must know that by deserting your husband and your children you forfeit all claims on his and their affection, and, I am bound to say, on mine as well. Whether Oliver, in Christian charity, will receive you at Carminowe again I cannot say, but I misdoubt it, fearing your pernicious influence upon his daughters, and for my own part I could not offer you protection at Bere, for Matilda, as Oliver's sister, has too much sympathy for her brother to offer hospitality to his erring wife. Indeed, she is in so sore a state since hearing you have deserted him that she could not countenance your presence amongst us with our five sons. It seems, therefore, there is only one course open to you, which is to seek refuge in the nunnery of Cornworthy here in Devon, the Prioress being known to me, and to remain there in seclusion until such time as Oliver, or some other member of the family, may be willing to receive you. I have every confidence that our kinswoman, Joanna, will permit her servants to escort you to Cornworthy.

"'Farewell, in the power of Christ,
      "'Your sorrowful brother,
          "'William Ferrers'"

The monk folded the letter and passed it across the table to Isolda. "You may see for yourself, my lady," he murmured, "that the letter is in Sir William's own handwriting, and bears his signature. There is no deception."

She barely glanced at it. "You are very right," she said "there is no deception."

Joanna smiled. "If William had known you were here and not at Trelawn, I doubt if he would have written so generously, nor would the Prioress at Cornworthy be willing to open her convent doors. However, you may count on me to keep it secret, and arrange your escort into Devon. Two days under my roof to make the necessary preparations, a change of attire, which I can see you need, and you can be on the road." She leant back in her chair, a look of triumph on her face. "I am told the air is mild at Cornworthy," she added. "The nuns there live to a great age."

"Then let us dwell behind convent walls together," replied Isolda. "Widows, when their sons marry, as your William does next year, must needs find new shelter, along with erring wives. We will be sisters in misfortune."

Proud and defiant, she stared at Joanna down the length of the trestle table, and the candlelight, throwing shadows on the wall, distorted both their figures, turning Joanna, because of her hooded cloak and widow's veil, to the likeness of some monstrous crab.

"You forget," she said, playing with her multitude of rings, slipping them from one finger to another, "I have a licence to remarry, and can do so whenever I choose to pick a new husband from a chain of suitors. You are still bound to Oliver, and furthermore disgraced. There is a second course open to you other than the nunnery at Cornworthy, if you prefer it, and that is to remain as drab here to my one-time steward, but I warn you the parish might serve you as they served my tenant this day in Tywardreath, and have you riding to do penance in the manor chapel on the back of a black ram."

She broke into a peal of laughter, and, turning to the monk who was standing behind her chair, she said, "What do you say, Frère Jean? We could mount the one on a ram and the other on a ewe, and have them jog-trot together or forfeit the Kylmerth land."

I knew it must happen, and it did. Roger seized the monk and threw him back against the wall. Then, bending to Joanna, he jerked her to her feet.

"Insult me as you please, not Lady Carminowe," he said. "This is my house, and you shall leave it."

"I will do so," she replied, "when she has made her choice. I have three servants only in your cow-house in the yard, but a score or more waiting by my carriage on the hill, only too willing to pay off ancient grudges."

"Then summon them," said Roger, freeing her. "Robbie and I can defend our home against every one of your tenants, the whole parish if you will."

His voice, raised in anger, had penetrated to the sleeping-room above, and Bess came running down the ladder, pale and anxious, to take her stand behind Isolda's bench.

"Who's this?" asked Joanna. "A third for the sheep-fold? How many other slatterns do you harbour in your loft?"

"Bess is Roger's sister, and so my own," answered Isolda, putting her arm round the frightened girl. "And now, Joanna, call your servants so that this household can be rid of you. God knows we've borne your insults long enough."

"We?" queried Joanna. "Then you count yourself one of them?"

"Yes, while I receive their hospitality," said Isolda.

"So you do not intend to travel with me to Trelawn?"

Isolda hesitated, glancing first at Roger, then at Bess. But before she could reply the monk stepped out of the shadows on the wall and stood beside them.

"There is a third choice yet for Lady Carminowe," he murmured. "I sail from Fowey, within twenty-four hours, to the parent house of St Sergius and Bacchus at Angers. If she and the girl care to accompany me to France, I know very well I could find asylum for them there. No one would molest them, and they would be safe from all pursuit. Their very existence would be forgotten once they were in France, and Lady Carminowe herself be at liberty to start life anew in pleasanter surroundings than behind convent walls."

The proposal was so obvious a trick to get both Bess and Isolda out of Roger's care and into his own charge, to dispose of them as he wished, that I expected even his patroness to round upon him. Instead, she smiled, and shrugged her shoulders.

"Upon my word, Frère Jean, you show true Christian feeling," she said. "What do you say, Isolda? Now you have three alternatives: seclusion at

Cornworthy, life in a pigsty at Kylmerth, or the protection of a Benedictine monk across the water. I know which I would choose."

She glanced about her as she had first done when he entered the house, and moving round the room touched the smoke-grimed walls, grimacing, then examined her fingers, wiping them with the handkerchief she carried, and finally paused by the ladder leading to the loft above, her foot upon one rung.

"One pallet amongst four, and louse-ridden?" she asked. "If you travel into Devon or to France, Isolda, I'll thank you to sprinkle your gown with vinegar first."

The singing started in my ears, and the thunder. Their figures began to fade. All but Joanna's, standing there at the foot of the ladder. She stared towards me, her eyes opening wide, and I did not care what happened afterwards, I wanted to put my hands round her throat and choke her before she vanished, like the others, out of sight. I crossed the room and stood beside her, and she did not fade. She began to scream, as I shook her backwards and forwards, my hands round her plump, white neck.

"Damn you," I shouted, "damn you . . . damn you . . ." and the screaming was all around me, and above as well. I loosened my grip and looked up, and the boys were crouching there on the landing at the top of the back stairs, and Vita had fallen against the banister beside me, and was staring at me, white-faced, terrified, her hands to her throat.

"Oh, my God!" I said. "Vita . . . darling . . . Oh, my God . . ."

I fell forwards on to the banister rail beside her, retching, seized by the uncontrollable, blasted vertigo, and she dragged herself away up the stairs to safety beside the boys, and they all started screaming once again.

CHAPTER TWENTY-THREE

THERE WAS NOTHING I could do. I lay there on the stairs, clinging to the handrail, arms and legs splayed out grotesquely, with walls and ceiling reeling above my head. If I shut my eyes the vertigo increased, with streaks of golden light stabbing the darkness. Presently the screaming stopped; the boys were crying, and I could hear the crying die away as they ran into the kitchen overhead, slamming both the doors.

Blinded by dizziness and nausea, I started to crawl upstairs, step by step, and when I had reached the top stood upright, swaying, and felt my way across the kitchen to the hall. The lights were on, the doors were open. Vita and the boys must have run up to the bedroom and locked themselves in. I staggered into the lobby and reached for the telephone, floor and ceiling blurring to become one. I sat there, holding the receiver in my hand, until the floor steadied, and the telephone directory, instead of being a jumble of black dots, straightened into words. I found Dr Powell's number at last and dialled it, and when he answered the tension inside me broke, and I felt the sweat pouring down my face.

"It's Richard Young from Kilmarth," I said. "You remember, the friend of Professor Lane."

"Oh yes?" He sounded surprised. After all, I was not one of his patients, and I must only be a face amongst hundreds of summer visitors.

"The most frightful thing has happened," I said. "I had a sort of black-out and tried to strangle my wife. I may have hurt her, I don't know."

My voice was calm, without emotion, yet all the time my heart was pounding, and the realisation of what had happened was clear and strong. There was no confusion. No merging of two worlds.

"Is she unconscious?" he asked.

"No," I said, "no, I don't think so. She's upstairs, with the boys. They must have locked themselves in the bedroom. I'm speaking to you from the lobby downstairs."

He was silent, and for one terrible moment I was afraid he was going to tell me it was none of his business and I had better call the police. Then, "All right, I'll be along straight away," he said, and rang off.

I put down the receiver and wiped the sweat off my face. The vertigo had subsided, and I was able to stand without swaying. I walked slowly upstairs and through the dressing-room to the bathroom door. It was locked.

"Darling," I called, "don't worry, it's OK. I've just telephoned the doctor. He's coming out at once. Stay there with the boys until you hear his car." She did not answer, and I called louder. "Vita," I shouted, "Teddy, Micky, don't be frightened, the doctor's coming. Everything's going to be all right."

I went back downstairs and opened the front door, and stood waiting there on the steps. It was a fine night, the sky ablaze with stars. There was no sound anywhere; the campers in the field across the Polkerris road must have turned in. I looked at my watch. It was twenty to eleven. Then I heard the sound of the doctor's car coming along the main road from Fowey, and I began to sweat again, not from fear but from relief. He turned down the drive and came to a standstill in the sweep before the house. I went through the garden to meet him.

"Thank God you've come," I said.

We went into the house together, and I pointed up the stairs. "First room at the top, on the right. That's my dressing-room, but she's locked the bathroom beyond. Tell them who you are. I'll wait for you down here."

He ran upstairs, two steps at a time, and I kept thinking that the silence from above meant that Vita was dying, that she was lying on the bed, and the boys were crouching beside her, too terrified to move. I went into the music-room and sat down, wondering what would happen if he told me Vita was dead. All of it was happening. All of it was true.

He was up there a long time, and presently I heard the sound of shifting furniture; they must be dragging the divan bed through the bathroom to the bedroom, and I could hear the doctor talking, and Teddy too. I wondered what the hell they were doing. I went and listened at the foot of the stairs, but they had gone through to the bedroom again and shut the door. I sat on in the music-room, waiting.

He came down just after the clock in the hall struck eleven. "Everything's under control," he said. "No panic stations. Your wife's all right, and so are your stepsons. Now what about you?"

I tried to stand up, but he pushed me back into the chair.

"Have I hurt her?" I asked.

"Slight bruising on the neck, nothing more," he said. "It may look a bit blue tomorrow, but it won't show if she wears a scarf."

"Did she tell you what happened?"

"Supposing you tell me?"

"I'd rather hear her version first," I said.

He took a cigarette out of a packet and lighted it. "Well," he said, "I gather you didn't want any dinner, for reasons known best to yourself, and she spent the evening in here with the boys, while you were in the library. Then they decided to go to bed, and she found you had gone to the kitchen and switched on the lights. There was bacon on the stove burnt to a frazzle, the stove still on, but nobody there. So she went down to the basement. It seems you were standing there, near the old kitchen, so she said, waiting for her to come downstairs, and as soon as you saw her you went straight across to the foot of the stairs and began swearing at her, and then you put your hands round her throat and tried to throttle her."

"That's right," I said.

He looked at me sharply. Perhaps he thought I would deny it. "She insists you were fighting drunk and didn't know what you were doing," he said, "but it was a pretty grim experience for all of them, and she and those boys were scared out of their wits. More so, as I gather you're not a drinking type."

"No," I said, "I'm not. And I wasn't drunk."

He did not answer for a moment. Then he came and stood in front of me, and taking some sort of flash thing from the bag he had with him he examined my eyes. Afterwards he felt my pulse.

"What are you on?" he asked abruptly.

"On?"

"Yes, what drug. Tell me straight, and I'll know how to treat you."

"That's just it," I said. "I don't know."

"Was it something Professor Lane gave you?"

"Yes," I replied.

He sat down on the arm of the sofa beside my chair. "By mouth or by injection?"

"By mouth."

"Was he treating you for something specific?"

"He wasn't treating me for anything. It was an experiment. Something I volunteered to do for him. I've never taken drugs in my life before I came down here."

He went on looking at me with his shrewd eyes, and I knew there was nothing for it but to tell him everything.

"Was Professor Lane on the same drug when he walked into that freight-train?" he asked.

"Yes."

He got off the sofa and began walking up and down the room, fiddling with things on tables, picking them up and putting them down again, as Magnus himself used to do when coming to a decision.

"I ought to get you into hospital for observation," he said.

"No," I said, "for God's sake . . ." I got up from my chair. "Look," I said, "I've got the stuff in a bottle upstairs. It's all there is left. One bottle. He told me to destroy everything I found here in his lab, and I did—it's all buried in the wood above the garden. I only kept the one bottle, and I used some of it today. It must be different in some way—stronger, I don't know—but you take it away, have it analysed, anything. Surely you realise, after what has happened tonight, I couldn't touch the stuff again? Christ! I might have killed my wife."

"I know," he said. "That's why you ought to be in hospital."

He did not know. He did not understand. How could he understand?

"Look," I said, "I never saw Vita, my wife, standing at the foot of the stairs. It wasn't her I tried to strangle. It was another woman."

"What woman?" he asked.

"A woman called Joanna," I said. "She lived six hundred years ago. She was down there, in the old farmhouse kitchen, and the others were with her too. Isolda Carminowe, and the monk Jean de Meral, and the man the farm belonged to, who used to be her steward, Roger Kylmerth."

He put out his hand and held my arm. "All right," he said, "steady on, I follow you. You took the drug, and then you went downstairs and saw these people in the basement?"

"Yes," I said, "but not only here. I've seen them in Tywardreath as well, at the old manor house below the Gratten, and at the Priory too. That's what the drug does. It takes you back into the past, straight into an older world."

I could hear my voice rising in excitement, and he kept a firm grip on my arm. "You don't believe me?" I persisted. "How can you possibly believe me? But I swear to you I've seen them, heard them talking, watched them moving, I've even seen a man, Isolda's lover Otto Bodrugan, murdered down in Treesmill creek."

"I believe you all right," he said. "Now supposing we go together and you hand over that remaining bottle?"

I led him upstairs to the dressing-room, and took the bottle out of the locked suitcase. He did not examine it, he just put it in his bag.

"Now I'll tell you what I'm going to do," he said. "I'm going to give you a pretty hefty sedative that will put you out until tomorrow morning. Is there some other room than this where you can sleep?"

"Yes," I said. "There's the spare-room along the landing here."

"Right," he said. "Collect a pair of pyjamas and let's go."

We went together into the spare-room, and I undressed and got into bed, feeling suddenly humble and subdued, like a child without responsibility.

"I'll do anything you say," I told the doctor. "Put me right out, if you like, so that I never wake again."

"I shan't do that," he answered, and for the first time smiled. "When you open your eyes tomorrow I shall probably be the first object you see."

"Then you won't pack me off to hospital?"

"Probably not. We'll talk about it in the morning."

He was getting a syringe out of his bag. "I don't mind what you tell my wife," I said, "as long as you don't tell her about the drug. Let her go on thinking I was crazy drunk. Whatever happens she mustn't know about the drug. She disliked Magnus—Professor Lane—and if she knew about this she'd dislike his memory even more."

"I dare say she would," he answered, wiping my arm with spirit before plunging his needle in, "and you could hardly blame her."

"The thing was," I said, "she was jealous. We'd known one another for so many years, he and I; we were at Cambridge together. I used to come and stay here in the old days, and Magnus seemed to take charge. We were always together, the same things intrigued us, the same things made us laugh, Magnus and I . . . Magnus and I . . ."

The depth of an abyss or the long sweet sleep of death, I did not mind. Five hours, five months, five years . . . in point of fact, so I learnt later, it was five days. The doctor always seemed to be there, when I opened my eyes, giving me another jab, or else sitting at the end of the bed swinging his legs, listening while I talked. Sometimes Vita looked in at the door with an uncertain smile, then disappeared. She and Mrs Collins between them must have made my bed, washed me, fed me—though I have no recollection of eating anything at all. Memory of those days is blotted out. I could have cursed, raved, torn the bedding, or merely slept. I understand I slept, and also talked. Not to Vita, not to Mrs Collins, but to the doctor. However many sessions it took between jabs I have no idea, nor do I know just what I said, but I gather I split, as the saying goes, the beans from start to finish, with the consequence that in the middle of the following week, when I was more or less back to normal and sitting around in a chair upstairs instead of lying in bed, body and mind felt not only rested but completely purged.

I told him so, over coffee which Vita had brought and left with us, and he laughed, saying a thorough clear-out never did any harm, and it was amazing the amount of stuff people locked away in attics and cellars they had forgotten about, which would be all the better if the light got through to it.

"Mind you," he added, "purging the soul comes easier to you than to others, because of your Catholic background."

I stared. "How did you know I was a Catholic?" I asked.

"It all came out in the wash," he said.

I felt strangely shocked. I had imagined that I had told him everything from start to finish about the experiment with the drug, and had described to him, in detail, the happenings of the other world. The fact that I had been born and bred a Catholic had no bearing on this at all.

"I'm a very bad Catholic," I said. "I couldn't wait to get away from Stonyhurst, and I haven't been to Mass for years. As to Confession . . ."

"I know," he said, "all in the attic or underground. Along with your dislike of monks, stepfathers, widows who remarry, and other little things along the same line."

I poured myself another cup of coffee, and one for him as well, throwing in too much sugar and stirring furiously.

"Look here," I said, "you're talking nonsense. I never give a thought to monks, widows or stepfathers—with the exception of myself—in my ordinary present-day life. The fact that these people existed in the fourteenth century, and I was able to see them, was entirely due to the drug."

"Yes," he said, "entirely due to the drug." He did his abrupt thing of getting up and walking round the room. "That bottle you gave me, I did what you ought to have done after the inquest. I sent it up to Lane's chief assistant, John Willis, with a brief word that you had been in trouble with it, and could I have a report as soon as possible? He was good enough to ring me up on the telephone as soon as he had my letter."

"Well?" I asked.

"Well, you're a very lucky man to be alive, and not only alive but here in this house and not in a loony-bin. The stuff in that bottle contained probably the most potent hallucinogen that has ever been discovered, and other substances as well which he isn't even sure of yet. Professor Lane was apparently working on this alone: he never took Willis fully into his confidence."

A lucky man to be alive, possibly. Lucky not to be in a loony-bin, agreed. But much of this I had told myself already, when I first started the experiment.

"Are you trying to tell me," I asked, "that everything I've seen has been hallucination, dug up from the murky waste of my own unconscious?"

"No, I'm not," he said. "I think Professor Lane was on to something that might have proved extraordinarily significant about the workings of the brain, and he chose you as guinea-pig because he knew you would do whatever he told you, and that you were a highly suggestible subject into the bargain." He wandered over to the table and finished his cup of coffee. "Incidentally, everything you've told me is just as secret as if you had split it into the Confessional. I had an initial struggle with your wife to keep you here, instead of sending you in an ambulance to some top chap in Harley Street who would have bunged you straight into a psychiatric home for six months. I think she trusts me now."

"What did you tell her?" I asked.

"I said you had been on the verge of a nervous breakdown, and suffering from strain and delayed shock owing to the sudden death of Professor Lane. Which, you may agree, is perfectly true."

I got up rather gingerly from my chair and walked over to the window. The campers had gone from the field across the way, and the cattle were grazing once again. I could hear our own boys playing cricket by the orchard.

"You may say what you like," I said slowly, "suggestibility, breakdown, Catholic conscience, the lot, but the fact remains that I've been in that other world, seen it, known it. It was cruel, hard, and very often bloody, and so were the people in it, except Isolda, and latterly Roger, but, my God, it held a fascination for me which is lacking in my own world of today."

He came and stood beside me at the window. He gave me a cigarette, and we both smoked awhile in silence.

"The other world," he said at last. "I suppose we all carry one inside us, in our various ways. You, Professor Lane, your wife, myself, and we'd see it differently if we all made the experiment together—which God forbid!" He smiled, and flicked his cigarette out of the window. "I have a feeling my own wife might take a dim view of an Isolda if I took to wandering about the Treesmill valley looking for her. Which is not to say I haven't done so through the years, but I'm too down to earth to go back six centuries on the off-chance that I might meet her."

"My Isolda lived," I said stubbornly. "I've seen actual pedigrees and historical documents to prove it. They all lived. I've got papers downstairs in the library that don't lie."

"Of course she lived," he agreed, "and what is more had two small girls called Joanna and Margaret, you told me about them. Little girls are more fascinating sometimes than small boys, and you have a couple of stepsons."

"And what the hell is that supposed to mean?"

"Nothing," he said, "just an observation. The world we carry inside us produces answers, sometimes. A way of escape. A flight from reality. You didn't want to live either in London or in New York. The fourteenth century made an exciting, if somewhat gruesome, antidote to both. The trouble is that day-dreams, like hallucinogenic drugs, become addictive; the more we indulge, the deeper we plunge, and then, as I said before, we end in the loony-bin."

I had the impression that everything he said was leading up to something else, to some practical proposition that I must take a grip on myself, get a job, sit in an office, sleep with Vita, breed daughters, look forward contentedly to middle-age, when I might grow cacti in a greenhouse.

"What do you want me to do?" I asked. "Come on, out with it."

He turned round from the window and looked me straight in the face.

"Frankly, I don't mind what you do," he said. "It's not my problem. As your medical adviser and father confessor for less than a week, I'd be glad to see you around for several years to come. And I'll be delighted to prescribe the usual antibiotics when you catch the 'flu. But for the immediate future I suggest that you get out of this house pretty quick before you have another urge to visit the basement."

I drew a deep breath. "I thought so," I said. "You've been talking to Vita."

"Naturally I've talked to your wife," he agreed, "and apart from a few feminine quirks she's a very sensible woman. When I say get out of the house I don't mean for ever. But for the next few weeks at least you'd be better away from it. You must see the force of that."

I did see it, but like a cornered rat I struggled for survival, and played for time.

"All right," I said. "Where do you suggest we go? We've got those boys on our hands."

"Well, they don't worry you, do they?"

"No . . . No, I'm very fond of them."

"It doesn't matter where, providing it's out of the pull of Roger Kylmerth."

"My alter ego?" I queried. "He and I are not a scrap alike, you know."

"Alter egos never are," he said. "Mine is a long-haired poet who faints at the sight of blood. He's dogged me ever since I left medical school."

I laughed, in spite of myself. He made everything seem so simple. "I wish you had known Magnus," I said. "You remind me of him in an odd sort of way."

"I wish I had. Seriously, though, I mean what I say about your getting away. Your wife suggested Ireland. Good walking country, fishing, crocks of gold buried under the hills . . ."

"Yes," I said, "and two of her compatriots who are touring around in the best hotels."

"She mentioned them," he said, "but I gather they've gone—got fed up with the weather and flown to sunny Spain instead. So that needn't worry you. I thought Ireland a good idea because it only means a three-hour drive from here to Exeter, and then you can fly direct. Hire a car the other side, and you're away."

He and Vita had the whole thing taped. I was trapped; there was no way out. I must put a brave face on it and admit defeat.

"Supposing I refuse?" I asked. "Get back into bed and pull the sheet over my head?"

"I'd send for an ambulance and cart you off to hospital. I thought Ireland was a better idea, but it's up to you."

Five minutes later he had gone, and I heard his car roaring up the drive. The sense of anti-climax was absolute: the purge had been very thorough. And I still did not know how much I had told him. Doubtless a hotch-potch of everything I had ever thought or done since the age of three, and, like all doctors with leanings towards psychoanalysis, he had put it together and summed me up as the usual sort of misfit with homosexual leanings who had suffered from birth with a mother complex, a stepfather complex, an aversion to copulation with my widowed wife, and a repressed desire to hit the hay with a blonde who had never existed except in my own imagination.

It all fitted, naturally. The Priory was Stonyhurst, Brother Jean was that silken bastard who taught me history, Joanna was my mother and poor Vita rolled into one, and Otto Bodrugan the handsome, gay adventurer I really longed to be. The fact that they all had lived, and could be proved to have lived, had not impressed Dr Powell. It was a pity he had not tried the drug himself, instead of sending bottle C to John Willis. Then he might have thought again.

Well, it was over now. I must go along with his diagnosis, and his holiday plans as well. God knows it was the least that I could do, after nearly killing Vita.

Funny he hadn't said anything about side-effects, or delayed action. Perhaps he had discussed this with John Willis, and John Willis had given the OK. But then Willis didn't know about the bloodshot eye, the sweats, the nausea and the vertigo. Nobody did, though Powell may have guessed, especially after our first encounter. Anyway, I felt normal enough now. Too normal, if the truth be told. Like a small boy spanked who had promised to amend his ways.

I opened the door and called for Vita. She came running up the stairs at once, and I realised, with a sense of shame and guilt, what she must have been through during the past week. Her face was drained of colour and she had lost weight. Her hair, usually immaculate, was swept back with a hasty comb behind her ears, and there was a strained, unhappy look in her eyes that I had never seen before.

"He told me you had agreed to come away," she said. "It was his idea, not mine, I promise you. I only want to do what's best for you."

"I know that," I said. "He's absolutely right."

"You're not angry, then? I was so afraid you'd be angry."

She came and sat beside me on the bed, and I put my arm round her.

"You must promise me one thing," I said, "and that is to forget everything that's happened up to now. I know it's practically impossible, but I do ask you."

"You've been ill. I know why, the doctor explained it all," she said. "He told the boys too, and they understand. We none of us blame you for anything, darling. We just want you to get well and to be happy."

"They're not frightened of me?"

"Heavens, no. They were very sensible about it. They've both been so good and helpful, Teddy especially. They're devoted to you, darling, I don't think you realise that."

"Oh, yes, I do," I said, "which makes it all the worse. But never mind that now. When are we supposed to be off?"

She hesitated. "Dr Powell said you'd be fit to travel by Friday, and he told me to go ahead and get the tickets."

Friday . . . The day after tomorrow.

"OK." I said, "if that's what he says. I suppose I'd better move about a bit to get myself in trim. Sort out some things to pack."

"As long as you don't overdo it. I'll send Teddy up to help you." She left me with the best part of week's mail, and by the time I'd been through it, and chucked most of it into the waste-paper basket, Teddy had appeared at the door.

"Mom said you might like some help with your packing," he said shyly.

"Good lad, I would. I hear you've been head of the house for the past week, and doing a fine job."

He flushed with pleasure. "Oh, I don't know. I haven't done much. Answered the phone a few times. There was a man called up yesterday, asked if you were better and sent his regards. A Mr Willis. He left his number, in case you wanted to ring him. And he left another number too. I wrote them both down."

He brought out a shiny black notebook and tore out a page. I recognised the first number—it was Magnus's lab—but the other one baffled me.

"Is this second one his home number, or didn't say?" I asked.

"Yes, he did say. It's someone called Davies, who works at the British Museum. He thought you might like to get in touch with Mr Davies before he went on holiday."

I put the torn page in my pocket, and went along with Teddy to the dressing-room. The divan bed had gone, and I realised what the dragging sound had signified the night the doctor came: the bed had been moved into the double room and put under the window.

"Micky and I have been sleeping in here with Mom," said Teddy. "She felt she wanted company."

It was a delicate way of putting that she wanted protection. I left him in the dressing-room pulling things out of the wardrobe, and picked up the telephone receiver beside the bed.

The voice that answered me, precise and rather reserved, assured me the owner's name was Davies.

"I'm Richard Young," I told him, "a friend of the late Professor Lane. You know all about me, I believe."

"Yes, indeed, Mr Young, I hope you are better. I heard through John Willis that you'd been laid up."

"That's right. Nothing serious. But I'm going away, and I gather you are too, so I wondered if you had anything for me."

"Unfortunately nothing very much, I'm afraid. If you'll excuse me a moment, I'll just get my notes and read them out to you."

I waited, while he put down the receiver. I had the uncomfortable feeling that I was cheating, and that Dr Powell would have disapproved.

"Are you there, Mr Young?"

"Yes, I'm here."

"I hope you won't be disappointed. They are only extracts from the Registers of Bishop Grandisson of Exeter, one dated 1334, the second 1335. The first relates to Tywardreath Priory, and the second to Oliver Carminowe. The first is a letter from the Bishop at Exeter to the Abbot of the sister-house at Angers, and reads as follows:

"John, etc., Bishop of Exeter, sends greeting with true kindness of thought in the Lord. Inasmuch as we expel from our fold the diseased sheep which is wont to spread its disorder, lest it should infect our other healthy sheep, so in the case of Brother Jean, called Meral, a monk of your monastery at present living in the Priory of Tywardreath in our diocese, which is ruled by a Prior of the Order of St Benedict, on account of his outrageous abandonment of all shame and decent behaviour, in spite of frequent kindly admonitions—and because, alas, as I am ashamed to say (not to mention his other notorious

offences), he has nevertheless become more hardened in his wickedness—
we have therefore, with all zeal and reverence for your order and for
yourself, arranged to send him back to you to be subjected to the discipline
of the monastery for this evil behaviour. May God Himself maintain you in
the rule of this flock in length of days and health."

He cleared his throat. "The original is in Latin, you understand. This is my
translation. I couldn't help thinking, as I copied it out, how the phrasing would
have appealed to Professor Lane."

"Yes," I said, "it would."

He cleared his throat again. "The second piece is very short, and may not
interest you. It is only that on April 21st, 1335, Bishop Grandisson received Sir
Oliver Carminowe and his wife Sybell, who had been clandestinely married
without banns or licence. They confirmed that they had erred through
ignorance. The Bishop relaxed the sentences imposed upon them and confirmed the marriage, which seems to have taken place at some previous date,
not stated, in Sir Oliver's private chapel at Carminowe, in the parish of
Mawgan-in-Meneage. Proceedings were taken against the priest who married
them. That's all."

"Does it say what had happened to the previous wife, Isolda?"

"No. I presume she died, possibly a short while before, and this other
marriage was clandestine because it took place so soon after her death. Perhaps
Sybell was pregnant, and a private ceremony seemed necessary to save face.
I'm sorry, Mr Young, but I haven't been able to turn up anything else."

"Don't worry," I said. "What you've told me is very valuable. Have a good
holiday."

"Thank you. The same to you."

I put down the receiver. Teddy was calling to me from the dressing-room.

"Dick?"

"Yes?"

He came through from the bathroom with Magnus's walking-stick in his
hands.

"Will you be taking this with you?" he asked. "It's too long to fit into your
suitcase."

I had not seen the stick since I had poured into it the colourless liquid from
bottle C nearly a week ago. I had forgotten all about it.

"If you don't want it," said Teddy, "I'll put it back in the cupboard where I
found it."

"No," I said, "give it to me. I do want it."

He pretended to take aim to me, smiling, holding it balanced like a spear,
then lobbed it gently in the air. I caught it and held it fast.

CHAPTER TWENTY-FOUR

W E SAT IN the lounge at Exeter airport waiting for our flight to be called. Take-off was twelve-thirty. The Buick was parked behind the airport, to remain there until our return, whenever that should be. I got sandwiches for all of us, and while we ate them cast an eye over our fellow-travellers. There were flights that afternoon for the Channel Isles as well as Dublin, and the lounge facing the airfield was filled with people. There were a number of priests returning from some convocation, a party of schoolchildren, family parties such as our own, and the usual sprinkling of holiday types. There was also a hilarious sextet who, from their conversation, were on their way to, or from, a riotous wedding.

"I hope," said Vita, "we aren't going to find ourselves beside that lot on the 'plane."

The boys were already doubled up with laughter, for one of the group had donned a false nose and a moustache, which he kept dipping into his glass of Guinness, to emerge beaded with froth.

"The thing to do," I said, "is to leap to our feet as soon as our flight is called, so that we can get right up to the front, well away from them."

"If that man with the false nose tries to sit beside me, I shall scream," said Vita.

Her remark set the boys off again, and I congratulated myself on having ordered generous rations of cider for the boys and brandy and soda—our holiday drink—for Vita and myself, because it was that, more than the wedding party, which was making the boys giggle and causing Vita to squint as she peered in her powder-compact. I kept a close watch on the plane on the runway, until I saw that it was loaded. They were pulling the baggage trucks away, and a hostess was walking across the tarmac to our door.

"Damn!" I said. "I knew it was a mistake to swill all that coffee and brandy. Look, darling, I must rush to the gents. If they call the flight go ahead and get seats in front, as I said. If I'm caught up in the mob I'll find myself a seat at the back and change places after take-off. As long as you three are together you'll be all right. Here—you take your boarding cards and I'll hang on to mine, just in case."

"Oh, Dick, honestly!" exclaimed Vita. "You might have gone before. How typical of you!"

"Sorry," I said. "Nature calls . . ."

I walked rapidly across the lounge as I saw the hostess enter the door, and waited inside the gents. I heard the flight number called over the loudspeaker, and after a few minutes, when I came out again, our party was walking with the hostess across to the aircraft, Vita and the boys in the van. As I watched, they disappeared into the plane, followed by the school-children and the priests. It was now or never. I went rapidly out of the main door of the airport building, and crossed over to the car park. In a moment I had started the Buick and pulled out of the airport entrance. Then I drew into the side of the road and listened. I could hear the sound of the engines before the plane taxied to the start, which must mean that everyone was aboard. If the engines ceased it would mean my plan had gone for nothing, and the hostess had discovered that I was missing. It was twelve thirty-five exactly. Then I heard the engines increase in pitch and in a few minutes, unbelievably, my heart pounding, I saw the silver streak of the aircraft speeding along the runway and take off, gain height and flatten out, and then it was away amongst the clouds and out of sight, and I was sitting there, at the wheel of the Buick, on my own.

They were due to touch down at Dublin at one-fifty. I knew exactly what Vita would do. She would put through a call from the airport to Dr Powell in Fowey, and find him out. He would be out because it was his half-day. He had told me so, when I had rung up after breakfast to say goodbye. He had said that, if it was fine, he was going to take his family over to the north coast to surf, and he would be thinking about us, and would I please send him a postcard from Ireland saying "Wish you were here".

I started to sing, as I turned into the main road and touched seventy. This was how a criminal must feel when he had just robbed a bank and got away with the loot in a stolen van. A pity I had not the whole day before me to explore at leisure, drive over to Bere and look up Sir William Ferrers and his wife Matilda, perhaps. I had found the spot on the map—it was only just across the Tamar in Devon—and I wondered if their house was standing still. Probably not, or, if it was, it had turned itself into a farm like Carminowe. I had located Carminowe on my map at the same time, when Teddy was up in my dressing-room packing my case, and had also found the reference to it in the old volume of *Parochial History* that had given me Tregesteynton. Carminowe was in Mawgan-in-Meneage, near the Loe Pool, and the writer said that the ancient mansion and chapel had fallen into decay in the reign of James I, along with the old burial ground.

I took the Launceston road after leaving Okehampton, for it was faster than the way we had come, and as I crossed from Devon into Cornwall, heading for Bodmin moor like a homing pigeon, I sang louder still, for even if Vita had beaten me to it, and was about to land in Dublin, I was safe from pursuit; she could not reach me now. This was my last trip, my final fling; and whatever became of me in the process I could not hurt either her or the boys, for they would be safe on Irish soil.

> "In such a night
> Stood Dido with a willow in her hand
> Upon the wild sea-banks, and wav'd her love
> To come again to Carthage."

The trouble was, Isolda's lover had died in Treesmill creek upon the strand, and I doubted if either the threat of convent walls, or Joanna's taunts, or the monk's promise of safe passage to some doubtful refuge in Angers would have made her turn to Roger in the end. The future was bleak, six hundred years ago, for wives who left their husbands, especially when the husband had an eye to a third bride. It would have suited Oliver Carminowe, and the Ferrers family too, if Isolda had simply disappeared, which she might well have done had she entrusted herself to Joanna's care; but to remain under Roger's roof was at best only a stop-gap measure, and could not have continued long.

As I drove across Bodmin moor, rejoicing that each mile brought me nearer home, exhilaration was tempered by the knowledge that not only must this be the last trip to the other world, but that when I entered it I had no choice of date or season. The thaw could have come and Lent be over, high summer have taken its place, Isolda herself, having made her choice, be languishing behind those convent walls somewhere in Devon, in which case she would have moved out of Roger's life, and mine as well. I wondered, had Magnus lived, whether he could have perfected the timing factor, thus leaving the awakening from present to past to the participant's own choice; so that today, by some infinitesimal alteration of the dose, I could have summoned up at will those figures in the basement where I had left them last. Never, in the few weeks of experiment, had it happened that way. There had always been a jump in time. Joanna's carriage would no longer be waiting on the top of the hill above Kylmerth; Roger, Isolda and Bess would have left the farmhouse kitchen. That single draught in the walking-stick could guarantee re-entry to my world, but not what I should find there when I did.

The halt-sign brought me up with a jerk on to the main Lostwithiel-St Blazey road. I had driven the last twenty miles like an automaton, and I remembered the side turning that would take me past Tregesteynton to the Treesmill valley. I drove down it with a strange nostalgic sense, and as I passed the present farmhouse of Strickstenton, and a black-and-white collie darted out on to the road barking, I thought of small Margaret, Isolda's younger child, who had wanted a riding-whip like Robbie's, and Joanna, the elder, preening in the looking-glass while her father chased Sybell up the stairs with the otter's paw.

I came down into the valley, and so intense was my identification with the past that I had forgotten, momentarily, that the river would no longer be there, and I looked for Rosgof's cottage by the side of the ford opposite the mill: but of course there was no river and no ford, only the road turning left and a few cows grazing in the marshy field.

I wished I was in the Triumph, for the Buick was too big and conspicuous. On sudden impulse I parked by the bridge below the mill, and, walking a short way up the lane, climbed over the gate into the field leading to the Gratten. I knew I must stand there once more amongst the mounds before returning home, for once back at Kilmarth the future would be uncertain; the last experiment might land me in some trouble unforeseen. I wanted to carry in my mind the image of the Treesmill valley as it looked today under the late August sun, letting imagination and memory do the rest, bringing back the winding river and the creek, and the anchorage below the long-vanished house. They had been harvesting in the Chapel Park fields behind the Gratten, but here where I walked beneath the hedge it was all grass, and cows were grazing. I came to the first of the gorse-bushes, climbing to the top of the high bank surrounding the site, and then looked down to the apron of grass which had once been a path under the hallway window, where Isolda and Bodrugan had sat holding hands.

A man was lying there, smoking a cigarette, his coat propped under his head as pillow. I stared hard, unbelieving, thinking that guilt and an uneasy conscience must have conjured his image out of the air; but I was not mistaken. The man who was lying there was very real, and it was Dr Powell.

I stood there a moment watching him, then deliberately, without malice but with total resolution, I unscrewed the top of Magnus's stick and took out the little measure. I swallowed my last dose, and replaced the measure once again inside the stick. Then I walked down the mound and joined him.

"I thought," I said, "you had gone surfing on the north coast?"

He sat up instantly, and I experienced, for the first time since knowing him, the immensely satisfying feeling that I had caught him unawares and at a disadvantage.

He recovered quickly, the look of astonishment giving place to an engaging smile. "I changed my mind," he said calmly, "and let the family go off without me. You seem to have done the same."

"So Vita beat me to it after all. She didn't lose much time," I told him.

"What's your wife got to do with it?"

"Well, she telephoned you from Dublin, didn't she?"

"No," he said.

Now it was my turn to look astonished and stare at him. "Then what the hell are you doing here waiting for me?"

"I wasn't waiting for you. Rather than brave the Atlantic breakers I decided to explore your piece of territory. A hunch that has apparently paid off. You can show me round."

My one-upmanship began to fade, my self-confidence desert me. He seemed to be playing my own game and getting away with it.

"Look," I said, "don't you want to know what happened at the airport?"

"Not particularly," he replied. "The 'plane took off, I know, because I rang through to Exeter and checked. Whether you were on it or not they couldn't tell me, but I knew that if you weren't you would head back for Kilmarth, and if I turned up there for a cup of tea I'd find you in the basement. Meanwhile, burning curiosity drove me to while away half an hour or so down here."

His cocksure attitude infuriated me, but I was even more angry with myself. If I had taken the other road, if I had not come through the Treesmill valley and allowed momentary sentiment to sway me, I should have been safely back at Kilmarth with at least half an hour or more in hand before he breezed in to take possession.

"All right," I said, "I know I've played a dirty trick on Vita and the boys, and she's probably ringing you from Dublin airport now and getting no reply. What staggers me is that you let me go knowing what might happen. It's almost as much your fault as mine."

"Oh, I agree," he answered. "I'm equally to blame, and we'll both apologise when we get her on the telephone. But I wanted to give you a chance, just to see if you could make it, instead of going by the rules."

"And what do the rules say?"

"Put your addict inside, once he's well and truly hooked."

I looked at him thoughtfully, and leant on Magnus's walking-stick for support. "You know very well," I said, "I gave bottle C to you, and that was the last; and you must have given the house a pretty thorough search when I was lying prone upstairs all the week."

"I did," he replied, "and searched it again today. I told Mrs Collins I was looking for buried treasure, and I think she believed me. Suspicious sort of chap, aren't I?"

"Yes. And you found nothing, because there was nothing there."

"Well, you may count yourself damn lucky that there wasn't. I've got Willis's final report in my pocket."

"What does it say?"

"Only that the drug contains a substance of some toxicity that could seriously affect the central nervous system, possibly leading to paralysis. No need to elaborate."

"Show it to me now."

He shook his head, and suddenly he was not there any more, and the walls were all around me, and I was standing in the hall of the Champernoune manor-house looking out of the casement window at the rain. Panic gripped me, for it was not meant to happen, at least not yet; I had counted on being home, behind my own four walls, with Roger acting as my usual guide-protector. He was not here, and the hall was empty, and had been altered since I had seen it last. There seemed to be more furniture, more hangings, and the curtain masking the doorway to the stair above was drawn aside. Someone was crying in the bedroom overhead, and I could hear the sound of heavy footsteps pacing the floor. I looked out of the casement window once again, and saw through the falling rain that it must be autumn, for the clump of trees on the opposite hill where Oliver Carminowe had concealed himself and his men, as they lay in ambush waiting for Bodrugan, was golden brown as it had been then. But today no wind blew, tossing the leaves on to the ground below; the steady mizzle made them hang dispirited, and a shroud of mist clung above Lanescot and the river's mouth.

The crying turned to a high-pitched laugh, and down the stairs came a cup and ball, rolling one behind the other, until they reached the floor of the hall itself, when the ball rolled slowly under the table. I heard a man's voice call anxiously, "Mind how you go, Elizabeth!" as someone, still laughing, came clumping down the stairs in search of the toy. She stood a moment, her hands clasped in front of her, her long dress trailing, an absurd little bonnet askew on her auburn hair. Her likeness to Joanna Champernoune was startling, then tragic, for this was an idiot girl, above twelve years old, with a full loose mouth, and eyes set high in her head. She nodded, laughing, then picked up the ball and cup and began to throw them in the air, screaming with delight. Suddenly, tiring of the game, she tossed them aside and started to spin round in circles until she became giddy, when she fell on to the floor and sat there motionless, staring at her shoes.

The man's voice from above called out again, "Elizabeth . . . Elizabeth", and the girl struggled clumsily to her feet and smiled, gazing at the ceiling. Footsteps came slowly down the stairs and the man appeared, wearing a long, loose robe to his ankles, and a night-cap. I thought, for a moment, I had travelled back in time and it was Henry Champernoune who stood there, weak and pale in his final illness, but it was Henry's son William, an adolescent when I saw him last, squaring up to take his place as head of the family when Roger broke the news of his father's death. Now he looked thirty-five or even more, and I realised, with a shock of dismay, that time had leapt ahead of me at least twelve years, and all the intervening months and years were buried in a past I should never know. The frozen winter of 1335 meant nothing to this William, who had been a minor and unmarried then. He was now master of his own house, although battling, it would seem, against sickness, and enmeshed as well in the inescapable net of some family flaw.

"Come, daughter, come, love," he said gently, holding out his arms, and she put her finger in her mouth and sucked it, shaking her shoulders, then, with a sudden change of mind, darted to the floor and picked up her cup and ball again and gave it to him.

"I'll toss it for you above, but not down here," he said. "Katie has been sick as well, and I must not leave her."

"She'll not have my toy, I won't let her," said Elizabeth, nodding her head up and down, and she put out her hand and tried to snatch it back.

"What? Not let your sister share it when she gave it to you? That's not my Lizzie speaking, surely? Lizzie's flown up the chimney and a bad girl has taken her place."

He clicked his tongue in reproof, and at the sound of it her full mouth drooped, her eyes filled with tears, and she flung her arms about him, crying bitterly, clinging to his long robe.

"There, there," he said. "Father did not mean it, Father loves his Liz, but she must not tease him, he is still weak and sick, and poor Katie too. Come, now, upstairs, and she can watch us from her bed, and when you toss the ball high she'll be the better for it, and maybe smile."

He took her hand and led her towards the stairs, and as he did so someone came through the door leading to the kitchen quarters. William heard the footsteps and turned his head.

"See that all the doors are fastened before you go," he said, "and bid the servants keep them so, and open them to no one. God knows I hate to give the order, but I daren't do otherwise. Sick stragglers bide their time, and wait for darkness before they walk abroad and knock on men's doors."

"I know it. There have been many so in Tywardreath, and death has spread because of it."

There was no doubt about the speaker who stood at the open door. It was Robbie, a taller, broader Robbie than the lad I knew, and his chin was bearded now like his brother's.

"Watch how you go upon the road, then," answered William. "The same poor demented wanderers might attempt to strike you down, thinking, because you ride, you have some magic property of health denied to them."

"I'll ride with care, Sir William, have no fear. I would not leave you for the night except for Roger. Five days since I was home, and he's alone."

"I know, I know. God keep you both, and watch over all of us this night."

He led his daughter up the stairs to the room above, and I followed Robbie to the kitchen quarters. Three servants sat there in dejected fashion, hugging the hearth, one with his eyes closed and his head resting against the wall. Robbie gave him William's message, and he echoed, "God be with us," without opening his eyes.

Robbie shut the door behind him and walked across the stable-court. His pony was tied to the stall inside the shed. He mounted and began riding slowly up the hill through the mizzling rain, passing the small cottages that formed part of the demesne, lining the muddied track. All the doors were fastened tight, and smoke came from the roofs of only two, the others seeming deserted. We reached the brow of the hill, and Robbie, instead of turning to the right on the road to the village, paused by the geld-house on the left, and, dismounting, tied his pony to the gate and walked up the path to the chapel alongside. He opened the door and entered, I following after. The chapel was small, hardly more than twenty feet in length and fifteen broad, with a single window facing east behind the altar. Robbie, making the sign of the Cross, knelt down before it, and bowed his head in prayer. There was an inscription in Latin beneath the window, which I read:

"Matilda Champernoune built this chapel in memory of her husband William Champernoune, who died in 1304."

A stone before the chancel steps was inscribed with her own initials and the date of her death, which I could not decipher. A similar stone, to the left, bore the initials H.C. There were no stained glass windows, no effigies or tombs built against the walls: this was an oratory, a memorial chapel.

When Robbie rose from his knees and turned away, I saw another stone before the chancel steps. The lettering read I.C.; the date was 1335. As I followed Robbie out into the rain and down towards the village, I knew of only one name that would fit, and it was not Champernoune.

Desolation was all about me, here by the geld-house and in the village too. No people on the green, no animals, no barking dogs. The doors of the small dwellings huddled close around the green were closed, like those on the demesne itself. A single goat, half-starved by its appearance, with ribs protruding from its lean body, was tethered by a chain near to the well, cropping the rough grass.

We climbed the hill-track above the Priory, and looking down on to the enclosure I could see no sign of life from behind the walls. No smoke came from the monks' quarters, nor from the chapter-house; the whole place seemed abandoned, and the ripening apples in the orchard had been left to cluster on the trees unplucked. And when we passed the plough-lands on the high ground I saw that the soil had not been turned, and some of the corn was not even harvested but lay rotting on the earth, as if some cyclone in the night had swept it down. As we came to the pasture-land on the lower slopes the Priory cattle, roaming loose, came lowing after us in desperation, as though in hope that Robbie, on his pony, might drive them home.

We crossed the ford with ease, for the tide was ebbing fast and the sands lay uncovered, flat and dirty brown under the rain. A thin wreath of smoke came from Julian Polpey's roof—he at least must have survived calamity—but Geoffrey Lampetho's dwelling in the valley looked as bare and deserted as those on the village green. This was not the world I knew, the world I had come to love and long for because of its magic quality of love and hate, its separation from a drab monotony; this was a place resembling, in its barren desolation, all the most hideous features of a twentieth-century landscape after disaster, suggesting a total abandonment of hope, the aftertaste of atomic doom.

Robbie rode uphill above the ford, and passing through the copse of straggling trees came down to the wall encircling Kylmerth yard. No smoke curled up from the chimney. He flung himself from his pony, leaving it to wander loose towards the byre, and running across the yard he opened the door.

"Roger!" I heard him call, and "Roger!" once again. The kitchen was empty, the turf no longer smouldered on the hearth. The remains of food lay untouched upon the trestle table, and as Robbie climbed the ladder to the sleeping-loft I saw a rat scurry across the floor and disappear.

There can have been no one in the loft, for Robbie came down the ladder instantly, and opened the door beneath it which gave access to the byre, revealing at the same time a narrow passage ending in a store-room and a cellar. Slits in the thickness of the wall allowed streaks of light to penetrate the gloom, and this was the only source of air as well. There was little draught to cleanse the atmosphere of sweet mustiness pervading, due to the rotting apples laid in rows against the wall. An iron cauldron, unsteady on three legs, and rusted from disuse, stood in the far corner, and beside it pitchers, jars, a three-pronged fork, a pair of bellows. This store-room was a strange choice for a sick man to make his bed. He must have dragged his pallet from the sleeping-loft and placed it here beside the slit in the wall, and then, from increasing weakness or lack of will, lain through the days and nights until today.

"Roger . . ." whispered Robbie, "Roger!"

Roger opened his eyes. I did not recognise him. His hair was white, his eyes sunk deep in his head, his features thin and drawn; and under the white furze that formed his beard the flesh was discoloured, bruised, with the same discoloured swellings behind his ears. He murmured something, water, I think it was, and Robbie rose from his side and ran into the kitchen, but I went on kneeling there beside him, staring down at the man I had last seen confident and strong.

Robbie returned with a pitcher of water, and, putting his arms round his brother, helped him to drink. But after two mouthfuls Roger choked, and lay back again on his pallet, gasping.

"No remedy," he said. "The swelling's spread to my throat and blocked the wind-pipe. Moisten my lips only, that's comfort enough."

"How long have you lain here?" asked Robbie.

"I cannot tell. Four days and nights, maybe. Not long after you went I knew it had me, and I brought my bed to the cellar so that you could sleep easy above when you returned. How is Sir William?"

"Recovered, thanks be to God, and young Katherine too. Elizabeth still escapes infection, and the servants. More than sixty died this week in Tywardreath. The Priory is closed, as you know, and the Prior and brethren gone to Minster."

"No loss," murmured Roger. "We can do without them. Did you visit the chapel?"

"I did, and said the usual prayer."

He moistened his brother's lips with water once again, and in rough but tender fashion tried to soften the swellings beneath his ears.

"I tell you, there's no remedy," said Roger. "This is the end. No parish priest to shrive me, no communal grave amongst the rest. Bury me at the cliff's edge, Robbie, where my bones will smell the sea."

"I'll go to Polpey and fetch Bess," said Robbie. "She and I can nurse you through this together."

"No," said Roger, "she has her own children to care for now, and Julian too. Hear my confession, Robbie. There's been something on my conscience now these thirteen years."

He struggled to sit up but had not strength enough, and Robbie, the tears running down his cheeks, smoothed the matted hair out of his brother's eyes.

"If it concerns you and Lady Carminowe, I don't need to hear it, Roger," he said. "Bess and I knew you loved her, and love her still. So did we. There was no sin in that for any of us."

"No sin in loving, but in murder, yes," said Roger.

"Murder?"

Robbie, kneeling by his brother's side, stared down at him, bewildered, then shook his head. "You're wandering, Roger," he said softly. "We all know how she died. She had been sick for weeks before she came here, and hid it from us; and then when they tried to carry her away by force she gave her promise she would follow in a week, and so they let her stay."

"And would have gone, but I prevented it."

"How did you prevent it? She died before the week had passed, here, in the room above, with Bess's arms about her, and yours too."

"She died because I would not let her suffer pain," said Roger. "She died because, had she kept her bargain and travelled to Trelawn and thence into Devon, there would have been weeks of agony ahead, even months, agony that our own mother knew and endured when we were young. So I let her go from us in sleep, knowing nothing of what I had done, and you and Bess in the same ignorance."

He put out his hand and felt for Robbie's, holding it tight. "Did you never wonder, Robbie, when in the old days I stayed at the Priory late at night, or on occasion brought de Meral here to the cellar, what it was I did?"

"I knew the French ships landed merchandise," said Robbie, "and you conveyed it to the Priory. Wine and other goods which the Prior lacked. And the monks lived well because of it."

"They taught me their secrets too," said Roger. "How to make men dream and conjure visions, rather than pray. How to seek a paradise on earth that would last for a few hours only. How to make men die. It was only after young Bodrugan perished in de Meral's care that I sickened of the game, taking no further part in it. But I had learnt the secret well, and so made use of it, when the time came. I gave her something to ease pain and let her slip away. It was murder, Robbie, and a mortal sin. And no one knows of it but you."

The effort of speaking had drained him of all strength, and Robbie, lost and frightened suddenly in the presence of death, let go his hand, and, stumbling to his feet, went blindly along the passage to the kitchen, in search, I think, of some additional covering to draw over his brother. I went on kneeling there, in the cellar, and Roger opened his eyes for the last time and stared at me. I think he asked for absolution, but there was no one there, in his own time, to grant it, and I wondered if, because of this, he had travelled through the years in search of it. Like Robbie, I was helpless, and six centuries too late.

"Go forth, O Christian soul, out of this world, in the name of God the Father Almighty, who created thee; in the name of Jesus Christ, the Son of the living God, who suffered for thee; in the name of the Holy Ghost, who sanctified thee . . ."

I could not remember any more, and it did not matter, because he had already gone. The light was coming through the chinks of the shuttered window in the old laundry, and I was kneeling there, on the stone floor of the lab, amongst the empty bottles and the jars. There was no nausea, no vertigo, no singing in my ears. Only a great silence, and a sense of peace.

I raised my head and saw that the doctor was standing by the wall and watching me.

"It's finished," I said. "Roger's dead, he's free. It's all over."

The doctor put out his hand and took my arm. He led me out of the room and up the stairs, and through to the front part of the house and into the library. We sat down together on the window-seat, staring out across the sea.

"Tell me about it," he said.

"Don't you know?"

I had thought, seeing him in the lab, that he must have shared the experience with me, then I realised it was impossible.

"I waited with you on the site," he told me, "then walked with you up the hill, and followed behind you in the car. You stopped for a moment in a field above Tywardreath, near where the two roads join, then down through the village and along the side-lane to Polmear, and so back here. You were walking quite normally, rather faster, perhaps, than I would have cared to do myself. Then you struck to the right through the wood, and I came down the drive. I knew I should find you below."

I got up from the window-seat and went to the bookshelf, and took down one of the volumes of the *Encyclopaedia Britannica*.

"What are you looking for?" he asked.

I turned the pages until I found the reference I sought.

"The date of the Black Death," I said, "1348. Thirteen years after Isolda died." I put the book back upon the shelf.

"Bubonic plague," he observed. "Endemic in the Far East—they've had a number of cases in Vietnam."

"Have they?" I said. "Well, I've just seen what it did in Tywardreath six hundred years ago."

I went back to the window-seat and picked up the walking-stick. "You must have wondered how I managed that last trip," I said. "This is how." I unscrewed the top and showed him the small measure. He took it from me and held it upside down. It was fully drained.

"I'm sorry," I said, "but when I saw you sitting there below the Gratten I knew I had to do it. It was my last chance. And I'm glad I did, because now the whole thing is done with, finished. No more temptation. No more desire to lose myself in the other world. I told you Roger was free, and so am I."

He did not answer. He was still staring at the empty measure.

"Now," I said, "before we put through a call to Dublin airport and ask if Vita is there, supposing you tell me what else was written in that report John Willis sent you?"

He picked up the stick, and replacing the measure screwed on the top and gave it back to me.

"I burnt it," he said, "with the flame from my lighter, when you were on your knees in the basement reciting that prayer for the dying. Somehow it seemed to me the right moment, and I preferred to destroy it rather than have it lying in the surgery amongst my files."

"That's no answer," I told him.

"It's all you're going to get," he replied.

The telephone started ringing from the lobby in the hall. I wondered how many times it had rung before.

"That will be Vita," I said. "Now for the count-down. I'd better get on my knees again. Shall I tell her I got locked in the gents and I'll join her tomorrow?"

"It would be wiser," he said slowly, "if you told her you hoped to join her later, perhaps in a few weeks' time."

"But that's absurd," I frowned. "There's nothing to hold me back. I've told you it's all over and I'm free."

He did not say anything. He just sat there staring at me.

The telephone went on ringing, and I crossed the room to answer it, but a silly thing happened as I picked up the receiver. I couldn't hold it properly; my fingers and the palm of my hand went numb, and it slipped out of my grasp and crashed to the floor.

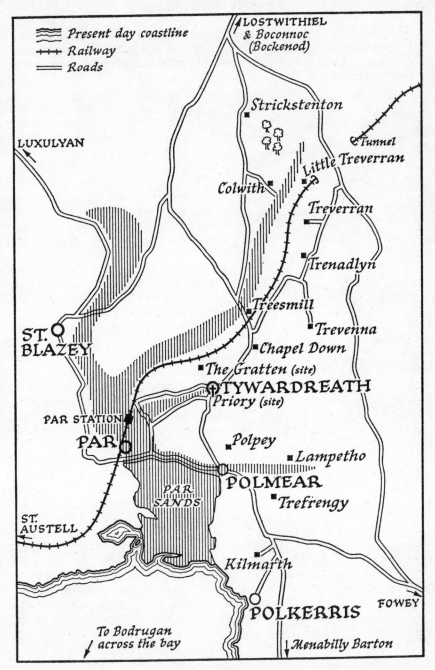

Part of Tywardreath parish. When Roger Kylmerth lived,
the shaded area was estuary.

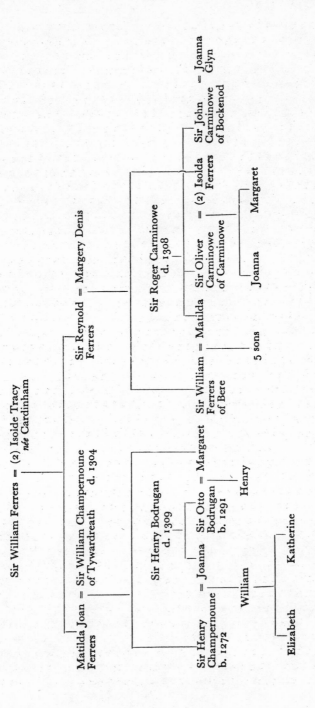